Maigret Triumphant

GEORGES SIMENON

Maigret Triumphant

COMPRISING

MAIGRET AND THE BURGLAR'S WIFE
MAIGRET'S REVOLVER
MY FRIEND MAIGRET
MAIGRET IN COURT
MAIGRET AFRAID

HAMISH HAMILTON

LONDON

First Published in Great Britain
by Hamish Hamilton Ltd. 1969
90 Great Russell Street London W.C.1

© 1969 by Georges Simenon

SBN 241 01810 2

PRINTED IN GREAT BRITAIN
BY EBENEZER BAYLIS AND SON, LTD.
THE TRINITY PRESS, WORCESTER, AND LONDON

MAIGRET AND THE BURGLAR'S WIFE

MAIGRET AND THE BURGLAR'S WIFE

(*Maigret et la Grande Perche*)
was first published in France in 1953
and in Great Britain in 1955
Translated from the French by J. Maclaren-Ross

MAIGRET AND THE BURGLAR'S WIFE

I

THE appointment-slip, duly filled in, and handed to Maigret by the office porter, bore the following text:

Ernestine Micou, alias 'Lofty' (now Jussiaume), who, when you arrested her seventeen years ago in the Rue de la Lune, stripped herself naked to take the mike out of you, requests the favour of an interview on a matter of most urgent and important business.

Maigret glanced quickly, out of the corner of his eye, at old Joseph, to see whether he'd read the message, but the white-haired 'boy' didn't move a muscle. He was probably the only one in the whole of Police Headquarters that morning who wasn't in shirt-sleeves, and for the first time in so many years the chief-inspector wondered by what official vagary this almost venerable man was compelled to wear a heavy chain with a huge seal round his neck.

It was the sort of day when one's apt to indulge in pointless speculation. The heat-wave may have been to blame. Perhaps the holiday spirit also prevented one from taking things very seriously. The windows were wide open and the muted roar of Paris throbbed in the room where, before Joseph came in, Maigret had been engaged in following the flight of a wasp that was going round in circles and bumping against the ceiling at invariably the same spot. At least half the plain-clothes section was at the seaside or in the country. Lucas went about wearing a straw hat which, on him, assumed the aspect of a native grass hat or a lampshade. The Chief himself had left the day before, as he did year after year, for the Pyrenees.

'Drunk?' Maigret asked the porter.

'Don't think so, sir.'

For a certain type of woman, having taken a drop too much, often feels impelled to make disclosures to the police.

'Jumpy?'

'She asked me if it'd take long, and I said I didn't even know if you'd see her. She sat herself down in a corner of the waiting-room and started to read the paper.'

Maigret couldn't recall the names Micou or Jussiaume, or even the

nickname Lofty, but he retained a vivid memory of the Rue de la
Lune, on a day as hot as this, when the asphalt feels elastic under one's
tread and fills Paris with a smell of tar.

It was down by the Porte Saint-Denis, a little street of shady hotels
and small sweetshops. He wasn't a chief-inspector in those days. The
women wore low-waisted frocks and had shingled hair. To find out
about this girl, he'd had to go into two or three of the neighbouring
bars, and it so happened he'd been drinking Pernod. He could almost
conjure up the smell of it, just as he could conjure up the smell of armpits and feet pervading the small hotel. The room was on the third or
fourth floor. Mistaking the door, he'd first of all found himself face to
face with a negro who, sitting on his bed, was playing the accordion;
one of the band in a *bal musette*, probably. Quite unperturbed, the negro
had indicated the room next door with a jerk of his chin.

'Come in!'

A husky voice. The voice of one who drank or smoked too much.
And, standing by a window that gave onto the courtyard, a tall girl in
a sky-blue wrap, cooking herself a chop on a spirit lamp.

She was as tall as Maigret, maybe taller. She'd looked him up and
down without emotion; she'd said straight away:

'You're a copper?'

He'd found a pocket-book and the bank-notes on top of the wardrobe
and she hadn't batted an eyelid.

'It was my girl friend who did the job.'

'What girl friend?'

'Don't know her name. Lulu, they call her.'

'Where is she?'

'Find out. That's your business.'

'Get dressed and come with me.'

It was only a case of petty theft, but Headquarters took a rather
serious view of it, not so much because of the sum involved, though this
was a pretty large one, as because it concerned a big cattle-dealer from
the Charentes, who had already started to stir up his local Deputy.

'It'd take more than you to stop me eating my chop!'

The tiny room contained only one chair. He'd remained standing
while the girl ate, taking her time; he might not have been there for all
the attention she paid to him.

She must have been rising twenty at the time. She was pale, with
colourless eyes, a long bony face. He could see her now, picking her
teeth with a matchstick, then pouring boiling water into the coffee-pot.

'I asked you to get dressed.'

He was hot. The smell of the hotel turned his stomach. Had she
sensed that he was not at his ease?

Calmly she'd taken off her wrap, her shift and pants, and, stark
naked, had gone and lain down on the unmade bed, lighting a cigarette.

'I'm waiting!' he'd told her impatiently, looking away with an effort.

'So am I.'

'I've a warrant for your arrest.'

'Well, arrest me then!'

'Get dressed and come along.'

'I'm all right like this.'

The whole thing was ludicrous. She was cool, quite passive, a little glint of irony showing in her colourless eyes.

'You say I'm under arrest. *I* don't mind. But you needn't ask me to give you a hand as well. I'm in my own place. It's hot, and I've a right to take my clothes off. Now, if you insist on my coming along with you just as I am, I'm not complaining.'

At least a dozen times he'd told her:

'Get your things on!'

And, perhaps because of her pallid flesh, perhaps because of the surrounding squalor, it seemed to him that he'd never seen a woman so naked as that. To no avail he'd thrown her clothes on the bed, had threatened her, then tried persuasiveness.

In the end he'd gone down and fetched two policemen, and the scene had become farcical. They'd had to wrap the girl forcibly in a blanket and carry her, like a packing-case, down the narrow staircase, while all the doors opened as they went by.

He'd never seen her since. He'd never heard her mentioned.

'Send her in!' he sighed.

He knew her at once. She didn't seem to have changed. He recognized her long pale face, the washed-out eyes, the big over-made-up mouth that looked like a raw wound. He recognized also, in her glance, the quiet irony of those who've seen so much that nothing's any longer important in their eyes.

She was simply dressed, with a light green straw hat, and she'd put on gloves.

'Still got it in for me?'

He drew on his pipe without answering.

'Can I have a seat? I heard you'd been promoted and in fact that's why I never ran into you again. Is it all right if I smoke?'

She took a cigarette from her bag and lit up.

'I want to tell you right away, with no hard feelings, that I was telling the truth that time. I got a year inside that I didn't deserve. There was a girl called Lulu all right, whom you didn't take the trouble to find. The two of us were together when we ran across that fat steamer. He picked us both up, but when he'd taken a good look at me, he told me to buzz off because he couldn't stand 'em skinny. I was outside in the passage when Lulu slipped me the pocket-book an hour after so's I could ditch it.'

'What became of her?'

'Five years ago she'd a little restaurant down South. I just wanted to show you everyone sometimes makes mistakes.'

'Is that why you came?'

'No. I wanted to talk to you about Alfred. If he knew I was here, he'd take me for a proper mug. I could've gone to Sergeant Boissier, who knows all about him.'

'Who's Alfred?'

'My husband. Lawfully wedded, too, before the mayor *and* the vicar, because he still goes to church. Sergeant Boissier pinched him two or three times, and one of those times he got Alfred five years in Fresnes.'

Her voice was almost harsh.

'The name Jussiaume doesn't mean much to you, perhaps, but when I tell you what they call him, you'll know who he is right away. There's been a lot about him in the papers. He's Sad Freddie.'

'Safe-breaking?'

'Yes.'

'You've had a row?'

'No. It's not what you'd think I've come for. I'm not that sort. So you see who Fred is now?'

Maigret had never set eyes on him, or, rather, only in the corridors, when the cracksman was waiting to be interrogated by Boissier. He called to mind vaguely a puny little man with anxious eyes, whose clothes seemed too big for his scrawny body.

'Of course, we don't look at him the same way,' she said. 'Poor blighter. There's more to him than you think. I've lived with him close on twelve years; I'm only starting to get to know him.'

'Where is he?'

'I'm coming to that, don't worry. I don't know where he is, but he's got in a proper jam without its being any of his fault, and that's why I'm here. Only you've simply got to trust me, and I know that's asking a lot.'

He was watching her with interest, because she spoke with appealing simplicity. She wasn't putting on airs, wasn't trying to impress him. If she took some time in coming to the point, it was because what she had to tell was genuinely complicated.

There was still a barrier between them, nevertheless, and it was this barrier that she was trying hard to break down, so that he wouldn't get a wrong idea of things.

About Sad Freddie, with whom he'd never had any personal dealings, Maigret knew little more than he'd heard at Headquarters. The man was a sort of celebrity, and the newspapers had tried their best to boost him into a romantic figure.

He'd been employed for years by the firm of Planchart, the safe-makers, and had become one of their most skilled workers. He was, even at that time, a sad, retiring youth, in poor health, throwing epileptic fits periodically.

Boissier would probably be able to tell Maigret how he had come to give up his job at Planchart's.

Whatever the cause, he had turned from installing safes to cracking them.

'When you first met him, had he still got a steady job?'

'Not likely. It wasn't me that sent him off the straight and narrow, in case that's what you've got in mind. He was doing odd jobs, sometimes he'd hire himself out to a locksmith, but it wasn't long before I saw what he was really up to.'

'You don't think you'd do better to see Boissier?'

'Housebreaking's his line, isn't it? But you deal with murder.'

'Has Alfred killed anybody?'

'Look, Chief-Inspector, I think we'll get along faster if you just let me talk. Alfred may be anything you'd like to call him, but he wouldn't murder for all the money in the world. May seem soppy to say so about a bloke like him, but he's sensitive, see? Why, he'd pipe his eye for the least little thing. I ought to know. Anyone else would say he was soft. But maybe it's because he's like that, that I fell in love with him.'

And she looked at him quietly. She'd uttered the word 'love' without particular emphasis, but with a sort of pride all the same.

'If one knew what was going on in his head, one wouldn't half get a surprise. Not that it matters. Far's you're concerned, he's just a thief. He got himself pinched once and did five years inside. I never missed going to see him a single visiting-day, and all that time I'd go back on my old beat, at the risk of getting in trouble, not having a proper card and those being the days when you still had to have one.

'He always hopes he'll pull off a big job and then we can go and live in the country. He's always dreamed of it ever since he was a nipper.'

'Where do you live?'

'On the Quai de Jemmapes, just opposite the Saint-Martin Lock. Know where I mean? We've two rooms above a café painted green, and it's very handy because of the 'phone.'

'Is Alfred there now?'

'No. I already told you I don't know where he is, and believe me I don't. He did a job, not last night, but the night before.'

'And he's cleared out?'

'Hang on, will you, Inspector! You'll see later on that everything I tell you's got its point. You know people that take tickets in the National Sweep at every draw, don't you? There are some of them that go without eating to buy them, because they reckon in a day or two they'll be in the money at last. Well, that's the way it is with Alfred. There're dozens of safes in Paris that he put in himself, and that he knows like the back of his hand. Usually, when you buy a safe, it's to put money or jewels away in.'

'He hopes to strike lucky one day?'

'You got it.'

She shrugged, as though speaking of a child's harmless craze. Then she added:

'He's just unlucky. Most times it's title-deeds it's impossible to sell or else business contracts he gets hold of. Only once there was real big dough, that he could've lived on quietly for the rest of his days, and that time Boissier pinched him.'

'Were you with him? Do you keep the look-out?'

'No. He never liked me to. At the start, he used to tell me where he was going to be on the job, and I'd fix it so I was nearby. When he spotted that, he gave up telling me anything.'

'For fear you'd get pulled in?'

'Maybe. Or it may have been because he's superstitious. See, even when we're living together, he's all alone really, and sometimes he doesn't say a word for two whole days. When I see him go out at night on his bicycle, I know what's up.'

Maigret remembered this characteristic. Some of the newspapers had dubbed Alfred Jussiaume the burglar-on-a-bike.

'That's another of his notions. He reckons that nobody, at night, is going to notice a man on a bike, specially if he's got a bag of tools slung over his shoulder. They'd take him for a bloke on his way to work. I'm talking to you like I would to a friend, see?'

Maigret wondered again why she had really come to his office and, as she took out another cigarette, he held a lighted match for her.

'We're Thursday today. On Tuesday night Alfred went out on a job.'

'Did he tell you so?'

'He'd been going out for several nights at the same time, and that's always a sign. Before breaking into a house or an office, he sometimes spends a week on the watch to get to know the people's habits.'

'And to make sure there'll be no one about?'

'No. That doesn't signify to him. I even think he'd rather work where there was somebody than in an empty house. He's a bloke that can get about without making a sound. Why, hundreds of times he's slipped into bed beside me at night and I never so much as knew he'd come home.'

'D'you know where he worked that night before last?'

'All I know, it was at Neuilly. And then I only found it out by chance. The day before, when I came in, he told me the police had asked to see his papers, and must've taken him for a dirty old man because they stopped him in the Bois de Boulogne, just by the place where women go and tidy up.

' "Where was it?" I asked him.

' "Behind the Zoo. I was coming back from Neuilly."

'Then, night before last, he took his bag of tools, and I knew he'd gone to work.'

'He hadn't been drinking?'

'Never touches a drop, doesn't smoke. He'd never be able to take it. He lives in terror of his fits, and he's that ashamed when it happens in the middle of the street, with masses of people who crowd round and feel sorry for him. He said to me before he set out:

' "I reckon this time we're really going down to live in the country." '

Maigret had begun to take notes which he was surrounding automatically with arabesques.

'What time did he leave the Quai de Jemmapes?'

'About eleven, like on the other nights.'

'Then he must have got to Neuilly round about midnight.'

'Maybe. He never rode fast, but then, at that time, there'd be no traffic.'

'When did you see him again?'

'I haven't seen him again.'

'So you think something may have happened to him?'

'He rang me up.'

'When?'

'Five in the morning. I wasn't asleep. I was worried. If he's always scared he'll have a fit in the street, I'm always scared it might happen while he's working, you see? I heard the 'phone ringing downstairs in the café. Our room's right up above. The owners didn't get up. I guessed it was for me, and I went down. I knew right away from his voice there'd been a hitch. He spoke very low

' "That you?"

' "Yes!"

' "Are you alone?"

' "Yes. Where are you?"

' "In a little café up by the Gare du Nord. Look, Tine," (he always calls me Tine), "I've simply got to make myself scarce for a bit."

' "Somebody see you?"

' "It's not that. I don't know. A bloke saw me, yes, but I'm not sure it was a policeman."

' "Got any money?"

' "No. It happened before I'd finished."

' "What happened?"

' "I was busy on the lock when my torch lit up a face in the corner of the room. I thought somebody'd come in silently and was watching me. Then I saw the eyes were dead." '

She watched Maigret.

'I'm sure he wasn't lying. If he'd killed anyone, he'd have told me. And I'm not going telling you any stories. I could tell he was near fainting at the other end. He's so scared of death. . . .'

'Who was it?'

'I don't know. He didn't make it very clear. He was going to hang up the whole time. He was scared someone'd hear him. He told me he was taking a train in a quarter of an hour. . . .'

'To Belgium?'

'Probably, as he was near the Gare du Nord. I looked up a time-table. There's a train at five forty-five.'

'You've no more idea what café he was 'phoning from?'

'I went on a scout round the district yesterday and asked some questions, but no good. They must've taken me for a jealous wife, and they weren't giving anything away.'

'So all he really told you was that there was a dead body in the room where he was working?'

'I got him to tell me a bit more. He said it was a woman, that her chest was all covered in blood, and that she was holding a telephone receiver in her hand.'

'Is that all?'

'No. Just as he was going to do a bunk—and I can imagine the state he was in!—a car drew up in front of the gate. . . .'

'You're sure he said the gate?'

'Yes. A wrought-iron gate. I remember it struck me particularly. Somebody got out and came towards the door. As the man went into the passage, Alfred got out of the house by the window.'

'And his tools?'

'He left them behind. He'd cut out a window-pane to get in. That I'm sure of, because he always does. I believe he'd do it even if the door was open, he's sort of faddy that way, or maybe superstitious.'

'So nobody saw him?'

'Yes. As he was going through the garden. . . .'

'He mentioned a garden as well?'

'I didn't make it up. As I say, just when he was going through the garden someone looked out of the window and shone a torch on him; maybe Alfred's own, which he hadn't taken with him. He jumped on his bike, went off without looking round, rode down as far as the Seine, I don't know exactly where, and threw the bike in, for fear they'd recognize him by it. He didn't dare come back home. He got to the Gare du Nord on foot and 'phoned me, begging me not to say a word. I pleaded with him not to clear off. I tried to reason with him. He finished up promising to write me *poste restante* saying where he'd be so I could go and join him.'

'He hasn't written yet?'

'There hasn't been time for a letter to get here. I went to the post office this morning. I've had twenty-four hours to think things over. I bought all the papers, thinking they'd surely say something about a murdered woman.'

Maigret picked up the telephone and called the police-station at Neuilly.

'Hello! Headquarters here. Any murder to report during the last twenty-four hours?'

'One moment, sir. I'll put you through to the desk. I'm only the duty constable.'

Maigret persisted for some time.

'No corpse found on the roads? No night calls? No bodies fished up from the Seine?'

'Absolutely nothing, Monsieur Maigret.'

'Nobody reported a shot?'

'Nobody.'

Lofty waited patiently, like someone making a social call, both hands clasped upon her bag.

'You realize why I came to you?'

'I think so.'

'First, I reckoned the police had maybe seen Alfred, and, in that case, his bike alone would have given him away. Then there were the tools he left behind. Now he's bolted over the frontier, no one'll ever believe his story. And he's no safer in Belgium or Holland than in Paris. I'd sooner see him in jail for attempted burglary, even if it meant five years all over again, than see him had up for murder.'

'The trouble,' Maigret retorted, 'is that there's no body.'

'You think he made it up or that I'm making it up?'

He didn't answer.

'It'll be easy for you to find the house he was working in that night. Maybe I shouldn't tell you this, but I'm sure you'll think of it yourself. The safe's bound to be one of those he put in at some time. Planchart's must keep a list of their customers. There can't be that many in Neuilly who bought a safe at least seventeen years back.'

'Apart from you, did Alfred have any girl-friends?'

'Ah! I guessed that was coming. I'm not jealous and, even if I was, I wouldn't come to you with a pack of lies to get my own back, if that's what you've got in mind. He hasn't a girl-friend because he doesn't want one, poor blighter. If he wanted to I'm the one who'd fix him up with as much as he liked.'

'Why?'

'Because life's not so much cop for him, as it is.'

'Have you any money?'

'No.'

'What are you going to do?'

'I'll get by, you know that all right. I only came here because I want it proved that Freddie didn't kill anyone.'

'If he wrote to you, would you show me his letter?'

'You'll read it before I do. Now that you know he's going to write me *post restante*, you'll have every post office in Paris watched. You forget that I know the racket.'

She had risen to her feet, very tall; she looked him over as he sat at his desk, from top to toe.

'If all the tales they tell about you are true, there's an even chance that you'll believe me.'

'Why?'

'Because otherwise you'd be a mug. And you're not one. Are you going to ring Planchart's?'

'Yes.'

'You'll keep me posted?'

He looked at her without replying, and realized that he couldn't restrain himself from smiling good-humouredly.

'Please yourself then,' she sighed. 'I could help you; you may know an awful lot, but there're things people like us understand better than you do.'

Her 'us' obviously stood for a whole world, the one that Lofty lived in, the world on the other side of the barrier.

'If Sergeant Boissier's not on holiday, I'm sure he'll bear me out in what I told you about Alfred.'

'He's not on leave. He's going tomorrow.'

She opened her bag, took from it a bit of paper.

'I'll leave you the 'phone number of the café underneath where we live. If by some fluke you need to come and see me, don't be scared that I'll start undressing. Nowadays, if it's left to me, I keep my clothes on!'

There was a touch of bitterness in her tone, but not much. A second later she was poking fun at herself:

'Much better for all concerned!'

It wasn't until he closed the door behind her that Maigret realized he had shaken, quite as a matter of course, the hand she'd held out to him. The wasp still buzzed in circles at ceiling level, as though seeking a way out, without thinking of the wide open windows. Madame Maigret had announced in the morning that she'd be coming round to the flower market and had asked him, if he were free about noon, to go and meet her there. It was noon now. He paused irresolute, leant out of the window from which he could see the splashes of vivid colour beyond the embankment of the quay.

Then he picked up the telephone with a sigh.

'Ask Boissier to drop in and see me.'

Seventeen years had slipped by since the absurd incident in the Rue de la Lune, and Maigret was now an important official in charge of the Homicide Branch. A funny notion came into his head, an almost childish craving. He picked up the telephone once more.

'The *Brasserie Dauphine*, please.'

As the door opened to admit Boissier, he was saying:

'Send me up a Pernod, will you?'

And, looking at the sergeant, who had large half-moons of sweat on his shirt underneath the arms, he changed it to:

'Make it two! Two Pernods, thank you.'

The blue-black moustache of Boissier, who came from Provence, twitched with pleasure, and he went over to sit on the window-sill, mopping his forehead.

II

AFTER swallowing a mouthful of Pernod, Maigret had to come to the point:

'Tell me, Boissier, old man, what d'you know about Alfred Jussiaume?'

'Sad Freddie?'

'Yes.'

And immediately the sergeant's brow had darkened, he'd shot Maigret a worried glance, had asked in a voice no longer the same, forgetting to take a sip of his favourite drink:

'Has he done a job?'

It was always like this with the sergeant, Maigret knew. He also knew why and, by using the utmost tact, had become the only chief-inspector to find favour in Boissier's eyes.

The latter, by rights, ought to have been one himself, and would have been a long time ago, had an absolute inability to spell and the handwriting of a first-form schoolboy not prevented his passing the simplest examinations.

For once, however, the administrative staff had not made a bloomer. They had appointed at the head of his branch Chief-Inspector Peuchet, an old has-been, always half-asleep and, save for drawing up the reports, it was Boissier who got through all the work and governed his colleagues.

That department wasn't concerned with homicide, as Maigret's was. It wasn't concerned with amateurs either, shop-assistants who run off one fine day with the till, or any tripe of that sort.

The customers Boissier and his men dealt with were professional thieves of every kind, from the jewel robbers who put up at the big hotels in the Champs-Élysées, to the bank-smashers and hustlers, who hid out mostly, like Jussiaume, in seedy neighbourhoods.

Because of this, they had an outlook quite different from that of the Special Division. In Boissier's line, they were all craftsmen, on both sides. The battle was a battle between experts. It wasn't so much a question of psychology, as of knowing, from A to Z, the little quirks and eccentricities of everyone.

It was not unusual to see the sergeant sitting quietly outside a café with a cat-burglar, and Maigret, for one, would have found it hard to hold a conversation of this sort with a murderer:

'Here, Julot, it's a long time since you did a job of work.'

'That's right, Sergeant.'

'When was the last time I pulled you in?'

'Must be going on six months, now.'

'Funds getting low, eh? I'll bet you're cooking something up.'

The idea that Sad Freddie might have done a bust without his knowledge put Boissier's back up.

'I don't know if he's really been on the job lately, but Lofty has just left my office.'

That was enough to reassure the sergeant.

'She doesn't know a thing,' he stated. 'Alfred's not the type to go blabbing his business to a woman, not even his own wife.'

The picture of Jussiaume that Boissier now set himself to draw was not unlike that previously outlined by Ernestine, even though he, the sergeant, tended rather to emphasize the professional angle.

'I get browned off with pinching a bloke like that and sending him to the nick. Last time, when they dished him out five years, I damn nearly gave his lawyer a piece of my mind for not knowing how to go about his job. He's wanting, that lawyer is!'

It was hard to define precisely what Boissier meant by 'wanting', but the point was plain enough.

'There's not another in Paris like Alfred for breaking into a house full of people without a sound and going to work there without even waking the cat. Technically, he's an artist. What's more, he doesn't need anyone to tip him off, keep a look-out and all that palaver. He works on his own, without ever getting jumpy. He doesn't drink, doesn't talk, doesn't go acting tough round the bars. With his talents he ought to have enough dough to choke himself with. He knows just where to find hundreds of safes that he put in himself, and exactly how they work, and you'd think he'd only have to go and help himself. Instead, every time he has a go, he comes a cropper or else gets a spell inside.'

Perhaps Boissier only spoke thus because he saw a parallel between Sad Freddie's career and his own, except that he himself enjoyed a constitution that could withstand any number of *apéritifs* imbibed on café terraces and nights spent standing to in all kinds of weather.

'The joke is that, if they put him away for ten years or twenty years, he'd start all over again directly he came out, even supposing he was seventy and on crutches by then. He's got it into his head that he only needs one lucky break, just one, and that he's earned it by this time.'

'He's had a nasty knock,' Maigret explained. 'It seems that he was just getting a safe open, somewhere at Neuilly, when he spotted a dead body in the room.'

'What'd I tell you? That could only happen to him. Then he cleared off? What'd he do with the bike?'

'In the Seine.'

'He's in Belgium?'

'I dare say.'

'I'll ring through to Brussels, unless you don't want him picked up?'

'I want him picked up most decidedly.'

'D'you know where this took place?'

'I know that it was at Neuilly, and that the house has a garden with a wrought-iron gate in front.'

'That'll be easy. Be back right away.'

Maigret had the grace to order, in his absence, two more Pernods from the *Brasserie Dauphine*. It brought back to him not only a whiff of the Rue de la Lune period, but a whiff of the South of France, particularly of a little dive in Cannes, where he'd once been on a case and, all of a sudden, the whole business was lifted out of the general rut, took on almost the aspect of a holiday task.

He hadn't definitely promised Madame Maigret to meet her in the flower market, and she knew that she ought never to wait for him. Boissier returned with a file, from which he produced, first of all, the official photographs of Alfred Jussiaume.

'That's what he looks like!'

An ascetic face, really, rather than that of a guttersnipe. The skin was stretched tight across the bones, the nostrils were long and pinched, and the stare had an almost mystical intensity. Even in these harshly lit photographs, full face and side view, collarless, with a protruding Adam's apple, the man's immense loneliness made itself felt, and his sadness that was still in no way aggressive.

Born to be fair game, it had been natural for him to be hunted.

'Would you like me to read you his record?'

'It's not necessary today. I'd rather go over the file with an open mind. What I'd like to have is the list.'

Boissier was pleased by this last sentence. Maigret knew that he would be, as he said it, for he intended it as a tribute to the sergeant.

'You knew I'd have it?'

'I was certain you would.'

For, in point of fact, Boissier really did know his job. The list in question was that, drawn from the books of Messrs. Planchart, of the safes installed in Alfred Jussiaume's time.

'Wait till I look up Neuilly. You're sure it's at Neuilly?'

'I've Ernestine's word for it.'

'You know, she wasn't really so dumb to come and look you up. But why you?'

'Because I arrested her, sixteen or seventeen years ago, and because she played me quite a dirty trick.'

This didn't surprise Boissier, it was all in the game. They both knew where they stood. From the glasses, the pale-coloured Pernod could already be smelt all over the office, inciting the wasp to a kind of frenzy.

'A bank . . . it's certainly not that . . . . . Freddie never took to banks, because he's windy of the burglar-alarms. . . . A petrol company that's been out of business for ten years. . . . A scent manufacturer . . . he went bankrupt a year ago.'

Boissier's finger came to a stop finally on a name, on an address.

'Guillaume Serre, dentist, 43b, Rue de la Ferme, Neuilly. You know it? It's just past the Zoo, a street parallel with the Boulevard Richard-Wallace.'

'I know.'

They looked at each other for a moment.

'Busy?' asked Maigret.

And in so doing he was again pandering deliberately to Boissier's self-esteem.

'I was classifying some files. I'm off to Brittany tomorrow.'

'Shall we go?'

'I'll get my coat and hat. Shall I 'phone Brussels first?'

'Yes. And Holland as well.'

'Right you are.'

They went there by bus, standing on the outside platform. Then, in the Rue de la Ferme, quiet and countrified, they found a little café-restaurant where there were four tables on the terrace between green potted plants, and sat down there for lunch.

There were only three bricklayers in white smocks inside, drinking red wine with their meal. Flies circled round Maigret and Boissier. Farther along, on the other side of the road, they could see a black wrought-iron gate that should correspond with No. 43b.

They weren't in any hurry. If there'd really been a dead body in the house, the murderer had had over twenty-four hours in which to get rid of it.

A waitress in a black dress and a white apron looked after them, but the proprietor came over to greet them.

'Nice weather, gentlemen.'

'Nice weather. Would you, by any chance, know of a dentist anywhere about here?'

A sidelong nod.

'There's one opposite, over there, but I don't know what he's like. My missus prefers to go to one in the Boulevard Sebastopol. This one'd be expensive, I'd say. He hasn't all that many patients.'

'D'you know him?'

'A wee bit.'

The proprietor paused, looked them over for a while, particularly Boissier.

'You'd be police-officers, eh?'

Maigret thought it better to say yes.

'Has he done anything?'

'We're just making a few enquiries. What does he look like?'

'Taller and bigger than you and me,' he said, looking this time at the chief-inspector. 'I weigh fifteen stone ten, and he must go all of sixteen.'

'How old?'

'Fifty? Round about, anyway. Not too well turned out, which is odd, him being a dentist. Seedy looking, like what old bachelors get.'

'He isn't married?'

'Wait a bit. . . . Matter of fact, if I remember rightly, he did get married, it'd be about two years ago. . . . There's an old woman living in the house, too—his mother, I suppose—who does the shopping every morning. . . .'

'No maid?'

'Only a charwoman. Mind you, I wouldn't be sure. I only know him because he comes in here now and then for a foxy drink.'

'Foxy?'

'In a manner of speaking. People like him don't come to places like this, as a rule. And when he does, he always takes a quick look round at his house, as if to make sure he can't be seen. And he looks sheepish, coming up to the counter.

' "Glass of red wine!" he'll say.

'Never takes anything else. I know right away not to put the bottle back on the shelf, because he's bound to have another. He drinks 'em at a gulp, wipes his mouth, and he's got the change all ready in his hand.'

'Does he ever get drunk?'

'Never. Just the two glasses. As he goes out, I see him slip a cachou or a clove into his mouth, so that his breath won't smell of wine.'

'What's his mother like?'

'A little old woman, very dried up, dressed in black, who never passes the time of day with anybody and doesn't look easy to get on with.'

'His wife?'

'I've scarcely seen her except when they go by in the car, but I've heard tell she's a foreigner. She's tall and stout like him, with a high colour.'

'D'you think they're away on holiday?'

'Let's see. I believe I still served him with his two glasses of red two or three days ago.'

'Two or three?'

'Wait a bit. It was the evening when the plumber came to mend the beer-pump. I'll go and ask my wife, to make sure I'm not talking through my hat.'

It was two days previously, in other words Tuesday, a few hours before Alfred Jussiaume discovered a dead woman's body in the house.

'Can you remember the time?'

'He comes, as a rule, about half-past six.'

'On foot?'

'Yes. They've got an old car, but that's the time of day he takes his constitutional. You can't tell me what this is all about?'

'It's not about anything at all. A check-up.'

The man didn't believe them, you could see it plainly in his eyes.

'You'll be back?'

And, turning to the chief-inspector: 'You're not Monsieur Maigret, by any chance?'

'Did someone say so?'

'One of the bricklayers thought he recognized you. If you are, my wife'd be very happy to meet you in the flesh.'

'We'll be back,' he promised.

They'd had a jolly good meal, and they'd drunk the Calvados which the proprietor, who came from Falaise, had offered them. Now they were walking together down the pavement on the shady side of the street. Maigret was taking little puffs at his pipe. Boissier had lit a cigarette, and two fingers of his right hand were stained brown with nicotine, coloured like a meerschaum pipe.

One might have been fifty miles outside Paris, in almost any small town. There were more private houses than buildings with flats, and some were big middle-class family mansions about a century or two old.

There was only the one gate in the street, a black wrought-iron gate beyond which a lawn was spread like a green carpet in the sunshine. On the brass plate was the legend:

GUILLAUME SERRE
Dental Surgeon

And, in smaller letters:

From 2 to 5 p.m.
By appointment only

The sun struck full on the façade of the house, warming its yellowish stone, and, except for two of the windows, the shutters were closed. Boissier could sense that Maigret was undecided.

'Are you going in?'

'What have we got to lose?'

Before crossing over, he cast a quick glance up and down the street and suddenly frowned. Boissier looked in the direction towards which Maigret was gazing so steadily.

'Lofty!' he exclaimed.

She'd just come from the Boulevard Richard-Wallace, and was wearing the same green hat as earlier that morning. Catching sight of Maigret and the sergeant, she paused for a moment, then made straight for them.

'Surprised to see me?'

'You've got hold of the address?'

'I 'phoned your office about half an hour ago. I wanted to tell you that I'd found the list. I knew it must be somewhere about. I've seen Alfred looking at it, and putting in crosses here and there. When I came out of your office this morning I thought of a place where Alfred might have hidden it.'

'Where?'

'Do I have to tell you?'

'It might be as well.'

'I'd rather not. Not right away.'

'What else did you find?'

'How d'you know I found anything else?'

'You'd no money this morning and you came here by cab.'

'You're right. There was some money.'

'A lot?'

'More than I'd have expected.'

'Where's the list?'

'I burnt it.'

'Why?'

'Because of the crosses. They might have marked the places where Alfred worked and, whatever else, I'm not going to give you evidence against him.'

She glanced at the house.

'You going in?'

Maigret nodded.

'D'you mind if I wait for you outside the café?'

She hadn't said a word to Boissier who, for his part, was staring at her rather sternly.

'Please yourself,' Maigret told her.

And, followed by the sergeant, he crossed from the shade into the sunlight, while the tall figure of Ernestine moved off towards the café terrace.

It was ten past two. Unless the dentist had gone on holiday, he ought, according to the brass plate, to be waiting for patients in his surgery. There was an electric bell-push on the right of the gateway. Maigret pressed it and the gate swung open automatically. They crossed the small garden and found another bell-push by the front door, which was not mechanically operated. After the peal of the bell inside, there was a long silence. The two men listened, both of them aware that someone was lurking on the other side of the panel, and looked at each other.

At last a chain was unhooked, the bolt withdrawn, a thin crack showed round the lintel of the door.

'Have you an appointment?'

'We'd like to speak to Monsieur Serre.'

'He only sees people by appointment.'

The crack did not widen. They could dimly make out, behind it, a silhouette, the thin face of an old woman.

'According to the brass plate . . .'

'The plate is twenty-five years old.'

'Would you tell your son that Chief-Inspector Maigret wishes to see him?'

The door remained for a moment longer without moving, then opened; it revealed a wide hallway with a black-and-white tessellated floor which resembled that of a convent corridor, and the old lady who stood back to let them enter would not have looked out of place dressed as a nun.

'You must excuse me, Chief-Inspector, but my son doesn't really care to receive casual patients.'

The woman was far from unpresentable. She'd an innate elegance and dignity which were remarkable. She was attempting to efface by her smile any bad impression that she might have created.

'Do please come in. I'm afraid that I'll have to ask you to wait a moment or two. For some years, my son has been accustomed, especially in summer, to take a siesta, and he's still lying down. If you'd care to come this way. . . . .'

She opened, on the left, a pair of polished oaken doors, and Maigret was reminded more than ever of a convent or, better still, a rich parsonage. Even the soft, insidious smell reminded him of something; he didn't know what, he tried to remember. The drawing-room that she showed them into was lit only by daylight seeping through the slots of the shutters, and to enter it from outside was like stepping into a cool bath.

The noises of the town, one felt, could never penetrate this far, and it was as if the house and everything in it had remained unchanged for more than a century, that the tapestried chairs, the occasional tables, the piano and the chinaware had always stood in the same place. Even the enlarged photographs on the walls, in black wooden frames, which looked like photographs from the time of Nadar. The man strapped into a collar of the last century, above the chimney-piece, wore bushy side-whiskers and, on the opposite wall, a woman of about forty, her hair parted in the middle, looked like the Empress Eugénie.

The old lady, who might almost have stepped herself out of one of those frames, hovered at their side, motioned them to seats, folded her hands like a Sister of Mercy.

'I don't wish to seem inquisitive, Chief-Inspector. My son has no secrets from me. We've never lived apart, although he's now past his fiftieth year. I haven't the slightest idea of your business or of what brings you here, and, before going to disturb him, I would like to know . . .'

She left the sentence unfinished, glancing from one to the other with a gracious smile.

'Your son is married, I believe?'

'He's been married twice.'

'Is his second wife at home?'

A shade of melancholy clouded her eyes, and Boissier began to cross and uncross his legs; this was not the sort of place he felt at home in.

'She's no longer with us, Chief-Inspector.'

She moved softly to close the door, and returning, sat down in the corner of a sofa, keeping her back very straight, as young girls are taught to hold themselves in convent schools.

'I hope she hasn't done anything silly?' she asked in a low voice.

Then, as Maigret remained silent, she gave a sigh, resigned herself to begin once more:

'If it's anything to do with her, I was right to question you before disturbing my son. It is about her that you've come, isn't it?'

Did Maigret make a vague sign of assent? He was not aware of doing so. He was too intrigued by the atmosphere of this house, and even more by this woman, behind whose meekness he could sense an indomitable strength of will.

Everything about her was in good taste: her clothes, her bearing and her voice. One might have expected to meet her in some château or, better still, in one of those enormous country houses that are like museums of a bygone age.

'After he became a widower, fifteen years ago, the thought of re-marrying didn't enter my son's head for a long time.'

'He did remarry, two years ago, if I'm not mistaken?'

She showed no surprise at finding him so well-informed.

'He did, indeed. Two and a half years ago exactly. He married one of his patients, a woman also of a certain age. She was then forty-seven. Of Dutch origin, she lived alone in Paris. I won't live for ever, Chief-Inspector. As you see me now, I am seventy-eight.'

'You don't look it.'

'I know. My mother lived to the age of ninety-two, and my grand-mother was killed in an accident at ninety-eight.'

'And your father?'

'He died young.'

She spoke as though this were of no importance, or rather as if men in general were doomed to die young.

'I almost encouraged Guillaume to marry again, by saying that thus he would not be left to live alone.'

'The marriage was unhappy?'

'I wouldn't say that. Not to begin with. I think that the trouble arose mainly from her being a foreigner. There are all sorts of little things that one cannot get used to. I don't quite know how to explain. Oh yes. Food, for instance! A preference for this or that dish! Perhaps, too, when she married my son she imagined him to be wealthier than he actually is.'

'She'd no income of her own?'

'A certain competence. She was not badly off, but, with the rising cost of living . . .'

'When did she die?'

The old woman's eyes opened wide.

'Die?'

'I'm sorry. I thought she was dead. You yourself speak of her in the past tense.'

She smiled.

'That's true. But not for the reason you imagine. She isn't dead; only for us it's as though she were, she's gone away.'

'After a quarrel?'

'Guillaume is not the kind of man who quarrels.'

'With you?'

'I am too old to quarrel now, Chief-Inspector. I've seen too much. I know life too well, and I let everybody . . .'

'When did she leave the house?'

'Two days ago.'

'Did she tell you she was going?'

'My son and I knew that she would go in the end.'

'She had talked to you about it?'

'Often.'

'Did she give you any reasons?'

She did not reply at once, seemed to be pondering.

'Do you want me to tell you frankly what I think? If I hesitate, it's because I fear you may laugh at me. I don't like to discuss such things in front of men, but I suppose that a police officer is rather like a doctor or a priest.'

'You are a Roman Catholic, Madame Serre?'

'Yes. My daughter-in-law was a Protestant. That made no difference. You see, she was at the awkward age for a woman. We all, more or less, have to go through a few years during which we are not our normal selves. We get upset over trifles. We are apt to see things out of perspective.'

'I understand. That's what it was?'

'That and other things, probably. In the end, she dreamed only of her native Holland, spent all day writing to friends that she had kept up with over there.'

'Did your son ever go to Holland with her?'

'Never.'

'So she left on Tuesday?'

'She went on the nine-forty from the Gare du Nord.'

'The night-train?'

'Yes. She had spent the whole day packing.'

'Your son went with her to the station?'

'No.'

'Did she take a taxi?'

'She went to fetch one from the corner of the Boulevard Richard-Wallace.'

'She hasn't got in touch with you since?'

'No. I don't suppose she feels it necessary to write to us.'

'Was there any question of a divorce?'

'I've told you that we are Catholics. Moreover, my son has no wish to get married again. I still do not understand why the police have seen fit to call upon us.'

'I would like to ask you, Madame, exactly what happened here on Tuesday night. One moment. You haven't a maid, have you?'

'No, Chief-Inspector. Eugénie, our charwoman, comes every day from nine till five.'

'Is she here today?'

'You have come on her day off. She'll come in again tomorrow.'

'She lives in the neighbourhood?'

'She lives at Puteaux, on the other side of the Seine. Above an iron-monger's shop, directly opposite the bridge.'

'I suppose she helped your daughter-in-law to pack?'

'She brought the cases downstairs.'

'How many cases?'

'One trunk and two leather suit-cases precisely. Then there was a jewel-box and a dressing-case.'

'Eugénie left at five as usual?'

'She did, indeed. Please forgive me if I seem disconcerted, but this is the first time I've ever been cross-questioned like this and I must confess . . .'

'Did your son go out that evening?'

'What time of evening do you mean?'

'Let's say before dinner.'

'He went out for his usual stroll.'

'I suppose he went to have an *apéritif*?'

'He doesn't drink.'

'Never?'

'Nothing except a glass of wine and water at meal-times. Still less those horrible things called *apéritifs*.'

It seemed then that Boissier, who was sitting on his best behaviour in his arm-chair, sniffed the smell of aniseed which still clung to his moustache.

'We sat down to table as soon as he came in. He always takes the same stroll. It became a habit with him in the days when we had a dog that had to be exercised at set times and, I declare, it's become second nature to him.'

'You haven't a dog nowadays?'

'Not for four years. Not since Bibi died.'

'Or a cat?'

'My daughter-in-law loathed cats. You see! I spoke of her again in the past tense, and it's because we really do think of her as belonging to the past.'

'The three of you had dinner together?'

'Maria came down just as I was bringing in the soup.'

'There was no quarrelling?'

'None. Nobody spoke during the meal. I could tell that Guillaume, after all, was a little upset. At first sight, he seems cold, but really he's a terribly sensitive boy. When one has lived on terms of intimacy with someone for over two years. . . .'

Maigret and Boissier had not heard a thing. But she, the old lady, was sharp of hearing. She bent her head as though she were listening. It was a mistake, for Maigret understood, rose to his feet, and went and opened the door. A man, undoubtedly taller, broader and heavier than the chief-inspector, stood there, slightly shamefaced, for he had plainly been eavesdropping for some time.

His mother had told the truth when she claimed that he'd been taking a siesta. His sparse hair, ruffled, clung to his forehead and he'd pulled on trousers over his white shirt, with his collar still unbuttoned. He wore carpet slippers on his feet.

'Won't you come in, Monsieur Serre?' asked Maigret.

'I beg you pardon. I heard voices. I thought . . .'

He spoke deliberately, turning his heavy, brooding stare upon each of them in turn.

'These gentlemen are police officers,' his mother explained, rising to her feet.

He didn't ask for any explanation, stared at them again, buttoned up his shirt.

'Madame Serre was telling us that your wife left the day before yesterday.'

This time he turned round to face the old lady, his brows together. His big frame was flaccid, like his face, but, unlike many fat men, he did not give an impression of agility. His complexion was very pale and sallow, tufts of dark hair sprouted from his nostrils, from his ears, and he had enormously bushy eyebrows.

'What exactly do these gentlemen want?' he asked, carefully spacing out the syllables.

'I don't know.'

And even Maigret felt at a loss. Boissier wondered how the chief-inspector was going to get out of the situation. These weren't the sort of people who could be put through the third degree.

'Actually, Monsieur Serre, the question of your wife merely cropped up in the course of conversation. Your mother told us that you were lying down, and we had a little talk while we were waiting for you. We're here, my colleague and myself'—the term 'colleague' gave Boissier so much pleasure!—'simply because we've reason to believe that you have been the victim of an attempted burglary.'

Serre was not the sort of man who is unable to look others in the face. Far from it, he stared at Maigret as though attempting to read his innermost thoughts.

'What gave you that idea?'

'Sometimes we come into possession of confidential information.'

'You are speaking, I suppose, of police informers?'

'Let's put it like that.'

'I'm sorry, gentlemen.'

'Your house hasn't been burgled?'

'If it had been, I would have lost no time in lodging a complaint myself with the local police.'

He wasn't trying to be civil. Not once had he shown even the vestige of a smile.

'You are, however, the owner of a safe?'

'I believe that I'd be within my rights in refusing to answer you. I don't mind telling you, however, that I have got one.'

His mother was attempting to make signs to him, advising him, probably, not to be so ill-tempered.

He realized this and remained obdurate.

'If I'm not mistaken, it's a safe installed by Messrs. Planchart about eighteen years ago.'

He remained unperturbed. He continued to stand, whilst Maigret and Boissier sat in semi-darkness, and Maigret saw that he had the same heavy jowl as the man in the portrait, the same eyebrows. The chief-inspector wondered whimsically what he'd look like with side-whiskers.

'I don't remember when I had it put in, nor is that anybody's business but mine.'

'I noticed, as we came in, that the front door is secured by a chain and a safety-lock.'

'So are lots of front doors.'

'You sleep on the first landing, your mother and yourself?'

Serre deliberately made no reply.

'Your study and surgery are on the ground floor?'

From a gesture on the part of the old lady, Maigret understood that these rooms led out of the drawing-room.

'Would you mind if I took a look round?'

He paused, opened his mouth, and Maigret felt certain it was to say no. His mother sensed this, too, for she intervened.

'Why not comply with these gentlemen's request? They will see for themselves that there has been no burglary.'

The man shrugged his shoulders, his expression as stubborn, as sullen, as ever, and he refrained from following them into the neighbouring rooms.

Madame Serre showed them first into a study as peaceful and old-fashioned as the drawing-room. Behind a black-leather-bottomed chair, stood a big safe, painted dark green, of a rather obsolete type. Boissier went up to it, smoothed the steel with a professional touch.

'You see that everything is in order,' said the old woman. 'You mustn't mind my son being in a bad temper, but . . .'

She stopped as she saw the latter, framed in the doorway, fixing them with the same morose stare.

Then, waving a hand towards the bound volumes which filled the shelves, she went on, with a strained sprightliness:

'Don't be surprised to see mostly books on law. They're part of my husband's library, who was a solicitor.'

She opened one last door. And here the furnishings were more commonplace; it might have been any dental surgery, with a mechanical chair and the usual instruments. Up to half the height of the window, the panes were frosted.

On their way back through the study Boissier crossed to one of the windows, again felt with his fingers on it, then gave Maigret a significant nod.

'Has this window-pane been put in recently?' asked the latter in his turn.

It was the old woman who answered immediately:

'Four days ago. The window was open during the big thunderstorm which I'm sure you remember.'

'Did you call in the glazier?'

'No.'

'Who replaced the pane?'

'My son. He likes doing odd jobs. He always sees to any of our little household repairs.'

At which Guillaume Serre said with a touch of irritation:

'These gentlemen have no right to pester us, Mamma. Don't answer any more questions.'

She turned so that her back was towards him, and smiled at Maigret in a way that meant plainly:

'Don't mind him. I did warn you.'

She showed them to the front door, while her son remained standing in the centre of the drawing-room, and leaned forward to whisper:

'If you have anything to say to me, come and call when he isn't here.'

They were outside in the sunlight again, which made the clothes cling immediately to their skin. Once outside the gate—its faint creak was reminiscent of a convent gate—they caught sight, on the opposite pavement, of Ernestine's green hat as she sat at a table outside the café-restaurant.

Maigret halted. They could have turned left and avoided her. If they joined her, it would look almost as though they had to give her an account of themselves.

Perhaps out of a sense of decency, the chief-inspector growled: 'Shall we go and have one?'

With an enquiring expression, she watched them come towards her.

III

'WHAT did you do today?' asked Madame Maigret, as they sat down to eat in front of the open window.

In the houses opposite also people could be seen eating, and, on every side, the same bright splashes of shirts showed where the men had taken off their jackets. Some of them, who'd finished dinner, were leaning on their elbows out of the window. Wireless music could be heard playing, babies crying, raised voices. A few concierges had brought their chairs out in front of their doorsteps.

'Nothing out of the way,' replied Maigret. 'A Dutchwoman who may have been murdered, but who's probably still alive somewhere.'

It was too early to talk about it. On the whole, he'd behaved slackly. They'd sat about for a long time outside the little café in the Rue de la Ferme, Boissier, Ernestine and himself, and of the three it was Ernestine who'd been the most worked up.

She took umbrage:

'He made out it wasn't true?'

The proprietor had brought them pints of beer.

'Actually he didn't say anything. It was his mother who did the talking. On his own, he'd have thrown us out.'

'He says there wasn't a corpse in the study?'

She'd obviously found out from the café owner about the residents in the house with the wrought-iron gate.

'Then why didn't he tell the police that somebody'd tried to burgle the place?'

'According to him no one tried to burgle him.'

Of course she knew all about Sad Freddie's little ways.

2

'Wasn't there a pane missing in one of the windows?'

Boissier looked at Maigret as if advising him to say nothing, but the chief-inspector took no notice.

'A pane has been mended recently; it appears that it got broken four or five days ago, on the night of the storm.'

'He's lying.'

'Somebody's lying, certainly.'

'You think it's me?'

'I didn't say so. It might be Alfred.'

'Why should he have told me all that story on the 'phone?'

'Perhaps he didn't,' interposed Boissier, watching her narrowly.

'And what should I have made it up for? Is that what you think, too, Monsieur Maigret?'

'I don't think anything.'

He was smiling vaguely. He felt comfortable, almost blissful. The beer was cool, and in the shade it smelt almost like the country, perhaps because the Bois de Boulogne was close by.

A lazy afternoon. They'd drunk two pints apiece. Then, so as not to leave the girl stranded so far from the centre of Paris, they gave her a lift in their taxi and dropped her at the Châtelet.

'Ring me up directly you get a letter.'

He felt she was disappointed in him, that she'd imagined him otherwise. She must be telling herself that he'd got old, had become like the rest of them, and couldn't be much bothered with her case.

'D'you want me to put back my leave?' Boissier had suggested.

'I suppose your wife's done all the packing?'

'The bags are at the station already. We were due to go on the six o'clock train tomorrow morning.'

'With your daughter?'

'Naturally.'

'Off you go.'

'Won't you be needing me?'

'You've trusted me with the file.'

Once alone in his office, he nearly dozed off in his chair. The wasp was no longer there. The sun had moved round to the other side of the quay. Lucas had been off duty since noon. He called Janvier, who had been the first to take his leave, in June, because of a wedding in some branch of his family.

'Sit down. I've got a job for you. You've made out your report?'

'I've just this minute finished it.'

'Right! Take a note of this. First you've got to look up, at the Town Hall in Neuilly, the maiden name of a Dutchwoman who, two and a half years ago, married a man called Guillaume Serre, residing at 43b Rue de la Ferme.'

'Easy.'

'I dare say. She must have been living in Paris for some time. You must try to find out where, what she did, what relatives she had, how much money, etc. . . .'

'Right you are, Chief.'

'She's supposed to have left the house in the Rue de la Ferme on Tuesday, between eight and nine in the evening, and to have taken the night-train to Holland. She went to fetch a taxi herself from the corner of the Boulevard Richard-Wallace to take her luggage.'

Janvier was writing words in columns on a page of his note-book.

'That all?'

'No. Get some help to save time. I want the people in the neighbourhood, tradesmen and so on, questioned about the Serres.'

'How many are there?'

'Mother and son. The mother's nearly eighty and the son's a dentist. Try to locate the taxi. Also make enquiries from the staff at the station and on the train.'

'Can I have transport?'

'You can.'

And that was about all he'd done that afternoon. He'd asked to be put through to the Belgian police, who had Sad Freddie's description but had not yet found him. He also had a long conversation with the passport inspector on the frontier, at Jeumont. The latter had himself gone over the train which Alfred was thought to have taken, and didn't remember any passenger resembling the expert safe-cracker.

That meant nothing. He just had to wait. Maigret signed a few papers on behalf of the Chief, went to have a drink at the *Brasserie Dauphine* together with a colleague in the Records Office, and then back home by bus.

'What shall we do?' asked Madame Maigret, when the table had been cleared.

'Let's go for a stroll.'

Which meant that they'd amble along as far as the main boulevards to finish up sitting at a café terrace. The sun had set. The air was becoming cooler, though gusts of warm air still seemed to rise up from the paving-stones. The bay-windows of the *brasserie* were open, and a depleted orchestra played inside. Most of the customers sat there without speaking, like them, at their tables, watching the passers-by, and their faces melted more and more into the dusk. Then the electric-light made them look quite different.

Like the other couples, they turned back towards home, Madame Maigret's hand crooked in her husband's arm.

After that it was another day, as clear and sunny as the one before.

Instead of going straight to Headquarters, Maigret made a detour by the Quai de Jemmapes, identified the green-painted café, near the

Saint-Martin Lock, with the sign 'Snacks served at all hours', and went in to lean against the counter.

'A white wine.'

Then he put the question. The Auvergnat who served him answered unhesitatingly:

'I don't know at what time exactly, but someone rang up. It was already daylight. My wife and I didn't get up, because, at that time, it couldn't have been for us. Ernestine went down. I heard her talking a long time.'

That was one thing at least she had not lied about.

'What time did Alfred go out, the night before?'

'Eleven, maybe? Maybe earlier. What I do remember is that he took his bike.'

A door led straight from the café into the passageway, from which a staircase mounted to the floors above. The wall of the staircase was whitewashed, as in the country. One could hear the racket made by a crane unloading gravel from a barge a little farther on.

Maigret knocked at a door, which half-opened; Ernestine appeared in her underclothes and merely said:

'It's you!'

Then she went at once to fetch her dressing-gown from the unmade bed, and slipped it on.

Did Maigret smile in memory of the Ernestine-that-used-to-be?

'You know, it's really a kindness,' she said frankly. 'I'm not a pretty sight these days.'

The window was open. There was a blood-red geranium. The bed-spread was red, too. A door stood open into a little kitchen, out of which came a good smell of coffee.

He didn't quite know what he'd come for.

'There was nothing at the *poste restante* yesterday evening?'

She answered, worried:

'Nothing.'

'You don't think it odd that he hasn't written?'

'Perhaps he's just being canny. He must be surprised to see nothing in the papers. He probably thinks I'm being watched. I was just going to the post office.'

An old trunk lay in a corner.

'Those are his belongings?'

'His and mine. Between the two of us, we don't own much.'

Then, with an understanding look:

'Like to make a search? Of course! I know. It's your duty. You'll find a few tools, because he's got a spare set, also two old suits, some dresses and a bit of linen.'

As she spoke, she was turning out the contents of the trunk onto the floor, opening the drawers of a dressing-table.

'I've been thinking it over. I've grasped what you were getting at yesterday. Of course somebody must have been lying. Either it's those people, the mother and her son, or it's Alfred, or it's me. You've no reason to believe any of us in particular.'

'Has Alfred no relatives in the country?'

'He's got no relatives anywhere now. He only knew his mother, and she's been dead twenty years.'

'You've never been anywhere together outside Paris?'

'Never farther than Corbeil.'

He couldn't be hiding out at Corbeil. It was too near. Maigret was beginning to think that he hadn't gone to Belgium either.

'There's no place he used to talk about, that he'd have liked to visit one day?'

'He always said the country, no special part. That summed it all up, to him.'

'Were you born in the country yourself?'

'Near Nevers, in a village called Saint-Martin-des-Prés.'

She took from a drawer a postcard that showed the village church, standing opposite a pond which served to water cattle.

'Did you show him this?'

She understood. Girls like Ernestine soon understand.

'I'd be surprised to find him there. He really was near the Gare du Nord when he 'phoned me.'

'How d'you know?'

'I found the bar, yesterday evening. It's in the Rue de Maubeuge, near a leather-goods shop. It's called the *Bar du Levant*. The owner remembers him because he was the first customer that day. He'd just lit the percolator when Alfred got there. Wouldn't you like a cup of coffee?'

He didn't like to refuse, but he'd just drunk white wine.

'No offence.'

He had some difficulty finding a taxi in those parts, eventually was driven to the *Bar du Levant*.

'A thin little chap, sad-looking, with eyes all red as if he'd been cry-ing,' they told him.

Unquestionably Alfred Jussiaume, who often had red-rimmed eyes.

'He talked a long time at the 'phone, drank two coffees without sugar and went off towards the station, looking round him as if he was scared of being followed. Has he done anything wrong?'

It was ten o'clock when Maigret at last climbed the staircase at Headquarters, where dust-motes still floated like a mist in the sunlight. Contrary to his usual custom, he didn't glance in through the glass partition of the waiting-room, and went past into the Duty Room, which was almost empty.

'Janvier not in yet?'

'He came about eight and went out again. He left a note on your desk.'

The note said:

The woman is called Maria Van Aerts. She is fifty-one and comes from Sneeck, in Friesland, Holland. I'm going to Neuilly, where she lived in a boarding-house, Rue de Longchamp. Haven't found the taxi yet. Vacher's looking after the station.

Joseph, the office-boy, opened the door.

'I didn't see you come in, Monsieur Maigret. A lady's been waiting for you half an hour.'

He held out an appointment-slip, on which old Madame Serre had inscribed her name in small, sharp handwriting.

'Shall I show her in?'

Maigret put on his jacket that he'd just taken off, went to open the window, filled his pipe and sat down.

'Yes, show her in.'

He wondered what she would seem like outside the framework of her home, but, to his surprise, she didn't look out of place at all. She wasn't dressed in black, as on the day before; she wore a frock with a white ground, on which dark patterns were traced. Her hat was not ludicrous. She moved forward with assurance.

'You were more or less expecting me to call, weren't you, Chief-Inspector?'

He had not been expecting it and refrained from telling her so.

'Do sit down, Madame.'

'Thank you.'

'The smoke doesn't worry you?'

'My son smokes cigars all day long. I was so upset yesterday at the way he received you! I tried to make signs to you not to persist, because I know him.'

She showed no nervousness, chose her words carefully, aimed at Maigret now and then a sort of conspiratorial smile.

'I think it is I who brought him up badly. You see, I had but the one child and, when my husband died, he was only seventeen years old. I spoilt him. Guillaume was the only man in the house. If you have any children . . .'

Maigret looked at her to try to sum up her background and did not succeed. Something made him ask:

'Were you born in Paris?'

'In the house that you came to yesterday.'

It was a coincidence to find in one case two people born in Paris. Almost invariably, the people he dealt with were more or less directly connected with the provinces.

'And your husband?'

'His father, before him, used to be a solicitor in the Rue de Tocque-ville, seventeenth *arrondissement*.'

That made three! To end up in the atmosphere, so absolutely pro-vincial, of the house in the Rue de la Ferme!

'My son and myself have almost always lived alone together, and I suppose that is what has made him a little unsociable.'

'I understood that he'd been married before.'

'He was. His wife didn't live long.'

'How many years after their marriage did she die?'

She opened her mouth; he guessed that a sudden thought made her pause. He even had the impression of seeing a slight flush mount to her cheeks.

'Two years,' she said at last. 'That's curious, is it not? It only struck me just now. He lived for two years with Maria, as well.'

'Who was his first wife?'

'A person of very good family, Jeanne Devoisin, whom we met one summer at Dieppe, at the time when we used to go there every year.'

'Was she younger than he?'

'Let me see. He was thirty-two. She was more or less the same age. She was a widow.'

'Had she any children?'

'No. I don't think she had any relatives, except a sister living in Indo-China.'

'What did she die of?'

'A heart attack. She had a weak heart and spent most of her time under the care of doctors.'

She smiled again:

'I haven't told you yet why I am here. I nearly telephoned to you yesterday, when my son went out for his evening stroll, then I thought it would be more polite to come and call on you. I wish to apologize for Guillaume's attitude towards you and to say that his ill-humour was not directed at you personally. He has such a fierce temperament.'

'So I saw.'

'At the very idea that you could suspect him of dishonest action. . . . He was like that even as a small boy. . . .'

'He lied to me?'

'I beg your pardon?'

The old lady's face expressed genuine surprise.

'Why should he have lied to you? I don't understand. You didn't really ask any questions. It's precisely to answer any which you should wish to put to me that I have come here. We have nothing to hide. I've no idea of the circumstances that have led you to bother about us. It must be some misunderstanding, or some neighbour's spitefulness.'

'When was the window-pane broken?'

'I told you or my son told you, I can't remember now: during the

thunderstorm last week. I was on the first floor and I hadn't had time
to shut all the windows when I heard a crash of glass.'

'Was it in broad daylight?'

'It must have been six o'clock in the evening.'

'Which means the charwoman, Eugénie, was no longer there?'

'She leaves us at five. I think I explained that to you also. I haven't
told my son that I was coming to see you. I thought that you might
like, perhaps, to visit the house, and it would be easier when he's not
there.'

'You mean during his late afternoon stroll?'

'Yes. You do understand that there's nothing to hide in our home,
and that, if it weren't for Guillaume's nature, everything would have
been cleared up yesterday.'

'You realize, Madame Serre, that you came here of your own free
will?'

'Yes, of course.'

'And that it's you who want me to question you?'

She nodded her head in confirmation.

'We'll go over your movements again, then, from the last meal that
you, your son and your daughter-in-law took together. Your daughter-
in-law's luggage was ready. In which part of the house was it?'

'In the corridor.'

'Who brought it down?'

'Eugénie brought down the suit-cases, and my son took charge of the
trunk, too heavy for her.'

'Is it a very big trunk?'

'What they call a cabin-trunk. Before her marriage, Maria travelled
a lot. She has lived in Italy and Egypt.'

'What did you have to eat?'

The question seemed both to amuse and surprise her.

'Let me see! As it's I who do the cooking, I should be able to remember. Vegetable soup, to start with. We always have vegetable soup, so
good for the health. Then I did grilled mackerel and potato purée.'

'And the sweet?'

'A chocolate custard. Yes. My son has always adored chocolate
custard.'

'No argument broke out at table? What time did the meal end?'

'About half-past seven. I put the dishes in the kitchen sink and went
upstairs.'

'So you weren't present at the departure of your daughter-in-law.'

'I wasn't very anxious to be. Moments such as those are painful, and
I prefer to avoid emotion. I said *au revoir* to her downstairs, in the
drawing-room. I've nothing against her. Everybody's as they are made
and . . .'

'Where was your son during that time?'

'In his study, I think.'

'You've no idea whether he had a last conversation with his wife?'

'It's unlikely. She'd gone upstairs again. I heard her in her room, getting ready.'

'Your house is very solidly built, like most old houses. I suppose that, from the first floor, it's hard to hear sounds coming from downstairs?'

'Not for me,' she answered, pursing her lips.

'What d'you mean?'

'That I have keen hearing. Not even a floorboard can creak without my hearing it.'

'Who went to fetch the taxi?'

'Maria. I told you so yesterday.'

'Did she stay out long?'

'Fairly long. There's no rank nearby, and one has to wait for a taxi to come cruising by.'

'Did you go to the window?'

She hesitated imperceptibly.

'Yes.'

'Who carried the trunk as far as the taxi?'

'The driver.'

'You don't know what company the cab belonged to?'

'How would I know that?'

'What colour was it?'

'Reddish-brown, with a coat-of-arms on the door.'

'Can you remember the driver?'

'Not very well. I think he was small and rather fat.'

'How was your daughter-in-law dressed?'

'She wore a mauve frock.'

'No coat?'

'She had it over her arm.'

'Was your son still in the study?'

'Yes.'

'What happened then? Did you go down?'

'No.'

'You didn't go to see your son?'

'It was he who came up.'

'Immediately?'

'Not long after the taxi drove away.'

'Was he upset?'

'He was as you have seen him. He's of a rather gloomy nature. I explained to you that he's really a highly sensitive man, likely to be affected by the smallest happenings.'

'Did he know that his wife was not coming back?'

'He suspected it.'

'She told him so?'

'Not exactly. She just hinted. She talked of the necessity to change her ideas, to see her own country again. Once over there, you understand. . . .'

'What did you do then?'

'I dressed my hair for the night.'

'Your son was in your room?'

'Yes.'

'He didn't leave the house?'

'No. Why?'

'Where does he garage his car?'

'A hundred yards away, where some old stables have been turned into private garages. Guillaume has hired one of them.'

'So he can take his car out and put it back without being seen?'

'Why should he want to hide?'

'Did he go downstairs again?'

'I have no idea. I think so. I go to bed early, and he usually reads until eleven o'clock or midnight.'

'In the study?'

'Or in his room.'

'His room is near yours?'

'Next door. There's a bathroom in between us.'

'Did you hear him go to bed?'

'Certainly.'

'At what time?'

'I didn't put on the light.'

'You didn't hear any noise later?'

'None.'

'I suppose that you're the first down in the morning?'

'In summer I come down at half-past six.'

'Did you go round all the rooms?'

'I went first into the kitchen to put some water on to boil, then I opened the windows, because that's the time when the air is still cool.'

'You went into the study then?'

'Probably.'

'You don't remember doing so?'

'I almost certainly did.'

'The broken pane was already repaired?'

'I suppose so . . . yes. . . .'

'Did you notice any disorder in the room?'

'None, except for some cigar ends, as always, in the ash-trays, and perhaps a book or two lying around. I don't know what all this means, Monsieur Maigret. As you see, I answer your questions frankly. I came especially to do so.'

'Because you were worried?'

'No. Because I was ashamed of the way Guillaume treated you. And also because I sense something mysterious behind your visit. Women aren't like men. In my husband's time, for instance, if there were a noise in the house at night, he never moved from his bed, and it was I who went to look. You understand? It's probably the same with your own wife. Really, it's in a way for the same reason that I'm here. You talked about burglary. You seemed preoccupied with the question of Maria.'

'You haven't had any news of her?'

'I don't expect to receive any. You're hiding certain facts and that makes me curious. It's the same with sounds in the night. I hold that mysteries don't exist, that one only has to look at things squarely for them to become perfectly simple.'

She was watching him, sure of herself, and Maigret had a slight feeling that she looked upon him as a child, as another Guillaume. She seemed to be saying:

'Tell me everything that's worrying you. Don't be frightened. You'll see that it'll all come right.'

He, too, looked her straight in the face.

'A man broke into your house that night.'

The old woman's eyes were incredulous, with a tinge of pity, as though he'd still believed in werewolves.

'What for?'

'To burgle the safe.'

'Did he do it?'

'He got into the house by cutting out a pane of glass to open the window.'

'The pane that was already broken in the thunderstorm? No doubt he put it back afterwards.'

She still refused to take what he was saying seriously.

'What did he take away?'

'He took nothing away, because at a certain moment his electric torch lit up something that he hadn't expected to find in the room.'

She was smiling.

'What sort of thing?'

'The dead body of a middle-aged woman, which may have been that of your daughter-in-law.'

'He told you that?'

He looked at the white-gloved hands that didn't tremble.

'Why don't you ask this man to come and repeat his accusations to me?'

'He's not in Paris.'

'Can't you make him come here?'

Maigret preferred to make no reply. He wasn't too pleased with himself. He was beginning to wonder if he too was not falling under the

influence of this woman who had the comforting serenity of a Mother
Superior.

She didn't get up, didn't fidget, didn't show indignation either.

'I have no idea what it's all about and I won't ask you. Perhaps you
have some good reason for believing in this man. He's a burglar, isn't
he? Whilst I am merely an old woman of seventy-eight who never did
anyone any harm.'

'Allow me, now that I know where we are, to invite you cordially to
come to our house. I will open every door for you, I will show you anything you may wish to see. And my son, once he's acquainted with the
facts, will not fail, in his turn, to answer your questions.'

'When will you come, Monsieur Maigret?'

Now she had risen to her feet still perfectly at ease, and there was
nothing aggressive in her manner, just a slight touch of bitterness.

'Probably this afternoon. I don't know yet. Has your son used the car,
these last few days?'

'You can ask him, if you like.'

'Is he at home now?'

'It's possible. He was there when I went out.'

'Eugénie as well?'

'She is certainly there.'

'Thank you.'

He showed her to the door. Just as they reached it, she turned round.

'I'd like to ask a favour,' she said gently. 'When I've gone, try for a
moment to put yourself in my place, forgetting that you have spent your
life in dealing with crime. Imagine that it's you who are suddenly being
asked the questions you put to me, you who are being suspected of
killing in cold blood.'

That was all. She only added:

'Until this afternoon, Monsieur Maigret.'

Once the door was closed, he stood for a full minute without moving
by the doorway. Then he went to look out of the window, soon caught
sight of the old lady walking with quick short steps, in full sunshine,
towards the Pont Saint-Michel.

He picked up the telephone.

'Get me the police-station at Neuilly.'

He didn't ask to be put through to the station officer, but to a
sergeant whom he knew.

'Vanneau? Maigret here. I'm well, thanks. Listen. It's a bit tricky.
Jump in a car and get round to 43b, Rue de la Ferme.'

'The dentist place? Janvier, who came here yesterday evening, spoke
to me about him. Something to do with a Dutchwoman, isn't it?'

'Never mind. Time's getting on. The chap's not easy to handle, and I
can't ask for a warrant just now. You've got to act quickly, before his
mother gets there.'

'Is she far away?'

'At the Pont Saint-Michel. I suppose she's going to take a cab.'

'What shall I do with the man?'

'Bring him in, on some excuse. Tell him whatever you like, that you need him as a witness. . . .'

'And then?'

'I'll be there. Just the time it takes to get downstairs and jump in a car.'

'Suppose the dentist's not at home?'

'You keep watch and grab him before he gets inside.'

'Bit irregular, eh?'

'Quite.'

As Vanneau was going to ring off, he added:

'Take somebody with you and put him to watch the stables that they've turned into garages in the same street. One of the garages is hired by the dentist.'

'Right you are.'

A moment later Maigret was hurrying down the stairs and climbing into one of the police-cars parked in the courtyard. As the car turned round towards the Pont Neuf, he thought he caught sight of Ernestine's green hat. He wasn't sure of it and preferred not to lose time. To tell the truth, he'd given way to a sudden fit of resentment against Lofty.

Once they'd crossed the Pont Neuf, he felt remorseful, but it was too late.

Couldn't be helped! She'd wait for him.

IV

THE police-station was on the ground floor of the Town Hall, an ugly square building that stood in the middle of a waste land, with sparse trees around and a dirty flag dangling. Maigret could have gone straight from outside into the Duty Rooms; so as not to come face to face with Guillaume Serre, he took a roundabout way through the draughty corridors, where he soon got lost.

Here too the slackness of summer held sway. Doors and windows were open, documents fluttered on tables in the empty rooms, while clerks in shirt-sleeves exchanged seaside gossip and an occasional tax-payer wandered disconsolately about in search of an endorsement or a signature.

Maigret finally managed to light upon a policeman who knew him by sight.

'Sergeant Vanneau?'

'Second on the left, third door along the passage.'

'Would you go and fetch him for me? There should be someone with him. Don't say my name out loud.'

A few moments later Vanneau joined him.

'Is he there?'

'Yes'

'How did it go off?'

'Middling. I'd taken good care to bring along a police summons. I rang. A servant answered and I asked to see her master. I had to wait about a bit in the passage. Then the bloke came down, and I handed him the paper. He read it, looked at me without saying anything.

' "If you'd like to come with me, I've a car outside."

'He shrugged his shoulders, took a Panama hat down from the hall-stand, shoved it on his head, and followed me out.

'Now he's sitting on a chair. He still hasn't uttered a word.'

A minute or two later, Maigret went into Vanneau's office, found Serre there smoking a very black cigar. The chief-inspector took up a seat in the sergeant's chair.

'I'm sorry to have troubled you, Monsieur Serre, but I'd like you to answer a few questions.'

As on the day before, the huge dentist surveyed him broodingly, and he had no trace of cordiality in his gloomy stare. Maigret, all of sudden, realized what the man reminded him of: the sort of sultan that one used to see pictures of at one time. He had the girth, the manifest weight; in all probability the strength, too. For, despite his fat, he gave the impression of being very strong. He had also the disdainful calm of those pashas that are depicted on cigarette packets.

· Instead of making some sign of agreement, uttering a polite common-place or even voicing a protest, Serre took a buff-coloured form from his pocket, cast his eye over it.

'I've been summoned here by the Police Superintendent of Neuilly,' he said. 'I look forward to hearing what this superintendent requires from me.'

'Am I to understand you refuse to answer my questions?'

'Emphatically.'

Maigret paused. He'd seen all sorts, the mutinous, the pig-headed, the wilful, the wily, but none had ever answered him back with such unruffled determination.

'I suppose it's no good arguing?'

'Not in my opinion.'

'Or trying to point out that your attitude doesn't show you in a good light?'

This time the other merely sighed.

'Very well. Wait. The superintendent will see you now.'

Maigret went in search of the latter, who did not at once understand what was expected of him, and only grudgingly agreed to play his part. His quarters were more comfortable, almost sumptuous in comparison with the rest of the offices, and there was a marble clock on the mantelpiece.

'Show Monsieur Serre in!' he told the man on duty.

He motioned him to a chair with a red velvet seat.

'Do sit down, Monsieur Serre. It's just a matter of a routine check-up, and I won't waste your time.'

The superintendent consulted a form which had just been brought to him.

'You are, I believe, the owner of a motor-vehicle registered under the number RS 8822 L?'

The dentist confirmed this with a nod. Maigret had gone over to sit on the window-sill and was watching him very thoughtfully.

'The vehicle in question is still in your possession?'

Another nod of assent.

'When was the last time you used it?'

'I believe I've the right to know the reason for this interrogation.'

The superintendent shifted in his chair. He didn't at all like the task which Maigret had entrusted to him.

'Just suppose that your car had been involved in an accident. . . .'

'Has it been?'

'Suppose the number had been notified to us as that of a car which had knocked somebody down?'

'When?'

The police officer threw Maigret a reproachful look.

'Tuesday evening.'

'Where?'

'Near the Seine.'

'My car didn't leave the garage on Tuesday evening.'

'Somebody might have used it without your knowledge.'

'I doubt it. The garage is locked up.'

'You're prepared to swear that you didn't use the car on Tuesday evening, or later during the night?'

'Where are the witnesses to the accident?'

Once again the superintendent looked anxiously to Maigret for support. The latter, realizing that this was leading nowhere, motioned to him not to take it any further.

'I've no further questions, Monsieur Serre. Thank you.'

The dentist rose, seemed for a moment to fill the room with his bulk, put on his Panama hat and left the room, after turning to stare fixedly at Maigret.

'I did what I could. As you saw.'

'I saw.'

'Did you get any lead out of it?'

'Perhaps.'

'That's a man who'll make trouble for us. He's a stickler for his rights.'

'I know'.

It seemed almost as if Maigret was unconsciously imitating the dentist. He had the same sombre, heavy expression. He, in turn, made for the door.

'What's he supposed to have done, Maigret?'

'I don't know yet. It may be that he's killed his wife.'

He went to thank Vanneau, and found himself outside once more, where the police-car awaited him. Before climbing in, he had a drink at the bar on the corner and catching sight of himself in the mirror, wondered what he'd look like wearing a panama hat. Then he smiled wryly at the thought that it was, in a way, a case of two heavy-weights engaged in a fight.

He said to the driver:

'Go round by the Rue de la Ferme.'

Not far from 43b, they caught sight of Serre walking along the pavement with long, rather indolent strides. As some fat men do, he straddled slightly. He was still smoking his long cigar. As he passed the garage he couldn't have failed to notice the plain-clothes man who was keeping a look-out there and had no means of taking cover.

Maigret was reluctant to stop the car at the house with the black wrought-iron gate. What good would it do? They probably wouldn't let him in.

Ernestine was waiting for him in the glass-panelled anteroom at Headquarters. He showed her into his office.

'Any news?' she asked him.

'Not a thing.'

He was in a bad temper. She didn't know that he rather liked feeling bad-tempered at the beginning of a difficult case.

'I had a card this morning. I brought it to you.'

She handed him a coloured postcard depicting the Town Hall at Le Havre. There was no inscription, no signature, nothing save Lofty's address, c/o *poste restante*.

'Alfred?'

'It's his handwriting.'

'He didn't go over to Belgium?'

'Doesn't look like it. He must have fought shy of the frontier.'

'D'you think he might try to get away by sea?'

'It isn't likely. He's never set foot on a boat. I'm going to ask you something, Monsieur Maigret, but you've got to give me a straight answer. Suppose he was to come back to Paris, what'd happen to him?'

'You want to know if he'd be detained?'

'Yes.'

'For attempted burglary?'

'Yes.'

'Nobody could detain him, because he wasn't caught red-handed, and, for another thing, Guillaume Serre hasn't laid a complaint, even denies that anybody broke into his house.'

'So they'd let him alone?'

'Unless he was lying and something quite different happened.'

'Can I promise him that?'

'Yes.'

'In that case, I'll put a notice in the Personal Column. He always takes the same paper, because of the crossword.'

She looked at him hard for a moment.

'You don't seem too sure about things.'

'What things?'

'The case. Yourself. I don't know. Did you see the dentist again?'

'Half an hour ago.'

'What did he say?'

'Nothing.'

She'd nothing more to say either and used the telephone ringing as an excuse to take her leave.

'What is it?' Maigret growled into the mouthpiece.

'It's me, Chief. Could I see you in your room?'

A few seconds later Janvier came into the office briskly, obviously very pleased with himself.

'I've got plenty of leads. Shall I give 'em to you right away? You got a bit of time to spare?'

His enthusiasm was a little damped by the behaviour of Maigret, who'd just taken off his coat and was loosening his tie to set his thick neck free.

'First, I went to the boarding-house I told you about. It's a bit like the hotels on the left bank, with potted palms in the hall and old ladies sitting around in cane chairs. There aren't many guests much under fifty. Most of 'em are foreigners. English women, Swiss and Americans, who go to museums and write endless letters.'

'Well?'

Maigret knew the kind of thing. It wasn't worth going on about.

'Maria Van Aerts lived there for a year. They remember her, because she made herself popular in the place. She seems to've been very gay and laughed a lot, shaking her great big bosom. She used to stuff herself with pastries, went to all the lectures at the Sorbonne.'

'That all?' said Maigret, meaning that he couldn't see what Janvier was so excited about.

'Nearly every day she used to write letters of eight to ten pages.'

The chief-inspector shrugged his shoulders, then examined the sergeant with more interest in his eye. He had caught on.

'Always to the same woman, a school friend who lives in Amsterdam and whose name I got hold of. This friend came to see her once. They shared a room for three weeks. I've an idea that even when married Maria Serre kept on writing. The friend's called Gertrude Oosting, she's the wife of a brewer. It shouldn't be hard to find out her address.'

'Ring through to Amsterdam.'

'Will you be wanting the letters?'

'The recent ones, if possible.'

'That's what I thought. Brussels still hasn't any news of Sad Freddie.'

'He's in Le Havre.'

'Shall I 'phone Le Havre?'

'I'll do it myself. Who's free next door?'

'Torrence came back to duty this morning.'

'Send him to me.'

Another heavy-weight, who wouldn't pass unnoticed on the pavement of an empty street.

'You go and stick yourself down in Neuilly, Rue de la Ferme, facing 43b, a house with a garden and an iron gate in front. Don't bother to take cover. Far from it. If you see a chap come out, bigger and taller than you, follow him so that he can see you.'

'Anything else?'

'Arrange to be relieved part of the night. There's a man from Neuilly on duty a bit farther on, opposite the garage.'

'What if the bloke goes off by car?'

'Take one of ours and park it along the kerb.'

He hadn't the energy to go home for lunch. It was hotter than the day before. There was thunder in the air. Most men were walking about with their jackets over their arms, and urchins were swimming in the Seine.

He went to have a bite at the *Brasserie Dauphine*, first having drunk, as if as a challenge, a couple of Pernods. Then he went to see Moers of the Technical Branch, under the overheated roof of the Palais de Justice.

'Let's say about eleven in the evening. Bring the things you need. Take someone with you.'

'Yes, Chief.'

He'd sent out a call to the police at Le Havre. Had Sad Freddie taken a train at the Gare du Nord after all, to Lille, for instance; or, having telephoned Ernestine, had he made a dash straight away for the Gare Saint-Lazare?

He must have gone to ground in some cheap lodging, or be wandering from bar to bar, drinking baby bottles of Vichy water, unless he was trying to stow away on board some ship. Was it as hot in Le Havre as it was in Paris?

They still hadn't found the taxi that was supposed to have picked up

Maria Serre and her luggage. The staff at the Gare du Nord had no recollection of her.

Opening the paper, about three o'clock, Maigret read Ernestine's message in the Personal Column:

Alfred.   Return Paris.   No danger.
All arranged.   Tine.

At half-past four he found himself still in his chair, the newspaper on his knee. He hadn't turned the page. He'd gone to sleep, and his mouth felt sticky, his back cricked.

None of the squad cars were in the courtyard and he had to take a taxi from the end of the quay.

'Rue de la Ferme, in Neuilly. I'll show you where to stop.'

He nearly dozed off again. It was five to five when he stopped the cab opposite the already familiar café. There was no one at the tables outside. Farther on the burly shape of Torrence could be seen, pacing up and down in the shade. He paid the driver, sat down with a sigh of relief.

'What can I get you, Monsieur Maigret?'

Beer, of course! He had such a thirst he could have swallowed five or six pints at a gulp.

'He hasn't been in again?'

'The dentist? No. I saw his mother, this morning, going down towards the Boulevard Richard-Wallace.'

The wrought-iron gate creaked. A wiry little woman started to walk along the opposite pavement and Maigret settled for his drink, caught her up just as she reached the edge of the Bois de Boulogne.

'Madame Eugénie?'

'What d'you want?'

The Neuilly household wasn't conspicuous for its affability.

'A little chat with you.'

'I've no time to chat. There's all the housework to do when I get home.'

'I'm a police officer.'

'That makes no odds.'

'I'd like to ask you a few questions.'

'Do I have to answer?'

'It would certainly be better to.'

'I don't like policemen.'

'You're not obliged to. D'you like your employers?'

'They stink.'

'Old Madame Serre as well?'

'She's a bitch.'

They were standing by a bus stop. Maigret raised his arm to stop a cruising taxi.

'I'm going to take you home.'

'I don't care all that much for being seen with a copper, but I suppose it's worth it.'

She climbed into the cab with dignity.

'What have you got against them?'

'What about you? Why are you sticking your nose into their business?'

'Young Madame Serre has gone away?'

'Young?' she said ironically.

'Let's say the daughter-in-law.'

'She's gone, yes. Good riddance.'

'Was she a bitch, too?'

'No.'

'You didn't like her?'

'She was always digging into the larder, and when it came to lunch-time, I couldn't find half what I'd got ready.'

'When did she go?'

'Tuesday.'

They were crossing the Pont de Puteaux. Eugénie tapped on the glass.

'Here we are,' she said. 'D'you need me any more?'

'Could I come up with you for a moment?'

They were on a crowded square, and the charwoman made towards an alleyway, to the right of a shop, began to climb a staircase that smelt of slops.

'If only you could tell them to leave my son alone.'

'Tell whom?'

'The other coppers. The ones from hereabouts. They never stop making trouble for him.'

'What does he do?'

'He works.'

'Doing what?'

'How should I know? Can't be helped if the housework isn't done for you. I can't clean up after others all day long and do my own as well.'

She went to open the window, for a strong, stuffy smell hung about, but it wasn't untidy and, except for a bed in one corner, the sort of drawing-cum-dining-room was almost dainty.

'What's all the to-do?' she asked, taking off her hat.

'Maria Serre can't be found.'

'Course not, as she's in Holland.'

'They can't find her in Holland either.'

'Why do they want to find her?'

'We've reason to believe that she's been murdered.'

A tiny spark kindled in Eugénie's brown eyes.

'Why don't you arrest them?'

'We haven't any proof yet.'

'And you're counting on me to get you some?'

She put some water to heat on the gas, came over to Maigret again.

'What happened on Tuesday?'

'She spent all day packing.'

'Wait a moment. She'd been married two and a half years, hadn't she? I suppose she had a good many things of her own.'

'She'd at least thirty dresses and as many pairs of shoes.'

'Was she smart?'

'She never threw anything out. Some of the dresses dated back ten years. She didn't wear them, but she wouldn't have given them away for all the money in the world.'

'Mean?'

'Aren't all rich people mean?'

'I was told that all she took with her was a trunk and two suitcases.'

'That's right. The rest went a week before.'

'You mean she sent other trunks away?'

'Trunks, packing-cases, cardboard boxes. A removal van came to fetch the lot, Thursday or Friday last.'

'Did you look at the labels?'

'I don't remember the exact address, but the stuff was booked for Amsterdam.'

'Did your employer know?'

'Of course he did.'

'So her departure had been decided on for some time?'

'Since her last attack. After each attack she'd talk of going back to her own country.'

'What kind of attacks?'

'Heart, so she said.'

'She'd a weak heart?'

'Seems like it.'

'Did a doctor come and see her?'

'Doctor Dubuc.'

'Did she take any medicine?'

'After each meal. They all did. The other two still do and they've each a little bottle of pills or drops beside their plate.'

'What's wrong with Guillaume Serre?'

'I don't know.'

'And his mother?'

'Rich people always have something wrong with them.'

'Did they get on well?'

'Sometimes they didn't speak to each other for weeks.'

'Maria Serre wrote a lot of letters?'

'Nearly from morning till night.'

'Did you ever happen to take them to the post?'

'Often. They were always to the same person, a woman with a funny name who lives in Amsterdam.'

'Are the Serres well off?'

'I reckon so.'

'What about Maria?'

'Sure. Otherwise he wouldn't have married her.'

'Did you work for them when they got married?'

'No.'

'You don't know who did the housework at that time?'

'They're always changing their daily help. It's my last week now. Soon as anybody begins to know the form, they pack in.'

'Why?'

'How would you like to see the lumps of sugar counted in the sugar-bowl and have a half-rotten apple picked out for your sweet?'

'Old Madame Serre?'

'Yes. Just because at her age she works all day, which is her own funeral, she's onto you like a shot if you're unlucky enough to be caught sitting down for a moment.'

'Does she tell you off?'

'She's never told me off. I'd like to see her! It's far worse. She's only too polite, she looks at you in a down-hearted sort of way as if it made her sad to see you.'

'Did anything strike you when you came to work on Wednesday morning?'

'No.'

'You didn't notice if a window had been broken during the night, or whether there was fresh putty round one of the panes?'

She nodded.

'You've got the wrong day.'

'Which day was it?'

'Two or three days before, when we had that big thunderstorm.'

'You're sure of that?'

'Certain. I even had to polish the floor of the study because the rain had come into the room.'

'Who put in the pane?'

'Monsieur Guillaume.'

'He went to buy it himself?'

'Yes. He brought back the putty. It was about ten o'clock in the morning. He had to go to the ironmonger's in the Rue de Longchamp. They never have a workman in if they can do without one, and Monsieur Guillaume unstops all the drains himself.'

'You're certain about the date?'

'Absolutely.'

'Thank you very much.'

Maigret had no further business there. There was really nothing more for him to do at the Rue de la Ferme either. Unless, of course,

Eugénie was merely repeating a piece that she'd been taught to say and, in that case, she was a better liar than most.

'You don't think they've killed her?'

He didn't answer, went on towards the door.

'Because of the window-pane?'

There was a slight hesitation in her tone.

'Does the window have to be broken on the day you said?'

'Why? Do you want to see them go to jail?'

'Nothing I'd like better. But now that I've told the truth. . . .'

She regretted it. For two pins she'd have gone back on her statement.

'You could always go and ask at the ironmonger's where he bought the glass and the putty.'

'Thank you for the tip.'

He stood for a moment in front of the shop outside, which happened in fact to be an ironmonger's. But it wasn't the right one. He waited for a taxi.

'Rue de la Ferme.'

There was no point in leaving Torrence and the plain-clothes man from Neuilly to kick their heels on the pavement any longer. The recollection of Ernestine playing her little joke in the Rue de la Lune came back to him, and he didn't find it at all funny, began to think about her. For it was she who'd started him off on this business. He'd been a fool to rush into it. Only this morning, in the police superintendant's office, he'd made a proper ass of himself.

His pipe tasted foul. He crossed and uncrossed his legs. The partition was open between himself and the driver.

'Go round by the Rue de Longchamp. If the ironmonger's is still open, stop there for a moment.'

It was a toss-up. This would be his last throw. If the ironmonger's was closed, he wouldn't bother to come back, Ernestine and Sad Freddie notwithstanding. Anyway, what proof was there that Alfred had ever really broken into the house in the Rue de la Ferme?

He'd gone off on his bike from the Quai de Jemmapes, agreed, and at daybreak he'd telephoned his wife. But nobody knew what they'd said to each other.

'It's open!'

Of course, the ironmonger's, where the hardware department could be seen inside. A tall youth in a grey smock came to meet Maigret between the galvanized tin pails and the brooms.

'Do you sell sheet glass?'

'Yes, sir.'

'And putty?'

'Certainly. Have you brought the measurements?'

'It's not for myself. Do you know Monsieur Serre?'

'The dentist? Yes, sir.'

'Is he a customer of yours?'

'He's got an account here.'

'Have you seen him recently?'

'*I* haven't, because I only got back from my holiday day before yesterday. He might have come in while I was away. I can easily tell you by looking up the book.'

The salesman didn't ask the reason why, but dived into the semi-darkness of the shop, opened a ledger that lay on a tall, raised desk.

'He bought a sheet of window-glass last week.'

'Could you tell me which day?'

'Friday.'

The thunderstorm had occurred on Thursday night. Eugénie had been right, and old Madame Serre as well!

'He bought half a pound of putty, too.'

'Thank you.'

It hung by a thread, by an unthinking gesture on the part of the young man in the grey smock who wouldn't be long in shutting up shop. He was turning over the entries in the ledger, more or less for form's sake. He said:

'He came back again this week.'

'What!'

'Wednesday. He bought a pane of the same size, forty-two by sixty-five, and another half-pound of putty.'

'You're sure?'

'I can even tell you that he was in early, because it's the first sale made that day.'

'What time d'you open?'

An important point since, according to Eugénie, who started work at nine, all the window-panes had been in good repair on Wednesday morning.

'Well, we get in at nine, but the boss comes down at eight to open the shop.'

'Thanks, old chap. You're a bright lad.'

The bright lad must have wondered for some time afterwards why this man, who had looked so depressed when he came in, now seemed to be in such high spirits.

'I suppose there's no danger of anyone destroying the pages in this ledger?'

'Why would anybody do that?'

'Why, indeed! All the same, I advise you to keep a look out. I'll send someone round tomorrow morning to photostat them.'

He took a card from his pocket, handed it to the young man, who read with astonishment:

Chief-Divisional-Inspector Maigret
Central Police Headquarters
Paris.

'Where to now?' asked the driver.

'Pull up for a moment in the Rue de la Ferme. You'll see a little café on your left. . . .'

This deserved a pint of beer. He nearly called Torrence and the plain-clothes man to have one with him, but finally merely asked the driver in.

'What'll you have?'

'Mine's a white wine and Vichy.'

The street was gilded by the sun. They could hear the breeze rustling through the big trees in the Bois de Boulogne.

There was a black wrought-iron gate farther up the road, a square of greensward, a house as serene and well-ordered as a convent.

Somewhere in this house there lived an old woman like a Mother Superior and a sort of sultan with whom Maigret had a score to settle.

It was good to be alive.

V

THE rest of the day went as follows. First of all, Maigret drank two pints of beer with the taxi-driver, who had only the one white wine and Vichy water himself. By that time it was beginning to get cooler and, as he climbed back into the cab, he'd the notion of driving round to the boarding-house that Maria Van Aerts had stayed in for a year.

There was nothing in particular for him to do there. He was simply following his habit of nosing round people's homes in order to understand them better.

The walls were cream-coloured. Everything was creamy, luscious, as in a dairy, and the proprietress with her floury face looked like a cake with too much icing on it.

'What a lovely person, Monsieur Maigret! And what a wonderful companion she must have made for her husband! She wanted to get married so much.'

'You mean she was looking for a husband?'

'Don't all young girls dream of a bridegroom?'

'She was about forty-eight when she lived here, if I'm not mistaken?'

'But she was still so young at heart! Anything could make her laugh.

Would you believe it, she loved to play practical jokes on her fellow-guests. Near the Madeleine, there's a shop I'd never noticed before I found out about it through her, that sells all sorts of joke-novelties, mechanical mice, spoons that melt in the coffee, gadgets that you slide under the table-cloth to lift someone's plate up all of a sudden while they're eating, glasses that you can't drink from, and I don't know what all! Well, she was one of its best customers! A very cultured woman, all the same, who'd been to every museum in Europe and used to spend whole days at the Louvre.'

'Did she introduce you to her prospective husband?'

'No. She was secretive by nature. Perhaps she didn't like to bring him here, for fear that some of the others might be envious. He was a man of very imposing presence, who looked like a diplomat, I believe.'

'Aha!'

'He's a dentist, she told me, but only sees a few patients, by appointment. He belongs to a very rich family.'

'And Mademoiselle Van Aerts herself?'

'Her father left her a good deal of money.'

'Tell me, was she mean?'

'Oh, you've heard about that? She was certainly thrifty. For instance, when she had to go into town, she'd wait until one of the other guests was going too so that they could share the taxi. Every week she'd argue over her bill.'

'Do you know how she came to meet Monsieur Serre?'

'I don't think it was through the matrimonial advertisement.'

'She put an advertisement in the papers?'

'Not in earnest. She didn't believe in it. More for fun really. I don't remember the exact wording, but she said that a distinguished lady, foreign, wealthy, wished to meet gentleman of similar circumstances, with a view to marriage. She had hundreds of replies. She used to make dates with the suitors at the Louvre, sometimes in one gallery, sometimes in another, and they had to carry a certain book in their hand, or wear a buttonhole.'

There were other women like her, from England, Sweden or America, sitting in the wicker arm-chairs of the lounge, from which the smooth hum of the electric fans could be heard.

'I hope she hasn't come to any harm?'

It was about seven o'clock when Maigret got out of the taxi at the Quai des Orfèvres. From the shady side of the street he'd caught sight of Janvier coming along, with a preoccupied expression, a parcel under his arm, and he'd waited to climb the stairs with him.

'How's things, Janvier, my boy?'

'All right, Chief.'

'What have you got there?'

'My dinner.'

Janvier didn't grumble, but he had a martyred look.

'Why don't you go home?'

'Because of that woman Gertrude, blast her.'

The offices were almost empty, swept by draughts, for a breeze had just got up and all the windows in the building were still open.

'I managed to track down Gertrude Oosting in Amsterdam. Or rather, I got her maid on the 'phone. I had to dig up a chap waiting for an identity-card in the Aliens Section, who was willing to interpret, because the maid doesn't speak a word of French, and then call her back.

'As luck would have it, the good lady Oosting had gone out with her husband at four in the afternoon. There's some open-air concert on today, over there, with a fancy-dress parade, and after that the Oostings are having dinner with friends, the maid doesn't know where. She's no idea when they'll be back either, and she'd been told to put the children to bed.

'And, talking of children . . .'

'What?'

'Nothing, Chief.'

'Come on, out with it!'

'Doesn't matter. Only that the wife's a bit disappointed. It's our eldest boy's birthday. She'd got a special little dinner ready. Never mind.'

'Did you find out from the maid if Gertrude Oosting can speak French?'

'She can.'

'Go on home.'

'What?'

'I told you to go home. Leave me those sandwiches and I'll stay on here.'

'Madame Maigret won't like that.'

Janvier needed a bit of pressure, but finally went rushing off to catch his train to the suburbs.

Maigret had eaten alone in his office, had gone down for a chat with Moers in the laboratory afterwards. Moers had not left until after nine, when darkness had completely fallen.

'Sure you know what to do?'

'Yes, Chief.'

He took a photographer with him, and masses of equipment. It wasn't strictly legal, but, ever since Guillaume Serre had bought two window-panes and not one, that no longer mattered.

'Get me Amsterdam, please. . . .'

At the other end the maid gabbled something and he understood her to mean that Madame Oosting still hadn't come in.

Then he called up his wife.

'You wouldn't mind coming down to have a drink at the *Brasserie Dauphine*? I've probably got another hour or so to fill in here. Take a cab.'

It wasn't a bad evening. The two of them were as comfortable as outside a café on the main boulevards, except that their view was blocked by the tall pale flight of steps leading to the Palais de Justice.

They ought to have got to work now, in the Rue de la Ferme. Maigret had given them instructions to wait until the Serres had gone to bed. Torrence was to mount guard in front of the house to prevent the others from being taken unawares while they broke into the garage, which couldn't be overlooked from the house, and gave the car a thorough overhaul. Moers and the photographer would take care of that. Everything would be gone into: fingerprints, samples of dust for analysis, the whole works.

'You look pleased with yourself.'

'I can't complain.'

He wasn't prepared to admit that, a few hours earlier, he was far from being in such a good mood, and now he began to have short drinks, while Madame Maigret stuck to barley-water.

He left her twice to go back and call Amsterdam from the office. Not until half-past eleven did he hear a voice which was not the maid's and which answered him in French:

'I can't hear you very well.'

'I said, I'm calling from Paris.'

'Oh! Paris!'

She'd a strong accent, which nevertheless was not unattractive.

'Police Headquarters.'

'Police?'

'Yes. I'm telephoning with reference to your friend Maria. You know Maria Serre, whose maiden name was Van Aerts, don't you?'

'Where is she?'

'I don't know. That's just what I'm asking you. She often wrote to you?'

'Yes, often. I was supposed to meet her at the station, Wednesday morning.'

'Did you go to meet her?'

'Yes.'

'Did she come?'

'No.'

'Had she wired or telephoned you that she couldn't keep the appointment?'

'No. I'm worried.'

'Your friend has disappeared.'

'What do you mean?'

'What did she tell you in her letters?'

'Lots of things.'

She began to speak in her own language to someone, probably her husband, who was evidently standing beside her.

'Do you suppose Maria is dead?'

'It could be. Did she ever write to you that she was unhappy?'

'She was distressed.'

'Why?'

'She didn't like the old lady.'

'Her mother-in-law?'

'Yes.'

'What about her husband?'

'It appears that he wasn't a man, but just an overgrown schoolboy who was terrified of his mother.'

'How long ago did she write you that?'

'Almost as soon as she got married. A few weeks after.'

'She already talked about leaving him?'

'Not then. After about a year or so.'

'And recently?'

'She'd made up her mind. She asked me to find her a flat in Amsterdam, near ours.'

'Did you find one for her?'

'Yes. And a maid.'

'So it was all arranged?'

'Yes. I was at the station.'

'Have you any objection to sending me copies of your friend's letters? Did you keep them?'

'I have kept all the letters, but it would be hard work to copy them, as they are very long. I can send you the ones that matter. You're sure something's happened to her?'

'I'm convinced of it.'

'Somebody's killed her?'

'Possibly.'

'Her husband?'

'I don't know. Listen, Madame Oosting, you could do me a great favour. Has your husband got a car?'

'Of course.'

'It would be kind of you to drive to Central Police Headquarters, which is open all night. Tell the duty officer that you were expecting your friend Maria. Show him her last letter. Then tell him you're very worried and that you'd like the matter gone into.'

'Should I mention your name?'

'It doesn't matter either way. What you must do is to insist upon an investigation.'

'I will do so.'

'Thank you. Don't forget the letters that you promised to send me.'

He rang Amsterdam again almost at once, asking this time for the number of Central Police Headquarters.

'In a few minutes, a Madame Oosting will be coming to see you about the disappearance of her friend, Madame Serre, *née* Van Aerts.'

'Did she disappear in Holland?'

'No, in Paris. In order to take action, I need an official complaint. Directly you've taken down her statement, I'd like you to send me a wire asking us to make enquiries.'

This took a bit of time. The duty officer at the other end couldn't understand how Maigret, in Paris, could have known that Madame Oosting was coming along.

'I'll tell you that later. All I must have is your wire. Send it priority. I should get it in less than half an hour.'

He went back to join Madame Maigret, who'd begun to get bored sitting about outside the *brasserie*.

'Have you done?'

'Not yet. I'll have one drink and then we'll be off.'

'Home?'

'To the office.'

That always impressed her. She'd only rarely been within the walls of Headquarters, and didn't know how to behave there.

'You look as if you were having fun. One'd think you were playing a joke on somebody.'

'I am in a way.'

'On whom?'

'A fellow who looks like a sultan, a diplomat and a schoolboy.'

'I don't understand.'

'Naturally not!'

He wasn't often in such high spirits. How many Calvados had he drunk? Four? Five? This time, before going back to the office, he swallowed a pint and took his wife's arm before crossing the couple of hundred yards of the quay to reach Police Headquarters.

'I only ask one thing: don't start telling me again that everything's covered in dust and that the offices need a good clean-out!'

On the telephone:

'Any telegrams come through for me?'

'Nothing, Chief-Inspector.'

Ten minutes later the whole squad, with the exception of Torrence, was back from the Rue de la Ferme.

'Did it go off all right? No hitches?'

'No hitches. Nobody disturbed us. Torrence insisted we should wait until the lights had all gone out in the house, and Guillaume Serre hung about for a long time before going to bed.'

'The car?'

Vacher, who'd nothing more to do, asked if he could go home. Moers and the photographer stayed behind. Madame Maigret, sitting on a chair as if paying a visit, assumed the abstracted expression of one who is not listening.

'We went over every bit of the car, which doesn't seem to have been taken out for two or three days. The petrol tank's about half-full. There are no signs of a struggle inside. In the boot, I found two or three more or less recent scratches.'

'As if a large heavy piece of luggage had been stowed in it?'

'That could be.'

'A trunk, for instance?'

'A trunk or a packing-case.'

'Were there any blood-stains inside?'

'No. Nor any loose hairs either. I thought of that. We took a flashlight along, and there's a power point in the garage. Emile is going to make enlargements of the photos.'

'I'm getting onto it right now,' the photographer said. 'If you could wait just twenty minutes. . . .'

'I'll wait. Did it look to you, Moers, as if the car had been cleaned lately?'

'Not on the outside. It hadn't been washed down by a garage. But it looked as if the inside had been carefully brushed. They must have even taken up the mat to be beaten, because I'd a job to find any dust in it. All the same, I've got several specimens for laboratory tests.'

'Was there a brush in the garage?'

'No. I looked. They must have taken it away.'

'So, except for the scratches . . .'

'Nothing out of the way. Can I go now?'

They were left alone, Madame Maigret and he, in the office.

'Aren't you sleepy?'

She said no. She'd her own special way of looking at the surroundings in which her husband had spent most of his life, of which she knew so little.

'Is it always like this?'

'What?'

'A case. When you don't come home.'

She must have thought it was easy, quiet work, more like a kind of game.

'Just depends.'

'Has there been a murder?'

'More than likely.'

'D'you know who did it?'

She turned her head away as he smiled at her. Then she asked:

'Does he know that you suspect him?'

He nodded.

'D'you suppose he's asleep?'

She added after a moment, with a slight shiver:

'It must be awful.'

'I don't suppose it was fun for the poor woman either.'

'I know. But probably that was quicker, don't you think?'

'Maybe.'

The telegram from the Dutch police came through on the 'phone, with a confirmatory copy promised for the next morning.

'Now then! We can go home.'

'I thought you were waiting for the photographs.'

He smiled once more. Really, she'd have liked to find out. She didn't feel now like going back to bed.

'They won't tell us anything.'

'Don't you think so?'

'I'm sure of it. Moers' laboratory tests won't either.'

'Why not? Because the murderer was too careful?'

He did not reply, put out the light and led his wife into the passage, where the cleaners were already at work.

'That you, Monsieur Maigret?'

He looked at the alarm clock, which said half-past eight. His wife had let him sleep on. He recognized Ernestine's voice.

'Did I wake you up?'

He preferred not to admit it.

'I'm at the post office. There's another card for me.'

'From Le Havre?'

'From Rouen. He doesn't say anything, still hasn't answered my advertisement. Nothing except my address at the *poste restante*, same as yesterday.'

There was a pause. Then she asked:

'You heard anything?'

'Yes.'

'What?'

'Something to do with window-panes.'

'Good?'

'Just depends for whom.'

'For us?'

'It may do Alfred and you some good.'

'You don't still think I've been telling lies?'

'Not at the moment.'

At Headquarters he picked Janvier to go with him, and the latter took the wheel of the little black police car.

'Rue de la Ferme.'

With the telegram in his pocket, he made the car stop outside the wrought-iron gate, through which the two of them passed looking their most official. Maigret rang. A window curtain moved on the first floor, where the shutters were not yet closed. It was Eugénie, in down-at-heel slippers, who came to the door, wiping her wet hands on her apron.

'Good morning, Eugénie. Monsieur Serre is at home and I'd like a word with him.'

Somebody leant over the banisters. The old woman's voice said:

'Show the gentlemen into the drawing-room, Eugénie.'

It was the first time that Janvier had been in the house, and he was impressed. They heard footsteps coming and going overhead. Then the door opened abruptly and the huge bulk of Guillaume Serre almost filled the entrance.

He was as self-possessed as on the day before, stared at them with the same calm insolence.

'Have you a warrant?' he asked, his lip twitching slightly.

Maigret deliberately took some time taking his wallet from his pocket, opening it, finding a document which he handed over politely.

'Here you are, Monsieur Serre.'

The man wasn't prepared for this. He read through the form, took it over to the window to decipher the signature, while Maigret was saying:

'As you see, it's a search warrant. Enquiries are being instituted into the disappearance of Madame Maria Serre, *née* Van Aerts, on a complaint lodged by Madame Gertrude Oosting, of Amsterdam.'

The old lady had entered on these last words.

'What is it, Guillaume?'

'Nothing, Mamma,' he told her in a curiously gentle voice. 'These gentlemen, I believe, would like to search the house. Go up to your room.'

She wavered, looked at Maigret as if to ask his advice.

'You'll keep your temper, Guillaume?'

'Of course, Mamma. Please leave us, I beg of you.'

Things weren't going exactly as Maigret had foreseen, and the chief-inspector frowned.

'I expect,' he said, when the old lady had reluctantly moved away, 'you'll want to consult your lawyer? I'll probably have a few questions to ask you later on.'

'I don't need a lawyer. Now that you have a warrant, I cannot object to your presence here. That's that.'

The shutters on the ground floor were closed. Until now they'd been in semi-darkness. Serre walked towards the nearest window.

'No doubt you'd prefer more light upon the scene?'

He spoke in a flat voice and if any expression at all could be read into his tone, it was a degree of contempt.

'Do your duty, gentlemen.'

It came almost as a shock to see the drawing-room in full daylight.

3

Serre went into his study next door, where he also opened the shutters, then into the surgery.

'When you wish to go up to the first floor, please let me know.'

Janvier was glancing in bewilderment at his Chief. The latter wasn't quite so buoyant as he'd been that morning or the night before. He seemed to be worried.

'May I use your telephone, Monsieur Serre?' he asked with the same cold courtesy the other had shown him.

'You have every right to.'

He dialled the number of Headquarters. Moers had made a verbal report that morning which, as the chief-inspector had expected, was more or less negative. The particles of dust had been analysed with no result. Or rather, almost none. Moers had only managed to scrape up, from the front of the car, by the driving-seat, a minute quantity of powdered brick.

'Give me the laboratory. That you, Moers? Can you come along to the Rue de la Ferme with your men and equipment?'

He was watching Serre who, engaged in lighting a long black cigar, didn't bat an eyelid.

'All the lot, eh? No, there's no body. I'll be here.'

Then turning to Janvier:

'You can get started.'

'On this room?'

'On any one you like.'

Guillaume Serre followed them up step by step and watched what they were doing without a murmur. He wore no tie and had slipped on a black alpaca jacket over his white shirt.

While Janvier was searching the drawers of the desk, Maigret himself was going through the dentist's private files and making entries in his large note-book.

Really, it had begun to border on farce. He'd have been hard put to it to say precisely what he was looking for. What it amounted to in the end was seeing whether, at any given moment, in any particular part of the house, Serre would show any sign of uneasiness.

When they had searched the drawing-room, for instance, he'd not moved a muscle, standing rigid and full of dignity, with his back to the brown marble chimney-piece.

Now, he was watching Maigret as if wondering what the latter could be searching for in his files, but it seemed to be more out of curiosity than fear.

'You certainly have very few patients, Monsieur Serre.'

He made no reply and shrugged his shoulders.

'I notice that there are far more women patients than men.'

The other's expression seemed to say, 'So what?'

'I also see that you first met Maria Van Aerts in your professional capacity.'

He found entries for five visits, spaced over two months, with details of the treatment given.

'Were you aware that she was wealthy?'

A further shrug.

'Do you know Doctor Dubuc?'

He nodded.

'He was your wife's doctor, unless I'm mistaken. Did you recommend him to her?'

Wonders never cease! He was talking at last!

'Doctor Dubuc was treating Maria Van Aerts before she became my wife.'

'You knew, when you married her, that she had heart trouble?'

'She told me about it.'

'Was it serious?'

'Dubuc will tell you if he considers it his duty.'

'Your first wife had a weak heart, too, hadn't she?'

'You'll find her death certificate in the files.'

Janvier was more ill at ease than anyone. He greeted with relief the arrival of the technical experts, who would start a bit of life in the house. As the car drew up in front of the gate, Maigret went to open the door himself, said to Moers under his breath:

'The whole show. Go over the house with a toothcomb.'

And Moers, who'd understood and spotted the bulky form of Guillaume Serre, muttered:

'You reckon that'll shake him?'

'It might end up by shaking someone.'

A few moments later, one might have thought that auctioneers had taken over the house and were preparing to put it up for public sale. The men from the Technical Branch left no corner untouched, taking down the pictures and the photographs, pushing back the piano and the arm-chairs to look underneath the carpets, piling up cupboard drawers, spreading out documents.

Once they caught sight of the face of Madame Serre who, having taken one glance through the doorway, had withdrawn with a look of distress. Then Eugénie came in grumbling:

'You'll put everything back where it was, I hope?'

She carried on even more when her kitchen was put through it and even the cupboards where she stored her brooms.

'If only you'd tell me what it is you're looking for.'

They weren't looking for anything in particular. Perhaps, when it came to the point, even Maigret wasn't looking for anything at all. All the time he was watching the man who followed in their tracks and never lost his poise for a second.

Why had Maria written to her friend that Serre was really nothing more than an overgrown schoolboy?

While his men continued to work, Maigret unhooked the telephone and got Dr. Dubuc on the line.

'You won't be going out for a while? Can I come and see you? No, it won't take long. Thanks, I'll tell the maid.'

Dubuc had five patients in his waiting-room and promised the chief-inspector to let him in by the back door. It was a stone's throw away, along the wharf. Maigret went there on foot, passed the ironmonger's, where the young assistant of the day before hailed him.

'Aren't you going to photograph the ledger?'

'Presently.'

Dubuc was a man of about fifty, with a ginger beard and glasses.

'You attended Madame Serre, didn't you, Doctor?'

'Young Madame Serre. Or rather, the younger of the two.'

'You never attended anyone else in the house?'

'Let me see. Yes! A charwoman who'd cut her hand, two or three years ago.'

'Was Maria Serre really ill?'

'She needed treatment, yes.'

'Heart?'

'An enlarged heart. Moreover, she ate too much, complained of dizziness.'

'Did she often call you in?'

'About once a month. Other times she came to see me.'

'Did you prescribe any medicine for her?'

'A sedative, in tablet form. Nothing toxic.'

'You don't think she could have had a heart attack?'

'Most unlikely. In ten or fifteen years, perhaps. . . . .'

'Did she do anything to get her weight down?'

'Every four or five months she'd decide to go on a diet, but her resolution never lasted for more than a few days.'

'You've met her husband?'

'Occasionally.'

'What did you think of him?'

'In what way? Professionally? One of my woman patients went to him for treatment and told me that he was very skilful and very gentle.'

'As a man?'

'I thought he seemed of retiring disposition. What is all this about?'

'His wife has disappeared.'

'Ah!'

Dubuc didn't give a damn, to tell the truth, and he merely sketched a vague gesture.

'These things happen, don't they? He was wrong to put the police on to find her, because she'll never forgive him.'

Maigret didn't argue the point. On his way back, he made a detour so as to pass the garage, which was no longer under observation. The house opposite had been divided into flats. The concierge was outside on the step, polishing the brass knob of the front door.

'Does your window look out on the street?'

'What's that got to do with you?'

'I'm a police officer. I wanted to find out whether you knew the person who keeps his car in the garage opposite, the first one on the right.'

'That's the dentist.'

'You see him now and again?'

'I see him when he comes to fetch his car.'

'Have you seen him this week?'

'Here! That reminds me — what was all that messing about in his garage yesterday night? Was it burglars? I said to my husband . . .'

'It wasn't burglars.'

'Was it you?'

'Never mind. Have you seen him take his car out this week?'

'I believe I did.'

'You don't remember which day? Or what time?'

'It was one night, pretty late. Hang on, I'd got up out of bed. Don't look at me like that. It'll come back to me.'

She seemed to be doing some mental arithmetic.

'I'd just got up out of bed, because my husband had toothache, and I'd given him an aspirin. If he was here he'd tell you straight away what day it was. I noticed Monsieur Serre's car coming out of the garage, and I remember saying what a coincidence.'

'Because your husband had toothache?'

'Yes. And there was a dentist opposite the house at that very moment. It was after midnight. Mademoiselle Germaine had come in. Right, then it was Tuesday, because she only goes out on Tuesday nights, to play cards round at some friends.'

'The car was coming out? It wasn't going in?'

'It was coming out.'

'Which way did it go?'

'Towards the Seine.'

'You didn't hear it stop a little farther on, for instance at Monsieur Serre's house?'

'I didn't take any more notice of it. I'd bare feet and the floor was cold, because we sleep with the window half-open. What's he done?'

What could Maigret have answered? He thanked her and moved away, crossed the little garden and rang. Eugénie opened the door, giving him a black, reproachful look.

'The gentlemen are upstairs,' she told him curtly.

They'd finished with the ground floor. From upstairs noisy footsteps could be heard, the rumble of furniture being dragged across the floor-boards.

Maigret went up, found old Madame Serre sitting on a chair in the middle of the landing.

'I no longer know where to go,' she said. 'It's like moving house. What can they be looking for, Monsieur Maigret?'

Guillaume Serre, standing in the centre of a room flooded with sun-light, was lighting a fresh cigar.

'My goodness, why did we let her go!' sighed the old lady. 'If I'd only known. . . .'

She did not state precisely what she would have done had she fore-seen the worries that her daughter-in-law's disappearance would bring down upon her.

VI

IT was twenty to four when Maigret made up his mind, twenty-five past four when the questioning began. But the fateful, almost dramatic moment was that when the decision was taken.

Maigret's behaviour had come as a surprise to those working with him in the house at the Rue de la Ferme. Ever since the morning, there'd been something unusual about the way in which the chief-inspector was directing operations. It wasn't the first search of this sort in which they'd taken part, but the more this one proceeded, the more it took on a different nature from any other. It was difficult to define. Janvier, because he knew his Chief better than the others, was the first to feel the change.

When he set them to work, there had been a slight, almost fierce flicker of glee in Maigret's eyes; he had loosed them on the house rather as he might have loosed a pack of hounds on a fresh scent, urging them on, not by his voice but by his whole attitude.

Had it become a personal issue between himself and Guillaume Serre? Or more precisely: would events have taken the same course, would Maigret have made the same decision, at the same moment, had the man from the Rue de la Ferme not been heavier than he, physically and morally?

He had seemed, from the start, impatient to get to grips with him.

At other times, one might have attributed different motives to him, wondered if he didn't take a more or less malicious pleasure in turning the house upside-down.

They had seldom been given the chance of working in a home like this, where everything was peaceful and serene, harmonious in a muted minor key, where even the most outdated objects were in no way ludicrous, and where, after hours of exhaustive searching, they hadn't come across even one questionable detail.

When he had made his pronouncement, at twenty to four, they still hadn't found anything. The search party was feeling a certain amount of discomfort, expecting the Chief to withdraw with apologies.

What was it that decided Maigret? Did he know himself? Janvier went so far as to suspect him of having drunk too many *apéritifs* when, about one o'clock, he'd gone to have a bite on the terrace of the café opposite. On his return, it was true, a smell of Pernod could be detected on his breath.

Eugénie hadn't laid the table for her employers. Several times she'd come up to whisper, now in the ear of Madame Serre, now in that of the dentist. At one moment, they'd caught sight of the mother eating, standing up, in the kitchen, as one might during a household removal, and not long after that, Guillaume having refused to come down, the charwoman took him up a sandwich and a cup of coffee.

They were working in the attic by then. This was the most personal part of the house, more personal than the bedrooms and the linen cupboards.

It was enormous, lit by dormer-windows that shed two large luminous rectangles upon the dingy floorboards. Janvier had opened two leather gun-cases, and a ballistics man had examined the weapons.

'These belong to you?'

'They belonged to my father-in-law. I have never done any shooting.'

An hour earlier, in Guillaume's room, they'd found a revolver, which had been examined, and which Maigret had placed on the pile of objects to be taken away for a subsequent check-up.

There was a bit of everything in that pile, including the dentist's professional records and, from an escritoire in the old lady's room, the death certificates of her husband and her first daughter-in-law.

There was also a suit of clothing on which Janvier had noticed a slight tear in the sleeve, and which Guillaume Serre claimed not to have worn for ten days.

They stumbled about among old trunks, packing-cases, pieces of broken-down furniture which had been taken up to the attic because they were no more use. In a corner stood a child's high chair of an old-fashioned type, with coloured knobs on either side of the tray, and also a rocking-horse, minus tail and mane.

They didn't stop working at lunch-time. The men took it in turns to knock off for a bite, and Moers was satisfied with a sandwich brought to him by the photographer.

Towards 2 p.m., they 'phoned through to Maigret, from the office, to tell him that a pretty heavy envelope had just come by air from Holland. He had them open it. Inside were Maria's letters, written in Dutch.

'Get hold of a translator and put him to work.'

'Here?'

'Yes. He's not to leave Headquarters until I come.'

Guillaume Serre's attitude had not altered. He followed them about, didn't miss a single action or gesture on their part, but not even once did he seem agitated.

He had a special way of staring at Maigret, and one could see that, for him, the others didn't count. It was indeed a match between the two. The plain-clothes men were merely lay figures. Even the police force didn't count. This was a more personal combat. And in the dentist's eyes one could see an indefinable expression that might have been one of reproach or of contempt.

In any case, he didn't allow this large-scale operation to intimidate him. He raised no more objections, submitted to this invasion of his home and privacy with lofty resignation, in which not the slightest trace of anxiety was perceptible.

Was he a weakling? A tough customer? The two theories were equally plausible. His torso was that of a wrestler, his behaviour that of a self-assured man, and yet, nevertheless, Maria's description of him as an overgrown schoolboy did not appear incongruous. His skin was pale, sickly-looking. In a drawer, they'd found a mass of doctor's prescriptions, pinned together in separate sheafs, some of them dating from twenty years back; the family's medical history could have been reconstructed with the help of these prescriptions, some of which were yellow with age. There was also, in the upstairs bathroom, a small white-painted cabinet containing phials of patent medicine, boxes of pills both new and old.

In this house nothing was ever thrown away, not even old brooms, which were stacked in a corner of the attic beside down-at-heel cracked leather shoes that would never be any use again.

Each time they left a room to launch an attack upon the next, Janvier gave his Chief a look which meant:

'Another wash-out!'

For Janvier still expected to make some discovery. Did Maigret, on the other hand, rely on their finding nothing? He didn't seem surprised, watched them go ahead, puffing lazily at his pipe, sometimes forgetting, for a whole quarter of an hour, to glance round at the dentist.

They realized his decision by implication, and that made it strike them even more forcibly.

Everybody was coming down from the attic, where Guillaume Serre had closed the dormer windows. His mother had just come out of her room to watch them go. They were standing on the landing, in an uneasy group.

Maigret had turned to Serre and said, as if it were the most natural thing in the world:

'Would you mind putting on a tie and a pair of shoes?'

Throughout the day, so far, the man had been wearing slippers.

Serre had grasped his meaning, had stared at him, undoubtedly surprised, but managing not to let it show. His mother had opened her mouth to speak, either to protest or to demand an explanation and Guillaume had clasped her arm, led her back into her room.

Janvier had asked under his breath:

'You arresting him?'

Maigret had made no reply. He didn't know. To tell the truth, he'd only just made up his mind, on the spur of the moment, here, on the landing.

'Come in, Monsieur Serre. Will you take a seat?'

The clock on the mantelpiece said four twenty-five. It was a Saturday. Maigret had only realized that from the bustle in the streets, as they crossed the city in a car.

The chief-inspector closed the door. The windows were open, and papers on the desk fluttered under the weights that prevented them from blowing away.

'I asked you to sit down.'

He himself went into the wall cupboard to hang up his hat and coat there and to rinse his hands under the enamel fountain.

For the next ten minutes he didn't say a word to the dentist, being too busy signing the things that were waiting on his desk. He rang for Joseph, gave him the file; then, slowly and deliberately, he filled the half-dozen pipes set out in front of him.

It was seldom that anyone in Serre's position could stand it for long without asking questions, losing his nerve, crossing and uncrossing his legs.

At last there was a knock at the door. It was the photographer who'd worked with them all day and been sent on a mission by Maigret. He handed the chief-inspector the still damp print of a document.

'Thank you, Dambois. Stay back there. Don't leave without letting me know.'

He waited until the door closed again, lit one of the pipes:

'Would you bring your chair nearer, Monsieur Serre?'

They were now facing each other, separated by the width of the desk, across which Maigret held out the document in his hand.

He added no comment. The dentist took the print, brought a pair of spectacles out of his pocket, examined it carefully and put it down on the table.

'I'm waiting.'

'I've nothing to say.'

3*

The photograph was that of a page from the ironmonger's ledger, the one recording the sale of the second sheet of glass and the second half-pound of putty.

'You realize what that implies?'

'Am I to understand that I'm charged?'

Maigret hesitated.

'No,' he decided. 'Officially, you're summoned as a witness. If you wish, however, I am ready to charge you, more exactly to ask the Director of Prosecutions to indict you, which would entitle you to have legal advice.'

'I've already told you that I don't want a lawyer.'

These were only the preliminary moves. Two heavy-weights were sizing each other up, taking each other's measure, feeling their way, in the office which had become a sort of ring, and silence reigned in the Duty Room, where Janvier had just put his colleagues in the picture.

'I reckon we're in for a long session!' he told them.

'Think the Chief'll go the limit?'

'He's got that look on his face.'

They all knew what that meant, and Janvier was the first to ring up his wife and tell her not to be surprised if he didn't come home that night.

'Have you a weak heart, Monsieur Serre?'

'An enlarged heart, like yourself, in all probability.'

'Your father died of heart trouble when you were seventeen, didn't he?'

'Seventeen and a half.'

'Your first wife died of heart trouble. Your second wife also had heart trouble.'

'According to statistics, about thirty per cent of people die of heart failure.'

'Your life's insured, Monsieur Serre?'

'Since I was a child.'

'Of course, I saw the policy earlier on. If I remember rightly, your mother is not insured.'

'That's correct.'

'Your father was?'

'I believe so.'

'And your first wife?'

'I saw you take the documents away.'

'Your second wife, as well?'

'It's quite a usual procedure.'

'What is less usual is to keep a sum of several million francs, in gold and currency, in a safe.'

'D'you think so?'

'Can you tell me why you keep this money at home, where it can bring no interest?'

'I imagine that thousands of people, nowadays, do the same. You forget the financial bills that have resulted several times in a panic, the excessive rate of taxation and the constant devaluations. . . .'

'I understand. You admit that your intention was to conceal your capital and defraud the Treasury?'

Serre was silent.

'Did your wife—I mean your second wife, Maria—know that this money was shut up in your safe?'

'She did.'

'You told her about it?'

'Her own money was in there as well a few days ago.'

He took his time before answering, weighed his words, let them fall one by one while keeping his eyes fixed gravely on the chief-inspector.

'I didn't find any marriage-contract among your papers. Am I to conclude that you were married under the joint-possession laws?'

'That is correct.'

'Isn't that odd, considering your ages?'

'I have already given you the reason. A contract would have obliged us to draw up a balance-sheet of our respective goods.'

'The joint-possession, however, had no existence in actual fact?'

'We each continued to retain control of our own affairs.'

And didn't all this seem quite natural?

'Was your wife wealthy?'

'She is wealthy.'

'As wealthy as you are, or wealthier?'

'About the same.'

'Does she have the whole of her money in France?'

'Only part of it. From her father, she inherited shares in a cheese factory in Holland.'

'In what form did she keep her other assets?'

'Mainly in gold.'

'Even before she met you?'

'I see what you're getting at. Nevertheless, I will tell you the truth. It was I who advised her to sell out her securities and to buy gold.'

'This gold was kept, with yours, in your safe?'

'It used to be.'

'Until when?'

'Tuesday. At the beginning of the afternoon, when she'd nearly finished packing, she came downstairs and I gave her what belonged to her.'

'Then this sum, when she left, was in one of the two suit-cases or in the trunk?'

'I suppose so.'

'She didn't go out before dinner?'

'I didn't hear her go out.'

'So, to your knowledge, she didn't go out?'

He nodded in confirmation.

'Did she telephone at all?'

'The only telephone in the house is in my study and she did not make use of it.'

'How am I to know, Monsieur Serre, that the money which I found in the safe is *yours alone*, and not yours *and* your wife's?'

Without emotion, still maintaining an expression of weariness or disdain, the dentist took from his pocket a green note-book which he handed to the chief-inspector. Its pages were covered with tiny figures. Those on the left-hand side were headed with the initial O; those on the right with the initial M.

'What does O stand for?'

'Ours. I mean my mother and myself. We've always shared everything, without making any distinction between what is hers and what is mine.'

'The M, I suppose, stands for Maria?'

'You are right.'

'I see a certain figure that occurs at regular intervals.'

'Her share of the household expenses.'

'Every month she paid you the cost of her bed and board?'

'If you like. Actually, she didn't pay me any money, because it was in the safe, but her account was debited with the amount.'

Maigret leafed through the note-book for a few minutes without speaking, got up and went into the room next door where, like schoolboys, the plain-clothes men immediately pretended to be busy.

He gave instructions to Janvier in a low voice, hesitated as to whether he should have beer sent up for himself, swallowed, as if automatically, the dregs of a glass which stood on Vacher's desk.

When he returned, Serre, who had not moved from his chair, had just lit one of his long cigars and murmured not without insolence:

'D'you mind?'

Maigret was loth to say yes, shrugged his shoulders.

'You've thought about this second window-pane, Monsieur Serre?'

'I haven't bothered to do so.'

'You're wrong. It'd be much better if you could find some reasonable explanation.'

'I'm not looking for one. . . .'

'D'you continue to maintain that you have only once replaced the pane in your study window?'

'The day after the thunderstorm.'

'Would you like us to have the weather-bureau confirm that there was no thunderstorm at Neuilly on Tuesday night?'

'It's pointless. Unless it would give you any satisfaction. I'm speaking of last week's thunderstorm.'

'The day after, you went to the ironmonger's in the Rue de Long-champ and you bought a sheet of glass and some putty.'

'I have told you that already.'

'You are prepared to swear that you haven't been back to the shop since then?'

And he pushed across the desk the photograph of the ledger entry.

'Why, in your opinion, should they have troubled to enter these purchases of glass and putty twice in their book?'

'I've no idea.'

'Why should the shopkeeper state that you came in on Wednesday, about eight o'clock in the morning?'

'That's his business.'

'When did you last use your car?'

'Last Sunday.'

'Where did you go?'

'We took a drive for two or three hours, my mother and I, as is our custom every Sunday.'

'In which direction?'

'Towards the forest of Fontainebleau.'

'Did your wife go with you?'

'No. She wasn't feeling well.'

'You'd decided to separate?'

'There was no question of a separation. She was tired, run down. She didn't always get on with my mother. By mutual agreement we decided that she should go back to her own country for a few weeks or a few months.'

'She took her money with her, all the same?'

'Yes.'

'Why?'

'Because there was a possibility that she wouldn't come back. We're no longer children. We're able to look at life calmly. It is a sort of experiment that we are making.'

'Tell me, Monsieur Serre, there are two frontiers to cross before you reach Amsterdam, aren't there? The French customs, on the way out, are fairly strict about the currency regulations. Wasn't your wife afraid that her gold would be discovered and impounded?'

'Am I obliged to answer?'

'I think it's in your own interests.'

'Even if I risk proceedings?'

'They'd probably be less serious than a charge of murder.'

'Very well. One of my wife's suit-cases was provided with a false bottom.'

'Specially for this trip?'

'No.'

'She'd already had occasion to use it?'

'Several times.'

'To cross the frontier?'

'The Belgian frontier and, once, the Swiss frontier. You're aware, I'm sure, that until recently it was easier and less expensive to procure gold in Belgium and especially in Switzerland.'

'You admit your complicity in these transfers of capital?'

'I do.'

Maigret got up, went back into the Duty Room.

'Mind coming here a moment, Janvier?'

Then, to Serre:

'My assistant will take down this part of our interview. Please repeat to him word for word what you've just told me. See that he signs his statement, Janvier.'

He went out, got Vacher to show him the office that had been assigned to the translator. He was a little man with glasses who was typing his translation straight onto the machine and pausing from time to time to consult the dictionary that he'd brought with him.

There were at least forty letters, most of them comprising several sheets.

'Where have you begun?'

'At the beginning. I'm onto the third letter. All three are dated about two and a half years ago. In the first one, the lady tells her friend that she's getting married, that her future husband is a distinguished man, of imposing appearance, belonging to the highest French professional class, and that his mother looks like I can't remember which painting in the Louvre. I can tell you the name of the painter.'

He turned over the pages.

'A Clouet. Painting is mentioned all the time in these letters. When she's saying what the weather's like, she cites Monet or Renoir.'

'I'd like you to begin at the end, from now on.'

'As you wish. You realize that if I spend all night at it, I won't have finished by tomorrow morning?'

'That's why I'm asking you to begin at the end. What's the date of the last letter?'

'Last Sunday.'

'Can you read it to me quickly?'

'I can give you some idea of it. Wait a moment.

'*Gertrude darling,*

'*Paris has never been so resplendent as this morning, and I very nearly went with G. and his mother to the forest of Fontainebleau, which must be adorned with all the glories of a Corot or a Courbet. . . .*'

'Is there a lot about the glories?'

'Shall I skip?'

'Please.'

The translator ran his eyes down a page and moved his lips silently as if in prayer.

'Here you are:

'*I wonder what effect returning once again to our Holland and its pastel shades will have upon me and now that the time comes near, I feel I'm being cowardly.*

'*After all that I've written to you about my life here, about G. and my mother-in-law, you must be wondering what has happened to me and why I am no longer happy.*

'*It's perhaps because of the dream I had last night, which has spoilt my day. Do you recall the little picture that hangs in The Hague museum and made us blush? It isn't signed. It's attributed to a painter of the Florentine School whose name I have forgotten, and depicts a faun carrying away over his shoulder a completely naked woman who is resisting. You remember?*

'*The faun, in my dream, had G.'s face, and his expression was so fierce that I awoke trembling and bathed in perspiration.*

'*Not with fear, that was the strangest thing. My memory is confused. There was some fear, certainly, but also another emotion. I'll try to explain it to you on Wednesday, when we'll at last be able to chat as we did so much when you came over on your last trip.*

'*I'm to leave on Tuesday night, it's settled. There's no doubt about it. So there are only two more days to wait. I've heaps of things to do during that time. It'll pass quickly. Nevertheless, it seems to me still far away, almost unreal.*

'*Sometimes I have the feeling, especially after that dream, that something will happen to prevent my departure.*

'*Don't worry. My decision is final. I shall follow your advice. I cannot stand this life here for much longer. But . . .*'

'You in here, Chief?'

It was Janvier, with sheets of paper in his hand.

'It's done. He's waiting for you.'

Maigret took the papers, left the translator to his task, crossed the Duty Room deep in thought.

Nobody, at that time, could have foretold how long the questioning would take. Guillaume Serre looked up at the chief-inspector, took a pen of his own accord from the desk.

'I suppose I have to sign?'

'Yes, here. Have you read it through?'

'I've read it. Might I trouble you for a glass of water?'

'You wouldn't prefer red wine?'

The dentist looked at him, gave the faintest of smiles, inscrutable, heavy with irony and bitterness.

'That, too?' he said disdainfully.

'That, too, Monsieur Serre. You're so afraid of your mother that you are reduced to drink in hiding.'

'Is that a question? I've got to answer?'

'If you wish to.'

'Allow me to inform you then that my mother's father was a drunkard, that her two brothers, who are now dead, were drunkards as well,

and that her sister ended her days in a lunatic asylum. My mother has
lived in fear of seeing me take to drink in my turn, for she refuses to
believe that this tendency is not hereditary. When I was a student, she
awaited my return with anxiety, and would even sometimes keep a
watch on the cafés in the Boulevard Saint-Michel where I was sitting
with my friends. There have never been any spirits in the house and
though there's wine in the cellar, she's kept the habit of carrying the
key on her.'

'She allows you a glass of wine and water at every meal, doesn't she?'
'I know that she called to see you and spoke to you.'
'Did she tell you what she said to me?'
'Yes.'
'Are you very fond of your mother, Monsieur Serre?'
The two of us have almost always lived together.'
'Rather like a married couple?'
He coloured slightly.
'I don't know what you mean.'
'Is your mother jealous?'
'I beg your pardon?'
'I'm asking you whether, as often happens with a widow and an only
son, your mother shows signs of jealousy towards the people you know.
Have you many friends?'
'Has this any connection with the alleged disappearance of my wife?'
'I didn't find in the house a single letter from a friend, or even one of
those group photographs that one sees in most homes.'
He didn't speak.
'Nor is there any photograph of your first wife.'
Still silence.
'Another thing that struck me, Monsieur Serre. The portrait hanging
over the mantelpiece is surely of your maternal grandfather?'
'Yes.'
'The one who drank?'
A sign of assent.
'In a drawer I came across a certain number of pictures of yourself as a
child and as a young man, also pictures of women and men who must
have been your grandmother, your aunt and your uncles. Always on
your mother's side. Doesn't it seem surprising to you that there isn't a
single portrait of your father or of his family?'
'It hadn't struck me.'
'Were they destroyed after your father's death?'
'My mother could answer that question better than I.'
'You don't remember if they were destroyed?'
'I was quite young.'
'You were seventeen. What memory have you of your father, Mon-
sieur Serre?'

'Is this part of your interrogation?'

'Neither my questions nor your answers, as you see, are being recorded. Your father was a solicitor?'

'Yes.'

'Did he take personal charge of his practice?'

'Not often. His chief clerk did most of the work.'

'Did he lead a very social life? Or was he exclusively devoted to the family circle?'

'He went about a great deal.'

'He had mistresses?'

'I couldn't tell you.'

'Did he die in his bed?'

'On the stairs, going up to his room.'

'Were you at home?'

'I'd gone out. When I came back, he'd been dead for nearly two hours.'

'Who attended him?'

'Doctor Dutilleux.'

'Is he still alive?'

'He died at least ten years ago.'

'Were you there when your first wife died?'

He drew his heavy brows together, staring at Maigret fixedly, and his lower lip was thrust out in a kind of disgust.

'Answer me, please.'

'I was in the house.'

'What part of the house?'

'In my study.'

'What time was it?'

'About nine p.m.'

'Did your wife keep to her room?'

'She'd gone up early. She didn't feel very well.'

'Had she felt ill for some time?'

'I don't remember.'

'Was your mother with her?'

'She was upstairs as well.'

'With her?'

'I've no idea.'

'Was it your mother who called you?'

'I think so.'

'When you got to the room, your wife was dead?'

'No.'

'Did she die a long time afterwards?'

'Fifteen or twenty minutes later. The doctor was ringing the doorbell.'

'Which doctor?'

'Dutilleux.'

'He was your family doctor?'

'He attended me when I was a child.'

'A friend of your father's?'

'Of my mother.'

'Did he have children?'

'Two or three.'

'You've lost sight of them?'

'I never knew them personally.'

'Why didn't you inform the police that somebody had tried to break open your safe?'

'I had nothing to inform the police.'

'What did you do with the tools?'

'What tools?'

'The ones the burglar left in the room when he made his getaway.'

'I saw neither tools nor burglar.'

'You didn't make use of your car on Tuesday night or early Wednesday morning?'

'I did not.'

'You were unaware that somebody used it?'

'I've had no reason, since then, to go into the garage.'

'When you garaged your car, last Sunday, were there scratches on the boot and the right mudguard?'

'I didn't notice anything.'

'Did you get out of the car, you and your mother?'

He didn't answer for a moment.

'I asked you a question.'

'I'm trying to remember.'

'It shouldn't be so difficult. You were driving along the road to Fontainebleau. Did you set foot to the ground?'

'Yes. We went for a walk in the country.'

'You mean on a country road?'

'A little path running between the fields on the right-hand side of the road.'

'Could you find this path again?'

'I think so.'

'Was it tarred?'

'I don't believe it was. No. That seems unlikely.'

'Where is your wife, Monsieur Serre?'

And the chief-inspector rose, not expecting any answer.

'Because we've got to find her, haven't we?'

VII

ABOUT five o'clock, already, Maigret had got up for a moment to open the communicating door between his office and the Duty Room and had winked at Janvier. A little later he'd got up again to go and shut the window, despite the heat, because of the noise from outside.

At ten to six he passed through the Duty Room, his jacket over his arm.

'All yours!' he told Janvier.

The latter and his colleagues had grasped the situation a long while ago. From the moment when, at the Rue de la Ferme, the chief-inspector had ordered Serre to come along, Janvier was pretty sure that he wouldn't get away from Headquarters very easily. What surprised him was that the Chief had made his decision so abruptly, without waiting to have all the evidence in his hands.

'She's in the waiting-room,' he said under his breath.

'Who?'

'The mother.'

Maigret stationed Marlieux, a young plain-clothes man, who knew shorthand, behind the door.

'Same questions?' asked Janvier.

'The same. And any others that come into your head.'

The idea was to wear down the dentist. The others could take it in turns, go out for a cup of coffee or a pint, make contact with the outside world again, while he would stay as long as need be in the same office, in the same chair.

Maigret began by calling in on the translator, who'd decided to take off his jacket and tie.

'What's she say?'

'I've translated the last four letters. There's a passage in the last but one that might interest you.

'*I've made up my mind, Gertrude dear, I am still wondering how it came about. Yet I had no dreams last night, or if I had, I have forgotten them.*'

'Does she say much about her dreams?'

'Yes. They're always coming into it. And she interprets them.'

'Go on.'

'*You've often asked me what has gone wrong and I answered that you were imagining things and that I was happy. The truth is that I was trying to persuade myself of it.*

'*Honestly, I've done all I could, for two and a half years, to try and believe that this house was my home and that G. was my husband.*

'*In my heart, you see, I knew that it wasn't true, that I'd always been a stranger here, more of a stranger than I was in the boarding-house you know, where we two spent so many happy hours.*

'*How did I suddenly come to see things as they really are?*

'*Do you remember, when we were little girls? We used to play at comparing everything we saw — people, streets, animals — with the pictures in our photograph albums. We wanted life to be like them. Then, later on, when we began to visit the museums, it was paintings that we used for comparison.*

'*I did the same here, but I did it on purpose, without believing in it, and this morning I suddenly saw the house as it really is, I saw my mother-in-law, I saw G. with a fresh vision, without illusions.*

'*I hadn't had any for some time — I mean illusions. You've got to understand me. I no longer had any, but I stubbornly refused to admit it.*

'*Now that's over. I made up my mind to leave on the spot. I haven't told anyone yet. The old lady hasn't any inkling. She still behaves the same towards me, meek and smiling, so long as I do everything she wants.*

'She's the most selfish woman I have ever known.

'Those words are underlined,' the translator remarked. 'Shall I go on?

'*As for G., I wonder whether it won't be a relief for him to see me go. He knows that from the beginning we had nothing in common. I could never get used to the feel of his skin, to his smell. Do you understand now why we've never shared the same room, which surprised you so much at the start?*

'*After two and a half years, it's exactly as though I'd just met him in the street or in the underground, and I have the same feeling of recoil whenever he comes to my room. Luckily it doesn't happen often.*

'*I even think, between ourselves, that he only comes because he believes it gives me pleasure, or because he feels it's his duty.*

'*Perhaps it's his mother who tells him to? It's possible. Don't laugh. I don't know how it is with your own husband, but G. has the crestfallen look of a schoolboy who's just been given a hundred lines. Can you see what I mean?*

'*I've often wondered if he was the same with his first wife. It's probable. He would be the same, I expect, with anyone. These people, you see, I mean the mother and son, live in a world of their own and have no need of anybody else.*

'*It seems astonishing that the old lady once had a husband of her own. They never speak about him at home. Besides themselves, there's nobody in the world except the people whose pictures are on the walls, people who are dead, but whom they talk about as if they were more alive than all the living.*

'*I can't stand it any longer, Gertrude. I'll talk to G. presently. I'll tell him that I feel the need to breathe the air of my own country, and he'll understand. What I'm wondering is, how he'll pluck up the courage to tell his mother. . . .*'

'Is there much more?' asked Maigret.

'Seven pages.'

'Go on translating. I'll be back.'

At the door he turned round:

'When you're hungry or thirsty, ring down to the *Brasserie Dauphine.* Get them to send up anything you want.'

'Thank you.'

From the corridor he saw, in the glass-panelled waiting-room, old

Madame Serre sitting on one of the green velvet chairs. She was bolt upright, her hands folded in her lap. When she caught sight of Maigret, she made as if to get up, but he passed on without stopping and went down the stairs.

The examination had barely begun and yet it already came as a surprise to see life still going on outside, in broad sunlight, people walking to and fro, taxis, buses with men reading the evening paper on the platform on their way home.

'Rue Gay-Lussac!' he told the driver. 'I'll tell you where to stop.'

The tall trees in the Luxembourg Gardens swayed in the breeze, and all the chairs were taken; there were a lot of bright dresses; some children were still playing along the paths.

'Is Maître Orin at home?' he asked the concierge.

'He hasn't been out for over a month, poor man.'

Maigret had suddenly remembered him. He was probably the oldest solicitor in Paris. The chief-inspector had no idea of his age, but he'd always known him as an old man, a semi-invalid, which didn't stop him from always having a smiling face and talking about women with a wicked twinkle in his eye.

He lived, together with a housekeeper almost as old as himself, in a bachelor flat cluttered up with books and prints, which he collected, and most of the prints dealt with bawdy subjects.

Orin was seated in an arm-chair in front of the open window, his knees covered by a rug, despite the weather.

'Well, m'lad? What a pleasant surprise! I'd begun to think everyone had forgotten me or thought that I'd been laid to rest in Père-Lachaise long ago. What's the trouble this time?'

He didn't try to deceive himself, and Maigret coloured slightly, since it was true that he'd seldom called on the lawyer for other than selfish reasons.

'I wondered just now if, by any chance, you would have known a man called Serre who, if I'm not mistaken, died thirty-two or thirty-three years ago.'

'Alain Serre?'

'He was a solicitor.'

'That'd be Alain.'

'What sort of man was he?'

'I suppose I'm not allowed to ask what it's all about?'

'About his son.'

'I never saw the boy. I knew there was a son, but I never met him. You see, Maigret, Alain and I belonged to a gay set, whose life didn't revolve round the family hearth. We were to be found mostly at the club or behind the scenes at variety shows, and we knew all the chorus girls by their Christian names.'

He added, with a ribald grin:

'If you see what I mean!'

'You didn't know his wife?'

'I must have been introduced to her. Didn't she live somewhere in Neuilly? For several years Alain went out of circulation. He wasn't the only one it happened to. There were even a few who looked down on us, once they got married. I didn't expect to see him again. And then, a long time afterwards . . .'

'About how long?'

'I don't know. Some years. Let me see. The club had already moved from the Faubourg Saint-Honoré to the Avenue Hoche. Ten years? Twelve years? Anyway, he came back to us. He behaved oddly at first, as if he thought we bore him a grudge for dropping us.'

'Then?'

'Nothing. He went the pace redoubled. Let's see. He went about for a long time with a little singer with a big mouth they used to call . . . We had a nickname for her. . . . Something smutty. . . . I can't call it to mind.'

'Did he drink?'

'Not more than anyone else. Two or three bottles of champagne occasionally. . . .'

'What became of him?'

'What becomes of us all in the end. He died.'

'That's all?'

'If you want to know the sequel, m'lad, you'll have to ask aloft. It's St. Peter's business and not mine. What misdeed has his son committed?'

'I don't know yet. His wife has disappeared.'

'A gay dog?'

'No. Quite the reverse.'

'Juliette! Bring us something to drink.'

Maigret had to stay another quarter of an hour with the old man who insisted on trying to find, among his prints, a sketch of the singer.

'I wouldn't swear that it's a good likeness. A very talented chap did it, one night when the whole gang of us were up in his studio.'

The girl was naked and walking on her hands, and her face could not be seen by reason of the fact that her hair was sweeping the floor.

'Come and see me again, Maigret my boy. If you'd had time to share my humble meal. . . .'

A bottle of wine was warming in a corner of the room and a pleasant smell of cooking filled the flat.

The police at Rouen hadn't been able to pick up Sad Freddie any more than those at Le Havre. Perhaps the expert safe-breaker was no longer in that town. Was he on his way back to Paris? Had he read Ernestine's message?

Maigret had sent a plain-clothes man on a mission along the river-bank.

'Where shall I start from?'

'As far upstream as you can.'

He'd also telephoned his wife that he wouldn't be back to dinner.

'D'you think I'll see you tonight?'

'Probably not.'

He wasn't hoping for too much. He, too, knew that he'd assumed a big responsibility by rushing matters and taking Guillaume Serre down to Headquarters before he had the slightest proof.

Now it was too late. He could no longer let him go.

He felt drowsy, glum. He sat down on the terrace of the *Brasserie Dauphine*, but, after reading right through the bill of fare, he ended by ordering a sandwich and a glass of beer, for he wasn't hungry.

He went slowly up the staircase at Headquarters. The lights had just come on, although it was still daylight. As his head reached the first-floor level, he glanced automatically at the waiting-room, and the first thing that caught his eye was a green hat that had begun to get on his nerves.

Ernestine was there, sitting opposite Madame Serre, with her hands in her lap like the old lady, and the same air of patience and resignation. She saw him straight away, and deliberately assumed a fixed stare, giving a slight shake of the head.

He understood that she was asking him not to recognize her. Immediately after, she began talking to the old lady as though the ice had been broken some time before.

He shrugged his shoulders, pushed open the door of the Duty Room. The shorthand writer was at work, a pad of paper on his knee. The weary voice of Janvier could be heard, punctuated by his footsteps as he paced up and down the room next door.

'According to you, Monsieur Serre, your wife fetched a taxi on the corner of the Boulevard Richard-Wallace. How long was she away?'

Before relieving him, he climbed up to Moers' attic, where the latter was busy filing documents.

'Tell me, my boy, apart from the brick dust, there were no traces of anything else in the car?'

'The car had been cleaned out very thoroughly.'

'You're sure?'

'It's only by chance that I found a little powdered brick in a fold of the mat, under the driver's seat.'

'Suppose the car hadn't been cleaned and that the driver had got out on a country road.'

'A tarred road?'

'No. Suppose, I'm saying, that he got out, also the person with him, that they'd both gone for a walk on the path and then climbed back into the car.'

'And that it hadn't been cleaned afterwards?'

'Yes.'

'There'd be marks left. Maybe not many. But I'd have found them.'

'That's all I wanted to know. Don't leave yet.'

'Right you are. By the way, I found two hairs in the room of the woman who's disappeared. She was a natural blonde, but gave herself henna rinses. I can tell you what face-powder she used, too.'

The chief-inspector went downstairs again, this time went into his office, throwing off his jacket. He smoked a pipe in there all afternoon. Janvier had smoked cigarettes, and Serre cigars. The air was blue with smoke that drifted in a haze up near the light.

'Aren't you thirsty, Monsieur Serre?'

'The sergeant gave me a glass of water.'

Janvier went out.

'You wouldn't prefer a glass of beer? Or wine?'

Still the same air of bearing Maigret a personal grudge for these little snares.

'Thank you all the same.'

'A sandwich?'

'D'you expect to keep me here much longer?'

'I don't know. Probably. It'll depend on you.'

He went to the door, called out to the plain-clothes men:

'Could one of you fetch me a road-map of the Fontainebleau district?'

He was taking his time. All this was just talk, it was merely scratching the surface.

'When you go for a meal, get them to send up some sandwiches and beer, Janvier.'

'Right you are, Chief.'

The road-map was brought to him.

'Show me the spot where you pulled up on Sunday.'

Serre searched for a moment, took a pencil from the desk, marked a cross where the main road met a country lane.

'If there's a farm with a red roof on the left, it'll be this lane here.'

'How long did you go on walking?'

'About a quarter of an hour.'

'Were you wearing the same shoes as today?'

He pondered, looked at his shoes, nodded.

'You're sure about that?'

'Certain.'

His shoes had rubber heels, on which concentric circles were stamped around the maker's name.

'Don't you think, Monsieur Serre, that it'd be simpler and less tiring for you to spill the beans? When did you kill your wife?'

'I didn't kill her.'

Maigret sighed, went to give fresh instructions next door. Couldn't be helped! It'll probably take hours more. The dentist's complexion was already slightly muddier than in the morning, and dark circles had begun to show beneath his eyes.

'Why did you marry her?'

'My mother advised me to.'

'For what motive?'

'For fear I'd be left to live alone one day. She thinks that I'm still a child and that I need someone to look after me.'

'And to stop you from drinking?'

Silence.

'I don't suppose that your marriage with Maria Van Aerts was a love match?'

'We were both nearing our fifties.'

'When did you start to quarrel?'

'We never quarrelled.'

'What did you do with your evenings, Monsieur Serre?'

'I?'

'You.'

'I mostly read, in my study.'

'And your wife?'

'Writing, in her room. She used to go to bed early.'

'Did your father lose much money?'

'I don't understand.'

'Have you ever heard that your father used to lead what they called in those days a fast life?'

'He went about a great deal.'

'Did he spend large sums?'

'I believe so.'

'Your mother made scenes?'

'We're not the sort of people who make scenes.'

'How much did your first marriage bring you in?'

'We don't speak the same language.'

'You and your first wife were married under the joint-possession law?'

'Correct.'

'And she had money. So you must have inherited.'

'Is that unusual?'

'So long as your second wife's body isn't found, you can't inherit from her.'

'Why shouldn't she be found alive?'

'You believe that, Serre?'

'I didn't kill her.'

'Why did you take your car out on Tuesday night?'

'I didn't take it out.'

'The concierge in the house opposite saw you. It was round about midnight.'

'You forget that there are three garages, three former stables, whose doors are adjacent. It was at night, you say so yourself. She may have got them confused.'

'The ironmonger, he couldn't have mistaken someone else for you, in broad daylight, when you went in to buy putty and another window-pane.'

'My word's as good as his.'

'Providing you didn't kill your wife. What did you do with the trunk and the suitcases?'

'That's the third time I've been asked that question. You've forgotten to mention the tools this time.'

'Where were you on Tuesday about midnight?'

'In bed.'

'Are you a light sleeper, Monsieur Serre?'

'No. My mother is.'

'Neither of you heard anything?'

'I seem to remember telling you that already.'

'And on Wednesday morning you found the house as usual?'

'I suppose that, since an enquiry has been opened, you've the right to question me. You've decided, haven't you, to put me through an endurance test? Your detective has already asked me all these questions. Now it's starting all over again. I can see that it's going to go on all night. To save time, I'll tell you once and for all that I didn't kill my wife. I also inform you that I will not answer any questions which have already been put to me. Is my mother here?'

'What makes you think that she is?'

'Does it seem peculiar to you?'

'She's sitting in the waiting-room.'

'D'you mean to let her spend the night there?'

'I shall make no attempt to prevent her. She's quite free.'

This time Guillaume Serre looked at him with hatred.

'I wouldn't like to have your job.'

'I wouldn't like to be in your shoes.'

They stared at each other in silence, each determined not to lower his gaze.

'You killed your wife, Serre. As you probably killed the first one.'

The other didn't move a muscle.

'You'll confess to it.'

A contemptuous smile curled the dentist's lips, and he threw himself back in his chair and crossed his legs.

Next door the waiter from the *Brasserie Dauphine* could be heard putting down plates and glasses on a desk.

'I wouldn't mind something to eat.'

'Perhaps you'd like to take off your coat?'

'No.'

He started to eat a sandwich slowly, while Maigret went to fill a glass with water from the fountain in the wall cupboard.

It was eight o'clock in the evening.

They could see the windows darkening gradually, the view dissolving into specks of light that seemed as far away as the stars.

Maigret had to send out for tobacco. At eleven o'clock, the dentist was smoking his last cigar and the air had got more and more thick. Twice the chief-inspector had gone out for a stroll through the building and had seen the two women in the waiting-room. The second time they'd drawn their chairs closer together and were gossiping together as if they'd known each other for years.

'When did you clean your car?'

'It was last cleaned a fortnight ago, in a garage at Neuilly, at the same time as they changed the oil.'

'It hasn't been cleaned again since Sunday?'

'No.'

'You see, Monsieur Serre, we've just performed a decisive experiment. One of my men who, like yourself, is wearing rubber heels, drove out to the crossing which you marked on the Fontainebleau road. As you stated that you did on Sunday with your mother, he got out of the car and went for a walk along the country lane. It hasn't a tarred surface. He got back in the car and returned here.

'The experts from our technical branch, who're supposed to know their job then examined the mats in the car.

'Here is the dust and gravel that they gathered up.'

He pushed a small paper bag across the desk.

Serre made no move to take it.

'We'd have found the same thing on the mat in your car.'

'That proves I killed my wife?'

'It proves that your car has been cleaned since Sunday.'

'Couldn't someone have got into my garage?'

'It's unlikely.'

'Didn't your men get in?'

'What are you insinuating?'

'Nothing, Chief-Inspector. I'm not accusing anyone – I'm merely pointing out to you that this operation was undertaken without witnesses, therefore without legal warranty.'

'Wouldn't you like to speak to your mother?'

'You'd love to know what I'd have to say to her? Nothing, Monsieur Maigret. I've nothing to say to her, and she has nothing to say to me.'

A thought suddenly crossed his mind.

'Has she had anything to eat?'

'I've no idea. I can only repeat that she's a free agent.'

'She won't leave as long as I'm here.'

'She may be in for a long stay.'

Serre lowered his eyes and his manner changed. After a long hesitation, he muttered, as if slightly ashamed:

'I suppose it would be asking too much to have a sandwich sent in to her?'

'That was done a long time ago.'

'Did she eat it?'

'Yes'

'How is she?'

'She talks all the time.'

'To whom?'

'To a certain person who happens also to be in the waiting-room. A girl who used to be on the streets.'

And again there was a gleam of hate in the dentist's eyes.

'You arranged that deliberately, didn't you?'

'Not at all.'

'My mother has nothing to tell.'

'All the better for you.'

They passed the next quarter of an hour in silence, then Maigret plodded into the next-door room, glummer than ever, motioned to Janvier who was dozing in a corner.

'Same routine, Chief?'

'Anything you like.'

The stenographer was worn out. The translator still worked on in his cubbyhole.

'Go and fetch Ernestine, the one with the green hat, and bring her to Lucas's office.'

When Lofty came in, she didn't look pleased.

'You oughtn't to have interrupted us. She'll start suspecting something.'

Perhaps because it was late at night. Maigret spoke to her more familiarly than usual, without noticing it.

'What've you been filling her up with?'

'How I didn't know why I'd been made to come here, how my husband's been missing two days and I had no news, how much I hate the police and the tricks they're always trying on.

' "They're just keeping me waiting here to try and shake me!" I told her. "They reckon they can get away with anything." '

'What did she say?'

'She asked me if I'd been here before. I said yes, I'd been put through it for a whole night, a year ago, because my husband had had a scrap in a café and they wanted to make out he'd knifed somebody. To start off with, she looked at me like she was sort of disgusted. Then, bit by bit, she began to ask me questions.'

'What about?'

'Mostly about you. I told her everything bad I could think up. I took good care to add that you always managed to make people talk, however tough you had to get with 'em.'

'What!'

'I know what I'm doing. I told her about the time when you kept somebody stark naked in your office for twenty-four hours, in midwinter, taking care the window was left wide open.'

'There's been no such thing.'

'It shook her. She's less sure of herself than she was when I got here. She spends all her time listening.

' "Does he beat people?" she asked me.

' "It's been known." '

'Would you like me to go back to her?'

'If you want to.'

'Only I'd like to be taken back to the waiting-room by one of the men, and have him be rough with me.'

'Still no news of Alfred.'

'You haven't had any either?'

Maigret had her taken back in the way that she'd asked for and the plain-clothes man returned grinning wryly.

'What happened?'

'Nothing much. When I passed by the old girl, she put up her arm as if she thought I was going to hit her. I'd hardly got out of the room when Lofty burst out crying.'

Madame Maigret rang up to find out if her husband had eaten anything.

'Shall I wait for you?'

'Certainly not.'

He had a headache. He was disgruntled with himself, with everybody else. Perhaps he was a bit uneasy as well. He wondered what would happen if they suddenly received a telephone call from Maria Van Aerts announcing that she'd changed her plans and had quietly settled down in some town or other.

He drank a pint already gone tepid, told them to send up some more before the *brasserie* closed and went back into his office, where Janvier had opened the window. The clamour of the city had subsided. Now and then a taxi crossed the Pont Saint-Michel.

He sat down, his shoulders drooping. Janvier went out. After a long pause, he said musingly:

'Your mother's got it into her head that I'm torturing you.'

He was surprised to see the other raise his head sharply, and for the first time he saw his face look anxious.

'What have they been telling her?'

'I don't know. It's probably the girl who's in there with her. These people like to make up stories so's to seem more interesting.'

'Could I see her?'

'Who?'

'My mother.'

Maigret pretended to hesitate, to weigh up the pros and cons, finally shook his head.

'No,' he said decisively. 'I think I'll question her myself. And I'm wondering if I shouldn't have Eugénie brought down, too.'

'My mother doesn't know anything.'

'Do you?'

'I don't either.'

'Then there's no reason why I shouldn't question her as I've questioned you.'

'Haven't you any pity, Inspector?'

'For whom?'

'An old woman.'

'Maria would have liked to become an old woman, too.'

He walked up and down the office, his hands behind his back, but what he was waiting for didn't come.

'Your turn, Janvier! I'm going to have a crack at the mother.'

Actually he didn't know yet whether he would do so or not. Janvier said later that he'd never known the Chief so tired and so surly as on that night.

It was one in the morning. Everybody at Headquarters had lost confidence, and chagrined glances were exchanged behind the chief-inspector's back.

VIII

MAIGRET was emerging from the Duty Room on his way to look in on the translator when one of the cleaners, who, half an hour before, had invaded the building, came up to tell him:

'There's a lady asking to speak to you.'

'Where?'

'It's one of the two who were in the waiting-room. Seems she's not feeling well. She came into the office I was sweeping out, white in the face like she'd come over queer, and asked me straight off to fetch you.'

'The old lady?' Maigret asked, frowning.

'No, the girl.'

Most of the doors that gave onto the corridor were open. In an office two doors away, the chief-inspector caught sight of Ernestine holding one hand to her breast, and strode quickly forward, scowling, his lips framing a question.

'Shut the door,' she whispered when he was within earshot.

And directly he'd done so:

'Phew! I couldn't stick it any longer and that's the truth, but I'm not sick. I put on an act so's to get away from her for a bit. Not that I'm feeling any too bright, either. You wouldn't have a stiff drink about the place?'

He had to go back to his office to get the bottle of brandy that he always kept in the cupboard. Not having any smaller glasses, he poured the spirit into a tumbler and she swallowed it at a gulp, with a shudder.

'I don't know how you manage to take the son. The mother's got me right down. In the finish, I reckoned I'd go crackers.'

'Did she talk?'

'She's wider than me. That's just what I wanted to tell you. To start off I made sure she'd swallowed all the bull I was stuffing her up with.

'Then, I don't know how it happened, she started to pop in a question here and there, all innocent-like. I've been third-degree'd before now and I reckoned I could hold my own.

'With her, I didn't have an earthly.'

'Did you tell her what you were?'

'Not right out. That woman's very, very clever, Monsieur Maigret. How could she have guessed I'd been on the beat? Tell me, does it still show? Then she says to me:

' "You're no stranger to these kind of people, are you?"

'It was your mob she was referring to.

'In the end, she's asking me what it's like in jail, and I'm telling her.

'If you'd told me, when I sat down there in front of her, that I'd give the game away, I'd have refused to credit it.'

'Did you tell her about Alfred?'

'In a way. Without saying exactly what his racket is. She thinks he's a kite-man. She's not all that interested. For three-quarters of an hour now, at least, she's been asking me about life in jail: what time you get up, what you have to eat, what the wardresses act like. . . . I thought you'd be interested to know and I made out I'd come over queer; I got up saying I was going to ask for a drink, that it wasn't human leaving women to hang about all night. . . .

'Mind if I have another drop?'

She really was worn out. The brandy brought the colour back into her cheeks.

'Her son won't talk?'

'Not yet. Has she said anything about him?'

'She harks to every sound, gets jumpy every time a door opens. Something else she asked me. She wanted to know if I'd met anybody who'd got guillotined. Now I feel better, I'll go back to her. I'll be on my guard this time, don't worry.'

She took the opportunity to put on some powder, looked at the bottle without venturing to ask for a third drink.

'What's the time?'

'Three o'clock.'

'I don't know how she sticks it. She doesn't look tired, and she's sitting up as straight as at the start of the evening.'

Maigret let her out, took a breath of air at a window opening on to the courtyard and swallowed a mouthful of brandy out of the bottle. As he crossed the office where the translator was working, the latter showed him a passage that he'd underlined in one of the letters.

'This dates back a year and a half,' he said.

Maria had written to her friend:

Yesterday I had a good laugh. G. came to my room, not for what you might think, but to talk to me about a scheme I'd proposed the day before to go and spend a couple of days in Nice.

They're terrified of travelling, these people. Only once in their lives have they ever been out of France. Their one trip abroad goes back to the time when the father was still alive and they all went over to London together. Incidentally, it appears that they were all seasick and had to call in the ship's doctor.

But that's nothing to do with the case.

Whenever I say something that doesn't suit them, they don't answer straight away. They just stop talking, and, as the saying goes, one can hear a pin drop.

Then, later on or next day, G. comes up to my room, looking distressed, beats about the bush, finally confesses what's worrying him. Briefly, it would seem that my notion of going to Nice for the Carnival was ludicrous, almost indecent. He made no bones about telling me that his mother had been shocked by it and pleaded with me to give up the idea.

Well, it so happened that the drawer of my bedside-table was open. He glanced into it by accident and I saw him turn pale.

'What's that?' he stammered, pointing at the little automatic with a mother-of-pearl butt that I bought during my trip to Egypt.

Do you remember? I wrote to you about it at the time. People had told me that a woman on her own was never safe in places like that.

I don't know why I'd put it in that drawer. I replied coolly:

'It's a pistol.'

'Is it loaded?'

'I don't remember.'

I picked it up. I looked in the magazine. There were no bullets in it.

'Have you any ammunition?'

'There must be some somewhere.'

Half an hour later, my mother-in-law came up on some excuse, for she never

*enters my room without giving a reason. She also beat about the bush for a while,
then explained to me that it was most unseemly for a woman to carry fire-arms.*

*'But it's more like a toy,' I retorted. 'I keep it as a souvenir, because the handle's
pretty and my initials are engraved on it. I don't think it could harm anybody
much, either.'*

*She gave in, finally. But not before I'd had to give her the box of ammunition
that was in the bottom of the drawer.*

*The funny part is that, no sooner had she gone, than I found in one of my
handbags another ammunition-clip that I'd forgotten about. I didn't tell her. . . .*

Maigret, who was holding the brandy bottle in his hand, poured
some out for the translator, then he went to give some to the typist and
the plain-clothes man who, to try to keep awake, was doodling on his
blotter.

When he went back into his office, which Janvier vacated automatically, the bell had gone for another round.

'I've been thinking, Serre. I'm beginning to believe that you haven't
been lying as much as I supposed.'

He'd dropped the 'Monsieur', as if so many hours alone together had
brought a sort of familiarity. The dentist merely regarded him mis-
trustfully.

'Maria wasn't meant to disappear any more than your first wife. Her
disappearance wasn't to your advantage. She'd packed her bags, announced her departure for Holland. She really intended to take the
night-train.

'I don't know if she was supposed to die in the house or not until she
got outside. What d'you say to that?'

Guillaume Serre made no reply, but his expression betrayed much
more concern.

'If you like it better, she was meant to die a natural death, by which I
mean a death that would *pass as natural*.

'This didn't take place, since, if it had, you'd have had no motive for
disposing of her body or her luggage.

'There's another thing that doesn't add up. You'd said good-bye to
each other. She'd no reason then to go back into your study. Yet her
dead body was lying there at a certain time that night.

'I'm not asking you to answer me, but to follow my reasoning. I've
only just found out that your wife owned a pistol.

'I'm ready to believe that you shot her in self-defence. After that you
got in a panic. You left the body where it had fallen, while you went to
get your car out of the garage. It was then, round about midnight, that
the concierge saw you.

'What I'm trying to find out, is what changed both your plans and
hers. You were in your study, weren't you?'

4

'I don't remember.'

'That's what you stated.'

'Possibly.'

'I'm convinced that your mother, however, was not in her room, but with you.'

'She was in her room.'

'So you remember that?'

'Yes.'

'Then you remember, also, that you were in your study? Your wife hadn't gone out to fetch a taxi yet. If she'd brought a cab back that night, we'd have found the driver. In other words, it was before leaving the house that she changed her mind and went to your study. Why?'

'I've no idea.'

'You admit that she came to see you?'

'No.'

'You're being unwise, Serre. There are very few instances, in criminal records, when a dead body hasn't been found sooner or later. We shall find hers. And I'm certain, now, that a post-mortem will reveal that she was killed by one or several bullet wounds. What I'm wondering is whether it was a shot fired by your gun or a shot fired by hers.

'The seriousness of your case will depend on that. If the bullet came from her pistol, the conclusion will be drawn that, for one reason or another, she took it into her head to go and settle some score with you and threaten you.

'Money perhaps, Serre?'

He shrugged his shoulders.

'You leaped at her, disarmed her and squeezed the trigger without meaning to. Another theory could be that she threatened your mother and not you. A woman's more likely to feel hatred for another woman than for a man.

'A final possibility, again, is that your own revolver was not in your room, where you put it soon after, but in the drawer of your desk.

'Maria comes in. She's armed. She threatens you. You pull the drawer open and shoot first.

'In either case, you're in no danger of execution. There can be no question of premeditation, since it's quite normal to keep a pistol in the desk of one's study.

'You can even plead self-defence.

'What remains to be explained is why your wife, on the point of leaving, should suddenly have rushed in to see you with a gun in her hand.'

He threw himself back and slowly filled a pipe, without taking his eyes off the other.

'What d'you say to that?'

'This can go on for ever,' said Serre in a tone of disgust.

'You still refuse to talk?'

'I'm answering your questions obediently.'

'You haven't told me why you shot her.'

'I didn't shoot her.'

'Then your mother did?'

'My mother didn't shoot her either. She was up in her room.'

'While you were quarrelling with your wife?'

'There was no quarrel.'

'Pity.'

'I'm so sorry.'

'You see, Serre, I've done my best to discover any reason your wife may have had for settling with you and threatening you.'

'She didn't threaten me.'

'Don't be too positive about it, because you may regret your claims later on. It's you who will plead with me or with the jury to believe that your life or your mother's was in danger.'

Serre smiled sardonically. He was tired, slumped in upon himself, his shoulders slightly hunched about his neck, but he hadn't lost any of his self-possession. His beard showed blue through the skin on his cheeks. The sky, beyond the window-panes, was already not quite so dark and the air in the room was becoming cooler.

It was Maigret who felt the cold first and went over to close the window.

'It wasn't to your advantage to have a corpse on your hands. *I mean a corpse that nobody could be allowed to see.* D'you follow me?'

'No.'

'When your first wife died, it was in such a manner that you were able to call in Doctor Dutilleux to make out the death certificate.

'That's how Maria was supposed to die, from apparently natural causes. She had a weak heart too. What had worked once could work again.

'But something went wrong.

'D'you see, now, what I'm getting at?'

'I didn't kill her.'

'And you didn't dispose of her body, together with her luggage and the burglar's tools?'

'There wasn't any burglar.'

'I'll probably confront you with him in a few hours.'

'You've found him?'

His tone was slightly uneasy, all the same.

'We were able to find his fingerprints in your study. You were careful to wipe over the furniture, but there's always some piece that gets forgotten. He happens to be an old offender, an expert in his way, well-known here, Alfred Jussiaume — "Sad Freddie", they call him. He told his wife what he'd seen. She is now out there in the waiting-room with your mother. As for Jussiaume, he's in Rouen and has no further reason to remain in hiding.

'We already have the concierge who saw you take your car out of the garage. We've also got the ironmonger who sold you a second sheet of glass at eight o'clock on Wednesday morning.

'The technical branch will prove that your car has been cleaned since that date.

'That makes quite a lot of evidence, doesn't it?

'When we have found the body and the luggage, my job will be over.

'Then, perhaps, you'll decide to explain why, instead of a, shall we say, lawful corpse, you found yourself landed with a body that you had to dispose of at once.

'There was some hitch.

'What was it, Serre?'

The man pulled a handkerchief out of his pocket, wiped his lips and forehead, but didn't open his mouth to reply.

'It's half-past three. I'm beginning to get fed up. Are you still determined not to talk?'

'I've nothing to say.'

'Very good,' said Maigret, getting up. 'I don't like having to bully an old woman. But I see that I am forced to question your mother.'

He expected a protest, at any rate some display of feeling. The dentist didn't bat an eyelid, and it seemed to Maigret that he even showed a kind of relief, that his nerves relaxed.

'You take over, Janvier. I'll get busy on the mother.'

It really was his intention; he was unable to put it into practice immediately, for Vacher had just appeared, in great excitement, a parcel in his hand.

'I've got it, Chief! Took me some time, but I think this is it.'

He undid the parcel wrapped in an old newspaper, revealing broken bits of brick, some reddish dust.

'Where?'

'On the Quai de Billancourt, opposite the Ile Seguin. If I'd started down-stream instead of starting up-stream, I'd have been here hours ago. I've been all over the wharves where they unload. Billancourt was the only place where a barge unloaded bricks lately.'

'When?'

'Last Monday. She sailed away about noon on Tuesday. The bricks are still there and kids must have been playing around, broken a fair amount of them. There's a red dust covering a good bit of the quay. Shall I take it up to Moers?'

'I'll go myself.'

As he went through the waiting-room, he looked at the two women sitting there in silence. It seemed, from their attitudes, as if there was now a chill between them.

Maigret entered the laboratory, where he felt he'd earned a cup of coffee, which Moers had just made.

'Have you got the sample of brick dust? Like to compare them?'

The colour was the same, the pattern seemed identical. Moers used magnifying slides and an electric projector.

'Does it add up?'

'Very likely. Comes from the same district, anyhow. It'll take me about thirty minutes or an hour to do the analysis.'

It was too late to have the Seine dragged. Nor would the river patrol be able to send a diver down until sunrise. Then, if they found Maria's body, or only the luggage and the tool-box, the circle would be closed.

'Hello! River Patrol? Maigret here.'

He still seemed to be in a bad temper.

'I'd like you to drag the Seine as soon as possible, Quai de Billancourt, at the place where a cargo of bricks was unloaded recently.'

'In an hour from now it'll be dawn.'

What stopped him from waiting? No jury would ask for further proof to find Guillaume Serre guilty even if he persisted in his denials. Without heeding the typist, who was staring at him, Maigret took a long pull at the bottle, wiped his mouth, went out into the passage and threw open purposefully the door of the waiting-room.

Ernestine thought he'd come for her and sprang quickly to her feet. Madame Serre, however, did not move.

It was the latter to whom Maigret spoke.

'D'you mind coming a moment?'

There was a large choice of empty offices. He pushed open a door at random, closed the window.

'Please take a seat.'

And he began to circle round the room, glancing at the old lady sourly from time to time.

'I don't much like to break bad news,' he growled at last. 'Especially to someone your age. Have you ever been ill, Madame Serre?'

'Except when we were seasick, crossing the Channel, I've never had to call in the doctor.'

'So, naturally, you don't suffer from heart trouble?'

'No.'

'Your son does, however?'

'He's always had an enlarged heart.'

'He killed his wife!' he shot out point-blank, raising his head and staring her in the face.

'Did he tell you so himself?'

He hated to use the old trick of a false confession.

'He still denies it, but that won't help. We've got proof.'

'That he's a murderer?'

'That he shot Maria, in his study.'

She had not moved. Her features had stiffened slightly; one had the impression that she'd stopped breathing, but she showed no other sign of emotion.

'What proof have you?'

'We've found the spot where his wife's body was thrown into the river, together with her luggage and the burglar's tools.'

'Ah!'

That was all she said. She was waiting, her hand stiffly folded on her dark dress.

'Your son refuses to plead self-defence. That's a mistake, because I'm convinced that, when his wife entered the study, she was armed and meant to do him harm.'

'Why?'

'That's what I'm asking you.'

'I've no idea.'

'Where were you?'

'In my room, as I told you.'

'You didn't hear anything?'

'Nothing. Only the door closing. Then the sound of a motor engine, in the street.'

'The taxi?'

'I thought it must be a taxi, since my daughter-in-law had said she was going to fetch one.'

'You're not sure? It might have been a private car?'

'I didn't see it.'

'Then it might easily have been your son's car?'

'He swore to me that he didn't go out.'

'You realize the discrepancy between what you're saying now and the statements that you made to me when you called here of your own accord?'

'No.'

'You stated positively that your daughter-in-law went away in a taxi.'

'I still think that she did.'

'But you're no longer certain about it. Are you so certain now that there was no attempted burglary?'

'I saw no sign of any.'

'What time did you come downstairs on Wednesday morning?'

'About half-past six.'

'Did you go into the study?'

'Not immediately. I got the coffee ready.'

'You didn't go and open the shutters?'

'Yes, I believe so.'

'Before your son came down?'

'Probably.'

'You wouldn't swear to it?'

'Put yourself in my place, Monsieur Maigret. For two days I've hardly known where I am. I've been asked all sorts of questions. I've been sitting in your waiting-room for I don't know how many hours. I'm tired. I'm doing my best to hold out.'

'Why did you come here tonight?'

'Isn't it natural for a mother to follow her son in such circumstances? I've always lived with him. He might be in need of me.'

'Would you follow him to prison?'

'I don't understand. I can't believe that . . .'

'Let me put it another way: if I made out a charge against your son, would you be willing to share the responsibility for what he did?'

'But since he hasn't done anything!'

'Are you sure of that?'

'Why should he have killed his wife?'

'You avoid giving me a straight answer. Are you convinced that he didn't kill her?'

'So far as I can tell.'

'Is there any chance that he did so?'

'He had no motive for it.'

'But he did!' he said harshly, staring her in the face.

She sat as if in suspended animation. She breathed:

'Ah!'

Then she opened her bag to take out her handkerchief. Her eyes were dry. She wasn't crying. She merely dabbed at her lips with the handkerchief.

'Might I have a glass of water?'

He had to hunt around for a moment, since he didn't know the office as well as his own.

'As soon as the Director of Prosecutions arrives at the Palais de Justice, your son will be indicted. I can tell you now that he hasn't the slightest change of getting away with it.'

'You mean that he . . .'

'He'll go to the guillotine.'

She didn't faint, but sat rigid on her chair, staring blankly ahead.

'His first wife's body will be exhumed. I dare say you know that traces of certain poisons can be found in a skeleton.'

'Why should he have killed them both? It isn't possible. It isn't true, Chief-Inspector. I don't know why you're telling me this, but I refuse to believe you. Let me speak to him. Allow me to talk to him in private and I'll find out the truth.'

'Were you in your room the whole of Tuesday evening?'

'Yes.'

'You didn't go downstairs at all?'

'No. Why should I have gone down, when that woman was leaving us at last?'

Maigret went over for a while to cool his forehead against the window-pane, then walked into the office next door, grabbed the bottle and drank from it the equivalent of three or four singles.

When he came back, he had assumed the heavy gait of Guillaume Serre and his obstinate glare.

IX

HE was sitting in a chair that wasn't his, both elbows on the table, his biggest pipe in his mouth, his eyes fixed upon the old lady whom he'd likened to a Mother Superior.

'Your son, Madame Serre, didn't kill either his first or his second wife,' he said, spacing out the words.

She frowned in surprise, but didn't look any the happier.

'Nor did he kill his father,' he added.

'What do you . . .?'

'Hush! . . . If you don't mind, we'll settle this as quickly as possible. We'll not bother about proof for the time being. That'll come in due course.

'We won't argue about your husband's case, either. What I'm almost certain of is that your first daughter-in-law was poisoned. I'll go further. I'm convinced that it wasn't done by arsenic or any of the strong poisons that are usually used.

'By the way, Madame Serre, I might tell you that, in nine cases out of ten, poison is a woman's weapon.

'Your first daughter-in-law, like the second, suffered from heart trouble. So did your husband.

'Certain drugs, which wouldn't seriously affect people in good health, can be fatal to cardiac cases. I wonder if Maria didn't provide us with the key to the problem in one of her letters to her friend. She speaks of a trip to England which you once took with your husband, and emphasizes that you were all so badly seasick that you had to be seen by the ship's doctor.

'What would be prescribed in such a case?'

'I've no idea.'

'That's very unlikely. They usually give you atropine in some form or other. Now, a fairly strong dose of atropine can be fatal to a person with a weak heart.'

'You mean that my husband . . .'

'We'll go into that another time, even if it's impossible to prove anything. Your husband, during his later days, was leading a disorderly life and throwing his money away. You've always been afraid of poverty, Madame Serre.'

'Not for myself. For my son. Which doesn't mean that I would have . . .'

'Later on, your son got married. Another woman came to live in your house, a woman who, overnight, bore your name and had as much right there as you.'

She compressed her lips.

'This woman, who also had a weak heart, was rich, richer than your son, richer than all the Serres put together.'

'You believe that I poisoned her, having first poisoned my husband?'

'Yes.'

She gave a little strained laugh.

'Doubtless I also poisoned my second daughter-in-law?'

'She was going away, discouraged, after having tried in vain to live in a house where she was treated like a stranger. Very likely she was taking her money with her. By coincidence, she had heart trouble too.

'You see, I wondered from the start why her body disappeared. If she'd simply been poisoned, you only had to call in a doctor who, given Maria's state of health, would have diagnosed a heart attack. Perhaps the attack itself was intended to come on later, in the taxi, at the station or on the train.'

'You seem very sure of yourself, Monsieur Maigret.'

'I know that something happened which obliged your son to shoot down his wife. Let's suppose that Maria, just as she was going to fetch a taxi or, more likely, as she was on the point of telephoning for one, felt certain symptoms coming on.

'She knew you both, having lived with you for two and a half years. She was a widely read woman, in all sorts of subjects, and it wouldn't surprise me if she had acquired some medical knowledge.

'Realizing that she'd been poisoned, she went into your husband's study while you were in there with him.'

'Why do you say that I was in there?'

'Because, unfortunately for her, she laid the blame on you. If you'd been in your room, she'd have gone upstairs.

'I don't know if she threatened you with her pistol or if she merely reached for the telephone to call the police. . . .

'There was only one way out for you: to shoot her down.'

'And, according to you, it was I who . . .'

'No. I've already told you that it's more likely to have been your son who fired, or, if you'd rather, finished your work for you.'

The drab light of dawn blended with the electric lamps. The lines in their faces were etched more deeply. The telephone bell rang.

'That you, Chief? I've done the test. It's ten to one the brick dust we found in the car came from Billancourt.'

'You can go home to bed, my boy. Your job's through.'

He got up once again, circled the room.

'Your son, Madame Serre, is determined to shoulder all the blame. I don't see any way of stopping him. If he's been able to keep his mouth shut all this time, he's capable of keeping it shut for good. Unless . . .'

'Unless . . .?'

'I don't know. I was thinking aloud. Two years ago I'd a man as tough as he is in my office and after fifteen hours we still hadn't got a word out of him.'

He threw open the window abruptly, in a kind of rage.

'It took twenty-seven and a half hours to break his nerve.'

'Did he confess?'

'He spilled everything in one long stream, as if it were a relief to get rid of it.'

'I didn't poison anybody.'

'The answer doesn't lie with you.'

'But with my son?'

'Yes. He's convinced that you only did it for his sake, partly out of fear that he'd be left penniless, partly out of jealousy.'

He had to restrain himself from raising his hand to her, despite her age, for the old woman's thin lips had just twitched in an involuntary smile.

'Which is a lie!' he said flatly.

Then, coming closer to her, his eyes on hers, his breath on the woman's face, he rapped out:

'It's not for his sake that you're afraid of poverty, it's for your own! It's not for his sake that you murdered, and if you came here tonight, it's because you were afraid he might talk.'

She tried to shrink away, threw herself back in her chair, for Maigret's face was thrust into hers, hard, menacing.

'Never mind if he does go to prison, or even if he's executed, so long as you can be sure of staying in the clear. You believe that you've still many years to live, in your house, counting your money. . . .'

She was frightened. Her mouth opened as if to call for help. Suddenly, with a violent, unexpected jerk, Maigret wrenched from her withered hands the bag that she was clinging to.

She gave a cry, shot forward to retrieve it.

'Sit down.'

He undid the silver clasp. Right at the bottom, beneath the gloves, the note-case, the handkerchief and the powder-compact, he found a folded paper which contained two white tablets.

A hush like that in a church or a cavern enclosed them. Maigret let his body relax, sat down, pressed a bell-push.

When the door opened, he said slowly, without a glance at the plain-clothes man who'd appeared:

'Tell Janvier to lay off him.'

And, as the detective still stood there, in amazement:

'It's all over. She's confessed.'

'I haven't confessed to anything.'

He waited until the door closed again.

'It comes to the same thing. I could have carried on the experiment to the end, let you have the private talk with your son that you wanted.

'Don't you think that you've caused enough deaths already for one old woman?'

'You mean that I would have . . .'

He was toying with the tablets.

'You'd have given him his medicine, or rather what he would have thought was his medicine, and there'd have been no danger of his ever talking again.'

The corners of the roof-tops had begun to be crested with sunlight. The telephone rang again.

'Chief-Inspector Maigret? River Patrol here. We're at Billancourt. The diver's just gone down for the first time and he's found a pretty heavy trunk.'

'The rest'll turn up as well!' he said indifferently.

An exhausted and astonished Janvier was framed in the doorway.

'They told me. . . .'

'Take her down to the cells. The man, too, as an accessory. I'll see the prosecutor directly he comes in.'

He'd no longer any business with either the mother or the son.

'You can go off to bed,' he told the translator.

'It's over?'

'For today.'

The dentist was no longer there when he entered his office, but the ash-tray was full of very black cigar-butts. He sat down in his chair and was about to doze off, when he remembered Lofty.

He found her in the waiting-room, where she'd gone to sleep, shook her by the shoulder and, instinctively, she put her green hat straight.

'That's the lot. Off you go now.'

'Has he confessed?'

'It was her.'

'What! It was the old girl who . . .'

'Later!' he murmured.

Then, turning round, since he was assailed by a twinge of remorse:

'And thanks! When Alfred comes back, advise him to . . .'

But what was the good? Nothing would cure the Sad Man of his mania for burgling the safes that he had once put in, or wean him from his belief that each would be the last and that this time he was really going to live in the country.

On account of her age, old Madame Serre was not executed and left the Court with the complacent air of one who is at last going to set the women's prison in order.

When her son came out of Fresnes jail, after two years, he made straight for the house in the Rue de la Ferme and, that very evening, took the same stroll round the neighbourhood that he'd been accustomed to take in the days when he had a dog to exercise.

He continued to go and drink red wine in the little café and, before entering, to look uneasily up and down the street.

Shadow Rock Farm,
Lakeville, Conn.
May 8, 1951

MAIGRET'S REVOLVER

MAIGRET'S REVOLVER

(*Le Revolver de Maigret*)
*was first published in France in 1954
and in Great Britain in 1956
Translated from the French by Nigel Ryan*

MAIGRET'S REVOLVER

I

WHEN, later on, Maigret thought about that case, it would always be as of something a little abnormal, linked in his mind with those illnesses which do not break out openly, but begin with vague aches and pains, symptoms too mild to claim one's attention.

There was, to start off with, no complaint to Police Headquarters, no emergency call, no anonymous information, but, to go as far back as possible, a banal telephone call from Madame Maigret.

The black marble clock on the office mantelpiece had stood at twenty to twelve; he saw again distinctly the angle of the hands on its face. The window was wide open, for it was June, and, beneath the hot sun, Paris had taken on its summer smell.

'That you?'

His wife had recognized his voice, obviously, but she still asked if it really was him speaking, not in doubt, but merely because she had always been awkward on the telephone. At the Boulevard Richard-Lenoir too the windows must have been open, Madame Maigret at that hour had finished the bulk of her housework. It was unusual for her to ring him up.

'It's me.'

'I wanted to ask if you expect to be back for lunch.'

It was even more unusual for her to telephone to ask him that question. He had frowned, not worried, but in surprise.

'Why?'

'Oh nothing. Or rather, there's someone here waiting to see you.'

'Who?'

'No one you know. It's nothing. Only if you weren't coming back I wasn't going to make him wait.'

'A man?'

'A young man.'

She had probably taken him into the drawing-room where they scarcely ever set foot. The telephone was in the dining-room, which they normally used, and where they entertained their friends. It was there that Maigret had his pipes, his armchair, Madame Maigret her sewing-machine. From the embarrassed way she spoke he realized that she hadn't dared to close the door between the two rooms.

'Who is it?'

'I don't know.'

'What does he want?'

'I don't know that either. It's personal.'

He attached no importance to the matter. If he took it up, it was rather because his wife was uncomfortable about it, and also because she seemed to have taken the visitor under her protection.

'I expect to leave the office about midday,' he said finally.

He had only one more person to see, a woman who had already been at him three or four times about threatening letters which some neighbour was sending her. He rang for the office-boy.

'Show her in.'

He lit his pipe, and leant back in his chair, resigned.

'Well, Madame, you've had another letter?'

'Two, Inspector. I've brought them with me. In one of them, as you'll see, she admits it was she who poisoned my cat and declares that if I don't move house, it will soon be my turn . . .'

The hands crept slowly round the dial of the clock. He had to make a show of taking the matter seriously. It lasted for a little under a quarter of an hour. Then, just as he was getting up to fetch his hat from the cupboard, there was a knock at the door.

'You busy?'

'You! What are you doing in Paris?'

It was Lourtie, once one of his detectives, who had been posted to the flying squad in Nice.

'Just on my way through. I felt like taking a look at the old place again and saying hello to you. Have we time to drink a *pastis* at the *Brasserie Dauphine*?'

'A quick one, then.'

He was fond of Lourtie, a big-boned, strapping fellow with a voice like a choir leader. In the *brasserie*, where they remained standing at the bar, there were several other detectives. They spoke of this and that. The taste of the *pastis* was exactly what was needed for a day like that. They drank one, then a second, a third.

'It's time I was getting along. I'm expected at home.'

'Can I walk some of the way with you?'

They had crossed the Pont-Neuf together, Lourtie and he, then walked as far as the Rue de Rivoli, where it had taken Maigret a good five minutes to find a taxi. It was ten to one when he had at last climbed the three floors of the Boulevard Richard-Lenoir, and, as usual, the door of his flat had opened before he had time to take the key from his pocket.

Straightaway he had noticed his wife's uneasy manner. Speaking low, on account of the open doors, he had asked:

'He's still waiting?'

'He's gone.'

'You don't know what he wanted?'

'He didn't tell me.'

But for something in Madame Maigret's manner, he would have shrugged his shoulders and muttered:

'Good riddance!'

But instead of going into the kitchen and serving lunch, she followed him into the dining-room with the air of someone who has excuses to make.

'Did you go into the drawing-room this morning?' she finally asked.

'Me? No. Why?'

Why in fact should he have gone into the drawing-room, which he loathed, before going to the office?

'It seemed all right to me.'

'Well?'

'Nothing. I was trying to remember. I looked in the drawer.'

'What drawer?'

'The one where you keep your revolver from America.'

Only then had he begun to suspect the truth. When he had gone to spend several weeks in the United States at the invitation of the F.B.I. there had been a great deal of talk about weapons. The Americans had presented him on his departure with a revolver of which they were very proud, a Smith and Wesson '45 special, with short barrel and highly sensitive trigger mechanism. His name had been engraved upon it.

To J.-J. Maigret
from his F.B.I. friends.

He had never used it. But only the day before he had taken it out of its drawer to show to a friend, or rather a colleague, whom he had asked in for a liqueur after dinner.

'Why J.-J. Maigret?'

He had asked the same question himself when he had been presented with the gun at a cocktail party in his honour. The Americans, who normally have two christian names, had found out his. The first two, luckily: Jules-Joseph. In fact there was a third: Anthelme.

'You mean my revolver has disappeared?'

'I'm just going to explain.'

Before letting her speak, he went into the drawing-room which still smelt of cigarette smoke, and glanced at the mantelpiece where he remembered having put the gun the evening before. It was no longer there. Yet he was sure he had not put it away in its place.

'Who's responsible for this?'

'Sit down first of all. Let me give you your meal, or the joint will be overdone. Don't be cross.'

He was.

'I think it's a bit much when you let a stranger make his way in here and . . .'

She left the room, came back with a plate.

'If you had seen him . . .'

'What age?'

'Quite a young man. Nineteen? Twenty perhaps?'

'What did he want?'

'He rang the bell. I was in the kitchen. I thought it was the gas man. I went and opened the door. He asked me if this was where Inspector Maigret lived. I gathered, from his manner, that he mistook me for the maid. He was nervous, frightened-looking.'

'And you showed him into the drawing-room?'

'Because he told me he simply had to see you to ask your advice. My advice was to go and see you at your office. It seems it was too private.'

Maigret kept his peevish look, but began to feel like smiling. He pictured the panic-stricken young man, on whom Madame Maigret had at once taken pity.

'What sort of young man?'

'A very nice boy. I don't know how to put it. Not very well off, but from a good family. I'm sure he'd been crying. He took some cigarettes from his pocket and then immediately apologized. So I told him: "You can smoke. I'm used to it." Then I promised to telephone you to make sure you'd be coming back.'

'The revolver was still on the mantelpiece?'

'I'm certain it was. I didn't notice it there at that moment, but I remember it was there when I did the dusting this morning about nine, and no one else has been in.'

If she hadn't replaced the revolver in the drawer it was, he knew, because she had never been able to get used to firearms. It made no difference her knowing the weapon wasn't loaded — she wouldn't have touched it for anything in the world.

He pictured the scene. His wife going into the dining-room, speaking to him in low tones on the telephone, then coming back to say:

'He'll be here in half an hour at the latest.'

Maigret asked:

'You left him alone?'

'Well, I had to see to the lunch.'

'When did he leave?'

'That's just what I don't know. At one point I had to fry some onions, and I closed the kitchen door so the smell wouldn't escape. Then I went to the bedroom to tidy up. I thought he was there all the time. Perhaps he still was. I didn't want to disturb him by going into the drawing-room. It was only just after half-past twelve that I decided

to go and ask him to be patient, and found he wasn't there any longer.
Are you cross with me?'

Cross with her about what?

'What do you think it's all about? He looked so unlike a thief!'

He certainly wasn't one, either! How could a thief have guessed that
on that particular morning there was a revolver on the mantelpiece in
Maigret's drawing-room?

'You look worried. Was the gun loaded?'

'No.'

'Well then?'

The question was a stupid one. Anyone who takes the trouble to get
hold of a revolver has more or less some intention of using it. Wiping
his mouth, Maigret got up and had a look in the drawer, where he
found the cartridges in their place. Before sitting down again he rang
up his office.

'That you, Torrence? Would you get on to the gunsmiths in town. . . .
Hullo! The gunsmiths, yes. . . . Ask them if anyone has been to buy
cartridges for a Smith and Wesson '45 special. . . . What? . . . '45 special.
. . . In case no one has been yet, if anyone does come this afternoon or
tomorrow, tell them to find an excuse to keep the customer there for a
moment and warn the nearest police station. . . . Yes. . . . That's all. . . .
I'll be at the office as usual. . . .'

When he arrived at Police Headquarters at about half-past two,
Torrence already had the answer. A young man had been in to a gunsmith's in the Boulevard Bonne-Nouvelle who had no ammunition of
the calibre asked for and had sent his customer to Gastinne-Renette.
The latter had sold him a box.

'Did the lad produce the gun?'

'No. He showed them a scrap of paper with the make and calibre
written on it.'

Maigret had had other things to attend to that afternoon. Towards
five o'clock he had gone up to the laboratory. Jussieu, the head, had
asked him:

'Are you going to the Pardons' this evening?'

'With a fish *brandade* for dinner!' Maigret had replied. 'Pardon rang
me up the day before yesterday.'

'Me too. I don't think Dr. Paul can come.'

There are, just like that, periods in the lives of households during
which one sees a lot of another household, and then loses sight of them
for no reason.

For about a year, every month, the Maigrets had dined with the
Pardons, or rather 'at the doc's'. It was Jussieu, the head of the police
laboratory, who had one evening brought the inspector round to Dr.
Pardon's house, in the Boulevard Voltaire.

'You'll see! He's a chap you'll take to. An able man besides, who could have become one of our biggest specialists. I should add, specialist in any field, since after being on the staff at the Val-de-Grace and an assistant of Lebraz, he then spent five years on the staff at Sainte-Anne.'

'And now?'

'He's become a G.P., by choice, works twelve or fifteen hours a day without bothering to find out if his patients are going to be able to pay him, and most of the time forgets to send in his bill. Apart from that his one passion is cooking.'

Two days later, Jussieu had rung him up.

'Do you like *cassoulet*?'

'Why?'

'Pardon has invited us for tomorrow. In his house, you just have one dish, a regional one for preference, and he likes to know in advance if his guests like it.'

'*Cassoulet* suits me.'

Since then there had been other dinners, the one with *coq au vin*, the *couscous* one, the *sole dieppoise*, and others besides.

This time it was to be *brandade de morue*. By the way, who was it again Maigret was going to meet at the dinner? Pardon had rung him up the day before.

'You free the day after tomorrow? You like *brandade*? Are you for or against truffles?'

'For.'

They had got into the habit of calling each other Maigret and Pardon, while the women called each other by their christian names. The couples were almost the same age. Jussieu was ten years younger. Dr. Paul, the police doctor, who often joined them, was older.

'Tell me, Maigret, would it bore you to meet one of my former schoolmates?'

'Why should it bore me?'

'I don't know. To tell you the truth, I wouldn't have invited him if he hadn't asked me to give him an opportunity to meet you. Just now he came to see me in my consulting-room, for he's one of my patients as well, and insisted on knowing if you were coming definitely.'

At half-past seven that evening Madame Maigret, who had bedecked herself in a flowered dress and a pretty straw hat, finished putting on her white cotton gloves.

'You ready?'

'I'm coming.'

'Still thinking about the young man?'

'Of course not.'

What was nice, among other things, about these dinners, was that the Pardons lived only five minutes' walk away. One could see the sunlight reflected in the top-floor windows. The streets smelt of warm dust. Children were still playing out of doors, and families were taking the air on the pavements, where they had brought their chairs.

'Don't walk too fast.'

He always walked too fast for her.

'You're sure it was he who bought the cartridges?'

Since that morning, especially since he had told her about Gastinne-Renette, she had had a load on her mind.

'You don't think he's going to kill himself?'

'Suppose we talk about something else?'

'He was so nervous! The cigarette ends in the ashtray were all picked to pieces.'

The air was warm, and Maigret went with his hat in his hand, like people who go for Sunday walks. They reached the Boulevard Voltaire and, just near the square, disappeared into the block where the Pardons lived. They took the narrow lift which always made the same noise as it set off, and Madame Maigret gave her usual little start.

'Come in. My husband will be here in a few minutes. He's just been called out on an urgent case, but it's only up the road.'

It was seldom that a whole dinner went by without the doctor being disturbed. He would say:

'Don't wait for me.'

And often, in fact, they went home without seeing him again.

Jussieu was already there, alone in the drawing-room where there was a grand piano and embroidery work on all the furniture. Pardon came bursting in a few minutes later, and at once plunged into the kitchen.

'Lagrange not here yet?'

Pardon was a little man, rather stout, with a very large head and bulging eyes.

'Wait a minute and I'll give you something that'll really make you sit up.'

In his house there was invariably a surprise, maybe some unusual wine, maybe a liqueur or, as in this case, a *pineau* from the Charentes, which a vineyard owner from Jonzac had sent him.

'Not for me!' protested Madame Maigret, who became tipsy after one glass.

They chatted on. Here again the windows were open, life idled past on the pavement and the air was gilded, the light a little more opaque and reddish.

'I wonder what Lagrange is doing.'

'Who is he?'

'A fellow I knew in the old days at the Lycée Henri IV. If I remember rightly, he must have left us about his third year. He lived in the Rue Cuvier at the time, opposite the Jardin des Plantes, and his father impressed me because he was a Baron, or pretended to be. I lost track of him for a long time, more than twenty years, and only a few months ago I saw him coming into my consulting-room after waiting his turn. However, I recognized him at once.'

He looked at his watch, then the clock.

'What surprises me is that he made such a fuss about coming and now isn't here himself. If he isn't here in five minutes we'll start dinner.'

He filled up the glasses. Madame Maigret and Madame Pardon did not speak. While Madame Pardon was thin and the chief-inspector's wife plump, they both had the same self-effacing attitude towards their husbands. It was rare during dinner for either of them to open their mouths, and it was not until afterwards that the two of them retired into a corner to whisper. Madame Pardon had a very long nose, much too long. You had to get used to it. At first it was embarrassing to look her in the face. Was it because of this nose, which her schoolmates must have laughed at, that she was so humble and looked at her husband as though to thank him for having married her?

'I bet everyone here,' Pardon was saying, 'at school, had a boy or a girl of the Lagrange type. Out of twenty boys, or thirty, it is rare for there not to be at least one who, at the age of thirteen, is already a fat lump with a baby face and great pink legs.'

'In my class it was me,' ventured Madame Maigret.

And Pardon, gallantly:

'With girls it adjusts itself. Indeed those are often the ones who turn out to be the prettiest in the end. We used to call François Lagrange "Baby Cadum", and there must have been thousands of them in all the schools of France given that nickname by their school-friends at the time when the streets were full of pictures of the monster baby in the advertisements.'

'He hasn't changed?'

'The proportions are no longer the same, naturally. But he's still a great wet. Ah well, let's eat!'

'Why not telephone him?'

'He hasn't got a telephone.'

'Does he live near here?'

'A few yards away in the Rue Popincourt. I wonder what he wants exactly. The other day, in my consulting-room, he came trailing in with a magazine with your photograph on the front page. . . .'

Pardon looked at Maigret.

'I'm sorry, old man. I don't know how I happened to let it out that I knew you. I must have added that you were a friend.'

' "Is he really like people say?" Lagrange asked me.'

'I said yes, that you were a man who . . .'

'Who what?'

'It doesn't matter. Anyway I said what I thought while I was examining him. He's diabetic. He also had glandular troubles. He comes in twice a week, he's so over-anxious about his health. On the next visit, he talked about you again, wanting to know if I saw you often, and I said that we dined together once a month. It was then that he insisted on being invited, which surprised me, because since we left the Henri-IV I've only seen him in my consulting-room. Let's sit down to dinner. . . .'

The *brandade* was a masterpiece, and Pardon had brought out a dry wine from somewhere round Nice, which went miraculously with the fish. After talking about fat people, they talked about redheads.

'It's true there's a redhead in every class, too.'

This steered the conversation on to the theory of types. They always ended up by talking medicine, and Madame Maigret knew this pleased her husband.

'Is he married?'

With the coffee, they had got back to Lagrange, goodness knows why. The blue of the sky, a deep velvety blue, had slowly prevailed over the red of the setting sun; but they had not put on the lights, and they could see, through the french windows, the balcony railings printing in inky black their wrought-iron arabesques. From a distant street corner came the strains of an accordion, and a couple on a neighbouring balcony were talking in low tones.

'He was, from what he told me, but his wife died a long time ago.'

'What does he do?'

'Business. Pretty vague sort of business, probably. His visiting-card says "Company Director" with an address in the Rue Tronchet. I rang up the address one day when I wanted to cancel an appointment, and was told the offices had ceased to exist years ago.'

'Any children?'

'Two or three. A daughter certainly, if I remember rightly, and a son he wants to find a steady job for.'

They came back to medicine. Jussieu, who had worked at Sainte-Anne, recalled memories of Charcot. Madame Pardon was knitting and explaining a complicated stitch to Madame Maigret. The lights were put on. There were several mosquitoes. It was eleven o'clock before Maigret got up.

They left Jussieu at the corner of the Boulevard, as he caught the underground at the Place Voltaire. Maigret felt a bit full on account of the *brandade* and perhaps also the Midi wine.

His wife, who had taken his arm, which she seldom did except when they were going home in the evening, wanted to say something. How was it that he sensed this? She hadn't opened her mouth, and yet he was waiting.

'What are you thinking about?' he finally grunted.

'You won't be annoyed?'

He shrugged his shoulders.

'I'm thinking about the young man this morning. I wonder if when we get back you could telephone to see *if there's been anything.*'

She used a roundabout way of talking, and he understood. She meant: '. . . to see if he's committed suicide.'

Oddly enough this was not the idea Maigret had in mind of what might happen. It was only a feeling, without any solid basis. It was not, in his case, a suicide that he was thinking of. He felt vaguely uneasy, without wishing to seem so.

'How was he dressed?'

'I didn't pay much attention to his clothes. I seem to remember he was in something dark, probably navy-blue.'

'His hair?'

'Fair. Blond, rather.'

'Thin?'

'Yes.'

'Good-looking boy?'

'Quite. To my mind.'

He would have sworn she was blushing.

'You know, I didn't look at him much! I remember more than anything else his hands, because he fiddled nervously with the brim of his hat. He didn't dare sit down. I had to bring a chair up for him. He seemed to be expecting me to turn him out.'

Back at home Maigret called the central police station where all emergency calls were put through.

'Maigret here. Anything to report?'

'Only some Bercy cases, sir.'

Which, on account of the *Halle aux Vins* in the Quai de Bercy, means drunks.

'Nothing else?'

'A free fight in the Quai de Charenton. Wait. Yes. Late in the afternoon, a drowned woman was taken out of the Saint-Martin canal.'

'Identified?'

'Yes. A prostitute.'

'No suicides?'

This to please his wife, who was listening, hat in hand, at the bedroom door.

'No. Not so far. Shall I call you if there's anything new?'

He hesitated. It annoyed him to appear interested in the affair, even and above all in front of his wife.

'If you like.'

He was not called again that night. Madame Maigret woke him with his coffee, and the bedroom windows were already open. Workmen could be heard loading crates onto a lorry in front of the warehouse opposite.

'You see, he hasn't killed himself!' he said, as though he were getting his revenge.

'Perhaps they don't know about it yet.'

He reached Police Headquarters at nine o'clock, met his colleagues at the conference in the Chief's office. Just routine matters. Paris was quiet. They had the description of the murderer of the woman fished out of the canal. His arrest was only a question of time. Probably he would be found dead drunk in some bar before the end of the day.

Around eleven o'clock, Maigret was called to the telephone.

'Who is it?'

'Doctor Pardon.'

The latter, on the end of the line, seemed hesitant.

'Excuse my disturbing you at your office. Yesterday I spoke to you about Lagrange, who had asked if he might be allowed to come to our dinner party. This morning, on my rounds, I went by his place in the Rue Popincourt. I went in on the off-chance, thinking he perhaps wasn't well. Hullo! Are you there?'

'I'm listening.'

'I wouldn't have telephoned you, only after you went my wife told me about the young man.'

'What young man?'

'The young man and the revolver. It seems Madame Maigret told my wife how, yesterday morning . . .'

'Yes. Well?'

'Lagrange would be furious if he knew I've gone and warned you. I found him in a curious state. First of all he let me knock for several minutes at the door of his lodgings without answering, and I began to be uneasy, as the concierge had told me he was in. In the end he came and let me in, in bare feet and shirt-sleeves, dishevelled-looking, and he seemed relieved to see it was me.

' "I'm sorry about yesterday evening . . ." he said, going back to bed. "I wasn't feeling well. I still don't feel well. Did you mention me to the inspector?" '

'What did you reply?' asked Maigret.

'I don't remember. I took his pulse, his blood pressure. He was not a pretty sight. He gave the impression of someone who's just had a shock. The place was in chaos. He hadn't eaten, or had any coffee. I asked him if he was alone, and that at once alarmed him.

' "You're afraid I may have a heart attack, aren't you?"

' "Of course not! I was only surprised . . ."

' "What about?"

' "Don't your children live here?"

' "Only my younger son. My daughter left as soon as she was twenty-one. The elder boy is married."

' "Does the younger one work?"

'Then he began to cry, and it was like a wretched great creature being deflated.

' "I don't know," he stammered. "He isn't here. He hasn't come back."

' "Since when?"

' "I don't know. I'm all alone. I'm going to die all alone . . ."

' "Where does your son work?"

' "I don't even know if he does work. He doesn't tell me anything. He's gone . . ." '

Maigret listened, with a serious face.

'Is that all?'

'Pretty well. I tried to cheer him up. He was rather pathetic. Usually he goes about looking rather grand; at any rate he still keeps up appearances. To see him in those shabby lodgings, sick in a bed that hasn't been made for several days . . .'

'His son is in the habit of sleeping out?'

'Not so far as I could see. It would be a pure fluke, obviously, if it were the same young man as . . .'

'Yes.'

'What do you make of it?'

'Nothing so far. Is the father really ill?'

'As I told you, he's had a severe shock. His heart's not too good. He's there, sweating in his bed, in a blue funk that he's going to die . . . .'

'You were quite right to telephone me, Pardon.'

'I was afraid you would laugh at me.'

'I didn't know my wife had told you the story of the revolver.'

'Have I put my foot in it?'

'Not at all.'

He rang for the office-boy.

'No one else for me?'

'No, sir. Apart from the loony.'

'Send him in to Lucas.'

A regular customer, this was, a harmless madman who came in once a week to offer his services to the police.

Maigret hesitated a moment longer. Mainly out of self-respect in actual fact. This story, seen in a certain light, was rather absurd.

On the embankment, he nearly took one of the Headquarters' cars, then, still slightly from shame, decided to go to the Rue Popincourt by taxi. It was less official. In this way, there would be no one to laugh at him.

II

THE lodge, on the right of the archway, was like a hole in the wall, lit all day by a yellowish bulb, which hung on the end of a wire, and practically the entire space was taken up with objects that gave the impression of fitting into place as in a child's set of bricks: a stove, a very high bed surmounted by a red eiderdown, a round table covered with an oil-cloth, an armchair with a big ginger cat in it.

The concierge didn't open the door, but watched Maigret through the glass, and as he didn't go away, resigned herself to opening the pane. Her head was then framed in the window like an enlarged photograph, a bad enlargement with blemishes, a bit faded, which might have been done at a fair. The black hair looked dyed, the rest was without colour or shape. She waited. He said:

'Monsieur Lagrange, please?'

She did not reply at once, and he might well have thought her deaf. In the end she uttered, in a voice of hopeless boredom:

'Third on the left the far side of the courtyard.'

'Is he in?'

It was not boredom, but indifference, perhaps contempt, perhaps even hatred for all that existed outside her aquarium. Her voice droned on.

'As the doctor came to see him this morning, he's probably in.'

'No one went up after Doctor Pardon?'

Mentioning the name gave the impression he knew all about it.

'He wanted me to go up there.'

'Who?'

'The doctor. He wanted to give me a little money to go and do the place out and get him something to eat.'

'Did you go?'

She shook her head, without explaining.

'Why?'

She shrugged her shoulders.

'You don't get on with Monsieur Lagrange?'

'I've only been here two months.'

'Does the last concierge still live round here?'

'She's dead.'

It was useless, he knew, to try and get any more out of her. The entire establishment, the six-storey building which gave onto the street, and the three-storey building on the far side of the courtyard, with its tenants, its workers, its children, its comings and goings – for her all this represented the enemy whose sole object in life was to disturb her peace.

As one emerged from the dark, cold archway the courtyard seemed almost gay, it even showed a bit of grass struggling up between the flag-stones; the sun was shining full on the yellowish plastered house-front at the far end, a carpenter in his workshop was sawing pleasant-smelling wood and in a pram a child was sleeping, while its mother looked down from time to time from a first-floor window.

Maigret knew the district, which was just near his own, where there were many houses like this. In the courtyard at the Boulevard Richard-Lenoir too, there was still a lavatory without a seat, with a door that was always half open, as in a country yard.

He climbed the three floors slowly, pressed an electric bell-push, and heard it ring in the lodging. Like Pardon he had to wait. Like him, too, he eventually heard light sounds, the slithering of bare feet on the floor, a cautious approach, and finally, he could have sworn, laboured breathing just near him on the other side of the latch. The door did not open. He rang again. Nothing moved this time, and bending down, he could see the gleam of an eye in the keyhole.

He coughed, wondering whether he ought to give his name, then just as he was going to open his mouth, a voice said:

'One moment, please.'

More steps, comings and goings, finally the click of the lock, the noise of a bolt. In the half-open doorway a tall man in a dressing-gown was surveying him.

'Did Pardon tell you . . .?' he stammered.

The dressing-gown was old, worn out, the slippers too. The man was unshaven, and his hair was dishevelled.

'I am Chief-Inspector Maigret.'

With a nod he was given to understand that he had been recognized.

'Come in! I am sorry about . . .'

He did not specify what. They went straight into an untidy living-room where Lagrange hesitated, and Maigret, pointing to the open door of a bedroom, said:

'Do go back to bed.'

'Thank you.'

Sunshine flooded the cheap rooms, which did not look like other ones, but more like a sort of camping-place, without it being possible to say exactly why.

'I'm sorry . . .' the man repeated, as he slipped into the unmade bed.

He was breathing with difficulty. His face glistened with sweat and his big eyes didn't know where to rest. Underneath, Maigret was not much more at ease himself.

'Take the chair here.'

Seeing there was a pair of trousers on it, Lagrange repeated again: 'Sorry.'

The chief-inspector didn't know where to put the trousers, in the end left them on the foot of the bed and began, steadying his voice:

'Doctor Pardon told us yesterday we should have the pleasure of meeting you . . .'

'I hoped so, yes. . . .'

'Were you in bed?'

He saw that the man was hesitating.

'In bed, yes.'

'When did you begin to feel ill?'

'I don't know. Yesterday.'

'Yesterday morning?'

'Maybe . . .'

'Heart?'

'And everything else. . . . Pardon has been looking after me a long time. . . . Heart as well. . . .'

'You're worried about your son?'

The man was looking at him just as the big schoolboy he had once been must have looked at his teacher when he didn't know what to reply.

'He hasn't come back home?'

Another moment's hesitation.

'No. . . . Not yet. . . .'

'You wanted to see me?'

Maigret tried to affect the indifferent tones of a visitor. Lagrange, for his part, sketched a vague polite smile.

'Yes, I'd said to Pardon . . .'

'Because of your son?'

He looked suddenly astonished, repeated:

'My son?'

Then straight away he shook his head.

'No. . . . I didn't know then . . .'

'You didn't know he was going away?'

Lagrange corrected him, as though the words were too emphatic:

'He hasn't been back.'

'For how long? Several days?'

'No.'

'Since yesterday morning?'

'Yes.'

'You had a quarrel?'

Lagrange was in torment, but still Maigret was determined to get to the bottom of it.

'In Alain's case, we've never quarrelled.'

He said this with a kind of pride, which hadn't escaped the chief-inspector.

'And with your other children?'

'They don't live here any more.'

'Before they left you?'

'That wasn't the same.'

'I suppose you'd be glad if we found your son?'

Fear showed, once again.

'What do you intend to do?' the man asked.

He had bouts of energy which made him seem almost like a normal person, then, all of a sudden, he would collapse, deflated, onto his bed.

'No. You mustn't. I think it's better not to. . . .'

'You're worried?'

'I don't know.'

'You're afraid of dying?'

'I'm ill. I've no strength left. I . . .'

He put his hand to his heart, and seemed to be feeling its beats anxiously.

'You know where your son worked?'

'Not recently. I didn't mean the doctor to talk to you about it.'

'Yet two days ago you insisted on his arranging you an interview with me.'

'I insisted?'

'You wanted to see me about something, didn't you?'

'I was interested in seeing you.'

'Nothing else?'

'I am sorry.'

It was the fifth time at least he had uttered those words.

'I am ill, very ill. There's nothing else.'

'However, your son has disappeared.'

Lagrange became impatient.

'Perhaps he has simply done the same as his sister.'

'What did his sister do?'

'When she was twenty-one, the very day of her coming of age, she left without a word, with all her belongings.'

'A man?'

'No, she works in an underwear shop, in the Champs-Élysées Arcade, and lives with a girl-friend.'

'Why?'

'I don't know.'

'You have another son, older?'

'Philippe, yes. He's married.'

'You don't think Alain's gone to him?'

'They don't see one another. It's nothing, I tell you. Except that I'm ill, and I'm left all alone. I'm ashamed you've been disturbed. Pardon oughtn't to have done it. I wonder why I told him about Alain. I suppose I was in a fever. Perhaps I still am. You mustn't stay here. It's all in a mess, and it must smell of the sick-bed. I can't even offer you a drink.'

'You haven't a charwoman?'

It was obvious that Lagrange was lying.

'She hasn't come.'

Maigret didn't like to ask if he had any money. It was very hot in the bedroom, a stagnant heat, and a disagreeable smell hung in the air.

'You don't want me to open the window?'

'No. There's too much noise. I have a headache. I ache all over.'

'Perhaps you'd better be taken to hospital?'

The word frightened him.

'Above all, not that! I want to stay here.'

'To wait for your son?'

'I don't know.'

It was strange. At one moment Maigret was moved to pity, and then immediately afterwards he felt irritated, with the impression that it was play-acting. Perhaps the man was ill, but not, it seemed to him, to the point of collapsing on his bed like a great slug, not enough to have tears in his eyes, and lips quivering like a baby going to cry.

'Tell me, Lagrange . . .'

As he broke off, he caught a sudden firmer look, one of those sharp looks which women in particular dart furtively at you when they think they have been found out.

'What?'

'You're sure that when you asked Pardon to invite you to meet me you had nothing to tell me?'

'I swear I just said that off-hand. . . .'

He was lying; that was why he found it necessary to swear. Just like a woman still.

'You have no information to give me which would enable us to find your son?'

The chest of drawers in one corner, and Maigret, who had risen, went over to it, all the time conscious of the other man's eyes fixed on him.

'I'm going to ask you all the same to let me have a photograph of him.'

Lagrange was about to reply that he hadn't got one. Maigret was so sure of this that, with an almost mechanical gesture, he opened one of the drawers.

'Is it here?'

Everything was to be found there, keys, an old wallet, a cardboard box containing buttons, jumbled papers, gas and electricity bills.

'Give it to me.'

'What?'

'The wallet.'

Afraid the inspector would examine the contents himself, he found the strength to raise himself on one elbow.

'Give it here. . . . I think I have a photo taken last year. . . .'

He was becoming feverish. His big podgy fingers were trembling. From a small fold, where he knew it was, he pulled out a photograph.

'Since you insist. I'm sure there's nothing to it. You mustn't publish it in the papers. You mustn't do anything.'

'I'll bring it back to you this evening or tomorrow.'

This frightened him again.

'There's no hurry.'

'What are you going to eat?'

'I'm not hungry. I don't need anything.'

'And this evening?'

'I shall probably be better and be able to go out.'

'And if you aren't better?'

He was on the verge of sobbing with agitation and impatience, and Maigret was not so cruel as to impose himself any longer.

'Just one question. Where has your son Alain been working recently?'

'I don't know the name. . . . It was in an office in the Rue Réaumur.'

'What sort of office?'

'Advertising. . . . Yes . . . it must have been an advertising office. . . .'

He made as if to get up and show his visitor out.

'Don't disturb yourself. Good-bye, Monsieur Lagrange.'

'Good-bye, Inspector. Don't hold it against me. . . .'

Maigret all but asked: 'What?'

But what was the use? He remained standing a moment on the landing, to relight his pipe, and he could hear the bare feet on the floor, then the key in the lock, the bolt, and probably also a sigh of relief.

Passing in front of the lodge he saw the concierge's head in its frame, hesitated, stopped.

'You'd better go up from time to time, as Doctor Pardon advised, to see if he needs anything. He really is ill.'

'He wasn't last night, when I thought he was doing a moonlight getaway.'

This had hung from a thread. Maigret, who had been on the point of going off, frowned, came back.

'He went out last night?'

'He was fit enough to carry his big trunk with the aid of a taxi-driver.'

'You spoke to him?'

'No.'

'What time was it?'

'About ten o'clock. I hoped the rooms were going to be empty!'

'You heard him come back?'

She shrugged.

'Of course, as he's up there.'

'With his trunk?'

'No.'

Maigret was too near home to take a taxi. As he passed in front of a café, he remembered the *pastis* of the day before, which suited the early summer so well, and he had one at the bar, gazing, without seeing them, at some workmen in white overalls having drinks next to him.

As he crossed his own boulevard, he lifted his head and saw Madame Maigret passing to and fro in the flat with the windows open. She must have seen him too. At any rate, she recognized his footsteps on the stairway, for the door opened.

'Still nothing happened to him?'

She was again thinking of her young man of the day before, and her husband took the photograph from his pocket, showed it to her.

'Is that him?'

'How did you get it?'

'It's him?'

'Certainly it's him! Is he . . .?'

She must already have been imagining him dead and was in a state about it.

'No, no. He's still alive and kicking. I've just come from his father.'

'The one the doctor told you about yesterday?'

'Lagrange, yes.'

'What did he say?'

'Nothing.'

'So you still don't know why he took your revolver?'

'To use it, presumably.'

He telephoned Headquarters, but nothing had happened that could be put down to Alain Lagrange. He ate a quick lunch, took a taxi for the Quai, went straight up to the photograph section.

'Print me enough copies of this for all the police in Paris.'

He nearly changed his mind, and had the photo circulated all over France, but wouldn't that have attached too much importance to the affair? What annoyed him was that in the last resort the only real fact was that someone had pinched his gun.

A little later on he called Lucas into his office. He had taken off his waistcoat, and was smoking his enormous pipe.

'I'd like you to get hold of the taxis which work at night around the Rue Popincourt. There's a rank in the Place Voltaire. That must be the one. At this time, the night drivers are generally at home.'

'What do I ask them?'

'If one of them, yesterday evening about ten o'clock, took a big trunk from a building in the Rue Popincourt. I should like to know where he delivered it.'

'That all?'

'Also ask if he took his fare back to the Rue Popincourt.'

'Right, Chief.'

Already at three o'clock the radio-cars were in possession of the photograph of Alain Lagrange; at four, it reached the police stations and posts with the legend: '*Warning! Armed!*' At six o'clock all the police in Paris, going out on their beats, would have it in their pockets.

As for Maigret, he was not too clear what to do. Shame prevented him from taking the affair too seriously, and at the same time he felt uncomfortable in his office. He felt he was wasting time and ought to have been doing something.

He would have liked to have a long conversation with Pardon about the Lagranges, but at that time the doctor's waiting-room would be full of sick people. The idea of interrupting the consultations disconcerted him. He didn't even know what questions he would have put.

He thumbed through the telephone directory, found three advertising agencies in the Rue Réaumur, jotted them down almost mechanically in his notebook.

'Anything for me, Chief?' Torrence came in and asked a little later on.

But for that he wouldn't have given him the agencies to do.

'Telephone all three and find out which of them employed a young man called Alain Lagrange. If you find him, go over and get all the information you can. Not so much from the employers, who never know anything, as from the rest of the staff.'

He lingered on another half-hour in his office, finishing off odd jobs of no importance. Then he saw a curate who complained that money had been stolen from the collection-boxes in his church. To receive the priest, he had put his jacket on. And on his own once more, he in turn went out, took one of the police cars waiting on the Quai.

'The Champs-Élysées Arcade.'

The pavements were overflowing with people. At the entrance to the Arcade there were more tourists, speaking any language, than there were Frenchmen. He didn't often go there, and was surprised to note that in a stretch of less than a hundred yards there were five women's underwear shops. It embarrassed him to have to go in. He felt the shopgirls were looking ironically at him.

'You haven't a young lady by the name of Lagrange here, have you?'

'Is it something private?'

'Yes . . . that's to say . . .'

'We have a Lajaunie, Berthe Lajaunie, but she's on holiday. . . .'

At the third shop a pretty girl lifted her head sharply and said, already on the defensive:

'That's me. What do you want?'

She did not look like her father; perhaps like her brother Alain, with a very different expression, and, without knowing why, Maigret felt sorry for the man who fell in love with her. At first sight, indeed, she was charming, especially when she put on her shop-assistant's smile. But behind the charm, he guessed that she was hard, exceptionally self-possessed.

'Have you seen your brother recently?'

'Why do you ask that?'

She glanced towards the back of the shop, where the manageress was in a fitting-room with a customer. Rather than talk in the air, Maigret preferred to show his badge.

'Has he done something wrong?' she asked in a low voice.

And he:

'It is Alain you're thinking of?'

'Who told you I work here?'

'Your father.'

She didn't stop to think for long.

'If you really have to talk to me, wait for me somewhere in half an hour's time.'

'I'll wait for you on the terrace of the café *Le Français.*'

She watched him go without stirring, her brows puckered, and Maigret spent thirty-five minutes seeing the crowd flowing past, and moving his legs out of the way every time a waiter or the passers-by knocked against them. She arrived, dressed in a light coat and skirt, looking determined. He was sure she would come. She was not the girl to leave him in the lurch, nor, once there, to show embarrassment. She sat in the chair he had kept for her.

'What will you have?'

'A port.'

She arranged the hair either side of her white straw toque, crossed her well-shaped legs.

'You know your father's ill?'

'He always has been.'

There was no pity, no emotion in her voice.

'He's in bed.'

'Very likely.'

'Your brother's disappeared.'

He saw that she was startled, that this piece of news took her aback more than she was willing to admit.

'That doesn't surprise you?'

'Nothing surprises me.'

'Why?'

'Because I've seen too much. What exactly do you want from me?'

It was difficult to reply point blank to such a straight question, and she calmly took a cigarette from a case and asked:

'Have you a light?'

He lit a match for her.

'I'm waiting.'

'How old are you?'

'I presume it wasn't just to find out my age that you took all this trouble. According to your badge, you aren't a plain sergeant, but a chief-inspector. In other words, someone important.'

Examinining him more closely:

'You're not the famous Maigret?'

'I'm Inspector Maigret, yes.'

'Has Alain killed someone?'

'Why do you think that?'

'Because for you to be on a case I imagine it must be serious.'

'Your brother could be the victim.'

'Has he really been killed?'

Still no emotion. True, she didn't seem to believe it.

'He's wandering about Paris somewhere with a loaded gun in his pocket.'

'There must be other people doing that.'

'He stole the revolver yesterday morning.'

'Where?'

'From where I live.'

'He went to your home? To your flat?'

'Yes.'

'When there was no one there? You mean he burgled you?'

This amused her. There was a sudden look of irony on her face.

'You're no more fond of Alain than of your father, are you?'

'I'm not fond of anybody, not even myself.'

'How old are you?'

'Twenty-one and seven months.'

'So that it's seven months since you left your father's house?'

'You call that a house? Have you been there?'

'Do you think your brother is capable of killing someone?'

Wasn't it to make herself interesting that she replied, as if to rile him:

'Why not? Everyone is capable of it.'

Anywhere but on this terrace, where a couple next to them were beginning to eavesdrop, he would probably have shaken her, so much did she exasperate him.

'Did you know your mother, mademoiselle?'

'Hardly — I was three when she died, immediately after Alain's birth.'

'Who were you brought up by?'

'My father.'

'He looked after his three children himself?'

'When he had to.'

'Which means what?'

'When he hadn't the money to pay for a maid. There was a time when we had two of them, but that didn't last. Sometimes it was a charwoman who looked after us, at others, a neighbour. You don't give the impression of knowing the family very well.'

'Have you always lived in the Rue Popincourt?'

'We've lived everywhere, even near the Bois de Boulogne. We went up, we went down, then up again a little bit, before finally going down-hill for good. Well, if you haven't anything more important to tell me, it's time I was getting along, as I've a date with my friend.'

'Where do you live?'

'A few yards away, in the Rue de Berry.'

'At the hotel?'

'No. We've got two rooms in a private house. I suppose you want to know the number?'

She gave it to him.

'Anyway, it's been interesting meeting you. One tends to get ideas into one's head about people.'

He didn't dare ask her what idea she had formed about him, nor more particularly what idea she now had. She was standing up, her suit showing off her figure, and some customers looked at her, then looked at Maigret, no doubt telling themselves he was in luck. He rose in turn and left her in the middle of the pavement.

'I'm much obliged to you,' he said grudgingly.

'Not at all. Don't worry too much about Alain.'

'Why not?'

She shrugged her shoulders.

'An idea, that's all. I've a feeling that even though you may be the great Maigret, you've still a lot to learn.'

Thereupon she set off hurriedly in the direction of the nearby Rue de Berry, and did not turn back. He had not kept the police car. He took the underground, which was packed, and gave him an opportunity of venting his ill-humour. He wasn't pleased with anyone, not excepting himself. If he had met Pardon he would have upbraided him for telling him about this Lagrange who looked like a great ghost puffed up with wind, and he nursed a grievance against his wife for the revolver busi-ness for which he wasn't far from holding her responsible.

All this was no concern of his. The underground smelt of laundry. The advertisements, always the same in the stations, nauseated him. Outside he found the sun almost burning, and he bore a grudge against the sun too, for making him sweat. Seeing him go by, the office-boy realized he was in a bad mood and confined himself to a discreet bow.

On his desk, well in evidence, protected against gusts of wind by one of his pipes which served for the occasion as a paper-weight, there was a note:

Please telephone the station police at the Gare du Nord as soon as possible.

It was signed: '*Lucas*.'

He picked up the telephone, asked for the number, still with his hat on, and, so as to light his pipe, held the receiver between his cheek and shoulder.

'Is Lucas still with you?'

Maigret had spent the grimmest two years of his life in the station police-post and he knew every side of it. He heard the voice of a sergeant saying:

'For you. Your chief.'

And Lucas:

'Hullo! I wondered if you would be going back by the office. I telephoned your house as well.'

'Did you find the driver?'

'A stroke of luck. He told me he was in a bar in the Place Voltaire yesterday evening, when a customer came and hunted him out, a great fat fellow, trying to look important, who had himself taken to the Gare du Nord.'

'To put a trunk in the left luggage office?'

'That's right. You've got it. The trunk is still here.'

'Have you opened it?'

'They won't let me.'

'Who?'

'The station people. They insist on the ticket, or else a search warrant.'

'Anything special?'

'Yes. It stinks!'

'You mean?'

'What you're thinking, yes. If it's not a stiff, the trunk is stuffed with rotten meat. Shall I wait?'

'I'll be there in half an hour.'

Maigret made his way to the police chief's office. The latter rang up the public attorney's office. The public attorney had already left, but one of his subordinates finally took the responsibility upon himself.

When Maigret came back through the duty room Torrence had not returned. Janvier was dictating a report.

'Take someone with you. Go to the Rue Popincourt and watch number 37b. There's a certain François Lagrange, who lives on the third floor on the left at the far end of the courtyard. Don't give yourselves away. He's a big fat chap, sickly-looking. Take the son's photo with you too.'

'What do we do with him?'

'Nothing. If by any chance the son returns and goes out again, follow him carefully. He's armed. If the father goes out, which would surprise me, follow him as well.'

Several minutes later Maigret was travelling in the direction of the Gare du Nord. He recalled what the Lagrange girl had said to him on the terrace in the Champs-Élysées:

'*Isn't everyone capable of it?*'

Something like that, anyway. And now it was a question of murder. He threaded his way through the crowd, found Lucas chatting quietly with a special service sergeant.

'You have the warrant, Chief? I may as well warn you right away that the bloke at the cloakroom is tough and the police don't count for anything with him.'

It was true. The man scrutinized the document, turned it over, turned it back, put on his glasses to examine the signature and the stamps.

'Seeing that I'm released from all responsibility . . .'

With a resigned but disapproving gesture he indicated a big grey trunk of old-fashioned design, its cloth torn in places, which had been tied up with rope. Lucas had exaggerated in saying it stank, but it gave out a stale smell that Maigret knew well.

'I presume you're not going to open it here?'

It happened to be the rush hour. The crowds were pressing around the ticket-office.

'Is there someone who could help us?' Maigret asked the railway-man.

'There are porters. You don't by any chance want me to lug it myself?'

The trunk would not fit into the small black Headquarters car. Lucas had it loaded into a taxi. All this was not very regular. Maigret wanted to get it over quickly.

'Where's it to go to, Chief?'

'The laboratory. That'll be best. Jussieu's probably still there.'

He met Torrence on the stairs.

'I say, Chief . . .'

'You've found him?'

'Who?'

'The young man.'

'No, but . . .'

'One minute then. . . .'

Sure enough, Jussieu was upstairs. There were four or five of them around the trunk, photographing it from all sides and trying various experiments before opening it.

Half an hour later, Maigret called the Commissioner's office.

'The Chief's just gone,' they replied.

He rang him at his home address, discovered he was dining that evening at a restaurant on the left bank. At the restaurant he hadn't yet arrived. It meant another ten minutes' wait.

'I'm sorry to trouble you, Chief. It's Maigret here, about the case I told you about. Lucas was right. I think you'd better come, as it's someone important, and it may cause a sensation. . . .'

A second's pause.

'André Delteil, the deputy. . . . I'm sure of it, yes. . . . Right. . . . I'll wait for you. . . .'

III

THE Chief of Police was attending a foreign press dinner at a big hotel in the Avenue Montaigne when the Headquarters Commissioner succeeded in getting through to him on the telephone. At first he only let out an exclamation:

'*M. . . .!*'

After which there was a silence.

'I trust the press isn't onto the case yet?' he finally murmured.

'Not so far. A reporter is hanging about in the corridor and realizes that something is going on. We won't be able to hide what it's all about for long.'

The journalist, Gérard Lombras, an old hand at petty scandals, who made his little trip to the Quai des Orfèvres every evening, was sitting on the bottom step of the stairs just opposite the laboratory door, patiently smoking his pipe.

'Do nothing, say nothing until I give the word,' cautioned the Chief of Police.

And in his turn, from one of the booths in the hotel, he called the Minister of the Interior. It was an evening of interrupted dinners, an exceptionally balmy evening, however, with languid strollers filling the streets of Paris. There were some on the Quais as well who must have wondered why, when night had not yet fallen, there were so many offices lit up in the old building of the Palais de Justice.

The Minister of the Interior, a native of Cantal who had kept his rough local accent and style of speech, exclaimed on hearing the news:

'Even dead, that fellow's a — — nuisance!'

The Delteils lived in a big house in the Boulevard Suchet, on the edge of the Bois de Boulogne. When eventually Maigret got permission to ring up, a manservant replied that Madame was not in Paris.

'You don't know when she'll be back?'

'Not before the autumn. She's in Miami. Monsieur is not here either.'

Maigret asked on the off-chance:

'Do you know where he is?'

'No.'

'Was he in Paris yesterday?'

A moment's hesitation.

'I don't know.'

'How do you mean?'

'Monsieur went out.'

'When?'

'I don't know.'

'The evening before last?'

'I think so, yes. Who is it speaking?'

'Police Headquarters.'

'I don't know anything. Monsieur is not here.'

'Has he relations in Paris?'

'His brother, Monsieur Pierre.'

'You know his address?'

'I think he lives just near the Étoile. I can give you his telephone number. One minute. . . . Balzac 51–02.'

'You weren't surprised not to see your master return?'

'No, sir.'

'Had he warned you he wouldn't be coming back?'

'No, sir.'

New figures began to fill the scientific laboratory. The examining magistrate, who had been sought out from the house of some friends where he had been playing bridge, had just arrived, as had the public attorney, and the two were conversing together in low tones. Paul, the police doctor, who had also been dining out, was one of the last to appear, the perpetual cigarette between his lips.

'Shall I take him away?' he said, indicating the open trunk where the corpse was still slumped.

'As soon as you've made your preliminary examination.'

'I can tell you straight away he's not fresh today. Good Lord! It's Delteil!'

'Yes.'

A 'yes' which spoke volumes. Ten years earlier, probably none of those who were present would have recognized the dead man. He was then a young lawyer more often to be met with at the Roland-Garros races or the bars of the Champs-Élysées than at the law courts, and was more like a young film star than a member of the bar.

A little later on he had married an American woman with a private fortune, had installed himself in the Boulevard Suchet, and three years afterwards was a candidate at the general election. Even his opponents, during the electoral campaign, had not taken him seriously.

He had none the less been elected, by a narrow majority, and from the very next day had begun to get himself talked about. He did not, strictly speaking, belong to any party, but became the terror of them all, continually interrupting, exposing abuses, plots, intrigues, without anyone ever being able to see exactly what he was hoping to get out of it. At the start of each important session, ministers and deputies could be heard to ask:

'Is Delteil there?'

And brows would knit. If in fact he was there, bronzed like a Holly-wood film star, with his little brown moustaches shaped like commas, it meant there would be some fun.

Maigret had his peevish look. He had called the brother's number, a

5*

furnished house in the Rue Ponthieu, where he had been advised to try *Le Fouquet's*. *Le Fouquet's* had put him on to *Maxim's*.

'Is Monsieur Delteil with you?'

'Who is it calling?'

'Tell him it's about his brother.'

He finally got onto him. They must have delivered his message wrongly.

'That you, André?'

'No. This is Police Headquarters. Will you take a taxi and come round here?'

'I've got my car at the door. What's it all about?'

'Your brother.'

'Has something happened to him?'

'Don't talk about anything until you've seen me.'

'But . . .'

Maigret hung up, cast an irritated look at the groups which were forming in the vast room, then, as he wasn't needed straight away, went down to his office. Lombras, the journalist, followed on his heels.

'You won't forget me, Inspector?'

'No.'

'In an hour it'll be too late for my edition.'

'I'll see you before then.'

'Who is it? A big bug, isn't it?'

'Yes.'

Torrence was waiting for him, but before speaking to him Maigret telephoned his wife.

'Don't expect me this evening, and more than likely not tonight at all.'

'I thought as much when you didn't come home.'

A silence. He knew what, or rather whom, she was thinking about.

'Is it he?'

'Anyhow, he hasn't committed suicide.'

'He's shot someone?'

'I just don't know anything.'

He hadn't told them everything, upstairs. He didn't feel like telling them everything. He still had probably about an hour ahead of him being bored by the big-wigs, after which he could take up his inquiry in peace once more.

He turned to Torrence.

'You've found the lad?'

'No. I saw his former employer and his colleagues. It's only three weeks ago that he left them.'

'Why?'

'He got thrown out.'

'In trouble?'

'No. It seems he's honest. But recently he was continually absent. At first they weren't annoyed. Everyone rather took to him. Then, as he took things more and more leisurely . . .'

'Did you find out anything about his habits?'

'Nothing.'

'No girl friend?'

'He never talked about his private affairs.'

'No flirting with the typists?'

'One of them, not a pretty one, blushed when she mentioned him, but I got the impression he took no notice of her.'

Maigret dialled a number on the telephone.

'Hullo! Madame Pardon? Maigret here. Is your husband in? Heavy day? Ask him to come to the telephone for a second, would you?'

He wondered if, by any chance, the doctor had gone back, late in the day, to the Rue Popincourt.

'Pardon? I'm very sorry to bother you, old man. Have you got patients to see this evening? Listen. Things are getting serious in connection with your friend Lagrange. . . . Yes. . . . I've seen him. . . . Something new has come up since I went to his place. I need your help. . . . That's right. . . . I should very much like you to come and pick me up here. . . .'

When he went upstairs again, still followed by Lombras, he caught sight of Pierre Delteil on the stairway, whom he recognized from his likeness to his brother.

'Was it you who called me here?'

'Ssh! . . .'

He pointed to the reporter.

'Follow me.'

He led him off upstairs, pushed the door to just as Dr. Paul, who had been making a preliminary examination of the body, was straightening up.

'Recognize him?'

Everyone was silent. The scene was made more painful by the resemblance between the two men.

'Who did that?'

'It's your brother all right?'

There were no tears, but clenched fists, set jaws, eyes which became fixed and hard.

'Who did it?' repeated Pierre Delteil, himself three or four years younger than the deputy.

'We don't know yet.'

Dr. Paul explained:

'The bullet entered through the left eye and lodged in the brain. It did not come out again. As far as I can judge, it's a small-calibre bullet.'

On one of the telephones the Commissioner of Police Headquarters spoke to the Chief of Police. When he came back to the group waiting for him, he passed on the instructions which came from the Minister.

'A simple statement to the press, announcing that André Delteil the deputy has been found dead in a trunk deposited in the cloakroom at the Gare du Nord. As few details as possible. There'll be time tomorrow.'

Rateau the magistrate drew Maigret into a corner.

'You think it's a political crime?'

'No.'

'An affair over a woman?'

'I don't know.'

'You suspect someone?'

'I shall know tomorrow.'

'I count on you to keep me posted. Telephone me, even at night, if there's anything new. I'll be in my office tomorrow from nine o'clock in the morning onwards.'

Maigret vaguely nodded his assent, went and had a few words with Dr. Paul.

'Right, old man.'

Paul went off to the morgue to proceed with the autopsy. All this had taken time. It was ten o'clock at night when dark silhouettes merged into one another on the badly lit stairway. The journalist did not leave the inspector's side.

'Come into my office a moment. You are right. It is a big bug. André Delteil the deputy has been murdered.'

'When?'

'We don't know yet. A bullet in the head. The body was found in a trunk deposited in the cloakroom at the Gare du Nord.

'Why was the trunk opened?'

The man had caught on straight away.

'Nothing else for today.'

'Have you got any clues?'

'Nothing else for today.'

'Are you going to spend all night on the case?'

'Possibly.'

'What if I followed you?'

'I should have you locked up on the first pretext to hand and leave you to cool off till tomorrow morning.'

'I see.'

'So that's settled.'

Pardon knocked at the door, came in. The reporter asked:

'Who's this?'

'A friend.'

'Mayn't we know his name?'

'No.'

They were left alone together at last, and Maigret began by taking off his jacket and lighting a pipe.

'Sit down. Before going over there, I should like to have a little talk, and it's better for it to be here.'

'Lagrange?'

'Yes. One question, to begin with. Is he really ill, and to what extent?'

'I was expecting that and I've been thinking about it all the way here, as it's not easy to answer categorically. Ill, yes, that's certain. He contracted diabetes some ten years ago.'

'Which doesn't stop him leading a normal life?'

'Hardly at all. I gave him insulin. I've taught him to give himself his own injections. When he eats away from home, he always has a little folding balance in his pocket so as to weigh certain foods. With insulin, it's important.'

'I know. Well?'

'Do you want a diagnosis in technical terms?'

'No.'

'All his life he's suffered from glandular trouble, which is the case with most people of his physical type. He's soft, impressionable, easily depressed.'

'And his present state?'

'It's here that it becomes more tricky. I was very surprised this morning to find him in the state you saw him in. I examined him carefully. Although hypertrophied, the heart's not bad, no worse than it was a week or two ago, when Lagrange was going around as usual.'

'You've considered the possibility of a sham?'

Pardon had considered it, that could be seen from his expression. A scrupulous man, he was picking his words with care.

'I presume you have good reason to ask me that?'

'Grave reasons.'

'His son?'

'I don't know. I'd better give you all the facts. Forty-eight hours ago, a man was killed, more than likely in the flat in the Rue Popincourt.'

'Has he been identified?'

'It's the deputy Delteil.'

'Did they know one another?'

'Our inquiries will tell us. The fact remains that yesterday evening while we were dining with you and talking about him, François Lagrange called a taxi to the front of his house and, with the aid of the driver, brought down a trunk containing the corpse, to take to the Gare du Nord and deposit it. Does that surprise you?'

'It would be a surprise any time.'

'You understand now why I am anxious to know if, when you

examined him this morning, François Lagrange was ill to the extent
he wanted people to believe, or if he was pretending.'

Pardon rose.

'Before answering, I should like to examine him again. Where is he?'

He expected that Lagrange had been taken off to one of the offices
in the Police Headquarters.

'Still at home, in bed.'

'Doesn't he know anything?'

'He doesn't know we've discovered the body.'

'What are you going to do?'

'Go over there with you, if you're prepared to come with me. Have
you a liking for him?'

Pardon hesitated, in the end replied frankly:

'No!'

'Sympathy?'

'Let's say pity. I wasn't pleased to see him come into my consulting-
room. Rather irritated, actually, as I always am in the presence of
weaklings. But I can't forget that he has had to bring up his three
children on his own, nor that when he talked about his younger son,
his voice trembled with emotion.'

'Skin-deep sentimentality?'

'I wondered about that. I don't like men who weep.'

'Did he ever cry in front of you?'

'Yes. Once in particular when his daughter deserted him, without
even leaving him her address.'

'I've seen her.'

'What does she have to say?'

'Nothing. She doesn't waste any tears! You coming with me?'

'I suppose it'll take some time?'

'Possibly.'

'Mind if I give my wife a ring?'

It was dark when they took their places in one of the official police
cars. All the way they were silent, each engrossed in his own thoughts,
each, probably, also apprehensive of the scene they were about to face.

'Stop at the corner of the road,' Maigret told the driver.

He recognized Janvier opposite 37b.

'A colleague of yours?'

'As a precaution I hid him in the courtyard of the building.'

'The concierge?'

'She won't taken any notice of us.'

Maigret rang, made Pardon go before him. The lodge was no longer
lit. The concierge didn't ask who they were but the chief-inspector
thought he could make out the light blur of her face behind the
window.

Way up, on the third floor, there was a light in one of the rooms.

'Let's go up.'

He knocked, failing to find the bell in the darkness, as the staircase lighting was not working. A shorter time elapsed than in the morning before a voice inquired:

'Who is it?'

'Inspector Maigret.'

'One moment please. . . .'

Lagrange must have been putting on his dressing-gown again. His hands were trembling, for he had trouble in turning the key in the lock.

'Have you found Alain?'

All of a sudden he saw the doctor in the semi-darkness and his face changed, turned still paler than usual. He stood there, without moving, no longer knowing what to do or say.

'May we come in?'

Maigret sniffed, recognized the smell which pervaded his nostrils, a smell of burnt paper. Lagrange's beard had grown a bit more since the chief-inspector's visit, and the bags under his eyes were more pronounced.

'Considering your state of health,' the chief-inspector began at last, 'I didn't want to come without being accompanied by your doctor. Pardon has consented to take the trouble. I presume you have no objection to his examining you?'

'He sounded my chest this morning. He knows I'm ill.'

'If you'll get back into bed, he'll examine you again.'

Lagrange was on the point of protesting, as could be seen from his expression, but in the end he resigned himself, went into the bedroom, removed his dressing-gown, and lay down.

'Uncover your chest,' Pardon said gently.

While he was being sounded, the man stared fixedly at the ceiling. As for Maigret, he paced to and fro in the room. There was a chimney with a black damper, which he lifted, and behind the shutter he found some paper ashes which had been carefully reduced almost to powder with a poker.

From time to time Pardon muttered professional phrases.

'Turn over. . . . Breathe in. . . . Breathe deeper. Cough. . . .'

There was a door not far from the bed, and the inspector pushed it, found an unoccupied room which must have belonged to one of the children, with an iron bedstead from which the mattress had been removed. He switched on the light. The room had become a sort of glory-hole. A pile of weekly papers lay in one corner, with tattered books, including school-books, a leather suitcase covered with dust. On the right, near the window, a patch of the floor the shape of the trunk found in the Gare du Nord was a lighter colour than the rest.

When Maigret came back into the adjoining room, Pardon was standing up, with a preoccupied look.

'Well?'

He did not reply at once, was avoiding Lagrange's eye which was fixed on him.

'In all conscience, I think he's in a fit state to reply to your questions.'

'You hear, Lagrange?'

The man was looking from one to the other of them in silence, and his eyes were a wretched sight, like those of a wounded beast staring at the men bending over it and trying to understand.

'You know why I am here?'

Lagrange must have come to a decision, probably during the examination, for he remained silent, and not a muscle of his face moved.

'Why not admit you know very well, that you've been expecting it since this morning, and that it's fear which is making you ill?'

Pardon had gone and sat in a corner, one elbow over the back of his chair, chin in hand.

'We have discovered the trunk.'

There was no shock. Nothing happened, and Maigret could not even have sworn that for the fraction of a second there had been an added intensity in those pupils.

'I'm not saying that you killed André Delteil. It's possible that you are innocent of the crime. I don't know anything, I admit, of what happened here, but I am certain it was you who took the corpse shut up in your trunk to the cloakroom. In your own interest it would be better for you to speak.'

Still no sound, no movement. Maigret turned to Pardon, at whom he shot a discouraged glance.

'I should even like to believe that you are ill, that the effort you made yesterday evening and the emotional upset have shaken you. All the more reason to answer me frankly.'

Lagrange closed his eyes, opened them again, but his lips did not part.

'Your son is on the run. If he did the killing, we shan't be long in getting our hands on him, and your silence doesn't help him at all. If it's not him, it's better, for his safety, that we should know. He's armed. The police are warned about it.'

Maigret had approached the bed, and perhaps leant over it a bit without realizing, and at last the man's lips moved, he stammered something.

'What did you say?'

Then, in a frightened voice. Lagrange cried out:

'Don't hit me! You've no right to hit me!'

'I have no intention of doing so, and you know it.'

'Don't hit me. . . . Don't . . .'

And all of a sudden he threw back the covers, cringed, made as if to ward off an attack.

'I don't want . . . I don't want to be hit. . . .'

It was ugly to see. It was painful. Once more, Maigret turned to Pardon as if to seek his advice. But what advice could the doctor give him?

'Listen, Lagrange. You are perfectly lucid. You're no longer a child. You understand me extremely well. And a short while ago, you weren't so ill, since you had the energy to burn some compromising papers. . . .'

A lull, as though the man were getting his breath, only to break out more violently than ever, to shout this time:

'Save me! . . . Help! . . . They're hitting me! . . . I don't want them to hit me! . . . Let me go!'

Maigret seized one of his wrists.

'That's enough of that, do you hear?'

'No! No! No!'

'Are you going to shut up?'

Pardon had risen, and in turn came over to the bed, looking intently at the sick man.

'I don't want . . . Leave me .. . . I shall wake the whole place up. . . . I shall tell them. . . .'

Pardon murmured in his ear:

'You won't get anything out of him.'

Hardly had they moved away from the bed before Lagrange became motionless and relapsed into his silence.

The two of them held council in the corner.

'You think his mind is really deranged?'

'I can't be positive.'

'It's a possibility?'

'It's always a possibility. He ought to be put under observation.'

Lagrange had slightly moved his head so as not to lose sight of them, and it was evident that he was listening. He must have understood the last few words. He seemed pacified. Nevertheless Maigret returned to the charge, not without weariness.

'Before you make any decision, Lagrange, I would like to warn you of one thing. I have a warrant of arrest out in your name. Downstairs two of my men are waiting. Unless I get satisfactory replies to my questions they are going to take you to the police infirmary.'

No reaction. Lagrange was gazing at the ceiling with such a far-away look that one might have wondered if he were listening.

'Doctor Pardon can assure you that there are almost infallible methods of exposing malingerers. You were not mad this morning. No more were you when you burnt your papers. You aren't now, I feel sure.'

Was there really a vague smile on the man's lips?

'I haven't struck you, and I'm not going to strike you. I'm just telling you again that the attitude you're adopting won't get you anywhere, and will only make people unsympathetic, if not worse. Have you made up your mind to answer?'

'I don't want them to hit me!' he repeated in a toneless voice, as if mumbling a prayer.

Maigret, with shoulders hunched, went and opened the window, leant out, called to the policeman waiting in the yard.

'Come up with Janvier!'

He closed the window again and began pacing up and down the room. Footsteps were heard on the stairs.

'If you want to dress you can. If not, they'll carry you as you are, wrapped up in a blanket.'

Lagrange merely went on moving his lips, repeating the same syllables so that they ended up by meaning nothing at all.

'I don't want them to hit me. . . . I don't want them . . .'

'Come in, Janvier. . . . You too. . . . Just take him to the infirmary. . . . No use dressing him, as he's quite capable of starting to struggle again. . . . Just in case, put the handcuffs on him. . . . Wrap him up in a blanket. . . .'

A door had opened on the floor above. A window was lighted on the other side of the courtyard, and they could see a woman leaning out of her window, and a man getting out of bed behind her.

'I don't want them to hit me! . . .'

Maigret didn't look, heard the click of the handcuffs, then heavy breathing, footsteps, bumps.

'I don't want them to . . . I . . . Help! Save me!'

One of the men must have put a hand over his mouth, or gagged him, for the voice became fainter, then ceased; the footsteps reached the staircase.

The silence, immediately afterwards, was uncomfortable. The chief-inspector's first move was to light his pipe. Then he looked at the unmade bed, from which a sheet trailed out into the middle of the room. The old slippers were still there, the dressing-gown on the floor.

'Your views, Pardon?'

'You'll have trouble.'

'I'm sorry to have mixed you up in this case. It wasn't a pretty sight.'

As though a detail had come back to him, the doctor muttered:

'He was always very frightened of dying.'

'Ah!'

'Every week he used to complain of new illnesses, questioned me at length to find out if they were serious. He used to buy medical books. We ought to find them about somewhere.'

Maigret in fact found them in the chest of drawers, and there were markers on certain pages.

'What are you going to do?'

'To start with, the police infirmary will see to him. As for me, I'm going on with the case. What I'd like more than anything would be to find his son.'

'You've got an idea it's him?'

'No. If Alain had done the killing, he wouldn't have needed to steal my revolver. Actually, by the time he was at my house, the crime had already been committed. The death dates back forty-eight hours at least, to Tuesday, in fact.'

'Are you staying here?'

'A few minutes. I'm waiting for the men I got Janvier to send. In an hour I shall have Doctor Paul's report.'

It was Torrence who came a little later on accompanied by two colleagues and some men from the Technical Branch complete with cameras. Maigret gave them instructions, while Pardon stood to one side, still looking worried.

'You coming?'

'I'm with you.'

'Can I drop you at home?'

'I should really like to ask your permission to go round to the Police Infirmary. But perhaps my colleagues over there would take a dim view?'

'On the contrary. Have you got an idea?'

'No. I should just like to see him again, perhaps try once more. He's a difficult case.'

It did them good to breathe the air in the streets once again. The two men reached the Quai des Orfèvres, and Maigret knew in advance that there would be more lighted windows than usual.

Pierre Delteil's sports car was still at the side of the road. The chief-inspector frowned. He found the reporter, Lombras, on guard in the waiting-room.

'The brother's waiting for you. Still nothing for me?'

'Still nothing, my boy.'

He spoke without thinking, for Gérard Lombras was almost his own age.

IV

PIERRE DELTEIL was aggressive from the start. For example, while Maigret was giving instructions to little Lapointe, who had just come on duty, he stood by the desk, his buttocks resting on its edge, playing a tattoo with the tips of his well-manicured fingers on a silver cigarette-case. Then, when Maigret changed his mind just as Lapointe was going

out, and asked him to order some sandwiches and beer, he deliberately
twisted his lips into a sardonic smile.

True, he had received a serious shock, and since then his nervousness
had continually increased, to a point where it became tiring to watch him.

'At last!' he cried, when the door had closed, and the chief-inspector
sat down at his desk.

And, as the latter was looking at him as though seeing him for the
first time:

'I suppose you're going to decide on a vice crime or some affair with
a woman? They must have given you instructions from above to hush
up the business? Let me tell you this . . .'

'Sit down, Monseiur Delteil.'

He would not sit down at once.

'I hate talking to a man standing up.'

Maigret's voice was a bit weary, a bit hollow. The ceiling light was
not on, and the desk lamp only diffused a green glow. Pierre Delteil
finally settled himself in the chair that was offered him, crossed, then
uncrossed his legs, opened his mouth to say something else disagreeable,
but didn't have time to utter a word.

'Pure formality,' Maigret interrupted him, reaching out a hand towards him without bothering to look at him. 'Would you show me your
identity card?'

He examined it with care, like a frontier policeman, turned it over
and back again in his hands.

'Cinema producer,' he read out finally, against the heading 'Profession'. 'Have you produced many films, Monsieur Delteil?'

'The fact is that . . .'

'Have you produced one?'

'It's not yet in production, but . . .'

'If I understand you correctly, you haven't produced anything at all.
You were at *Maxim's* when I got you on the telephone. A little while
before you were at *Le Fouquet's*. You live in a furnished flat in a pretty
expensive block in the Rue de Ponthieu and you own a magnificent car.'

He now examined him from head to foot, as though to appraise the
cut of the suit, the silk shirt, the shoes which came from the best shoe-
maker.

'You have private means, Monsieur Delteil?'

'I don't see the point of these . . .'

'These questions,' the inspector finished, placidly. 'None. What did
you do before your brother became a deputy?'

'I worked at his election campaign.'

'And before that?'

'I . . .'

'Just so. In short, for several years, you've more or less been your
brother's grey eminence. In return, he provided for your needs.'

'Are you trying to humiliate me? Is that part of the instructions you've received? Why not admit that those people know perfectly well it's a political crime and they've told you to suppress the truth at all costs. It's because I realized that, up there, that I waited for you. Let me inform you . . .'

'You know the murderer?'

'Not necessarily, but my brother was becoming a nuisance, and it had been arranged for . . .'

'You may light your cigarette.'

This time there was no reply.

'I suppose, in your eyes, there is no solution other than a political crime?'

'Do you know the culprit?'

'Here, Monsieur Delteil, it's I who ask the questions. Had your brother any mistresses?'

'It's common knowledge. He made no secret of it.'

'Not even from his wife?'

'He had still less reason to conceal it as they were getting divorced. That's one of the reasons why Pat is now in the States.'

'Is it she who's asking for the divorce?'

Pierre Delteil hesitated.

'For what reason?'

'Probably because she has got bored with it all.'

'Your brother?'

'You know the Americans?'

'I've met one or two.'

'Rich ones?'

'Some.'

'In that case you must know that they marry as a sort of game. Eight years ago, Pat was passing through France. It was her first visit to Europe. She decided to stay, to have her own mansion in Paris, to live the life of Paris . . .'

'And to have a husband playing a part in that same Parisian life. Was it she who pushed your brother into politics?'

'He always had an idea of taking it up.'

'So he simply took advantage of the means which the marriage placed at his disposal. You mean that, fairly recently, his wife had enough of it and went back to the States to demand a divorce. What would have become of your brother?'

'He would have continued with his career.'

'What about money? Usually rich Americans take the precaution of marrying under a separate maintenance arrangement.'

'All the same, André would never have accepted her money. Anyhow, I don't see where these questions . . .'

'Do you know this young man?'

Maigret handed him the photograph of Alain Lagrange. Pierre
Delteil looked at it uncomprehendingly, raised his head.

'Is that the murderer?'

'I'm asking if you've seen him before.'

'Never.'

'Do you know a man called Lagrange, François Lagrange?'

He began to search in his memory as though the name were not
entirely unknown to him and he was trying to place it.

'I think, in certain circles,' Maigret prompted him, 'he is called
Baron Lagrange.'

'Now I know whom you're talking about. Most of the time people
just say the Baron.'

'You know him well?'

'I meet him from time to time at *Fouquet's* or other places. I occasionally say hello. I must have drunk an *apéritif* with him . . .'

'Did you have any business relations?'

'Thank the Lord, no.'

'Your brother saw him often?'

'Same as me, probably. Everybody knows the Baron, more or less.'

'What do you know about him?'

'Practically nothing. He's an idiot, a soft idiot, a great wet who tries
to worm his way in.'

'What's his profession?'

And Pierre Delteil, more naïvely than he would have wished:

'Does he have a profession?'

'I presume he must have means of support?'

Maigret almost added: 'Not everyone's lucky enough to have a
deputy for a brother.'

He didn't do so, because it was no longer necessary. Young Delteil
was coming to heel, without noticing his own change of attitude.

'He's in some vague sort of business. At least, I suppose so. He isn't
the only one in his position. He's the kind of man who buttonholes you
and tells you he's just pulling off a deal involving several hundred
millions, and ends up by asking you to lend him the price of a dinner
or a taxi.'

'He must have got round to touching your brother?'

'He tried to touch everybody.'

'You don't think your brother could have made use of him?'

'Certainly not.'

'Why?'

'Because my brother distrusted idiots. I don't see what you're driving
at. I get the impression you know something you don't intend to tell
me. What I still don't understand is how they knew that a trunk, left in
the cloakroom at the Gare du Nord, contained André's body.'

'They didn't know.'

'It was just chance?'

He was beginning to sneer again.

'Almost sheer chance. One more question. What reason would a man like your brother have had to pay a visit, at his home, to a man like the Baron?'

'Did he pay him a visit?'

'You haven't answered me.'

'It doesn't seem likely to me.'

'A crime, at the start of the investigation, never seems likely.'

As there was someone knocking at the door, he called out:

'Come in!'

It was the waiter from the *Brasserie Dauphine* with the sandwiches and beer.

'Would you like some, Monsieur Delteil?'

'Thank you, but . . .'

'No thank you?'

'I was just having dinner when . . .'

'I shan't keep you any longer. I've got your telephone number. Maybe I shall need you, tomorrow or the day after.'

'In fact, you altogether discount the idea of a political crime?'

'I discount nothing. As you see, I'm working on it.'

He picked up the telephone, to make quite clear that the interview was over.

'Hullo! Is that you, Paul?'

Delteil hesitated, finally went to get his hat and made for the door.

'At any rate, you can be sure I shan't let it rest . . .'

Maigret waved a hand at him:

'Good night! Good night!'

The door closed once again.

'Maigret here. . . . Well? . . . Yes, as I suspected. . . . In your opinion he was killed on Tuesday evening, perhaps during the course of the night? . . . Does that tally? . . . Roughly speaking. . . .'

It was on Tuesday, too, but in the afternoon, that François Lagrange had telephoned for the last time to the doctor to make sure that Maigret would be at the dinner the following day. At that time he still wanted to meet the chief-inspector, and it was more than likely it was not out of mere curiosity. He couldn't then have been expecting the deputy's visit, but perhaps he foresaw it for one of the next few days?

On the Wednesday morning his son, Alain, appeared at the Boulevard Richard-Lenoir so nervous, looking so frightened according to Madame Maigret, that she felt sorry for him and took him under her protection.

What did the young man come there for? To ask advice? Had he seen the murder? Had he discovered the body, which was probably not yet in the trunk?

The fact remained that the sight of Maigret's gun made him change his mind, that he took the weapon, left the flat on tiptoe, and dashed into the first gunmaker's he came across to buy ammunition.

So he had some idea in his head.

The same evening his father was not at the Pardons' dinner party. Instead, he got hold of a taxi-driver and, with his help, went and deposited the body at the Gare du Nord, after which he retired to bed and became ill.

'The bullet, Paul?'

As he expected, it had not been fired from his American revolver, since the weapon, at the time of the murder, was still at his home, but from a small-calibre gun, a 6.35, which would not have done much harm if the shot, hitting the left eye, had not entered the brain.

'Anything else to report? The stomach?'

The latter contained the remains of a copious dinner, and digestion had only just begun. That put the crime, according to Dr. Paul, at about 11 o'clock in the evening, Delteil the deputy not being one of those who dine early.

'Thanks, old man. No, the problems which I've still got to solve aren't in your province.'

He began to eat, all alone in his office, where there was still only a greenish light. He was uncomfortable, ill at ease. He found the beer tepid. He hadn't thought of ordering coffee and, wiping his lips, he went and fetched the bottle of cognac which he kept in his cupboard, and poured himself out a glass.

'Hullo! Get me the police infirmary.'

He was surprised to hear Journe's voice. The professor had gone out of his way in person.

'You've had time to look at my customer? What do you think of him?'

A definite answer would have eased his mind a bit, but old Journe was not the man for definite answers. He delivered, down the telephone, a lecture studded with technical terms, from which it emerged that there was about a 60 per cent chance that Lagrange was a fraud, but that short of a mistake on his part weeks could pass before they had any scientific proof of it.

'Is Doctor Pardon still with you?'

'He's just on the point of leaving.'

'What's Lagrange doing?'

'Absolutely quiet. He let himself be put to bed and began talking to the nurse in a childish voice. He told her in tears that people had wanted to beat him, that everyone was set against him, that it had been like that all his life.'

'Can I see him in the morning?'

'Whenever you like.'

'I'd like a word with Pardon.'

And, to the latter:

'Well?'

'Nothing new. I'm not altogether of the Professor's opinion, but he's more of an expert than I, and it's a long time since I gave up psychiatry.'

'What's your personal opinion?'

'I'd rather have a few hours to think it over before saying. It's too serious a matter to give an opinion lightly. Aren't you going home to bed?'

'Not yet. I probably won't get any sleep tonight.'

'You don't need me any more?'

'No, old man. Thanks very much. Apologize to your wife for me again.'

'She's used to it.'

'So's mine, fortunately.'

Maigret rose, with the idea of going round to the Rue Popincourt to see how his men were getting on. On account of the burnt papers in the fireplace, he was not too hopeful that they'd find a clue, but he wanted to poke about in the corners of the rooms.

Just as he was getting his hat the telephone rang.

'Hullo! Inspector Maigret? Faubourg Saint-Denis police station here. I was told to telephone you just in case. It's Constable Lecœur speaking.'

The man was plainly very excited.

'It's about the young man in the photograph they sent us. I've got a character here . . .'

He corrected himself:

'. . . person here who's just had his wallet pinched in the Rue de Maubeuge . . .'

The victim must have been listening, causing Constable Lecœur to pick his words.

'It's a business man from the provinces. . . . Hold on . . . from Clermont-Ferrand. . . . He was going along the Rue de Maubeuge, about half an hour ago, when a man came out of the darkness and brandished a large gun under his nose . . . a young man to be more precise . . .'

Lecœur spoke to someone standing beside him.

'He says a very young man, almost a boy. . . . It seems his lips were trembling, so it was all he could do to say: "Your wallet, please." . . .'

Maigret frowned. Ninety-nine times out of a hundred an assailant simply says: 'Your wallet!'

And in that alone could be recognized the amateur, the beginner.

'When the gentleman spoke about a young man,' Lecœur went on, not without a touch of self-satisfaction, 'I at once thought of the photo issued to us yesterday, and I showed it to him. He recognized it without hesitating. . . . What? . . .'

It was the Clermont-Ferrand business man talking, whose voice
Maigret could hear stating emphatically:

'I'm absolutely certain of it!'

'What did he do then?' Maigret asked.

'Who?'

'The assailant.'

Two voices again, as when a wireless is not properly tuned in, two
voices saying the same thing:

'He ran away.'

'In which direction?'

'Boulevard de la Chapelle.'

'How much money was there in the wallet?'

'About 30,000 francs. What shall I do? You want to see him?'

'The man? No. Take down his statement. One moment. Just put
him on the line.'

The man immediately said:

'My name is Grimal, Gaston Grimal, but I'd rather my name . . .'

'Of course. I only want to ask you if anything struck you about the
behaviour of your assailant. Give yourself a moment to reflect.'

'I've been reflecting for half an hour. All my papers . . .'

'There is a good chance of recovering them. Your assailant?'

'He seemed to me like a young man of good family, not a thug.'

'Were you far from a street lamp?'

'Not very far. The same as here to the next room. He looked as
frightened as I was. So much so that I very nearly . . .'

'Resisted?'

'Yes. Then I thought that accidents easily happen and . . .'

'Anything else? What sort of a suit was he wearing?'

'A dark suit, probably navy-blue.'

'Crumpled?'

'I don't know.'

'Thank you, Monsieur Grimal. I'd be very surprised if between now
and the morning a patrol doesn't find your wallet on the pavement.
Without the money, of course.'

It was a detail that Maigret hadn't thought of, and he reproached
himself. Alain Lagrange had got hold of a revolver, but he could have
had very little money in his pocket, to judge by the kind of life that was
led in the Rue Popincourt.

He left his office abruptly and went into the Radio Section, where
there were only two men on duty.

'Put out a general call for me to police stations and cars.'

Less than half an hour later all the stations in Paris were listening in.

*Report to Chief-Inspector Maigret any armed hold-up or attempted hold-up
taking place in the past twenty-four hours. Urgent.*

He repeated it, gave the description of Alain Lagrange.

Probably still in the Gare du Nord and Boulevard de la Chapelle area.

He did not return directly to his office, but went through to the Hotels Section.

'Just have a look and see if you haven't got the name Alain Lagrange somewhere. Probably in a second-class hotel.'

It was worth trying. Alain hadn't given his name to Madame Maigret. There was a chance that he had slept somewhere the previous night. Since his identity wasn't known, why should he not have written his real name on the register?

'Will you wait, Inspector?'

'No. Let me have the answer upstairs.'

The technical men had returned from the Rue Popincourt with their cameras, but the detectives had remained over there. At half-past midnight Maigret had a telephone call from the Chief of Police.

'Anything doing?'

'Nothing definite, so far.'

'What about the papers?'

'They'll only publish the bulletin. But once the first editions are out, I'm expecting a flood of reporters.'

'What do you think, Maigret?'

'Nothing yet. The Delteil brother was determined it was a political crime. I politely dissuaded him.'

The Headquarters Commissioner telephoned as well, and even Rateau the magistrate. They all slept badly that night. As for Maigret, he had no intention of going to bed.

It was a quarter past one when he received a more surprising call.

This one didn't come from the Gare du Nord area, nor even from the centre of the city, but from the Neuilly constabulary.

Over there they had just been speaking about Maigret's call to a constable returning from his beat, and the constable, scratching his head, had finally mumbled:

'Perhaps I'd better ring him up.'

He had told his story to the sergeant on duty. The sergeant had encouraged him to call up the chief-inspector. It was a young constable who had only been in uniform a few months.

'I don't know if it will interest you,' he said, much too close to the instrument so that his voice vibrated. 'It was this morning, or rather yesterday morning, seeing it's past midnight. . . . I was on duty in the Boulevard Richard-Wallace, on the edge of the Bois de Boulogne, almost opposite the Bagatelle, as it's only from this evening that I'm on nights. . . . There was a row of buildings, all the same. It was about ten o'clock. . . . I had stopped to look at a big car of some foreign make which had a number-plate I didn't know. . . . A young man, behind me, came out of a building, the one with the number 7b. . . . I didn't pay any attention, as he was walking naturally in the direction of the

street corner. . . . Then I saw the concierge coming out with an odd
look on her face.

'As it happens I know her a bit. I had a chat with her one day when I
was taking a summons to someone who lives in the block. . . . She
recognized me. . . .

' "You look worried," I said to her. And she replied: "I wonder
what that fellow wanted in my house?" She was looking in the direction
of the young man who was just turning the corner.

' "He just passed by the lodge without asking for anyone," she went
on. "He went towards the lift, hesitated, then went up the stairs. As
I'd never seen him before I ran after him. 'Who do you want?' He had
already gone up several steps. He turned round in surprise, as if he was
afraid, and stood there a good while without replying.

' "All he could find to say to me was: 'I must have come to the wrong
building.' "

The constable went on: 'The concierge declares he stared at her in
such a funny way that she didn't dare press him. But when he left she
followed him. Being interested, I went myself to the corner of the Rue
de Longchamp, where there wasn't anybody any longer. The young
man must have taken to his heels. It's only just now that they've shown
me the photo. I'm not sure, but I'd swear it's him. I was probably
wrong to phone you. The sergeant told me . . .'

'You've done perfectly right.'

And the young policeman, who had his wits about him, added:

'My name is Emile Lebraz.'

Maigret called Lapointe.

'Tired?'

'No, Chief.'

'Stay in my office and take any messages. I hope to be back here in
three-quarters of an hour. If there's anything urgent, call me at the
Boulevard Richard-Wallace, in Neuilly. Number 7b. With the concierge, who should have a telephone. In fact, it would save time if you'd
ring up and warn her I want to talk to her for a moment. Then she'll
have time to get up and put on a dressing-gown before I arrive.'

The run through the deserted streets took little time, and when he
rang he found the lodge lit, the concierge not in a dressing-gown, but
fully dressed to receive him. It was a handsome building, and the lodge
was a sort of drawing-room. In the next room, to which the door was
open, they could see a child asleep.

'Monsieur Maigret?' stammered the good woman, quite overcome at
receiving him in person.

'I am very sorry to have woken you up. I should just like you to look
at these photographs and tell me if the young man you caught on the
stairs yesterday morning looks like any of them.'

He had taken the precaution of bringing a handful of photographs of young men of about the same age. The concierge took no longer than the business man from Clermont.

'That's him!' she said, pointing to Alain Lagrange.

'You're quite sure about it?'

'There's no mistaking him.'

'When you caught him up, he didn't threaten you at all?'

'No! It's odd that you should ask me that, as I've thought about it. It's more an impression, if you see what I mean. I don't want to state as a fact what I'm not certain of. When he had turned round he didn't move, but I had an odd feeling inside me. In point of fact, it seemed to me he was wondering whether to go for me. . . .'

'How many tenants have you in the building?'

'There are two flats to each floor. That makes fourteen flats for the seven floors. But there are two empty at the moment. One family left for Brazil three weeks ago—they are actually Brazilians from the Embassy—and the gentleman on the fifth died twelve days ago.'

'Can you let me have a list of your tenants?'

'That's easy. I've got one already made up.'

Water was boiling on a gas cooker, and after handing a piece of typed paper to the chief-inspector, the concierge set about making some coffee.

'I thought you'd like a cup. At this hour. . . . My husband whom I had the misfortune to lose last year, wasn't exactly in the police, but he was in the Republican Guard.'

'I see two names on the ground floor, the Delvals and the Trélos.'

She smiled.

'The Delvals, that's right. They are importers, with offices in the Place des Victoires. But Monsieur Trélo is all alone. Don't you know him? He's the film comedian.'

'Anyway, it's not them the young man was after, because, after hesitating by the lift, he headed for the stairs.

'On the first floor, to the left, Monsieur Desquiens, whom you see on the list, is away at the moment. He's on holiday with his children, who have a place in the Midi.'

'What does he do?'

'Nothing. He's rich. He's a widower, very polite and quiet.'

'On the right, Rosetti?'

'Italians. She's a very beautiful person. They have three maids, plus a nurse for the baby, which is just over a year old.'

'Profession?'

'Monsieur Rosetti's in motor-cars. It was actually his car the constable was looking at when I came out behind the young man.'

'On the second floor? I'm sorry to keep you up so late.'

'Not at all. Two lumps of sugar? Milk?'

'No milk. Thanks. Mettetal. Who's that?'

'Rich people too, but they can't keep their maids, because Madame Mettetal, who's in bad health, goes for everybody.'

Maigret was writing notes in the margin of the list.

'On the same floor I see: Beauman.'

'Diamond brokers. They are travelling. It's the season. I forward their mail to them in Switzerland.'

'Third floor on the right, Jeanne Debul. Single woman?'

'A single woman, yes.'

The concierge had said this in the tone women generally use to speak of another woman against whom they have a grudge.

'What type of person?'

'You can hardly call her a type. She left yesterday about midday for England. I was really rather surprised she hadn't mentioned it.'

'To whom?'

'To her maid, a good girl who tells me everything.'

'Is the maid up there now?'

'Yes. She spent part of the evening in the lodge. She wasn't in a hurry to go to bed as she's nervous and has a horror of sleeping by herself in the flat.'

'You say she was surprised?'

'The maid, yes. The night before Madame Debul came home in the small hours, as often happens with her. You notice how they say Madame, but I'm convinced she's never been married.'

'What age?'

'The real one, or the one she pretends to be?'

'Both.'

'The real one I know, seeing I had her papers through my hands when she took out her lease.'

'How long ago.'

'About two years. Before that she lived in the Rue Notre-Dame-de-Lorette. The fact is she's forty-nine and pretends to be forty. In the morning she looks her age. In the evening, why heavens . . .'

'Has she a lover?'

'It's not exactly what you might think. Otherwise she wouldn't be kept on in the place. The management is very strict on that point. I don't quite know how to put it.'

'Try.'

'She's not the same class as the other residents. Even so, she's not a person who gives a bad impression, if you see what I mean. Not a kept woman, for example. She's got money. She gets letters from her bank, from her stockbroker. She could be a widow or a divorcée having a good time.'

'Does she entertain?'

'Not gigolos, if that's what you've got in mind. Her business manager comes from time to time. Women friends as well. Sometimes couples.

But she's more a woman who goes out than one who entertains at home. In the morning she stays in bed till midday. In the afternoon she sometimes goes into town, always extremely well dressed, rather quietly even. Then she comes back to put on her evening dress, and I don't pull the cord to let her in till well after midnight. There's another odd thing besides, which her maid Georgette tells me. She spends a lot of money. Her furs alone are worth a fortune, and she always wears a diamond ring on her finger as big as that. Even so, Georgette says she's mean, and spends a large part of her time going over the household accounts.'

'When did she leave?'

'About half-past eleven. That's what surprised Georgette. At that time, her mistress ought still to have been in bed. She was asleep when she had a telephone call. Straight afterwards, she had a railway timetable brought to her.'

'This was a short time after the young man tried to get into the house?'

'A little after, yes. She didn't wait for her breakfast and she packed herself.'

'Large cases?'

'Only suitcases. No trunks. She's been around a lot.'

'Why do you say that?'

'Because there were labels all over the cases, nothing but big hotels in Deauville, Nice, Naples, Rome, and other foreign places besides.'

'She didn't say when she would be back?'

'Not to me. Georgette doesn't know anything about it either.'

'She didn't ask her to have her letters forwarded?'

'No. She just rang up the Gare du Nord to reserve a seat on the Calais express.'

Maigret was struck by the persistence with which the words Gare du Nord had recurred since the beginning of the case. It was at the cloakroom of the Gare du Nord that François Lagrange had deposited the trunk containing the body of the deputy. Again it was in the neighbourhood of the Gare du Nord that his son had held up the manufacturer from Clermont-Ferrand.

This same Alain had slipped up the stairs of a block of flats in the Boulevard Richard-Wallace, and a little while later, a resident in the block had set off for the Gare du Nord. Coincidence?

'You know if you have the slightest desire to question Georgette, she would be absolutely delighted. She's so afraid of being on her own that it would be a pleasure for her to have company.'

And the concierge added:

'And especially company like yours!'

Before anything else Maigret wanted to finish with the residents in the house, and he pointed to them patiently, one after the other. There was a cinema producer on the fourth floor, a genuine one this time, whose name was to be seen on walls all over Paris. Directly above him was a film director, well known too, and, as though by chance, on the seventh floor there lived a script-writer who did his daily dozen on the balcony every morning.

'Do you want me to go and warn Georgette?'

'I should like to make a telephone call first.'

He rang up the Gare du Nord.

'Maigret here, from Police Headquarters. Tell me, do you have a train for Calais around midnight?'

It had been about half-past eleven when the business man was held up in the Rue de Maubeuge.

'At twelve-thirteen.'

'Express?'

'It connects with the Dover mail at half-past five. It doesn't stop on the way.'

'You don't remember issuing a ticket to a young man by himself?'

'The clerks who were in the booking-offices then have gone to bed.'

'Thank you.'

He called the harbour police at Calais, gave the description of Alain Lagrange.

'He's armed!' he added, just in case.

Then, without expecting too much, he announced, after emptying his cup of coffee:

'I'll go up and see Georgette. Warn her.'

To which the concierge replied with a malicious smile:

'You be careful. She's a pretty girl!'

She added:

'And she likes handsome men!'

V

SHE was rosy-complexioned, with ample breasts, in her pyjamas of candy-pink crepon, washed so often that they allowed dark shadows to show through them. One would have said that her body, too rounded everywhere, was still not fully developed, and with her complexion, too fresh for Paris, she reminded one of a gosling which has not yet lost its down. When she opened the door to him, he had caught the smell of her bed, of armpits.

He had let the concierge telephone her to wake her and say he was on his way up. She couldn't have got through straight away because, when he reached the third floor, the bell was still ringing in the flat.

He had waited. The telephone was too far from the landing for him to hear her voice. There had been footsteps on the moquette, and she had opened the door for him, not in the least embarrassed, without having taken the trouble to put on a dressing-gown. Perhaps she hadn't one? When she got up in the morning it was in order to set to work, and when she undressed at night it was to go to bed. She was blonde, her hair all untidy, and there were still traces of lipstick on her lips.

'Sit down there.'

They had crossed the hall, and she had switched on only a large standard lamp in the drawing-room. She had chosen for herself a large sofa of delicate green, where she was half stretched out. The air coming in through the high french window billowed out the curtains. She was watching Maigret with the solemnity of a child examining an important grown-up people have told them a lot about.

'I didn't picture you quite like that,' she finally admitted.

'How had you pictured me?'

'I don't know. You are better.'

'The concierge told me you wouldn't mind if I came up and asked you a few questions.'

'About Madame?'

'Yes.'

That didn't surprise her. Nothing could have surprised her.

'How old are you?'

'Twenty-two years old, six of them in Paris. You can go ahead.'

He began by showing her the photograph of Alain Lagrange.

'You know him?'

'I've never seen him.'

'You're sure he's never come to see your mistress?'

'At any rate, not since I've been with her. Young people aren't her type, whatever you might think.'

'Why should people think the opposite?'

'Because of her age.'

'Have you been in service with her long?'

'Since she set up house here. That makes it nearly two years.'

'You didn't work for her when she was living in the Rue Notre-Dame-de-Lorette?'

'No. I applied the day she moved out.'

'Had she still got her previous maid?'

'I didn't even meet her. She started afresh, as you might say. The furniture, the bits and pieces, everything was new.'

For her, this seemed to have one meaning, and Maigret thought he interpreted her innuendo correctly.

'You don't like her?'

'She's not the kind of woman one can like. Besides it's all the same to her.'

'How do you mean?'

'She's good enough for herself. She doesn't take the trouble to be nice. When she talks to you, it's not for your benefit, but just because she wants to talk.'

'You don't know who telephoned her when she suddenly decided to leave for London?'

'No. She answered the telephone herself. She didn't mention any name.'

'Did she seem surprised, annoyed?'

'If you knew her, you'd realize she never shows what she feels.'

'You don't know anything about her past?'

'Except that she lived in the Rue Notre-Dame-de-Lorette, that she's familiar with me and that she goes through all the accounts with a tooth-comb.'

From the way she spoke, that explained everything, and this time again, Maigret had the impression he understood her meaning.

'In fact, in your opinion, she's not a lady?'

'Certainly not. I've worked with real ladies and I know the difference. I've also worked in the Place Saint-Georges area with a kept woman.'

'Has Jeanne Debul been kept?'

'If she has been, she isn't any longer. She's certainly rich.'

'Did men come to see her?'

'Her masseur came every other day. She was on easy terms with him as well and called him Ernest.'

'Anything between them?'

'She's not interested.'

Her pyjama top was of the kind you slip over your head, very short, and as Georgette was lying back in the cushions, her skin showed in a band above her belt.

'You don't mind if I smoke?'

'I'm sorry,' he said, 'but I haven't any cigarettes.'

'There are some on the table. . . .'

She found it natural for him to get up and offer her a packet of Egyptian cigarettes belonging to Jeanne Debul. While he held the match, she puffed inexpertly at the cigarette, blowing out the smoke like a beginner.

She was pleased with herself, pleased at having been woken up by a man as important as Maigret, who was listening to her with attention.

'She's got plenty of men and women friends, but they seldom come here. She rings them up, mostly calls them by their christian names. She sees them in the evening at cocktail parties, or in restaurants and night clubs. I've often wondered if she didn't keep a house before. You see what I mean?'

'And the people who do come here?'

'Her business manager, chiefly. She sees him in her study. He's a lawyer, Maître Gibon, who doesn't come from this neighbourhood, but lives in the ninth arrondissement. So she knew him before when she was in the same district. Then there's a slightly younger man who's in the bank and she discusses her investments with him. He's the one she rings up when she has instructions to give about her shares.'

'You never see a man called François Lagrange?'

'Carpet Slippers!'

She broke off with a laugh.

'It's not me who calls him that. It's the mistress. When I tell her he's here, she grumbles:

' "That old Carpet Slippers again!" '

'That's another sign, don't you think? He always says, to announce himself:

' "Ask Madame Debul if she can see Baron Lagrange." '

'Does she see him?'

'Nearly always.'

'Which means often?'

'Say about once a week. There are some weeks when he doesn't come at all, others when he comes twice. Last week he came twice on the same day.'

'About what time?'

'Always in the morning, about eleven o'clock. Apart from Ernest the masseur, he's the only one she sees in her bedroom.'

And, as he registered her point:

'It's not what you think. Even for the lawyer she dresses. I must say she dresses well, in a very quiet way. It's actually what struck me right away: what she's like in bed, in her room, and what she's like when she's dressed. It's two different people. She doesn't speak in the same way: you might say that even her voice changes.'

'Is she more common in bed?'

'Yes. Not only common. I can't think of the word.'

'Is François Lagrange the only one she receives like that?'

'Yes. She shouts to him, no matter what state she's in:

' "Come in, you!" As if they were old friends. . . .'

'. . . or accomplices?'

'If you like. Until I go out, they don't talk about anything important. He sits down timidly on the edge of an easy chair, as though afraid of creasing the satin.'

'Does he have papers, a brief-case, with him?'

'No. He's a proper gentleman. He's not my type, but I think he's so distinguished.'

'You've never overheard their conversations?'

'It isn't possible with her. She guesses everything. She's got sharp ears. It's she that does most of the listening at doors in this house. When

I happen to be telephoning, I can be almost sure that she's somewhere about spying on me. If I'm taking a letter to the post she says to me:

'"Who are you writing to now?"'

'And I know she looks at the address. You know the type?'

'I see.'

'There's something you haven't seen yet which may give you a surprise.'

She jumped to her feet, threw the butt of her cigarette into the ash-tray.

'Come with me. Now you've seen the drawing-room. It's furnished in the same style as all the other drawing-rooms in the building. One of the best decorators in Paris took on the job. Here's the dining-room, in modern style as well. Wait till I put on the light.'

She pushed open a door, turned on a switch, stood out of the way to let him see a bedroom entirely in white satin.

'Now here's how she dresses in the evening.'

In an adjoining room, she opened some cupboards, and ran her hands over the silk of a neat array of dresses.

'Right. Now come this way!'

She went before him into a corridor, and the crepon of her pyjamas was caught between her buttocks. She opened another door, turned on another switch.

'There!'

It was a little office at the back of the apartment, which might have belonged to a business man. Not the least feminine trace was to be found. There was a metal filing cabinet painted green and behind the revolving armchair there was an enormous safe of fairly recent design.

'It's here that she spends part of her afternoons and sees the lawyer and the man from the bank. Look . . .'

She was pointing to a pile of papers: *The Stock Exchange Courier.* True, Maigret noticed a racing paper beside them.

'Does she wear glasses?'

'Only in this room.'

There was a pair of them, big round glasses with tortoise-shell rims, on a blotting-pad with leather corners.

Mechanically he tried to open the filing cabinet, but it was locked.

'Every night when she comes in she goes and puts her jewels in the safe.'

'What else does it contain? Have you ever seen inside?'

'Deeds mostly. Papers. Then there's a little red diary she often looks at.'

From the desk Maigret picked up one of those indexes in which people jot down the telephone numbers they use often, and set about going through its pages. He read out the names in an undertone. Georgette explained:

'The milkman. . . . The butcher. . . . The ironmonger in the Avenue de Neuilly. . . . Madame's shoemaker. . . .'

When, instead of a surname, there was only a christian name she would smile, satisfied.

'Olga . . . Nadine . . . Marcelle . . .'

'What did I tell you?'

Men's christian names, too, but fewer of them. Then some names the maid did not know. Under the heading 'banks' there were no less than five establishments entered, including an American bank in the Place Vendôme.

He searched, without finding it, for the name Delteil. There were certainly an André and a Pierre somewhere. Did these refer to the deputy and his brother?

'After seeing the rest of the flat and the wardrobe, were you expecting to find this?'

He said no, to please her.

'Aren't you thirsty?'

'The concierge was kind enough to make me some coffee.'

'You won't have a little something?'

She led him back to the drawing-room, turning out the lights behind her, and, as if the interview was likely to last a lot longer, took her place on the sofa again, since he had refused a drink.

'Does your mistress drink?'

'Like a man.'

'Which means a lot?'

'I've never seen her drunk, except once or twice coming home in the small hours. But she pours herself a whisky straight after her morning coffee and has two or three others in the course of the afternoon. That's why I say she drinks like a man. She takes her whisky almost neat.'

'She hasn't told you which hotel in London she will be stopping at?'

'No.'

'Nor how long she expects to stay?'

'She told me nothing. She didn't take half an hour over her packing and dressing.'

'How was she dressed when she left?'

'In her grey suit.'

'Did she take any evening dresses with her?'

'Two.'

'I don't think I've any more questions to ask you and I'll let you go to bed.'

'Already? Are you in a hurry?'

She deliberately uncovered a bit more of her body between the two parts of her pyjamas, deliberately, too, crossed her legs in a certain way.

'Do you often have to do your investigations at night?'

'Sometimes.'

'You really don't want anything to drink?'

She sighed.

'Personally, now that I'm awake, I shan't be able to go to sleep again. What time is it?'

'Getting on for three o'clock.'

'At four it starts to get light, and the birds begin to sing.'

He got up, sorry to disappoint her, and perhaps she still had hopes that he was not intending to leave, but only to come over to her. It wasn't until she saw him going towards the door that she got up in turn.

'You'll be coming back?'

'Possibly.'

'You'll never bother me. Just give two little rings, then one long one. I'll know it's you and I'll open the door. When I'm alone I don't always open it.'

'Thank you, mademoiselle.'

Once again he caught the smell of bed, of armpits. One of the large breasts brushed against his sleeve with a certain insistence.

'Good luck!' he called to her softly, when he was on the stairs.

And she leant over the banisters to watch him go down.

At Headquarters he found Janvier waiting, having spent several hours at the rooms in the Rue Popincourt, and he looked worn out.

'How did it go, Chief? Did he talk?'

Maigret shook his head.

'I left Houard over there just in case. We turned the flat upside down, without getting much out of it. I've only got this to show you.'

Maigret first poured himself a glass of brandy, then passed the bottle to the detective.

'You'll see. It's rather odd.'

In a rough paper cover, which had been torn from the back of a school exercise-book, were some press cuttings, some of them illustrated with photographs.

Frowning, Maigret read the headings and ran through the texts, while Janvier watched him with a curious expression.

All the articles, without exception, were about the chief-inspector, and some dated back seven years. They were reports of cases, published on the same day, with, often, a summary of the court proceedings.

'Notice anything, Chief? While I was waiting for you, I took the trouble to read from beginning to end.'

Maigret noticed something he preferred not to mention.

'You could swear, couldn't you, that they've chosen the cases where you seemed to be more or less defending the guilty party.'

One of the articles was headed: *The Kind-hearted Inspector.*

Another was devoted to a statement of Maigret's at the High Court, a statement in the course of which all his replies showed his sympathy for the young man who was being tried.

Even more clear was another article, appearing the previous year in a weekly, which did not deal with any particular case, but the question of guilt in general, and which was entitled: *Maigret's Humanity*.

'What do you think of it? This file proves the fellow has been following you for a long time, has got some interest in what you do or say, in your character.'

Some words were underlined in blue chalk, among others the words *'leniency'* and *'understanding'*.

Finally a passage was entirely ringed round — one where a journalist described the last morning of a man condemned to death, and revealed that after refusing a priest the condemned man asked for the favour of a last interview with Chief-Inspector Maigret.

'You don't like it?'

He had in fact become more grave, more intent as though this discovery was opening up new horizons for him.

'You found nothing else?'

'Some bills. Unpaid, of course. The Baron owes money all round. The coal merchant hasn't been paid for last winter. Here's a photo of his wife with his first child.'

The print was a bad one. The dress dated it, and so did the hair style. The young woman posing for it had a melancholy smile. Perhaps it was the period when that was the fashion, so as to look distinguished. Yet Maigret felt certain that, simply through seeing the photo, anyone would have realized this woman was not destined for happiness.

'In a wardrobe, I found one of her dresses, in pale blue satin, and a boxful of baby clothes, too.'

Janvier had three children, the youngest of them not a year old.

'My wife only keeps their first pair of shoes.'

Maigret picked up the telephone.

'Police Infirmary!' he said in a low voice. 'Hullo! Who's that speaking?'

It was the nurse, a redhead, whom he knew.

'Maigret here. How's Lagrange? What d'you say? I can't hear you properly.'

She was saying that her patient, who had been given an injection, had gone off to sleep almost immediately after the doctor's departure. Half an hour later she had heard a slight noise and had gone over on tiptoe to see.

'He was crying.'

'Didn't he speak to you?'

'He heard me, and I put on the light. The tears were still shining on his cheeks. He looked at me in silence for a while and I got the impression he was hesitating whether to confide in me.'

'Did he seem to you to be in his senses?'

She, too, hesitated.

'It's not for me to judge,' she countered, beating a retreat.

'Then what?'

'He made a move to take my hand.'

'Did he take it?'

'No. He started whimpering, and kept on repeating, always the same words: "You won't let them hit me, will you? . . . I don't want to be hit." '

'That all?'

'In the end, he became excited. I thought he was going to jump out of bed, and he began to cry out: "I don't want to die! . . . I don't want to! . . . I mustn't be left to die!" . . .'

Maigret hung up, turned to Janvier, opposite him, who was fighting against sleep.

'You can go home to bed.'

'And you?'

'I've got to wait up till half-past five. I want to know if the boy actually took the Calais train.'

'Why should he have taken it?'

'To catch up with someone in England.'

On the Wednesday morning, Alain had stolen his gun from him, and had provided himself with ammunition. On Thursday he went to the Boulevard Richard-Wallace, and half an hour later Jeanne Debul, who knew his father, had a telephone call and set off in a hurry for the Gare du Nord.

What was the young man doing during the afternoon? Why didn't he leave at once? Couldn't it only be presumed to be for lack of money?

To get some, by the only means at his disposal, he had to wait till nightfall.

It so happened he attacked the business man from Clermont-Ferrand not far from the Gare du Nord, a short time after the departure of the Calais train.

'By the way, I was forgetting to tell you there was a call about the wallet. It's been found in the street.'

'Which street?'

'Rue de Dunkerque.'

Still near the station.

'Without the money, of course.'

'Before you leave, get the passport office on the line. Ask them if they've ever issued a passport in the name of Alain Lagrange.'

In the interval he went and planted himself in front of the window. It was not yet day, but that grey, cold hour which comes before sunrise. In a sort of dull green mist the Seine flowed by, almost black, and a bargee was washing down the deck of his boat, moored to the jetty. A tug was going silently downstream, on its way to fetch its string of barges.

'He applied for a passport eleven months ago, Chief. He wanted to go to Austria.'

'So his passport is still valid. You don't need a visa for England. You didn't find it among his things?'

'Nothing.'

'No change of clothes?'

'He can only have one decent suit and he's got that on. There was another in his wardrobe, worn to threads. All the shoes we saw had holes in them.'

'Go to sleep.'

'You're sure you don't need me any longer?'

'Certain. Besides, there are still two men in the office.'

Maigret wasn't conscious of dozing off in his armchair, and when he suddenly opened his eyes, because the tug he had noticed a short while ago was returning upstream and whistling before negotiating the bridge with its seven barges behind it, the sky was pink and gleams of reflected light could be seen from various rooftops. He looked at his watch, picked up the telephone.

'Harbour police, Calais!'

This took a little time. The harbour police would not reply at once. The sergeant who eventually came to the telephone was out of breath.

'Maigret, Paris Police Headquarters, here.'

'I know what you're after.'

'Well?'

'We've just finished examining the passports. The boat hasn't left the quayside yet. My colleagues are still there.'

Maigret heard the siren-blasts from the mail-boat which was about to depart.

'Young Lagrange?'

'We haven't found anything. No one resembling him. There were very few passengers and it was easy to check up.'

'Have you still got a list of the people who sailed yesterday?'

'I'll go and fetch it from the office next door. Will you hold on?'

When he spoke again, it was to say:

'I don't see any Lagrange on yesterday's departures, either.'

'It's not Lagrange I want. Look for a Madame Jeanne Debul.'

'Debul . . . Debul . . . D . . . D . . . Here we are. . . . Daumas . . . Dazergues . . . Debul, Jeanne Louise Clementine, forty-nine, living at Neuilly-sur-Seine, 7b Boulevard. . . .'

'I know. What destination address does she give?'

'Savoy Hotel, London.'

'Thank you. You're sure that Lagrange . . .'

'You may rest assured, Inspector.'

Maigret was hot, perhaps through not having slept. He was in a bad mood, and it was as if to get his own back that he seized hold of the

6*

bottle of brandy. Then all of a sudden he picked up the telephone again, grunted:

'Le Bourget.'

'I beg your pardon?'

'I asked you to put me through to Le Bourget.'

His tone was offensive; the operator made a wry face and acted quickly.

'Maigret here, from Police Headquarters.'

'Sergeant Mathieu.'

'Is there a plane to London during the course of the night?'

'There's one at ten o'clock in the evening, another at twelve forty-five and then the first of the morning took off a few seconds ago. I can still hear it gaining height.'

'Will you get a passenger list?'

'Which flight?'

'Twelve forty-five.'

'One moment.'

It was seldom that Maigret was so unfriendly.

'You there?'

'Yes.'

'Look for Lagrange.'

'Right. . . . Lagrange, Alain François Marie.'

'Thank you.'

'That all?'

Maigret had already hung up. On account of that cursed Gare du Nord, which had hypnotized him, he hadn't thought of the plane, so that by now Alain Lagrange, with his loaded revolver, had already been in London for some time.

His hand hovered over the desk for a moment before grasping the telephone receiver.

'Savoy Hotel, London.'

He got through almost at once.

'Savoy Hotel. Reception speaking. . . .'

He was getting tired of repeating his patter, his name and office.

'Can you tell me if a Madame Jeanne Debul arrived at your hotel yesterday?'

This took less time than with the police. The reception clerk had the list of guests for each day within his reach.

'Yes, sir. Room 605. You wish to speak to her?'

He hesitated.

'No. See if you had an Alain Lagrange last night.'

This took hardly any longer.

'No, sir.'

'I presume you ask for the passports of travellers on their arrival?'

'Certainly. We follow the regulations.'

'So Alain Lagrange couldn't be staying with you under another name?'

'Only if he had a false passport. They are checked every night by the police, remember.'

'Thanks.'

He still had one call to make, and this one he particularly disliked, all the more because he was going to be obliged to use the not very good English he had learnt at school.

'Scotland Yard.'

It would have been a miracle if Inspector Pyke, whom he had entertained in France, were on duty at such an hour. He had to be content with a stranger who was slow to understand who he was, and answered him in a nasal voice.

'A Madame Jeanne Debul, aged forty-nine, is staying at the Savoy, room 605. . . . I should like to have her discreetly watched for the next few hours. . . .'

The far-away voice had a mania for repeating Maigret's last words, but with the right accent, as though to correct him.

'It's possible a young man may try to pay her a visit or waylay her. I'll give you his description. . . .'

The description provided, he added:

'He's armed; a Smith and Wesson special. That gives you an excuse to detain him. I'm having his photograph sent to you by telephoto in a few minutes.'

But the Englishman seemed unable to grasp what he was talking about, and Maigret was obliged to spell things out, to repeat the same thing three or four times.

'Now what exactly do you want us to do?'

Faced with so much obstinacy, Maigret was sorry he had taken the precaution of ringing up the Yard, and felt like replying: 'Nothing at all!'

He was bathed in sweat.

'I shall be there as soon as possible,' he finished by saying.

'You mean you're coming to Scotland Yard?'

'I'm coming to London, yes.'

'What time?'

'I don't know at all. I haven't got the air time-table in front of me. . . .'

'You're coming by air?'

He finally hung up, exasperated, calling down every sort of curse on this civil servant he didn't know, who was probably really a very good man. What would Lucas have replied to a Yard inspector ringing him up at six o'clock in the morning to tell him a story of the same type in bad French?

'It's me again! Get me Le Bourget once more.'

An aeroplane was leaving at eight-fifteen. That gave him time to go round to the Boulevard Richard-Lenoir to change and even to shave and swallow his breakfast. Madame Maigret was careful not to ask him questions.

'I don't know when I'll be back,' he said grumpily, with the vague intention of making her angry with him, so as to be able to blame his temper onto someone else. 'I'm off to London.'

'Ah!'

'Get my little case ready with a change of clothes and my toilet things. There ought to be a few English pounds at the bottom of the drawer.'

The telephone rang. He was in the middle of putting on his tie.

'Maigret? Rateau here.'

The examining magistrate, bright and early, who had spent the night in bed, who was doubtless delighted at being woken by brilliant sunshine and who, as he ate his croissants, was asking for news.

'What do you say?'

'I said I haven't got time: I'm taking the plane to London in thirty-five minutes.'

'To London?'

'That's right.'

'But what have you found out that . . .'

'I'm sorry to ring off; the aeroplane won't wait.'

He was in such a state of mind that he added:

'I'll send you some picture postcards.'

By then, of course, the receiver was back on its rest.

VI

THERE were clouds as they approached the French coast and they flew above them. Through a large break, a little while later, Maigret had a chance of glimpsing the sea which sparkled like fishes' scales, and fishing-boats trailing their foamy wake behind them.

His neighbour leant over in a friendly way to point out some chalky cliffs to him, explaining:

'Dover . . . *Douvres* . . .'

He thanked him with a smile, and soon there was nothing more than an almost transparent mist between the earth and the plane. Only now and then did they fly into a large, luminous cloud, from which they emerged almost immediately, to find beneath them once more fields of pasture dotted with tiny cows.

Finally the landscape rocked, and it was Croydon. It was also Mr.

Pyke. For Mr. Pyke was there, awaiting his French colleague. Not on the airstrip itself, as he doubtless would have had the right to be, not away from the crowd, but with it, wisely, behind the barrier separating passengers from relations and friends waiting for them.

He made no gesticulations, didn't wave his handkerchief. When Maigret looked in his direction he merely nodded his head, as he must have done every morning on meeting his colleagues at the office.

It was years since they had seen one another, and twelve or thirteen years since the chief-inspector had set foot in England.

He followed the queue, his case in his hand, into a building where he had to go through the immigration office, then through the customs, and Mr. Pyke was still there, behind a glass panel, with his dark grey suit which looked a little too tight for him, his black felt hat, a carnation in his buttonhole.

He could have come in here as well, told the immigration official: 'It's Chief-Inspector Maigret who's come to see us. . . .'

Maigret would have done that for him at Le Bourget. He did not mind, however, understanding that it was, on the contrary, a sort of tact on his part. Actually, he felt rather ashamed of his anger that morning over the policeman at the Yard. The fact that Mr. Pyke was there showed that the man had not done his job so badly, had even showed initiative. It was only half-past ten. To reach Croydon in time Pyke must have left London almost as soon as he arrived at his office.

Maigret was coming out of the room. The dry, hard hand was extended.

'How are you?'

Pyke went on, in French, which was a sacrifice on his part, since he spoke it with difficulty and hated making mistakes:

'*J'espère que vous allez* . . . enjoy . . . How d'you say it? . . . *Jouir.* . . . Oui, jouir de cette journée resplendissante.*'

It was in fact the first time Maigret had been in England in summer and he wondered if he had ever seen London in real sunshine.

'I thought you would rather travel up by car than in the company coach.'

He did not speak to him about his case, made no reference to it, and that was again all part of his sort of tact. They took their seats in a Yard Bentley, driven by a chauffeur in uniform, and the latter, scrupulously respecting the speed limits, didn't shoot any traffic lights.

'Pretty, isn't it?'

Pyke was pointing to some rows of small red-brick houses, which under grey skies would have looked gloomy, but which, in the sunshine, were trim, rather gay, each with a square patch of lawn slightly larger than a sheet, between the front door and the fence. One could tell how he relished this prospect of suburban London, where he lived himself.

The red-brick houses were succeeded by yellow houses, then brown houses, then more red-brick ones. It was beginning to be very hot, and in some gardens automatic hoses were playing.

'I was forgetting to let you have this.'

He handed Maigret a piece of paper on which there were notes written in French.

Alain Lagrange, aged nineteen, business employee, booked in at 4 a.m. at the Gilmore Hotel, opposite Victoria Station, without luggage.

Slept till eight o'clock, then went out.

First went to the Astoria Hotel and made inquiries about Madame Jeanne Debul.

Then went to the Continental Hotel, then to Claridge's, still asking the same question.

Appears to be following an alphabetical list of the big hotels.

Has never been to London before. Does not speak English.

Now it was Maigret who merely nodded his thanks, and he was more annoyed with himself than ever for his unkind thoughts about the policeman that morning.

After a long silence and several rows of identical houses, Pyke began to speak:

'I took the liberty of reserving you a hotel room as we have a lot of tourists at the moment.'

He handed his colleague a ticket bearing the name 'Savoy' and the number of the room. Maigret very nearly paid no attention to it. The number struck him: 604.

So they had thought of putting him just opposite Jeanne Debul.

'Is that woman still there?' he asked.

'She was when we left Croydon. I had a report by telephone just as your plane was beginning to fly over the airfield.'

Nothing else. He was satisfied, not so much with having proved to Maigret that the English police are efficient as with showing him England beneath an indisputable sun.

When they entered London and passed the big red buses, when they saw women in light frocks on the pavements, he could not help murmuring:

'That's really something, isn't it?'

And, as they approached the Savoy:

'If you aren't busy, could I come and pick you up for lunch at about one? From now until then I shall be at my office. You can ring me up.'

That was all. He let him go into the hotel alone, while the chauffeur in uniform handed his suitcase over to one of the porters.

Did the reception clerk recognize him after twelve years? Did he know him purely by his photographs? Or was it just flattery? Or the fact that his room had been booked through Scotland Yard?'

'Did you have a good journey, Monsieur Maigret?'

'Very good, thank you.'

The immense hall, where at every hour of the day and night there were people in deep armchairs, always overawed him a little. On the right, flowers were being sold. Every man had one in his buttonhole, and probably under the influence of Pyke's good-humour, Maigret bought himself a red carnation.

He remembered that the bar was on the left. He was thirsty. He went towards the glass-panelled door, tried in vain to open it.

'At half-past eleven, sir!'

His face clouded. It was always the same abroad. Details which enchanted him, then, all of a sudden, others which infuriated him. Why the devil hadn't he the right to have a drink before half-past eleven? He hadn't been to bed all the night before. His head felt thick and the sun was making him slightly giddy. Perhaps it was the motion of the aeroplane as well?

As he was going up towards the lift, a man he didn't know came up to him.

'The lady has just had her breakfast taken up. Mr. Pyke told me to keep you informed. Should I wait in case you want me?'

It was a man from the Yard. Maigret thought him elegant, not out of place in this luxurious hotel, and he, too, wore a flower in his buttonhole. His was white.

'The young man hasn't appeared?'

'No so far, sir.'

'Would you watch the hall and warn me the moment he arrives?'

'It'll be some time now before he gets to the letter S, sir. I think Inspector Pyke has posted one of my colleagues at the Lancaster Hotel.'

The room was vast, with a pearl-grey lounge adjoining, and the windows gave onto the Thames, where just as that moment a boat was passing, of the same kind as the river steamers of Paris with two decks covered with tourists.

Maigret was so hot that he decided to take a shower and change. He all but rang up Paris for news of the Baron, changed his mind, dressed again, half-opened the door. 605 was opposite. The sunlight could be seen under the door, which meant the curtains had been drawn. Just as he was going to knock, he heard the noise of water in the bathroom, and he began to pace up and down the corridor smoking his pipe. A chambermaid passing by looked at him curiously. She must have mentioned him at the office, for a boy in uniform came and had a look at him too. Then, seeing from his watch that it was eleven twenty-four, he took the lift and was at the door of the bar at the very second it was being opened. Other men as well, who must have been waiting for this moment in the armchairs in the hall, were in an equal hurry.

'Whisky?'

'All right.'

'Soda?'

His pout must have shown that he thought the drink hadn't got much taste, for the barman suggested:

'A double, sir?'

Things were better already. He had never suspected it could be so hot in London. He went to get some fresh air for a few minutes in front of the big revolving doors, looked at the time again and went over to the lift.

When he knocked at the door of 605, a woman's voice inside called: '*Entrez!*'

Then, probably thinking it was the boy coming to take away her tray:

'Come in!'

He turned the handle, and the door opened.

He found himself in a room bright with sunshine, where a woman in a house-coat was seated before her dressing-table. She didn't look at him straight away. She went on brushing her brown hair, and she had hairpins between her teeth. It was in the looking-glass that she saw him. Her brows contracted.

'What do you want?'

'Chief-Inspector Maigret, of Police Headquarters.'

'Does that give you the right to walk into other people's rooms?'

'It was you who asked me to come in.'

It was hard to tell her age. She must have been very beautiful once, and something of it remained. In the evening, with the lights on, she would probably give that impression, especially if her mouth didn't take on the hard twist it had at the moment.

'You can start by taking your pipe out of your mouth.'

He did so awkwardly. He hadn't thought about his pipe.

'Then, if you have something to say, get it over quickly. I don't see what business the French police can have with me. Especially here.'

She was still not facing him, and it was disquieting. She must have known it, and lingered at her dressing-table, watching him in the looking-glass. Standing up he felt too big, too massive. The bed was not made. There was a tray with the remains of breakfast, and to sit on he could only see a small armchair, in which he could scarcely accommodate his large thighs.

He announced, looking at her himself by means of the glass:

'Alain is in London.'

Either she was very strong-minded or else this christian name meant nothing to her, for she did not falter.

He went on in the same tone:

'He's armed.'

'Did you cross the Channel just to tell me that? I presume you've come from Paris? What name did you say? I mean yours.'

He was convinced she was play-acting, in the hopes of annoying him.

'Chief-Inspector Maigret.'

'Which district?'

'Police Headquarters.'

'You're looking for a young man whose christian name is Alain? He's not here. Search the room if that would reassure you.'

'It's he who's looking for you.'

'Why?'

'That's just what I'd like to ask you.'

This time she got up, and he saw that she was almost as tall as he was. She was wearing a dressing-gown of thick salmon-coloured silk which showed a still attractive figure. She went to get a cigarette from a side-table, lit it, rang for service. For a moment he thought it was with the intention of having him thrown out, but when the waiter appeared she simply said:

'A Scotch. Without ice. With water.'

Then, when the door had closed, she turned towards the chief-inspector.

'I've nothing to say to you. I'm sorry.'

'Alain is the son of Baron Lagrange.'

'Possibly.'

'Lagrange is one of your friends.'

She shook her head, as though she felt sorry for him.

'Listen, Chief-Inspector. I don't know what you've come here to do, but you're wasting your time. Probably there is some mistake over the person concerned.'

'You really are Jeanne Debul?'

'That's my name. You want to see my passport?'

He made a sign that there was no need.

'Baron Lagrange has been in the habit of paying visits to your flat in the Boulevard Richard-Wallace, and before that probably in the Rue Notre-Dame-de-Lorette.'

'I see that you are well informed. Tell me now, how does the fact that I've known Lagrange explain your pursuing me to London?'

'André Delteil is dead.'

'You mean the deputy?'

'Was he one of your friends as well?'

'I don't think I ever met him. I've heard people talk about him, like everyone else, because of his questions in parliament. If I have seen him, it was in some restaurant or night club.'

'He's been murdered.'

'Judging by his political methods, he must have made himself a certain number of enemies.'

'The murder was committed in François Lagrange's flat.'

There was a knock at the door. It was the waiter with the whisky. She drank one straight off, like a person used to taking alcohol every day at the same time, and, glass in hand, went over and sat on the easy chair, crossed her legs, pulled the cords of her dressing-gown.

'That all?' she asked.

'Alain Lagrange, the son, got hold of a gun and some ammunition. He went round to your house yesterday, a short while before you left so abruptly.'

'Say that word again.'

'Ab-rupt-ly.'

'Because you know, I suppose, that the evening before I had no intention of coming to London?'

'You hadn't told anyone.'

'Do you tell your plans to your maid? Presumably it was Georgette you questioned?'

'It's unimportant. Alain went to your house.'

'No one told me about it. I didn't hear the bell ring.'

'Because on the stairs he was caught by the concierge and did an about-turn.'

'He told the concierge it was me he wanted to see?'

'He said nothing.'

'Can you be serious, Inspector? Was it really just to tell me these fancy tales that you made the journey?'

'You had a telephone call from the Baron.'

'Really!'

'He put you in the picture about what had happened. Or perhaps you were already in the picture?'

He was hot. She wasn't giving him any opening, still as calm, as fresh as ever in her appearance for the morning. From time to time she would sip from her glass, without thinking of offering him anything to drink, and she left him standing, feeling awkward.

'Lagrange is under arrest.'

'That's his affair and yours, isn't it? What does he have to say about it?'

'He tries to make out he's mad.'

'He always has been a little mad.'

'He's none the less a friend of yours?'

'No, Inspector. You can save your ingenuity. You won't make me talk, for the excellent reason that I have nothing to say. If you care to examine my passport you will see that I do sometimes spend a few days in London. Always at this hotel, where they will confirm it. As for Lagrange, poor man, I've known him for some years.'

'Under what circumstances did you meet him?'

'That's none of your business. Under the most banal circumstances, I will say however, as a man and woman do meet one another.'

'He was your lover?'

'You are a man of the utmost delicacy.'

'Was he?'

'Suppose he was, for an evening or a week, or even a month, it was twelve or fifteen years ago. . . .'

'You remained good friends?'

'Ought we to have quarrelled or fought?'

'You used to receive him the mornings, in your bedroom, when you were still in bed.'

'It's morning now, my bed's unmade, and you're in my room.'

'You did business with him?'

She smiled.

'What business, for Heaven's sake? Don't you really know that all the business affairs that old Carpet Slippers talked about only existed in his imagination? Didn't you take the trouble to find out about him? Go to *Fouquet's* to *Maxim's*, to any bar in the Champs-Élysées, and they'll put you in the know. It wasn't worth taking the boat or the plane just for that.'

'Did you give him money?'

'Is that a crime?'

'A lot?'

'You will observe that I am patient. I could have had you thrown out a quarter of an hour ago, for you've no right to be here or to question me. I want, however, to repeat, once and for all, that you are on the wrong track. I knew Baron Lagrange once, when he was still handsome and made a show. I met him again later in the Champs-Élysées, and he treated me as he does everybody.'

'Which means?'

'He sponged. Ask anyone about him. He's the sort of man who's everlastingly short of a few hundred francs in order to bring off the most stupendous deal and make himself rich in a few days. Which means he hasn't enough to pay for the *apéritif* he's drinking at the moment or for the underground to get home. I behaved like the others.'

'And he badgered you at your home?'

'That's all.'

'Nevertheless his son is on your track.'

'I've never seen him.'

'He's been in London since last night.'

'In this hotel?'

This was the only occasion when her voice was a little less firm, betraying a certain anxiety.

'No.'

He hesitated. He had to choose between two solutions and he inclined for the one he thought would be better.

'The Gilmore Hotel, opposite Victoria Station.'

'How can you be sure it's me he's looking for?'

'Because all this morning he has been turning up at a whole string of hotels and asking for you. He seems to be going in alphabetical order. In less than an hour he will be here.'

'Then we'll find out what he wants from me, won't we?'

There was a slight quaver in her voice.

'He is armed.'

She shrugged her shoulders lightly, got up, looked at the door.

'I suppose I should thank you for having the kindness to watch over me.'

'There's still time.'

'For what?'

'For talking.'

'We've been doing nothing but that for the last half-hour. Now I must ask you to leave me alone so that I can dress.'

She added, in a voice that did not ring altogether true, with a little laugh:

'If this young man is really coming to pay me a visit, I'd better be ready!'

Maigret left without saying anything more, his shoulders rounded, annoyed with himself and with her, for he had got nothing out of her and he had a feeling that throughout the interview, Jeanne Debul had kept the upper hand. With the door closed again, he paused in the corridor. He would have liked to know if she was telephoning or showing signs of sudden activity.

Unfortunately a chambermaid, the same one who had seen him prowling about the corridor earlier on, came out of a nearby room and stared at him. Feeling disconcerted, he began to walk towards the lift.

In the hall he rejoined the Yard man installed in one of the armchairs, his eyes riveted on the swing doors. He sat down next to him.

'Any sign?'

'Not yet.'

At that hour there were many arrivals and departures. Cars drew up incessantly in front of the hotel, bringing not only travellers but Londoners coming to lunch, or simply to have a drink at the bar. They were all very gay. They all had the same look of delight as Pyke at such an exceptional day. Groups began to form. There were constantly three or four people round the reception desk. Women, in armchairs, were waiting for their escorts, whom they then followed into the dining-room.

Maigret remembered another way out of the hotel giving onto the Embankment. If he had been in Paris. . . . It would all have been so easy! Pyke had put himself at his disposal in vain; he did not want to abuse his offer. The fact was, here, he was always afraid of making himself look ridiculous. Did Inspector Pyke have the same humiliating sensation during his stay in France?

Upstairs in the corridor, for example, in France the presence of a maid would not have perturbed him. He would have told her some story, probably that he was from the police, and would have continued his vigil.

'Lovely day, sir!'

Even that was beginning to jar on him. These people were too pleased with their exceptional sun. Nothing else would count any more. The passers-by in the street were walking as though in a dream.

'D'you think he'll come, sir?'

'It's likely, isn't it? The Savoy is on the list.'

'I'm a bit afraid Fenton may have been clumsy.'

'Who's Fenton?'

'My colleague, whom Inspector Pyke sent to the Lancaster. He was to sit down like me opposite the reception desk and wait. Then, when the young man left, to follow him.'

'He's no good?'

'He's not bad, sir. He's a very good man. Only he is red-haired and he has a moustache. So that once he's been seen, he's easily recognized.'

The detective looked at his watch, sighed.

Maigret himself was watching the lifts. Jeanne Debul came out of one of them, wearing a pretty two-piece spring frock. She appeared completely at her ease. On her lips she had the slight smile of a woman who knows she is pretty and well dressed. Several men followed her with their eyes. Maigret had noticed the big diamond she was wearing on her finger.

In the most natural way in the world, she took a few steps in the hall looking at the faces around her, then put her key on the reception desk, and hesitated.

She had seen Maigret. Was it for his benefit that she was taking the stage?

There were two places you could lunch in: the big dining-room on one side, which adjoined the hall, and whose bay windows gave out onto the Thames, and on the other hand the grill, less vast, less solemn, where there were more people and the windows allowed one to see the hotel entrance. It was the grill she made for in the end. She said a few words to the *maître d'hôtel*, who showed her promptly to a little table near a window.

At the same moment the Yard man was saying, next to Maigret:

'That's him. . . .'

The chief-inspector looked quickly into the street through the swing doors, saw no one resembling the photograph of Alain Lagrange, opened his mouth to ask a question.

Before he even framed it, he understood. A small man with very red hair and a flamboyant moustache was nearing the door.

It was not Alain who was referred to, but the detective Fenton. In the hall he looked around for his colleague, went up to him, and ignoring the presence of Maigret, asked:

'He hasn't come?'

'No.'

'He came to the Lancaster. So I followed him. He went into the Montreal. I wonder if he noticed me. He had turned round once or twice. Then, all of a sudden, he jumped into a taxi. I lost a minute finding one for myself. I tried at five other hotels. He hadn't . . .'

One of the page boys was leaning towards Maigret:

'The reception manager would like a word with you,' he murmured in a low voice.

The reception manager, in a morning coat with a flower in his buttonhole, was holding a telephone receiver in his hand.

He winked at Maigret, a sign the chief-inspector thought he understood. Then he said into the instrument:

'I'll pass you the man on duty.'

Maigret took the receiver.

'Allo!'

'*Vous parlez Français?*'

'*Oui*. . . . Yes . . . I speak French. . . .'

'I'd like to know if Madame Jeanne Debul is stopping at your hotel.'

'Who is calling?'

'One of her friends.'

'You wish to speak to her? I can have you put through to her room.'

'No. . . . No. . . .'

The voice seemed far away.

'Her key is not on the board. So she must be in. I imagine she will be down before long.'

'Thank you.'

'Can I . . .'

Alain had already hung up. He wasn't such a fool, after all. He must have realized that he was being followed. Rather than show himself in person at various hotels, he had adopted the device of telephoning from a call-box or a bar.

The reception manager was holding another receiver in his hand.

'Another for you, Monsieur Maigret.'

This time it was Pyke, asking him to have lunch with him.

'I'd better stay here.'

'Have my men been successful?'

'Not entirely. It's not their fault.'

'Have you lost track of him?'

'He's definitely coming here.'

'Anyway, they are at your disposal.'

'I'll keep the one who's not called Fenton, if you don't mind.'

'Keep Bryan. Excellent. He's intelligent. Perhaps this evening?'

'Perhaps this evening.'

He rejoined the two men who were still chatting and fell silent on his arrival. Bryan must have told Fenton who he was, and the red-haired fellow was looking contrite.

'Thank you, Mr. Fenton. I've picked up the tracks of the young man. I shan't need you any more today. Will you have a drink?'

'Never on duty.'

'You, Mr. Bryan, I should like you to go and lunch in the grill, near that women wearing a two-piece frock with small blue flowers. If she leaves, try and follow her.'

A faint smile stole over Bryan's lips, as he watched his companion depart.

'Count on me.'

'You can charge the bill up on my account.'

Maigret was thirsty. He had been thirsty for more than half an hour. As the too deep armchairs were making him hot he rose, wandered about the hall, ill at ease in the midst of people speaking English who all had a reason to be there.

How many times did he see the doors revolve, each time sending a reflection of sunlight across one of the walls? Yet again. There was a constant coming and going. Cars were stopping, driving off, old London taxis, comfortable and picturesque, Rolls Royces or Bentleys with impeccable chauffeurs, small machines modelled like racing cars.

Thirst was parching his throat and from where he was he could see the bar full of people drinking, and the pale Martinis which, from afar, looked so fresh in their ice-cold glasses, the whiskies which the customers standing at the bar were holding in their hands.

If he went over there he would lose sight of the door. He approached it, went away again, regretted having dismissed Fenton who could at any rate have taken over the watch for a few minutes.

As for Bryan, he was busy eating and drinking. Maigret was beginning to feel hungry as well.

He sat down again, sighing, as an old gentleman with white hair, in the chair next to his, pressed an electric bell which Maigret hadn't noticed. A few moments later a waiter in a white jacket was bending towards him.

'A double Scotch with ice!'

There! It was as simple as that. It had never occurred to him that he could be served in the hall.

'The same for me. I suppose you haven't any beer?'

'Yes, sir. What sort of beer would you like?'

The bar had every kind of beer, Dutch, Danish, German and even a French export beer which Maigret had never heard of.

In France he would have ordered two glasses at a time, he was so dry. Here he didn't dare. And it infuriated him not to dare. It was humiliating to be thus intimidated.

Were the waiters, the *maîtres d'hôtel*, the page boys, the porters, more imposing than those in a big Paris hotel? It seemed to him that everyone was watching him, that the old gentleman, his neighbour, was studying him with a critical eye.

Was Alain Lagrange going to make up his mind one way or the other, to come or not?

It wasn't the first time this had happened to him: Maigret all of a sudden, without any plausible reason, was losing confidence in himself. What was he doing there, in actual fact? He had passed the night without sleeping. He had been to drink coffee in a concierge's lodge, then he had listened to the tales of a big girl in rose-coloured pyjamas who showed him a patch of her stomach and tried hard to make herself interesting.

What else? Alain Lagrange had lifted his revolver, threatened a passer-by in the street, and stolen his wallet before taking the plane to London. At the Police Infirmary the Baron was acting like a madman.

What if he really was mad?

Supposing Alain did appear at the hotel, what was Maigret going to do? Accost him politely? Tell him he wanted an explanation?

What if he tried to escape, if he showed fight? What sort of a figure would he cut, in front of all these Englishmen smiling at their sunshine, attacking a young lad? Perhaps it would be he whom they would lay hold of?

It had happened to him once in Paris, when he was a young man, though, and still doing his beat. Just as he was putting his hand to the shoulder of a thief in the line of people coming out of the underground, the fellow started shouting: 'Help!' And it was Maigret whom the crowd had held until the arrival of the police.

He was still thirsty, hesitated to ring, then finally pressed the white button, convinced that his white-haired neighbour thought him an ill-bred fellow who drank glasses of beer one after the other.

'A ...'

He thought he recognized a profile outside, said, without thinking: 'A whisky and soda.'

'Certainly, sir.'

It wasn't Alain. From near to, it didn't look like him at all, and besides he joined a girl waiting for him at the bar.

Maigret was still there, thoroughly torpid, with an unpleasant taste in his mouth, when Jeanne Debul came out of the grill in fine form, and reached the swing-doors.

Outside she waited for one of the porters to whistle for a taxi. Bryan was following, looking sprightly himself, and winked at Maigret as he passed.

He seemed to be saying: 'Don't worry!' He got into a second taxi.

If Alain Lagrange had been considerate, he would have arrived now.

Jeanne Debul was no longer there. So there was no danger of his charging at her and firing his revolver. The hall was quieter than it had been for the past half-hour. The people had eaten. Looking more pink-faced, they went off one after the other about their business, or to walk down Piccadilly or Regent Street.

'Same again, sir?'

'No. This time I should like a sandwich.'

'I'm sorry, sir. We are not allowed to serve anything to eat in the hall.'

He could have wept with rage.

'Well give me anything you like. Same again, then!'

Too bad, on top of everything else. It wasn't his fault.

VII

At three o'clock, at half-past three, at four Maigret was still there, as uncomfortable as when, after days and days of stormy heat, people look irritably at one another, so over-wrought that one expects to see them open their mouths to breathe like fish out of water.

The difference was that he was the only one in this state. There was not the slightest storm in the air. The sky above the Strand remained a pretty, airy blue, without any trace of violet, with occasionally a little white cloud which floated in space like a feather escaped from an eiderdown.

At odd moments he caught himself examining his neighbours as though to vow them a personal hatred. At others an inferiority complex weighed on his stomach and gave him a shifty look.

They were all too smart, too sure of themselves. The most exasperating of all was still the reception manager, with his smooth morning coat, his collar which no drop of sweat would ever soften. He had shown friendliness towards Maigret, or perhaps it was pity, and from time to time he gave him a smile at once conspiratorial and encouraging.

He seemed to be saying, above the coming and going of the anonymous travellers: 'We are both victims of professional duty. Can't I do anything for you?'

Maigret would probably have replied: 'Bring me a sandwich.'

He was sleepy. He was hot. He was hungry. When, a few minutes after three, he had rung for another glass of beer, the waiter looked as shocked as if he had taken off his coat in church.

'I'm sorry, sir. The bar is closed until half-past five, sir!'

The chief-inspector muttered something like:

'Savages!'

And ten minutes later, discomfited, he had gone up to a page boy, the youngest and least imposing one.

'Could you go and buy me a bar of chocolate?'

He was unable to last any longer without eating and so it was that he consumed, in little morsels, a bar of milk chocolate concealed in the depths of his pocket. Mustn't he look, in the hall of this palatial hotel, like one of those caricatures of a French detective, whom the Parisian journalists call 'hob-nail socks'? He caught himself looking in the mirrors, found himself ugly, ill-dressed. Pyke, well, he didn't look like a policeman, but a bank manager. Or rather an assistant manager. Or a trusted clerk, a meticulous clerk.

Would Pyke wait, as Maigret was doing, without even knowing that anything was going to happen?

At twenty to four the reception manager made a sign to him.

'Paris on the line for you. I expect you would prefer to take the call here?'

Some telephone boxes stood in a row in a room to the right of the hall, but from there he wouldn't be able to watch the entrance.

'That you, Chief?'

It was good to hear old Lucas's voice.

'What's the latest, old man?'

'The revolver's been found. I thought I'd better tell you.'

'Go ahead.'

'Just before midday I went and paid a call at the old man's place.'

'Rue Popincourt?'

'Yes. I started poking about in the corners on the off-chance. I couldn't find anything. Then I heard a baby crying in the courtyard, so I leant out of the window. The rooms, you remember, are on the top floor, with rather a low ceiling. A gutter collects the water from the roof, and I noticed that you could reach this gutter with your hand.'

'The gun was in the gutter?'

'Yes. Just below the window. A small revolver, Belgian make, a very nice job, initialled A.D.'

'André Delteil.'

'Exactly. I made inquiries at the station. The deputy had a licence to carry weapons. The numbers coincide.'

'It's the weapon that was used?'

'The expert has just sent in his report by telephone. I was waiting for it before calling you. The answer is yes.'

'Any finger-prints?'

'The dead man's and François Lagrange's.'

'Has anything happened?'

'The evening papers have long accounts. The corridors are swarming with reporters. I think one of them, who got wind of your going to

London, has taken a plane. The magistrate Rateau has rung up two or three times to find out if you'd sent any news.'

'That all?'

'It's wonderful weather.'

Him as well!

'Have you lunched?'

'Very well, Chief.'

'I haven't! Hullo! Don't cut us off, miss. Are you listening, Lucas? I want you, just in case, to keep an eye on the building at number 7b in the Boulevard Richard-Wallace. Also question the taxi-drivers to find out if any of them drove Alain Lagrange. . . . Listen! It's the son, you've got his photo.'

'I understand.'

'Find out, as I was saying, if one of them took him on Thursday morning to the Gare du Nord.'

'I thought he didn't leave till during the night, by air.'

'Doesn't matter. Tell the Chief I'll call him as soon as I have some news.'

'You haven't found the lad?'

He thought it best not to reply. He didn't much like to admit that he had had Alain on the telephone, that for hours his movements had been followed, minute by minute, through the streets of London, but that they were no further ahead.

Alain Lagrange, with the large revolver stolen from Maigret in his pocket, was somewhere about, probably not far away, and all the chief-inspector could do was wait, and watch the crowd coming and going around him.

'I'll ring off.'

His eyelids were prickling. He didn't dare sit down in an armchair for fear of dropping off to sleep. The chocolate turned his stomach.

He went for a breath of air outside the main entrance.

'Taxi, sir?'

He no longer had the right to take a taxi, nor the right to go for a walk, the right to do anything, except stay there and act the fool.

'Lovely weather, sir!'

Scarcely had he gone back into the hall when his arch-enemy, the reception manager, called him again, a smile on his lips, a telephone in his hand.

'For you, Monsieur Maigret.'

It was Pyke.

'I've just received some news from Bryan by telephone and am passing it on to you.'

'Thanks very much.'

'The lady had herself dropped at Piccadilly Circus and went up Regent Street to look at the shop-windows. She didn't appear to be in a hurry. She went into two or three shops to buy a few things, which she had sent to the Savoy. Would you like the list?'

'What sort of things?'

'Underwear, gloves, shoes. Then she went through to Old Bond Street to come back down Piccadilly, and half an hour ago went into a cinema with a continuous programme. She's there now. Bryan is still watching her.'

Another detail which would not have struck him at any other time, but which put him in a bad temper: instead of telephoning to him, Maigret, Bryan had telephoned his own chief in the hierarchy.

'Are we dining together?'

'I'm not sure. I'm beginning to doubt it.'

'Fenton is very upset about what happened.'

'It's no fault of his.'

'If you need one of my men, or several of them . . .'

'Thanks.'

What on earth was that Alain creature doing? Was Maigret to believe he had been mistaken from beginning to end?

'Can you get me the Gilmore Hotel?' he asked, when Pyke rang off.

By the expression on the reception manager's face, he gathered that it was not a first-class hotel. This time he had to speak English, as the man on the other end of the line did not understand a word of French.

'Has Monsieur Alain Lagrange, who came to your hotel very early this morning, been in during the day?'

'Who is it speaking?'

'Chief-Inspector Maigret of Paris Police Headquarters.'

'One moment, please.'

Someone else was called, with a more impressive voice, who was obviously more important.

'Can I help you? This is the manager of the Gilmore speaking.'

Maigret repeated his patter.

'May I ask you why you are making the inquiry?'

He launched out into an involved explanation, for want of the right English words. The reception manager finally took the receiver from his hands.

'Can I help?'

It only took him a couple of sentences, in which the words 'Scotland Yard' were mentioned. When he hung up, he was delighted with himself.

'These people always distrust foreigners a bit. The manager of the Gilmore was just wondering if he ought to warn the police. The young man took his key and went up to his room about one o'clock. He didn't stay there very long. Later a chambermaid, who was cleaning out a room on the same floor, reported that her skeleton key, which she had left in the door, had disappeared. Does that tell you anything?'

'Yes.'

The episode actually somewhat altered the idea he had formed of young Alain. The boy's wits had been at work all that morning. He had realized that if a maid's skeleton key opens all the doors of one hotel, there is a good chance that it will open the doors of another hotel as well.

Maigret went and sat down. When he looked at the time it was five o'clock. He went back suddenly to the reception desk.

'Do you think a skeleton key of the Gilmore Hotel would open the doors here?'

'It's unlikely.'

'Would you mind checking that none of your maids has lost her skeleton keys?'

'I imagine they would have informed the floor manager, who would herself have . . . One moment . . .'

He saw to a gentleman who wanted to change his suite because there was too much sun in his, then disappeared into an office nearby, where several telephone bells could be heard ringing.

When he came back, he was no longer quite so patronizing, and his brow was furrowed.

'You're right. A bunch of keys has disappeared from the sixth floor.'

'In the same way as at the Gilmore?'

'In the same way. While they're doing the rooms the staff have a mania, despite the regulations, for leaving the keys in the door.'

'How long ago did this happen?'

'Half an hour. Do you think this means trouble for us?'

And the man looked at the hall with the same anxious expression as a captain who is responsible for his ship. Must he not, at all costs, avoid the smallest incident which would dull the splendour of so fine a day?

In France Maigret would have said to him: 'Give me another skeleton key. I'm going upstairs. If Jeanne Debul comes back, keep her there for a moment and warn me.'

Not so here. He was sure they wouldn't let him enter a suite taken by someone else without a warrant.

He was prudent enough to wander about the hall for a while. Then he decided to wait for the bar to open, as it was only a matter of minutes, and omitting to watch the revolving doors, he propped himself up there long enough to drink a couple of glasses of beer.

'You're thirsty, sir.'

'Yes.'

That 'yes' was glum enough to wipe out the smiling barman.

He manoeuvred so as to leave the hall without being seen from the reception desk, took the lift, worried by the idea that his whole plan from now on depended on the mood of a male or female servant.

The long corridor was empty when he started down it, and he slowed up and stopped completely until he saw a door open and a valet in a striped waistcoat appear, a pair of dancing pumps in his hand.

Then, with the self-assurance of a resident without any ulterior motive, whistling between his teeth, he headed towards number 605, fumbled in his pockets, looked disconcerted.

'Valet, please.'

'Yes, sir?'

He was still fumbling. It wasn't the same valet as in the morning. The relief shift must have taken over.

'Would you mind opening my door for me, to save me going down for my key?'

The other suspected nothing.

'With pleasure, sir.'

Having opened the door he did not look inside, where he would have seen a woman's dressing-gown hanging up.

Maigret closed the door again carefully, mopped his brow, walked into the middle of the room, where he said in his normal voice, as if he were making conversation:

'Well, now!'

He hadn't gone into the bathroom, of which the door was ajar, nor looked in the cupboards. He was disturbed, underneath, far more than he let it appear or his voice let it be suspected.

'Here we are, my boy. Now we're going to have a little chat together.'

He sat down heavily in the easy chair, crossed his legs, drew a pipe from his pocket and lit it. He was convinced Alain Lagrange was hiding somewhere, perhaps in one of the hanging cupboards, perhaps under the bed.

He also knew that the young man was armed, that he was highly strung, that his nerves must be at breaking-point.

'All I ask you is not to do anything silly.'

It was from the direction of the bed that he thought he heard a slight sound. He wasn't quite sure of it, didn't lean forward.

'Once upon a time,' he went on, as if he were telling a story, 'I was an eye-witness at an extraordinary scene, just near my home, in the Boulevard Richard-Lenoir. It was in summer, too, one evening when it had been very hot, when it was still hot and the whole neighbourhood was out of doors.'

He was speaking slowly, and anyone coming in at the moment would have taken him at the very least for an eccentric.

'I don't know who saw the cat first. I seem to remember it was a little girl who ought to have been in bed at that hour. Night was beginning to fall. She pointed to a dark shape in a tree. As always the passers-by stopped. From my window, where I was leaning out, I could see them gesticulating. Others joined the group. In the end there were a hundred people at the foot of the tree, and I finally went to see for myself as well.'

He broke off to remark:

'Here, we are alone: that makes it easier. What was drawing the bystanders on the boulevard was a cat, a big tabby cat crouched right at the end of a branch. It seemed frightened at finding itself there. It can't have realized that it had climbed so high. It didn't dare make a move to turn round. It didn't dare jump either. The women, with their noses in the air, felt sorry for it. The men were trying to devise a way of getting it out of its unfortunate predicament.

' "I'll go and fetch a double ladder!" said a workman, who lived opposite.

'They put up the ladder. He climbed it. It was three feet too short for him to reach the branch. But even so, at the sight of his outstretched arm the cat hissed with rage and tried to claw him.

'A lad suggested: "I'll climb up."

' "You can't. The branch isn't strong enough."

' "I'll shake it, and all you'll have to do is hold out a sheet."

'He must have seen the fire brigade on the films.

'It had become a real occasion. A concierge brought a sheet. The boy shook the branch, and the poor brute at the end of it hung on with all his claws and cast panic-stricken glances around him.

'Everyone felt sorry for him.

' "If we had a longer ladder . . ."

' "Watch out! Perhaps he's angry. There's blood round his mouth."

'It was true. They were sorry and they were afraid as well, you understand? No one wanted to go to bed without seeing the end of this business with the cat. How to get it into his head that he could let himself fall into the outstretched sheet without danger? Or that all he had to do was turn round?'

Maigret was almost expecting a voice to ask:

'What happened?'

But there wasn't any question, and he went on by himself:

'They got him in the end; a tall thin fellow crept along the branch and, with the aid of a stick, managed to make the cat fall into the sheet. When they opened it the animal jumped out so quickly that you could scarcely see it cross the street and disappear into a grating. That's all. . . .'

This time he was sure there had been a movement under the bed.

'The cat was afraid because he didn't know that no one wished him any harm.'

Silence. Maigret drew at his pipe.

'I don't wish you any harm either. It isn't you who killed André Delteil. As for my gun, it's not a very serious matter. Who knows? At your age, in the state you were in, I would perhaps have done the same. It's my fault, after all. Oh yes. If, that day, I hadn't gone and had an *apéritif* before lunch, I would have got home half an hour earlier, when you were still there.'

He was talking in a negative, almost sleepy tone of voice.

'What would have happened? You would have told me straight out what you meant to tell me. After all, it was to speak to me that you came to my house. You couldn't know a revolver was lying about on the mantelpiece. You wanted to tell me the truth and ask me to save your father.'

He was silent rather longer this time, to give his words time to sink into the young man's head.

'Don't move yet. It isn't necessary. We are quite all right as we are. I only advise you to be careful with the gun. It's a special model, which the American police are very proud of. The trigger is so sensitive that you hardly have to touch it to set it off. I've never used it. It's a souvenir, you see?'

He sighed.

'Now, I wonder what you would have said to me if I had come in to lunch a little earlier. You would have had to tell me about the body. . . . Wait. . . . We're in no hurry. . . . First of all, I imagine you weren't in on Tuesday evening when Delteil paid your father a visit. If you had been there things would have turned out differently. You must have come in when it was all over. Probably the body was hidden in the bedroom you use as a junk-room, perhaps already in the trunk. Your father said nothing to you. I bet you don't talk much to each other, you two?'

He caught himself waiting for a reply.

'Right! Perhaps you suspected something, perhaps not. Be that as it may, in the morning you discovered the body. You kept quiet. It's difficult to broach a subject like that with one's father.

'Yours was dead beat, sick.

'Then you thought of me, because you read newspaper cuttings your father collected.

'Well! Here's more or less what you'd have said to me:

' "*There's a body in our flat, I don't know what happened, but I know my father. To start off with there's never been any weapon in the house.*"

'For I bet there never has been one, isn't that so? I don't know your father very well, but I'm sure he's very scared of revolvers.

'You would have gone on:

' "*He's a man who couldn't do harm to anyone. That won't stop him being the one they're going to accuse. He won't tell the truth because a woman is involved.*"

'If it had happened like that I would have helped you, of course. We would have found out the truth together.

'By this time it's almost certain that woman would be in prison.'

Was he hoping it would happen there and then? He mopped his brow, watching for a reaction that did not come.

'I had a longish talk with your sister. I don't think you like her very much. She's an egoist, who thinks only of herself. I haven't had time to see your brother Philippe, but he must be even harder than she is. Both of them have a grudge against your father for the childhood they had,

whereas your father actually did all he could. It's not given to everyone
to be strong. You, you understood . . .'

Under his breath, he was saying to himself: 'Don't let her come back
just yet, Lord!'

For then it would probably be like the cat in the Boulevard Richard-
Lenoir with the whole population of the Savoy round an adolescent at
the end of his tether.

'You see, there are some things which you know and I don't know,
but there are others that I know and you don't. Your father at this
moment is in the Police Infirmary. That means he is under arrest, but
people are wondering if he is in his right mind. When all's said and done,
as usual, the psychiatrists disagree. They never do agree. What must be
worrying him most is not knowing what's happened to you, nor what
you are going to do. He knows you, realizes you are capable of going
through with your plans.

'As for Jeanne Debul, she's at the cinema.

'It wouldn't help anyone for her to be killed coming back into her
room. To start off with it would be rather a bore because it would be
impossible to question her, and also because you would fall into the
hands of the law of England which in all probability would end up by
hanging you.

'There you are, young fellow.

'It's horribly hot in this room, and I'm going to open the window.
I'm not armed; it's a mistake to imagine that all police sergeants and
inspectors are armed. Actually they have no more right to be than
other citizens.

'I'm not looking under the bed. I know you are there. I know almost
everything you are thinking. It's difficult, of course! It's less spectacular
than shooting at a woman and playing executioner!'

He went over to the window, which he opened, leant on it, his ears
pricked, looking out. Nothing moved behind him.

'You haven't made up your mind?'

He became impatient, facing into the room again.

'You'll make me believe you are less intelligent than I thought!
Where will it get you staying there? Speak up, idiot! After all, you are
nothing but a young idiot. You haven't understood the first thing about
this affair, and if you go on like this, it's you who'll end up by getting
your father condemned. Leave my gun alone, do you hear? I forbid
you to touch it. Put it on the floor. Now come out of there.'

He seemed really angry. Perhaps in fact he was. In any case he was
in a hurry to get this unpleasant scene over.

As with the cat, so now, a false move would be enough, an idea passing through the young man's head.

'Hurry up. She's not going to be much longer coming back. It
wouldn't be very smart to let her find us like this, you under the bed,

me trying to make you come out. I shall count up to three. . . . One . . .
two . . . If at three you are not standing up, I shall telephone to the
hotel detectives and . . .'

Then, at last, two feet appeared, worn-down soles, then cotton socks,
the lower half of a pair of trousers Alain had ruffled up by crawling.

To make it easier for him Maigret turned back to the window, from
where he heard a slithering on the floor, then the light noise of someone
standing up. He didn't forget the young man was armed, but he was
waiting to give him time to recover himself.

'Is it all over?'

He turned right round. Alain was standing before him, with dust on
his blue suit, his tie askew, his hair in disorder. He was very pale, his
lips were trembling, his eyes seemed to want to wander over the room.

'Give me back my gun.'

Maigret held out his hand, and the young man fumbled in his right-
hand pocket, held out his hand in turn.

'Don't you think it's better that way?'

There was a faint:

'Yes.'

Then straight away:

'What are you going to do?'

'First of all, eat and drink. Aren't you hungry?'

'Yes. I don't know.'

'Well, I'm very hungry and there's an excellent grill-room on the
ground floor.'

He made for the door.

'Where have you put the skeleton key?'

He pulled out not one, but a whole bunch from his other pocket.

'It would be better for me to hand them in to the reception as they
might make a scene about it.'

In the corridor he stopped in front of his own door.

'We'd better tidy ourselves up a bit.'

He didn't want a crisis. He knew that it was only hanging from a
thread. That was why he was keeping the other's mind busy with small
material details.

'Have you a comb?'

'No.'

'You can use mine. It's quite clean.'

That almost won him a smile.

'Why are you doing all this?'

'All what?'

'You know what I mean.'

'Perhaps because I was a young man once as well. And had a father.
Give yourself a brush. Take off your coat. The bed-springs haven't been
cleaned for a long time.'

He himself washed his hands and face in cold water.

'I wonder if I shan't change my shirt again. I've sweated such a lot today!'

He did so, so that Alain saw him bare-chested, with his braces hanging over his thighs.

'Of course you haven't got any luggage?'

'I don't think I could go into the grill as I am.'

He examined him with a critical eye.

'Your clothes are certainly not very clean. Did you sleep in your shirt?'

'Yes.'

'I can't lend you one of mine. It would be too big.'

This time Alain smiled more openly.

'It's just too bad if the *maître d'hôtel* doesn't like it. We'll chat in a little corner and try to get them to give us a little white wine, nice and cold. Perhaps they've got that.'

'I don't drink.'

'Never?'

'I tried once, and I was so ill I didn't start again.'

'Have you got a girl friend?'

'No.'

'Why?'

'I don't know.'

'Are you shy?'

'I don't know.'

'Have you ever wanted to have a girl friend?'

'Perhaps. I think so. But I'm not very keen.'

Maigret did not insist. He had understood. And, as he went out of the room, he just put his big hand on his companion's shoulder.

'You gave me a fright, you little wretch.'

'What about?'

'Would you have fired?'

'At whom?'

'At her.'

'Yes.'

'And yourself?'

'Perhaps. Afterwards, I think I'd have done it.'

They passed the valet, who turned round to look at them. Perhaps he had seen them coming out of number 604, whereas Maigret had gone into number 605?

The lift deposited them on the ground floor. Maigret had his key in his hand as well as the bunch of pass keys. He went over to the reception desk. He was hoping for a little triumph over his arch-enemy in the too well-cut morning clothes. How would it strike him seeing them together and receiving the skeleton keys?

Alas! It wasn't he who was standing behind the desk but a tall pale fair-haired young man, who wore an identical morning coat and buttonhole. He didn't know Maigret.

'I found this bunch of keys in the corridor.'

'Thanks very much,' he said, unconcernedly.

When Maigret turned round, Bryan was standing in the middle of the hall. From the look in his eyes he seemed to be asking the chief-inspector if he could have a word with him.

'Will you excuse me?' he asked Alain.

He went over to the English detective.

'You've found him? It's really him?'

'It's him.'

'The lady has just come in.'

'Has she gone up to her room?'

'No. She's in the bar.'

'Alone?'

'She's chatting to the barman. What shall I do?'

'Can you bear to keep an eye on her for another hour or two?'

'Easily.'

'If she looks like going out, warn me straight away. I'll be in the grill-room.'

Alain hadn't tried to run away. He was waiting, a little awkwardly, a little embarrassed, at the edge of the crowd.

'Enjoy your meal, sir.'

'Thanks.'

He rejoined the young man, whom he led towards the grill, saying: 'I'm ravenous.'

And he caught himself adding, as he passed through a ray of sunshine slanting through the wide bay-window:

'What wonderful weather!'

VIII

'You like lobster?'

Only Maigret's eyes appeared above the immense menu which the *maître d'hôtel* had put in his hand, and Alain didn't know what to do with his, which, out of tact, he didn't look at.

'Yes, sir,' he answered, as if at school.

'Well then, we'll treat ourselves to a lobster *à l'Américaine*. Before that I should like a plateful of hors d'oeuvres. Waiter!'

His order given:

'When I was your age, I preferred tinned lobster, and when I was told this was heretical I would reply that it had more taste. We didn't open a tin of lobster in six months, only on special occasions, as we weren't rich.'

He leant back a little.

'You've suffered from not being rich, haven't you?'

'I don't know, sir. I would have liked my father not to have had to worry so much about bringing us up.'

'You really don't want anything to drink?'

'Only water.'

Nevertheless, Maigret ordered himself a bottle of wine, a Rhine wine, and glasses the colour of absinthe were set before them with high stems of a darker hue.

The grill-room was lighted, but the sunlight lingered on outside. The room was filling rapidly, with *maîtres d'hôtel* and waiters in tails moving about noiselessly.

What fascinated Alain were the trolleys. They had brought one up, laden with hors d'oeuvres, near to their table, and there were others, particularly the trolleys of pastries and dessert. Best of all was the enormous dome-shaped silver one, which opened like a box.

'Before the war it used to hold a roast quarter of beef,' explained Maigret. 'I think it's here that I've eaten the best roast beef. Anyway, the most impressive. Now they've put a turkey in it. Do you like turkey?'

'I think so.'

'If you've any appetite left after the lobster, we can have turkey.'

'I'm not hungry.'

They must have looked, the two of them together at their little table, like a rich uncle from the provinces giving a gala dinner to his nephew at the end of term.

'I lost my mother very young, too, and it was my father who brought me up.'

'Used he to take you to school?'

'He couldn't. He had to work. It was in the country.'

'When I was very small my father used to take me to school and came to fetch me home. He was the only man waiting at the door among the women. When he got back home, it was he who made the supper for us all.'

'There must have been times when you had servants?'

'Did he tell you that? Have you talked to him?'

'I've talked with him.'

'Is he worried about me?'

'I shall ring up Paris presently so they can reassure him.'

Alain didn't realize that he was eating with a good appetite and he drank a large gulp of the wine which the wine waiter had served as a matter of course. He didn't pull a face.

'That never lasted long.'

'What?'

'Servants. My father so much wanted to change it all that he acted as if his wishes had come true from time to time. "From now on, children," he would announce, "we're going to live like everyone else. Tomorrow, we move house." '

'Did you move house?'

'Sometimes. We would go into a new flat, where there was still no furniture. They would bring it when we were already there. We saw new faces, women my father had engaged at the employment bureau, and we called them by their christian names. Then almost at once the tradesmen would begin to troop in, bailiffs who would wait for hours thinking my father was out when he was only hiding in one of the rooms. In the end they cut off the gas and the electric light. It's not his fault. He's very intelligent. He has heaps of ideas. Listen.'

Maigret bent his head to hear better, his face relaxed, his eyes full of sympathy.

'There were years of that. . . . I remember that for a long time, perhaps two years, he went round all the offices with a scheme for enlarging and modernising a Moroccan port. All he got was promises. If that had come off we would have gone to live over there and we'd have been very rich. When the plan reached the higher authorities they shrugged their shoulders. They all but treated my father as mad for wanting to establish a big port at that point. Now it's the Americans who have done it.'

'I understand.'

Maigret knew that type of man so well! But could he show him up to his son for what he was? What was the point? The other two, the elder son and the daughter, had long ago seen the truth and had left, without any gratitude for the big, weak, soft man who, after all, had brought them up. He couldn't look to those two for pity.

There was only Alain left to believe in him. It was odd, for Alain looked so like his sister that it was disturbing.

'A few more mushrooms?'

'No thank you.'

Looking outside was not without its fascination for him. It was the hour at which, as at lunch, cars followed one another without respite, waiting their turn to halt for a moment beneath the awning, where a porter in mouse-grey livery would hurry to the door. The difference from mid-day was that the people who came out of the cars were nearly all in evening dress. There were plenty of young couples, and whole families as well. Most of the women wore orchids in their dress.

The men were in dinner jackets, some in tails, and through the windows they could be seen coming and going in the hall before taking their places in the main dining-room, from which filtered the strains of the orchestra.

It was, to the very end, a marvellous day, with still enough light from the setting sun to lend an unreal hue to people's faces.

'Until what age did you go to school?'

'Fifteen and a half.'

'Lycée?'

'Yes. I finished my third year and then left.'

'Why?'

'I wanted to earn some money to help my father.'

'Were you good at work?'

'Fairly. Except maths.'

'Did you find a job?'

'I went into an office.'

'Did your sister give your father the money she earned?'

'No. She used to pay for her board and lodging. She had it worked out exactly, without counting the rent, or the heating or the light. It was she who used up most electricity reading in bed part of the night.'

'You handed over everything to him?'

'Yes.'

'You don't smoke?'

'No.'

The arrival of the lobster interrupted them for a while. Alain seemed relaxed now. From time to time, however, as he was sitting with his back to the door, he would turn round in that direction.

'What are you looking at?'

'To see if she's coming.'

'You think she will come?'

'I saw you talking to someone and glancing towards the bar. I gathered from that that she was there.'

'You know her?'

'I've never spoken to her.'

'And does she know you?'

'She'll recognize me.'

'Where has she seen you?'

'Two weeks ago in the Boulevard Richard-Wallace.'

'You went up to her flat?'

'No. I was opposite, on the other side of the railings.'

'Had you been following your father?'

'Yes.'

'Why?'

Maigret had gone too fast. Alain was withdrawing.

'I don't see why you are doing all this.'

'All what?'

With a glance, he indicated the grill, the table, the lobster, the luxuries which the man who ought logically to have clapped him in jail was lavishing on him.

'We had to eat, hadn't we? I haven't had anything since this morning. What about you?'

'A sandwich, in a milk bar.'

'So we're having dinner. Afterwards we'll see.'

'What'll you do?'

'We'll very likely take the plane to Paris. D'you like flying?'

'Not much.'

'Have you been abroad before?'

'Only this once. Last year I was to have spent two weeks in Austria
in a holiday camp. An organization works an exchange scheme for
young people of the two countries. I put my name down. They told me
to get a passport. Then, when my turn came, I had sinus trouble and
was in bed.'

A silence.

He had returned to the thought that was uppermost in their minds,
and it only remained for him to bring it up again himself.

'Have you spoken to that person?'

'To whom?'

'To her.'

'This morning, in her bedroom.'

'What did she say?'

'Nothing.'

'It's she that ruined my father, but you'll see, nothing can be done to
her.'

'You think not?'

'You wouldn't dare arrest her, would you?'

'Why?'

'I don't know. It's always like that. She's taken her precautions.'

'You know all about her dealings with your father?'

'Not exactly. It's only a few weeks ago that I learnt what she is.'

'Yet he's known her for a long time.'

'He's known her since just after my mother died. At that time he
didn't hide her from us. I don't remember anything about it myself,
because I was only a baby, but Philippe told me. Father had told him
he was going to marry again, which would be better for everybody, as
there would be a woman to look after us. It didn't happen. Now that
I've seen her, and know the sort of woman she is, I'm sure she was making a fool of him.'

'Very possibly.'

'Philippe says father was miserable about it, that he often cried in
bed at night. He went years without seeing her. Perhaps she had left
Paris. Or changed her address without telling him.

'Then about two years ago I noticed a change in my father.'

'In what way?'

'It's difficult to say exactly. His whole attitude was no longer the

same. He was more gloomy and particularly worried. When anyone
came up the stairs he would tremble and seem relieved when it was a
tradesman, even one coming to dun him.

'My brother wasn't with us any longer by then. My sister had announced she would be leaving on the day she was twenty-one. It didn't
all happen at once, you see. It was only now and again that I noticed
the difference.

'In the old days, even in bars where I used to go and meet him to do
errands for him, he used only to drink bottles of Vichy. He started having *apéritifs*, and some evenings he came back very sodden, saying he
had a headache.

'He didn't look at me in the same way any more, seemed embarrassed
by my presence, and spoke impatiently to me.'

'Eat up.'

'I'm sorry; I'm not hungry any more.'

'A sweet?'

'All right.'

'It was then that you began to follow him?'

He hesitated before replying, and looked closely at Maigret, frowning, and at that moment he looked so like his sister that Maigret turned
away his eyes.

'It was quite natural for you to try and find out what was happening.'

'Even so, I don't know anything!'

'Quite. You only know that he often went to see this woman, especially in the late morning. You followed him to the Boulevard Richard-
Wallace, you admitted just now. You were down below, behind the
railings of the Bois de Boulogne. Your father and the woman must have
gone near the window in the flat. Did she notice you?'

'Yes. She pointed at me with her finger. Probably because I was looking in the direction of the window.'

'Your father told her who you were. Did he speak to you about it
afterwards?'

'No. I was expecting him to speak, but he didn't.'

'And you?'

'I didn't dare.'

'You found the money?'

'How do you know?'

'Isn't it true that in the evening you sometimes searched your father's
wallet, not to take money, but to find out?'

'Not his wallet. He used to put it under his shirts, in the drawer.'

'A lot?'

'Sometimes a hundred thousand francs, sometimes more, sometimes
only fifty thousand.'

'Often?'

'It varied. Once or twice a week.'

7*

'And the day after these evenings he would go round to the Boulevard Richard-Wallace?'

'Yes.'

'Then the money wasn't there any more?'

'She left him a few small notes.'

Alain saw a gleam in Maigret's eye as he watched the door, but he had enough strength of mind not to turn round. He was not unaware that it was Jeanne Debul coming in.

Behind her Bryan made a questioning gesture to the chief-inspector, who in turn gave him to understand that he could stop trailing her.

If it was so late it was because on leaving the bar she had gone up to change. Though she was not in evening dress she was wearing a fairly formal one which came from a first-class dressmaker. On her wrist she had a wide diamond bracelet, and more diamonds at her ears.

She hadn't seen the inspector, nor Alain, and was following the head-waiter, while most of the women looked her up and down.

She was placed less than six yards away from them, at a little table almost facing them, and she sat down, glanced round as they handed her the menu, met Maigret's eye, and at once looked hard at his companion.

Maigret was smiling the smile of a man who has dined well, his mind at rest. Alain, blushing scarlet, didn't dare turn in her direction.

'Has she seen me?'

'Yes.'

'What's she doing?'

'She's just defying me.'

'How do you mean?'

'She's pretending to be at her ease, lighting a cigarette and leaning over to examine the hors d'oeuvres on a trolley beside her. Now she's talking with the head waiter and making her diamonds sparkle.'

'You won't arrest her!' he said with bitterness and a touch of defiance.

'I shan't arrest her today because, you see, if I were foolish enough to do so, she would get out of it.'

'She'll always get out of it, while my father . . .'

'No. Not always. Here in England I am at a disadvantage, as I should have to prove that she has committed one of the crimes covered by the extradition laws. She won't stay in London for ever. She needs Paris. She'll go back, and I shall have had time to see about her. Even if it isn't straight away, her turn will come. Sometimes we leave people at large for months, even years, under the impression that they are fooling us. You can look at her. You don't have to be ashamed. She's just showing off. Still, she'd rather be in your shoes than her own.

'Suppose I had left you under the bed. She would have gone up. By now . . .'

'Don't.'

'You would have fired?'

'Yes.'

'Why?'

Alain muttered between his teeth:

'Because!'

'Are you sorry?'

'I don't know. There's no justice!'

'Oh yes, there's a sort of justice, and it does what it can. Obviously if I were God the Father this evening, instead of being at the head of the Special Force and having to account to my superiors, to the magistrate, the attorney, even the press, I should arrange this differently.'

'How?'

'First of all, I should forget you pinched my revolver. That I can still do. Then I should arrange for a certain business man, from I can't remember where, to forget that he didn't lose his wallet, but was forced to hand it over with a gun under his nose.'

'It wasn't loaded.'

'Are you sure?'

'I'd taken good care to remove the cartridges. I needed the money for getting to London.'

'You knew the Debul woman was there?'

'I had followed her that morning. First of all I tried going up to her flat. The concierge . . .'

'I know.'

'When I came out of the building there was a policeman at the entrance, and I guessed it was for me. I went round the block. On my return the policeman wasn't there any longer. I hid in the park, waiting for her to come out of the house.'

'To shoot her?'

'Perhaps. She must have telephoned for a taxi. I couldn't get near her. I was lucky enough to find another taxi coming from Puteaux. I followed her as far as the station. I saw her get on the Calais train. I hadn't enough money left to pay for my ticket.'

'Why didn't you kill her when she was standing at the carriage door?'

Alain shook, looked at him to see if he was being serious, mumbled:

'I didn't dare.'

'If you didn't dare shoot when you were in a crowd, you probably wouldn't have shot her in her bedroom either. You had been following your father for several weeks, hadn't you?'

'Yes.'

'Have you a list of people he went to see?'

'I could make one up from memory. He went several times to a little bank in the Rue Chauchat, and also to a newspaper office where he saw the assistant editor. He made a lot of telephone calls and kept turning round all the time to make sure he wasn't being followed.'

'Did you realize what was going on?'

'Not straight away. I happened to read a novel about it.'

'About what?'

'You know perfectly well.'

'Blackmail?'

'It was her.'

'Of course. And that's why it'll take some time to get her. I don't know what kind of life she led before she moved into the Boulevard Richard-Wallace. She probably got about and knew all sorts of people. A woman is better than a man at finding out little secrets, especially shameful secrets. When she was no longer young enough to carry on her sort of life, she got the idea of making money out of her bits and pieces of information.'

'She made use of my father.'

'Precisely. She wasn't the one who went and sought out the victims to demand money from them. It was a man-about-town who had no definite profession. People weren't over-surprised. They almost expected it.'

'Why do you say that?'

'Because you must face the facts. Perhaps your father was still in love? I think he was. He's the sort of man to remain faithful to an infatuation like that. Jeanne Debul more or less provided his keep. He lived in fear of being caught. He was ashamed of himself. He didn't dare look you in the face any more.'

Alain turned a hard face, with eyes full of hate, in the direction of the woman, who wore a thin, contemptuous smile.

'One strawberry tart, *maître d'hôtel*.'

'Aren't you having any?' protested Alain.

'I seldom eat any sweet. Coffee and a *fine* for me.'

He pushed his chair back a little, pulled his pipe from his pocket. He was busy filling it when the head waiter leant towards him, and said a few words in a low voice, waving an apology with his hands.

Then Maigret stuffed his pipe back into his pocket and stopped a passing trolley of cigars.

'Aren't you going to smoke your pipe?'

'Not allowed here! By the way, have you paid for your hotel room?'

'No.'

'Have you still got the pass key you took from the corridor? Hand it over to me.'

He passed it to Maigret under the table.

'Is the tart good?'

'Yes . . .'

His mouth was full of it. He was just a child now, unable to resist sweet things, and for that moment, he was entirely engrossed in his tart.

'Did he often see Delteil?'

'I saw him go round to his office twice.'

Was it necessary to discover the whole truth? It was more than likely that the deputy, whose wife was petitioning for a divorce and who was going to find himself without a penny, obliged to leave his big house in the Avenue Henri-Martin, was trading on his influence. It was more serious for him than anyone else, as he had built up his political career by denouncing scandals and intrigues.

Had Jeanne Debul gone too far? Maigret had another idea on the subject.

'Your father didn't talk any longer about finishing with your kind of life?'

Despite the strawberry tart Alain lifted his head in sudden distrust.

'What do you mean?'

'In the old days, he used to announce periodically that everything was going to change. Then there was a time when he seemed to lose faith in his stars.'

'Even so, he still hoped.'

'Less strongly though?'

'Yes.'

'And recently?'

'He spoke three or four times about going to live in the Midi.'

Maigret didn't go on. This was his affair. There was no point in explaining to the son what he deduced from it. Hadn't François Lagrange, who had been doing commissions for the Debul woman for two years and only picking up the crumbs, got it into his head to work on his own account?

Supposing Jeanne Debul ordered him to extract a hundred thousand francs from Delteil, who was a big shot. . . . And the Baron had demanded a million? Or more? He was a man who liked talking in big figures, who had spent his life juggling with imaginary fortunes. . . .

Delteil decided not to pay.

'Where were you, on Tuesday night?'

'I went to the cinema.'

'Did your father encourage you to go out?'

He paused to think. This idea had come to him for the first time.

'I think he did. . . . He said to me . . . I seem to remember he spoke to me about a film being shown exclusively at the Champs-Élysées and . . .'

'When you came back, he'd gone to bed?'

'Yes. I went to say good night, as I always do; he wasn't well. He promised me he would see the doctor.'

'That struck you as quite normal?'

'No.'

'Why?'

'I don't know. I was worried. I couldn't get to sleep. There was a strange smell in the house, a smell of American cigarettes. In the morning I woke up when it was hardly daybreak. I went round the flat. My father was asleep. I noticed that the box-room, which was my bedroom when I was small, was locked and the key wasn't in the door. I opened it.'

'How?'

'With a hook. It's a trick I learnt from my friends at school. You twist a thick bit of wire in a special way and . . .'

'I know. I've done it too.'

'I always kept one of those hooks in my drawer. I saw the trunk in the middle of the room and I lifted the lid.'

It was best to move quickly now.

'Did you speak to your father?'

'I couldn't.'

'You left at once?'

'Yes. I walked about the streets. I wanted to call on that woman.'

There was one scene whose details would never be known unless the Baron gave up playing the madman, and that was the one enacted in the flat between François Lagrange and André Delteil. It didn't concern Alain. There was no point in shattering the picture he had formed of his father.

The chances were very small that the barrister had come with the intention of killing him. More than likely he intended, if necessary by means of threats, to recover the documents which were being used to blackmail him.

Weren't the sides rather unevenly matched? Delteil was full of punch. He was a man used to fighting, and all he had to oppose him was a big funk trembling in his skin.

The documents were not in the flat. Even if he had wanted, Lagrange would have been unable to return them.

What had he done? He had probably wept, begged, asked to be forgiven. He had promised . . .

All the time, he was being hypnotized by the revolver that was threatening him.

It was he, by virtue of his very weakness, who had ended by winning the fight. How had he got hold of the weapon? By what ruse had he distracted the deputy's attention?

However it came about, the fact remained that he no longer trembled. His turn now to speak loudly, to threaten.

Probably he hadn't pulled the trigger on purpose. He was too much of a coward, too used, ever since his schooldays, to walking about hanging his head and receiving kicks in the behind.

'In the end I went to your flat.'

Alain turned towards Jeanne Debul, who was trying in vain to catch some of their conversation. The sounds that filled the grill-room, the noise of crockery, knives, forks, the hum of conversation, the laughter and the music coming from the big room prevented her hearing.

'Shall we be going . . .?'

There was a protest in Alain's eyes:

'Are you going to leave her there?'

The woman, too, was surprised to see Maigret pass in front of her without saying a word to her. It seemed too easy for her. Perhaps she had hoped for a scene, which would have given her plenty of scope.

In the hall where he finally took his pipe from his pocket and triumphantly stubbed out his cigar in the sand of a monumental ashtray, Maigret murmured:

'Will you wait here a second?'

He went up to the doorman.

'What time is there a plane for Paris?'

'There is one in ten minutes, but you obviously can't catch that. The next is half-past six in the morning. Shall I book you a seat?'

'Two.'

'What names?'

He gave them. Alain hadn't moved and was looking at the lights of the Strand.

'Just a moment. A telephone call to make.'

He no longer had to do it from the reception desk: he could go into one of the boxes.

'That you, Pyke? I'm sorry I couldn't lunch or dine with you. I shan't see you tomorrow, either. I'm going back during the night.'

'On the half-past six plane? I'll drive you there.'

'But . . .'

'See you then.'

It was better to let him do it; otherwise he would never be happy. Strange as it was, Maigret was no longer sleepy.

'Shall we have a stroll out of doors?'

'If you like.'

'Otherwise I shan't even have set foot on the London pavements during my entire visit.'

It was true. Was it because he was conscious of being abroad? The street lamps seemed to him to have a different sort of light from the ones in Paris, another colour, and even the air had a different smell.

The two of them walked along unhurriedly, looking at the cinema entrances, the bars. After Charing Cross there was an enormous square with a column in the middle.

'Did you come this way this morning?'

'I think so. I seem to recognize it.'

'Trafalgar Square.'

It was pleasant, before leaving, to come across sights which he recognized, and he took Alain as far as Piccadilly Circus.

'It only remains for us to go to bed.'

Alain could have run away. Maigret wouldn't have lifted a finger to stop him. But he knew the young man wouldn't do so.

'Still, I should like a glass of beer. Do you mind?'

It wasn't so much the beer as the atmosphere of a pub that Maigret was looking for. Alain didn't drink anything, but waited in silence.

'You like London?'

'I don't know.'

'Perhaps you'll be able to come back in a few months. It shouldn't really take as much as a few months.'

'Shall I see my father?'

'Yes.'

A little further on he sniffed, and Maigret pretended not to notice.

As they came back into the hotel, the chief-inspector slipped a little money and the pass-key into an envelope with the address of the Gilmore Hotel.

'I was going to take it off to France.'

Then to Alain, who didn't know what to do:

'You coming?'

They took the lift. There was a light on in Jeanne Debul's room; perhaps she was expecting a visit from Maigret. She would have to wait a long time.

'Come in! There are twin beds.'

And, as his companion seemed embarrassed:

'You can go to bed in all your clothes if you prefer.'

He arranged to be called at half-past five, slept deeply without a shadow of a dream. As for Alain, the telephone bell didn't wake him from his sleep.

'Up you get, lad!'

Used François Lagrange to wake his son?

Right to the very end, it wasn't like any other case.

'Still, I'm very glad.'

'About what?'

'That you didn't shoot. Don't let's talk about that any more. . . .'

Pyke was waiting for them in the hall, exactly the same as the day before, and it was another glorious morning.

'Nice day, isn't it?'

'Splendid!'

The car was at the door. Maigret realized that he had forgotten to introduce them.

'Alain Lagrange. Mr. Pyke, a friend from Scotland Yard.'

Pyke made a sign that he understood, and didn't ask any questions. The whole way he talked about the flowers in his garden and the wonderful shade of the hydrangeas which he had obtained after long years of experiment.

The aeroplane took off, without a cloud in the sky, nothing but a fine morning haze.

'What are those?' the young man asked, pointing to the cardboard receptacles put there for the convenience of passengers.

'In case anyone feels sick. . . .'

Was it on account of this that, a few minutes later, Alain went pale, then green, and, with a despairing look, leant over his receptacle?

He would have given so much not to be ill, especially in front of Chief-Inspector Maigret!

IX

IT had all happened as usual, except that a month had not elapsed since the last dinner; in fact it was a good deal less. First of all, Pardon's voice on the telephone.

'Are you free tomorrow evening?'

'Probably.'

'With your wife, of course.'

'Yes.'

'Do you like *tête de veau en tortue?*'

'Don't know it.'

'Do you like calf's head?'

'Rather.'

'Then you'll like it mock turtle. It's a dish discovered on a visit to Belgium. You'll see. But, frankly, I don't know what wine to serve with it. . . . Perhaps some beer?'

At the last moment Pardon, as he explained with almost scientific precision, had decided on a light Beaujolais.

Maigret and his wife had walked there and had avoided looking at one another as they passed the Rue Popincourt. Jussieu, from the police laboratory, was present, and Madame Maigret said he was a confirmed old bachelor.

'I wanted to invite Professor Journe. He said he never dines in town. It's twenty years since he had a meal outside his own house.

The french windows were open, and the wrought-iron balcony traced its arabesques against a sky of deepening blue.

'Isn't it a wonderful evening?'

Maigret gave a little smile which the others could not understand. He had two helpings of *tête de veau*. Over the coffee Pardon, who was passing round the cigars, absentmindedly handed the box to Maigret.

'No thanks. Only at the Savoy.'

'You smoked a cigar at the Savoy?' His wife was astonished.

'I had to. They came and whispered in my ear that pipes were forbidden.'

Pardon had arranged the dinner solely in order to talk about the Lagrange affair, and everyone was being careful not to steer the conversation onto that topic. They talked about everything else, idly, except that one subject which was in everyone's mind.

'Did you pay a visit to Scotland Yard?'

'I didn't have time.'

'How do you get on with them?'

'Excellently. They're the most tactful people in the world.'

He meant it; he kept a soft spot for Mr. Pyke, who had raised his hand in farewell the moment the aeroplane took off, and who had, perhaps, at heart, been rather touched.

'Much work at Headquarters just now?'

'Just the usual stuff. Much illness in the district?'

'The usual, too.'

Then there was a little talk about illnesses. So that it was ten o'clock when Pardon finally made up his mind to murmur:

'Have you seen him?'

'Yes. Have you seen him too?'

'I've been there twice?'

The women, tactfully, were pretending not to listen. As for Jussieu, the affair was out of his hands, and he was looking out through the window.

'Was he confronted with his son?'

'Yes.'

'Did he say anything?'

Maigret shook his head.

'Same old story?'

For François Lagrange was sticking to his original attitude, curling up in himself like a frightened animal. The moment anyone approached him he cowered against the wall, an arm crooked over his face to protect himself.

'Don't hit me. . . . I don't want to be hit. . . .'

He even managed to make his teeth chatter.

'What does Journe think about it?'

This time it was Maigret who asked the question.

'Journe is a clever man, probably one of our best psychiatrists. He's also a man worried to death by his responsibilities.'

'I understand.'

'Furthermore he has always been opposed to capital punishment.'

Maigret made no comment, drew slowly at his pipe.

'One day, when I was talking to him about fishing, he looked at me with a shocked expression. He doesn't even kill fish.'

'So that . . .?'

'If François Lagrange keeps it up for another month . . .'

'Will he keep it up?'

'He's frightened enough to do so. Unless someone forces the issue. . . .'

Pardon was staring intently at Maigret. This was the reason for the dinner, the question he had long waited to ask, which he only expressed with a look.

'As far as I am concerned,' murmured the chief-inspector, 'it's nothing to do with me now. I have handed in my report. Rateau the magistrate, for his part, will follow the experts.'

Why did Pardon seem to be saying thank you? It was embarrassing. Maigret was a little put out with him for this indiscretion. It was true to say that it was nothing to do with him now. He could, obviously, have . . .

'I have other fish to fry,' he sighed, rising to his feet, 'among others a certain Jeanne Debul. She returned to Paris yesterday. She's still brazening it out. Within the next two months I hope to have her in my office for a cosy chat.'

'Anyone would think you had a private quarrel with her,' remarked Madame Maigret, although she had not seemed to be listening.

Nothing more was said about it. A quarter of an hour later, in the darkness of the street, Madame Maigret took her husband's arm.

'It's odd,' he said. 'The street-lamps in London, though they're really almost the same . . .'

And, as they went along, he began to tell her about the Strand, Charing Cross, Trafalgar Square.

'I thought you hardly had time to eat.'

'I went out for a few minutes in the evening after dinner.'

'By yourself?'

'No. With him.'

She didn't ask whom he meant. As they approached the Boulevard Richard-Lenoir, he must have remembered the pub where he had drunk a glass of beer before going to bed. It made him thirsty.

'You don't mind if . . .'

'Of course not! Go and have a drink. I'll wait for you.'

For it was a little bar where she would have felt in the way. When he came out, wiping his mouth, she took his arm again.

'Beautiful night.'

'Yes.'

'With lots of stars.'

Why did the sight of a cat which, as they came by, dived into a grating, cloud his face for a moment?

Shadow Rock Farm,
Lakeville, Conn.
June 1952.

MY FRIEND MAIGRET

MY FRIEND MAIGRET

(*Mon Ami Maigret*)
*was first published in France in 1949
and in Great Britain in 1956
Translated from the French by Nigel Ryan*

MY FRIEND MAIGRET

I

'YOU were standing in the doorway of your club?'

'Yes, officer.'

It was no good remonstrating with him. Four or five times Maigret had tried to make him say 'inspector'. What did it matter anyway? What did all this matter?

'A grey sports car stopped for a moment and a man got out, with a flying leap almost, that's what you said, isn't it?'

'Yes, officer.'

'To get into your club he must have passed close to you and even brushed against you. Now there's a luminous neon sign above the door.'

'It's purple, officer.'

'So what?'

'So nothing.'

'Just because your sign is purple you are incapable of recognizing the individual who a moment later tore aside the velvet curtain and emptied his revolver into your barman?'

The man was called Caracci or Caraccini (Maigret was obliged to consult the dossier each time). He was short, but with high heels, a Corsican head (they still bear a faint resemblance to Napoleon) and he wore an enormous yellow diamond on his finger.

This had been going on since eight o'clock in the morning and it was now striking eleven. In actual fact it had been going on since the middle of the night, as all the people who had been rounded up in the Rue Fontaine, at the club where the barman had been shot down, had spent the night in the police station. Three or four detectives, including Janvier and Torrence, had already been working on Caracci, or Caraccini, without getting anything out of him.

It was May, but for all that the rain was falling as in the heaviest of autumn downpours. It had been raining like this since four or five o'clock, and the roofs, window ledges and umbrellas made reflections similar to the water of the Seine, which the chief-inspector could see by twisting his neck.

Mr. Pyke did not move. He remained seated on his chair, in a corner, as rigid as if he was in a waiting-room, and it was beginning to be exasperating. His eyes travelled slowly from the chief-inspector to the little man and from the little man to the chief-inspector, without it being possible to guess what was going on in his English official's mind.

'You realize, Caracci, that your attitude could cost you dear, and that your club might well be closed down for good and all?'

The Corsican, unimpressed, gave Maigret a conspiratorial wink, smiled, smoothed the ends of his black moustache with his ringed finger.

'I've always gone straight, officer. Try asking your colleague, Priollet.'

Although there was a corpse, it was actually Chief-Inspector Priollet, chief of the Vice Squad, that the case concerned, owing to the particular circumstances in which it had all started. Unfortunately Priollet was in the Jura at the funeral of some relation.

'In short, you refuse to speak?'

'I don't refuse, officer.'

Maigret, heavily, looking disgruntled, went and opened the door.

'Lucas! Work on him a bit longer.'

Oh, the way Mr. Pyke stared at him! Mr. Pyke might be the nicest man on earth, but there were moments when Maigret caught himself hating him. Exactly the same as with his brother-in-law, who was called Mouthon. Once a year in the spring, Mouthon got off the train at the Gare de l'Est with his wife, who was Madame Maigret's sister.

He, too, was the nicest man on earth; he would never have hurt a fly. As for his wife, she was gaiety personified, and from the moment she arrived in the flat in the Boulevard Richard-Lenoir, she would call for an apron to help with the housework. On the first day it was perfect. The second day, it was almost as perfect.

'We're leaving tomorrow,' Mouthon would then announce.

'I won't hear of it!' Madame Maigret would protest. 'Why leave so soon?'

'Because we'll be getting in your way.'

'Not on your life!'

Maigret would also declare with conviction:

'Not on your life!'

On the third day, he would hope that some unexpected job would prevent his dining at home. Now never, since his sister-in-law had married Mouthon and the couple had been coming to see them every year, never, ever, had one of those cases which keep you out of doors for days and nights on end cropped up at that moment.

From the fifth day onwards his wife and he would exchange agonized glances, and the Mouthons would stay for nine days, invariably pleasant, charming, thoughtful, as discreet as could be, so that one felt more guilty than ever for coming to detest them.

It was the same with Mr. Pyke. However, it was now only three days that he had been accompanying Maigret wherever he went. One day, during the holidays, they had said to Mouthon, idly:

'Why not come and spend a week in Paris, in the spring? We have a guest room which is always empty.'

They had come.

Similarly, a few weeks back, the Chief of Police had paid an official visit to the Lord Mayor of London. The latter had had him shown round the offices of the famous Scotland Yard, and the Chief had been agreeably surprised to discover that the senior officers of the English police knew Maigret by repute and were interested in his methods.

'Why don't you come and see him at work?' the worthy man had said.

They had taken him at his word. Just like the Mouthons. They had sent over Inspector Pyke, and for the last three days the latter had followed Maigret about everywhere, as discreet, as self-effacing as could be. He was none the less there.

In spite of his thirty-five or forty years he looked so young that he reminded one of a serious-minded student. He was certainly intelligent, perhaps even acutely so. He looked, listened, reflected. He reflected so much that one seemed to be able to hear him reflecting, and it was beginning to be wearing.

It was a little as though Maigret had been placed under observation. All his acts, all his words were carefully sifted in the cranium of the impassive Mr. Pyke.

For three days now there had been nothing interesting to do. Just routine. Red tape. Uninteresting interrogations, like the one with Caracci.

They had come to understand one another, Pyke and he, without anything being said. For example, the moment the night-club owner had been led off to the sergeants' room, where the door had been carefully closed, there was no mistaking the question in the Englishman's eyes:

'Rough stuff?'

Probably, yes. You don't put on velvet gloves to deal with people like Caracci. So what? It was of no importance. The case was without interest. If the barman had been done in it was probably because he hadn't been playing straight, or because he had belonged to a rival gang. Periodically, these characters settle their accounts, kill one another off, and in the long run, it is a good riddance.

Whether Caracci talked or held his peace, there would sooner or later be someone who would take the bait, very likely a police informer. Did they have informers in England?

'Hullo! . . . Yes. . . . It's me. . . . Who? . . . Lechat? . . . Don't know him. . . . Where do you say he's calling from? . . . Porquerolles? Put him through. . . .'

The Englishman's eye was still riveted upon him like the eye of God in the story of Cain.

'Hullo! . . . I can't hear very well. . . . Lechat? . . . Yes. . . . Right. . . . I got that. . . . Porquerolles. . . . I got that too. . . .'

With the receiver to his ear he was looking at the rain which was streaming down the window-panes and thinking that there must be sunshine at Porquerolles, a small island in the Mediterranean off Hyères and Toulon. He had never been there, but he had often been told about it. People came back from it as brown as Bedouins. In fact it was the first time anyone had telephoned to him from an island and he told himself that the telephone wires must pass under the sea.

'Yes. . . . What? . . . A short fair-haired fellow, at Luçon? . . . Ah yes, I remember. . . .'

He had met an Inspector Lechat when, as a result of some rather complicated administrative postings, he had been sent for a few months to Luçon, in the Vendée.

'You're at present with the flying squad at Draguignan, right. And you're ringing from Porquerolles. . . .'

There was a crackling noise on the line. Every now and then the girls could be heard interrupting from one town to another.

'Hallo! Paris . . . Paris . . . Hallo! Paris . . . Paris . . .'

'Hallo! Toulon . . . Are you Toulon, dearie? Hallo! Toulon . . .'

Did the telephone work better on the other side of the Channel? Impassive, Mr. Pyke listened and looked at him, and for appearance's sake Maigret toyed with a pencil.

'Hallo! . . . Do I know a Marcellin? . . . What Marcellin? . . . What? . . . A fisherman? . . . Try to make yourself clear, Lechat. . . . I can't understand what you're talking about. . . . A character who lives in a boat. . . . Right. . . . Go on. . . . He claims to be a friend of mine? . . . What? . . . He used to claim? . . . He's dead? . . . He was killed last night? . . . That's nothing to do with me, Lechat, old man. . . . It's not my area. . . . He had talked about me all evening? . . . And you say that is why he's dead? . . .'

He had dropped his pencil and was trying, with his free hand, to relight his pipe.

'I'm making a note, yes. . . . Marcel. . . . It's not Marcellin any more. . . . As you say. . . . P for Paul . . . A for Arthur . . . C for cinema . . . yes . . . Pacaud. . . . You've sent off fingerprints? . . . A letter from me? . . . Are you sure? . . . Headed paper? . . . What heading? . . . *Brasserie des Ternes*. It's possible. . . . And what did I say? . . .'

If only Mr. Pyke hadn't been there and hadn't been looking at him so earnestly!

'I'm writing it down, yes. . . . "Ginette leaves tomorrow for the sanatorium. She sends her love. Sincerely . . ." It's signed Maigret? . . . No, it's not necessarily a forgery . . . I seem to remember something. . . . I'll go and look on the files. . . . Go down there? . . . You know perfectly well it's no business of mine. . . .'

He was just going to ring off, but he couldn't resist asking one question, at the risk of shocking Mr. Pyke.

'Is the sun shining down there? . . . *Mistral?* . . . But there's sun as well? . . . Okay. . . . If I've any news I'll call you back. . . . I promise. . . .'

If Mr. Pyke asked few questions, he had a way of looking at you that obliged Maigret to speak.

'You know the island of Porquerolles?' he said, lighting his pipe. 'It's supposed to be very beautiful, as beautiful as Capri and the Greek islands. A man was killed there last night, but it's not in my district. They found a letter from me in his boat.'

'It really was from you?'

'Quite likely. The name Ginette seems to ring a bell. Are you coming upstairs with me?'

Mr. Pyke already knew all the departments of Police Headquarters, which he had been shown round. One behind the other they walked up to the attics, where files are kept on everyone who has had dealings with the police. On account of the Englishman, Maigret was suffering from a sort of inferiority complex, and he was ashamed of the antiquated clerk in long grey overalls, who was sucking cough sweets.

'Tell me, Langlois . . . By the way, is the wife better?'

'It's not the wife, Monsieur Maigret. It's my mother-in-law.'

'Oh yes! Sorry. Has she had her operation?'

'She went back home yesterday.'

'Would you have a look and see if you've got anything under the name Marcel Pacaud? With a "d" at the end.'

Was it any better in London? You could hear the rain hammering on the roof, cascading into the gutters.

'Marcel?' asked the clerk, perched on a ladder.

'That's right. Pass me his file.'

Besides fingerprints, it contained a photograph, full face, and a profile, without collar or tie, under the crude light of the identity department.

'Pacaud, Marcel-Joseph-Etienne, born in Le Havre, seaman . . .'

Frowning, Maigret tried to remember, his eyes fixed on the photographs. The man, at the time they had been taken, was thirty-five. He was thin, sickly-looking. A black bruise below the right eye seemed to indicate that he had been interrogated thoroughly before being handed over to the photographer.

There followed a long list of convictions. At Le Havre, aged seventeen, assault and battery. At Bordeaux, a year later, assault and battery again, with drunkenness on the public way. Resisted arrest. Assault and battery again in a house of ill-repute in Marseilles.

Maigret held the file so as to let his English colleague read at the same time as himself, and Mr. Pyke showed no surprise, seemed to say:

'We have that over the other side as well.'

'Living on immoral earnings . . .'

Did they have that too? That meant Marcel Pacaud had been a pimp. And, in the usual way, he had been sent off to do his military service in the Africa Battalions.

'Assault and battery, at Nantes . . .'

'Assault and battery, at Toulon . . .'

'A thug,' Maigret said simply to Mr. Pyke.

Then it became more serious.

'Paris. Inveigling.'

The Englishman asked:

'What's that?'

Imagine having to explain that to a man who belongs to a race with the reputation of being the most tight-laced in the world!

'It's a sort of theft, but a theft committed in special circumstances. When a gentleman accompanies an unknown lady to a more or less disreputable hotel and then goes and complains that his wallet has been stolen, it's called inveigling. Nearly always the prostitute has an accomplice. You follow me?'

'I understand.'

There were three convictions for acting as accomplice to inveigling on Marcel Pacaud's file, and on each occasion, there was a certain Ginette in the case.

Then things became worse still, for there was an incident involving a knife wound which Pacaud was supposed to have inflicted on a recalcitrant gentleman.

'They're what you call *mauvais garçons*, I believe?' Mr. Pyke insinuated gently; his French was terribly impregnated with nuances, so much so that it became ironical.

'Precisely. I wrote to him, I recall. I don't know how you deal with them in your country.'

'Very correctly.'

'I don't doubt it. Here we sometimes knock them around. We're not always gentle with them. But the odd thing is that they seldom hold it against us. They know we're only doing our job. From one interrogation to the next, we get to know each other.'

'This is the one who called himself a friend of yours?'

'I'm convinced he was sincere. I particularly remember the girl and what I remember still better is the headed paper. If we have the chance I'll show you the *Brasserie des Ternes*. It's very comfortable and the sauerkraut is excellent. Do you like sauerkraut?'

'On occasions,' replied the Englishman, without enthusiasm.

'Every afternoon and evening there are a few women sitting round a table. It's there that Ginette used to work. A Breton girl, who came from a village in the St. Malo area. She started off as a maid of all work with a local butcher. She adored Pacaud, and when he talked to her, tears would come into her eyes. Does that surprise you?'

Nothing surprised Mr. Pyke, whose expression betrayed no emotion whatsoever.

'I became rather interested in them, at one time. She was riddled with T.B. She hadn't wanted to have herself cured because that would have taken her away from her Marcel. When he was in prison, I persuaded her to go to see one of my friends, a specialist on consumption, and he got her into a sanatorium in Savoie. That's all.'

'That's what you wrote to Pacaud?'

'That's right. Pacaud was at Fresnes and I hadn't time to go there myself.'

Maigret gave the file back to Langlois and started down the stairs.

'How about going to eat?'

This was another problem, almost a case for his conscience. If he took Mr. Pyke for his meals into too luxurious restaurants he risked giving his colleagues from across the Channel the impression that the French police spend most of their time junketing. If, on the other hand, he took him to places where only set meals are served, perhaps they would accuse him of stinginess.

Same with *apéritifs*. To drink them or not to drink them?

'Are you expecting to go to Porquerolles?'

Did Mr. Pyke want to make a trip to the Midi?

'It's not up to me to decide. In theory I don't operate outside Paris and the department of the Seine.'

The sky was grey, a lowering, hopeless grey, and even the word *mistral* took on a tempting allure.

'Do you like tripe?'

He took him to the Market, and made him eat *tripes à la mode de Caen* and *crêpes Suzettes* which were brought to them on attractive copper chafing-dishes.

'This is what we call an empty sort of day.'

'So do we.'

What could the Scotland Yard man be thinking of him? He had come to study 'Maigret's methods' and Maigret had no method. He found only a large, rather clumsy man who must appear to him to be the prototype of the French public servant. How long would he go on following him about like that?

At two o'clock they were back at the Quai des Orfèvres, and Caracci was still there, in the kind of glass cage that served as a waiting-room. That meant they had got nothing out of him and they were going to question him again.

'Has he eaten?' Mr. Pyke asked.

'I don't know. Possibly. Sometimes they have a sandwich brought up for them.'

'And otherwise?'

'They let them fast a little to prompt the memory.'

'The Chief is asking for you, Inspector.'

'Will you excuse me, Mr. Pyke?'

That was something to the good. The other wouldn't follow him into the Chief's office.

'Come in, Maigret. I've just had a call from Draguigan.'

'I know what that's about.'

'Lechat has of course been in touch with you. Have you much work at the moment?'

'Not too much. Apart from my guest . . .'

'Does he get in your way?'

'He's the soul of discretion.'

'Do you remember the man called Pacaud?'

'I remembered him when I looked up his file.'

'Don't you find the story rather odd?'

'I only know what Lechat told me on the telephone and he was so eager to explain that I didn't understand very much.'

'The Commissioner talked to me at great length. He insists on your going for a trip down there. According to him it's because of you that Pacaud was killed.'

'Because of me?'

'He can't see any other explanation for the murder. For several years Pacaud, better known under the name of Marcellin, had lived at Porquerolles in his boat. He had become a popular figure. As far as I could gather he was more like a tramp than a fisherman. In the winter he lived without doing anything. In the summer he took tourists out fishing round the islands. No one had anything to gain by his death. He wasn't known to have had enemies. Nothing was stolen from him, for the very good reason that there was nothing to steal.'

'How was he killed?'

'That's just what intrigues the Commissioner.'

The Chief consulted several notes which he had made during his telephone conversation.

'As I don't know the place, it's difficult for me to get an accurate picture. The evening before last . . .'

'I thought I was told it was yesterday . . .'

'No, the day before. A number of people were gathered at the *Arche de Noé*. That must be an inn or a café. At this time of year, it seems, only the habitués are to be seen there. Everyone knows everyone else. Marcellin was there. In the course of an almost general conversation he mentioned you.'

'Why?'

'I've no idea. People talk freely about celebrities. Marcellin claimed you were a friend of his. Perhaps some people had cast doubts on your professional abilities? The fact remains that he defended you with uncommon vigour.'

'Was he drunk?'

'He was always more or less drunk. There was a strong *mistral* blowing. I don't know what effect the *mistral* has down there, but as far as I can gather, it is of some importance. It was chiefly on account of this *mistral*, that Marcellin, instead of sleeping in his boat, as he normally did, went off in the direction of the hut which stands near the harbour, where the fishermen spread out their nets. When he was found, the next morning, he had received several shots in the head, fired at point-blank range, and one in the shoulder. The murderer emptied his gun on him. Not content with that he hit him in the face with a heavy instrument. It seems he put an extraordinary ferocity into it.'

Maigret looked at the Seine, outside, through the curtain of rain, and thought of the Mediterranean sun.

'Boisvert, the Commissioner, is a pleasant fellow, whom I've known for ages. He doesn't usually get carried away. He's just arrived on the scene, but he has to leave again this evening. He agrees with Lechat in thinking it was the conversation about you which started the thing off. He's not far from saying that it was you, in a sort of way, that was being aimed at through Marcellin. See what I mean? A man who has a big enough grudge against you to go for anyone who claims to be a friend of yours and sticks up for you.'

'Are there people like that at Porquerolles?'

'That's what's puzzling Boisvert. On an island everyone is known. No one can land and go off again without it being known. So far there isn't the remotest suspect. Or else they'll have to suspect people without any grounds. What to you think?'

'I think Mr. Pyke would like a trip to the Midi.'

'And you?'

'I think I'd like it too if it was a question of going by myself.'

'When will you be leaving?'

'I'll take the night train.'

'With Mr. Pyke?'

'With Mr. Pyke!'

Did the Englishman imagine the French police had powerful motor-cars at their disposal to take them to the scenes of crimes?

He must think, at any rate, that Police Headquarters detectives have unlimited expenses for their movements. Had Maigret done right? Alone, he would have been content with a *couchette*. At the Gare de Lyon he hesitated. Then at the last moment he took two *wagon-lit* places.

It was sumptuous. In the corridor they found de luxe travellers, with impressive-looking luggage. An elegant crowd, laden with flowers, was seeing a film star onto the train.

'It's the Blue Train,' Maigret mumbled, as if to excuse himself.

If only he had been able to know what his fellow policeman was thinking! Into the bargain they were obliged to undress in front of one another and, the next morning, they would have to share the minute washing compartment.

'Well,' said Mr. Pyke, in dressing-gown and pyjamas, 'so a case is under way.'

Just what did he mean by that? His French had something so precise about it that he always looked for a hidden meaning.

'It's a case, yes.'

'Did you take a copy of Marcellin's file?'

'No. I confess I never thought of it.'

'Have you concerned yourself at all about what has become of the woman: Ginette, I believe?'

'No.'

Was there a reproach in the look Mr. Pyke shot at him?

'Have you brought an open arrest warrant with you?'

'Not that either. Only an interrogation permit, which entitles me to summon people and question them.'

'Do you know Porquerolles?'

'I've never set foot there. I hardly know the Midi. I was on a case there, once, at Antibes and Cannes, and I remember particularly it was over-poweringly hot and I felt permanently sleepy.'

'Don't you like the Mediterranean?'

'In general, I dislike places where I lose the desire to work.'

'That's because you like working, is it?'

'I don't know.'

It was true. On the one hand he railed every time a case came along to interrupt his daily routine. On the other hand as soon as he was left in peace for several days he would become restless, as though anxious.

'Do you sleep well on trains?'

'I sleep well anywhere.'

'The train doesn't help you think?'

'I think so little, you know!'

It embarrassed him to see the compartment filled with smoke from his pipe, the more so as the Englishman didn't smoke.

'So you don't know what line you are going to start on?'

'Quite right. I don't even know if there is a line.'

'Thank you.'

One could feel that Mr. Pyke had registered Maigret's every word, had carefully arranged them in order in his brain, for use later on. It could not have been more off-putting. One could imagine him, on his return to Scotland Yard, gathering his colleagues round him (why not in front of a blackboard?) and announcing in his precise voice:

'A case conducted by Chief-Inspector Maigret . . .'

And what if it was a flop? If it was one of those stories where one flounders about and only finds out the solution ten years later, by the merest fluke? If it was a humdrum affair, if tomorrow Lechat rushed up to the carriage door, announcing:

'All over! We've arrested the drunkard who did it! He's confessed.'

What if . . . Madame Maigret hadn't put a dressing-gown in his suitcase. She hadn't wanted him to take the old one, which looked like a monk's habit, and he had been meaning to buy a new one for the last two months. He felt indecent in his nightshirt.

'How about a nightcap?' suggested Mr. Pyke, offering a silver whisky flask and cup. 'That's what we call the last whisky before going to bed.'

He drank a cupful of whisky. He didn't like it. Perhaps, equally, Mr. Pyke didn't like the calvados that Maigret had been making him take for the last three days?

He slept and was conscious of snoring. When he woke, he saw olive trees on the edge of the Rhône and knew they had passed Avignon.

The sun was shining, a light golden mist above the river. The Englishman, freshly shaved, immaculate from head to foot, was standing in the corridor, his face pressed to the window. The washing compartment was as clean as if he had never used it and there lurked a discreet smell of lavender.

Not yet sure if he was in a good temper or a bad one Maigret grumbled as he fumbled in his suitcase for his razor:

'Now we must be careful not to make a balls of this.'

Perhaps it was the impeccable correctness of Mr. Pyke that made him coarse. . . .

II

AND so the first round had been fairly successfully concluded. Which does not mean that there had been any competition between the two men, at least not on professional grounds. If Mr. Pyke was more or less participating in Maigret's activities as a policeman, it was purely in the role of spectator.

Yet Maigret was thinking in terms of 'first round', aware that it was not quite accurate. Hasn't one the right to use one's own private language, in one's own mind?

When he had joined the English detective in the Pullman corridor, for example, there was no doubt that the latter, taken by surprise, had time to efface the expression of wonder which quite transfigured him. Was it simply shame, because a Scotland Yard official is not supposed

to give his attention to the sunrise on one of the most beautiful land-
scapes in the world? Or was the Englishman reluctant to show outward
signs of admiration, considering it indecent in the presence of an alien
witness?

Maigret had inwardly chalked up a point to himself, without a
moment's hesitation.

In the restaurant car, he had to admit, Mr. Pyke had scored one in
his turn. A mere nothing. A slight contraction of the nostrils on the
arrival of bacon and eggs, which were indisputably not so good as in his
country.

'You don't know the Mediterranean, Mr. Pyke?'

'I usually spend my holidays in Sussex. I once went to Egypt though.
The sea was grey and choppy, and it rained all the way.'

And Maigret, who in his heart of hearts didn't like the Midi very
much, felt himself spurred by the desire to defend it.

A questionable point: the head-waiter, who had recognized the
chief-inspector, whom he must have served elsewhere, came up and
asked, in an insinuating voice, immediately after his breakfast:

'Something to drink, as usual?'

Now the day before, or the day before that, the Yard inspector had
commented, with the air of one who never touches it, that an
English gentleman never had strong drinks before the end of the
afternoon.

The arrival at Hyères was without question a round in Maigret's
favour. The palm-trees, round the station, were motionless, transfixed
in a Sahara sun. It was likely that there had been an important market
that morning, a fair or a fête, for the carts, vans and heavy lorries were
mobile pyramids of early vegetables, fruits and flowers.

Mr. Pyke, just like Maigret, found his breath coming a little more
quickly. There was a real sense of entering another world, and it was
uncomfortable to do so in the dark clothes which had suited the previous day in the rainy streets of Paris.

He ought, like Inspector Lechat, to have worn a light suit and a shirt
with an open collar, and shown a red patch of sunburn on his forehead.
Maigret had not immediately recognized him, for he remembered his
name rather than his face. Lechat, who was threading his way through
the porters, looked almost like a boy from the district, small and thin,
hatless, with espadrilles on his feet.

'This way, Chief!'

Was this a good mark? For though this devil Mr. Pyke noted everything down, it was impossible to tell what he classified in the good
column and what he put into the bad one. Officially Lechat ought to
have called Maigret 'Chief-Inspector', for he was not in his department.
But there were few detectives in France who could deny themselves the
pleasure of calling him 'Chief' with affectionate familiarity.

'Mr. Pyke, you already know about Inspector Lechat. Lechat, let me introduce Mr. Pyke, from Scotland Yard.'

'Are they in on it too?'

Lechat was so taken up with his Marcellin case that it didn't surprise him at all that it should have become an international affair.

'Mr. Pyke is in France on a study tour.'

While they walked through the crowd Maigret wondered at the curious way Lechat was walking sideways, twisting his neck around.

'Let's hurry through,' he was saying. 'I've got a car at the entrance.'

It was the small official car. Once inside the inspector heaved a sigh:

'I thought you'd better be careful. Everyone knows it's you *they've got it in for.*'

So just now, in the crowd, it was Maigret the tiny Lechat was trying to protect!

'Shall I take you straight to the island? You haven't anything to do on Hyères, have you?'

And off they went. The land was flat, deserted, the road lined with tamarisks, with a palm-tree here and there, then white salt marshes on the right. The change of scene was as absolute as if they had been transported to Africa — with a blue porcelain sky, and the air perfectly still.

'And the *mistral*?' Maigret asked, with a touch of irony.

'It stopped quite suddenly yesterday evening. It was high time. It's blown for nine days and that's enough to drive everyone mad.'

Maigret was sceptical. The people from the North — and the North begins around Lyons — have never taken the *mistral* seriously. So Mr. Pyke was excused for displaying indifference as well.

'No one has left the island. You can question everyone who was there when Marcellin was murdered. The fishermen were not at sea that night because of the storm. But a torpedo boat from Toulon and several submarines were doing exercises in the lee of the island. I rang up the Admiralty. They are positive. No boat made the crossing.'

'Which means the murderer is still on the island?'

'You'll see.'

Lechat was playing the old boy, who knows his way around and the people. Maigret was the new boy, which is always rather a distasteful role. The car, after half an hour, was slowing to a halt at a rocky promontory on which there was nothing to be seen except a typical Provençal inn and several fishermen's cottages painted pink and pale blue.

One mark for France, for the mouth fell open. The sea was an incredible blue, such as one normally only sees on picture postcards, and over on the horizon an island stretched lazily in the middle of the rainbow-like surface, with bright green hills, and red and yellow rocks.

At the end of the wooden landing-stage, a fishing boat was waiting, painted pale green picked out in white.

'That's for us. I asked Gabriel to bring me over and wait for you. The boat which does the regular service, the *Cormorant*, only comes at eight in the morning and five in the evening. Gabriel is a Galli. Let me explain. There are Gallis and Morins. Almost everyone on the island belongs to one of the two families.'

Lechat was carrying the luggage, which seemed to grow larger at the end of his arms. The engine was already turning over. It was all a little unreal and it was hard to believe that they were there solely to concern themselves with a dead man.

'I didn't suggest showing you the body. It's at Hyères. The post-mortem took place yesterday morning.'

There were about three miles between Giens Point and Porquerolles. As they advanced over the silky water the contours of the island became more distinct, with its peaks, its bays, its ancient fortresses in the greenery and, right in the middle, a small group of light-coloured houses and the white church tower which might have come from a child's building set.

'Do you think I might be able to get hold of a bathing-costume?' the Englishman asked Lechat.

Maigret hadn't thought of that and, leaning over the rail, he suddenly discovered, with a sense of vertigo, the bottom of the sea which was slipping away under the boat. It was a good thirty feet below, but the water was so clear that the minutest details of the underwater landscape were visible. And it really was a landscape, with its plains covered in greenery, its rocky hills, its gorges and precipices, among which shoals of fish trooped like sheep.

A little put out, as though he had been surprised playing a child's game, Maigret looked at Mr. Pyke, but only to score another point: the Scotland Yard inspector, almost as moved as himself, was also gazing at the bottom of the water.

It is only after a while that one begins to take in the atmosphere of a place. At first everything seemed strange. The harbour was tiny, with a jetty on the left, a rocky promontory, covered with sea-pines, on the right. In the background some red roofs, white and pink houses among the palm-trees, the mimosas and the tamarisks.

Had Maigret ever seen mimosas before outside the flower girls' baskets in Paris? He couldn't remember whether the mimosas had been in flower at the time of the case he had conducted in Antibes and Cannes, a few years before.

On the jetty a handful of people were waiting. There were also some fishermen in boats painted like Christmas decorations.

They were watched as they disembarked. Perhaps the people, on the

island, consisted of various groups? Maigret needn't bother about these
details until later. For example, a man dressed in white, with a white
cap on his head, greeted him with a hand to his forelock, and he didn't
recognize him at first.

'That's Charlot!' Lechat whispered in his ear.

The name, for the moment, conveyed nothing to him. A sort of
colossus with bare feet piled the luggage onto a barrow without uttering
a word, and pushed it in the direction of the village square.

Maigret, Pyke and Lechat followed. And behind them the locals
followed in turn; all this in an odd silence.

The square was vast and deserted, enclosed by eucalyptus trees and
coloured houses, with, to crown it, the little yellow church and its white
tower. They could see several cafés with shaded terraces.

'I could have booked you rooms at the Grand Hotel. It has been open
for a fortnight.'

It was a fair-sized block overlooking the harbour, and a man dressed
like a cook stood in the doorway.

'I thought it better to put you into the *Arche de Noé*. Let me explain.'

There were already a lot of things for the inspector to explain. The
terrace of the *Arche*, on the square, was wider than the others, bounded
by a small wall and green plants. Inside it was cool, a little dark, which
was in no way disagreeable, and one was at once struck by the pronounced smell of cooking and of white wine.

Yet another man dressed as a cook, but without the chef's cap. He
advanced with outstretched hand, a radiant smile on his face.

'Delighted to welcome you, Monsieur Maigret. I have given you
the best room. Of course you will have a glass of our local white
wine?'

Lechat whispered:

'That's Paul, the proprietor.'

There were red tiles on the floor. The bar was a proper *bistrot* bar,
made of metal. The white wine was cool, a little young, but a good
strong one.

'Your health, Monsieur Maigret. I never dared to hope that I should
one day have the honour of having you to stay.'

It didn't occur to him that it was to a crime that he owed the honour.
No one seemed to bother about Marcellin's death. The groups they had
just seen near the jetty were now in the square and imperceptibly
approaching the *Arche de Noé*. Some of them were even sitting down on
the terrace.

In short, what really mattered was Maigret's arrival, in flesh and
blood, just as if he had been a film star.

Was he cutting a good figure? Did the Scotland Yard people have
more self-assurance at the beginning of an investigation? Mr. Pyke
looked at everything and said nothing.

'I should like to go and clean up a bit,' Maigret sighed after a while, having drunk two glasses of white wine.

'Jojo! Will you show Monsieur Maigret up to his room? Will your friend be going up too, Inspector?'

Jojo was a small dark servant girl, dressed in black, with a broad smile and small pointed breasts.

The whole house smelt of *bouillabaisse* and saffron oil. Upstairs, where there was red flooring as in the bar, there were only three or four rooms and they had in fact reserved the best for the chief-inspector, the one with one window looking onto the square and the other onto the sea. Ought he to offer it to Mr. Pyke? It was too late. They had already indicated another door for the latter.

'Is there anything you want, Monsieur Maigret? The bathroom is at the end of the corridor. I think there's some hot water.'

Lechat had followed him up. It was natural. It was normal. But he didn't ask him in. It seemed to him that it would be a sort of discourtesy towards his English colleague. The latter might imagine they were hiding something from him, that they weren't letting him in on the *whole* case.

'I'll be down in a few minutes, Lechat.'

He would have liked to find a kindly word for the inspector, who was looking after him with such care. He seemed to recall that at Luçon his wife had come into the picture a lot. Standing in the doorway, he asked, in a friendly and familiar manner:

'How is your charming Madame Lechat?'

And the poor fellow could only stammer:

'Didn't you know? She left me. It's eight years ago now since she left.'

What a gaffe! It all came back to him suddenly. If people talked so much about Madame Lechat at Luçon, it was because she deceived her husband for all she was worth.

In his bedroom he did nothing except take off his coat, wash his hands, teeth and face, stretch in front of the window and lie on the bed for a few minutes as if to try out the springs. The furnishing was antiquated, agreeable, with always the good smell of southern cooking which pervaded every corner of the house. He hesitated about whether to go down in shirt-sleeves, for it was hot, but decided that it would look too much like a holiday and put on his coat again.

When he arrived downstairs there were several people at the bar, mostly men in fishermen's clothes. Lechat was waiting for him in the doorway.

'Would you like a stroll, Chief?'

'We'd better wait for Mr. Pyke.'

'He's already gone out.'

'Where?'

'Into the water. Paul lent him a bathing-costume.'

They headed unconsciously for the harbour. The slope of the ground led them there of its own accord. One felt that everyone was bound inevitably to take the same path.

'I think you'd better be very careful, Chief. Whoever killed Marcellin has a grudge against you and will try to get you.'

'We'd better wait until Mr. Pyke is out of the water.'

Lechat pointed to a head which emerged on the far side of the boats.

'Is he on the case?'

'He's following it. We mustn't give the impression of plotting behind his back.'

'We would have been quieter at the Grand Hotel. It's closed in the winter. It has only just opened and there's no one there. Only it's at Paul's that everyone meets. It's there that it all began, because it was there that Marcellin mentioned you and claimed you were a friend of his.'

'Let's wait for Mr. Pyke.'

'Do you want to question people in his presence?'

'I shall have to.'

Lechat made a wry face, but did not dare to protest.

'Where are you thinking of summoning them? There's hardly anywhere except the town hall. A single room with benches, a table, flags for the 14th of July and a bust of the Republic. The mayor keeps the grocer's shop, next to the *Arche de Noé*. That's him you can see over there, pushing a wheelbarrow.'

Mr. Pyke was now coming back into his depth once more near a boat attached to a chain, was walking in the water, peacefully splashing in the sun.

'The water's marvellous,' he said.

'If you like, we'll wait here while you go and get dressed.'

'I'm very comfortable as I am.'

This time it was a point to him. He was in fact just as much at his ease in bathing-trunks, with drops of salt water trickling down his long, thin body, as in his grey suit.

He pointed to a black yacht, not in the harbour, but at anchor, several cables out. The English flag was discernible.

'Who's that?'

Lechat explained:

'The boat is called the *North Star*. It comes here almost every year. It belongs to a Mrs. Ellen Wilcox: that's also the name of a whisky, I believe. She's the owner of Wilcox whisky.'

'Is she young?'

'She's fairly well preserved. She lives on board with her secretary, Philippe de Moricourt, and a crew of two. There's another Englishman

on the island, who lives here all the year round. You can see his house
from here. It's the one with the minaret beside it.'

Mr. Pyke didn't look particularly enthusiastic at coming across
fellow-countrymen.

'It's Major Bellam, but the locals simply call him the Major, and
sometimes Teddy.'

'I suppose he's an Indian Army major?'

'I don't know.'

'Does he drink a lot?'

'Yes, a lot. You'll see him tonight at the *Arche*. You'll see everyone
at the *Arche*, including Mrs. Wilcox and her secretary.'

'Were they present when Marcellin spoke?' asked Maigret, for the
sake of something to say, for in actual fact he was no longer interested in
anything.

'They were. Practically everyone was at the *Arche*, as they are every
evening. In a week or two the tourists begin to pour in and life will be
different. For the moment it's not entirely the life of the winter, when
the inhabitants are alone on the island, and it's not quite what is called
the season. Only the regulars have arrived. I don't know if you follow
me. Most of them have been coming here for years, and know everybody. The major has been living at the Minaret for eight years. The
villa next to it belongs to Monsieur Emile.'

Lechat looked at Maigret with a hesitant air. Perhaps, in the presence
of the Englishman, he, too, was overcome with a sort of patriotic shame.

'Monsieur Emile?'

'You know him. At any rate, he knows you. He lives with his mother,
old Justine, who is one of the most widely known women on the Riviera.
She's the proprietor of the *Fleurs*, at Marseilles, the *Sirènes* at Nice, two
or three houses at Toulon, Béziers, Avignon . . .'

Had Mr. Pyke realized what sort of houses they were?

'Justine's seventy-nine years old. I thought she was older, for Monsieur Emile admits to being sixty-five. It appears she had him when she
was fourteen. She told me so yesterday. They're very quiet, the two of
them, and don't see anyone. Look. That's Monsieur Emile you can see
in his garden, in the white suit, with the topee. He looks like a white
mouse. He has a little boat, like everyone else, but he hardly ever
ventures beyond the end of the jetty, where he spends hours happily
fishing for *girelle*.'

'What's that?' asked Mr. Pyke, whose skin was beginning to dry.

'*Girelle?* An extremely attractive little fish, with red and blue on its
back. It's not bad fried, but it's not a serious fish, if you see what I
mean.'

'I see.'

The three of them walked on the sand, along the backs of the houses
which faced onto the square.

'There is another local character. We shall probably eat at the next table to him. It's Charlot. Just now, when we landed, he said hello to you, Chief. I asked him to stay, and he didn't object. It's curious, actually, that nobody asked to leave. They are all being very calm, very sensible.'

'And the big yacht?'

There was indeed an enormous white yacht, not very beautiful, made entirely of metal, which almost filled the harbour.

'The *Alcyon*? It's there all the year round. It belongs to a Lyons businessman, Monsieur Jaureguy, who only uses it for one week in the year, and then it's to go and bathe, all by himself, a stone's throw from the island. There are two sailors on board, two Bretons, who have a pretty easy life.'

Was the Englishman expecting to see Maigret taking notes? He watched him smoking his pipe, looking lazily around him, and listening absently to Lechat.

'You see the small green boat, to one side, which has such an odd shape? The cabin is minute, yet there are two people, a man and a girl, living there. They have fixed up a tent by means of the sail, over the deck, and most of the time that's where they sleep. They do their cooking and washing there. Those two aren't regulars. They were found one morning, tied up where you see them now. The man is called Jef de Greef and is Dutch. He's a painter. He's only twenty-four. You'll see him. The girl is called Anna and isn't his wife. I had their papers in my hands. She's eighteen. She was born at Ostend. She's always half-naked and sometimes more than half. As soon as night falls, you can see both of them bathing at the end of the jetty without a stitch of clothing.'

Lechat was careful to add for Mr. Pyke's benefit:

'It's true that Mrs. Wilcox, if you can believe the fishermen, does the same round her yacht.'

They were being watched, from a distance. Always little knots of people who gave the impression of having nothing else to do all day.

'Another fifty yards farther on you can see Marcellin's boat.'

From this point the harbour was no longer flanked with the backs of the houses in the square, but with villas, most of them surrounded by vegetation.

'They are empty, all except two,' Lechat was explaining. 'I'll tell you who they belong to. This one belongs to Monsieur Emile and his mother. I've already told you about the Minaret.'

A supporting wall divided the gardens from the sea. Each villa had its little landing-stage. At one of these, a local craft, pointed at both ends, about eighteen feet long, was tied up.

'That's Marcellin's boat.'

It was dirty, its deck in disorder. Against the wall was a sort of hearth

8*

composed of large stones, a saucepan, some pots blackened by smoke, empty wine bottles.

'Is it true that you knew him, Chief? In Paris?'

'In Paris, yes.'

'What the local people refuse to believe is that he was born in Le Havre. Everyone is convinced he was a real Southerner. He had the accent. He was a queer fish. He lived in his boat. Now and then he would go for a trip to the continent as he would call it, which means that he would go and tie his boat up to the jetty at Giens, Saint-Tropez or Le Lavandou. When the weather was too bad, he would sleep in the hut you can see just above the harbour. That's where the fishermen boil their nets. He had no wants. The butcher would give him a bit of meat occasionally. He didn't fish much, and then only in summer, when he took tourists out. There are a few others like him along the coast.'

'Do you have types like that in England, too?' Maigret asked Mr. Pyke.

'It's too cold. We only have the dockside loafers, at the ports.'

'Did he drink?'

'White wine. When people needed him to give a hand, they paid him with a bottle of white wine. He used to win it at bowls, too, for he was an expert bowls player. It was in the boat that I found the letter. I'll give it back to you presently. I've left it at the town hall.'

'No other papers?'

'His army book, a photograph of a woman, that's all. It's strange that he should have kept your letter, don't you think?'

Maigret didn't find it so very surprising. He would have liked to talk about it with Mr. Pyke, whose bathing-trunks were drying in patches. But that could wait.

'Do you want to see the hut? I've shut it, but I've got the key in my pocket; I shall have to give it back to the fishermen, as they need it.'

No huts for the moment. Maigret was hungry. And he was also anxious to see his English colleague in less informal attire. It made him feel awkward, for no very definite reason. He was not accustomed to conducting a case in the company of a man in a swimming-costume.

He needed another drink of white wine. It was decidedly a tradition on the island. Mr. Pyke went upstairs to dress and returned without a tie, with open collar, like Lechat, and he had found time to procure, probably at the mayor's grocery, a pair of blue canvas espadrilles.

The fishermen, who would have liked to speak to him, still didn't dare. The *Arche* had two rooms: the room where the bar was, and a smaller one with tables covered with red check table-cloths. These were laid. Two tables away Charlot was busy sampling sea-urchins.

Once again he raised a hand in salute as he looked at Maigret. Then he added, idly:

'How goes?'

They had spent several hours, perhaps an entire night, alone together
in Maigret's office, five or six years before. The chief-inspector had
forgotten his real name. Everyone knew him as Charlot.

He did a little bit of everything, procuring girls for licensed brothels
in the Midi, smuggling cocaine and certain other goods; he dabbled in
racing too, and at election time became one of the most active election-
eering agents on the coast.

He was meticulous in his personal appearance, with measured gestures, and imperturbable calm, an ironical little twinkle in his eye.

'Do you like Mediterranean cooking, Mr. Pyke?'

'I don't know it.'

'Do you want to try it?'

'With pleasure.'

And Paul, the proprietor, suggested:

'Some small birds, to start with? I've a few cooked on the spit,
brought in this morning.'

They were robins, Paul unfortunately announced as he served the
Englishman, who could not help gazing tenderly at his plate.

'As you see, Inspector, I've been a good boy.'

From where he sat Charlot, without stopping eating, was addressing
them in an undertone.

'I've waited for you without being impatient. I haven't even asked
the inspector's permission to leave.'

A lengthy silence.

'I'm at your service, whenever you like. Paul will tell you that I didn't
leave the *Arche* that evening.'

'Are you in such a hurry?'

'What about?'

'To clear yourself.'

'I'm just clearing the ground a little, that's all. I'm doing my best to
stop you swimming too far out to sea. Because you soon will be swimming. I swim well, but I come from these parts.'

'Did you know Marcellin?'

'I've had a drink with him hundreds of times, if that's what you mean.
Is it true you've brought someone from Scotland Yard with you?'

He examined Mr. Pyke cynically, like some strange object.

'This is no case for him. It's not a case for you either, if you'll forgive
me saying what I think. You know I've always kept clean. We've already had things out between us. There's no hard feelings on either
side. What's the fat little sergeant in your office called again? Lucas!
How's he getting on, Lucas? Paul! Jojo! . . . Hey! . . .'

As there was no reply, he went towards the kitchen and came back
after a few minutes with a plate smelling of garlic mayonnaise.

'I'm not stopping you talking?'

'Not at all.'

'If I am, you can just ask me politely to shut my trap. I'm just thirty-four years old. To be exact, it was my birthday yesterday, which means I'm just beginning to feel my age. In my time I've had several chats with your colleagues, either in Paris, or Marseilles, or elsewhere. They haven't always been very polite to me. We haven't always got on together, but there's one thing everyone will tell you: Charlot's never got his hands dirty.'

It was true, if one took that to mean he had never killed anyone. He must have had a round dozen convictions to his credit, but for relatively harmless offences.

'Do you know why I come here regularly? I like the place, obviously, and Paul's a good chap. But there's another reason. Look in the corner, on the left. The fruit machine. It's mine, and I've got around fifty of them from Marseilles to Saint-Raphael. They aren't exactly legal. From time to time, some of your gentlemen turn nasty and remove one or two of them.'

Poor Mr. Pyke, who had eaten his little birds to the bitter end, in spite of the softness of his heart! Now he was sniffing the garlic mayonnaise with ill-concealed apprehension.

'You're wondering why I am talking so much, aren't you?'

'I haven't wondered anything yet.'

'It's not a habit of mine. But I'll tell you anyway. Here, I mean on the island, there are two characters who are bound to get blamed for the whole affair. They're Emile and me. We've both seen trouble. People are very decent with us, more so as we are open-handed with drinks. They wink at one another. They whisper:

' "They're regular crooks!"'

'Or sometimes:

' "Take a look at him. He's quite a lad!"'

'Just the same, the moment there's any dirty work it's us they go for.

'I realized that, and that's why I took it easy. I've some pals waiting for me on the coast and I haven't even tried to telephone them. Your little inspector with the dainty manner has been keeping his eye on me and for the last two days has been itching to put me inside. Well! I'll tell you straight, to save you making a blunder: it'd be a big mistake.

'That's all. After which, I'm at your service.'

Maigret waited for Charlot to go out, a toothpick at his lips, to ask quietly of his Scotland Yard colleague:

'Does it ever happen over there, that you make friends among your clients?'

'Not in quite the same way.'

'How do you mean?'

'We haven't a lot of people like that. Certain things don't happen in quite the same way. Do you follow me?'

Why did Maigret think of Mrs. Wilcox and her young secretary? Indeed certain things did not happen in quite the same way.

'For example, I had dealings, you might call them cordial, for a long time with a notorious jewel thief. We have a lot of jewel thieves. It's something of a national speciality of ours. They are nearly always educated men who come from the best schools, and belong to the smartest clubs. We have the same difficulty as you do with people like this man, or the one called Monsieur Emile: it is to catch them in the act. For four years I kept on the track of the thief I was telling you about. He knew it. We often had a whisky at the bar together.

'We played a number of games of chess together, too.'

'And did you get him?'

'Never. In the end we came to a gentleman's agreement. You know the expression? I got rather in his way, so much so, in fact, that last year he wasn't able to try anything on, and he was genuinely hard up. On my side, I wasted a lot of time on his account. I advised him to go and exercise his talents elsewhere. Is that how you say it?'

'Did he go and steal jewels in New York?'

'I rather think he's in Paris,' Mr. Pyke corrected him calmly, selecting a toothpick in his turn.

A second bottle of the island's wine, which Jojo had brought without being asked, was more than half-empty. The *patron* came over to suggest:

'A little *marc*? After the garlic mayonnaise, it's essential.'

It was balmy, almost cool in the room, while a heavy sun, humming with flies, beat down on the square.

Charlot, probably for the sake of his digestion, had just begun a game of *pétanque* with a fisherman, and there were half a dozen others to watch them play.

'Will you be doing your interrogations at the town hall?' inquired little Lechat, who didn't seem at all sleepy.

Maigret all but answered:

'What interrogations?'

But he mustn't forget Mr. Pyke, who was swallowing his *marc* almost without distaste.

'At the town hall, yes . . .'

He would have preferred to go and take a siesta.

III

MONSIEUR FÉLICIEN JAMET, the mayor (of course people just called him Félicien), came along with his key to open the town hall door for them. Twice before, seeing him cross the square, Maigret had asked himself what it was about his appearance that was abnormal, and he suddenly realized: perhaps because he also sold lamps, paraffin, galvanized wire and nails, Félicien, instead of wearing a grocer's yellowish apron, had taken to the ironmonger's grey smock. He wore it very long, almost down to his ankles. Was he wearing trousers underneath? Or did he leave them off, on account of the heat? The fact remained that if the trousers were there, they were too short to project below the smock, so that the mayor looked as if he were in a nightshirt. More precisely—and the species of skull cap he sported added to the impression—he had something medieval about him, and one had the impression of having seen him before somewhere in a stained-glass window.

'I presume you won't be needing me, gentlemen?'

Standing in the doorway of the dusty room, Maigret and Mr. Pyke looked at one another in some surprise, then looked at Lechat, and finally at Félicien. For on the table, the one used for council meetings and elections, was laid a deal coffin which seemed to have lost something of its brand-newness.

In the most natural way in the world, Monsieur Jamet said to them:

'If you like to give me a hand, we can shove it into its corner.'

'What is this coffin?' Maigret asked, in surprise.

'It's the municipal coffin. We are obliged by law to provide burial for destitutes and we've only got one carpenter on the island; he's very old and works slowly. In summer, with the heat, the bodies can't be kept waiting.'

He spoke of it as of the most banal thing in the world, and Maigret studied the Scotland Yard man out of the corner of his eye.

'Have you many destitute people?'

'We've got one, old Benoît.'

'So that the coffin is destined for Benoît?'

'Theoretically. However, last Wednesday it was used to take Marcellin's body to Hyères. Don't worry. It's been disinfected.'

There were only some very comfortable folding chairs in the room.

'May I leave you now, gentlemen?'

'Just a moment. Who is Benoît?'

'You must have seen him, or you soon will: he wears his hair down to his shoulders, with a shaggy beard. Look: through that window, you can see him having his siesta on a bench, near the bowls players.'

'Is he terribly old?'

'Nobody knows. Nor does he. According to him he's getting on for a hundred, but he must be boasting. He hasn't any papers His real name isn't known. He landed on the island a very long time ago, when Morin-Barbu, who keeps the café on the corner, was still a young man.'

'Where did he come from?'

'That's not known either. From Italy, for certain. Most of them came from Italy. You can usually tell from their way of speaking whether they come from Genoa or the Naples area, but Benoît has a language of his own; he's not easy to understand.'

'Is he simple?'

'I beg your pardon?'

'Is he a bit mad?'

'He's as sly as a monkey. Today he looks like a patriarch. In a few days when the summer trippers begin to arrive, he'll shave his beard and head. He does it every year at the same time. And he starts fishing *mordu*.'

Everything had to be learnt.

'*Mordu?*'

'*Mordus* are worms with very hard heads which you find in the sand, on the seashore. Fishermen use them in preference to other bait because they stay on the hook. They fetch a high price. All summer Benoît fishes *mordu* up to his thighs in the water. He used to be a builder, in his young days. It was he that built a good number of the houses on the island. There's nothing else you want, is there, gentlemen?'

Maigret hurriedly opened the window to let the close, musty smell out of the room: it could not have been aired except for the 14th of July, at the same time as they brought out the flags and the chairs.

The chief-inspector didn't know exactly what he was doing there. He had no desire to proceed with the interrogations. Why had he said 'yes' when Inspector Lechat had suggested it to him? Through cowardice, on account of Mr. Pyke? Isn't it usual, when one starts a case, to question people? Isn't that the way they do it in England? Would he be taken seriously if he wandered about the island like a man who has nothing else to do?

However, it was the island which interested him at the moment, and not such and such a person in particular. What the mayor had just been saying, for example, set in motion a whole train of thought, so far still nebulous. These men in their little boats who came and went along the coasts, as though quite at home, as though along a boulevard! This did not fit into the picture one had of the sea. It seemed that here the sea had something intimate about it. A few miles from Toulon one met people from Genoa or Naples, perfectly naturally, people in boats, who fished on the way over. Rather like Marcellin. They stopped, and if it suited them, they stayed, perhaps even wrote home for their wife or fiancée to come out?

'Would you like me to bring them in one by one, Chief? Who do you want to start with?'

It was all the same to him.

'I see young de Greef crossing the square with his girl friend. Shall I go and get him?'

He was being rushed, and he didn't dare protest. He had the consolation of noting that his colleague was as sluggish as he was.

'These witnesses you are going to interview,' he asked, 'are they summoned officially?'

'Not at all. They come because they are willing to. They have the right to reply or not. Most of the time they prefer to reply, but they could always demand the presence of a lawyer.'

It must have been spread around that the chief-inspector was at the town hall, for groups of people, as in the morning, were forming on the square. Some way away, beneath the eucalyptus trees, Lechat was in animated conversation with a couple, who finally followed him. A mimosa was growing just beside the door and its sweet scent mingled strangely with the musty smell which pervaded the room.

'I suppose, with you, all this is more formal?'

'Not always. Often, in the country or in small towns, the coroner's inquest is held in the backroom of an inn.'

De Greef seemed all the more fair because his skin was as bronzed as a Tahiti native's. All he wore in the way of clothes was a pair of light-coloured shorts and espadrilles, while his companion had a sunsuit tight around her body.

'You wish to speak to me?' he asked, suspiciously.

And Lechat, reassuringly:

'Come in! Chief-Inspector Maigret has to question everyone. It's just routine.'

The Dutchman spoke French with hardly any accent. He had a net bag in his hand. The two of them were probably going shopping, at the Co-operative, when the inspector had interrupted them.

'Have you been living long aboard your boat?'

'Three years. Why?'

'No reason. You're a painter, they tell me? Do you sell your pictures?'

'When the occasion presents itself.'

'Does it often do so?'

'It's rather rare. I sold a canvas to Mrs. Wilcox last week.'

'Do you know her well?'

'I met her here.'

Lechat came over to speak to Maigret in a low voice. He wanted to know if he should go and fetch Monsieur Emile, and the chief-inspector nodded his assent.

'What sort of person is she?'

'Mrs. Wilcox? She's fantastic.'

'What does that mean?'

'Nothing. I might have met her in Montparnasse, for she passes through Paris every winter. We found we had friends in common.'

'Have you often been to Montparnasse?'

'I lived in Paris for a year.'

'With your boat?'

'We tied up at the Pont Marie.'

'Are you rich?'

'I haven't a bean.'

'Tell me: exactly how old is your girl friend?'

'Eighteen and a half.'

The latter, her hair falling over her face, her sunsuit moulded to her figure, looked like a young savage, as she watched Maigret and Mr. Pyke with a blazing eye.

'You aren't married?'

'No.'

'Do her parents object?'

'They know she's been living with me.'

'How long for?'

'Two and a half years.'

'In other words, she was only just sixteen when she became your mistress?'

The word didn't shock either of them.

'Have her parents ever tried to get her back?'

'They've tried several times. She came back.'

'So they've given up?'

'They prefer not to think about it any more.'

'What did you live on in Paris?'

'Selling a picture or a drawing now and then. I had friends.'

'They lent you money?'

'Sometimes. Other times I was a porter at the vegetable market. Or else I distributed prospectuses.'

'Did you already have an urge to come to Porquerolles?'

'I didn't even know of the existence of this island.'

'Where were you planning to go?'

'Anywhere, provided there was sun.'

'And you expect to go where?'

'Farther on.'

'Italy?'

'Or somewhere else.'

'Did you know Marcellin?'

'He helped to recaulk my boat when it leaked.'

'Were you at the *Arche de Noé* the night he died?'

'We are there almost every night.'

'What were you doing?'

'We were playing chess, Anna and I.'

'May I inquire, Monsieur de Greef, what is your father's profession?'

'He's a magistrate at Groningen.'

'You don't know why Marcellin was killed?'

'I'm not curious.'

'Did he speak to you about me?'

'If he did, I didn't hear.'

'Do you possess a revolver?'

'What for?'

'You have nothing to say to me?'

'Nothing at all.'

'And you, mademoiselle?'

'Nothing, thank you.'

He called them back just as they were about to leave.

'One more question. Just now, have you got any money?'

'I told you, I've sold a picture to Mrs. Wilcox.'

'You've been aboard her yacht?'

'Several times.'

'What do people do aboard yachts?'

'I don't know.'

And de Greef added with a hint of contempt:

'You drink. We drank. Is that all?'

Lechat cannot have had to go far to find Monsieur Emile, for the two men were standing in a patch of shade, a few yards from the little town hall. Monsieur Emile looked older than his sixty-five years and he gave an impression of extreme frailty, only moving with great care, as if he were afraid of breaking. He spoke low, economizing every grain of energy.

'Come in, Monsieur Emile. We've met before, I think?'

As Justine's son was eyeing a chair, Maigret went on:

'You can sit down. Did you know Marcellin?'

'Very well.'

'You were in constant touch with him? Since when?'

'I couldn't say quite how many years. My mother should be able to remember exactly. Since Ginette's been working for us.'

There was a brief silence. It was very strange. One might have thought a bubble had just burst in the peaceful air of the room. Maigret and Mr. Pyke looked at one another. What had Mr. Pyke said as they left Paris? He had mentioned Ginette. He had been surprised — discreetly, as in all things — that the chief-inspector had not inquired what had become of her.

Now there was no need for inquiries, or ruses. Quite simply, in his opening remarks, it was Monsieur Emile who mentioned the woman whom, once upon a time, Maigret had sent to a sanatorium.

'You say she works for you? That means, I suppose, in one of your houses.'

'At the one in Nice.'

'Just a minute, Monsieur Emile. It's a good fifteen years since I met her at the *Ternes*, and she wasn't a young girl then. If I'm not mistaken, she was well past thirty, and tuberculosis wasn't making her any younger. Now she must be . . .'

'Between forty-five and fifty.'

And Monsieur Emile added in the most natural way imaginable:

'It's she who runs the *Sirènes*, at Nice.'

It was better not to look at Mr. Pyke, whose expression of disapproval must have been as ironical as his good education allowed. Hadn't Maigret blushed? At any rate he was conscious of being perfectly ridiculous.

For the fact was that he had on this occasion played the moral reformer. After sending Marcellin to prison, he had turned his attention to Ginette and, just as might happen in a popular novel, had 'snatched her from the gutter' to have her put into a sanatorium.

He saw her again clearly, so thin that one wondered how men could allow themselves to be tempted, with feverish eyes and slack mouth.

He said to her:

'You must have treatment, my girl.'

And she answered, docilely:

'I'm quite willing, Chief-Inspector. Don't think I enjoy it!'

With a touch of impatience, Maigret now asked, looking Monsieur Emile straight in the face:

'You're sure it's the same woman? At that time she was riddled with consumption.'

'She kept up her cure for a few years.'

'Did she stay with Marcellin?'

'She hardly saw him, you know. She's very busy. She sent him a money order from time to time. Not large sums. He didn't need them.'

Monsieur Emile took a eucalyptus pill from a small box, and sucked it gravely.

'Used he to go and see her in Nice?'

'I don't think so. It's a high-class establishment. You probably know it.'

'Was it because of her that Marcellin came to the Midi?'

'I don't know. He was a queer fish.'

'Is Ginette in Nice at the moment?'

'She rang us up from Hyères this morning. She saw what happened from the papers. She's in Hyères seeing to the funeral.'

'Do you know where she's staying?'

'At the *Hôtel des Palmes*.'

'You were at the *Arche* the evening of the murder?'

'I went there for my *tisane*.'

'Did you leave before Marcellin?'

'Certainly. I never go to bed after ten o'clock.'

'Did you hear him speaking of me?'

'Perhaps. I paid no attention. I'm a bit hard of hearing.'

'What are your relations like with Charlot?'

'I know him, but I don't see a lot of him.'

'Why?'

Monsieur Emile was visibly striving to explain a delicate matter.

'We don't move in the same circles, if you see what I mean?'

'He's never worked for your mother?'

'He may once or twice have found staff for her.'

'Has he been going straight?'

'I think so.'

'Did Marcellin find people for you too?'

'No. He didn't go in for that.'

'You know nothing?'

'Nothing at all. I hardly concern myself with business matters any longer. My health won't allow me.'

What was Mr. Pyke thinking of all this? Are there Monsieur Emiles in England as well?

'I think I might go and have a chat with your mother.'

'You'll be very welcome, Inspector.'

Lechat was outside, this time in the company of a young man in white flannel trousers, a blue striped blazer, and a yachting cap.

'Monsieur Philippe de Moricourt,' he announced. 'He was just landing with the dinghy.'

'You wish to speak to me, Inspector?'

He was in his thirties, and contrary to what one might have expected, he wasn't even good-looking.

'I presume this is mere formality?'

'Sit down.'

'Is it essential? I loathe sitting down.'

'Stay standing up then. You're Mrs. Wilcox's secretary?'

'A nominal title, of course. Let us say that I am her guest and that, as between friends, I sometimes act as her secretary.'

'Is Mrs. Wilcox writing her memoirs?'

'No. Why do you ask?'

'Does she have anything to do with her whisky firm herself?'

'Nothing whatever.'

'Do you write her private letters?'

'I can't see what you are driving at.'

'At nothing at all, Monsieur Moricourt.'

'De Moricourt.'

'If you insist. I was only trying to get some idea of your work.'

'Mrs. Wilcox is no longer young.'

'Exactly.'

'I don't get you.'

'Never mind. Tell me, Monsieur de Moricourt – that's right, isn't it? – where you made Mrs. Wilcox's acquaintance?'

'Is this an interrogation?'

'It's whatever you like to call it.'

'Am I obliged to answer?'

'You can wait until I summon you formally.'

'Am I regarded as a suspect?'

'Everyone is suspect, and no one is.'

The young man considered for a few moments, threw his cigarette through the open doorway.

'I met her at the Casino at Cannes.'

'A long time ago?'

'A little over a year.'

'Are you a gambler?'

'I used to be. That's how I lost my money.'

'Did you have a lot?'

'The question strikes me as indiscreet.'

'Did you have a job before?'

'I was attached to the office of a minister.'

'Who was doubtless a friend of your family's?'

'How did you know?'

'Do you know young de Greef?'

'He's been on board several times, and we bought a canvas from him.'

'You mean that Mrs. Wilcox bought a canvas from him?'

'That's right. I beg your pardon.'

'Has Marcellin been on board the *North Star* as well?'

'Occasionally.'

'As a guest?'

'It's difficult to explain, Inspector. Mrs. Wilcox is a very generous person.'

'I imagine so.'

'Everything interests her, expecially in the Mediterranean which she loves, and it abounds in colourful characters. Marcellin was undeniably one himself.'

'He was given drinks?'

'Everyone is given drinks.'

'You were at the *Arche* on the night of the crime?'

'We were with the major.'

'Another colourful character, no doubt?'

'Mrs. Wilcox used to know him in England. It was a social connection.'

'Were you drinking champagne?'

'The major drinks nothing but champagne.'

'Were the three of you very merry?'

'We behaved perfectly well.'

'Did Marcellin join in with your party?'

'Everyone more or less joined in. You haven't met Major Bellam yet?'

'Doubtless it won't be long before I have that pleasure.'

'He's generosity itself. When he comes to the *Arche* . . .'

'And he often goes there?'

'That is correct. As I was saying, he seldom fails to offer drinks all round. Everyone comes to have a drink with him. He's been living on the island such a long time that he knows the children by their christian names.'

'So Marcellin came over to your table. He drank a glass of champagne.'

'No. He had a horror of champagne. He used to say it was only fit for girls. We had a bottle of white wine fetched up for him.'

'Did he sit down?'

'Of course.'

'There were other people seated at your table? Charlot for example?'

'Oh yes.'

'You know his profession, if one can use the term?'

'He doesn't try to hide the fact that he is a crook. He's a character too.'

'And, in that capacity, he was sometimes invited on board?'

'I don't think, Inspector, that there's anyone on the island who hasn't been.'

'Even Monsieur Emile?'

'Not him.'

'Why?'

'I don't know. I don't think we've ever even spoken to him. He's something of a hermit.'

'And he doesn't drink.'

'That's so.'

'Because you drink a lot, on board, don't you?'

'At times. I presume it's allowed?'

'Was Marcellin at your table when he started talking about me?'

'Probably. I don't remember exactly. He was telling stories, as usual. Mrs. Wilcox liked to hear him tell stories. He talked about his years in a penal settlement.'

'He never went to a penal settlement.'

'In that case, he invented it.'

'To amuse Mrs. Wilcox. So he talked about prison. And I was brought into the story? Was he drunk?'

'He was never entirely sober, especially in the evening. Wait. He said he had been convicted because of a woman.'

'Ginette?'

'Maybe. I seem to recall the name. It was then, I think, that he claimed that you had looked after her. Someone murmured:

' "Maigret—he's just a copper like the rest of them." Forgive me.'

'Not at all. Carry on.'

'That's all. At that he started singing your praises, saying you were a friend of his and that for him a friend was sacred. If I remember rightly, Charlot teased him and he became even more worked up.'

'Can you tell me exactly how it finished?'

'It's difficult. It was late.'

'Who was the first to leave?'

'I don't know. Paul had closed the shutters a long time before. He was sitting at our table. We had a final bottle. I think we left together.'

'Who?'

'The major left us in the square to go back to his villa. Charlot, who sleeps at the *Arche*, stayed behind. Mrs. Wilcox and I went off to the landing-stage, where we had left the dinghy.'

'Did you have a sailor with you?'

'No. We usually leave them on board. There was a strong *mistral* blowing and the sea was choppy. Marcellin offered to take us.'

'So he was with you when you set off?'

'Yes. He stayed on shore. He must have gone back to the hut.'

'In short, you and Mrs. Wilcox were the last people to see him alive?'

'Apart from the murderer.'

'Did you have difficulty getting back to the yacht?'

'How did you know?'

'You told me the sea was rough.'

'We arrived soaking wet, with six inches of water in the dinghy.'

'Did you go straight to bed?'

'I made some grog to warm us up, after which we played a game of gin rummy.'

'I beg your pardon?'

'It's a card game.'

'What time was this?'

'Around two in the morning. We never go to bed early.'

'You didn't hear or see anything unusual?'

'The *mistral* prevented us from hearing anything.'

'Are you thinking of coming to the *Arche* this evening?'

'Probably.'

'Thank you.'

Maigret and Mr. Pyke remained alone together for a moment or two, and the chief inspector gazed at his colleague with large, sleepy eyes. He had the feeling that it was all futile, that he ought to have tackled it differently. For example, he would have liked to be on the square, in the sunshine, smoking his pipe and watching the bowls players, who had started a big match; he would have liked to roam about the harbour watching the fishermen repairing their nets; he would have liked to know all the Gallis and the Morins whom Lechat had just touched on in conversation with him.

'I believe that in your country, Mr. Pyke, investigations are carried out in a very orderly fashion, aren't they?'

'It all depends. For example, after a crime committed two years ago near Brighton, one of my colleagues stayed eleven weeks in an inn, spending his days fishing and his evenings drinking ale with the locals.'

That was exactly what Maigret would have liked to do, and what he was not doing on account of this very Mr. Pyke! When Lechat came in, he was in a bad temper.

'The major wouldn't come,' he announced. 'He's in his garden, doing nothing. I told him you asked him to step along here. He replied that if you wanted to see him, you had only to go and drink a bottle with him.'

'He's within his rights.'

'Who do you want to question now?'

'Nobody. I'd like you to telephone to Hyères. I presume there is a telephone at the *Arche*? Ask for Ginette, at the *Hôtel des Palmes*. Tell her from me that I would be glad if she would come and have a chat with me.'

'Where shall I find you?'

'I don't know. Probably at the harbour.'

They walked slowly across the square, Mr. Pyke and he, and people followed them with their eyes. One might have thought it was with some distrust, but it was only that they didn't know how to behave in the presence of the famous Maigret. The latter, on his side, felt an *estranger*, as they say locally. But he knew that it would not take much for every one of them to start talking freely, perhaps too freely.

'Don't you find you have the impression of being miles away, Mr. Pyke? Look! That's France you can see over there, twenty minutes away by boat, and I'm as lost as if I were in the heart of Africa or South America.'

Some children stopped playing, so as to examine them. They reached the Grand Hotel, came in sight of the harbour, and Inspector Lechat was back with them already.

'I couldn't get her on the line,' he announced. 'She's left.'

'Has she gone back to Nice?'

'Probably not, as she told the hotel that she'd be back tomorrow morning in time for the burial.'

The jetty, the small boats of all colours, the big yacht blocking the harbour, the *North Star*, far out, near a rocky promontory, and people watching another boat arriving:

'That's the *Cormorant*,' Lechat explained. 'In other words, it's just on five o'clock.'

A youth, with a cap bearing the words *Grand Hôtel* in gold letters, was waiting for the guests-to-be beside a barrow intended for luggage. The small white boat approached, with silvered moustaches given it by the sea, and Maigret was not long in spotting, in the bows, a female figure.

'Probably Ginette, coming to meet you,' the inspector said. 'Every-one at Hyères must know you are here.'

It was a strange sensation to see the people in the boat, slowly grow-ing in size, becoming more clearly defined as on a photographic plate. Above all, it was distressing to see a woman, with Ginette's features, very fat, very respectable, all in silk, all made up, and, no doubt, heavily scented.

Truth to tell, when Maigret had met her in the *Brasserie des Ternes*, was he not himself more slim, and wasn't she feeling at that moment just as disappointed as he, while she watched him from the deck of the *Cormorant*?

She had to be helped down the gangway. Apart from her there was no one on board besides Baptiste, the captain, except the dumb sailor and the postman. The lad with the gold-braided cap tried to take possession of her luggage.

'To the *Arche de Noé*!' she said.

She went up to Maigret, hesitated, perhaps on account of Mr. Pyke, whom she didn't know.

'They told me you were here. I thought you might like to speak to me. Poor Marcel! . . .'

She didn't say Marcellin, like the others. She didn't affect any great sorrow. She had become a mature person, sober and calm, with a glimmer of a slightly disillusioned smile.

'Are you staying at the *Arche* as well?'

It was Lechat who took her case. She seemed to know the island and walked quietly, without haste, like one who easily gets out of breath, or who isn't made for the open air.

'*Le Petit Var* says it's because he mentioned you that he was killed. Do you believe it?'

Now and again she cast a glance, at once curious and anxious, at Mr. Pyke.

'You can talk in front of him. He's a friend, an English colleague who's come to stay a few days with me.'

She gave the Scotland Yard man a very ladylike smile and sighed with a glance at the stout profile of the chief-inspector:

'I've changed, haven't I?'

IV

It was strange to see her overcome with a feeling of modesty, and holding her dress tight against her because the stairway was steep and Maigret was coming up behind her.

She had come into the *Arche* as she would into her own house, had said in the most natural way in the world:

'Have you a room left for me, Paul?'

'You'll have to put up with the little room beside the bathroom.'

Then she had turned to Maigret.

'Would you like to come up for a moment, Inspector?'

These words would have had a double meaning in the house she ran at Nice, but not here. None the less she showed her scorn for Maigret's hesitation, who was keeping up his game of hiding nothing of the case from Mr. Pyke. For a moment, her smile was almost professional.

'I'm not dangerous, you know.'

For some extraordinary reason, the Scotland Yard inspector spoke English, perhaps out of delicacy. He said only one work, to his French colleague.

'*Please. . . .*'

On the stairway Jojo went in front with the suitcase. She wore a very short dress and you could see the pink slip enveloping her little behind. No doubt that was what had given Ginette the idea of holding her dress tightly against her.

Apart from the bed there was only a straw-bottomed chair to sit on, for it was the smallest of the rooms, poorly lighted by one attic window. Ginette took off her hat, sank onto the edge of the bed with a sigh of relief and immediately removed her extremely high-heeled shoes, and through the silk of her stockings, caressed her aching toes.

'Are you annoyed that I asked you to come upstairs? There's no place to talk downstairs, and I hadn't the energy to walk. Look at my ankles: they're all swollen. You can smoke your pipe, Inspector.'

She was not completely at her ease. It was obvious that she was talking for the sake of talking, to gain time.

'Are you very cross with me?'

Although he understood, he gained time himself as well, by countering:

'What about?'

'I know perfectly well that you're disappointed. But it isn't really my fault. Thanks to you, I spent the happiest years of my life in the san. I didn't have anything to worry about. There was a doctor rather like you who was extremely kind to me. He brought me books. I used to read all day. Before going there I was ignorant. Then, when there was something I couldn't understand, he would explain it to me. Have you got a cigarette? Never mind. Besides, it's better for me not to smoke. . . .

'I stayed five years at the san, and I had come to believe I'd spend my whole life there. I liked the idea. Unlike the others, I had no desire to go out.

'When they told me I was cured and could go, I can tell you I was more afraid than glad. From where we were, we could see the valley almost always covered with a kind of mist, sometimes with thick clouds, and I was afraid of going down into it again. I would have liked to have stayed as a nurse, but I hadn't the necessary knowledge, and I wasn't strong enough to do the housework or be a kitchen maid.

'What could I have done, down there? I had got into the habit of having three meals a day. I knew that with Justine I should have that.'

'Why did you come today?' asked Maigret in a rather cold voice.

'Haven't I just told you? I first went to Hyères. I didn't want the poor Marcel to be buried without anyone to follow the hearse.'

'Were you still in love with him?'

She showed slight embarrassment.

'I think I really was in love with him, you know. I talked about him a lot to you, in the old days, when you took me up after his arrest. He wasn't a bad man, you know. Underneath he was really rather innocent, I'd even say shy. And just because he was shy he wanted to be like the others. Only he exaggerated. Up there I understood everything.'

'And you stopped loving him?'

'I didn't love him any more in the same way. I saw other people. I could make comparisons. The doctor helped me to understand.'

'Were you in love with the doctor?'

She laughed, a little nervously.

'I think in a sanatorium people are always more or less in love with their doctors.'

'Did Marcel write to you?'

'Now and then.'

'Was he hoping to take up the old life with you again?'

'At first, yes, I think so. Then he changed, too. We didn't change in the same way, the two of us. He grew old very quickly, almost overnight. I don't know if you saw him again. Before, he was smart, particular about his appearance. He was proud. It all started when he came to the Riviera, quite by chance.'

'Was it he who made you go into service with Justine and Emile?'

'No. I knew Justine by name. I applied to her. She took me on trial, as an assistant manageress, as I wasn't fit for anything else. I was operated on four times up there, and my body is covered with scars.'

'I asked you why you had come today.'

He came relentlessly back to this question.

'When I found out that you were on the case, I thought you would remember me and try to get hold of me. That would probably have taken some time.'

'If I understand you correctly, since you came out of the sanatorium you had no further relations with Marcel, but you sent him money orders?'

'Occasionally. I wanted him to enjoy himself a little. He wouldn't show it but he went through some bad patches.'

'Did he tell you so?'

'He told me he was a failure, that he always had been a failure, and that he hadn't even been able to become a real crook.'

'Was it in Nice that he told you this?'

'He never came to see me at the *Sirènes*. He knew it was forbidden.'

'Here?'

'Yes.'

'Do you often come to Porquerolles?'

'Nearly every month. Justine's too old, now, to inspect her establishments herself. Monsieur Emile has never liked travelling.'

'Do you sleep here, at the *Arche*?'

'Always.'

'Why doesn't Justine give you a room? The villa is large enough.'

'She never has women sleeping under her roof.'

He sensed that he was reaching the sensitive spot, but Ginette wasn't giving in completely yet.

'Is she afraid for her son?' he asked jokingly, as he lit a fresh pipe.

'Strange though it may seem, it's the truth. She has always made him live tied to her apron strings and that is why he has got a girl's character rather than a man's. At his age she still treats him like a child. He can't do anything without her permission.'

'Does he like women?'

'He's more afraid of them. I mean in general. He's not keen, you know. He's never had good health. He spends his time looking after himself, taking pills, reading medical books.'

'What else is there, Ginette?'

'What do you mean?'

'Why have you come here today?'

'But I've told you.'

'No.'

'I thought you would be wondering about Monsieur Emile and his mother.'

'Explain.'

'You aren't like the other detectives, but even so! When something fishy happens, it's always people of a certain type that are suspected.'

'And you intended to tell me that Monsieur Emile has nothing to do with Marcel's death?'

'I wanted to explain to you . . .'

'Explain what?'

'We remained good friends, Marcel and me, but there was no question of living together. He no longer thought about that. I don't think he even wanted it. Do you understand? He was enjoying the kind of life he had made for himself. He no longer had any relations with the underworld. Look, I saw Charlot, just now . . .'

'You know him?'

'I've met him here several times. We even ate occasionally at the same table. He's found girls for me.'

'Were you expecting him to be at Porquerolles today?'

'No. I swear I'm speaking the truth. It's your way of putting questions that upsets me. Before, you used to trust me. You were even a little sorry for me. It's true I've no longer anything to be sorry about, have I? I haven't got T.B. now!'

'Do you make a lot of money?'

'Not as much as you might think. Justine is very tight-fisted. So is her son. I don't go without anything, of course. I even put a little aside, but not enough to retire on.'

'You were telling me about Marcel.'

'I can't remember what I was saying. Oh yes! How can I explain? When you knew him he used to try to play the tough guy. In Paris he was always going to bars where you meet people like Charlot, and even killers. He wanted to look as though he belonged to their gangs and they didn't take him seriously . . .'

'He was a half-in-half, eh?'

'Well, he grew out of it. He grew up seeing those types, and lived in his boat or in his hut. He drank a lot. He always found some means of getting a drink. My money orders used to help him. I know what people think when a man like him is killed . . .'

'That is?'

'You know it, too. People imagine it's an underworld affair, a settling of accounts, or a revenge. But that isn't the case.'

'That's what you really came to say, isn't it?'

'For the last few minutes I've lost my train of thought. You've changed so much! I'm sorry. I don't mean physically . . .'

He smiled, in spite of himself, at her confusion.

'In the old days, even in your office in the Quai des Orfèvres, you didn't remind one of a policeman.'

'You're really afraid that I'm going to suspect the old lags? You aren't in love with Charlot, by any chance?'

'Certainly not. I'd be pretty hard put to it to be in love with anyone after all the operations I've been through. I'm not a woman any more, if you must know. And Charlot doesn't interest me any more than the others.'

'Tell me the rest now.'

'What makes you think there is anything else? I give you my word of honour that I don't know who killed poor Marcel.'

'But you know who didn't kill him.'

'Yes.'

'You know whom I might be led to suspect.'

'After all, you'll find out for yourself one of these days, if you haven't already done so. I would have said so to start off with if you hadn't questioned me so dryly. I'm going to marry Monsieur Emile. There!'

MY FRIEND MAIGRET

'When?'

'When Justine dies.'

'Why do you have to wait until she isn't there any more? '

'I tell you she's jealous of all women. It's because of her that he hasn't married or ever been known to have any mistresses. When, from time to time, he needed a woman, it was she who chose him the least dangerous one, and she never ceased giving him advice. Now all that's over.'

'For whom?'

'For him, of course!'

'And yet he's still contemplating marriage?'

'Because he has a horror of being left alone. As long as his mother is alive, he is content. She looks after him like a baby. But she hasn't much time left. A year at the outside.'

'Did the doctor say so?'

'She's got cancer and she is too old to have an operation. As for him he always imagines he's going to die. He has fits of breathlessness several times a day, doesn't dare stir, as if the least movement might be fatal . . .'

'So he's asked you to marry him?'

'Yes. He made sure I was fit enough to look after him. He's even had me examined by several doctors. Needless to say Justine knows nothing, or she would have thrown me out a long time ago.'

'And Marcel?'

'I told him.'

'What was his reaction?'

'None. He thought I was right to provide for my old age. I think it pleased him to know that I would come to live here.'

'Monsieur Emile wasn't jealous of Marcel?'

'Why would he have been jealous? I've already told you there was nothing between us any more.'

'In short, this is what you were so anxious to talk to me about?'

'I thought of all the assumptions you would arrive at which don't correspond with reality.'

'For example that Marcel might have been able to blackmail Monsieur Emile, and the latter, to get him out of the way . . .'

'Marcel never blackmailed anyone, and Monsieur Emile would rather die of hunger than strangle a chicken!'

'Of course you haven't been onto the island these last few days?'

'It's easy to check up.'

'Because you hadn't left the house in Nice, had you? It's an excellent alibi.'

'Do I need one?'

'According to what you said just now, I am speaking as a policeman. Marcel, despite everything, could have been in your way. Especially as

Monsieur Emile is a big fish, a very big fish. Supposing he does marry you, he would leave you, on his death, a considerable fortune.'

'Quite considerable, yes! I wonder now if I was right to come. I wasn't expecting you to speak to me like that. I've admitted everything to you, frankly.'

Her eyes were shining, as though she were on the verge of tears, and it was an old face, badly patched up and disfigured with a childish pout, that Maigret beheld.

'You can do what you like. I don't know who killed Marcel. It's a catastrophe.'

'Especially for him.'

'For him too, yes. But he's at rest. Are you going to arrest me?'

She had said this with the shadow of a smile, although one could feel that she was anxious, more serious than she wanted to appear.

'For the moment I have no such intention.'

'Can I go to the funeral tomorrow morning? If you like, I'll come straight back afterwards. All you have to do is send a boat for me at Giens Point.'

'Perhaps.'

'You won't say anything to Justine?'

'Not before it's strictly necessary and I don't envisage the necessity.'

'Are you cross with me?'

'Of course not.'

'Yes. I felt it straight away, before leaving the *Cormorant*, from the moment I saw you. I recognized you. I was moved, because it was a whole period of my life coming back to me.'

'A period you regret?'

'Perhaps. I don't know. I sometimes wonder.'

She rose with a sigh, without putting on her shoes again. She wanted to unlace her stays and was waiting for the chief-inspector to leave before doing so.

'You must do as you wish,' she sighed finally, as he was putting his hand to the door knob.

And he felt something like a pang at leaving her all alone, aging, anxious, in the little bedroom into which the setting sun penetrated through the attic window, casting everywhere, on the painted wallpaper and the counterpane, a pink hue, like rouge.

'A white wine, Monsieur Maigret!'

Noise, all of a sudden, and movement. The bowls players, who had finished their game on the square, were crowding round the bar and speaking at the tops of their voices, with strong accents. In the corner of the dining-room, near the window, Mr. Pyke was at a table opposite Jef de Greef, and the two men were deeply engrossed in a game of chess.

Beside them, on the bench, Anna was sitting smoking a cigarette at the end of a long cigarette-holder. She had dressed. She wore a little cotton frock under which one sensed she was as naked as beneath her sunsuit. She had a well-rounded body, extremely feminine, so expressly made for caressing that despite oneself one imagined her in bed.

De Greef had put on a pair of grey flannel trousers and a sailor's jersey with blue and white stripes. On his feet he wore rope-soled espadrilles, like practically everyone else on the island, and they were the first thing that strict Mr. Pyke had bought.

Maigret looked round for the inspector, but didn't see him. He was obliged to accept the glass of wine which Paul was pushing towards him, and the people at the bar squeezed themselves together to make room for him.

'Well, Inspector?'

They were appealing to him, and he knew that in a few minutes the ice would be broken. Probably the islanders had been waiting ever since the morning for this particular moment to make his acquaintance? There was quite a crowd of them, about ten at the least, most of them in fishermen's clothes. Two or three had a more bourgeois look, probably retired on a modest income.

Never mind what Mr. Pyke might think. He had to have a drink.

'You like our island wine?'

'Very much.'

'But the papers claim you only drink beer. Marcellin said it wasn't true, that you didn't pull a face at a jug of calvados. Poor Marcellin! Your health, Inspector . . .'

Paul, the *patron*, who knew how these things develop, kept the bottle in his hand.

'It's true, he was a friend of yours?'

'I knew him once, yes. He wasn't a bad fellow.'

'Certainly not. Are the papers right, too, when they say he came from Le Havre?'

'Certainly.'

'With his accent?'

'When I knew him, some fifteen years ago, he hadn't got any accent.'

'You hear that, Titin? What have I always said?'

Four rounds . . . five rounds . . . and words being bandied about rather at random, for the sake of saying them, like children throwing balls into the air.

'What do you feel like eating this evening, Inspector? There is *bouillabaisse*, of course. But perhaps you don't like *bouillabaisse*?'

He swore that he liked nothing better, and everyone was delighted. It wasn't the moment to get to know personally the people who surrounded him and formed a rather confused mass.

'You like *pastis* as well, the real stuff, which is banned? A *pastis* all round, Paul! I insist! The inspector won't say anything . . .'

Charlot was sitting on the terrace, with a *pastis* in front of him, busy reading a paper.

'Have you got any ideas yet?'

'Ideas about what?'

'Well, about the murderer! Morin-Barbu, who was born on the island and hasn't left it for seventy-seven years, has never heard of anything like it. There have been people drowned. A woman from the North, five or six years back, tried to do away with herself by swallowing sleeping tablets. An Italian sailor, in the course of an argument, stabbed Baptiste in the arm. But a crime, never, Inspector! Here even the bad ones become as gentle as lambs.'

Everybody there was laughing, trying to talk, for what counted was to talk, to say anything, chat over your drink with the famous inspector.

'You'll understand better when you've been here a few days. What you ought to do is to come and spend your holidays here with your wife. We'd teach you to play bowls. Isn't that right, Casimir? Casimir won the *Petit Provençal* championship last year, and you know what that means.'

From the pink it had been a short while ago, the church at the far end of the square was becoming violet; the sky was gently turning a pale green and the men began to depart one after the other; now and again a shrill woman's voice could be heard calling in the distance:

'Hey, Jules! . . . The soup's ready . . .'

Or else a small boy would come boldly in to look for his father and pull him by the hand.

'Well, aren't we going to have a game?'

'It's too late.'

It was explained to Maigret that after the game of bowls it was cards, but that the latter hadn't taken place because of him. The sailor from the *Cormorant*, a dumb colossus with immense bare feet, who smiled at the chief-inspector with all his teeth, now and again raised his glass and made a strange gobbling noise which took the place of: '*Here's to you!*'

'Do you want to eat straight away?'

'Have you seen the inspector?'

'He went out while you were upstairs. He didn't say anything. That's his way. He's marvellous, you know. In the three days he's been ferreting about the island, he knows almost as much as I do about all the families.'

Leaning forward, Maigret could see that the de Greefs had left and the Englishman was alone in front of the chessboard.

'We eat in half an hour,' he announced.

Paul asked him in a low voice, indicating the Scotland Yard detective:

'Do you think he likes our cooking?'

A few minutes later Maigret and his colleague went out for a walk and, quite naturally, walked towards the harbour. They had fallen into

9

the habit. The sun had disappeared, and there was a feeling, as it were, of an immense release in the air. The noises were no longer the same. One could hear the faint lapping of the water against the stone of the jetty, and the stone had become a harder grey, like the rocks. The greenery was dark, almost black, mysterious, and a torpedo boat with a huge number painted in white on the hull slid silently towards the open sea, at what appeared to be a giddy speed.

'I just beat him,' Mr. Pyke had declared at the outset. 'He's very good, very much his own master.'

'It was he that suggested the game?'

'I had taken the chessmen, to practise' (he didn't add: while you were upstairs with Ginette), 'not expecting to find an opponent. He sat down at the next table with his girl friend and I realized, from his way of looking at the pieces, that he wanted to pit his wits against mine.'

After this there had been a long silence and now the two men were strolling along the jetty. Near the white yacht there was a little boat, the name of which could be seen on the stern: '*Fleur d'amour.*'

It was de Greef's boat, and the couple were on board. There was a light under the roof, in a cabin just wide enough for two, where it was impossible to stand up. A noise of spoons and crockery was coming from within. A meal was in progress.

When the detectives had passed the yacht, Mr. Pyke spoke again, slowly, with his habitual precision.

'He's the sort of son good families hate to have. Actually you can't have many specimens in France.'

Maigret was quite taken aback, for it was the first time, since he had known him, that his colleague had expressed general ideas. Mr. Pyke seemed a little embarrassed himself, as though overcome with shame.

'What makes you think we have hardly any in France?'

'I mean not of that type, exactly.'

He picked his words with great care, standing still at the end of the jetty, facing the mountains which could be seen on the mainland.

'I rather think that in your country, a boy from a good family can commit some *bêtises*, as you say, so as to have a good time, to enjoy himself with women or cars, or to gamble in the casino. Do your bad boys play chess? I doubt it. Do they read Kant, Schopenhauer, Nietzsche and Kierkegaard? It's unlikely, isn't it? They only want to live their life without waiting for their inheritance.'

They leant against the wall which ran along one side of the jetty, and the calm surface of the water was occasionally troubled by a fish jumping.

'De Greef does not belong to that category of bad characters. I don't think he even wants to have money. He's almost a pure anarchist. He has revolted against everything he has known, against everything he's been taught, against his magistrate of a father and his bourgeois mother, against his home town, against the customs of his own country.'

He broke off, half-blushing.

'I beg your pardon . . .'

'Go on, please.'

'We only exchanged a few words, the two of us, but I think I have understood him, because there are a lot of young people like that in my country, in all countries, probably, where morals are very strict. That's why I said just now that one probably doesn't come across a vast number of that type in France. Here there isn't any hypocrisy. Perhaps there isn't enough.'

Was he alluding to the surroundings, the world the two of them had been plunged in since their arrival, to the Monsieur Emiles, the Charlots, the Ginettes, who lived among the others without being singled out for opprobrium?

Maigret felt a little anxious, a little piqued. Without being attacked, he was stung by an urge to defend himself.

'By way of protest,' pursued Mr. Pyke, 'these young people reject everything *en bloc*, the good and the bad. Look, he has taken a young girl away from her family. She's sweet, very desirable. I don't think, however, that it was from desire for her that he did it. It was because she belonged to a good family, because she was a girl who used to go to Mass every Sunday with her mother. It was because her father is probably an austere and high-minded gentleman. Also because he was taking a big risk in carrying her off. But, of course, I may be quite wrong.'

'I don't think so.'

'There are some people who, when in a clean and elegant setting, feel the need to defile. De Greef feels the need to defile life, to defile anything. And even to defile his girl friend.'

This time Maigret was astounded. He was bowled over, as they say, for he realized that Mr. Pyke had been thinking the same thing as he had. When de Greef had admitted having been several times on board the *North Star*, it had immediately occurred to him that it was not only to drink, but that more intimate and less admissible relations existed between the two couples.

'They are very dangerous fellows,' Mr. Pyke concluded.

He added:

'Perhaps they are very unhappy too?'

Then, probably finding the silence a little too solemn, he said in a lighter tone:

'He speaks perfect English, you know. He hasn't even got an accent. I shouldn't be surprised if he went to one of our public schools.'

It was time to go to dinner. It was long past the half-hour. The darkness was almost complete, and the boats in the harbour were swaying to the rhythm of the sea's breathing. Maigret emptied his pipe and knocked it against his heel, hesitated to fill another. Going past, he studied the Dutchman's little boat closely.

Had Mr. Pyke just spoken for the sake of speaking? Had he, in his own way, wanted to convey some sort of message?

It was difficult, if not impossible, to tell. His French was perfect, too perfect, and yet the two men did not speak the same language, their thoughts followed different channels in their passage through the brain.

'They're very dangerous, those fellows,' the Scotland Yard inspector had emphasized.

There was no doubt that he would not have wished, for anything in the world, even to appear to be intervening in Maigret's case. He hadn't asked him any questions about what had happened in Ginette's room. Was he under the impression that his colleague was hiding something from him, that Maigret was trying to cheat? Or worse still, after what he had just said about the customs of the French, did he imagine that Maigret and Ginette . . .?

The chief-inspector grunted:

'She told me of her engagement to Monsieur Emile. It has to be kept secret, because of old Justine, who would attempt to stop the marriage, even after her death.'

He noticed that by contrast with the telling phrases of Mr. Pyke his speech was vague, his ideas even vaguer.

In a few words the Englishman had said what he had to say. From half an hour spent with de Greef, he had formulated definite ideas, not only about the latter, but on the world in general.

As for Maigret he would have been hard put to it to express a single idea. It was quite different. He sensed something. He sensed a whole heap of things, as he always did at the start of a case, but he couldn't have said in what form this mist of ideas would sooner or later resolve itself.

It was rather humiliating. It was a loss of face. He felt himself heavy and dull-witted beside the clear silhouette of his colleague.

'She's a strange girl,' he mumbled, in spite of everything.

That was all he could find to say of someone he had met before, whose whole life-story he almost knew, and who had spoken to him openly.

A strange girl! She attracted him in some ways, and in others, she disappointed him, as she had herself sensed perfectly well.

Perhaps, later on, he would have a definite opinion about her?

After a single game of chess and a few remarks exchanged over the board, Mr. Pyke had made a definitive analysis of his opponent's character.

Was it not as though the Englishman had won the first rubber?

V

He had thought about the smell straight away, when he still imagined he was going to go to sleep at once. In actual fact, there were several smells. The principal one, the smell of the house, which one sniffed immediately on crossing the threshold of the café, he had been trying to analyse since that morning, for it was a smell which was unfamiliar to him. It struck him every time as he went in, and, each time, he would dilate his nostrils. There was a basis of wine of course, with a touch of *anis*, then the kitchen odours. And, since it was a Mediterranean kitchen, with foundations of garlic, red peppers, oil and saffron, this made it differ from the usual smells.

But what was the point of worrying about all this? His eyes closed, he wanted to sleep. It was no use calling to mind all the Marseillais or Provençal restaurants where he happened to have eaten, in Paris or elsewhere. The smell wasn't the same, let it rest at that. All he had to do was sleep. He had had enough to drink to plunge into a leaden sleep.

Hadn't he been to sleep, immediately after lying down? The window was open and a noise had intrigued him; he had finally realized it was the rustling of leaves in the trees on the square.

Strictly speaking, the smell downstairs could be compared with that of a small bar, in Cannes, kept by a fat woman, where he had once been on a case and had idled away many hours.

The one in the bedroom was unlike anything. What was there in the mattress? Was it, as in Brittany, seaweed, which gave off the iodized smell of the sea? Other people had been in the bed before him, and he thought at odd moments that he could detect the smell of oil with which women smear themselves before sunbathing.

He turned over heavily. It was at least the tenth time, and there was still someone about, opening a door, walking down the passage and going into one of the lavatories. There was nothing extraordinary about that, but it seemed to him that far more people were going there than there were in the house. Then he began counting the occupants of the *Arche*. Paul and his wife slept over his head, in an attic which one reached by a sort of ladder. As for Jojo, he didn't know where she slept. At any rate there was no room for her on the first floor.

She, too, had a special smell of her own. It came partly from her oiled hair, partly from her body and clothes, and it was at once vague and spicy, not at all disagreeable. This smell had distracted him while she was talking to him.

Another case where Mr. Pyke might have thought Maigret was cheating. The chief-inspector had gone up to his bedroom for a moment, after dinner, to wash his teeth and hands. He had left the door open, and without his hearing, her feet making no sound on the floor, Jojo had come in and stood framed in the doorway. How old could she be? Sixteen? Twenty? She had the look, at once admiring and timorous, of girls who go to the stage-doors of theatres to beg for autographs. Maigret impressed her, because he was famous.

'Have you got something to say to me, my girl?'

She had closed the door behind her, which he hadn't liked, for you never know what people will think. He was not forgetting that there was an Englishman in the house.

'It's about Marcellin,' she went on to say, blushing. 'He talked to me one afternoon when he was very drunk and took his siesta on the café bench.'

Well! Not so long ago, too, when the *Arche* was empty, he had seen someone stretched out on the same bench, a newspaper over his face, taking a short nap. It was evidently a cool spot. An odd house, even so! As for the smell . . .

'I thought it might be of some use to you. He told me that, if he wanted, he could have a pile as big as that.'

'A pile of what?'

'Of bank-notes, of course.'

'A long time ago?'

'I think it was two days before what happened.'

'There wasn't anyone else in the café?'

'I was alone, polishing the counter.'

'Did you tell anyone about it?'

'I don't think so.'

'He didn't say anything else?'

'Only: "*What would I do with it, my little Jojo? It's so nice here.*" '

'He never made love to you, never made any proposals?'

'No.'

'And the others?'

'Nearly all of them.'

'When Ginette was here — she came almost every month, didn't she? — did Marcellin ever happen to go up to see her in her bedroom?'

'Certainly not. He was very respectful towards her.'

'Can I speak to you like a grown-up, Jojo?'

'I'm nineteen, you know.'

'Good. Did Marcellin have relations with women, now and again?'

'Certainly.'

'On the island?'

'With Nine, to start with. That's my cousin. She does it with every-body. It seems she can't help it.'

'On board his boat?'

'Anywhere. Then with the widow Lambert, who keeps the café on the other side of the square. He would sometimes spend the night with her. Whenever he caught some sea-wolves, he would bring them to her.'

I suppose, now he's dead, I can tell you: Marcellin fished with dyna-
mite.'

'There was never any question of his marrying the widow Lambert?'

'I don't think she wants to remarry.'

And Jojo's smile let it be understood that the widow Lambert was no
ordinary person.

'Is that all, Jojo?'

'Yes. I'd better be going down again.'

Ginette wasn't asleep either. She lay in the next room, just behind the
partition, so that Maigret had the impression that he could hear her
breathing. It made him feel uncomfortable because when he turned
over, half-asleep, he sometimes banged the partition with his elbow
and each time that must have made her jump.

It had been a very long time before she went off to sleep. What could
she have been doing? Seeing to her face or her toilet? The silence at
times was so profound in her bedroom that Maigret wondered if she
was in the middle of writing something. Especially as the attic window
was too high for her to be able to lean out and breathe the fresh air.

The famous smell again. . . . It was, quite simply, the smell of
Porquerolles. He had caught it at the end of the jetty, a short while ago,
with Mr. Pyke. There were whiffs of smells from the water, overheated
by the sun during the day and others coming from the land, with the
breeze. Weren't the trees in the square eucalyptus? There were probably other natural scents on the island.

Who was it going down the passage again? Mr. Pyke? It was the
third time. Paul's cooking, for which he was so ill acclimatized, must
have upset him.

He had drunk a lot, had Mr. Pyke. Was it from choice, or because he
had been unable to do otherwise? At all events he liked champagne and
Maigret had never thought of offering him any. He had drunk it all
evening with the major. They got on so well together from the start,
that one might have thought they had always known one another. They
had settled themselves in a corner. On instructions, Jojo had brought
champagne.

Bellam didn't drink it in champagne glasses, but in large ones, like
beer glasses. He was so perfect that he looked like a drawing in *Punch*,
with his silvery grey hair, his rosy complexion, large clear eyes swimming in liquid, and the huge cigar which never left his lips.

He was an old boy of seventy or seventy-two years, with a mis-
chievous twinkle in his eye. His voice, probably because of the champagne and the cigars, was husky. Even after several bottles, he maintained an affecting dignity.

'May I introduce Major Bellam?' Mr. Pyke had said at a certain
moment. 'It turns out we were at the same school.'

Not the same year, at all events, nor the same decade. One could feel that this gave them both pleasure. The major called the chief-inspector 'Monsieur Maigrette'.

From time to time he would give an almost imperceptible signal to Jojo or Paul, which was enough for them to bring fresh champagne to the table. At other times, a different sign would bring Jojo, who would pour out a glass, and take it over to someone in the room.

This might have had something haughty or condescending about it. The major did it so charmingly, so naïvely, that it gave no offence. He looked a little as if he were distributing good marks. When the glass had arrived at its destination, he raised his own and drank a silent toast from where he sat.

Everyone, or almost everyone, dropped in. Charlot, almost the whole evening, had been working the crane. He had started off by playing with the fruit machine and he could allow himself to spend as much as he liked since it was he who collected the kitty. The crane must have belonged to him as well. He fitted a coin into the slot, and with sustained concentration turned the knob, directing the small chromium pincers towards a cheap cigarette-case, or a pipe, or a wallet from a bazaar.

Was Ginette not sleeping because she was worried? Had Maigret been too harsh with her? In the bedroom, yes, he had been hard. It was not out of spite, as might have been thought. Had she thought it was out of spite?

It is always ridiculous to play the Good Samaritan. He had picked her up in the Place des Ternes and had sent her off to the sanatorium. He had never told himself he was saving a soul, that he was 'snatching a girl from the gutter'.

Someone else, 'who was like him', as she had told him, had looked after her in his turn: the doctor at the sanatorium. Had he been hoping for something?

She had become what she had become. That was her affair. He had no reason to take offence, to resent it with bitterness.

He had been hard because it had been a necessity, because that type of woman, even the least wicked of them, lie as they breathe, sometimes without any need, without any reason. And she hadn't told him everything yet, he was sure. So much so that she couldn't get to sleep. There was something on her mind.

Once, she got up. He heard her bare feet on the floor of the room. Was she going to come and find him? There was nothing impossible about that, and Maigret had prepared himself mentally to hurry into his trousers which he had left lying on the floor.

She hadn't come. There had been the clink of a glass. She was thirsty. Or else she had taken a sleeping pill.

He had only drunk one glass of champagne. The rest of the time he had drunk mostly wine, then, God knows why, *anisette*.

Who had ordered *anisette*? Oh yes, it was the dentist. A retired dentist, to be precise, whose name escaped him. Another phenomenon. There were nothing but phenomena on the island, at the *Arche* at any rate. Or perhaps was it they who were right and the people on the other side of the water, on the mainland, who were wrong to behave otherwise?

He must once have been very respectable, very well groomed, for he had a dentist's surgery in one of the smartest districts of Bordeaux, and the people of Bordeaux are particular. He had come to Porquerolles by chance, on holiday, and since then he had only left for a week, the time it took to go and wind up his affairs.

He wore no collar. It was one of the Morins, a fisherman, who cut his hair once a month. That Morin was called Morin-Coiffeur. The ex-dentist's beard was at least three days old, and he neglected his hands, he neglected everything, didn't do anything, except read, in a rocking chair, in the shade of his veranda.

He had married a girl on the island who had perhaps been pretty but who had very quickly become enormous, with the shadow of a moustache on her lip and a strident voice.

He was happy. Or so he claimed. He would say with a disconcerting assurance:

'You'll see! If you stay long enough, you'll be bitten, like the others. And then you won't go away again.'

Maigret knew that, on certain of the Pacific islands, white people sometimes let themselves go like that, go native, as they say, but he didn't know it was possible three miles from the French coast.

When someone was mentioned to the dentist, he only judged them in terms of the extent to which they had gone native. He called it something else. He said: Porquerollitis.

The doctor? For there was a doctor, too, whom Maigret had not yet met, but Lechat had mentioned him. Infected to the bone, according to the dentist.

'I presume you are friends?'

'We never see one another. We pass the time of day, at a distance.'

True, the doctor had arrived with his preoccupations. He was very ill and had only settled in the island to cure himself. He was a bachelor. He lived alone in a poky little house with a garden full of flowers and he did his own housework. Indoors, it was very dirty. On account of his health, he didn't go out in the evenings, even in cases of emergency, and, in winter, if it happened to be really cold, which was rare, days and sometimes weeks would go by without his white nose being seen.

'You'll see! You'll see!' the dentist insisted with a sarcastic smile. 'Besides, you've already got some idea of what it is by looking around you. Just think, it's the same every evening.'

And it was indeed a curious spectacle. It wasn't quite the atmosphere of a café, nor was it that of a drawing-room. The disorder called to mind a soirée in an artist's studio.

9*

Everyone knew everyone else and people didn't stand on ceremony for each other. The major, who came from a leading English school, was here on the same footing as a dockside loafer like Marcellin, or as a Charlot.

From time to time, someone would change places, or partners.

To start with, Monsieur Emile and Ginette had remained still and quiet at the same table, near the counter, like a long-married couple waiting for a train in a railway station. Monsieur Emile had ordered his usual *tisane*, Ginette a greenish liqueur in a minute glass.

Now and then they would exchange a word or two, in a low voice. Nothing could be heard. Only the movement of their lips could be seen. Then Ginette had risen with a sigh and gone off to fetch a game of draughts from a cabinet under the gramophone.

They played. One felt that it might have been like that every day, for years on end, that the people could grow old without changing their places, without attempting any actions other than the ones they were to be seen making now.

No doubt in five years Maigret would find the dentist in front of the same *anisette*, with an identical smile, at once savage and satisfied. Charlot was working the crane with the movements of an automaton, and there was no reason for that to stop at a given moment.

The engaged couple moved the men about on the draughts-board, which they contemplated with unreal gravity between each move, and the major emptied glass after glass of champagne, whilst he recounted stories to Mr. Pyke.

No one was in a hurry. No one seemed to think that tomorrow existed. When she hadn't any customer to serve, Jojo went and leant on the counter and, with her chin on hand, gazed thoughtfully in front of her. Several times Maigret felt her eyes fixed on him, but the moment he turned his head she would look away.

Paul, the *patron*, still in his cook's attire, went from table to table, and at each he offered a round of drinks. It must have cost him a lot, but it is to be presumed that he made it up in the long run.

As for his wife, a small person with faded blond hair, hard-faced, who was scarcely noticed, she had settled down by herself at a table and was doing the day's accounts.

'It's like this every evening,' Lechat had told the chief-inspector.

'And the islanders, the fishermen I mean?'

'They hardly ever come after dinner. They go out to sea before daybreak and retire early to bed. At any rate, in the evening, they wouldn't come to the *Arche*. It's a sort of tacit agreement. In the afternoon, the morning as well, everyone mixes. After dinner, the islanders, the real inhabitants, prefer to go to the other cafés.'

'What do they do?'

'Nothing. I've been to see them. Sometimes they listen to the wireless, but that's fairly unusual. They have a small drink in silence, staring in front of them.'

'Is it always as calm here?'

'It all depends. Listen. It can happen from one moment to another. It takes a mere nothing, a remark in the air, a round of drinks offered by one person or another, and everyone groups together, and starts talking at once.'

It hadn't happened, perhaps because of the presence of Maigret.

It was hot, in spite of the open window. It had become an obsession to listen to the noises of the house. Ginette was still not asleep. There were occasional footsteps above his head. As for Mr. Pyke, he had to go a fourth time to the end of the passage and, each time, Maigret waited with a sort of anguish for the racket caused by the plug, before attempting to go back to sleep. For he must have been sleeping between the interruptions, a sleep not deep enough to efface his thoughts completely, but sufficient to distort them.

Mr. Pyke had played a dirty trick on him when he had spoken about the Dutchman at the end of the jetty. From now on the chief-inspector could see de Greef in the light of the peremptory phrases of his British colleague.

However, the portrait which Pyke had sketched of the young man did not satisfy him. He, too, was there, with Anna, who must have been sleepy and who, as time passed, allowed herself to lean more and more on her companion's shoulder.

De Greef did not speak to her. He cannot have been in the habit of speaking to her often. He was the male, the leader, and she had only to follow, to await his pleasure.

He was watching. With his very thin face he called to mind a lean animal, a wild beast.

The others probably weren't lambs, but indisputably de Greef was a wild beast. He sniffed like a wild beast. It was a mannerism. He would listen to what was being said and then he would sniff. That was his only perceptible reaction.

In the jungle the major would probably have been a pachyderm, an elephant, or better still a hippopotamus. And Monsieur Emile? Something furtive, with pointed teeth.

It was absurd. What would Mr. Pyke have thought if he had been able to read Maigret's thoughts? True the chief-inspector had the excuse of having had too much to drink and being half-asleep. If he had foreseen his insomnia he would have accounted for a few more glasses, in order to plunge at once into a dreamless slumber.

All in all Lechat was a very good man. So good that Maigret would have liked to have had him in his service. Still a little young, a little excitable. He was easily agitated, like a gun dog which runs in all directions around its master.

He knew the Midi already, as he had been in the squad at Draguig-nan, but he had only had occasion to visit Porquerolles once or twice; he had only really got to know the island during the last two or three days.

'The people from the *North Star* don't come every evening?'

'Almost every evening. They sometimes arrive late. Usually, when the sea is calm, they come by moonlight in a dinghy.'

'Are Mrs. Wilcox and the major friends?'

'They studiously avoid speaking to one another, and each looks at the other as though they didn't exist.'

After all, it was understandable. They both had the same back-ground. Both, for one reason or another, had come here to let their hair down.

The major must have been very embarrassed becoming drunk under the eye of Mrs. Wilcox, for in his country, gentlemen do that among themselves, behind closed doors.

As for her, in front of the retired Indian Army officer, she cannot have been very proud of her Moricourt.

They had arrived about eleven o'clock in the evening. As nearly always happens, she was nothing like the idea the chief-inspector had formed of her in his mind.

He had imagined a lady, and she was a red-head — of an artificial red — rather a stout woman on the wane, whose broken voice recalled that of Major Bellam, only it was louder. She was wearing a linen dress, but she had round her neck three strings of pearls which were perhaps genuine, and a large diamond on her finger.

Straight away she had singled out Maigret. Philippe must have told her about the chief-inspector and from the moment she sat down she hadn't ceased sizing him up and discussing him in a low voice with her companion.

What was she saying? Did she, on her side, find him heavy and vulgar? Had she pictured him as a film star? Perhaps she thought he didn't look very intelligent?

The two of them were drinking whisky, with very little soda. Philippe waited on her hand and foot and the chief-inspector's attention irritated him; he evidently didn't like being seen in the exercise of his functions. As for her, she was doing it on purpose. Instead of summoning Jojo or Paul, she would send her beau to change her glass which she didn't find clean enough, or made him get up again to go and fetch her some cigarettes from the counter. Another time, God knows why, she sent him outside.

She had to assert her power over the heir of the Moricourts, and perhaps, by the same token, to show that she was unashamed.

As they passed, the couple had greeted the young de Greef and his companion. Very vaguely. Rather in the way that masonic signs are exchanged.

The major, contrary to Maigret's expectations, had been the first to leave, dignified but uncertain in his bearing, and Mr. Pyke had gone some of the way with him.

Then the dentist, in his turn, had left.

'You'll see. You'll see!' he had repeated to Maigret, as he predicted for him a speedy onset of Porquerollitis.

Charlot, who had had enough of the crane, had gone to sit jockey-style on a chair, next to the draughts players, and, silently, had pointed out one or two moves to Ginette. Once Monsieur Emile had left, he had gone up to bed. As for Ginette, she seemed to be waiting for Maigret's permission. In the end she had come over to his table and murmured, with a little smile:

'Still cross with me?'

She was visibly tired, and he had advised her to go up to bed. He had gone up straight away after her, because the idea had come to him that she might be going to join Charlot.

At one moment, when he was trying to go to sleep — but perhaps he was already asleep and it was only a dream? — he had had the impression that he had discovered a really important fact.

'I mustn't forget it. It is essential that I should remember it tomorrow morning.'

He had all but got up and made a note of it on a piece of paper. It had come to him in a flash. It was very odd. He was pleased. He kept repeating to himself:

'Above all, I mustn't forget it in the morning!'

And the pulling of the plug once more set the *Arche* resounding with its racket. Afterwards there were ten minutes of listening to the water slowly flowing back into the cistern. It was exasperating. The noise was becoming louder. There were explosions. Maigret sat up in bed, opened his eyes, and found the room bathed in sunlight, with, just in front of him, framed in the open window, the belfry of the little church.

The explosions were coming from the port. It was the engines of the boats being started up and coughing. All the fishermen were leaving at the same time. One of the motors kept on stopping after several efforts, and a silence followed, then again the coughing sound, so that one wanted to go and help to get it going properly once and for all.

He felt like getting dressed and going out of doors, then looked at the time by his watch, which he had put on the bedside table and found it was only half-past four in the morning. The smell was still more pronounced than on the day before, probably because of the damp of the dawn. There was no sound in the house, no sound in the square, where the foliage of the eucalyptus trees was motionless in the rising sun. Only the motors, in the harbour, an occasional voice, then even the thrumming of the motors died away in the distance, and, for a very long time, was no more than a vibration in the air.

When he opened his eyes once more, another smell reminded him of all the mornings since his early childhood, the smell of fresh coffee, and from most parts of the house came the buzz of activity, footsteps could be heard on the square, brooms frisking against the stones in the roadway.

He was at once aware that there was something of vital importance that he had to remember, but could bring back to mind no distinct memory. His mouth was lined with fur, because of the *anisette*. He felt for a bell button in the hope of having some coffee sent up. There was none. Then he put on his trousers, his shirt, his slippers, ran a comb through his hair and opened his door. A strong smell of scent and soap was issuing from Ginette's room, where she must have been busy at her toilet.

Wasn't it about her that he had made, or thought he had made, a discovery? He went down and, in the main room, found the chairs in pyramids on the tables. The doors were open and the chairs on the terrace were similarly stacked up. There was nobody about.

He went into the kitchen, which seemed dark to him, and had to accustom his eyes to the half-light.

'Good morning, Chief-Inspector. Did you sleep well?'

It was Jojo, with her black dress, which was too short and literally clung to her body. She hadn't yet washed either, and she seemed to be naked underneath.

'Will you have some coffee?'

For a second he thought of Madame Maigret who at that hour would be preparing the breakfast in their flat in Paris, with the windows open on to the Boulevard Richard-Lenoir. It struck him that it was raining in Paris. When he had left it was almost as cold as in winter. From here it seemed incredible.

'Shall I clear a table for you?'

What for? He was perfectly all right in the kitchen. She was cooking some vine-stalks on the kitchen stove, and it smelt good. When she lifted her arms he could see the small brown hairs of her armpits.

He was still searching his mind for the discovery of the night before, uttering words without thinking, perhaps because he was embarrassed to be alone with Jojo.

'Isn't Monsieur Paul up yet?'

'He's already been at the harbour a good while. He goes every morning to buy his fish from the boats as they come back.'

She glanced at the clock.

'The *Cormorant* leaves in five minutes.'

'Is anyone else up?'

'Monsieur Charlot.'

'Not with his luggage, I presume?'

'No. He's with Monsieur Paul. Your friend has gone out too, at least a quarter of an hour ago.'

Maigret contemplated the expanse of the square through the open windows.

'He's probably in the water. He was wearing a bathing-costume, with his towel under his arm.'

It had something to do with Ginette. But it was also linked in his mind with Jojo. He remembered that, in his half-sleep, he had recalled Jojo at the moment she was going up the stairs. Now this wasn't an erotic thought. The legs she disclosed were only incidental to it. Let's see! Later on, she had come into his room.

The day before, he had persistently asked Ginette:

'Why have you come?'

And she had lied several times. At first she had said that it was to see him, because she had learnt that he was on the island and had assumed he would send for her.

A little later, she was admitting that she was in a sort of way engaged to Monsieur Emile. This meant admitting at the same time that she had come to clear him, to assure the chief-inspector that her employer was in no way concerned with Marcellin's death.

He hadn't been so very wrong to be hard with her. She had yielded some ground. But she hadn't yet yielded enough.

He was drinking his coffee in small sips, standing in front of the stove. By a curious coincidence, the cup of common china, but of an old-fashioned design, was almost a replica of the one he used during his childhood, which he then imagined to be unique.

'Aren't you having anything to eat?'

'Not now.'

'In a quarter of an hour, there will be fresh bread at the baker's.'

In the end he relaxed, and Jojo must have wondered why he began to smile. He had remembered.

Hadn't Marcellin mentioned to Jojo a 'packet' which he could have had? He was drunk, certainly, but he often was drunk. For how long had the possibility of laying his hands on this 'packet' been here? It wasn't necessarily recent. Ginette used to visit the island practically every month. She had come the month before. It was easy to check up. Marcellin, on the other hand, could have written to her.

If he was able to get hold of a packet, it was probable that someone else could get it in his place, for instance by knowing what he knew.

Maigret stayed where he was, cup in hand, staring at the brightly lit rectangle of the door and Jojo kept darting curious glances at him.

Lechat claimed that Marcel had died because he had talked too much about 'his friend Maigret' and, at first sight, this appeared to make sense.

It was odd to see Mr. Pyke, almost naked, come out into the light, his soaked towel in his hand, his hair stuck to his forehead.

Instead of greeting him, Maigret murmured:

'Just a moment . . .'

He almost had it. A slight effort and his ideas would fall into place. Starting off, for example, with the notion that Ginette had come because she knew why Marcellin had died.

She hadn't necessarily put herself out to prevent the discovery of the guilty party. Once she had married Monsieur Emile she would be rich, certainly. Only old Justine wasn't dead yet, she might linger on for years, despite the doctors. If she discovered what was afoot, she was quite capable of playing a dirty trick so as to prevent her son marrying anyone after her death.

Marcellin's 'packet' was to be had straight away. Perhaps it was still there to be got? In spite of the presence of Maigret and Inspector Lechat?

'I beg your pardon, Mr. Pyke. Did you sleep well?'

'Very well,' replied the Englishman imperturbably.

Was Maigret to admit that he had counted the times the plug was pulled? It was not necessary and, after his bathe, the Scotland Yard inspector was as fresh as a fish.

Presently, while he was shaving, the chief-inspector would have time to think about the 'packet'.

VI

THERE is something to be said for the English. Would a French colleague, in Mr. Pyke's place, have been able to resist the desire to score a point? And hadn't Maigret, who was not especially given to teasing, all but made a discreet allusion, just now, to the plug which the Yard inspector had pulled so many times during the night?

Perhaps more alcohol had flowed that evening than either of them had imagined? At all events it was rather unexpected. There were still the three of them, Maigret, Pyke and Jojo, in the kitchen with the door left open. Maigret was finishing his coffee, and Mr. Pyke, in his bathing-costume, was standing between him and the light, while Jojo was trying to find some bacon for him in the larder. It was exactly three minutes to eight and then, looking at the clock, Maigret declared in that innocent, inimitable voice, that comes to one in moments of gaffes:

'I wonder if Lechat is still sleeping off his wine from last night.'

Jojo started, but managed not to turn round As for Mr. Pyke, all his good education failed to prevent the round look of astonishment being seen to light up his face It was, however, with perfect simplicity that he uttered:

'I've just seen him taking his place on board the *Cormorant*. I presume it will wait for Ginette.'

Maigret had done nothing more or less than forget all about Marcellin's funeral. Worse still, it suddenly came back to him that the day before he had talked about it for a long time, with even a little too much insistence, to the inspector. Was Mr. Pyke present at that conversation? He couldn't have said, but he could picture himself again, seated on the bench.

'You go with her, old man, you get the idea? I don't say it'll lead anywhere. Perhaps she will show some reaction, perhaps not. Perhaps someone will try to speak to her on the sly? Perhaps recognizing a face in the congregation may tell you something? One should always go to funerals, it's an old principle that has often succeeded. Keep your eyes skinned. That's all.'

He seemed even to recall that, while chatting away to the inspector, he had related one or two stories of funerals which had put him on the track of criminals.

He understood now why Ginette had made so much noise in her bedroom. He heard her opening her door and calling out from upstairs:

'Pour me out a cup of coffee, Jojo. How much time have I got?'

'Three minutes, madame!'

Just at that moment, the sound of a siren was announcing the *Cormorant*'s imminent departure.

'I'll come as far as the landing-stage,' the chief-inspector announced.

In his slippers and with no collar, for he hadn't time to go up and get dressed. He wasn't the only one in that attire. There were little groups in the neighbourhood of the boat, still the same ones as had been there the day before when the chief-inspector had landed. They must have attended all the departures and all the arrivals. Before starting the day they would come to watch the *Cormorant* leaving the harbour, after which, delaying their morning toilet a little longer, they would have a glass of white wine at Paul's or in one of the cafés.

The dentist, less discreet than Mr. Pyke, looked hard at Maigret's slippers and his state of undress, and his satisfied smile was saying unambiguously:

'I warned you! It's started!'

Porquerollitis, presumably, in which he himself was steeped to the marrow. Aloud, he contented himself with asking:

'Slept well?'

Lechat, already on board, petulant, impatient, went ashore again to have a word with his chief.

'I didn't want to wake you up. Isn't she coming? Baptiste says that if she doesn't come at once, they'll go off without her.'

There were others making the crossing for Marcellin's funeral, fishermen in their Sunday best, the builder, the tobacconist. Maigret couldn't

see Charlot around and yet he had spotted him just now in the square.
Nothing was moving aboard the *North Star*. At the moment the dumb
sailor was about to cast off, Ginette appeared, half-walking, half-
running, dressed in black silk with a black hat and a veil, leaving a
rustling and scented wake behind her. She was whisked on board as
though by a conjuring trick, and it was not until she was seated that she
saw the chief-inspector on the jetty and wished him good morning with
a little nod of her head.

The sea was so smooth, so luminous, that when one stared at it for
long one could no longer distinguish, for a moment or two, the shape of
things. The *Cormorant* described a silver curve on the water. The people
waited another moment watching her, from habit and tradition, then
set off, slowly, towards the square. A fisherman, who had just spiked an
octopus with his harpoon, was skinning it and the tentacles were coiling
round his tattooed arm.

At the *Arche*, Paul, bright-eyed, was serving out white wine from
behind his counter, and Mr. Pyke, who had had time to dress, was at a
table eating bacon and eggs. Maigret drank a glass of wine, like the
others, and a little later, while he was busy shaving in front of his
window, with his braces hanging over his thighs, there was a knock at
the door.

It was the Englishman.

'Am I in the way? May I come in?'

He sat in the only chair, and the silence was a long one.

'I spent part of the evening chatting with the major,' he said finally.
'Do you know he was one of our best polo players?'

He must have been disappointed with the reaction, or to be more
precise, with the lack of reaction on the part of Maigret. The latter had
only a vague notion of the game of polo. All he knew was that it was
played from horseback and that somewhere, in the Bois de Boulogne
or at St. Cloud, there was a very aristocratic polo club.

Mr. Pyke, with a guileless air, stretched out a helping hand.

'He's a younger son.'

For him, this meant a lot. In England, in great families, isn't it the
eldest son alone who inherits title and fortune, which obliges the others
to make a career for themselves in the army or the navy?

'His brother is a member of the House of Lords. The major chose the
Indian Army.'

The same phenomenon must take place, in reverse, when Maigret
made allusions to his English colleague about people like Charlot, or
Monsieur Emile, or Ginette. But Mr. Pyke was being patient, dotting
his *i*'s with an exquisite discretion, almost without touching them.

'People with a certain name are reluctant to remain in London unless
they have the means to cut a fine figure there. The great passion of the
Indian Army is horses. To play polo a stable of several ponies is essential.'

'The major's never got married?'

'Younger sons seldom marry. In taking charge of a family Bellam would have had to give up his horses.'

'And he preferred the horses!'

This did not seem at all surprising to Mr. Pyke.

'In the evening, out there, the bachelors gather at the club and have no distraction besides drink. The major has drunk a lot in his time. In India it was whisky. It was only here that he took to champagne.'

'Did he tell you why he chose to live in Porquerolles?'

'He had an appalling tragedy, the worst that could have befallen him. As a result of a bad fall from his horse, he was immobilized in bed for three years, half of the time in plaster, and, when he was on his feet again, he realized that his riding days were over.'

'That's the reason he left India?'

'That's why he's here. I'm sure that almost everywhere in climates like this, in the Mediterranean or the Pacific, you will find old gentlemen of the same type as the major, who are considered eccentrics. Where else could they go?'

'Don't they have any desire to go back to England?'

'Their means won't permit them to live in London according to their rank, and the habits they have adopted would be frowned upon in the country in England.'

'Did he tell you why he doesn't speak to Mrs. Wilcox?'

'There was no need for him to tell me.'

Should he persist? Or would Mr. Pyke, too, prefer not to hear too much about his compatriot? Mrs. Wilcox, to put it in a nutshell, was not as a woman what the major was as a man.

Maigret wiped his cheeks, hesitated about putting on his jacket. The Yard inspector had not put on his. It was already hot. But the chief-inspector could not allow himself, like his slim colleague, not to wear braces, and a man in braces always looks like a shopkeeper on a picnic.

He put his jacket on. They had nothing else to do in the room, and Mr. Pyke murmured as he rose:

'The major, despite everything, has remained a gentleman.'

He followed Maigret down the stairs. He didn't ask what he intended to do, but he was following him, and that was enough to spoil the chief-inspector's day.

He had vaguely promised himself, expressly on Mr. Pyke's account, to behave that morning like a high police official. In theory, a Police Headquarters chief-inspector does not run around streets and bars looking for murderers. He is an important man, who spends most of his time in his office, and like a general in his H.Q., directs a small army of sergeants, inspectors and technicians.

Maigret had never been able to resign himself to this. Like a gun dog, he had to ferret things out for himself, to scratch and sniff the smells.

The first two days, Lechat had got through a considerable amount of work and had handed over to Maigret an account of all the interrogations he had carried out. The whole island had been put through it, the Morins and the Gallis, the sick doctor, the priest, whom Maigret hadn't seen, and the women as well.

Maigret would have installed himself in a corner of the dining-room, which was empty all the morning, and he would have zealously studied these reports, marking them with a blue or red pencil.

With an uneasy glance, he asked Mr. Pyke:

'Does it happen at the Yard for your colleagues to run about the streets like novices?'

'I know at least three or four who are never to be seen in their offices.'

So much the better, for he had no desire to remain sitting down. He was beginning to understand why the people of Porquerolles were always to be found in the same places. It was instinctive. Despite oneself one was to some extent affected by the sun, by the landscape. Now, for example, Maigret and his companion were taking a walk out of doors, without any definite direction, and hardly noticing that they were going down towards the harbour.

Maigret was sure that if, by chance, he was obliged to spend the rest of his days on the island, he would take the same walk every morning and that the pipe he smoked then would always be the best pipe of the day. The *Cormorant*, over there, on the other side of the water, at Giens Point, was disgorging its passengers, who were piling into an old bus. Even with the naked eye one could make out the boat as a tiny white dot.

The mute would be about to load up some crates of vegetables and fruit for the mayor and for the Co-operative, meat for the butcher, and the post-bags. People would embark perhaps, as Maigret and Mr. Pyke had embarked the day before, and would no doubt experience the same feeling of vertigo on discovering the underwater landscape.

The sailors on the big white yacht were washing down the deck. They were middle-aged men who from time to time went for a drink, without mixing with the locals, at Morin-Barbu's.

To the right of the harbour a footpath ran up the steep slope, like a cliff, and ended at a hut, with the door open.

A fisherman, sitting in the doorway, was holding a net stretched out between his bare toes, and his hands, as nimble as a seamstress's, were passing a netting hook in and out of the holes.

It was here that Marcellin had been killed. The two policemen glanced at the interior. The centre was occupied by a huge cauldron, like the ones used in the country for boiling pig swill. Here it was the nets that were put to boil in a brown mixture which protected them against the action of the sea water.

Marcellin must have used old sails as a mattress, and in the corners there were pots of paint scattered about, oil or paraffin cans, pieces of scrap iron, patched-up oars.

'Do other people ever sleep here?' Maigret asked the fisherman.

The latter raised his head indifferently.

'Old Benoît, sometimes, when it's raining.'

'And when it's not raining?'

'He prefers to sleep out of doors. It depends. Sometimes it's in a cove or on the deck of a boat. Sometimes on a bench in the square.'

'Have you seen him today?'

'He was over there just now.'

The fisherman pointed at the footpath which continued beside the sea at a certain height and which, on one side, was bordered with pine trees.

'Was he alone?'

'I think the gentleman from the *Arche* joined up with him a little farther on.'

'Which one?'

'The one with a linen suit and a white cap.'

It was Charlot.

'Did he come back this way?'

'A good half-hour ago.'

The *Cormorant* was still no more than a white dot in the blue of the world, but the white dot, now, was clearly separated from the shore. Other boats were dotted about on the sea, some motionless, some progressing slowly, leaving a luminous wake behind them.

Maigret and Mr. Pyke went down to the harbour once more, followed along the jetty, as on the previous evening, mechanically watched a boy fishing for conger eels with a short line.

When they passed in front of the Dutchman's little boat, Maigret glanced inside and was somewhat surprised to see Charlot in conversation with de Greef.

Mr. Pyke was still following him, silently. Was he expecting something to happen? Was he trying to guess Maigret's thoughts?

They went to the end of the pier, retraced their steps, came once more past the *Fleur d'Amour*, and Charlot was still in the same place.

Three times they covered the hundred yards of the pier, and the third time Charlot climbed onto the deck of the little yacht, turned round to say good-bye and stepped onto the plank which served as a gangway.

The two men were just near to him. They were going to pass one another. Maigret, after hesitating stopped. It was the time when the bus from Giens should be arriving at Hyères. The people for the funeral would go and have a drink before heading for the morgue.

'I say, I was looking for you this morning.'

'As you can see, I didn't leave the island.'

'That's just what I wanted to talk to you about. I see no reason for keeping you here any longer. You told me, I think, that you had only come for two or three days and that but for Marcellin's death, you would have left by now. The inspector thought it right to make you stay. I'll set you free again.'

'Thank you.'

'I only ask that you tell me where I can find you in case I need you.'

Charlot, who was smoking, studied the end of his cigarette for a moment as though reflecting.

'At the *Arche*!' he finally said.

'You aren't going away then?'

'Not for the moment.'

And, lifting his head again, he looked the chief-inspector in the eye.

'Does that surprise you? One might think you were annoyed to see me stay. I suppose it's allowed?'

'I can't stop you. I admit I should be curious to know what made you change your mind.'

'I haven't got a particularly absorbing profession, have I? No office or factory or business premises, no employees or workers waiting for me. Don't you find it pleasant here?'

He made no attempt to conceal his irony. They could see the mayor, still in his long grey smock, coming down towards the harbour pushing his wheelbarrow. The page from the Grand Hotel was there as well, and the porter with the uniform cap.

The *Cormorant* was now just midway in the crossing and would reach the disembarkation point in a quarter of an hour.

'You've had a long conversation with old Benoît?'

'When I saw you just now near the hut, I thought you would ask me that. You'll question Benoît in your turn. I can't stop you, but I can tell you in advance that he knows nothing. At any rate, that's what I gathered, for it's not easy to interpret his language. Perhaps, after all, you'll be luckier than I was.'

'You are trying to find out something?'

'Perhaps the same thing as you.'

It was a challenge almost, thrown out with good humour.

'What makes you think it could be of interest to you? Did Marcellin talk to you?'

'No more than to the others. He was always a little embarrassed in front of me. The half-and-halfs are never at their ease in front of the *caïds*.'

Presently the word *caïd* would be explained to Mr. Pyke, who was visibly setting it to one side in a compartment of his brain.

Maigret joined in the game, spoke also in an undertone, lightly, as though uttering words of no consequence.

'You know why Marcellin was killed, Charlot?'

'I know almost as much as you. And, indeed, I probably draw the same conclusions, but with different ends.'

He smiled, crinkling up his eyelids in the sun.

'Has Jojo talked to you?'

'To me? Haven't you been told that we hate one another like cat and dog?'

'Have you done something to her?'

'She didn't want me to. That's just what's kept us apart.'

'I wonder, Charlot, if you wouldn't do better to return to Pont du Las.'

'And I, with all due respect for your advice, prefer to remain.'

A dinghy was detaching itself from the *North Star*, and on it Moricourt's silhouette could be recognized as he sat at the oars. He was the only person aboard. Like the others, he was doubtless coming over for the arrival of the *Cormorant*, and would go up as far as the post-office to collect his mail.

Charlot, following Maigret's gaze, seemed at the same time to be following his thoughts. As the chief-inspector had turned towards the Dutchman's boat, he declared:

'He's a strange fellow, but I don't think it's him.'

'You mean Marcellin's murderer?'

'One can hide nothing from you. Mark you, the murderer doesn't interest me in himself. Only, except in the course of a fit, one doesn't kill someone without any reason, does one? Even and above all if that someone proclaims to whoever wants to hear that he's a friend of Chief-Inspector Maigret.'

'You were at the *Arche* when Marcellin mentioned me?'

'Everyone was there. I mean, all the people you are busying yourself with. And Marcellin, especially after a few drinks, had a pretty piercing voice.'

'Do you know why he said that, on that particular evening?'

'There you are. As you may imagine that was the first question I asked myself when I learnt that he was dead, I wondered who the poor fellow was speaking to. Do you understand?'

Maigret understood perfectly.

'Did you find a satisfactory reply?'

'Not so far. If I had found one, I should have returned to Pont du Las by the next boat.'

'I didn't know you liked playing amateur detectives.'

'You're joking, Inspector.'

The latter still persisted, with an air of utter indifference, in trying to make the other say something he was refusing to say.

It was a strange sort of game, in the sun on the jetty, with Mr. Pyke playing the part of umpire and remaining strictly neutral.

'So you definitely start from the idea that Marcellin was not killed without good reason?'

'As you say.'

'You suppose the murderer was trying to appropriate something which Marcellin had in his possession.'

'Neither you nor I suppose anything of the sort, or else your reputation is damned overrated.'

'Someone wanted to shut his mouth?'

'You're getting very warm, Inspector.'

'He had made a discovery which could endanger someone?'

'Why are you so anxious to know what I think when all the time you know as much about it as I do?'

'Including the "big money"?'

'Including the "big money".'

After which, lighting a fresh cigar, Charlot threw out:

'Big money has always interested me; do you catch on now?'

'That's why you visited the Dutchman this morning?'

'He's flat broke.'

'Which means it's not him?'

'I don't say that. All I say is that Marcellin couldn't have hoped to get money out of him.'

'You're forgetting the girl.'

'Anna?'

'Her father is very rich.'

That made Charlot think, but he finally shrugged his shoulders. The *Cormorant* was passing by the first rocky promontory and entering the harbour.

'Will you excuse me? I'm probably meeting someone.'

And Charlot touched his cap ironically and headed for the jetty.

While Maigret was stuffing his pipe, Mr. Pyke declared:

'I think he's a highly intelligent fellow.'

'It's pretty hard to succeed in his job without being.'

The page boy from the Grand Hotel was taking the luggage of a young married couple. The mayor, who had gone aboard, was examining the labels on the packages. Charlot was helping a young woman ashore, and was taking her towards the *Arche*. So he really was waiting for someone. He must have telephoned the day before.

As a matter of fact, where had Inspector Lechat telephoned Maigret from, two days before, to tell him about it all? If it was from the *Arche*, where the wall telephone was just beside the bar, everyone had overheard him. He must remember to ask him.

The dentist was there again, in the same clothes as in the morning, unshaven, perhaps unwashed, an old straw hat on his head. He was watching the *Cormorant*, and that was enough for him. He seemed happy to be alive.

Were Maigret and Mr. Pyke to follow the general movement, stroll up to the *Arche*, make for the bar and drink the white wine which would be served up without their being asked what they wanted?

The chief-inspector studied his companion from the corner of his eye, and on his side Mr. Pyke, though impassive, seemed to be studying him. Why not follow the others, after all? Marcellin's burial was in progress in Hyères. Behind the bier Ginette was taking the place of the family and she would be mopping her brow with her handkerchief, screwed tightly into a ball. There was a heavy heat in the air over there, in the avenues lined with motionless palms.

'Do you like the island white wine, Monsieur Pyke?'

'I should be very happy to drink a glass.'

The postman was crossing the bare expanse of the square pushing a barrow piled with the mail-bags. Lifting his head, Maigret saw the windows of the *Arche* wide open and, in one of the frames on the first floor, Charlot leaning on the window-sill. Behind him in the gilded half-light, a young woman was in the act of removing her dress, which she was slipping over her head.

'He talked a lot and I wonder if he was hoping to get more out of me.'

That would emerge later. People like Charlot cannot easily resist adopting an advantageous position. Just as Maigret and Mr. Pyke were sitting down on the terrace they saw Monsieur Emile, more of a little white mouse than ever, advancing onto the square with short steps, a panama hat on his head, and heading diagonally for the post office — situated to the left of the church, at the top. The door was open. Four or five people were waiting, while the postmistress sorted the mail.

It was Saturday. Jojo was giving the red tiles of the dining-room a good wash; her feet were bare, the rivulets of dirty water were draining onto the terrace.

Paul brought not two glasses of white wine, but a whole bottle.

'Do you know the woman who went up to Charlot's room?'

'That's his girl friend.'

'Is she in service?'

'I don't think so. She's some sort of a dancer or singer in a Marseilles night club. It's the third or fourth time she's been here.'

'He telephoned to her?'

'Yesterday afternoon, while you were in your room.'

'Do you know what he said?'

'He simply asked her to come and spend the week-end. She accepted at once.'

'Were Charlot and Marcellin friends?'

'I don't remember having seen them together; I mean just the two of them.'

'I would like you to try to remember exactly. When, that evening, Marcellin mentioned me . . .'

'I know what you mean. Your inspector put the same question to me.'

'I suppose at the start of the evening the customers were at different tables, like yesterday evening?'

'Yes. It always starts off like that.'

'Do you know what happened next?'

'Someone put on the gramophone. I don't recall who. The Dutchman and his girl friend began to dance. It comes back to me because I noticed that she let herself go limp in his arms like a rag doll.'

'Did other people dance too?'

'Mrs. Wilcox and Monsieur Philippe. He's a very good dancer.'

'Where was Marcellin at that moment?'

'I seem to picture him at the bar.'

'Very drunk?'

'Not very, but fairly. Wait. A detail. He insisted on asking Mrs. Wilcox to dance . . .'

'Marcellin?'

Was it deliberate that when his compatriot was mentioned Mr. Pyke suddenly looked blank?

'Did she accept?'

'They danced a few steps. Marcellin must have stumbled. He liked to act the clown when there were a lot of people present. It was she who stood the first round of drinks. Yes. There was a bottle of whisky on their table. She doesn't like being served by the glass. Marcellin drank some and asked for white wine.'

'And the major?'

'I was just thinking of him. He was in the opposite corner and I'm trying to remember who he had with him. I think it was Polyte.'

'Who's Polyte?'

'A Morin. The one with the green boat. In the summer he takes tourists right round the island. He wears a proper captain's cap.'

'Is he a captain?'

'He did his service in the navy and he must hold the rank of quartermaster. He often accompanies the major to Toulon. The dentist was drinking with them. Marcellin started going from one table to the other, with his glass, and, if I am not mistaken, he was mixing whisky with his white wine.'

'How was it he began talking about me? Who to? Was it at the major's table, or Mrs. Wilcox's?'

'I'm doing my best. You saw for yourself how it is, and yesterday was a quiet evening. The Dutch couple were near Mrs. Wilcox. I think it was at that table that the conversation began. Marcellin was standing up, in the middle of the room, when I heard him declare:

' "*My friend Chief-Inspector Maigret . . . Just so, my friend, and I know what I'm talking about . . . I can prove it . . .*" '

'He produced a letter?'

'Not to my knowledge. I was busy, with Jojo, serving.'

'Was your wife in the room?'

'I think she'd gone up. She normally does go up when she has finished the accounts. She's not very strong and needs plenty of sleep.'

'In short Marcellin might just as well have been addressing Major Bellam as Mrs. Wilcox or the Dutchman? And even Charlot, or someone else? The dentist, for example? Monsieur Emile?'

'I suppose so.'

He was called inside and, excusing himself, left them. The people coming out of the post office began to saunter across the sunny patch of the square where, in one corner, a woman was standing behind a table on which vegetables were on sale. The mayor, to one side of the *Arche*, was unpacking his crates.

'You're wanted on the telephone, Monsieur Maigret.'

He penetrated into the semi-darkness of the café, picked up the receiver.

'That you, Chief? Lechat here. It's all over. I'm in a bar near the cemetery. The woman, you know who, is with me. She hasn't left me since the *Cormorant*. She has had time to tell me her life story.'

'How did it go off?'

'Very well. She bought some flowers. Other people from the island placed some on his grave. It was very hot in the cemetery. I don't know what to do. I think I shall have to ask her to lunch.'

'Can she hear you?'

'No. I'm in a telephone box. I can see her through the window. She's powdering her nose and looking into a pocket mirror.'

'She hasn't met anyone? Or telephoned?'

'She hasn't left me for a second. I even had to go with her to the florist and, behind the hearse, as I was walking beside her, I looked as though I was part of the family.'

'Did you take the bus to get from Giens to Hyères?'

'The only thing I could do was to ask her to come with me in my car. Everything going all right, on the island?'

'Everything's all right.'

When he came back onto the terrace, Maigret found the dentist sitting beside Mr. Pyke and apparently waiting to share the bottle of white wine.

Philippe de Moricourt, a pile of newspapers under his arm, was hesitating whether to come into the *Arche*.

Monsieur Emile, with cautious steps, was heading towards his villa where old Justine would be waiting for him, and, as on any other day, the smell of *bouillabaisse* floated out from the kitchen.

VII

It wasn't a nickname. The fat girl hadn't done it on purpose. She really
had been called Aglaé at her christening. She was very fat, especially
the bottom half, deformed like a woman of fifty or sixty who has become
fat with age and, by contrast, her face only looked the more infantile, for
Aglaé was twenty-six years old at most.

Maigret had discovered, that afternoon, a whole new section of
Porquerolles when, still accompanied by Mr. Pyke, he had walked right
across the square for the first time to pay a visit to the post office. Was
there really a smell of incense coming from the church, where the
services could not have been very frequent?

It was the same square as the one opposite the *Arche*, and yet one
would have sworn that, at the top, the air was hotter and more dense.
Some small gardens, in front of two or three houses, were a riot of
flowers and bees. The noises from the harbour reached them muted.
Two old men were playing bowls, *Pétanque* style, that is without sending the jack more than a few yards from their feet, and it was strange to
see the precautions they took in bending down.

One of them was Ferdinand Galli, the patriarch of all the Gallis on
the island, who kept a café in his corner of the square, a café which the
chief-inspector had never seen anyone enter. It must only have been
frequented by neighbours, or by the Gallis of the tribe. His partner was
a retired man, natty, completely deaf, wearing a railwayman's cap, and
another octogenarian, sitting on the post office bench, was watching
them sleepily.

For beside the open door of the post office there was a green painted
bench on which Maigret was to spend a part of his afternoon.

'I wondered if you would come up here in the end!' Aglaé exclaimed,
seeing him come in. 'I expected you would need to use the telephone
and wouldn't want to do it from the *Arche*, where so many people can
hear what you are saying.'

'Will it take long to get Paris, mademoiselle?'

'With a priority call I can get you through in a few minutes.'

'In that case, get Police Headquarters for me.'

'I know the number. It was me that put your inspector through when
he called you.'

He all but asked:

'And you listened in?'

But she would not be long in revealing this herself.

'Who do you wish to speak to at Police Headquarters?'

'Sergeant Lucas. If he's not there, Inspector Torrence.'

A few seconds later he had Lucas on the line.

'What's the weather like with you, old man? Still raining? Showers? Good! Listen, Lucas. Do your best to get me everything you can as soon as possible on someone called Philippe de Moricourt. Yes. Lechat has seen his papers and says it's his real name. His last address in Paris was a furnished house on the left bank, Rue Jacob, 17b. . . . What do I want to know exactly? I've got no preconceived ideas. Everything you can find out. I don't think he's got a dossier in the Records, but you can always check. Do all you can by telephone and then call me back here. No number. Just Porquerolles. I would also like you to telephone the police at Ostend. Ask if they know a certain Bebelmans who, I think, is an important shipbuilder. Same thing. Everything you can find out. That's not all. Don't cut us off, mademoiselle. Have you any acquaintances in Montparnasse? See what they say about a certain Jef de Greef, who is a sort of painter and spent a certain amount of time on the Seine, in his boat moored near the Pont Marie. Have you made a note of that? That's all, yes. Don't wait for all the information before ringing me back. Put as many people on to it as you like. Everything all right, at the office? . . . *Who's* had a baby? . . . Janvier's wife? . . . Give him my congratulations.'

When he came out of the telephone box, he saw Aglaé, without a trace of embarrassment, taking the earphones off her head.

'You always listen in to conversations?'

'I stayed on the line in case it was cut off. I don't trust the Hyères operator; she's an old cat.'

'Do you do the same for everyone?'

'In the morning I haven't time because of the mail, but in the afternoon it's easier.'

'Do you take note of the calls made by the islanders?'

'I have to.'

'Could you make me out a list of all the calls you have put through in the last few days? Say the last eight days.'

'Right away. It'll take me a few minutes.'

'You're the person who receives the telegrams as well, aren't you?'

'There aren't many, except in the season. I had one this morning which is sure to interest you.'

'How do you know?'

'It's a telegram which someone sent from here, someone who appears to be interested in one of the people, at least, about whom you've been asking for information.'

'Have you a copy?'

'I'll find it for you.'

A moment later she was handing a form to the inspector, who read:

Fred Masson, c/o Angelo, Rue Blanche, Paris.

Like complete information on Philippe de Moricourt address Rue Jacob Paris stop *Please telegraph Porquerolles. Regards.*

Signed: CHARLOT.

Maigret gave it to Mr. Pyke to read, and the latter confined himself to a nod.

'Will you prepare a list of the calls for me, mademoiselle? I'll wait outside with my friend.'

So it was that, for the first time, they went and sat on the bench, in the shade of the eucalyptus trees round the square, and the wall at their backs was pink and hot. Somewhere there was an invisible fig-tree, and they inhaled its sweet smell.

'In a few minutes,' said Mr. Pyke, looking at the church clock, 'I shall ask your permission to leave you for a moment, if you don't mind.'

Was it from politeness that he pretended to believe that Maigret would grieve over it?

'The major has invited me for a drink at about five o'clock. I should have hurt his feelings by refusing.'

'That's perfectly all right.'

'I thought you would probably be busy.'

Hardly time for the chief-inspector to smoke a pipe, as he watched the two old men playing bowls, before Aglaé was calling out in her shrill voice, over the counter:

'Monsieur Maigret! It's ready!'

He went and took the piece of paper which she was holding out to him, and went and sat once more beside the man from the Yard.

She had done her work conscientiously, in the laboured writing of a schoolgirl, with three or four spelling mistakes.

The word *butcher* recurred several times on the list. Apparently he telephoned every day to Hyères to order his meat for the next day. Then there was the Co-operative, with calls as frequent but more varied.

Maigret made a mark a little more than halfway down the list, thus separating the calls made before Marcellin's death from those made afterwards.

'Are you taking notes?' Mr. Pyke asked, seeing his companion opening a large note-book.

Didn't this imply that for the first time he was seeing Maigret behaving like a real chief-inspector?

The name which occurred most often on the list was Justine's. She called Nice, Marseilles, Béziers, Avignon, and in one week there were four calls to Paris.

'We'll see about that presently,' said Maigret. 'I suppose the post-mistress took care to listen in. Is that done in England too?'

'I don't think it's legal, but it's possible that it sometimes happens.'

The day before, Charlot had telephoned Marseilles. Maigret knew that already. It was to summon his girl friend, whom they had seen landing from the *Cormorant* and with whom he was now playing cards on the terrace of the *Arche*.

For the *Arche* could be seen in the distance, with human forms bustling around it. From where they were, where all was so calm, it looked as active as a hive of bees.

The most interesting thing was that Marcellin's name occurred on the list. He had called a number in Nice, just two days before his death.

Suddenly Maigret rose and went into the post office, and Mr. Pyke followed him in.

'Do you know what this number is, mademoiselle?'

'Certainly. It's the house where the lady works. Justine calls it every day; you can see it on the list.'

'Have you listened in to Justine's conversations?'

'Often. I no longer bother, because it's always the same.'

'Does she do the talking, or her son?'

'She talks and Monsieur Emile listens.'

'I don't understand.'

'She's deaf. So Monsieur Emile holds the receiver to his ear, and repeats what is being said to her. Then she shouts so loud into the mouthpiece that it's difficult to distinguish her syllables. The first thing she says is always:

' "How much?" '

'They give her the figure for the takings. Monsieur Emile, standing by her, notes it down. She calls up her houses one after the other.'

'I suppose it's Ginette who answers in Nice?'

'Yes, seeing that she's the manageress.'

'And the Paris calls?'

'There are fewer of them. Always to the same person, a certain Monsieur Louis. And always to ask for girls. He gives the age and the price. She answers yes or no. Sometimes she does her business as though she were at the village market.'

'You haven't ever noticed anything odd about her conversations recently? Monsieur Emile hasn't telephoned privately?'

'I don't think he'd dare.'

'Doesn't his mother allow him?'

'She hardly allows him to do anything.'

'And Marcellin?'

'I was just going to tell you about him. It was unusual for him to come to the post office, and then it was only to cash money orders. I should say that in a year he would only telephone three times.'

'To whom?'

'Once, it was to Toulon to order a part of a motor, which he needed for his boat. Another time it was to Nice . . .'

'To Ginette?'

'It was to say that he hadn't been able to cash the order. He received one almost every month, did you know? She had made a mistake. The sum in words wasn't the same as the sum in figures, and I couldn't pay him. She sent another by the next post.'

'How long ago was this?'

'About three months. The door was closed, which means it was cold, so it was winter.'

'And the last call?'

'I started to listen, as usual, then Madame Galli came in to buy some stamps.'

'Was it a long conversation?'

'Longer than usual. It's easy to check up.'

She turned over the pages of her book.

'Two three-minute periods.'

'You heard the start. What did Marcellin say?'

'Something like this:

' *"Is that you? . . . It's me . . . yes. No, it's not money. . . . Money, I could have as much of that as I wanted. . . ."* '

'Did she say anything?'

'She murmured:

' *"You've been drinking again, Marcellin."*

'He swore he was practically sober. He went on:

' *"I want you to do something for me. . . . Is there a big Larousse in the house?"*

'That's all I know. At that moment Madame Galli came in and she's not easy to please. She says it's she who pays for civil servants with her taxes and she's always talking of complaining.'

'As the call only lasted six minutes, it's unlikely that Ginette had time to look up the Larousse encyclopaedia, come back to the telephone and give Marcellin a reply.'

'She sent the reply by telegram. Look. I have it here for you.'

She gave him a yellow form on which he read:

Died in 1890.

It was signed: *Ginette.*

'It would have been too bad for you if you hadn't come up to see me, wouldn't it? I shouldn't have come down, and you would have found out nothing.'

'Did you notice Marcellin's face when he read this telegram?'

'He re-read it two or three times, to make sure he had got it right, then he went off whistling.'

'As though he had received some good news?'

'Exactly. And also, I think, as if he had suddenly been struck with admiration for somebody.'

'Did you listen to Charlot's conversation yesterday?'

'With Bébé?'

'I beg your pardon?'

'He calls her Bébé. She must have arrived this morning. You want me to repeat his words?

'He said to her: "How goes, Bébé? I'm fine, thanks. I've got to stick around here a few more days and I'd like a little bit of fun. So come on over." '

'And she came,' Maigret finished. 'Thank you very much, mademoiselle. I'm on the bench outside, with my friend, and I'm waiting for my call from Paris.'

Three-quarters of an hour was passed, watching the bowls; the young married couple came to send off postcards; the butcher in turn came to make his daily call to Hyères. Mr. Pyke looked at the church tower from time to time. Occasionally he opened his mouth as well, perhaps to ask a question, but each time he changed his mind.

They were both of them oppressed by the heavily scented heat. From afar they could see the men gathering for the big bowls match, the one between about ten players, fought out across the entire square until time for *apéritifs* and dinner.

The dentist was taking part. The *Cormorant* had left the island for Giens Point from whence it would bring back Inspector Lechat and Ginette.

Finally Aglaé's voice summoned him in.

'Paris!' she announced.

It was the good Lucas who must, as usual during Maigret's absences, have taken over the latter's office. Through the window Lucas could see the Seine and the Pont Saint-Michel, while the chief-inspector was looking vaguely at Aglaé.

'I've got part of the information, Chief. I'm expecting the rest from Ostend presently. Who shall I start with?'

'Whichever you like.'

'Right, the Moricourt fellow. That wasn't difficult. Torrence remembered the name through having seen it on the cover of a book. It's his real name all right. His father, who was a cavalry captain, died a long while ago. His mother lives at Saumur. As for as I could gather they haven't any private means. Several times Philippe de Moricourt tried to marry heiresses, but didn't succeed.'

Aglaé was listening unashamedly, and through the glass, was winking at Maigret, to underline the bits she liked.

'He passes himself off as a man of letters. He published two volumes of poetry with a publisher on the left bank. He used to frequent the *Café de Flore*, where he was fairly well known. He has also worked occasionally on several newspapers. Is that what you want to know?'

'Go on.'

'I've hardly any other details as I did it all by telephone, to save time; but I sent someone to find out and you'll have some more snippets this evening or tomorrow. There's never been any charge against him, or rather there was one, five years ago, but it was withdrawn.'

'I'm listening.'

'A woman, who lives in Auteuil, whose name I should be able to get, had given him a rare edition to sell, after which she waited for several months without hearing of him. She lodged a complaint. It was found that he had sold the book to an American. As for the money, he promised to pay it back in monthly instalments. I got its former owner on the telephone. Moricourt was habitually two or three payments behind, but he paid up in the end, bit by bit.'

'Is that all?'

'Almost. You know the type. Always well-dressed, always impeccably correct.'

'And with old women?'

'Nothing definite. He had dealings of which he made a great mystery.'

'And the other one?'

'Did you know they knew one another? It seems de Greef is quite somebody; some people claim that, if he wanted, he could be one of the best painters of his generation.'

'And he doesn't want to be?'

'He ends by quarrelling with everybody. He went off with a Belgian girl of very good family.'

'I know.'

'Good. When he arrived in Paris, he held an exhibition of his works in a small room in the Rue de Seine. On the last day, as he hadn't sold anything, he burnt all the canvases. Some say veritable orgies took place on board his boat. He has illustrated several erotic works which are sold under the counter. It's mainly off this that he lived. There you are, Chief. I'm waiting for Ostend to call. Everything all right, down there?'

Through the glass, Mr. Pyke was showing Maigret his watch, and as it was five o'clock, he went off in the direction of the major's villa.

The chief-inspector felt quite light-headed about it, regarding it like a spell of holidays.

'Did you convey my congratulations to Janvier? Ring up my wife and tell her to go and see his and take something along, a present or some flowers. But not a silver mug!'

He found himself back with Aglaé, separated from her by the grilled partition. She seemed very amused. She admitted without shame:

'I'd like to see one of his books. Do you think he has some on board?'

Then, without stopping:

'It's strange! Your job's a lot simpler than people think. Information pours in from all sides. Do you think it's one of those two?'

There was a large bunch of mimosa on her desk, and a bag of sweets, which she offered to the chief-inspector.

'Things happen so seldom here! About Monsieur Philippe, I forgot

to tell you that he writes a lot. I don't read his letters, naturally. He
shoves them in the box and I recognize his writing and his ink, as he
always uses green ink, I don't know why.'

'Who does he write to?'

'I forget the names, but it's nearly always to Paris. Now and then he
writes to his mother. The letters to Paris are much thicker.'

'Does he get much post in return?'

'Quite a lot. And reviews, and newspapers. Every day there's printed
matter for him.'

'Mrs. Wilcox?'

'She writes a lot as well, to England, Capri, Egypt. I particularly
remember Egypt because I took the liberty of asking her for the stamps
for my nephew.'

'Does she telephone?'

'She has been along to telephone two or three times from the box,
and each time it was London she was calling. Unfortunately I don't
understand English.'

She added:

'I'm going to shut up. I should have shut at five. But if you want to
wait for your call . . .'

'What call?'

'Didn't Monsieur Lucas say he would call back about Ostend?'

She probably wasn't dangerous; yet Maigret would have preferred,
if only because of the people near by, not to remain too long alone with
her. She was all curiosity. She asked him, for example:

'Aren't you going to telephone your wife?'

He told her he would be on the square, not far from the *Arche* in case
a call came for him, and he went down quietly, smoking his pipe, in
the direction of the bowls match. He no longer needed to watch his
behaviour, as Mr. Pyke was not there to observe him. He really wanted
to play bowls and several times he asked about the rules of the game.

He was extremely surprised to discover that the dentist, whom everyone familiarly addressed as Léon, was a first-class player. At twenty
yards, after three bounding strides he would strike his opponent's ball
and send it rolling away into the distance, and each time he at once
affected a little modest air as though he considered the achievement to
be quite natural.

The chief-inspector went to have a glass of wine and found Charlot
busy working the fruit machine while his companion on the bench was
engrossed in a film magazine. Had they had their 'little bit of fun'?

'Isn't your friend with you?' asked Paul in surprise.

For Mr. Pyke as well, it must have been like a holiday. He was with
another Englishman. He could speak his own language, use expressions
which only meant something to two men from the same school.

It was easy to foretell the arrival of the *Cormorant*. Each time the same phenomenon took place. Outside there was a sort of downward current. People could be seen passing by, all making for the harbour. Then, once the boat was moored, the ebb would begin. The same people would pass by in the opposite direction, with, in addition, the new arrivals carrying suitcases or packages.

He followed the downward current, not far from the mayor who was pushing his eternal wheelbarrow. On the boat-deck he at once saw Ginette and the inspector, who looked like a couple of friends. There were also fishermen coming back from the funeral and two old ladies, tourists for the Grand Hotel.

In the group of people watching the disembarkation, he recognized Charlot who had followed him and who, like him, seemed to be going through a ritual without really believing in it.

'Nothing new, Chief?' asked Lechat, no sooner had he set foot on land. 'If you knew how hot it was over there!'

'Did it go off all right?'

Ginette stayed with them, quite naturally. She appeared tired. Her look betrayed a certain anxiety.

The three of them set off towards the *Arche*, and Maigret had the feeling that he had been taking this walk daily for a very long time.

'Are you thirsty, Ginette?'

'I could do with an *apéritif*.'

They drank together, on the terrace, and Ginette was uncomfortable every time she felt Maigret's gaze fall upon her. He looked at her dreamily, heavily, like a person whose thoughts are far away.

'I'll go up and wash,' she announced when her glass was empty.

'May I come with you?'

Lechat, who sensed something new in the air, was trying to guess. He didn't dare question his chief. He remained alone at the table, while the latter, behind Ginette, climbed the stairs.

'You know,' she said, when they were finally in the bedroom, 'I really want to change my life.'

'That doesn't worry me.'

She pretended to joke.

'And supposing it worried me?'

None the less she removed her hat, then her dress, which he helped her to unfasten at the back.

'This has sort of done something to me,' she sighed. 'I think he was happy here.'

On the other evenings Marcellin, at this hour, would have been taking part in the game of bowls on the square, in the setting sun.

'Everyone's been very kind. He was well liked.'

She hastily removed her corsets, which had left deep marks on her milky skin. Maigret, facing the attic window, had his back to her.

'Do you remember the question I asked you?' he said in a neutral voice.

'You repeated it enough times. I would never have believed you could be so hard.'

'On my side I would never have believed that you would try to hide anything from me.'

'Have I hidden something from you?'

'I asked you why you had come here, to Porquerolles, when Marcel's body was already in Hyères.'

'I answered you.'

'You told me a lie.'

'I don't know what you mean.'

'Why didn't you tell me about the telephone call?'

'What telephone call?'

'The one Marcellin made you the day before he died.'

'I didn't remember it.'

'Nor the telegram?'

He didn't have to turn to discover her reaction, and kept his gaze fixed on the game of bowls in progress opposite the terrace, from where there came a murmur of voices. The clink of glasses could be heard.

It was very soft, very reassuring, and Mr. Pyke wasn't there. As the silence continued, behind him, he asked:

'What are you thinking about?'

'I'm thinking that I was wrong, as you know perfectly well.'

'Are you dressed?'

'Just going to put on my dress.'

He went and opened the door, to make sure there was nobody in the corridor. When he came back to the middle of the room, Ginette was busy rearranging her hair in front of the glass.

'You didn't mention the Larousse?'

'Who to?'

'I don't know. Monsieur Emile for example. Or Charlot.'

'I wasn't so stupid as to mention it.'

'Because you were hoping to step into Marcel's shoes? Do you know, Ginette, you are a terribly calculating woman.'

'That's what people always say about women when they try to provide for the future. And they fall on them when misery drives them into a job they haven't chosen.'

There was a sudden bitterness in her voice.

'I thought you were going to marry Monsieur Emile?'

'On condition Justine makes up her mind to die and doesn't make last-minute arrangements preventing her son from marrying. Perhaps you think that makes me feel gay!'

'In short, if Marcel's tip was a good one and you succeeded, you wouldn't marry?'

'Certainly not that piece of creeping sickness.'

'Would you leave the house at Nice?'

'Without a moment's hesitation, I assure you.'

'What would you do?'

'I'd go and live in the country, anywhere. I'd keep chickens and rabbits.'

'What did Marcellin say to you on the telephone?'

'You'll say I'm lying again.'

He stared at her for a long while, and then said quietly:

'Not any more.'

'Good! It's not a moment too soon. He said he had accidentally discovered an extraordinary thing. Those are the words he used. He added that it could mean big money, but he wasn't yet sure.'

'Did he make any reference to anyone?'

'No. I have never known him so mysterious. He needed some information. He asked if we had a big Larousse, the one in I don't know how many volumes, in the house. I said we didn't keep one. Then he insisted on my going to the town library to look it up.'

'What did he want to know?'

'It's just too bad, isn't it? Now you've got so far, I haven't a chance of course.'

'None at all.'

'Even though I didn't understand a thing about it. I thought I'd get some idea when I reached here.'

'Who died in 1890?'

'You've seen my telegram? Didn't he destroy it?'

'The post office, as usual, kept a copy.'

'A certain Van Gogh, a painter. I read that he committed suicide. He was very poor and today people fight over his pictures which are worth I don't know what. I wondered if Marcel had got hold of one.'

'And it wasn't that?'

'I don't think so. When he telephoned me he didn't even know the gentleman concerned was dead.'

'What did you think?'

'I don't know, I promise. Only I told myself that if Marcel could make money with this information, it was possible that I could do so too. Especially when I learnt that he had been killed. People don't kill for fun. He had no enemies. There was nothing to steal from him. You understand?'

'You assume the crime has a connection with the Van Gogh in question?'

Maigret spoke without a trace of irony. He took small puffs at his pipe and gazed out of the window.

'No doubt you were right.'

'Too late, since you're here and it's no more use to me. Is there any further reason to keep me on the island? You see it's a holiday for me here, and as long as you keep me here, the old cat can't say anything.'

'In that case, stay.'

'Thank you. You are becoming almost like you were when I knew you in Paris.'

He didn't trouble to return the compliment.

'You have a rest.'

He went downstairs, passed near to Charlot who surveyed him with a bantering eye, and went and sat beside Lechat, on the terrace.

It was the most luscious hour of the day. The whole island was relaxed and the sea around it, the rocks, the ground of the square which seemed to breathe to another rhythm after the heat of the daytime.

'Have you found out anything, Chief?'

Maigret's first thought was to order a drink from Jojo who was passing near by and who looked as if she were cross with him for having closeted himself with Ginette in the bedroom.

'I'm afraid so,' he sighed finally.

And, as the inspector was looking at him in surprise:

'I mean that I shall probably not have much longer to stay here. It's a good place, don't you think? On the other hand, there's Mr. Pyke.'

Wasn't a quick success better, on account of Mr. Pyke and what he would say at Scotland Yard?

'There's a call from Paris for you, Monsieur Maigret.'

It was probably the information from Ostend.

VII

SUNDAY lay so heavily in the air as to become almost nauseating. Maigret used to claim openly, half seriously, half in fun, that he had always had the knack of sensing a Sunday from his bed, without even having to open his eyes.

Here there was an unprecedented noise of bells. They were not proper church bells, but small, high-pitched ones, like chapel or convent bells. One was led to the belief that the quality, the density of the air was not the same as elsewhere. One could distinctly hear the hammer striking the bronze, which gave out some sort of a note, but it was then that the phenomenon would begin: a first ring would carry into the pale and still cool sky, would extend hesitantly, like a smoke ring, becoming a perfect circle out of which other circles would form by magic, ever increasing, ever purer. The circles passed beyond the square and the houses, stretched over the harbour and a long way out to sea where small boats were anchored. One felt them above the hills and rocks, and they hadn't ceased to be perceptible before the hammer struck the metal once more and other circles of sound were born so as to reproduce themselves, then others, which one listened to in innocent amazement, as one watches a firework.

Even the simple sound of footsteps on the rough surface of the square had something Paschal about it, and Maigret, glancing out of the window, was expecting to see first communicants with their small legs becoming caught up in their veils.

As on the previous day he put on his slippers and trousers, and slipped his jacket over his nightshirt with the red embroidered collar, went downstairs and, going into the kitchen, was thoroughly disappointed. Subconsciously he had been hoping to repeat the previous early morning, to find himself beside the stove again with Jojo preparing the coffee, and the clear rectangle of the door open to the outside. But today there were four or five fishermen there. They must have been given some liquor which was strongly pervading the air. On the floor of the room a basket of fish had been upset: pink hog-fish, blue and green fish of which Maigret didn't know the name, a sort of sea-serpent with red and yellow blotches, which was still alive and coiling itself round the foot of a chair.

'Do you want a cup of coffee, Monsieur Maigret?'

It wasn't Jojo who served him but the *patron*. Perhaps because it was Sunday. Maigret felt like a thwarted child.

It sometimes happened to him, especially in the morning, expecially when he approached the looking-glass to shave. He would look at the broad face, the huge eyes often underlined with pouches, the thinning hair. He would become stern, deliberately, as though to frighten himself. He would tell himself:

'That's the divisional chief-inspector!'

Who would have dared not to take him seriously? Heaps of people, who did not have easy consciences, trembled at the mention of his name. He had the power to question them until they cried out with anguish, to put them in prison, send them to the guillotine.

In this very island, there was now someone who, like himself, heard the sound of the bells, who breathed the sabbath air, someone who was drinking in the same room as himself the previous evening and who, in a few days, would be shut up once and for all within four walls.

He swallowed down his cup of coffee, poured himself out another, which he carried up to his room, and he had some difficulty in realizing that all this could be serious: it was not so very long ago that he was wearing short trousers and walking across his village square, on chilly mornings, his fingertips numb with cold, to go and serve Mass in the small church lit only by wax candles.

Now he was a grown-up: everyone believed what he said, and there was only himself whom, from time to time, it was hard to convince.

Did other people have the same experience? Did Mr. Pyke, for example, sometimes wonder how other people could take him seriously? Did he, be it ever so rarely, have the impression that it was all a game, that life was just a joke?

Was the major anything more than an overgrown schoolboy, like the ones there are in every class, one of those fat and sleepy boys whom the master cannot resist making fun of?

Mr. Pyke had said a terrible thing the previous evening, shortly before the Polyte episode. It was downstairs, at the moment when, as on the evening before and every other evening, almost everybody was gathered at the *Arche*. Naturally, the Yard inspector had sat at the major's table, and at that moment, despite the difference in age and rotundity, they had a sort of family resemblance.

They must have been drinking, late in the afternoon, when Mr. Pyke had been to see his fellow-countryman at the villa. Enough to have a dulled eye and thick tongue, but too little to lose their dignity. Not only had they been taught the same manners at school, but later, heaven knows where, they had learnt to hold liquor in the same way.

They were not sad, but nostalgic rather, a little far away. They gave the impression of being two gods gazing down on the agitation of the world with a condescending melancholy, and, just as Maigret sat down next to him, Mr. Pyke had sighed:

'*She's been a grandmother since last week.*'

He did not look at the person in question, whose name he always avoided mentioning, but it could only be Mrs. Wilcox. She was there, on the far side of the room, sitting on the bench in Philippe's company. The Dutchman and Anna were at the next table.

Mr. Pyke had allowed a certain time to elapse, then had added in the same neutral voice:

'Her daughter and son-in-law don't allow her to set foot in England. The major knows them extremely well.'

Poor old woman! For all of a sudden. Mrs. Wilcox was revealed as really an old woman. One stopped laughing at her make-up, her dyed hair — with the white roots visible — and her artificial animation.

She was a grandmother, and Maigret remembered that he had conjured up his own in his thoughts; he had tried to imagine his reactions as a child if he had been shown a woman like Mrs. Wilcox and told:

'Go and kiss your granny!'

She was forbidden to live in her own country and she made no protest. She knew perfectly well that she wouldn't have the last word, that it was she who was in the wrong. Like drunkards, who are given a bare minimum of pocket money, and who try to cheat, and cadge a drink here and there.

Did she, like drunks too, sometimes become emotional over her misfortunes, weep in a corner by herself?

Perhaps when she had had a lot to drink? For she used to drink as well. Her Philippe saw to the filling of her glass whenever the need arose, while Anna, on the same bench, was only thinking of one thing: the moment when she could finally go off to bed.

Maigret was shaving. He hadn't been able to get into the only bathroom, which Ginette was occupying.

'In five minutes!' she had called out to him through the door.

From time to time he glanced out onto the square which was not the same colour as on other days, even now that the bells had ceased. The priest was in the middle of saying the first Mass. The one in his village used to rattle it off so quickly that young Maigret had scarcely time to get in the responses as he ran about with the cruets.

An odd sort of job, his! He was only a man like the others, and he held the fate of other men in his hands.

He had looked at them one by one, the evening before. He hadn't drunk much, just enough to exaggerate his feelings ever so slightly. De Greef, with his clear-cut profile, stared at him from time to time in silent irony and seemed to be challenging him. Philippe, despite his fine name and his ancestors, was of a coarser stock, and he tried hard to cut a figure each time Mrs. Wilcox ordered him about like a servant.

He must have got his revenge at other moments, granted, but he was none the less obliged to swallow insults in public.

The one he swallowed was fair-sized, so much so in fact that everyone felt uncomfortable about it. Poor Paul, who fortunately didn't know where the source of the trouble had been, took infinite pains afterwards to bring the party back to life.

They must be talking about it, down there. They would talk about it on the island all day. Would Polyte keep the secret? Just then it hardly mattered.

Polyte was at the counter, his captain's cap on his head, and he had already consumed a good many short drinks; he spoke so loud that his voice was drowning the various conversations. On Mrs. Wilcox's orders, Philippe had crossed the room to start up the gramophone, as often happened.

Then, with a wink at Maigret, Polyte had headed in turn towards the machine and stopped it.

Then he had turned to Moricourt and looked at him sarcastically, straight in the eye.

Philippe, without protesting, had pretended not to notice.

'I don't like people looking at me like that!' Polyte had then shouted out, advancing a few paces.

'But . . . I'm not even looking at you . . .'

'So you're too grand to look at me?'

'I didn't say that.'

'You think I don't understand?'

Mrs. Wilcox had murmured something in English to her companion. Mr. Pyke had frowned.

'I'm not good enough for you, perhaps, you little rat?'

Very red in the face, Philippe still didn't move, making an effort to look elsewhere.

'Try saying again that I'm not good enough for you.'

At the same moment de Greef had looked at Maigret, sharply, in a particularly pointed way. Had he understood? Lechat, who had understood nothing at all, had wanted to get up and interrupt, and Maigret had been obliged to seize his wrist under the table.

'What would you say if I pushed your pretty face in, eh? What would you say?'

Polyte, who judged that the ground was sufficiently prepared, then brought his fist flying over the table, at Philippe's face.

The latter put his hand up to his nose. But that was all. He didn't try to defend himself, nor to attack in his turn. He stammered:

'I've done nothing to you.'

Mrs. Wilcox was calling out, facing the bar:

'Monsieur Paul! Monsieur Paul! Will you throw this hooligan out? It's an outrage.'

Her accent gave a special flavour to the words *hooligan* and *outrage*.

'As for you . . .' Polyte began, turning to the Dutchman.

The reaction was different. Without leaving his place, de Greef stiffened, growled:

'That's enough, Polyte!'

One could feel that he wouldn't let himself be trifled with, that he was ready to spring, with all his muscles tensed.

Paul finally interposed.

'Calm down, Polyte. Come into the kitchen for a moment. I want a word with you.'

The captain let himself be led off, protesting for the sake of appearances.

Lechat, who still hadn't understood, had however asked, dreamily:

'Was it you, Chief?'

Maigret had not replied. He had assumed as benign an air as possible when the Scotland Yard inspector had looked him in the eye.

Paul had made his apologies in the correct way. Polyte was put out of the back door and seen no more. Today he would act like a hero.

The fact remained that Philippe hadn't defended himself, that his face, for one moment, had sweated with fear, a physical fear which seizes the pit of the stomach and is not to be overcome.

After that he had drunk to excess, with a cloudy look on his face, and Mrs. Wilcox had finally taken him off.

Nothing else had happened. Charlot and his dancing girl had gone up to bed rather early, and when Maigret had in turn gone up, they were still not asleep. Ginette and Monsieur Emile had chatted in undertones. No one had offered drinks all round, perhaps on account of the incident.

'Come in, Lechat,' the chief-inspector called out through the door. The inspector was already fully dressed.

'Has Mr. Pyke gone for a bathe?'

'He's downstairs, busy eating his bacon and eggs. I went down to see the *Cormorant* off.'

'Nothing to report?'

'Nothing. It seems that on Sundays lots of people come over from Hyères and Toulon, people who rush for the beaches and strew them with sardine tins and empty bottles. We'll be able to see them landing in an hour.'

The information from Ostend contained nothing unexpected. Monsieur Bebelmans, Anna's father, was an important figure, who had been mayor of the town for a long time and had once stood for Parliament. Since his daughter's departure, he had forbidden her name to be mentioned in his presence. His wife was dead, and Anna hadn't been told of it.

'It seems that everyone who has come off the rails for one reason or another has landed up here,' Maigret observed as he put on his coat.

'It's the climate that's responsible!' riposted the inspector, who was not troubled by such questions. 'I went to see another revolver this morning.'

He carried out his job conscientiously. He had taken pains to find out all the revolver owners. He went to see them one after the other, examined their weapons, without too much hope, simply because that was part of the routine.

'What are we doing today?'

Maigret, making for the door, avoided replying, and they found Mr. Pyke in front of the red check table-cloth.

'I presume you are a Protestant?' he said to him. 'In which case you wouldn't go to High Mass?'

'I am a Protestant and I went to Low Mass.'

Perhaps he would have been just the same if there had only been a synagogue, so as to attend a service, whatever it was, because it was Sunday.

'I don't know whether you'll want to come with me. This morning I have to pay a call on a lady you aren't anxious to meet.'

'You're going aboard the yacht?'

Maigret nodded, and Mr. Pyke pushed his plate away, rose and picked up the straw hat he had bought the day before at the mayor's shop, for he was already sunburnt enough to make his face almost as red as the major's.

'Are you coming with me?'

'You may need a translator.'

'Shall I come too?' asked Lechat.

'I'd like you to, yes. Can you row?'

'I was born at the seaside.'

They walked as far as the harbour, once again. It was the inspector who asked a fisherman permission to use a boat without a motor, and the three men took their places in it. They could see de Greef and Anna breakfasting on the deck of their little boat.

The sea, too, as though in honour of the Sabbath, had put on a shot-satin appearance, and at every stroke of the oar pearls sparkled in the sun. The *Cormorant* was on the other side of the water, at Giens Point, waiting for the passengers to alight from the bus. One could see the bottom of the sea, the violet urchins in the hollow of the rocks and an occasional brightly coloured sea-wolf which would flee like an arrow. The bells were ringing to announce High Mass, and all the houses must have smelt of the scent the women put on their best dresses, in addition to the morning coffee.

The *North Star* seemed much bigger, much higher from alongside, and as nobody was stirring, Lechat called out, raising his head:

'Hello there, on board!'

After a fairly long pause, a sailor leant over the rail, one cheek covered with frothy soap, an open razor in his hand.

'Can we see your mistress?'

'Couldn't you come back in an hour or so?'

Mr. Pyke was visibly uncomfortable. Maigret hesitated a moment, thinking of the 'grandmother'.

'We'll wait on deck if necessary,' he said to the seaman. 'Up you go, Lechat.'

They climbed the ladder, one behind the other. There were round copper portholes in the cabin, and Maigret saw a woman's face pressed against one for an instant, and then disappear into the semi-darkness.

A moment later the hatch opened, and Philippe's head appeared, his hair uncombed, his eyes still puffy with sleep.

'What do you want?' he asked, sullenly.

'A word with Mrs. Wilcox.'

'She's not up yet.'

'That's not true. I've just seen her.'

Philippe was wearing silk pyjamas, with blue stripes. There were a few steps to go down in order to enter the cabin, and Maigret, heavy and obstinate, was not waiting to be invited.

'May we come in?'

It was a strange mixture of luxury and disorder, of the refined and the sordid. The deck was meticulously scrubbed and all the brasswork gleamed, the ropes were carefully coiled, the captain's bridge, with its compass and nautical instruments, was as clean as a Dutch kitchen.

Going down the steps, the visitors immediately found themselves in a cabin with mahogany panelling, a table fixed to the floor, two benches with red leather upholstery, but with bottles and glasses lying about on the table, and there were slices of bread, a half-eaten tin of sardines, playing cards; a nauseating smell hung in the air, a mixture of alcohol and beds.

The door of the next cabin, which served as a bedroom, must have been shut in a hurry, and in her flight, Mrs. Wilcox had left a satin slipper upon the floor.

'Please excuse the intrusion,' Maigret said politely to Philippe. 'You were probably in the middle of breakfast?'

He was looking, without irony, at the half-empty bottles of English beer, a piece of bread which had been bitten into, a scrap of butter in some paper.

'Is this an official search?' questioned the young man, running his fingers through his hair.

'It's whatever you want it to be. Just now, as far as I am concerned, it's a straightforward visit.'

'At this hour?'

'At this hour there are some people who are already tired!'

'Mrs. Wilcox is in the habit of rising late.'

The sound of water could be heard on the other side of the door. Philippe would have liked to go away and put on something decent, but that would have meant revealing the too intimate disorder of the second cabin. He had no dressing-gown to hand. His pyjamas were crumpled. Mechanically he swallowed a mouthful of beer. Lechat had remained on deck, following the chief-inspector's instructions, and must then have been busy with the two sailors.

The latter were not English, as one might have supposed, but came from Nice, probably of Italian origin, to judge by their accents.

'You can sit down, Mr. Pyke,' said Maigret, since Philippe omitted to invite them.

Maigret's grandmother always used to go to the first Mass, at six o'clock in the morning, and when everyone else got up they found her in a black silk dress, with a white bonnet on her head, a fire blazing in the hearth, and breakfast served on a starched table-cloth.

Old women had been to the first Mass here, and others would now be making their way diagonally across the square, heading for the open door of the church, with its smell of incense.

As for Mrs. Wilcox, she had already had a drink of beer and in the morning more of the white roots must have been visible in her dyed hair. She went to and fro on the other side of the partition, without being able to be of any assistance to her secretary.

The latter, his cheek slightly swollen where the evening before Polyte had struck him with his fist, looked like a sulky schoolboy in his striped pyjamas. For just as there is in every class a fat boy who resembles an indiarubber ball, there is invariably the pupil who spends his free time silently preening himself in his corner while his schoolmates say:

'He's a drip!'

On the walls were hung engravings, but the chief-inspector was unable to pronounce on their quality. Some of them were fairly erotic, but without exceeding the limits of good taste.

They looked, Mr. Pyke and himself, rather as though they were in a waiting-room, and the Englishman was holding his straw hat between his knees.

Maigret finally lit his pipe.

'How old is your mother, Monsieur de Moricourt?'

'Why do you ask me that?'

'No reason. Judging by your age she must be in her fifties?'

'Forty-five. She had me very young. She married at sixteen.'

'Mrs. Wilcox is older than her, isn't she?'

Mr. Pyke lowered his head. Anyone might have thought the chief-inspector was doing it deliberately to make everyone feel more uncomfortable. Lechat was more at ease, outside, seated on the rail, chatting with one of the two sailors who was cleaning his nails in the sun.

In the end there was a noise from the door which opened and Mrs. Wilcox appeared, shutting it again hastily behind her so as not to let the chaos be seen.

She had found time to dress, and make up, but her features, under the thick cosmetics, remained puffed, her eyes anxious.

She must have been pitiable in the morning when she tried to clear her hang-over with a bottle of strong beer.

'Grandmother . . .' thought Maigret, in spite of himself.

He rose, greeted her, introduced his companion.

'Perhaps you know Mr. Pyke? He's a fellow-countryman of yours, who works at Scotland Yard. He's not here on business. Excuse my disturbing you at such an early hour, Mrs. Wilcox.'

She remained, in spite of everything, a lady, and a glance was enough to give Philippe to understand that his attire was indecent.

'Will you excuse me while I go and dress?' he murmured with a nasty look at the chief-inspector.

'Perhaps you will feel more at your ease.'

'Sit down, gentlemen. Is there anything I can offer you?'

She saw the pipe that Maigret was allowing to go out.

'Do go on smoking. Besides, I'm going to light a cigarette myself.'

She forced a smile.

'You must forgive the mess here, but a yacht isn't a house and space is limited.'

What was Mr. Pyke thinking at that particular moment? That his French colleague was a brute, or a boor?

Very possibly. Maigret was anyhow not exactly proud of the job he had to do.

'I believe you know Jef de Greef, Mrs. Wilcox?'

'He's a clever young man, and Anna's sweet. They've been on board several times.'

'He's said to be a talented painter.'

'I believe he is. I've had occasion to buy a canvas from him and I would have been happy to show it to you, only I've sent it off to my villa in Fiesole.'

'You've got a villa in Italy?'

'Oh, it's quite a modest little villa. But it's magnificently situated, on a hill, and from the windows you have a view over the whole of Florence. Do you know Florence, Inspector?'

'I haven't that pleasure.'

'I live there for part of the year. I send everything there that I happen to buy during the course of my wanderings.'

She thought she had found firm ground.

'You really don't want anything to drink?'

She was thirsty herself, and eyed the bottle she hadn't had time to finish earlier on, not daring to drink alone.

'Won't you really try some of this beer, which I have sent straight from England?'

He said yes, to please her. She went over to a cupboard which had been turned into an ice-box to look for some bottles. Most of the walls of the cabin were actually cupboards, just as the benches concealed chests.

'You've bought a lot of things on your travels, I gather?'

She laughed.

'Who told you that? I buy for the pleasure of buying, it is true. In Istanbul, for example, I always allow myself to be tempted by the salesmen at the bazaar. I come back on board with absolute horrors. At the time, they seem beautiful. Then, when I get back to the villa and find those things . . .'

'Did you meet de Greef in Paris?'

'No. Here only, not so long ago.'

'And your secretary?'

'He's been with me for two years now. He's a very cultured boy. We got to know each other at Cannes.'

'Was he working?'

'He was reporting for a Paris newspaper.'

Moricourt must have had his ear glued to the partition.

'You speak French perfectly, Mrs. Wilcox.'

'I was partly educated in Paris. My governess was French.'

'Did Marcellin often come on board?'

'Certainly. I think almost everyone on the island has been on board.'

'Do you remember the night he died?'

'I think so.'

He looked at her hands, which were not trembling.

'He talked a lot about me, that evening.'

'That's what I was told. I didn't know who you were. I asked Philippe.'

'And did Monsieur de Moricourt know?'

'It appears that you're well known.'

'When you left the *Arche de Noé* . . .'

'Go on.'

'Had Marcellin gone already?'

'I couldn't tell you. What I do know is that we went down to the harbour hugging the houses, the *mistral* was so strong. I was even afraid we shouldn't manage to get back on board.'

'Did you set off straight away in the boat, Monsieur de Moricourt and yourself?'

'Straight away. What else could we have done? That reminds me that Marcellin came with us as far as the dinghy.'

'You didn't meet anyone?'

'There can't have been anybody out at that hour.'

'Had de Greef and Anna returned to their boat?'

'Possibly. I can't remember. Wait . . .'

Then Maigret was astounded to hear the precise voice of Mr. Pyke, who, for the first time, was allowing himself to intervene in his investigation. The Yard man said deliberately, yet without appearing to attach too much importance to it:

'At home, Mrs. Wilcox, we should be obliged to remind you that anything you say may be used in evidence against you.'

She looked at him, dumbfounded, then looked at Maigret, and there was a sort of panic in her eyes.

'Is this an interrogation?' she asked. 'But . . . tell me, Chief-Inspector . . . I presume you don't suspect us, Philippe and me, of having killed this man?'

Maigret was silent for a moment, examining his pipe with deliberation.

'I suspect nobody *a priori*, Mrs. Wilcox. However, this is certainly an interrogation and you have the right not to reply.'

'Why shouldn't I reply? We came back straight away. Even though we shipped water in the dinghy and had to cling to the ladder to climb on board.'

'Philippe didn't go out again?'

There was a hesitation in her eyes. The presence of her fellow-countryman made her feel uncomfortable.

'We went straight to bed and he couldn't have left the boat without my hearing.'

Philippe chose this moment to make his appearance, in white flannels, his hair smoothed down, a freshly lit cigarette at his lips. He wanted to appear bold. He addressed himself directly to Maigret.

'You have some questions to put to me, Inspector?'

The latter pretended not to notice him.

'Do you often buy paintings, madame?'

'Fairly often. It's one of my hobbies. Without having exactly what you might call a picture gallery, I have some pretty good ones.'

'At Fiesole?'

'At Fiesole, yes.'

'Italian masters?'

'I don't rise to that. I'm more modest and content myself with fairly modern works.'

'Cézannes or Renoirs, for example?'

'I've a charming little Renoir.'

'Dégas, Manet, Monet?'

'A Dégas drawing, a dancer.'

'Van Gogh?'

Maigret was not looking at her, but stared straight at Philippe, who appeared to swallow hard and whose gaze became completely rigid.

'I've just bought a Van Gogh.'

'How long ago?'

'A few days. What day did we go to Hyères to send it off, Philippe?'

'I don't remember exactly,' the latter replied in a colourless voice.

Maigret prompted them.

'Wasn't it the day before or two days before Marcellin's death?'

'Two days before,' she said. 'I remember it now.'

'Did you find the picture here?'

She didn't stop to think, and a moment later she bit her lip.

'It was Philippe,' she said, 'who through a friend . . .'

She understood, by the silence of the three men, looked at them in turn, then cried:

'What is it, Philippe?'

She had risen with a start, was advancing towards the chief-inspector.

'You don't mean? . . . Explain to me! Speak! Why don't you say something? Philippe? What's . . .?'

The latter still didn't stir.

'Excuse me, madame, but I must take your secretary away.'

'Are you arresting him? But I tell you he was here, he didn't leave me all night, that . . .'

She looked at the door of the cabin which served as a bedroom and one could feel that she was on the point of throwing open the door, showing the double bed and shouting:

'How could he have gone without my knowing?'

Maigret and Mr. Pyke had risen as well.

'Will you come with me, Monsieur de Moricourt?'

'Have you a warrant?'

'I shall ask for one from the examining magistrate if you insist, but I don't think that will be the case.'

'Are you arresting me?'

'Not yet.'

'Where are you taking me?'

'Somewhere where we can have a quiet conversation. Don't you think it would be better that way?'

'Tell me, Philippe . . .' Mrs. Wilcox began.

Without realizing she began to speak to him in English. Philippe wasn't listening to her, or looking at her, or thinking about her any more. As he climbed onto the deck, she was not even give a look of farewell.

'This won't get you very far,' he said to Maigret.

'That's very possible.'

'Perhaps you're going to handcuff me?'

It was still Sunday and the *Cormorant*, moored to the jetty, was dis-gorging its passengers in their bright-coloured clothes. Already some tourists, perched on rocks, were busy fishing.

Mr. Pyke left the cabin last, and when he took his place in the dinghy, he was very red. Lechat, surprised to see another passenger, didn't know what to say.

Maigret, seated at the stern, allowed his left hand to trail in the water, as he used to do when he was small and his father took him in a boat on the pond.

The bells were still sending their circles of sound into the air.

IX

THEY stopped outside the grocer's to ask the mayor for the key. He was busy serving customers and he shouted something to his wife, who was small and pale, with a bun at the nape of her neck. She searched for a long while. During all this time Philippe remained waiting, be-tween Maigret and Mr. Pyke, his face set obstinately in a sulky

expression, and it resembled more than ever a school scene, with the
punished schoolboy and the heavy, implacable headmaster.

One would never have believed that so many people could have
come off the *Cormorant*. True, other boats had made the crossing that
morning. Until the trippers had had time to stream off to the beaches,
the square looked like an invasion.

Anna could be seen, in the semi-obscurity of the Co-operative, with
her net bag, wearing her sunsuit, while de Greef was sitting with Charlot on the terrace of the *Arche*.

These two had seen Philippe passing by between the detectives. They
had followed them with their eyes. They were free themselves, with a
table in front of them and a bottle of cool wine on the table.

Maigret had said a few words in an undertone to Lechat who had
stayed behind.

The mayor's wife finally brought the key and a few minutes later
Maigret was pushing open the door of the town hall, and immediately
opened the window on account of the dust and mustiness.

'Sit down, Moricourt.'

'Is that an order?'

'Precisely.'

He pushed over to him one of the folding chairs used for the July 14th
celebrations. Mr. Pyke appeared to have understood that on these
occasions the chief-inspector didn't like to see people standing, for he
unfolded a chair in his turn and settled himself in a corner.

'I suppose you have nothing to say to me?'

'Am I under arrest?'

'Yes.'

'I didn't kill Marcellin.'

'What else?'

'Nothing. I shall say nothing more. You can question me to your
heart's content and use all the vile methods you have at your command
to make people speak, but I'll still say nothing.'

How like a vicious child! Perhaps because of the impressions of that
morning, Maigret couldn't manage to take him seriously, to get it into
his head that he was dealing with a man.

The chief-inspector didn't sit down. He walked up and down aimlessly, touching a rolled-up flag or the bust of the Republic, stood for a
moment in front of the window and saw some little girls in white crossing
the square in the care of two nuns with winged bonnets. He hadn't
been so far out just now in being reminded of a first communion.

The islanders were wearing clean trousers that morning, made of
cloth, of a blue that became deep and rich in the sunlight of the square,
and the white of their shirts was dazzling. A game of bowls was already
starting. Monsieur Emile was making for the post office with his careful
tread.

'I suppose you realize you're a little rat?'

Maigret, enormous beside Philippe, looked him up and down, and the young man instinctively raised his hands to protect his face.

'I said a little rat, a rat who's afraid, who's a coward. There are people who break into flats and take risks. Others only go for old ladies, pinch rare books from them to resell them, and when they are caught, start crying, begging forgiveness and talking about their poor mothers.'

Mr. Pyke appeared to be making himself as small and as motionless as possible so as in no way to obstruct his colleague. One couldn't even hear him breathing, but the sounds from the island came in through the open window and mingled oddly with the chief-inspector's voice.

'Who first got the idea of the forged paintings?'

'I shall only reply in the presence of a lawyer.'

'So that your unfortunate mother will have to bleed herself white to pay for a well-known barrister for you! You'll have to have a well-known one, won't you? You're a repugnant creature, Moricourt!'

He stalked up and down, with his hands behind his back, more like a headmaster than ever.

'At my school we had a boy who was rather like you. Like you he was a drip. From time to time he needed a beating up, and when we gave him one, our teacher took care to turn his back or else to leave the playground. You had one yesterday evening and you didn't budge, you stayed there, pale and trembling in your place, beside the old woman who keeps you alive. It was I who asked Polyte to give you a hiding because I wanted to know your reactions, because I wasn't yet sure.'

'Are you intending to hit me again?'

He was trying to sneer, but one could tell that he was transfixed with fear.

'There are various species of rat, Moricourt, and unfortunately there are some that one somehow never manages to send to prison. I tell you straight away that I shall do all in my power to get you there.'

Ten times he turned back towards the young man in his chair, and each time the latter made an instinctive gesture to protect his face.

'Admit that the idea of the pictures was yours. You'll end by confessing, even if I have to spend three days and three nights at it. I've met a tougher nut than you. He sneered too, when he arrived at the Quai des Orfèvres. He was well-dressed like you. It was a long business. There were five or six of us taking it in turns. After thirty-six hours do you know what happened to him? Do you know how we discovered that he was giving in at last? By the smell! A smell as foul as himself! He had just relieved himself in his trousers.'

He looked at Moricourt's beautiful white trousers, then ordered him point blank:

'Take off your tie.'

'Why?'

'Do you want me to do it myself? Good! Now, undo your shoes. Remove the laces. You'll see, in a few hours you'll begin to look a bit more guilty.'

'You haven't the right . . .'

'I'll take it! You wondered how to squeeze more money from the mad old woman you had attached yourself to. Your lawyer will probably plead that it's immoral to allow fortunes to remain in the hands of women like her and will claim that it's an irresistible temptation. That doesn't concern us for the moment. All that's a matter for the jury. Because she bought pictures and didn't know anything about them you told yourself that there was big money to be made, and you got together with de Greef. I wonder whether it wasn't you that made him come to Porquerolles.'

'De Greef is a little saint, isn't he?'

'Another kind of rat. How many forgeries did he make for your old woman?'

'I've told you I shall say nothing.'

'The Van Gogh can't have been the first. Only it happens that somebody spotted that particular one, probably when it wasn't quite finished. Marcellin used to wander around almost anywhere. He used to climb on board de Greef's yacht as well as the *North Star*. I suppose he caught the Dutchman in the middle of signing a canvas with a name that wasn't his own. Then he saw the same canvas in Mrs. Wilcox's possession and he tumbled to it. It took him a bit of time to find out how the system was worked. He wasn't sure. He had never even heard of Van Gogh and he telephoned a girl friend to find out about him.'

Philippe was staring fixedly at the floor, a peevish look on his face.

'I don't say it was you who killed him.'

'I didn't kill him.'

'You're probably too much of a coward for that sort of a job. Marcellin told himself that as the two of you were getting fat off the old woman's bank balance there was no reason why he shouldn't be a third. He put it to you. You wouldn't play. Then, to dot all the *i*'s, he began to talk about his friend Maigret. How much did Marcellin ask?'

'I shan't answer.'

'I've plenty of time. That night, Marcellin was killed.'

'I have an alibi.'

'Namely that at the time of his death you were in the grandmother's bed.'

One could smell, even from the small town-hall room, the *apéritifs* that were being served on the terrace at the *Arche*. De Greef must still be there. Probably Anna had joined him with her provisions. Lechat, at a neighbouring table, was watching him, and if necessary would stop him going away.

As for Charlot, he had surely realized by now that, at all events, he was too late. He was another who had been hoping to have his cut!

'Are you intending to talk, Philippe?'

'No.'

'Note that I'm not trying to make you do so by telling stories. I'm not telling you that we've got proof, that de Greef has taken the bait. You'll talk in the end, because you're a coward, because you're poisonous. Give me your cigarettes.'

Maigret took the packet the young man handed to him and threw it out of the window.

'May I ask you to do me a service, Mr. Pyke? Will you go and ask Lechat, who is on the terrace at the *Arche*, to bring in the Dutchman? Without the girl. I'd also like Jojo to bring us a few bottles of beer.'

As though from scruple, he did not utter a word during his colleague's absence. He went on walking up and down, his hands behind his back, and the Sunday life continued on the other side of the window.

'Come in, de Greef. If you had a tie, I should tell you to take it off, and the same with your shoe-laces.'

'Am I under arrest?'

Maigret contented himself with a nod.

'Sit down. Not too near your friend Philippe. Give me your cigarettes and throw away the one you've got stuck in your mouth.'

'Have you a warrant?'

'I'm going to send for one by telegraph, in your two names, so there'll be no more doubt on the subject.'

He sat down in the place the mayor must have occupied for marriages.

'One of you two killed Marcellin. To tell the truth it doesn't much matter which, since you're each as guilty as the other.'

Jojo came in, with a tray covered with bottle and glasses, then stood nonplussed in front of the two young men.

'Don't be afraid, Jojo. They're just two dirty little killers. Don't start talking about it outside immediately or we'll have the whole population at the window and the Sunday trippers into the bargain.'

Maigret was taking his time, looking at the two young men in turn. The Dutchman was much the calmer and there was no trace of bravado about him.

'Perhaps I'd do better to leave you to settle it between the two of you? When all's said and done, it concerns one of you. There is in fact one person who will probably have his head lopped off or else will spend the rest of his days in a penal settlement, while the other will get away with a few years in prison. Which?'

Already the 'drip' was shifting in his chair and one might have thought he was going to put up his hand, as if at school.

'Unfortunately the law cannot take into account true responsibility. For my part I would happily put the two of you in the same bag, with this difference, however, that I should have a tiny scrap of sympathy for de Greef.'

Philippe was still shifting, ill at ease, visibly discontented.

'Admit, de Greef, that you didn't do it just for the money! You don't want to answer, either? As you wish. I bet that you've been amusing yourself painting forgeries for quite some time, just to prove you're no spare-time painter, no mere dauber. Have you sold a lot?

'Never mind! What a revenge on the people who don't understand you if you had one of your works, signed with a famous name, hanging in line at the Louvre, or an Amsterdam museum!

'We shall be seeing your latest works. We'll have them sent from Fiesole. At the trial the experts will argue over them. You're going to live through some great moments, de Greef!'

It was almost amusing to see Philippe's expression, at once disgusted and angry, during this little speech. The two of them looked more and more like schoolboys. Philippe was jealous of the words Maigret was addressing to his classmate and had to hold himself in so as not to protest.

'Admit, Monsieur de Greef, that you aren't really annoyed that it hasn't come off!'

Even down to the 'Monsieur', which wounded Moricourt to his very soul.

'When no one else knows but yourself, it's not much fun in the end. You don't love your life, Monsieur de Greef.'

'Nor yours, nor the one people wanted me to lead.'

'You don't love anything.'

'I don't love myself.'

'Nor do you love that little girl whom you only carried off out of defiance, to infuriate her parents. Since when have you been wanting to kill one of your fellow-creatures? I don't say from necessity, to gain money or to suppress an embarrassing witness. I'm speaking for the sake of killing, to see what it's like, what reactions one has. And even to hit the body afterwards with a hammer to prove that one has strong nerves.'

A thin smile twisted the Dutchman's lips, and Philippe was furtively watching him, without understanding.

'Would you like me to predict now what's going to happen! You've decided, both of you, to keep silent. You are convinced that there is no proof against you. There was no witness of Marcellin's death. Nobody, on the island, heard the shot, because of the *mistral*. The weapon hasn't been found; probably it's safe at the bottom of the sea. I haven't taken the trouble to make a search. Fingerprints won't tell us anything more. It will be a long inquiry. The magistrate will question you patiently, will find out about your antecedents, and the newspapers will talk a lot about you. They won't fail to splash the fact that you are both of good family.

'Your Montparnasse friends, de Greef, will emphasize that you are talented. You will be represented as a fantastic, misunderstood being.

'People will also talk about the two slim volumes of verse which Moricourt has had published.'

It may be imagined how delighted the latter was to see a good point awarded him at last!

'The reporters will go and interview the judge at Groningen, and Madame de Moricourt at Saumur. The gutter press will laugh at Mrs. Wilcox and no doubt her embassy will make representations for her name to be mentioned as seldom as possible.'

He drank half a glass of beer at a gulp and went and sat on the window-sill, his back turned to the sunny square.

'De Greef will remain silent, because it's in his temperament, because he's not afraid.'

'And I'll talk?' sneered Philippe.

'You'll talk. Because you're a drip through and through, because in the eyes of the world, you'll be the nasty piece of work, because you'll try to worm your way out of it, because you're a coward and you'll convince yourself that by talking you'll save your precious skin.'

De Greef turned to his companion, an indefinable smile on his lips.

'You'll talk, tomorrow probably, when you find several hefty chaps, in a real police station, questioning you with their fists. You don't like being hit, Philippe.'

'They haven't the right.'

'Nor have you the right to swindle a poor woman who no longer knows what she's doing.'

'Or who knows only too well! It's because she's got money that you go to her defence.'

Maigret didn't even have to advance towards him for him to lift up his hands again.

'You'll talk all the more when you see that de Greef has a better chance of getting off than you have.'

'He was on the island.'

'He had an alibi, as well. If you were with the old woman, he was with Anna . . .'

'Anna will say . . .'

'Will say what?'

'Nothing.'

Lunch had begun at the *Arche*. Jojo cannot have remained altogether silent or else people could smell something in the air, for silhouettes could be seen from time to time roving round the town hall.

Presently there would be a whole crowd.

'I've a good mind to leave the two of you alone. What do you think, Mr. Pyke? With someone to watch them, of course, or otherwise we'd risk finding them in small pieces. Will you stay, Lechat?'

The latter went and settled himself, his elbows on the table, and, for want of an *apéritif* or a white wine, poured himself a glass of beer.

Maigret and his British colleague found themselves outside once more in the sun, which was at its hottest, and strolled a few yards in silence.

'Are you disappointed, Mr. Pyke?' asked the chief-inspector finally, watching him from the corner of his eye.

'Why?'

'I don't know. You came to France to find out our methods and you discover there are none. Moricourt will talk. I could have made him talk straight away.'

'By employing the method you spoke of?'

'That one or another. Whether he talks or not, it's of no real importance. He'll retract. He'll confess again, then retract again. You'll see doubt being insinuated into the minds of the jury. The two lawyers will argue like cat and dog, each whitening his own client, each placing the entire responsibility on his colleague's client.'

They didn't need to raise themselves on tiptoe to see the two young men, through the town hall window, sitting on their chairs. On the terrace of the *Arche*, Charlot was eating his lunch, with his girl friend on his right, and on his left Ginette, who seemed to be explaining from afar to the chief-inspector that she hadn't been able to refuse the invitation.

'It's more pleasant to deal with professionals.'

Perhaps he was thinking of Charlot.

'But those are seldom the ones who kill. Real crimes occur partly by accident. These lads started by playing, without attempting to find out where it was leading them. It was almost like a good joke. To unload pictures signed with famous names on a dotty old woman, worth thousands! And then one fine morning some odd character called Marcellin climbs onto the deck of the boat at an inopportune moment . . .'

'Do you feel sorry for them?'

Maigret shrugged, without replying.

'You'll see how the psychiatrists will discuss their respective degrees of responsibility.'

Mr. Pyke, screwing up his eyes on account of the sun, gazed at length at his colleague, as though he were trying to plumb his thoughts, then said simply:

'Ah!'

The chief-inspector didn't ask whether he had just arrived at a conclusion. He spoke of something else, asking:

'Do you like the Mediterranean, Mr. Pyke?'

And as Mr. Pyke, hesitating, was preparing his answer, he went on:

'I wonder whether the air isn't too strong for me. We shall probably be able to get off this evening.'

The white church tower had become set against the sky, at once hard and transparent. The mayor, intrigued, was looking in from outside the window of his hall. What was Charlot doing? He could be seen rising from his table and setting off hurriedly for the harbour.

Maigret watched him for a moment, frowning, then grunted:

'As long as . . .'

He rushed off in the same direction, followed by Mr. Pyke, who didn't understand.

When they arrived within sight of the jetty, Charlot was already on the deck of the small yacht, ironically christened: 'Flower of Love.'

He paused for a moment, leaning on the rail, examining the interior, disappeared, then returned onto the deck carrying someone in his arms.

When the two men arrived in their turn, Anna was stretched out on the deck, and Charlot, without any shame, took off her sunsuit, laying bare in the sun a full and heavy bosom.

'Didn't it occur to you?' he said, bitterly.

'Veronal?'

'There's an empty tube on the cabin floor.'

There were five, then ten, then a whole crowd round the body of Mademoiselle Bebelmans. The island doctor came up slowly, and said in a broken voice:

'I've brought an emetic, in case there's a chance.'

Mrs. Wilcox was on the deck of her yacht, accompanied by one of her sailors, and they were handing a pair of binoculars to one another.

'So you see, Mr. Pyke, I make mistakes as well. She realized that de Greef had nothing to fear except her evidence and she was afraid of talking.'

He pushed through the crowd that had gathered in front of the town hall. Lechat had closed the window. The two young men were still in their places, the bottles of beer on the table.

Maigret started to prowl up and down the room like a bear, stopped in front of Philippe de Moricourt and, suddenly, without any warning whatever, this time without the young man having time to protect himself, he struck him full in the face with his hand.

It relieved him. In an almost calm voice, he murmured:

'I beg your pardon, Mr. Pyke.'

Then to de Greef, who was watching him and trying to understand:

'Anna is dead.'

He didn't bother to question them that day. He tried not to see the coffin which was still in its corner, the famous coffin of old Benoît, which had already been used for Marcellin and which was to be used for the young girl from Ostend.

Ironically, Benoît's hirsute head, well in evidence, was distinguishable among the crowd.

Lechat and the two men, handcuffed by their wrists, set off for Giens Point in a fishing boat.

Maigret and Mr. Pyke took the *Cormorant* at five o'clock, and Ginette was there, likewise Charlot and his dancing girl, and all the trippers who had spent the day on the beaches of the island.

The *North Star* was riding at anchor at the harbour entrance. Maigret, scowling, was smoking his pipe and as his lips moved, Mr. Pyke leant towards him to ask:

'I beg your pardon? You were saying?'

'I said: dirty wretches!'

With which he quickly turned away his head and gazed into the depths of the water.

Stud Barn,
Tumacacori, Arizona.
2 February, 1949

MAIGRET IN COURT

MAIGRET IN COURT

(*Maigret aux Assises*)
*was first published in France in 1960
and in Great Britain in 1961
Translated from the French by Robert Brain*

*Copyright © 1960 Georges Simenon
Translation copyright © 1961 by Hamish Hamilton Ltd*

TO DENISE

MAIGRET IN COURT

I

HAD he been there two hundred times? three hundred times? or even more? He had no desire to count them, nor to recall each individual case, even the most famous of them, those which had found a place in legal history, since this was the most unpleasant part of his profession.

Yet did not most of his investigations lead in the end to the Assize Court, like today, or to the police court? He would have preferred not to know about it, at least to keep out of these last rites, to which he had never altogether become habituated.

In his office at the Quai des Orfèvres, the conflict, which most often was not decided until the small hours of the morning, was still a battle of one man against another, more or less on equal terms.

Go along a few corridors, a few staircases, and it was a different setting, another world, where words no longer held the same meaning, an abstract, hieratic universe, pompous and preposterous at the same time.

With other witnesses, he had just left the courtroom with its solemn panelling, where the light from the electric globes mingled with the greyness of a rainy afternoon. The usher, whom Maigret would have sworn had always looked as old as he did now, led them to a smaller room, like a schoolmaster leading his pupils, and gestured to the benches fastened to the walls.

Most of them went and sat down obediently and, respecting the judge's instructions, did not utter a word, even hesitated to look at their companions.

They looked straight in front of them, tense, withdrawn, saving up their secrets until that solemn moment when, quite soon now, alone in the centre of an awesome space, they would be questioned.

It was rather like being in the vestry. As a little boy, when he had gone each morning to serve Mass at the village church, Maigret used to feel a similar nervousness as he waited to follow the priest towards the altar, lit by flickering candles. He could hear the footsteps of the unseen faithful going to their pews, the sacristan walking up and down.

In the same way now, he was able to follow the ritual ceremony which was being performed beyond the door. He could recognize the voice of Judge Bernerie, the most meticulous, the fussiest of magistrates, but also perhaps the most scrupulous and the most passionate seeker of the truth. Thin and in poor health, his eyes feverish, with a dry cough, he resembled a saint in a stained-glass window.

Then came the voice of Aillevard, the procurator, who sat in the public prosecutor's bench.

Finally steps approached, those of the court usher, who opened the door a crack and called:

'Detective-Inspector Segré.'

Segré, who had not sat down, glanced across at Maigret and went into the courtroom, in his overcoat, a grey hat in his hand. The eyes of the rest followed him for a moment, thinking that it would be their turn soon and anxiously wondering how they would acquit themselves.

A small patch of colourless sky was visible through some inaccessible windows, placed so high up that they were only opened or closed with the help of a cord, and the electric light sculpted the faces beneath with blank eyes.

It was warm, but it would not have been proper to take his overcoat off. There was this ritual, to which everyone on the other side of the door paid strict attention, and it made no difference that Maigret came only from next door, along the corridors of the gloomy Law Courts: he wore an overcoat, like the rest, and carried his hat in his hand.

It was October. The chief-inspector had only returned two days ago from his holidays, to a Paris drowning in apparently interminable rain. Back in the Boulevard Richard-Lenoir, then in his office, he would have found his feelings hard to define and there was certainly as much pleasure as sadness in coming home.

In a short while, when the judge asked him his age, he would answer: 'Fifty-three.'

And that meant that, according to regulations he would be retired in two years' time.

He had often thought about it and often looked forward to it. But this time, on his return from his holidays, retirement was no longer a vague or distant prospect; it was a logical conclusion, ineluctable, practically immediate.

Their future, during the three weeks they had spent on the Loire, had begun to materialize when the Maigrets finally bought the house where they would spend their declining days.

It had happened almost against their will. As in previous years, they had stayed at an hotel in Meung-sur-Loire where they had formed their own habits and the landlord and his wife, the Fayets, treated them as members of the family.

Notices on the walls of the little town announced the sale by auction of a house on the edge of the country. They went to see it, he and

Madame Maigret. It was a very old building which, with its garden surrounded by a grey wall, reminded them of a presbytery.

They had been captivated by the blue flagged passages, the kitchen with its huge beams, three steps down from ground level, which still had its pump in one corner; the drawing-room smelt like the parlour of a convent, and throughout the house the windows, with their tiny panes, mysteriously dissected the sun's rays.

At the sale the Maigrets, standing at the back of the room, had received several curious looks, and people had been surprised when the chief-inspector had raised his hand while the villagers turned round to look. . . . Going . . . Going . . . Gone!

For the first time in their lives they were property-owners and, the very next day, they arranged for the plumber and the carpenter to call.

During the last few days they had even begun to tour the local antique-shops. They had bought, among other things, a wooden chest with the arms of Francis I, which they had placed in the downstair-passage, near the drawing-room door, where there was a stone chimney piece.

Maigret had not mentioned anything about it to Janvier, nor to Lucas, not to a soul, rather as if he were ashamed to be planning his future in this way, as if it were a treasonable offence in respect of the Quai des Orfèvres.

The previous day, his office had no longer looked quite the same to him, and this morning, in the witnesses' room, listening to the echoes from the courtroom, he was beginning to feel a stranger.

In two years' time he would be going fishing, and probably playing *belote* on winter afternoons with a few cronies in the corner of a café where he had already begun to go regularly.

Judge Bernerie was putting precise questions, which the inspector from the IXth arrondissement police station was answering with no less precision.

On the benches, around Maigret, the witnesses, men and women, had all passed through his office and some of them had spent several hours in it. Was it because they were overwhelmed by the solemn atmosphere of the place that they seemed not to recognize him?

It was not he who would question them this time, it was true. They would not be appearing, this time, before a man like themselves, but in front of an impersonal machine, and it was even uncertain whether they would understand the questions that would be put to them.

The door half-opened. It was his turn. Like his colleague from the IXth he held his hat in his hand, and without looking to left or right, he walked up to the semi-circular balustrade of the witnesses' stand.

'Your surname, Christian names, age and profession . . .'

'Maigret, Jules, fifty-three, divisional chief-inspector at Police Head-quarters, Paris.'

'You are neither related to nor employed by the accused . . .? Raise your right hand. . . . Swear to tell the truth, nothing but the truth . . .'

'I swear . . .'

He saw, on his right, the figures of the jury, their faces standing out more clearly than others in the half-light, and on the right, behind the black gowns of the barristers, the accused man, sitting between two uniformed warders, his chin on his clasped hands, staring intently at him.

They had spent long hours on their own together, the two of them, in the overheated office at the Quai des Orfèvres, and they had sometimes broken off the interrogation to eat sandwiches and drink some beer, chatting like old friends.

'Listen, Meurant . . .'

Perhaps Maigret had occasionally used '*tu*' to him?

Here, an insurmountable barrier separated them and Gaston Meurant's look was as non-committal as the chief-inspector's.

Judge Bernerie and Maigret were also acquainted, not only because they had chatted together in the corridors, but because this was the thirteenth time the one had been interrogated by the other.

It had left no trace. Each played his part as if they had been strangers, officiating in a ceremony as ancient and ritualistic as the Mass.

'It was you, Divisional Chief-Inspector, who conducted the investigations into the facts of which the court has now been apprised?'

'Yes, your honour.'

'Please turn to the members of the jury and tell them all you know.'

'On February 28th last, at about one o'clock in the afternoon, I was in my office on the Quai des Orfèvres when I received a telephone call from the station officer of the IXth arrondissement. He informed me that a crime had just been discovered in the Rue Manuel, not far from the Rue des Martyrs, and that he was on his way to the scene. A few minutes later I had a call from the public prosecutor's department requiring me to go along as well and to send Technical Branch and laboratory experts there.'

Maigret heard a few coughs behind him, shoes scraping on the floor.

It was the first case of the law sitting and all the seats were occupied. There were probably spectators standing at the back, near the big door guarded by uniformed policemen.

Judge Bernerie belonged to that minority of magistrates who, applying the penal code to the letter of the law, do not content themselves with hearing a résumé in the Assize Court of the examining magistrate's findings, but go over it all again in its smallest details.

'You found the public prosecutor's staff on the premises?'

'I arrived several minutes before his surrogate. I found Inspector Segré on the spot with his assistant and two detectives from the district. Nothing whatever had been touched by any of them.'

'Tell us what you saw.'

'The Rue Manuel is a quiet street, middle-class, with little activity in it, which runs into the bottom of the Rue des Martyrs. The house, number 27a, is situated almost half-way along the street. The concierge's lodge is not on the ground floor, but on the landing above. The inspector, who was waiting for me, took me up the second floor where I saw two doors opening off the landing. The one on the right was ajar and on a small copper plaque was the name: Madame Faverges.'

Maigret was aware that for Judge Berneries every point counted, and that he must omit nothing or he would be drily called to order.

'In the hall, lit by an electric lamp of frosted glass, I noticed no disorder.'

'One moment, please! Were there, on the door, any signs of its having been forced?'

'No. Experts examined it later. The lock has been removed. It has been established that no instrument, of the type generally used to force locks, was employed on it.'

'Thank you. Please proceed.'

'The flat consists of four rooms, apart from the entrance-hall. Opposite the front door is a drawing-room; the glass door into it is hung with cream curtains. It was in this room, which leads through another glass door into the dining-room, that I saw the two bodies.'

'Where were they exactly?'

'That of the woman, who I afterwards learnt was named Léontine Faverges, was lying on the carpet, her head turned towards the window. Her throat had been cut by means of some weapon which was no longer in the room, and on the carpet there was a pool of blood more than twenty inches across. As for the child's body . . .'

'You mean, do you, the young Cécile Perrin, the four-year-old girl who normally lived with Léontine Faverges?'

'Yes, your honour. The body was curled up on a Louis Quinze sofa, her face buried beneath some silk cushions. According to the local doctor, and shortly afterwards Dr. Paul as well, after an attempt to strangle her, the child was smothered by those cushions . . .'

A murmur ran through the room, but the judge had only to raise his head, run his eyes along the rows of spectators, for silence to reign again.

'After the appearance of the members of the public prosecutor's department, you stayed on in the flat with your colleagues until the evening?'

'Yes, your honour.'

'Tell us what conclusions you reached.'

Maigret hesitated only a few seconds.

'From the first, I was struck by the furnishings and the interior decoration. According to her papers, Léontine Faverges had no profession.

She had a small private income and looked after Cécile Perrin, whose mother, a cabaret entertainer, could not do so herself.'

The mother, Juliette Perrin, he had noticed as he entered the room, seated in the front row of the body of the court, since she was claiming damages. Her hair was dyed red and she was wearing a fur coat.

'Tell us exactly what surprised you about the flat.'

'An unusual elegance, a special style which reminded me of certain flats in the days before the laws on prostitution. The drawing-room, for example, was over-padded, over-ripe, with a profusion of rugs, cushions and sentimental prints on the walls. The blinds were of delicate shades, as they were also in the two bedrooms, which had more mirrors than one might ordinarily expect. I gathered, in due course, that Léontine Faverges had indeed formerly kept her flat as a place of assignation. After the new laws were passed she carried on for a while. The Vice Squad had had to take notice of her and she only gave up and ceased all activity after being fined several times.'

'Were you able to discover what financial resources she had?'

'According to the concierge, women-neighbours and everybody who knew her, she had put money aside, since she had never been a spend-thrift. Her maiden name was Meurant; a sister of the accused's mother, she arrived in Paris when she was eighteen and worked for a time as a sales-woman in a department store. At twenty she married a man called Faverges, a commercial traveller, who died three years later in a motor accident. The couple were then living in Asnières. For several years the young woman was to be seen frequenting the restaurants in the Rue Royale and the Vice Squad had a record of her.'

'Have you made enquiries, among people she knew at that time, for anyone who might have remembered her recently and decided to attack her?'

'She was a solitary person, apparently, which is rather unusual amongst her sort. She saved her money, which enabled her, later on, to set herself up in the Rue Manuel.'

'She was sixty-two years of age when she died?'

'Yes. She had grown fat, but as far as I could judge she had retained a kind of youthful appearance and a coquettish way about her. Accord-ing to the witnesses I questioned she was very attached to the little girl, whom she boarded, less for the slight income it procured her, it seems, than for fear of loneliness.'

'Did she have a bank or savings-bank account?'

'No. She had no faith in loan societies, trustees, or investments of any sort, and kept everything she had at home.'

'Was the money found?'

'Very little, some change, some notes of small denomination in a handbag, and some more change in a kitchen drawer.'

'Was there a hiding-place and did you discover it?'

'Apparently there was. When Léontine Faverges was ill, which happened two or three times over the last few years, the concierge would go up to do her housework and look after the child. On a chest of drawers in the drawing-room there was a Chinese vase with a bunch of artificial flowers in it. One day the concierge wanted to dust the flowers so she took them out of the vase and found in the bottom a linen purse which she thought contained gold pieces. From its size and weight the concierge says there must have been more than a thousand. A test was carried out in my office with a linen bag and a thousand pieces. It was apparently conclusive. I questioned the staffs of various banks in the neighbourhood. At a branch of the Crédit Lyonnais they remembered a woman, whose description corresponded to that of Léontine Faverges, who they said bought bearer-bonds at various times. One of the cashiers, named Durat, officially recognized her from a photograph.'

'So it is likely that these bonds, like the gold pieces, would have been in the flat somewhere. But you did not discover anything?'

'No, your honour. We naturally searched for fingerprints on the Chinese vase, on the drawers and more or less all over the flat.'

'With no result?'

'Only the fingerprints of the two residents and, in the kitchen, those of a delivery boy whose movements have been checked. His last delivery was on the morning of the 27th. And, according to Dr. Paul, who performed the autopsy on both bodies, the crime was not committed earlier than the evening of February 27th between five and eight o'clock.'

'Have you questioned all the occupants of the building?'

'Yes, your honour. They confirmed what the concierge had already told me, in other words that Léontine Faverges had no men visitors apart from her two nephews.'

'You mean the accused, Gaston Meurant, and his brother Alfred?'

'According to the concierge, Gaston Meurant came to see her fairly regularly, once or twice a month, and his last visit had occurred about three weeks before. As for his brother, Alfred Meurant, he only put in rare appearances at the Rue Manuel because he was not in favour with his aunt. By questioning her neighbour across the landing, Madame Solange Lorris, a dressmaker, I learnt that a customer of hers had come to see her for a fitting on February 27th, at about half-past five. This person is named Madame Ernie and lives in the Rue Saint-Georges. She states that just as she was going up the stairs, a man came out of the dead woman's flat and that when he saw her, he seemed to change his mind. Instead of going downstairs he went up towards the third floor. She was unable to see his face clearly, because the staircase is badly lighted. According to her the man was wearing a navy suit and a maroon, belted raincoat.'

'Tell us how you first got into touch with the accused.'

'While my men and I were examining the flat, on the afternoon of February 28th, and were starting to question the other tenants, the evening papers came out with news of the crime and printed a certain number of details.'

'One moment. How was the crime discovered?'

'About noon that day, I mean February 28th, the concierge was surprised not to have seen either Léontine Faverges, or the little girl, who usually attended a kindergarten nearby. She went and rang the door-bell. Receiving no answer she went up again a little later, still without result, and eventually she telephoned the police. But to get back to Gaston Meurant, the concierge only knew that he was a picture-framer and that he lived near Père-Lachaise. I had no need to start a search for him because the next morning . . .'

'That's March 1st . . .'

'Yes. The next morning, as I was saying, he turned up of his own accord at the IXth arrondissement police station saying that he was the murdered woman's nephew, and the station sent him along to me . . .'

Judge Bernerie was not one of those judges who take notes, or during a hearing deal with their correspondence. Still less did he drowse off, and his eyes darted incessantly from the witness to the accused, with an occasional brief glance at the jury.

'Tell the court as exactly as possible of this first interview you had with Gaston Meurant.'

'He was wearing a grey suit and a fairly old fawn raincoat. He seemed slightly overawed at being in my office and I got the impression that it was his wife who had persuaded him to pay that visit.'

'Did she accompany him?'

'She stayed outside in the waiting-room. One of my inspectors came and informed me she was there, so I asked her to come in. Meurant told me he had read the newspapers, that Léontine Faverges was his aunt, and that, as he believed that he and his brother were the only near relations the murdered woman had, he thought he had better make himself known. I asked him how he got on with the old lady and he replied that they got on very well together. Still in answer to my queries, he added that his last visit to the Rue Manuel had been on January 23rd. He was unable to give me his brother's address since he no longer kept in touch with him.'

'So, on March 1st the accused categorically denied that he was at the Rue Manuel on February 27th, the day of the crime.'

'Yes, your honour. Asked about his movements he told me that he had been working, in his studio in the Rue de la Roquette, until half past six that evening. I visited this studio in due course, and the shop as well. The shop has only a rather narrow window and is crammed with frames and engravings. A suction-bracket, at the back of the glass door, is used to hang a notice which reads: "If not here apply at the end of the yard." An unlighted passage leads down, and there at the end is the workshop where Meurant constructed his picture-frames.'

'Is there a concierge?'

'No. The house has only two upper floors which you reach by a staircase leading off the yard. It is a very old building squeezed in between two blocks of tenements.'

One of the judge's assessors, whom Maigret did not know since he had recently arrived from the provinces, was staring straight ahead of him at the public with an air of not hearing a thing. The other, on the contrary, rosy-cheeked, white-haired, was nodding his head approvingly at Maigret's every sentence, some of which, God knows why, drew a smile of contentment from him. As for the jury, they stayed as still as if they had been, for example, the painted plaster figures around a Christmas crib.

Counsel for the defence, Pierre Duché, was a young man and this was his first important case. Nervous, appearing always about to jump to his feet, he bent over his file from time to time, covering it with notes.

Meurant alone, it might have been thought, showed a complete lack of interest in anything that was going on around him, or, more exactly, was watching this performance as if it were no concern of his.

He was a man of thirty-eight, relatively tall, broad-shouldered, with reddish-blond curly hair, blue eyes and the complexion that often goes with red hair.

All the witnesses described him as a gentle, mild-mannered person, not very gregarious, whose life was divided between his studio in the Rue de la Roquette and his flat in the Boulevard de Charonne, through the windows of which one could see the tombstones of the Père-Lachaise cemetery.

He was a pretty fair representative of the solitary artisan type, and the one thing surprising about him was the wife he had chosen.

Ginette Meurant was petite, with an excellent figure; she had that look about her, that way of pouting her lips, that kind of body which makes one automatically think of sex.

Ten years younger than her husband, she seemed even younger, and she had the childlike habit of fluttering her eyelashes as if she did not understand.

'How did the accused account for his movements between five o'clock and eight o'clock on February 27th.'

'He told me that he had left his studio at about half-past six, put out the shop lights and gone home on foot as he usually did. His wife was not in the flat. She had gone to the cinema, to the five o'clock showing, which was quite a common habit of hers. We have the box-office's evidence to this effect. It was a cinema in the Faubourg Saint-Antoine, where she regularly goes. When she got back, a little before eight o'clock, her husband had laid the table and prepared the evening meal.'

'Was this usual?'

'Apparently.'

'The concierge at the Boulevard de Charonne saw her tenant come in?'

'She doesn't remember. There are a score of flats in the building and at the end of the afternoon people are coming in and going out pretty frequently.'

'Did you mention the vase, the gold pieces and the bearer-bonds to the accused?'

'Not that day, but the next, March 2nd, when I summoned him to my office. I had only just then heard about the money from the concierge in the Rue Manuel.'

'Did the accused appear to know about it?'

'After some hesitation he eventually admitted that he did.'

'His aunt had taken him into her confidence?'

'Indirectly. I shall have to launch into a digression here. About five years ago, Gaston Meurant, apparently at his wife's prompting, gave up his trade to buy a café-restaurant property in the Rue de Chemin-Vert.'

'Why do you say "at his wife's prompting"?'

'Because, when Meurant first met her, eight years ago, she was a waitress in a restaurant in the Faubourg Saint-Antoine. It was through taking his meals there that Meurant got to know her. He married her and, according to her, insisted that she stop working. Meurant admits this too. Ginette Meurant's ambition was nevertheless to be the proprietress of a café-restaurant some day, and when the opportunity arose, she persuaded her husband. . . .'

'Things went badly for them?'

'Yes. Within the first few months Meurant was forced to approach his aunt and borrow money from her.'

'Did she lend him any?'

'Several times. According to her nephew, there was, in the Chinese vase, beside the bag of gold pieces, also an old wallet containing bank-notes. The sums she handed over to him were taken from this wallet. She used to laugh and call the vase her Chinese safe.'

'Have you traced the accused's brother, Alfred Meurant?'

'I hadn't done so then. I simply knew from our files that he lived an irregular sort of existence and that he had twice been convicted for procuring.'

'Had witnesses stated that they had seen the accused in his studio on the afternoon of the crime, after five o'clock?'

'Not at that time.'

'Was he wearing a blue suit and a maroon raincoat, according to his statement?'

'No. His every-day suit, which is grey, and a light fawn gabardine which he generally puts on to go to work.'

'If I understand you aright, there was no precise piece of evidence enabling you to charge him?'

'That is correct.'

'Can you tell us what direction your investigations took during the days following the crime?'

'First of all, the past life of the murdered woman, Léontine Faverges, and the men she had known. We were also interested in the activities of the child's mother, Juliette Perrin, who, being aware of the contents of the Chinese vase, might have mentioned it to friends.'

'These enquiries produced nothing new?'

'No. We questioned everyone living in the street, as well, and all those who might have seen the murderer walk past.'

'Without result?'

'Without result.'

'So that, on the morning of March 6th, your investigations had still got nowhere?'

'That is correct.'

'What happened on the morning of March 6th?'

'I was in my office at about ten o'clock when I received a telephone call.'

'Who was it from?'

'I don't know. The caller was unwilling to give his name and I motioned to Inspector Janvier, who was standing beside me, to try and trace the call.'

'Were they successful?'

'No. The conversation was too brief. I only recognized the characteristic click of a public callbox.'

'Was it a man or a woman who spoke to you?'

'A man. I'd have sworn that he was speaking through a handkerchief to disguise his voice.'

'What did he say to you?'

'His actual words were: "If you want to trace the Rue Manuel murderer, ask Meurant to show you his blue suit. You'll find bloodstains on it."'

'What did you do?'

'I went along to the examining magistrate, who provided me with a search warrant. Accompanied by Inspector Janvier, I reached the Boulevard de Charonne at ten-past eleven, and on the third floor I rang the bell of the Meurants' flat. Madame Meurant opened the door. She was in her dressing-gown, wearing slippers. She told us her husband was at his studio and I asked if he owned a navy-blue suit.

' "Yes, indeed," she answered. "His Sunday suit."'

'I asked to see it. The flat is comfortable, smart, with a gay look about it, but even at that time it was still untidy.

' "Why do you want to see this suit?"'

11*

' "Just a simple check-up . . ."

'I followed her into the bedroom, where she took a navy-blue suit from the wardrobe. Then I showed her the search warrant. The suit was packed away in a special bag I had brought, and Inspector Janvier filled in the usual receipts.

'Half an hour later the suit was in the hands of laboratory experts. During the course of the afternoon I was informed that it did in fact bear blood-stains on the right sleeve and on the lapel, but I had to wait until the next day before I knew if it was human blood. From noon, however, I arranged a discreet watch to be kept on Gaston Meurant and his wife.

'The next morning, March 7th, two of my men, Inspectors Janvier and Lapointe, armed with a warrant for arrest, presented themselves at the studio in the Rue de la Roquette and proceeded to arrest Gaston Meurant.

'He seemed surprised. He said, without resisting:

' "There must be some misunderstanding."

'I was waiting for him in my office. His wife, in another office near-by, seemed more upset than he was.'

'Are you able, without the help of notes, to repeat, as closely as possible, the interview you had with the accused that day?'

'I think I can, your honour. I was sitting at my desk and I had left him standing. Inspector Janvier was standing beside him, whereas Inspector Lapointe was sitting ready to take down the interrogation in shorthand.

'I was busy signing letters and that took some time. Eventually I looked up and said, reproachfully:

' "That was not a very nice thing to do, Meurant. Why did you lie to me?"

'His ears had reddened. His lips moved.

' "Until now," I went on, "I didn't think you could have been guilty, not even suspected of it. But what can you expect now I know you went to the Rue Manuel on February 27th? What did you go there for? Why did you keep quiet about it?" '

The judge was leaning forward, so as to miss nothing of what would follow.

'What was his answer?'

'He mumbled, his head lowered:

' "I am innocent. They were already dead." '

II

THE judge must have made a discreet sign beckoning the court usher, who moved quietly round to behind the bench and leant over him, while Duché, the young counsel for the defence, pale and tense, tried to guess what was going on.

The judge uttered a few words only and everyone in the room gazed after him as he stared up at the windows, placed high in the walls, with cords hanging from them.

The radiators were scorching. An invisible fug, smelling increasingly of human bodies, rose from the hundreds of people, pressed elbow to elbow, from their damp clothes, their breathing.

The usher, moving like a sacristan, made his way towards one of the cords, tried to open a window. It wouldn't budge. He tugged three times more, and everyone waited in suspense, their eyes following his every movement; there was eventually a nervous laugh when he decided to try the next window.

This incident made people aware of the external world once more, seeing trickles of rain on the window-panes, clouds beyond, hearing all at once more distinctly the sound of motor-cars and buses braking. At this very moment, as if to punctuate the pause, there even came the noise of an ambulance or police-car siren.

Maigret was waiting, worried, concentrating. He had taken advantage of the respite to glance across at Meurant, and, as their eyes met, he had thought he read a look of reproach in the blue eyes of the prisoner.

Not for the first time, at this same bar, the chief-inspector was feeling a kind of despondency. In hs office at the Quai des Orfèvres he was still in touch with reality, and even when he was composing his report, he could believe that his sentences adhered to the truth.

Then months would pass, sometimes a year, if not two, before he found himself one fine day shut up in the witnesses' room with the people he had questioned ages ago, who were now no more than a memory to him. Were they really the same human beings, concierges, passers-by, tradesmen, who now sat there, staring vacantly, on the vestry-like benches?

Was it the same man, after months in prison, now in the dock?

They had suddenly been plunged into a depersonalized world where every-day phrases seemed no longer to be current, where the most commonplace actions were translated into cut-and-dried formulas. The judges' black robes, the ermine, the red gown of the advocate-general further increased this feeling of some ceremony with changeless ritual, where the individual counted for nothing.

Judge Bernerie, however, conducted the proceedings with the maximum of patience and humanity. He never pestered the witnesses to finish, never interrupted them when they seemed bogged down in useless detail.

Other magistrates, more rigorous, often made Maigret clench his fists with anger and powerlessness.

Even today he knew he was only giving a lifeless, sketchy semblance of the reality. Everything he had just said was true, but he had not been able to convey the weight of things, their density, their tiniest stirrings, the smell of them.

It seemed to him indispensable, for example, that those who were about to sit in judgment on Gaston Meurant should be made to perceive the atmosphere of the Boulevard de Charonne flat as it was when he had first found it.

His description, in two sentences, was of no earthly use. He had been struck, from the start, by the couple's living quarters, in that huge building full of homes and children, overlooking the cemetery.

Whose ideas had been imposed on the rooms, their decoration, their furnishing? In the bedroom, instead of the proper bed there was one of those three-cornered divans surrounded by shelves of the kind called 'cosy corners'. It was covered in orange satin.

Maigret tried to imagine the picture-frames, the craftsman busy all day in his studio, at the end of a courtyard, returning from work and coming home to this magazine-like setting: the lighting almost as sub-dued as in the Rue Manuel, the furniture too fragile, too smart, the pastel colours . . .

Nevertheless the books on the shelves certainly belonged to Meurant, nothing but volumes bought second-hand from bookshops or the em-bankment stalls: Tolstoy's *War and Peace*; eighteen bound volumes of the *History of the Consulate and the Empire*, in an old edition which already smelt of musty paper; *Madame Bovary*; a work devoted to wild animals, and next to it, a *History of the Religions of the World*. . . .

Here was clearly a believer in self-education. In the same room were piles of sentimental newspapers, glossy magazines, cinema reviews, romantic novels, obviously constituting Ginette Meurant's fare, like the records, near the gramophone, which all bore the titles of popular songs.

How did they spend the evenings, she and he, and all day Sunday? What words did they exchange? What were their activities?

Maigret also realized he had not given an exact idea of Léontine Faverges nor of her flat where gentlemen with families and reputations used once to pay discreet visits and where, in order to prevent their meeting each other, they were whisked out of sight behind heavy curtains.

'*I am innocent. They were already dead.* . . .'

In the courtroom, packed like a cinema, that sounded like a desperate lie, since the public, who were acquainted with the case only through the newspapers, and probably the jury too, looked on Gaston Meurant as a

murderer who had not hesitated to put to death a little girl, first trying
to strangle her and then, nervous because she would not die quickly
enough, suffocating her beneath silk cushions.

It was barely eleven o'clock in the morning, but had these people
here any notion now of the time, or even of their own private lives?
Among the jurymen there was a birdseller from the Quai de la Megis-
serie and a plumber who had a little business in which he worked himself with his two mates.

Was there also someone here who had been married to a woman like
Ginette Meurant, and whose reading-matter, in the evenings, was
similar to that of the accused?

'Please continue, Chief-Inspector.'

'I asked him to give me an exact account of his movements on the
afternoon of February 27th. At two o'clock, as usual, he opened his
shop and hung up the card behind the door to ask people to call at
the studio. He went through to there, worked on several frames. At
four o'clock he turned on the lights and went back to the shop to light
up the window. According to him still, he was in his studio when,
shortly after six o'clock, he heard steps in the yard. Somebody tapped on
the window.

'It was an old man, whom he says he had never seen before. He was
looking for a flat, decorated frame, about sixteen inches by twenty-two,
for an Italian gouache he had just bought. Meurant says he showed him
mouldings in various sizes. After asking about the price the old man is
then said to have left.'

'Has this witness been found?'

'Yes, your honour. Only three weeks afterwards. He is called Germain
Lombras, a piano teacher, who lives in the Rue Picpus.'

'Have you questioned him personally?'

'Yes, your honour. He states that he did indeed go to Meurant's
studio a little after six o'clock one evening. He had happened to walk
past the shop the very day after he had bought a Neapolitan landscape
from an antique shop.'

'Did he tell you what the accused was wearing?'

'Apparently Meurant was wearing grey trousers under an unbleached
working-smock and had taken his tie off.'

Aillevard, the procurator, in the public prosecutor's seat, who was
following Maigret's testimony in a file open in front of him, was about
to ask permission to speak when the chief-inspector hastened to add:

'The witness found it impossible to state exactly whether this scene
took place on Tuesday or Wednesday, that's to say on February 26th
or 27th.'

Now it was defending counsel's turn to become agitated. The young
lawyer, for whom everyone was predicting a brilliant future, was
virtually staking it on this case. At all costs, he had to give the impression

of a man sure both of himself and the cause he was defending, and he was trying very hard to keep his hands still and not let them betray him.

Maigret went on, his voice impersonal:

'The accused claims that after this visit he shut up the studio, then the shop, before going off in the direction of the bus-stop.'

'Which would place his departure at about six-thirty?'

'Near enough. He got off the bus at the bottom of the Rue des Martyrs and made his way to the Rue Manuel.'

'Did he have any special reason for visiting his aunt?'

'At first he told me he hadn't, that it was just an ordinary visit, such as he was in the habit of making at least once a month. Two days later, however, when we discovered about the unhonoured bill of exchange, he went back on his statement.'

'Tell us about this bill of exchange.'

'On the 28th Meurant was due to honour a fairly substantial bill of exchange. He did not possess the necessary funds.'

'Was this bill of exchange presented?'

'Yes.'

'Was it met?'

'No.'

The advocate-general gestured as if to sweep away this argument in Meurant's favour, while Pierre Duché turned to the jury with the air of calling them to witness.

The fact had worried Maigret, too. If the accused, after cutting his aunt's throat and suffocating little Cécile Perrin, had taken away the gold pieces and the notes hidden in the Chinese vase, if he had appropriated the bearer-bonds as well, at a time when he was still not under suspicion and might well think he never would be, why had he not met the bill and avoided the risk of being declared bankrupt?

'My detectives have calculated the time it takes to get from the Rue de la Roquette to the Rue Manuel. By bus you would have to reckon about half an hour at that time of day, and by taxi you need twenty minutes. Enquiries amongst taxi-drivers have led to nothing; nor have those amongst bus conductors. Nobody remembers seeing Meurant.

'According to his subsequent statements, which he has signed, he arrived at the Rue Manuel at a few minutes before seven. He met nobody on the stairs, did not see the concierge. He knocked on his aunt's door, was surprised, after getting no answer, to see the key in the lock.

'He went in and found the scene previously described.'

'Were the lights on?'

'The main standard-lamp in the drawing-room, with its salmon-pink shade, was on. Meurant thinks there were lights on in other rooms, but it is simply an impression he got, because he did not enter them.'

'How does he explain his behaviour? Why didn't he trouble to call a doctor, to warn the police . . .?'

'For fear of being accused. He noticed a drawer in the Louis Quinze desk open and he shut it. In the same way he put back in the Chinese vase the artificial flowers which were lying on the floor. As he was about to leave he realized that through what he had done he had probably left fingerprints and he wiped the piece of furniture, then the vase, with his handkerchief. He also wiped the doorhandle and, finally, before going down the stairs, he took the key away with him.'

'What did he do with it?'

'He threw it down a drain.'

'How did he get home?'

'By bus. The route for the Boulevard de Charonne runs through quieter streets, and apparently he was in his flat by twenty-five to eight.'

'His wife was not there?'

'No. As I have said, she had gone to a local cinema for the five o'clock showing. She went to the cinema a lot, nearly every day. Five box-office girls remembered her on seeing her photograph. While he waited for her Meurant started reheating the remains of a joint and some runner beans, then laid the table.'

'Was that a common occurrence?'

'Quite common.'

He had the feeling, even with his back to the public, that everybody, especially amongst the women, was smiling.

'How many times have you interrogated the accused?'

'Five times, once for eleven hours. Once his statements were no longer inconsistent, I wrote out my report, which I handed to the examining magistrate, and since then I've had no opportunity of seeing him again.'

'He didn't write to you, when he was in prison?'

'Yes, he did. The letter has been entered in the file. He affirms, once again, that he is innocent and asks me to look after his wife.'

Maigret noticed Meurant make a slight movement and avoided meeting his eye.

'He didn't tell you what he meant by that, nor what he was afraid of on her account?'

'No, your honour.'

'Did you find his brother?'

'A fortnight after the crime in the Rue Manuel, on March 14th, to be precise.

'In Paris?'

'At Toulon, where, although he does not reside there permanently, he spends most of his time, with frequent trips along the Riviera, sometimes to Marseilles, sometimes to Nice and Menton. He was first examined by the Toulon police, on a rogatory commission. Then, when summoned to my office, he duly came, but not without insisting that his travelling expenses should be paid in advance. According to him, he hadn't set foot in Paris since January and he gave us the names of three witnesses with whom he played cards, at Bandol, on February 27th. The witnesses have been heard. They belong to the same sort of world as Alfred Meurant; the underworld, as you might put it.'

'What was the date when you submitted your report to the examining magistrate?'

'The final report, together with the various statements signed by the accused, was delivered on March 28th.'

They were reaching the tricky moment. Only three of them were aware of it, amongst those playing major roles. First the procurator, Justin Aillevard, whom Maigret had visited in the public prosecutor's office at five o'clock the day before. Then, apart from the chief-inspector himself, Judge Bernerie, who had also been informed the day before, later in the evening, by the advocate-general.

But there were others, unsuspected by the general public, who were also awaiting this moment: five detectives Maigret had chosen from among those less well known, some who belonged to that part of the Vice Squad generally known as the Society Section.

Since the opening of the trial they had been in the courtroom, scattered amongst the crowd at strategic points, watching the faces, keeping an eye on their reactions.

'Officially, therefore, Chief-Inspector, your investigations came to an end on March 28th.'

'That is true.'

'Nevertheless, have you, since that date, concerned yourself with the actions and movements of persons closely or distantly connected with the accused?'

At once counsel for the defence rose ready to protest. He was probably about to point out that it was not in order to admit further evidence, against his client, which had not been entered in the depositions.

'Please be calm, *maître*,' the judge said to him. 'You will see in a moment that if I am using my discretionary powers to admit an unexpected development in this case, it is not with the intent to damage the prisoner's cause.'

The advocate-general, for his part, looked across at the young defence lawyer somewhat ironically, rather as if to protect him.

'I repeat my question. Did Chief-Inspector Maigret, after all, continue his investigations unofficially?'

'Yes, your honour.'

'On your own account?'

'With the consent of the Director of Police Headquarters.'

'You kept the public prosecutor's office informed?'

'Not until yesterday, your honour.'

'Did the examining magistrate know that you were continuing to be concerned in the case?'

'I did mention it to him by the way.'

'You were not, however, acting on his instructions, nor on those of the Attorney-General?'

'No, your honour.'

'It is essential that this should be clearly established. That is why I have referred to this, in some ways, complementary investigation as an unofficial one. What was your motive, Chief-Inspector, in continuing to employ your detectives on enquiries which the transfer of the case to the Grand Jury of the Assize Court no longer rendered necessary?'

The quality of the silence in the room had changed. Not the slightest cough could now be heard, not a single shoe shifted on the floor.

'I was not satisfied with the results obtained,' Maigret growled in a surly voice.

He couldn't say what he most deeply felt. The verb 'to satisfy' only partly expressed his thoughts. The facts, to his mind, did not cohere with the characters. How could he explain this in the solemn setting of the Assizes, where they expected precise sentences from him?

The judge had had just as long experience of criminal cases as himself, longer even. Each evening he took back files to peruse in his flat on the Boulevard Saint-Germain, where the light in his study often remained on until two o'clock in the morning.

He had seen men and women of all sorts pass in and out of the dock and the witness box.

Yet weren't his contacts with life always theoretical? He had not been himself into the studio in the Rue de la Roquette, nor into the odd flat in the Boulevard de la Charonne. He did not know the swarming life that went on in those buildings, nor in the crowded streets, the bistros, the local dance-halls.

Prisoners were brought before him between two policemen and all he knew about them he had found in the pages of a file.

Facts. Sentences. Words. But all around them — what of that?

His assessors were in the same position. The advocate-general as well. The very dignity of their functions isolated them from the rest of the world, in which they formed a little island apart.

Among the members of the jury, among the spectators, there were probably some who were better equipped to understand the character of a Meurant, but these people had no title in the matter or knew nothing of the complicated instrument of the law.

Was Maigret not, himself, on both sides of the fence at the same time?

'Before allowing you to continue, Chief-Inspector, I would like you to tell us what was the result of the analysis of the blood-stains. I am referring to those which were discovered on the blue suit belonging to the defendant.'

'It was human blood. Minute laboratory tests later showed that this blood and that of the victim possess a sufficient number of similar characteristics for it to be scientifically certain that they were from one and the same body.'

'In spite of that you proceeded with your investigation?'

'Partly because of that, your honour.'

The young lawyer, who had prepared to dispute Maigret's statement, could not believe his ears, remained restless, while the chief-inspector went steadily rumbling on.

'The witness who saw a man in a blue suit and a maroon raincoat leave Léontine Faverges' flat about five o'clock is positive about the time. The time has been checked besides by a shopkeeper in the neighbourhood on whom this person called before going to her dressmaker in the Rue Manuel. If one accepts Lombras's testimony, although he is less definite about the date of his visit to the Rue de la Roquette, the accused was still in his studio, wearing his grey trousers, at six o'clock. We have calculated the time necessary to get from that studio to the Boulevard de la Charonne, then the time needed to change and finally go to the Rue Manuel. It takes, at the lowest estimate, fifty-five minutes. The fact that the bill of exchange, which fell due the next day, was not met also struck a wrong note with me.'

'So you turned your attention to Alfred Meurant, the prisoner's brother?'

'Yes, your honour. At the same time my colleagues and I entered upon other enquiries.'

'Before allowing you to give us the result of them, I must be certain that they are strictly connected with the present case.'

'They are, your honour. For several weeks detectives from the Hotels Section showed certain photographs around a large number of Paris lodging-houses.'

'What photographs?'

'Alfred Meurant's, first. Then one of Ginette Meurant.'

It was the prisoner who leapt to his feet this time, indignant, and his counsel had to rise in turn to calm him and force him to sit down again.

'Give us your conclusions as briefly as possible.'

'Alfred Meurant, the prisoner's brother, is well known in certain districts, particularly around the Place des Ternes and the neighbourhood of the Porte Saint-Denis. We found his registration-cards at a small hotel in the Rue de l'Étoile, among others, where he has often stayed, but there is nothing to show that he has been in Paris after January 1st.

'Finally, although he has been seen about with numerous women, nobody remembers having met him in his sister-in-law's company, at least during a period that goes back more than two years.'

Maigret sensed Meurant looking at him hostilely; the man had clenched both his fists, and his lawyer was continually glancing round at him for fear of an outburst.

'Please continue.'

'Ginette Meurant's photograph was recognized immediately, not only by the staffs of the cinemas, particularly the local cinemas, but also at the dance-halls both around La Chapelle and in the Rue de Lappe. She has frequented these places for many years, always in the afternoon, and the last dance-hall she has attended to date was one in the Rue des Gravilliers.'

'Used she to go to them alone?'

'She has had a certain number of boy-friends at them, never for long. However, during the last few months before the murder she was not often to be seen.'

Didn't all this evidence explain the atmosphere in the Boulevard de Charonne, the magazines and records, their contrast with the books Meurant went to buy at second-hand booksellers?

'When I left for my holidays, a little less than a month ago now,' Maigret went on, 'the various departments of Police Headquarters had discovered nothing further.'

'During this case has Madame Meurant been under surveillance by the police?'

'Not constant surveillance, in the sense that she was not followed every time she went out, and there was not always a detective outside her door at night.'

Laughter in court. A sharp look from the judge. Silence once again. Maigret wiped his brow, embarrassed by the hat he still held in his hand.

'Was this surveillance, even though sporadic,' the judge was asking, not without irony, 'the result of the letter the prisoner sent you from gaol and was it intended to protect his wife?'

'I wouldn't say that.'

'You were trying, if I understand you correctly, to discover her habits and contacts?'

'First of all I wanted to know whether she ever met her brother-in-law in secret. Then, since I obtained no positive results, I wondered whom she went about with and what she did with her time.'

'One question, Chief-Inspector. You examined Ginette Meurant at Police Headquarters. She stated to you, if I remember correctly, that she returned home on February 27th at about eight o'clock in the evening and found dinner ready to be served. Did she tell you which suit her husband was wearing?'

'Grey trousers. He had no jacket on.'

'And when he left her after lunch?'

'He was in a grey suit.'

'At what time did she herself leave the flat in the Boulevard de Charonne?'

'About four o'clock.'

'So that Meurant might have come and changed afterwards, gone out, changed again when he returned, without her knowing?'

'It's physically possible.'

'Let's return to the subsequent investigations you had embarked upon.'

'Following Ginette Meurant revealed nothing. After her husband's imprisonment, she stayed at home most of the time, only going out to do her shopping, to visit the prison, and two or three times a week to go to the cinema. The surveillance, as I have said, was not a continuous one. It was laid on from time to time. Its results only confirm what we have been told by neighbours and tradesmen. The day before yesterday I returned from my holidays and found a report on my desk. It might be just as well to explain that the police never completely lose touch with a case, so that sometimes an arrest is made, fortuitously, two or three years after the crime or the offence.'

'In other words, during the past months, no further *systematic* investigations of the actions and movements of Ginette Meurant had been carried out?'

'That's correct. Detectives from the Hotels Section and the Vice Squad, as well as my own detectives, always carried her photograph in their pockets, however, as well as one of her brother-in-law. They would show them from time to time. It was in this manner that, on September 26th, a witness recognised one of his regular clients in the photograph of the young woman.'

Meurant grew excited again and it was the judge's turn, this time, to give him a stern look. From the body of the court someone was protesting, probably Ginette Meurant.

'This witness is Nicolas Cajou, manager of a small hotel in the Rue Victor-Massé, round the corner from the Place Pigalle. He is normally in the office of his establishment and through the glass door he can keep an eye on people going in and out.'

'Wasn't he questioned last March or April, like the other hotel proprietors?'

'He was in hospital at that time, having an operation, and his sister-in-law was there in his place. Subsequently he spent three months convalescing in the Morvan, where his family come from, and it was not until the end of September that a man from the Hotels Section, just by chance, showed him the photograph.'

'Ginette Meurant's photograph?'

'Yes. He recognized her at first glance, saying that, up until he left for hospital, she used to go there with a man he did not know. One of the chamber-maids, Geneviève Lavancher, also recognized the photograph.'

At the press table they turned to each other, then turned to the judge in surprise.

'I suppose the companion you alluded to is not Alfred Meurant?'

'No, your honour. Yesterday, in my office, where I asked Nicolas Cajou and the chamber-maid to come, I showed them several hundred identification pictures in order to be satisfied that Ginette Meurant's companion is not on our records. The man is short, thick-set, with very dark brown hair. He dresses carefully and wears a ring with a yellow stone. He is said to be about thirty years old and he smokes American cigarettes, which he chain-smokes, so that after each of his visits to the Rue Victor-Massé the ashtray was always piled with butts, only a few of which had lipstick on them.

'I haven't had the requisite time, before the trial, to undertake a thorough investigation. Nicolas Cajou went into hospital on February 26th. On the 25th he was still at the office in the hotel and he states that the couple paid a visit that day.'

There was a stir in the courtroom, unseen by Maigret, and the judge raised his voice, something he did very rarely, and pronounced:

'Silence, or I shall clear the court.'

A woman's voice tried to make itself heard:

'Your honour, I . . .'

'Silence!'

As for the prisoner, his jaw tightly set, he was looking at Maigret with hatred.

III

NOBODY stirred while the judge leaned across towards each of his assessors in turn and spoke to them in undertones. A three-way colloquy took place, which again recalled a religious rite since one could see their lips moving noiselessly as if for responses, their heads nodding in a curious rhythm. At one stage the advocate-general, in his red robe, left his seat to put in his own words, and a little later it seemed as if the young counsel for the defence was about to follow his example. He was visibly hesitating, worried, not yet quite sure of himself, and he was almost on his feet when Judge Bernerie rapped on the bench with his gavel and each magistrate resumed his position, as in a tableau.

Xavier Bernerie announced, in a low voice:

'The court thanks the witness for his testimony and asks him not to leave the courtroom.'

Still like an officiating priest, he felt around for his cap, donned it and, rising to his feet, concluded his recital:

'The hearing is adjourned for a quarter of an hour.'

The next second there was a din as of school being let out, almost an explosion, scarcely muffled at all, of sounds of all sorts jumbled together. Half the spectators left their seats; some were standing in the aisles, gesticulating; others were jostling each other in an endeavour to reach the main door which the guards had just opened, while the policemen whisked away the prisoner through an exit which was hardly distinguishable from the panelling of the walls, Pierre Duché had a struggle to follow him, and the jurors, on the other side, also disappeared behind the scene.

Barristers in gowns, most of them young, including a woman barrister who might have been a cover-girl on a magazine, formed a black and white cluster by the witnesses' entrance. They were discussing articles 310, 311, 312 and so on in the code of criminal procedure, and some of them were talking excitedly of irregularities in the conduct of the hearings, which would inevitably lead to an appeal.

An elderly barrister, with yellow teeth, in a shiny gown, an unlit cigarette hanging from his lower lip, was calmly invoking precedents, citing two cases, one at Limoges in 1885, the other at Poitiers in 1923, when not only had the preliminary investigation been entirely recast at the public trial, but had taken a new turning as a result of unexpected testimony.

Of all this, Maigret, a motionless block, saw only jostling figures, heard only scraps of conversation, and he hadn't had time to locate in the courtroom, where there were now several empty spaces, more than a couple of his men before he was surrounded by reporters.

The same over-excitement reigned as at the theatre, on a first night, after the first act.

'What do you think about this bombshell you've just dropped, Chief-Inspector?'

'What bombshell?'

He was filling his pipe methodically and he felt thirsty.

'You believe Meurant's innocent?'

'I don't believe anything.'

'You suspect his wife?'

'Gentlemen, you'll have to forgive me, but I've nothing to add to what I said in the box.'

The pack only stopped pestering him abruptly when a young reporter suddenly dashed across to Ginette Meurant who was trying to reach the exit and the rest were afraid they might miss some sensational statement.

Everybody watched the group moving along. Maigret took advantage of it to slip through the witnesses' door, came upon men smoking cigarettes in the corridor and others, unfamiliar with the building, looking for the lavatories.

He knew that the magistrates were deliberating in the Judge's Chamber; he saw an usher leading young Duché, whom they had sent for, in that direction.

It was almost noon. Bernerie obviously wanted to have the matter cleared up during the morning's hearing in order to resume the ordinary course of the trial that afternoon, hoping for a verdict the same day.

Maigret reached the gallery, lit his pipe at last, beckoned to Lapointe, whom he saw leaning against a pillar.

He was not the only one wanting to take advantage of the adjournment to have a glass of beer. Outside, people could be seen running across the street in the rain, with their collars turned up, to dive into the cafés round about.

At the Palais bar an impatient crowd, in a hurry, was disturbing those lawyers and their clients who, a few moments ago, were quietly discussing their particular business.

'Beer?' he asked Lapointe.

'If you can get any, Chief.'

They thrust their way between the backs and elbows. Maigret made a sign to a waiter he had known for twenty years and a few seconds later two nicely foaming glasses of beer were passed to him over the heads of the other customers.

'See if you can find out where she has lunch, who with, who she speaks to, and who it is if she telephones to anyone.'

The tide was already ebbing and people were hurrying to get back to their seats. When the chief-inspector arrived at the courtroom, it was too late to reach the rows of benches and he had to lean against the small door, amongst the lawyers.

The jury were in their places, the prisoner as well, between his guards, his counsel lower down in front of him. The judges entered and sat down with dignity, probably conscious, like the chief-inspector, of the change that had taken place in the atmosphere.

A short time ago they had been here to deal with a man accused of having cut the throat of his aunt, a sixty-year-old woman, and having stifled, after attempting to strangle, a little four-year-old girl. Wasn't it natural that there had been a grim and somewhat stifling sense of seriousness in the air?

Now, after the interval, everything was changed. Gaston Meurant had now left the limelight and even the double crime had lost some of its importance. Maigret's evidence had introduced a new element, posed a new problem, suggestive, shocking, and the whole room now showed no interest in anything except the young woman whom the occupants of the back rows were trying in vain to glimpse.

This alone caused a buzz of noise and the judge could be seen scanning the crowd sternly, as if he were searching for the trouble-makers. This lasted a long time, but as the seconds passed the noises died down, finally disappeared altogether, silence reigned again.

'I warn the general public that I shall not tolerate any disturbance, and if there is any incident whatsoever I shall have the court cleared.'

He coughed, murmured a few words in the ears of his assessors.

'By virtue of the discretionary powers conferred upon me and in agreement with the counsels for the prosecution and the defence, I have decided to hear three new witnesses. Two are in the courtroom, and the third, the aforesaid Geneviève Lavancher, who has been summoned by telephone, will appear at this afternoon's hearing. Sergeant, will you call Madame Ginette Meurant.'

The old usher advanced, across the empty space, to meet the young woman who, sitting in the front row, rose, hesitated, then allowed herself to be led to the witness-box.

Maigret had talked to her several times at the Quai des Orfèvres. He had then had before him a young woman whose sexiness was vulgar and occasionally aggressive.

In honour of the Assize Court, she had bought herself a black tailored suit, a skirt with a threequarter-length jacket; the only touch of colour was provided by a straw-coloured jumper.

The chief-inspector was convinced that it was also to smarten her appearance for the occasion that she was wearing a model hat which lent a kind of mystery to her face.

She seemed to be playing two roles at the same time, the naïve girl and the smart young wife, lowering her head, raising it to rest timid, docile eyes on the judge.

'Your name is Ginette Meurant, maiden name Chenault?'

'Yes, your honour.'

'Speak up and please face the jury. You are twenty-seven years old and were born at Saint-Sauveur in the Nièvre?'

'Yes, your honour.'

'You are the wife of the prisoner?'

She replied again in the same good schoolgirl voice.

'Article 322 precludes your testimony being accepted as evidence, but, with the consent of the prosecution and the defence, the court has the right to hear you for its information.'

And, as she was raising her hand in imitation of the previous witnsses, he stopped her.

'No! You do not have to take the oath.'

Between other people's heads Maigret caught a glimpse of the pale face of Gaston Meurant staring steadfastly in front of him, his chin resting in his hands. From time to time he clamped his jaws so tightly together that the bones protruded.

His wife avoided turning in his direction, as though that were prohibited, and her eyes were fastened steadily on the judge.

'You knew the murdered woman, Léontine Faverges?'

She seemed to hesitate before murmuring:

'Not very well.'

'What do you mean by that?'

'That she and I never visited each other.'

'But you have met her?'

'The first time, before our marriage. My fiancé had insisted on introducing me to her, saying that she was all the family he had.'

'So you have been to the Rue Manuel?'

'Yes. One afternoon, about five o'clock. She gave us hot chocolate and cakes. I felt straight away that she had taken a dislike to me and that she would urge Gaston not to marry me.'

'Why was that?'

She shrugged her shoulders, searched for words, finally spoke out:

'We just weren't the same sort.'

A look from the judge halted the laughter which was about to break out.

'She did not attend your wedding?'

'Yes, she did.'

'And Alfred Meurant, your brother-in-law?'

'He, too. In those days he was living in Paris and was still on good terms with my husband.'

'What was his profession then?'

'Commercial traveller.'

'He had regular work?'

'How should I know? He gave us a coffee set as a wedding present.'

'Did you see Léontine Faverges after that?'

'Four or five times.'

'Did she come to your flat?'

'No. We used to go and see her. I never wanted to go because I hate imposing myself on people who dislike me, but Gaston maintained that I couldn't get out of it.'

'Why?'

'I don't know.'

'Was it by chance because of her money?'

'Probably.'

'When did you stop going to the Rue Manuel?'

'Ages ago.'

'Two years? Three years? Four years?'

'About three years, I suppose.'

'So you knew about the Chinese vase which was kept in the drawing-room?'

'I've seen it and I've even said to Gaston that artificial flowers ought to be kept for funeral wreaths.'

'You knew what it contained?'

'Flowers, as far as I was concerned.'

'Your husband never said anything to you?'

'What about? The vase?'

'The gold pieces.'

For the first time she turned round to the dock.

'No.'

'He did not confide in you, either, that his aunt, instead of putting her money in the bank, kept it at home?'

'I don't remember anything about that.'

'You can't be sure?'

'Oh yes. . . . Yes . . .'

'During the period when you still paid visits to the Rue Manuel, no matter how seldom, was little Cécile Perron already in the house?'

'I never saw her. No. She would have been too small.'

'You've heard about her from your husband?'

'He must have mentioned something about it. Wait a minute! I'm positive now. I remember I was surprised that anybody would let a woman like her look after a baby.'

'Did you know that the prisoner fairly often went to his aunt to ask for money?'

'He didn't always tell me what he was doing.'

'But you knew about it, vaguely?'

'I knew he wasn't much of a businessman, that he could be taken in by anybody, like when we opened a restaurant in the Rue du Chemin-Vert, which might have done very nicely.'

'What did you do in the restaurant?'

'I waited on the customers.'

'And your husband?'

'He worked in the kitchen, with the help of an old woman.'

'Did he know about cooking?'

'He used a book.'

'Were you on your own in the dining-room with the customers?'

'We had a young waitress at the beginning.'

'And when things started going badly, didn't Léontine Faverges help pay off the creditors?'

'I suppose she did. I think we still owe money.'

'Did your husband seem worried towards the end of February?'

'He was always worried.'

'Did he talk to you about a bill of exchange falling due on the 28th?'

'I didn't notice. There were bills of exchange every month.'

'He didn't tell you he would be going to see his aunt to ask for help once again?'

'I don't remember it.'

'It wouldn't have struck you?'

'No. I was used to it.'

'After the restaurant was closed, you didn't suggest finding a job?'

'I did nothing else. Gaston would not allow it.'

'Why not?'

'Because he was jealous probably.'

'Did he make jealous scenes with you?'

'Not scenes.'

'Please face the jury.'

'I forgot. I'm sorry.'

'On what sort of things do you base your statement that he was a jealous man?'

'First of all, he refused to let me go out to work. Later on, in the Rue du Chemin-Vert, he kept coming up from the kitchen to spy on me.'

'Has he ever followed you?'

Pierre Duché was shifting restlessly on his bench, unable to see what the judge was driving at.

'I haven't noticed that.'

'Used he to ask you in the evenings where you'd been?'

'Yes.'

'What would you reply?'

'That I had been to the cinema.'

'Are you certain that you never talked to anybody about the Rue Manuel or Léontine Faverges?'

'Only to my husband.'

'Not to a girl friend?'

'I have no girl friends.'

'What people did you and your husband know?'

'Nobody.'

If these questions were flummoxing her, she gave no sign of it.

'Do you remember which suit your husband was wearing at lunch-time on February 27th?'

'His grey suit. It was his every-day one. He only ever put on the other one on Saturday nights, if we went out, and on Sundays.'

'And when he visited his aunt?'

'Sometimes he wore his blue suit, I think.'

'He did so on that day?'

'I can't say. I wasn't in the house.'

'You don't know whether he returned to the flat during that afternoon?'

'How could I know that? I was at the cinema.'

'Thank you.'

She was still standing there, disconcerted, unable to believe that it was over, that she was not going to be asked the questions everybody was expecting.

'You may go back to your seat.'

And the judge carried on:

'Will Nicolas Cajou come forward.'

There was a feeling of disappointment in the air. The public felt that there had just been some trickery, that a scene had been cut which they had a right to watch. Ginette Meurant sat down again, almost

regretfully, and a lawyer standing by Maigret was whispering to his
colleagues:

'Lamblin got his claws into her in the corridor during the adjournment. . . .'

Maître Lamblin, with a profile like that of a half-starved dog, was a
figure who came in for quite a lot of discussion at the Palais, rarely to
the good, and several times his suspension from the Bar had been
mooted. As if by chance, here he was stationed beside the young woman
and he was speaking to her in a low voice, as if congratulating her.

The man who was approaching the witness-box, limping, was a
completely different specimen of humanity. If Ginette Meurant, underneath all her make-up, had the paleness of women who live in a hot-
house atmosphere, this man was not merely pallid but his substance
seemed soft and unhealthy.

Had he got so thin as a result of his operation? The fact remained that
his clothes floated, much too big for him around his body which had
lost all its spring and suppleness.

One could better imagine him nestling, in his slippers, in his hotel
office, with its frosted windows, than walking along the city pavements.

He had bags under his eyes, loose skin under his chin.

'You are Nicolas Cajou, sixty-two years old. You were born in
Marillac, in the Cantal, and you now keep a hotel in Paris, in the Rue
Victor-Massé?'

'Yes, your honour.'

'You are not related to the prisoner, nor a friend of his, nor his
employee. . . . You swear to tell the truth, the whole truth, nothing but
the truth. . . . Raise your right hand. . . . Say: I swear . . .'

'I swear . . .'

One of the assessors leaned towards the judge to make an observation
which must have had some pertinence, for Bernerie seemed to be struck
by it, pondered for a good while, finally shrugged his shoulders. Maigret
who had not missed any of this scene, guessed what was going on.

Witnesses who have been convicted with loss of civil rights, in fact, or
who indulge in immoral activities, are not entitled to be sworn in. Now,
was not this hotel-keeper indulging in an immoral practice, since he
admitted couples to his establishment under circumstances forbidden
by law? Were they sure that his police record carried no convictions?

It was too late to check up and the judge gave a small cough before
asking, in an impartial voice:

'Do you normally keep a register of the visitors to whom you let rooms?'

'Yes, your honour.'

'Of *all* visitors?'

'All those who stay the night in my hotel.'

'But you do not register the names of those who only stop there during
the course of the day?'

'No, your honour. The police can tell you that . . .'

That he was a law-abiding citizen, naturally, that there had never been a scandal at his place, and that occasionally he furnished the Hotels Section or Vice Squad detectives with clues they needed.

'Have you looked carefully at the witness who preceded you in the box?'

'Yes, your honour.'

'Did you recognize her?'

'Yes, your honour.'

'Tell the members of the jury of the circumstances in which you have previously seen this young woman.'

'In the usual circumstances.'

A look from Bernerie stifled the laughter.

'Which means?'

'Which means that she often appeared in the afternoon in the company of a gentleman who hired a room.'

'What do you mean by often?'

'Several times a week.'

'How many times, would you say?'

'Three or four times.'

'Her companion was always the same?'

'Yes, your honour.'

'Would you recognize him again?'

'Certainly.'

'When did you see him for the last time?'

'The day before I went into hospital, that's to say February 25th. I remember the date because of my operation.'

'Describe him.'

'Not tall. . . . Rather short. . . . I suspect that, like others who are unfortunately short, he wore special shoes. . . . Always well-dressed, a bit of a toff really. . . . We know the sort round our way. . . . That's just what surprised me. . . .'

'What do you mean?'

'Because those gentlemen, as a rule, don't make a habit of spending their afternoons in the hotel, specially not with the same woman. . . .'

'I suppose you know all the fauna of Montmartre more or less by sight?'

'Pardon?'

'I mean the men you are talking about . . .'

'I see them go by.'

'However, you have never seen this one except in your hotel?'

'No, your honour.'

'And you haven't heard of him before?'

'I only know he's called Pierrot.'

'How do you know that?'

'Because the lady who used to come with him sometimes called him that in front of me.'

'Did he have any accent?'

'Not strictly speaking. But I always thought that he came from the south, or maybe that he was Corsican.'

'Thank you.'

This time again, disappointment was evident on people's faces. They had expected a dramatic identification and nothing happened except an apparently innocent exchange of questions and answers.

The judge looked up at the clock.

'The hearing is adjourned and will be resumed at half-past two.'

The same hubbub as before, with the difference that this time the whole room was emptying and people were forming in two ranks to see Ginette Meurant pass between. It seemed to Maigret from where he was standing, at some distance, that Maître Lamblin was still following in her wake and that she kept turning around to make sure he was behind her.

The chief-inspector had hardly got outside the door when he bumped into Janvier, looked at him interrogatively.

'We've got them, Chief. They're both at the Quai.'

It took the chief inspector quite a while to realize that this referred to another case, an armed robbery at a branch of a bank in the Xth arrondissement.

'How did it happen?'

'Lucas arrested them at one of the boys' mother's place. The other had been hiding under the bed and the mother never knew. They hadn't been outside for three days. The poor woman thought her son was ill and kept making him hot grogs. She's the widow of a railwayman and works in a local chemist's. . . .'

'How old?'

'The son, eighteen. His pal, twenty.'

'They deny it?'

'Yes. But I don't think you'll have much trouble with them.'

'What about having lunch with me?'

'I warned my wife I wouldn't be coming home, as it happened.'

It was still raining as they crossed the Place Dauphine to make their way to the brasserie which had become a kind of annex of Police Head-quarters.

'How's it going at the Palais?'

'Nothing definite yet.'

They stopped at the bar, while waiting for a table to become vacant.

'I'll have to 'phone the judge to get his permission not to attend the trial.'

Maigret had no wish to spend the afternoon sitting motionless in the crowd, in the humid heat, listening to witnesses who, from now on, would spring no more surprises. He had heard these witnesses, all of them, in the quiet of his office. Most of them he had seen in their homes, in their proper surroundings, as well.

The Assize Court had always constituted the most unpleasant, most depressing part of his functions, and each time he had the same feeling of misery.

Was not everything distorted there? Not through any fault of the judges, the jury, the witnesses, nor on account of the criminal code or the procedure, but because human beings were suddenly reduced, if one can so put it, to a few words, a few sentences.

He had sometimes discussed it with his friend Pardon, the local G.P. with whom he and his wife had got into the habit of dining once a month.

Once when his surgery had been full all day, Pardon had displayed a touch of discouragement, almost of bitterness.

'Twenty-eight patients in the afternoon alone! Hardly time to let them sit down, ask them a few questions. What is it you feel? Where does it hurt? How long has it been going on? The others are waiting, staring at the padded door, and wondering if their turn will ever come. Show me your tongue! Take off your clothes! In most cases an hour wouldn't be sufficient to find out everything one should know. Each patient is a separate case, and yet I have to work on the conveyor-belt system . . .'

Maigret had then told him of the end-result of his own work, in other words the Assize Court, since most investigations anyway come to their conclusion there.

'Historians,' he had remarked, 'scholars, devote their entire lives to the study of some figure of the past on whom there already exist numerous works. They go from library to library, from archives to archives, search for the least item of correspondence in the hope of grasping a little more of the truth . . .

'For fifty years or more they've been studying Stendhal's letters to get a clearer idea of his character . . .

'Isn't a crime almost always committed by someone out of the ordinary, in other words less easy to comprehend than the man in the street? They give me a few weeks, sometimes only a few days, to steep myself in a new atmosphere, to question ten, twenty, fifty people I knew nothing at all about till then, and, if possible, to sift out the true from the false.

'I've been reproached for going myself onto the scene instead of sending my detectives. You wouldn't believe it, but it's a miracle that I'm still allowed this privilege!

'The examining magistrate, following on from me, has hardly any more scope and he only sees people, detached from their private lives, in the neutral atmosphere of his office.

'All he has in front of him, in fact, are men already reduced to mere diagrams.

'He also has only a limited time at his disposal; hounded by the press, by public opinion, his initiative restricted by a maze of regulations, submerged by administrative formalities which occupy most of his time, what is he likely to find out?

'If it is mere disincarnate beings who leave his office, what is left for the Assizes, and on what basis are the jury going to decide the fate of one or more of their own kindred?

'It's no longer a question of months or weeks, scarcely of days. The number of the witnesses is reduced to the minimum, as are the questions that are put to them.

'They come and repeat before the court a condensed version, a *digest*, as people say nowadays, of everything they have said beforehand.

'The case is merely sketched in with a few strokes, the people concerned are no more than outlines, caricatures almost . . .'

Hadn't he had that feeling once again this morning, even when he was giving his own evidence?

The press would report that he had spoken *at length* and perhaps be surprised at it. With any other judge than Xavier Bernerie, it was true, he would have been allowed only a few minutes to speak, whereas he had stayed in the witness-box for almost an hour.

He had done his best to be precise, to communicate a little of what he himself felt to those who listened to him.

He glanced through the cyclostyled menu and passed it to Janvier.

'I think I'll have the *tête de veau* . . .'

A group of detectives were standing by the bar. He noticed two lawyers in the restaurant.

'Did I tell you my wife and I have bought a house?'

'In the country?'

He had promised himself to keep quiet about this, not for the sake of making a mystery of it, but from a scruple of decency because a connection would inevitably be drawn between this purchase and his retirement which was no longer so far off.

'At Meung-sur-Loire?'

'Yes. . . . It's a bit like a presbytery . . .'

In two years he would be done with the Assize Court, except perhaps on the third page of the newspapers. There he would read of the testimony of his successor, *Chief-Inspector* . . .

Who would, in fact, succeed him? He had no idea. They were probably starting to discuss it in higher places, but they would obviously avoid mentioning it in his presence.

'What kind of lads are these two?'

Janvier shrugged his shoulders.

'Just like the rest of them nowadays.'

Through the window-panes Maigret watched the falling rain, the grey parapet along the Seine, the motor-cars sending up a bow wave of dirty water.

'How was the judge?'

'Not so bad.'

'What about her?'

'I've put Lapointe on her tracks. She's fallen into the clutches of a pretty shady lawyer, Lamblin . .'

'Did she confess to having a lover?'

'She wasn't asked to. Bernerie is cautious.'

It was just as well to remember, in fact, that it was the trial of Gaston Meurant that was taking place at the Assizes, not that of his wife.

'Cajou recognized her?'

'Of course.'

'How did the husband take that?'

'I think he would gladly have murdered me at that moment.'

'Will he be acquitted?'

'It's too soon to tell.'

Steam rose from the plates, smoke from cigarettes, and the names of recommended wines were painted in white on the mirrors around the room.

There was one small wine from the Loire, from quite near Meung and the house like a presbytery.

IV

AT two o'clock Maigret, still accompanied by Janvier, climbed the great staircase at the Quai des Orfèvres, which even in summer, on the gayest of mornings, managed to be gloomy and dim. Today a draught of damp air swept around it and the marks of wet shoes on the steps refused to dry.

Even on the first landing they could hear a faint noise from the first floor, then voices, the sound of people going to and fro could be distinguished, a sure sign that the press had been alerted and were there, with the photographers and probably television teams, perhaps cinema-newsreel men.

A case was finishing or appeared to be finishing at the Palais. A fresh one was beginning here. At one end there was already a crowd, at the other only the specialists were left.

At the Quai des Orfèvres there was also a sort of witnesses' room, the glassed-in waiting-room known as the glass cage, and the chief-inspector paused on his way past to glance in at the six people sitting there under the photographs of policemen who had died in the performance of their duty.

Was it true that all witnesses look alike? The ones here came from the same walks of life as those at the Palais de Justice, ordinary folk, modest working-class people, and two women amongst them who stared straight in front of them, their hands on their leather handbags.

The reporters charged towards Maigret, who calmed them with a movement of his hand.

'Take it easy now! Take it easy! Remember, gentlemen, that I am still in the dark about all this and I haven't even see these lads . . .'

He pushed open his office door, promised:

'In two or three hours, maybe, if I have some news for you . . .'

He shut the door, said to Janvier:

'Go and see if Lapointe has arrived.'

He was resuming the same old habits as before his holidays, almost as much of a ritual for him as was the ceremonial of the Assizes for the magistrates. Taking off his coat and hat, he hung them in the cupboard, where there was an enamel basin where he might wash his hands. Then he sat down at his desk, fondled his pipes a little before choosing one and filling it.

Janvier returned with Lapointe.

'I'll see your two idiots in a couple of minutes.'

And to young Lapointe:

'Well, what did she get up to?'

'All the way along the corridors and down the big staircase she was surrounded by a mob of journalists and photographers, and there were others waiting for her outside. There was even a cinema-newsreel van parked by the pavement. As far as I was concerned, I could only catch a glimpse of her face once or twice through the crowd. She seemed frightened and was obviously begging them to leave her in peace.

'Suddenly Lamblin elbowed his way through the crowd, seized hold of her arm and dragged her to a taxi he had had time to go off and find. He showed her into it and the cab moved off towards the Pont Saint-Michel.

'This all happened like a conjuring trick. Unable to find a taxi myself, I couldn't follow them. However, a few minutes ago, Mace, from the *Figaro*, arrived back at the Palais. He had been lucky enough to have his car parked near-by, which meant he was able to trail the taxi.

'According to him, Maître Lamblin took Ginette Meurant to a restaurant in the Place de l'Odéon which specializes in sea-food and *bouillabaisse*. They lunched there on their own together, taking their time.

'And now everybody's back in their seats in the courtroom and just waiting for the Bench to arrive.'

'Go back there. Give me a ring now and then. I'd like to know whether the chambermaid's evidence provokes any incident . . .'

Maigret had been able to get in touch with the judge by telephone and had been given permission by him not to waste his time at the Palais that afternoon.

The five detectives who had been planted about the courtroom during the morning had discovered nothing. They had studied the public with the trained eye that practised judges of facial expression cast over gambling-rooms. None of the men present answered to the description furnished by Nicolas Cajou of Ginette Meurant's companion. As for Alfred Meurant, the prisoner's brother, he was not in the Palais, nor in Paris, as Maigret had now learnt from a telephone call to the Toulon flying squad.

Apart from Lapointe, who was returning to the next building by way of the internal corridors, two detectives were staying on in the court-room, just in case.

Maigret called Lucas, who was dealing with the bank robbery.

'I though I'd better not start questioning them until you'd had a look at them, Chief. I've just arranged it so that the witnesses could catch a glimpse of them as they walked past.'

'Did they recognize both of them?'

'Yes. Particularly the one who had lost his mask, of course.'

'Bring the younger one in.'

His hair was too long, his face pimply, and he looked unhealthy and unwashed.

'Remove his handcuffs. . . .'

The boy shot him a glance of defiance, obviously determined not to fall into the trap which he knew was being set for him.

'Leave me alone with him now.'

In cases like this, Maigret preferred to remain alone with the suspect, and there was plenty of time, later on, for his statement to be taken down in writing and for him to be made to sign it.

He puffed away gently at his pipe.

'Sit down.'

He pushed a packet of cigarettes across to him.

'Do you smoke?'

His hand trembled. At the ends of his long, blunt fingers the nails were bitten away like a child's.

'You've lost your father?'

'It wasn't me!'

'I'm not asking whether it was you or wasn't you who organized this caper. I'm asking whether your father's alive still.'

'He's dead.'

'How did it happen?'

'In the sanatorium.'

'So your mother's keeping you?'

'I've got a job too.'

'What doing?'

'I'm a french polisher.'

It would take time. Maigret knew from experience that it was better to tackle it slowly.

'How did you get hold of the gun?'

'I've got no gun.'

'Do you want me to call in the witnesses straight away? They're waiting outside.'

'They're liars, the lot of them.'

The telephone was ringing already. It was Lapointe.

'Geneviève Lavancher has given her evidence, Chief. She was asked roughly the same questions as her boss, plus one extra. The judge asked her, in fact, whether she had noticed anything special about the couple's behaviour on February 25th and she replied that she was indeed surprised to see that the bed had not been touched.'

'Are the officially listed witnesses going through yet?'

'Yes. Things are really moving fast now. They hardly get a hearing.'

It took forty minutes to break the boy's resistance; he finally burst out sobbing.

So he had been the one armed with the gun. There had been three of them, not two, for an accomplice had been waiting at the wheel of a stolen car, who had apparently planned the hold-up and had then cleared off without the others as soon as he heard the cries for help.

Nonetheless this lad, who was called Virieu, refused to give his name.

'He's older than you?'

'Yes. He's twenty-three and married.'

'He's done this sort of thing before, hasn't he?'

'That's what he said.'

'I'll have a chat with you again later, after I've heard what your chum has got to say for himself.'

Virieu was taken away. They brought in Giraucourt, his friend, who also had his handcuffs removed, and the two boys had the opportunity to exchange looks as they passed each other.

'Did he spill the beans?'

'Did you think he'd be able to keep his mouth shut?'

Just routine. The hold-up had misfired. No one had been killed, nobody hurt, not even any damage done, except one window-pane.

'Who had the idea of the masks?'

It hadn't been a very original idea in any case. Professional gangsters in Nice had used carnival masks when they robbed a mail van a few months ago.

'You weren't armed?'

'No.'

'Were you the one who called out when the bank-clerk came to the window: "Shoot now, you fool . . ."?'

'I don't know what I said. I lost my head . . .'

'Don't forget that your chum did what you said and pressed the trigger.'

'He didn't shoot anyone.'

'But that was only because the gun luckily failed to go off. Perhaps there wasn't a round up the spout? Perhaps the gun was faulty?'

The bank staff, together with a woman customer, had stood with their hands up. It was ten o'clock in the morning.

'It was you who called out as you went in:

' "Hands up; everyone against the wall. This is a hold-up!"'

'Apparently you added:

' "This is serious." '

'I said that because a lady started to laugh.'

A woman clerk of forty-five, who was now waiting in the glass cage with the others, had seized a paper-weight and thrown it out of the window, calling for help as she did so.

'Have you been convicted before?'

'Once.'

'What for?'

'For stealing a camera from a car.'

'You know what you'll cop this time?'

The young man shrugged his shoulders, trying hard to be brave.

'Five years, my lad. As for your friend, whether his gun was jammed or not, it's quite likely that he won't get away with less than ten years . . .'

This was true. The third fellow would be found some day or other. The examining magistrate would soon be on the case and since, this time, there would be no legal recess to hold up the course of justice, in three or four months' time Maigret would again be testifying before the Assize Court.

'Take him away, Lucas. There's no longer any reason to keep him separated from his friend. Let them gossip away as much as they like. Send in the first witness.'

It was only a matter of formalities now, a lot of bumph to be got through. And according to Lapointe, on the telephone, things were moving even more swiftly at the Palais, where certain of the witnesses, after only about five minutes in the box, found themselves, to their amazement, and somewhat to their disappointment, back in the crowd, trying to find a place for themselves.

At five o'clock Maigret was still working on the bank robbery, and his office, with the lights now on, was filled with smoke.

'The claim for damages is just being heard. Maître Lioran has made a short statement. In view of the unexpected developments, he is prepare to associate himself in advance with the advocate-general's closing speech.'

'And the advocate-general's speaking now?'

'He began about two minutes ago.'

'Call me back when he's finished.'

Half an hour later, Lapointe telephoned through quite a detailed account of this speech. The procurator, Aillevard, had said, in effect:

'We are here to try the prisoner, Gaston Meurant, accused of having, on February 27th, cut the throat of his aunt, Léontine Faverges, then suffocated to death a four-year-old girl, Cécile Perrin, whose mother is claiming damages.'

The mother, with her henna'd hair, still wearing her fur coat, had cried out loud and had to be led, shaken with sobbing, from the courtroom.

The advocate-general had continued:

'From the witness-box we have heard some unexpected evidence which we do not need to take into account as far as this case is concerned. The charges brought against the prisoner have not altered and the questions which the jury must answer still remain the same.

'Was it humanly possible for Gaston Meurant to commit this double crime and to steal the life-savings of Léontine Faverges?

'It has been established that he was aware of the Chinese vase's secret and that his aunt on several occasions took money from it to give him.

'Had he a sufficient motive?

'The day following the murder, February 28th, a bill of exchange, which he had signed, fell due and he did not have the necessary funds to meet it, with the result that he was faced with bankruptcy.

'Finally do we have proof of his presence in the flat on the Rue Manuel that afternoon?

'Six days later there was discovered, in a cupboard at his flat in the Boulevard de Charonne, a navy-blue suit belonging to him, which bore, on the sleeve, and the lapel, spots of blood the origin of which he was at a loss to explain.

'According to the experts, it was human blood, and more likely than not was the blood of Léontine Faverges.

'There remains some evidence which appears to contradict this, though no aspersion is cast on the witnesses' honesty by my so putting it.

'Madame Ernie, a customer of the victim's neighbour from across the landing, saw a man dressed in a navy suit leave Léontine Faverges' flat at five o'clock that afternoon and she is almost prepared to swear that this man had very dark hair.

'On the other hand you have heard a piano teacher, Monsieur Germain Lombras, tell you that at six o'clock that evening he was with the prisoner in his studio off the Rue de la Roquette. Monsieur Germain

Lombras has nevertheless admitted to us that he has a slight doubt as to the exact date of this visit.

'We have to consider a heinous crime, committed in cold blood by a man who not only attacked a defenceless woman, but did not shrink from murdering a little girl.

'There can therefore be no question of mitigating circumstances, but simply of the supreme penalty.

'It is for the jury to say, in their own hearts and minds, whether they believe Gaston Meurant to be guilty of this double crime.'

Maigret, who had at last finished with his would-be gangsters, was resigning himself to opening the door and facing the journalists.

'Have they confessed?'

He nodded his head.

'Not too much publicity, please, gentlemen. Above all don't make too much of a fuss of them! Don't let others, who might be tempted to imitate them, get the impression that these young kids have done something big. They're a wretched pair, believe me . . .'

He answered the questions, shortly, feeling heavy and tired. His mind was still half in the Assize Court, where it was the young counsel for the defence's turn to speak.

He felt tempted to push open the glass door which led through to the Palais and go and join Lapointe. But what would be the point? He could imagine the defence's final plea, which would begin like a popular novel.

Wouldn't Pierre Duché dig up as much of the past as possible?

A Le Havre family, poor, swarming with children who had to start fending for themselves as early as possible. At fifteen or sixteen the girls entered into domestic service, or rather they left home for Paris, where they were supposed to be entering into service. Had the parents the time or the means to keep an eye on them? They would write once a month, a painful scrawl with spelling mistakes, sometimes enclosing a modest postal order.

Two sisters had left home in this way, first Léontine Faverges, who had become a salesgirl in a big department store and had married soon afterwards.

Hélène, the younger, had worked in a dairy, then in a haberdasher's in the Rue d'Hauteville.

The first girl's husband had died. As for the second, she was soon finding her way about the local dance-halls.

Had they kept in touch with each other? It was doubtful. When her husband was killed in an accident, Léontine Faverges had begun to hang around the cafés in the Rue Royale and the boarding-houses round the Madeleine before setting up on her own in the Rue Manuel.

Her sister Hélène had had two children by unknown fathers and had brought them up as best she could for three years. Then she had been

taken off to hospital for an operation one evening and had never left
there alive.

'My client, members of the jury, educated in the Poor Schools . . .'

It was true, and Maigret could have furnished the lawyer with some
interesting statistics on this subject, the percentage, for example, of
pupils who went to the bad and eventually turned up in the dock in
court.

These were the rebels, the ones who had a grudge against society for
their humiliating circumstances.

But, contrary to what one might expect, to what the jury probably
imagined, they constitute a minority.

No doubt many of the others are also affected in some way. Throughout their lives they suffer from a feeling of inferiority. But, in fact, their
reaction to this is to prove to themselves that they are as good as the
next man.

They have been taught a trade and they do their best to become first-
class workers.

Their ambition is to have a family of their own, a proper, normal
family with children to take out for a walk on Sundays.

And what sweeter revenge than to start a small firm one day, to set
up on their own?

Had Pierre Duché thought about it? Was that what he was now
telling them, in the courtroom where people's faces were already showing signs of fatigue?

During the long examination Maigret had been through that morning, he had left something out and now he regretted it. The conversation was, of course, all down in the file. But it was only an unimportant
detail.

The third time Ginette Meurant had come to his office, at Police
Headquarters, the chief-inspector had asked her incidentally:

'You have never had a child?'

She was apparently not expecting such a question, for she looked
surprised.

'Why do you ask me that?'

'I don't know. . . . I just have the feeling that your husband is the
sort of man who would want to have children. . . . Am I wrong?'

'No.'

'He did hope you would have some?'

'In the beginning, yes.'

He had sensed a hesitation, something slightly obscure, and he had
delved more deeply:

'You are not able to have them?'

'No.'

'He knew this when he married you?'

'No. We had never talked about that.'

'When did he find out?'

'After a few months. Since he was always hoping and kept asking me the same question every month, I thought it better to tell him the truth. . . . Not quite the whole truth. . . . But the main point. . . .'

'Which is?'

'That I was ill, before I met him, and had to have an operation . . .'

It had lasted like that for seven years. Though Meurant had wanted a family, they had remained simply a couple.

He had set up on his own. Later, giving in to his wife's pestering, he had tried for a while another trade than his own. As one might have expected, it had turned out disastrously. Nevertheless he had patiently built up his small picture-framing business once more.

This completed the picture for Maigret, who, rightly or wrongly, suddenly began to attach a great deal of importance to this matter of children.

He was not going so far as to maintain that Meurant was innocent. He had seen equally unobtrusive men, as quiet and gentle on the outside, become violent.

Almost always, in such cases, this was because at one time or another they had been hurt deep down, by something.

Meurant, driven by jealousy, was certainly capable of committing a *crime passionel*. It was also possible that he would have attacked a friend who had humiliated him.

Perhaps even, if his aunt had refused him money which he urgently needed . . .

Anything was possible, except, so it seemed to the chief-inspector, for a man who had so desperately wanted children, that he should slowly suffocate a little four-year-old girl.

'Hello, Chief . . .'

'Yes?'

'He's finished. The Bench and the jury have retired. Some people expect they'll be out a long time. Others, though, are convinced the die is already cast.'

'How is Meurant?'

'The whole of the afternoon you might have thought it no longer concerned him. He seemed far away, his eyes clouded. When his lawyer said something to him on two or three occasions, he simply shrugged his shoulders. At the end, when the judge asked him if there was any statement he wanted to make, he didn't appear to understand. The question had to be repeated. He simply shook his head.'

'Did he look at his wife at all?'

'Not once.'

'Thank you. Now listen: did you spot Bonfils in the courtroom?'

'Yes. He's keeping close to Ginette Meurant.'

'Go and tell him to make sure he doesn't lose sight of her on the way

out. In fact, to make doubly certain that he isn't given the slip, tell him
to get Jussieu to help him. One of the two of them can arrange to have a
car ready.'

'I understand. I'll give them your instructions.'

'She'll probably go home eventually and there must be a man permanently outside the house, in the Boulevard de Charonne.'

'And what if . . .'

'If Meurant's acquitted, Janvier, whom I'm going to send over, can
look after him.'

'Do you think he . . .?'

'I couldn't say at all, my lad.'

True enough. He had done his best. He was trying to find out the
truth, but there was nothing to prove that he had found it, or even part
of it.

The investigation had been conducted in March, then at the beginning of April with many hours of sunshine over Paris, light clouds, a few
showers to suddenly dampen the cool mornings.

The other end of the proceedings was now taking place in an early
spell of autumn weather, overcast, with rain, a low spongy sky, gleaming pavements.

To kill time, he signed some documents, went to take a look in the
duty room, where he gave Janvier some instructions.

'See that you keep me informed, even in the middle of the night.'

In spite of his seeming lack of concern, he was tense, suddenly anxious, as if he were blaming himself for having undertaken too heavy a
responsibility.

When the telephone rang in his office, he dashed to it.

'All over, Chief!'

He could hear not only Lapointe's voice, but many different noises,
quite a hubbub.

'There were four questions, two concerning each of the victims. The
answer is no to all four. His lawyer, at this moment, is trying to lead
Meurant through to the clerk's office, despite the crowd which . . .'

Lapointe's voice was lost for a moment in the din.

'I'm sorry, Chief. . . . I grabbed the first telephone I could get at. . . .
I'll be along at the office as soon as possible. . . .'

Maigret started walking up and down again, stuffing his pipe,
changing it for another because that one didn't draw properly, opening
and shutting his door again three times over.

The corridors of Police Headquarters were deserted again, and only a
regular, a casual informer, sat waiting in the glass cage.

When Lapointe arrived there was still an aura of Assize Court
excitement about him.

'A great many people predicted it, but it was quite a moment all the
same. . . . The whole room stood up. . . . The little girl's mother, who

had returned to her seat, fainted away and was almost trodden under foot . . .'

'Meurant?'

'He didn't seem to understand. He allowed himself to be led away without really knowing what was happening to him. The journalists who were able to get close enough didn't get a word out of him. So they descended on his wife again, with Lamblin playing her bodyguard.

'Immediately after the verdict, she tried to rush across to Meurant, as if to throw her arms around him. . . . He had already turned his back on the courtroom . . .'

'Where is she?'

'Lamblin led her off to some office or other, near the barristers' robing-room. . . . Jussieu's taking charge of her. . . .'

It was half-past six. Police Headquarters was beginning to empty, lights were being switched out.

'I'm off home to dinner.'

'What am I supposed to do now?'

'You go home to dinner too, and get some sleep.'

'Do you think anything will happen?'

The chief-inspector, who was opening his cupboard to get out his overcoat and hat, simply shrugged his shoulders.

'Do you remember the house search?'

'Clearly.'

'You're sure there were no firearms in the flat?'

'Positive. I'm convinced that Meurant has never possessed a gun in his life. He didn't even do military service, because of his eyesight . . .'

'See you tomorrow, my lad.'

'Okay, Chief.'

Maigret caught a bus, then walked along past the façades of the houses in the Boulevard Richard-Lenoir, his back bent, his collar raised. When he reached the landing on his floor, the door opened, forming a rectangle of warm light and letting smells of cooking drift out.

'Happy?' Madame Maigret asked him.

'Why?'

'Because he's been acquitted.'

'How did you know?'

'I just heard it on the wireless.'

'What else did they say?'

'That his wife was waiting for him at the exit and that they took a taxi and went home.'

He ensconced himself in his familiar world, got back into his habits, his slippers.

'Are you very hungry?'

'I don't know. What's for dinner?'

He was thinking of another flat, where another couple lived, in the

Boulevard de Charonne. There could be no dinner prepared over there, but probably some ham and cheese in the larder.

In the street two detectives would be walking up and down in the rain, unless they had found shelter in some doorway.

What would be happening? After living seven months in prison, what would Gaston Meurant have said to his wife? How would he be looking at her? Had he tried to kiss her, place his hand on hers?

Would she swear to him that everything they had said about her was untrue?

Or would she ask his forgiveness, swearing that she loved no one but him?

Would he go back to his shop the next day, to his picture-framing studio at the end of the court-yard?

Maigret was eating mechanically and Madame Maigret knew this was no time to ask him questions.

The telephone rang.

'Hello, yes . . . It's me . . . Vacher? . . . Is Jussieu with you?'

'I'm 'phoning from a bar near-by to give you my report. . . . I've nothing special to tell you, but I guessed you'd like to know. . . .'

'Have they gone home?'

'Yes.'

'Alone?'

'Yes. A few minutes later, the lights were switched on on the third floor. I saw shadows passing to and fro behind the curtain. . . .'

'And then?'

'About half an hour later his wife came down, carrying an umbrella. Jussieu followed her. She didn't go far. She went to a delicatessen, next a baker's, then she went back upstairs. . . .'

'Did Jussieu see her close to?'

'Quite close, through the delicatessen window.'

'How does she seem?'

'She looked as though she'd been crying. Her cheeks were flushed, her eyes shining . . .'

'She didn't seem upset?'

'Not according to Jussieu.'

'And since then?'

'I suppose they had something to eat. I saw Ginette Meurent's silhouette again, in the room which seems to be the bedroom . . .'

'Is that the lot?'

'Yes. Shall we both stay here?'

'I think it would be wisest. I should like one of you to go upstairs and keep watch inside the building in a little while. The tenants probably go to bed early. Perhaps Jussieu could install himself on the landing, as soon as people have stopped coming in and out. He can tell the concierge, but ask her to keep quiet about it.'

'Right, Chief.'

'Ring me back here in two hours, no matter what happens.'

'So long as the bar is still open.'

'If not I may call around there myself.'

There was no gun in the flat, certainly, but hadn't Léontine Faverges' murderer used a knife, which, moreover, had not been recovered? An extremely sharp knife, the experts maintained, and they thought it was probably a butcher's knife.

All the Paris cutlers, all the hardware shops had been questioned, and of course it had proved useless.

Come to think of it, they knew nothing, except that a woman and a little girl were dead, that a certain navy-blue suit belonging to Gaston Meurant had spots of blood on it, and that the man's wife, at the time of the crime, was meeting a lover several times a week in a boarding-house in the Rue Victor-Massé.

That was all. For lack of proof, the jury had just acquitted the frame-maker.

They had found it impossible to declare him guilty, but they had found it equally impossible to declare him innocent.

While her husband had been in prison, Ginette Meurant had led an exemplary life, hardly ever leaving home, never meeting anyone suspicious.

There was no telephone in their flat. Her mail had been watched, with no result.

'Are you serious about going over there tonight?'

'Just to have a little walk before going to bed.'

'Are you afraid something will happen?'

What answer could he give? That both of them were so ill-suited, living together in the strange flat where the *History of the Consulate and the Empire* stood on the shelves of the cosy-corner next to the silk dolls and the film stars' confessions.

V

AT about eleven-thirty, Maigret had stopped for a moment in a taxi in the Boulevard de Charonne. Jussieu, wearing the blank expression of men on night duty, had appeared silently out of the shadows, had pointed above them to a lighted window on the third floor. It was one of the few lights still on in the neighbourhood, a district where people leave for work early in the morning.

Rain was still falling, but the drops were well spaced and there were the beginnings of a silver glow between the clouds.

'That window up there is the dining-room,' the detective had explained, smelling strongly of cigarette smoke. 'The light's been off in the bedroom for the past half-hour.'

Maigret waited a few minutes, hoping to catch a glimpse of life behind the curtain. As nothing stirred, he went home to bed.

From reports and telephone calls next day, he was to reconstruct, then follow hour by hour, every movement of the Meurants.

At six o'clock in the morning, when the concierge was bringing in the dustbins, two other detectives went to take over, although this time one did not go inside the house, for it was no longer possible to stay on the stairs during the daytime.

Vacher, who had spent the night there, sometimes sitting on a step, sometimes, if there was a sound of movement in the flat, leaning against the door, made a report that was a little disturbing.

Quite early, after a meal during which the couple had hardly exchanged a word, Ginette Meurant had gone into the bedroom to get undressed; Jussieu, who had seen her, from out in the street, pulling her dress off over her head, as if in a Chinese lantern show, confirmed this.

Her husband had not followed her. She had gone to him to say something, but then apparently went to bed while he remained sitting in an armchair in the dining-room.

Later on, several times he got up, walked around the room, stopping and starting repeatedly, only to sit down again.

Towards midnight his wife had come in and spoken to him again. From the landing Vacher could not make out what they were saying, but he recognized their voices. From the tone they were not quarrelling. It was a kind of monologue from the young woman, with an occasional very brief sentence, or just a single word, from her husband.

She had gone back to bed, still by herself, seemingly. The light still burned in the dining-room and at about half-past two Ginette had returned to the charge once more.

Meurant was not asleep, since he had replied at once, laconically. Vacher thought she had wept. He had certainly heard a monotonous complaining, punctuated by characteristic sniffling.

Still without any sign of anger, the husband sent her back to bed and probably dozed off at last in the armchair.

Later, a baby had woken up on the floor above; there had been muffled footsteps, then from about five o'clock the occupants of the house had started to get up, turn on the lights; the smell of coffee had spread onto the staircase. At half-past five one man was already leaving for work and looked inquisitively at the detective, who had no means of hiding, then looked at the door and seemed to understand.

It was Dupeu and Baron who took over, outside, at six o'clock. The rain had stopped. The trees were dripping. The fog reduced visibility to about twenty yards.

The light in the dining-room was still on, the one in the bedroom off. It was not long before Meurant left the house, unshaven, his clothes crumpled, like those of a man who has spent the night fully clothed, and he had set off to the tobacconist's bar on the corner where he had drunk three cups of black coffee and eaten some croissants. Just as he was turning the door-handle to leave, he had changed his mind and, going back to the zinc counter, had ordered a cognac which he had swallowed in one gulp.

The investigations, in the spring, revealed that he was not much of a drinker, that he hardly took anything except a little wine with his meals and an occasional glass of beer in the summer.

He went by foot to the Rue de la Roquette, did not turn round to see if he was being followed. When he arrived at his shop he stopped outside a moment in front of the closed shutters, did not go in, but turned into the yard, and unlocked the door of his glass-fronted studio.

He remained standing inside for quite a time, doing nothing, just staring about him at the work-bench, the tools hooked on the wall, the hanging frames, the boards and the shavings. Water had seeped in under the door and formed a little puddle on the cement floor.

Meurant had opened the stove door, put in some kindling wood, some nuts of coal that were still left, then as he was about to strike a match he had changed his mind, gone outside again and locked the door behind him.

He had walked quite a long way, with no apparent destination. At the Place de la République he had gone into another bar where he had drunk a second brandy while the waiter kept staring at him, seemingly wondering where he had seen that face before.

Did he realize it? Two or three passers-by had also turned round to look at him, since his photograph was appearing in the papers that very morning under the headline:

'GASTON MEURANT ACQUITTED'

He might have seen the headline, the photograph, on all the news-paper-stands, but he did not have the curiosity to buy himself a paper. He took a bus, got out twenty minutes later at the Place Pigalle, and walked in the direction of the Rue Victor-Massé.

Finally he stopped in front of the small hotel kept by Nicolas Cajou, the Hôtel du Lion, and stood there a long time, staring at the façade.

When he began his tour again, it was to go back down towards the Grands Boulevards, walking in a vague way, sometimes stopping at crossroads as if he were not sure where to go, buying a packet of cigarettes en route . . .

Going along the Rue Montmartre, he had reached Les Halles and the detective almost lost track of him in the throng. At the Châtelet he had drunk a third cognac, in one gulp as before, and he had finally arrived at the Quai des Orfèvres.

Now that the sun had risen, the yellowy fog was becoming less thick. Maigret, in his office, received a telephone report from Dupeu, who had remained on guard at the Boulevard de Charonne.

'The wife got up at ten to eight. I saw her open the curtains, then the window, and gaze out into the street. She looked as though she was searching for her husband. She probably didn't hear him go out and was surprised to find the dining-room empty. I think she noticed me, Chief . . .'

'Never mind. But if she goes out as well, make sure she doesn't give you the slip.'

On the quayside, Gaston Meurant was hesitating, looking at the windows of Police Headquarters in the same way as he had looked at those of the hotel a short while before. It was half-past nine. He walked on as far as the Pont Saint-Michel, was about to cross the bridge when he retraced his steps and, going past the policeman on duty, at last came into the entrance-hall.

He was familiar with the place. He was seen to climb the grey staircase slowly, stopping, not for breath, but because he was still uncertain.

'He's on his way up, Chief!' Baron telephoned, from an office on the ground floor.

And Maigret repeated to Janvier, who was with him in his office:

'He's on his way up.'

They both waited. It took a long time. Meurant could not make up his mind, wandered along the corridor, stopped outside the chief-inspector's door, as if he were about to knock on it without having himself announced.

'What are you looking for?' Joseph, the old porter, asked him.

'I'd like to speak to Inspector Maigret.'

'Come along then. You'll have to fill in a form.'

Pencil in hand, he was pondering again whether to give up and go, just when Janvier came out of Maigret's office.

'Have you come to see the chief-inspector? Follow me.'

The whole thing must have been like a nightmare for Meurant. He had the face of someone who had hardly slept, his eyes red-rimmed, and he smelt of stale smoke and alcohol. Yet he was by no means drunk. He followed Janvier. The latter opened the door for him, ushered him in ahead, and then closed it again, without going in himself.

Maigret, at his desk, apparently deep in the perusal of a file, waited for a while without raising his head, then he turned towards his visitor, without any sign of surprise, murmured:

'One moment . . .'

He wrote some notes on a document, then another, murmured distractedly:

'Sit down.'

Meurant did not sit down, did not even come forward into the centre of the room. At the end of his patience, he announced:

'I suppose you think I've come to thank you?'

His voice was not entirely natural. He was a little hoarse and he tried to put some sarcasm into his reproach.

'Sit down,' Maigret repeated, without looking at him.

This time Meurant came forward three steps, grasped the back of a chair with its seat upholstered in green velvet.

'Did you do that to save me?'

The chief-inspector finally surveyed him, calmly, from top to toe.

'You look tired, Meurant.'

'I'm not concerned with myself, but with what you did yesterday.'

His voice was more hollow, as though it was an effort for him to control his temper.

'I've come here to tell you that I don't believe a word of what you said, that you lied, like those others lied, that I'd sooner be in prison, that it was a dirty trick you played . . .'

Was it the alcohol which made him somewhat disjointed? Possibly. Yet, once again, he was not drunk, and these sentences must have been running around in his head for a good part of the night.

'Sit down.'

At last! He complied, against his will, as if he smelt a trap.

'You may smoke if you wish.'

As a protest, so as not to be obliged to the chief-inspector for anything, he did not do so, much though he wanted to, and his hand was trembling.

'It's easy for you to make people like that say what you want them to; they depend on the police . . .'

He obviously meant Nicolas Cajou, letting rooms by the hour in his hotel, and the chambermaid.

Maigret lit his pipe slowly, waited.

'You know as well as I do that it's untrue . . .'

His anguish brought out drops of sweat on his forehead. Maigret spoke at last.

'You mean to tell me that you murdered your aunt and little Cécile Perrin?'

'You know very well I didn't.'

'I don't *know* it, but I am almost convinced that you didn't. Why, do you suppose?'

Surprised, Meurant could not think of an answer.

'There are a lot of children in the building where you live in the Boulevard de Charonne, aren't there?'

Meurant said yes, mechanically.

'You hear them coming in and going out. Sometimes when they

come back from school they play on the stairs. Do you talk to them sometimes?'

'I know them all right.'

'You know the school hours, although you've no children yourself. That made quite an impression on me, from the beginning of the investigations. Cécile Perrin used to attend kindergarten. Léontine Faverges went to collect her every day, except on Thursdays, at four o'clock in the afternoon. Until four o'clock therefore, your aunt was alone in the flat.'

Meurant was doing his best to follow.

'You had a large bill falling due on February 28th, we know. It is possible that the last time you borrowed money from her Léontine Faverges let you know that she would not fork out again. Supposing you planned to kill her, to get your hands on the money in the Chinese vase and the bonds . . .'

'I did not kill her.'

'Let me finish. Just suppose, I'm saying, that you had conceived this idea, there would have been absolutely no point in your going to the Rue Manuel after four o'clock and consequently being obliged to kill two people instead of one. Criminals who murder children unnecessarily are very rare and they fall into a well-defined category.'

It seemed as though Meurant, his eyes misting over, was on the point of bursting into tears.

'The murderer of Léontine Faverges and the child either was not aware of the existence of the latter or was forced to do the deed in the late afternoon. Well, if he knew of the secret of the vase and the drawer with the bearer-bonds in it, it is more than likely that he also knew of Cécile Perrin's presence in the flat.'

'What are you getting at?'

'Please have a cigarette.'

Automatically the man obeyed, but continued to look at Maigret with suspicion in his eyes, even if the anger was now dimmed.

'We're still just supposing, aren't we? The murderer knows that you're due to arrive at the Rue Manuel at about six o'clock. He is not unaware of the fact that police doctors — the newspapers have said so often enough — are capable of pinpointing the time of death in most cases to within an hour or two.'

'Nobody knew that . . .'

His voice had altered too and he was now looking away from the chief-inspector's face.

'If he committed the crime at about five o'clock the murderer was pretty well sure that you would be suspected. He could not foresee that a customer would turn up at your studio at six o'clock and, anyhow, the music teacher was not able to supply any absolute evidence, since he isn't positive about the date.'

'Nobody knew . . .' repeated Meurant mechanically.

Maigret changed the subject suddenly.

'Do you know your neighbours at the Boulevard de Charonne?'

'I say good morning to them on the stairs.'

'They never call on you, even for a cup of coffee? You don't visit their flats? You are not on more or less friendly terms with any of them?'

'No.'

'So the chances are that they have never heard your aunt mentioned.'

'They have now!'

'But not before. Did you and your wife have many friends in Paris?'

Meurant replied with bad grace, as if he were afraid that if he conceded one point he would have to give in all along the line.

'What difference does that make?'

'Did you sometimes dine out with friends?'

'No.'

'Who did you go out with on Sundays?'

'With my wife.'

'And she has no relations in Paris. Nor have you, apart from your brother, who lives mostly in the south, and with whom you broke off all contact two years ago.'

'There was no quarrel.'

'Nevertheless you stopped seeing him.'

And once again Maigret seemed to change the subject.

'How many keys are there to your flat?'

'Two. My wife has one, I have the other.'

'It never happens that either of you leaves the key with the concierge or a neighbour when you go out?'

Meurant preferred to keep quiet, realizing that Maigret never said anything without reason, but unable to see what he was driving at now.

'On that day the lock had not been forced, so the experts say who examined it. Yet, if you did not commit the murder, somebody entered your flat twice, the first time to get your blue suit from the wardrobe in the bedroom, and the second time to put it back, neatly enough for you to notice nothing amiss. Do you admit this?'

'I admit nothing. All I know is that my wife . . .'

'When you first met her, seven years ago, you were a lonely man. Or am I mistaken?'

'I worked all day, and in the evening I used to read, sometimes went to the cinema.'

'Did she fling herself at you?'

'No.'

'Didn't other men, other customers at the restaurant where she was a waitress, make advances to her?'

He clenched his fists.

'So what?'

'How long did it take you before she finally agreed to go out with you?'

'Three weeks.'

'What did you do, that first evening?'

'We went to the cinema, then she wanted to go dancing.'

'Are you a good dancer?'

'No.'

'Did she tease you about it?'

He didn't answer, more and more disconcerted by the turn the interview had taken.

'Afterwards you took her back to your place?'

'No.'

'Why not?'

'Because I was in love with her.'

'And the second time?'

'We went to the cinema again.'

'Afterwards?'

'To a hotel.'

'Why not to your flat?'

'Because I was living in a badly furnished room at the end of a yard.'

'Were you already intending to marry her and afraid you might put her off?'

'I wanted her to be my wife from the start.'

'Were you aware that she had many friends?'

'That's nobody's business but her own. She was free.'

'Did you talk to her about your job, your shop? You already had a shop in the Faubourg Saint-Antoine, unless I'm mistaken.'

'Naturally I talked to her about it.'

'Did you not have the idea at the back of your head that it might tempt her? By marrying you she would become the wife of a shop-keeper.'

Meurant was blushing.

'Do you realize now that it was you who wanted to get her and that you were prepared to cheat a little with that in view? Were you in debt?'

'No.'

'Any savings?'

'No.'

'Didn't she say anything to you about her wish to own a restaurant one day?'

'Several times.'

'What did you reply to that?'

'That it was a possibility.'

'Did you have any intention of giving up your job?'

'Not at thàt time.'

'You only decided to later, after two years of marriage, when she took up the cudgels again and mentioned an exceptional opportunity for it.'

He was distressed and Maigret went on, implacably:

'You were jealous. It was your jealousy which forced her to stay at home instead of going out to work as she wanted to. You were living in a small two-room flat then, in the Rue de Turenne. Every evening you insisted that she account for her movements during the day. Were you really convinced that she loved you?'

'I thought so.'

'Without any misgivings?'

'They didn't exist.'

'You saw quite a lot of your brother, I believe?'

'He was living in Paris.'

'Did he take your wife out?'

'We sometimes went out together, the three of us.'

'They never went alone?'

'Occasionally.'

'Your brother was living in a hotel, in the Rue Bréa, near the Place des Ternes. Did your wife ever visit his room there?'

Racked, Meurant almost screamed:

'No!'

'Did she once own a pullover, the sort people wear ski-ing, a pullover made of thick, white wool, hand-knitted, with reindeer designs in black and brown on it? Did she ever go out in it, in winter, wearing a pair of black slacks tight around the ankle?'

Frowning, he stared intently at Maigret.

'What are your trying to get at?'

'Answer me.'

'Yes. But only seldom. I didn't like her going out in the street in trousers.'

'Have you often met women in the streets of Paris dressed like that?'

'No.'

'Read this, Meurant.'

Maigret extracted a sheet of paper from a file, the evidence of the manageress of the hotel in the Rue Bréa. She distinctly remembered having had a guest called Alfred Meurant, who took a room in her place by the month for quite a long time, and sometimes came back for a few days since. He brought lots of women to his room. Without hesitation she recognized the photograph which was shown her, the one of Ginette Meurant. She even recalled seeing her in an unusual get-up . . .

There followed the description of the pullover and the slacks.

Had Ginette Meurant been back to the Rue Bréa recently?

The proprietress's reply: Less than a year ago, when Alfred Meurant was in Paris on a brief trip.

'It's untrue!' the man protested, pushing away the paper.

'Would you like me to give you the whole file to read? There are at least thirty statements, all from hotel proprietors, including one from Saint-Cloud. Did your brother once own a sky-blue convertible?'

Meurant's face provided the answer.

'He was not the only one. At the dance-hall in the Rue Gravilliers your wife was known to have had about fifteen lovers.'

Maigret, heavy and sombre, was filling another pipe, and it was with a gloomy heart that he had given this twist to the interview.

'It's not true!' muttered the husband once more.

'She did not ask to be your wife. She did nothing to help it. She took three weeks before she made up her mind to go out with you, perhaps because she didn't want to hurt your feelings. She went with you to the hotel when you asked her, since for her that was of little importance. You flashed before her eyes a picture of a pleasant, easy existence, security, a step up into a more or less middle-class world. You half-promised her that one day you would make her dream of owning a small restaurant come true.

'Out of jealousy, you stopped her working.

'You didn't dance. You weren't very fond of the cinema.'

'We used to go once a week.'

'The rest of the time she was forced to go by herself. In the evenings, you used to read.'

'I've always been keen on educating myself.'

'And she's always been keen on something different. Are you beginning to understand?'

'I don't believe you.'

'Nevertheless, you are sure that you spoke to nobody about the Chinese vase. And on February 27th you were not wearing your blue suit. You and your wife were the only ones with keys to the flat in the Boulevard de Charonne.'

The telephone rang. Maigret lifted the receiver.

'Yes, it's me . . .'

It was Baron at the other end of the line.

'She went out about nine o'clock, four minutes to, to be precise, and set off to the Boulevard Voltaire.'

'Wearing what?'

'A floral dress and a brown woollen coat. No hat.'

'What happened?'

'She went into a shop that sells travelling goods and bought a cheap suitcase. She came back to the flat carrying the case. It must be warm in there because she's opened the window. Now and then I see her walking to and fro and I presume she's packing her bags.'

While he listened, Maigret was watching Meurant, who suspected that they were talking about his wife, and looked worried.

'Has anything happened to her?' he even asked at that moment.

Maigret shook his head.

'The concierge has a telephone,' Baron went on, 'so I sent for a taxi, which is now parked a hundred yards down the street in case she wants to call one.'

'Very good. Keep me in touch.'

And, to Meurant:

'Just a moment . . .'

The chief-inspector went into the duty room, spoke to Janvier:

'You had better take one of the cars and go over there, to the Boulevard de Charonne, as quickly as you can. It looks as if Ginette Meurant's about to do a bunk. Perhaps she suspects that her husband has come along here? She must be pretty scared.'

'What's his reaction?'

'I'd sooner not be in his shoes.'

Maigret would sooner have had nothing to do with the whole business.

'You're wanted on the telephone, Chief-Inspector.'

'Put it through here.'

It was the public prosecutor, whose conscience was also troubling him a little.

'Has anything happened?'

'They went home. Apparently they slept in separate rooms. Meurant went out early and at the moment he's in my office.'

'What have you told him? I presume he can't hear what you're saying?'

'I'm in the duty room. He's not yet sure whether to believe me. He's struggling. He's beginning to realize that he had better face reality.'

'You're not afraid he'll . . .'

'It's more than likely that he won't find her home when he gets back. She's packing her bags now.'

'And what if he does find her?'

'After the dose I've been forced to inflict on him, it's not so much her he's going to have a grudge against.'

'He's not the suicidal type?'

'Not so long as he hasn't got to the bottom of it all.'

'Are you planning to reveal it to him?'

Maigret said nothing, shrugged his shoulders.

'As soon as you have any news . . .'

'I'll telephone you or come round to your office, sir.'

'Have you read the papers?'

'Only the headlines.'

Maigret hung up. Janvier had already left. It would be wise to hold on to Meurant for a while, to prevent him catching his wife in the midst of her preparations for departure.

If he found her later on, it would be less serious. The most dangerous moment would be over. This explained why Maigret, pipe in mouth, paced up and down, strolled into the long corridor, which was not so overheated, for a while.

Then, glancing at his watch, he went into his office and found Meurant calmer, looking thoughtful.

'There is one possibility which you haven't mentioned,' Ginette's husband objected. 'One person, at least, must have known the secret of the Chinese vase.'

'The child's mother?'

'Yes: Juliette Perrin. She often visited Léontine Faverges and Cécile. Even if the old lady had said nothing to her about her money, the child might have seen . . .'

'Do you imagine that I've not thought of this?'

'Then why have you made no investigations there? Juliette Perrin works in a night-club. She hangs around with all sorts of people . . .'

He was clinging to this hope desperately and Maigret felt unhappy about disillusioning him. Nevertheless it was necessary.

'We've made enquiries about all her contacts, without result.

'Besides there is something which neither Juliette Perrin, nor her casual or regular lovers could have procured without the very definite complicity of someone else.'

'What?'

'The blue suit. You know the child's mother?'

'No.'

'You never met her at the Rue Manuel?'

'No. I knew that Cécile's mother was a night-club hostess, but I never had the chance to see her with my own eyes.'

'Don't forget either that her daughter was killed.'

For Meurant yet another way out had been closed. He was still looking for a solution, feeling around, determined not to admit the truth.

'My wife might have mentioned it without thinking.'

'To whom?'

'I can't think.'

'And given away the key to your flat, still without thinking, before she went to the cinema?'

Telephone. Janvier this time, a little out of breath.

'I'm 'phoning from the concierge's, Chief. The person concerned left in a taxi with the suitcase and a rather full brown hand-bag. I took the cab number in any case. It's from a Levallois company and it will be easy to find it again. Baron's following her in another taxi. Shall I wait here?'

'Yes.'

'Is he still with you?'

'Yes.'

'I suppose I'd better stay put when he arrives.'

'It would be wise.'

'I'll park the car near one of the gates of the cemetery. It will be less noticed there. Are you reckoning on letting him go soon?'

'Yes.'

Meurant was still trying to puzzle it out and the effort required made the blood rush to his head. He was almost dropping with tiredness, with despair as well, but he succeeded in keeping going, and even almost in smiling.

'That my wife they're keeping their eye on?'

Maigret nodded his head.

'I suppose they'll be keeping the same sort of eye on me?'

A vague gesture from the chief-inspector.

'I haven't got a gun, I promise you!'

'I know.'

'I'm not intending to kill anyone, not even myself.'

'I know that, too.'

'Not now, at any rate.'

He got to his feet, hesitating, and Maigret realized that he was reaching the point of crisis, that the man was keeping a hold on himself so that he wouldn't burst into tears, sob, bang the walls with his clenched fists.

'Cheer up, son.'

Meurant turned his head away, walked towards the door, trying to keep his balance. The chief-inspector placed a hand on his shoulder for a second, gently.

'Come and see me when you want to.'

Meurant left the room at last without showing his face, without saying thank-you, and the door shut behind him.

Baron was waiting on the quayside, ready to start shadowing him again.

VI

AT mid-day, when he was getting ready to go home for lunch, Maigret heard his first news of Ginette Meurant.

It came through Dupeu, who telephoned from a bar in the Rue Delambre, in the Montparnasse area, near the Rue de la Gaité. Dupeu was an excellent detective, who had only one fault: he recited his reports in a monotonous voice, as if he would never come to an end, amassing so many details that you eventually listened to him with only half an ear.

'Get on! . . . Get on with it! . . .' was what you always wanted to say to him.

If you unfortunately went so far as to do so, he would appear so miserable that you immediately regretted it.

'I'm in a bar called the Pickwick, Chief, a hundred yards from the Boulevard Montparnasse, and about ten minutes ago she arrived at the Hôtel de Concarneau opposite. It's a decent enough hotel which prides itself on having hot and cold running water, a bathroom on each floor. She has room 32 and she doesn't seem likely to leave in a hurry since she argued about the prices and has taken her room on a weekly basis. Unless that's all a blind.'

'She knows she's been followed?'

'I'm positive she does. In the taxi she looked round several times. As soon as they left the Boulevard de Charonne, she showed the driver a visiting-card she took out of her handbag. When we reached the Boulevard Saint-Michel, one behind the other, she leant forward to the driver. I could see her clearly through the window at the back. He immediately swung right, into the Faubourg Saint-Germain, then drove around, for nigh on ten minutes, in the little streets of Saint-Germain-des-Prés.

'I suppose she was hoping to throw me off. When she realized that wasn't possible, she gave further directions and before long her taxi drew up outside a building in the Rue Monsieur-le-Prince.'

Maigret was listening patiently, without interrupting.

'She told the cab to wait and went in. I went in a little after her and questioned the concierge. The person Ginette Meurant went to see is none other than Maître Lamblin, who lives on the first floor. She stayed in the house about twenty minutes. When she emerged, she didn't look very reassured and she immediately told the driver to bring her here. I suppose I'm to go on keeping a look-out?'

'Until someone comes to relieve you.'

Now Janvier was probably still at the Boulevard de Charonne, keeping an eye on the husband, together with Baron.

Had Ginette Meurant called on the lawyer merely to ask for his advice? Maigret suspected otherwise. Before leaving Headquarters, he gave Lucas some instructions, then made his way towards the 'bus station.

Seven months before, on February 27th, the Meurants had hardly any money, since they were in no position to meet the bill of exchange which would fall due the next day. Apart from this, they had unpaid accounts with the neigbouring tradesmen, but that, it was true, was not unusual for them.

A few days later, when the examining magistrate had asked Meurant

to name a lawyer, the frame-maker had objected that he did not have
the means to pay for one and Pierre Duché had been appointed by the
court.

What had Ginette Meurant been living on in the meantime? As far
as the police knew — and they had watched her incoming mail — she had
received no money orders. Nor had she apparently cashed any cheques.
Although she had incurred very few expenses, had led a retired existence in her flat, she had still had to eat, and, before the trial, she had
bought the skirt and black coat which she wore at the Assizes.

Perhaps the answer was that she had been putting money aside herself, without her husband knowing, cheating him of some of the house-
keeping money, as quite a few wives do?

Lamblin, at the Palais, had fastened upon her. The lawyer was smart
enough to recognize that the case would have spectacular repercussions,
and to know that it would bring him a great deal of publicity if he then
represented the young woman.

Maigret might have been making a mistake; but he was convinced
that Ginette Meurant had gone to the Rue Monsieur-le-Prince to get
hold of some money, rather than to ask for advice.

Lamblin's reputation being what it was, he must have given her some
money, but only in dribs and drabs. He had probably also advised her
not to leave Paris but to stay calmly where she was and wait for new
developments.

The Montparnasse neighbourhood had not been chosen by chance.
Neither Meurant nor Ginette had lived round there or were known
there, and it was most unlikely that Meurant would look for his wife in
that area.

The chief-inspector returned to the peaceful atmosphere of his flat,
had lunch alone with Madame Maigret, and when he arrived back at
the Quai, at two o'clock, he had a telephone call from Janvier to say
that Meurant had not left the flat, where everything was quiet.

He had to go to a meeting with the Commissioner to discuss a disagreeable case which had political implications, and it was four o'clock
before Janvier called again.

'Things are on the move, Chief. I can't say what's going to happen,
but there will be a development soon, I'm sure. He left home at two
forty-five, carrying a number of large parcels. Although they seemed
heavy, he didn't call a taxi. Still, he hadn't far to go. A little later he
went into a second-hand shop, on the Boulevard de Ménilmontant, and
stayed there some time talking to the owner.'

'Did he see you?'

'Probably. It was hard to keep out of sight, since the neighbourhood
was pretty deserted. He sold his watch, the gramophone, some records,
a pile of books. Then he went back home, came out again, this time with
an enormous bundle wrapped up in a sheet.

'He returned to the same shop, where he sold some clothes, linen, blankets and some brass candlesticks.

'He's at home now. I don't think it'll be for long.'

In fact Janvier rang back in fifty minutes' time.

'He left the house once again and went to the Faubourg Saint-Antoine, to another frame-maker's. They had quite a long conversation, then the man took Meurant in his van to the Rue de la Roquette where they stopped opposite the shop you know.

'They inspected the frames one by one. The man from the Faubourg Saint-Antoine loaded a number of them into his van and handed over some bank-notes to Meurant.

'I forgot to tell you that he's shaved now. I don't know what he's up to in his studio, but the car's only a few yards away, just in case . . .'

At six o'clock Maigret received his last telephone call from Janvier, who was calling from the Gare de Lyon.

'He's due to leave in twelve minutes, Chief. He took a second-class ticket for Toulon. He's only got one small bag with him. At the moment he's drinking a brandy in the bar; I can see him through the window of the 'phone box.'

'Is he watching you?'

'Yes.'

'How does he seem?'

'Like a man who's got no time for anything else but one idea he's got fixed in his mind.'

'Make sure he really gets on that train and come back here.'

The train only stopped at Dijon, Lyons, Avignon and Marseilles. Maigret put through trunk calls to the police officers at each of the stations, gave them the frame-maker's description, specified the number of the carriage he was in. Then he called the flying squad at Toulon.

The chief-inspector in charge there was called Blanc and he was about the same age as Maigret. They knew each other well, because, before entering the Sûreté, Blanc had been at the Quai des Orfèvres.

'Maigret here. Look, old man, I hope you're not too busy. I'm arranging for the public prosecutor's department to send you a judicial warrant tomorrow, but I thought I'd better put you in the picture as soon as possible. What time does the six-seventeen from Paris arrive at Toulon?'

'Eight-thirty-two.'

'Good. In carriage number 10, that's presuming that he hasn't changed his seat during the journey, you will find a man by the name of Meurant.'

'I've been reading the papers.'

'I'd like him to be shadowed as soon as he steps off the train.'

'That's easy. Does he know the town?'

'I don't think he's ever been to the south before, but I may be mistaken. Meurant has a brother called Alfred.'

'I know the one. I've had quite a bit of trouble with him.'

'Is he at Toulon at the moment?'

'I can let you know in an hour or two. Shall I ring you back?'

'Yes, please, at my home.'

He gave his number at the Boulevard Richard-Lenoir.

'What do you know about Alfred Meurant's activities lately?'

'He normally lives at a boarding-house called "Les Eucalyptus", outside the town, quite a way out, on the hill between the Faron and La Vallette.'

'What sort of place is it?'

'The sort we keep an eye on. There are quite a few like it along the coast between Marseilles and Menton. The proprietor is a man named Lisca, known as Freddo, who was for a long time a barman in Montmartre, in the Rue de Douai. Freddo married a pretty kid, a former strip-tease dancer, and they bought "Les Eucalyptus".

'Freddo does the cooking and they say he's marvellous at it, too. The house is off the main road, at the end of a lane that leads nowhere. In summer they eat outside under the trees.

'Quite respectable people from Toulon, doctors, civil servants, magistrates, go there for a meal from time to time.

'But the bulk of the customers are the crooks who live along the Coast and periodically go up to Paris.

'A few tarts too, who come down for a rest-cure.

'Get the setting?'

'I get it.'

'Two frequent customers, almost all-year-round boarders are Falconi and Scapucci.'

Two men with a string of convictions behind them, who cropped up periodically around Pigalle.

'They are great friends of Alfred Meurant's. The three of them go around openly, putting gambling-machines in local bars. They also provide them with none-too-virtuous barmaids, whom they collect from all over the place.

'They have several cars at their disposal and change them pretty frequently. For some time now I've been suspecting them of selling cars in Italy which have been stolen and repainted in Paris and the suburbs.

'I've got no proof yet. My men are on to it.'

'I've good reason to think that Gaston Meurant will try and contact his brother.'

'If he asks at the right places, he won't have much trouble finding him, unless his brother's covering his tracks.'

'If my Meurant should buy a gun or try to get hold of one, I should like to be informed immediately.'

'Right, Maigret. We'll do our best. What's the weather like up there?'

'Grey and cold.'

'Sun's shining nicely here. By the way, I was almost forgetting some-one. Among Freddo's customers at the moment is a fellow called Kubik.'

Twelve years before, Maigret had arrested him after a jewel robbery in the Boulevard Saint-Martin.

'It's more than likely he's involved in the jewel-theft last month on the Cours Albert-Premier in Nice.'

Maigret was also familiar with the underworld down there, and he envied Blanc a little. Like most of his colleagues, he preferred to deal with professionals, since one knew at once with them the kind of ground on which the match would be played and there were definite rules to the game.

How was Gaston Meurant, alone in a corner of his compartment, going to cope with people like that?

Maigret spent some time with Lucas, whom he put in charge of organizing the watch being kept in the Rue Delambre, and appointing detectives to go there in relays.

Ginette Meurant had spent the afternoon in her hotel bedroom, more than likely asleep. As the notice stated on the outside of the building, there was a telephone in each room, but all calls had to go through the switchboard.

According to the proprietor, who came from the Auvergne, she had not used the telephone, and he was positive that nobody at the hotel had put a call through to the south. Nonetheless there was a special operator tapping the line at the listening-post.

Ginette had stuck it out a long time. Either she had been extra-ordinarily cunning, since the murder in the Rue Manuel, or she had not once tried to communicate with the man who had been accompanying her to the Rue Victor-Massé for several months, up to and including February 26th.

It was almost as if this man, suddenly from one day to the next, had ceased to exist. Nor did he, for his part, seem to have made any attempt to get in touch with her.

The police had envisaged the possibility of prearranged signals. They had kept a close watch on the windows in the Boulevard de Charonne, studied the position of the curtains, which might have carried some significance, the lights in the flat, the movements of people on the opposite pavement.

Nor had the man put in any appearance at the Assizes or in the neighbourhood of the Palais de Justice.

It was so remarkable that Maigret was very impressed by all this.

Now, she was going out at last, looking for a cheap restaurant in this district new to her, eating alone at a table, reading a magazine. Then

she was off to buy some more at the corner of the Boulevard Montparnasse, plus a few romantic novels, climbed back up to her room
where the light remained on until past midnight.

Gaston Meurant was still in the moving train. At Dijon, then at
Lyons, a detective walked along the corridors, ascertained that he was
still in his corner, and the information was telephoned to the Boulevard
Richard-Lenoir, where Maigret stretched his arm out in the dark to
pick up the receiver.

Another day was beginning. Past Montélimar, Meurant was discovering the climate of Provence, and probably his nose was soon pressed
against the window, as he watched a strange landscape pass by in the
sunshine.

Marseilles . . . Maigret was shaving when he had the call from the
Gare Saint-Charles.

Meurant was still on the train, which was now on its way again. He
had not tricked them. He really was going to Toulon.

At Paris the weather remained grey, and, in the bus, people's faces
were downcast or sullen. On his desk, a pile of administrative mail
awaited him.

A detective — Maigret had lost track of who it was — telephoned from
the bar in the Rue Delambre.

'She's asleep. The curtains are closed at any rate, and she hasn't
ordered any breakfast.'

The train arrived at Toulon. Gaston Meurant, his bag in his hand, a
policeman on his heels, wandered around the main square, disorien-
tated, and eventually walked into the Hôtel des Voyageurs, where he
chose their cheapest room.

A little later, they were convinced that he did not know the town,
when he began to lose himself in the streets, after some trouble reached
the Boulevard de Strasbourg, where he went into a large café. He
ordered coffee this time, not brandy, asked several questions of the
waiter, who did not seem able to furnish the required information.

At noon he had not found what he was after and, funnily enough, it
was Chief-Inspector Blanc who was getting impatient.

'I wanted to have a glimpse of your fellow myself,' he said to Maigret
on the telephone. 'I found him in a bar on the Quai Cronstadt. He
could not have slept much in the train. He looked like some poor bloke
absolutely knocked out by lack of sleep, but still obsessed by some crazy
idea. He's not setting about it the right way. Up till now he's been in
about fifteen cafés and bars. Each time he orders mineral water. He
looks so much like a man scrounging for something that they look at
him askance. He always asks the same question:

' "Do you know Alfred Meurant?"'

'Barmen and waiters are immediately suspicious, specially the ones
who do know him. Some just make a vague gesture in reply. Others ask:

' "What's he do?" '

' "I don't know. He lives at Toulon." '

'My detective who's trailing him is beginning to feel sorry for him and almost wants to tip him off.

'At the rate Meurant's going, this may last for ages and he'll make himself sick on mineral water.'

Maigret was familiar enough with Toulon to know of at least three places where Meurant would have found some news of his brother. The frame-maker was now, however, reaching the right end of the town at last. If he went further on into the back-streets which flank the Quai Cronstadt, or again if chance took him on to Le Mourillon, he would doubtless eventually pick up the information he was hunting for so stubbornly.

In the Rue Delambre, Ginette Meurant had opened her curtains, ordered coffee and croissants and had gone back to bed to read.

She telephoned neither Maître Lamblin nor anyone else. Nor did she make any attempt to find out what was happening to her husband, or if the police were still on her own tracks.

Wouldn't she collapse under the strain sooner or later?

As for the lawyer, he took no steps, but went on with his usual activities.

Maigret had an idea, went into the duty room and walked up to Lucas.

'What time did she go and see her lawyer yesterday?'

'About eleven o'clock, if I remember rightly. I can look up my report.'

'No need. In any case, she still had time to put an advertisement in the evening papers. Get hold of all yesterday's papers, this morning's as well, and later on the evening editions. Go through the private ads.'

Lamblin did not have the reputation of being a very scrupulous man. If Ginette Meurant asked him to insert an advertisement, would he hesitate? It was unlikely.

If Maigret's hunch was a good one, it would mean that she did not know the present address of her former lover.

On the other hand, if she knew it, and if he had not moved since March, wouldn't Lamblin have telephoned him for her? Might she not have done it herself, during the twenty minutes she spent in the lawyer's office?

One detail had struck the chief-inspector ever since the spring, when the case had begun. The liaison between the young woman and the man described by Nicolas Cajou had lasted for many months. Throughout the winter they had met several times a week, which seemed to indicate that her lover lived in Paris.

Yet, nonetheless, they always met in a small hotel.

Didn't it seem likely that, for one reason or another, the man was unable to receive his mistress at his home?

Was he married? Perhaps he did not live alone?

Maigret had not found the right answer.

'It's a long shot,' he said to Lucas, 'but try to find out if a telephone call was made to Toulon yesterday from Lamblin's building.'

There was nothing else for him to do now but wait. At Toulon, Gaston Meurant was still searching and it was not until half-past four, in a little café outside which men were playing bowls, that he at last got the information he was after.

The waiter pointed out the hill to him, launched into complicated directions.

Maigret already knew, by that time, that the brother, Alfred, was indeed at Toulon and had not left 'Les Eucalyptus' for over a week.

He gave Chief-Inspector Blanc his instructions.

'Have you got amongst your detectives some lad who wouldn't be recognized by those people?'

'My men never remain unknown for long, but I've one who only arrived three days ago. He comes from Brest, since his main job is to look after the naval docks. They've certainly not cottoned on to him yet.'

'Send him out to "Les Eucalyptus".'

'Right. He'll be there before Meurant; the poor chap is either trying to save money or he's got no idea of the distance, because he's set out on foot. As he'll probably get lost two or three times on those lanes up the hill . . .'

It was agony for Maigret not to be on the spot. In spite of frequent and precise reports, they only provided second-hand information.

Two or three times, during the day, he was tempted to go along to the Rue Delambre and renew contact with Ginette Meurant. He had the feeling, for no special reason, that he was beginning to get to know her better. Perhaps, now, he would find the right questions which she might finally answer?

It was still too early. If Meurant had gone off to Toulon like that without hesitating, he must have had his reasons.

During the investigation, the police had got nothing out of the brother, but that did not mean that there was nothing to be got from him.

Gaston Meurant was unarmed; this was already an established fact, and for the rest they would have to wait.

He went home, grumpy. Madame Maigret was careful not to question him, and he had dinner, in his slippers, plunged in the papers, then switched on the wireless, hunted for a less talkative station, and when he failed to find one, turned it off with a comfortable sigh.

At ten o'clock at night, they rang through from Toulon. It wasn't

Blanc, who was attending a banquet, but the young detective from
Brest, called Le Goënec, whom the chief-inspector of the flying squad
had sent out to 'Les Eucalyptus'.

'I'm telephoning from the station.'

'Where is Gaston Meurant?'

'In the waiting-room. He's taking the night-train in an hour and a
half. He's paid for his hotel room.'

'Did he got to "Les Eucalyptus"?'

'Yes.'

'He saw his brother?'

'Yes. When he arrived, at about six o'clock, three men were playing
cards with the proprietor's wife in the bar. There were Kukib, Falconi
and Alfred Meurant, all three of them rather merry. I had arrived
before him and asked if I could dine and sleep the night. The proprietor
had come out of the kitchen to inspect me and finally said I could. I was
wearing a haversack and told them I was hitch-hiking through the
Riviera looking for work.'

'Did they believe you?'

'I don't know. While waiting till it was dinner time, I sat down in a
corner, ordered some white wine and started reading. They looked
across at me from time to time, but they didn't seem to worry about me
much. Gaston Meurant arrived a quarter of an hour after me. It was
already dark. I saw the glass-door open from the garden and he remained standing on the threshold looking around him like an owl.'

'How did his brother take it?'

'He stared hard at the newcomer, stood up, threw his cards on the
table, and went over to him.

' "What do you think you're doing here, boy? Who tipped you off I
was here?"

'The others pretended not to be listening.

' "I must speak to you, Alfred," said Gaston Meurant.

'He added quickly:

' "Don't be afraid. I'm not after you."

' "Come on!" ordered his brother and went off towards the staircase
leading to the bedrooms.

'I couldn't follow them straight away. The others had stopped talking
and seemed worried; they began to look at me differently. They were
probably starting to link my arrival with Meurant's.

'At all events I went on drinking my wine and reading.

'The little house, although recently repainted, is quite old, badly
built, and every sound is audible.

'The two brothers shut themselves in a bedroom on the first floor and
Alfred Meurant's voice was harsh and loud at first. You couldn't make
out the words, but it was obvious he was very angry.

'Then the other, the one from Paris, began to speak, in a much softer voice. This lasted some time, almost without interruption, as if he was telling some prepared story.

'After winking at the men, the landlady came and set my table, as if she was trying to create a diversion. Then the others ordered *apéritifs*. Kubik went out to look for Freddo in the kitchen and I didn't see him again.

'I imagine that, with an eye to the main chance, he cleared out, because I heard a car engine starting up.'

'You've no idea what went on upstairs?'

'Only that they remained shut up there for an hour and a half. In the end, it seemed that it was Gaston Meurant, the one from Paris, who had the upper hand, while his brother spoke in a low voice.

'I had finished eating when they came downstairs. Alfred Meurant looked rather black, as if things hadn't worked out the way he planned, while the other fellow, on the contrary, seemed more relaxed than he had when he arrived.

' "You'll have a drink then?" Alfred proposed.

' "No. Thanks all the same."

' "You're going straight back?"

' "Yes."

'Then they both looked across at me, frowning.

' "I'll drive you down town in the car."

' "No, don't bother."

' "Do you want me to ring for a taxi?"

' "No, thanks."

'They were both talking in undertones and it was obvious that they only spoke to fill in an awkward gap.

'Gaston Meurant went out. His brother shut the door, was about to say something to the proprietress and Falconi when he caught sight of me and changed his mind.

'I wasn't sure what I should do then. I didn't dare telephone the chief and ask for further instructions. I thought the best thing to do was to follow Gaston Meurant. I went outside as if I were just going to get some fresh air after dinner, leaving my haversack behind.

'I caught up with my man, who was walking steadily down the road towards the town.

'He stopped to have a bite to eat in the Boulevard de la République. Then he went to the station, and found out the times of the trains. Last of all, he went to the Hôtel des Voyageurs, picked up his bag and paid his bill.

'Since then he's been waiting. He's not reading the newspapers, doing nothing except to stare in front of him, his eyes half closed. You can't say he looks jolly, but he doesn't exactly appear displeased with himself.'

'Wait till he gets into the train and ring me back with the number of the carriage.'

'Okay. Tomorrow morning, I'll give the chief-inspector my report.'

Inspector Le Goënec was about to hang up when Maigret thought of something.

'I'd like someone to make sure that Alfred Meurant does not leave "Les Eucalyptus".'

'Do you want me to go back there? You don't think they've rustled me?'

'All I want is for one of you to keep an eye on the house. I'd like the telephone tapped, too. If they call Paris, or any long-distance number, let me know as quickly as possible.'

The routine was starting to repeat itself, but in reverse order this time: Marseilles, Avignon, Lyons, Dijon were all alerted. Gaston Meurant was allowed to travel alone, like a grown-up, but in a way he was being passed hand from hand.

He wouldn't be arriving in Paris until half-past eleven the next morning.

Maigret went to bed, felt as though he had just dozed off when his wife woke him with his first cup of coffee. The sky was clean at last and there was sunshine on the roof-tops opposite. The people in the street were walking with a springier step.

'Will you be home to lunch?'

'I doubt it. I'll give you a ring before noon.'

Ginette Meurant hadn't left the Rue Delambre. She was still spending the greater part of her time in bed, only went down to eat and to stock up with magazines and novelettes.

'Nothing new, Maigret?' asked the public prosecutor, anxiously.

'Nothing definite yet, but I shouldn't be surprised if there was a development very shortly.'

'What's Meurant up to?'

'He's in the train.'

'Which train?'

'The one from Toulon. He's on his way back. He's been to see his brother.'

'What went on between them?'

'They had a long conversation, a bit violent at first apparently, but then calmer. The brother is unhappy about it. Gaston Meurant, on the other hand, appears to know where he is going at last.'

What else could Maigret have said? He had no definite information to give the public prosecutor's office. For two days he had been groping his way round in a sort of fog, but, like Gaston Meurant, he nonetheless felt that things were coming to a head.

He was tempted to go along to the station presently and meet the frame-maker himself. Wasn't it better that he should remain at the centre of operations? And if he started following Gaston Meurant through the streets, wasn't there a risk he might spoil everything?

He chose Lapointe, knowing he would be pleased, then another detective, Neveu, who had not had anything to do with the case so far. For ten years Neveu had worked on the streets of Paris and specialized in pickpockets.

Lapointe left for the station unaware that Neveu would soon be following him.

Maigret had to give him some precise instructions beforehand.

VII

FOR years Gaston Meurant, with his fresh complexion, his red hair, his blue eyes, his sheeplike expression, had been a timid man, maybe, but above all a patient, determined man, who had exerted himself, in the midst of the three million denizens of Paris, to construct some small measure of happinesss.

He had mastered his craft to the best of his ability, a delicate craft which required taste and precision, and one could readily conceive how, the day on which he had set up in business on his own, even though only at the end of a yard, he had felt the satisfaction of having overcome the most difficult obstacle.

Had it been his timidity, or his cautiousness, the fear of making a mistake, that had made him for a long time keep his distance from women? During the course of his interrogations, he had admitted to Maigret that, until Ginette, he had managed with little, with the very minimum, with furtive contacts of which he found himself ashamed, apart from an affair he had had when he was about eighteen with a woman much older than himself, which had only lasted a few weeks.

When the day came on which, blushing, he had at last asked a woman to marry him, he was well over thirty, and as luck would have it, she was a girl who, a few months later, when he was impatiently expecting news of a forthcoming birth, admitted to him that she could not have a baby.

He had not rebelled. He had accepted it, as he accepted the fact that she was unlike the companion he had dreamt of.

When all was said and done, they were a married couple. He was no longer on his own, even if there wasn't always a light in the window when he came home in the evening, even if it was often he who had to get the dinner ready, and although, afterwards, they had nothing to say to each other.

Her dream, on the other hand, had been of a life spent in the midst of all the activity of a restaurant of which she would be the proprietress, and he had let her have her way, without illusions, knowing perfectly well that the experiment could only come to grief.

Then, without a sign of bitterness, he had returned to his studio and his picture-frames, compelled, every so often, to go and ask his aunt for her help.

During those years of married life, as in the years which had preceded them, there had been no trace of anger, no trace of impatience.

He would go his own way with gentle determination, bowing his big red head when he had to, holding it high again the moment fate seemed to look more kindly on him.

All told, he had built up a little world of his own around his love and he was doing everything in his power to cling onto it.

Did not all this explain the hatred which had suddenly hardened his eyes when Maigret had given his evidence at the Assizes, replacing the image he had formed for himself of Ginette, with another one?

Acquitted against his will, as it were, freed on acount of the suspicions which would thenceforth hang over his companion, he had yet nonetheless left the Palais de Justice with her, at her side; without linking arms, they had returned to their flat on the Boulevard de Charonne.

They had not slept in their bed together, however. Twice, three times, she had gone to speak to him, perhaps doing her utmost to tempt him, but she had gone to sleep alone in the end, while he spent most of the night awake in the dining-room.

At that time, however, he was still struggling, striving not to believe it. Perhaps he might have been able to recover confidence. But would it have lasted long? Would life have been able to start all over again as before? Wouldn't he have undergone a series of painful makeshifts, before the ultimate crisis?

He had gone by himself, without shaving, to look at the front of an hotel. To lend himself courage, he had drunk three brandies. He had hesitated once more before entering the chilly hall of the Quai des Orfèvres.

Had Maigret been wrong to speak to him in that brutal way, setting up the reaction which would have been set up anyway sooner or later?

Even had he wanted to, the chief-inspector could not have acted otherwise. With Meurant acquitted, Meurant not guilty, there was somewhere, at liberty, a man who had cut the throat of Léontine Faverges and then suffocated a little girl aged four, a murderer with enough cold blood and cunning to send another man to trial in his stead, who had been on the verge of succeeding in his plan.

Maigret had struck while the iron was hot, forcing Meurant in one shock to open his eyes, to look truth in the face at last, and it had been a new man who had left his office, a man for whom nothing mattered any longer from now on but one fixed idea.

He had gone straight ahead, feeling neither hunger nor fatigue, moving from one train into another, incapable of stopping until he should reach his objective.

Did he have any inkling that the chief-inspector had established a whole network of surveillance around him, that he had been expected at every railway station he stopped at and that there was continually someone on his heels, possibly to intervene at the last moment?

He did not seem to be concerned about it, convinced that all the wiles of the police could not prevail against his will.

Telephone call came in after telephone call, report after report. Lucas had minutely examined the private advertisements in vain. The listening-post, which was waiting for any calls Ginette Meurant might eventually make, still in the room in the Rue Delambre, had nothing to report.

There had been no call from the lawyer, Lamblin, to the south, nor to any local number.

At Toulon, Alfred Meurant, the brother, had not left 'Les Eucalyptus', and had telephoned to nobody either.

They faced a blank void, a void in the midst of which there was just one silent man moving as if in a dream.

At eleven-forty, Lapointe telephoned from the Gare de Lyon.

'He's just got in, Chief. He's now eating some sandwiches in the buffet. He's still got his case with him. Was it you who sent Neveu to the station?'

'Yes. Why?'

'I wondered whether you wanted him to take over. Neveu's in the buffet, too, quite close to Meurant.'

'Don't worry about him. You carry on.'

A quarter of an hour later, it was Inspector Neveu's turn to give his account.

'I did it, Chief. I jostled him at the exit. He didn't notice anything. He's got a gun. A big revolver, probably a Smith and Wesson, in the right-hand pocket of his jacket. It doesn't show too much, thanks to his mackintosh.'

'Has he left the station?'

'Yes. He caught a bus and I saw Lapointe get on behind him.'

'You can come back now.'

Meurant had not called at any gunsmith's. It must necessarily have been at Toulon that he had obtained the revolver, which could therefore only have been supplied to him by his brother.

What exactly occurred between the two men, upstairs in the curious family *pension* which was used as a crooks' meeting-place?

Gaston Meurant knew now that his brother, too, had had an intimate relationship with Ginette, and yet he had not gone in order to settle accounts with him on that score.

Hadn't he hoped, in visiting Toulon, to get information about the

short, very dark-haired man who, several times a week, had been used
to taking his wife to the Rue Victor-Massé?

Had he some reason to think that his brother would know about it?
And had he eventually found what he wanted, a name, a clue, which
the police, for their part, had been searching for in vain, for several
months past?

It was possible. It was probable, since he had compelled his brother
to hand over a gun to him.

If Alfred Meurant had talked, in any case, it couldn't have been out
of brotherly affection. Had he been scared? Had Gaston threatened
him? With some disclosure or other? Or with doing him in one fine
day?

Maigret asked for Toulon on the line, succeeded, after some trouble,
in getting Chief-Inspector Blanc on the other end.

'It's me again, old man. I'm sorry for all the trouble I'm giving you.
We may need Alfred Meurant any time now. We can't be sure of finding him when the time comes, since I shouldn't be surprised if he took
it into his head to go off on a trip somewhere. At present, I've nothing to
pin on him. Couldn't you have him hauled in on some more or less
plausible excuse and keep him for a few hours?'

'Right you are. That's not difficult. I've always got a question or two
I can ask any of his crowd.'

'Thanks. See if you can find out if he had a pretty powerful revolver
and whether it's still in his room.'

'Okay. Any news?'

'Not yet.'

Maigret almost added that it wouldn't be long. He had just warned
his wife that he wouldn't be home to lunch, and, feeling disinclined to
leave his office, he had ordered some sandwiches from the *Brasserie
Dauphine*.

He still felt sorry not to be outside, following Gaston Meurant in
person. He was smoking pipe after pipe, impatient, ceaselessly watching
the telephone. The sun was shining brightly and the yellowing leaves of
the trees lent an air of gaiety to the Seine quaysides.

'That you, Chief? I must be quick. I'm at the Gare de l'Est. He's
deposited his case at the left-luggage office and he's just bought a ticket
to Chelles.'

'In Seine-et-Marne?'

'Yes. The diesel's due to leave in a few minutes. I'd better get cracking. I'm to go on following him, aren't I?'

'What do you think!'

'No special instructions?'

What was at the back of Lapointe's mind? Had he guessed the reason
for Neveu's presence at the Gare de Lyon?

The chief-inspector grunted:

'Nothing particular. Do what you think best.'

He knew Chelles, over a dozen miles outside Paris, on the banks of the canal and the Marne. He remembered there was a big caustic-soda works in front of which you could always see loaded barges, and once when he had gone through the neighbourhood on a Sunday morning, he had noticed a whole flotilla of canoes.

The temperature had altered in the past twenty-four hours, but whoever was in charge of the central heating in the offices of Police Headquarters had not regulated the boiler accordingly, so that the warmth was stifling.

Maigret was eating a sandwich, standing in front of the window, gazing vaguely at the Seine. From time to time he took a swig of beer, cast a questioning glance at the telephone.

The train, which stopped at all stations, would be bound to take half an hour at least, perhaps an hour, to reach Chelles.

It was the detective on duty in the Rue Delambre who rang first.

'Same as before, Chief. She's just gone out and is having her lunch in the same restaurant, at the same table, as if she already had her set habits.'

As far as one could tell, she still had the courage not to get into touch with her lover.

Had he given her, as long ago as February, even before the double murder in the Rue Manuel, her instructions for the future? Was she afraid of him?

Of the two of them, which was it who had had the idea of the telephone call which brought about the incrimination of Gaston Meurant?

For, at the start, he had not been suspected. He had presented himself of his own accord to the police and introduced himself as the nephew of Léontine Faverges, whose death he had just read about in the paper.

They had had no grounds for searching his home.

But someone grew impatient. Someone had been in a hurry to see the investigation take a definite direction.

Three days, four days had passed before the anonymous telephone call which revealed what would be found in a wardrobe in the Boulevard de Charonne, a certain blue suit with blood-stains on it.

Lapointe still gave no signs of life. It was Toulon which rang.

'He's in my duty room. We're asking him a few minor questions and we'll keep him until you give us further notice. We'll find some pretext all right. His room's been searched thoroughly, without a gun being found in it. Even so, my men maintain that he often carried a revolver, which has led him to be convicted twice.'

'Has he had other convictions?'

'Never anything serious, apart from proceedings for procuring. He's too clever.'

'Thanks very much. Goodbye for now. I must ring off, as I'm expecting an important call any moment now.'

He went through into the next-door office where Janvier had just arrived.

'You had better keep yourself on hand ready to leave and make sure there's a car free in the yard.'

He was beginning to regret that he had not told Lapointe everything he knew. He called to mind a film about Malaya. It had shown a native who had suddenly run amok, that's to say he had been seized in a matter of seconds by a kind of sacred madness, and walking straight ahead of him, his pupils dilated, a kris in his hand, he had killed every living thing in his path.

Gaston Meurant was not a Malay nor had he run amok. Nevertheless, for more than twenty-four hours now, had he not been pursuing a fixed idea and was he not capable of disposing of anyone who might happen to stand in his way?

At last, the telephone. Maigret leapt over to it.

'Is that you, Lapointe?'

'Yes, Chief.'

'At Chelles?'

'Beyond it. I don't know exactly where I am. Between the canal and the Marne, about a mile and a half from Chelles. I can't be certain, since we took a complicated route.'

'Did Meurant seem to know the way?'

'He didn't ask anybody anything. He must have been given precise directions. He stopped now and then to look at signposts and eventually he took a lane leading to the edge of the river. Where this lane joins the former towpath, which is now only a track, there's an inn, which is where I'm telephoning you from. The innkeeper's wife has warned me that in winter she doesn't serve meals nor let rooms. Her husband's the ferryman. Meurant went past the front of the house without stopping.

'Two hundred yards upstream you can just see a tumbledown cottage around which geese and ducks are waddling freely.'

'Is that where Meurant has gone?'

'He hasn't gone in. He spoke to an old woman who pointed to the river.'

'Where is he at the moment?'

'Standing at the edge of the water, leaning against a tree. The old woman's over eighty. She's known as Mother Goose. The innkeeper's wife maintains she's half mad. Her name is Joséphine Millard. Her husband's been dead a long time. Ever since, she's always worn the same black dress and it's rumoured locally that she doesn't even take it off to go to bed. When she needs anything she goes to the market on Saturday to sell a goose or a duck.'

'Has she had children?'

'That takes us back so long ago that the innkeeper's wife can't remember As she says, it was before her time.'

'Is that all?'

'No. There's a man living with her.'

'Permanently?'

'For the past few months, yes. Before that, he used to disappear for several days at a time.'

'What does he do?'

'Nothing. He cuts wood. He reads. He fishes. He's patched up an old canoe. Just now, he's doing a spot of fishing. I've seen him, from a distance, in the boat moored to some stakes, at the bend in the Marne.'

'What sort of man is he?'

'I couldn't make out. According to the innkeeper's wife, he's dark, thick-set, with a hairy chest.'

'Short?'

'Yes.'

There was a silence. Then, hesitantly, as if embarrassed, Lapointe asked:

'Are you coming, Chief?'

Lapointe was not afraid. Was he not feeling, however, that he would have to take responsibilities beyond his powers?

'By car, it would take you less than half an hour.'

'I'll be along.'

'What am I to do, while I wait?'

Maigret hesitated, eventually decided to say:

'Nothing.'

'Shall I stay in the inn?'

'Can you see Meurant from where you are?'

'Yes.'

'In that case, stay there.'

He went into the office next door, made a sign to Janvier who was waiting. Just as he was going out, he changed his mind, went across to Lucas.

'Go up to Records and see if there's anything under the name of Millard.'

'Okay, Chief. Shall I telephone you somewhere?'

'No. I don't know exactly where I'm going. The far side of Chelles, somewhere on the banks of the Marne. If you have some urgent news for me, ask at the local police station for the name of an inn about a mile and a half upstream.'

Janvier took the wheel of the small black car, since Maigret had never been inclined to learn to drive.

'Anything new, Chief?'

'Yes.'

The detective did not like to press him, and after a long silence the chief-inspector muttered gloomily:

'But I don't know what exactly.'

He wasn't sure that he was in such a hurry to arrive there. He would rather not admit it, not even to himself.

'Do you know the way?'

'I once went there for lunch on a Sunday with the wife and kids.'

They drove through the suburbs, past the first vacant lots, then the first fields. At Chelles they pulled up hesitantly at a crossroads.

'If it's upstream, we should turn right.'

'Let's try it.'

Just as they were leaving the town, a police car, with its siren blazing overtook them, and Janvier looked at Maigret without speaking.

The chief-inspector did not say anything either. Much further on, he said, chewing the stem of his pipe:

'I suppose it's all over.'

For the police car had turned off towards the Marne, which they could now glimpse between the trees. To the right, there appeared an inn, built in yellow-painted brick. A woman, who seemed highly excited, was standing on the doorstep.

The police car, unable to get any further, had parked by the side of the lane. Maigret and Janvier emerged from theirs. The woman, gesticulating, was calling out something to them which they couldn't catch.

They walked towards the cottage surrounded by geese and ducks. The local police, who had reached it before them, were challenging two men who seemed to have been waiting for them. One of them was Lapointe. The other, from a distance, looked like Gaston Meurant.

There were three local policemen, including one officer. An old woman on the doorstep was looking at all these people, nodding her head, without seeming to understand exactly what was going on. Nobody, anyway, really understood, except perhaps Meurant and Lapointe.

Automatically, Maigret glanced around to look for a body, but could see none. Lapointe said to him:

'In the water . . .'

But there was nothing to be seen in the water either.

As for Gaston Meurant, he was calm, almost happy, and when the chief-inspector finally decided to look him in the face, it was as if the picture-framer were silently thanking him.

Lapointe was explaining, both for the benefit of his chief and for that of the local police:

'The man gave up fishing, and shoved his boat off from the stakes you can see over there.'

'Who is he?'

'I don't know his name. He was wearing denim trousers and a roll-necked seaman's sweater. He began to row across the river against the current.'

'Where were you?' the local police officer enquired.

'At the inn. I was watching the scene from the window. I had just been on the 'phone to Chief-Inspector Maigret . . .'

He gestured to his chief, and the officer, in confusion, stepped towards him.

'I beg your pardon, Chief-Inspector. I never expected to see you here, that's why I didn't recognize you. Your inspector got the innkeeper's wife to telephone us, and all she said was that a man had just been killed and had fallen in the water. I immediately alerted the flying squad . . .'

They heard the sound of a car engine on the other side of the inn.

'There they are!'

The newcomers added to the chaos and the bewilderment. They were not in the Seine-et-Marne department and Maigret had no official standing in this case.

Nevertheless everybody turned towards the chief-inspector.

'Shall we put the handcuffs on him?'

'That's up to you, Lieutenant. If I were in your place, however, I shouldn't think it necessary.'

Meurant's fever had subsided. He listened vaguely to what was being said as if it was of no concern to him. Mostly he stared at the swirling waters of the Marne, downstream.

Lapointe went on with his explanation:

'While he was rowing, the man who was in the boat had his back turned to the bank. So he couldn't see Meurant, who was standing near this tree.'

'Did you know he was going to shoot?'

'I didn't know he was armed.'

Maigret's face remained impassive. Nevertheless, Janvier cast him a quick glance, as if he had suddenly begun to understand.

'The bow of the boat touched the bank. The rower stood up, seized the painter, and as he turned round he found himself face to face with Meurant, who was hardly three yards away from him.

'I can't say whether they exchanged words or not. I was too far away.

'Almost immediately, Meurant drew a revolver from his pocket and stretched out his right arm.

'The other man, standing ready to disembark, must have been hit by the two bullets, shot one after the other. He let go of the painter. His hands beat the air and he fell into the water head first . . .'

Everybody was now looking at the river. The rain, during the last few days, had swollen the water, which had a yellowish colour and in certain places there were swirling eddies.

'I asked the innkeeper's wife to notify the police and I ran across to here . . .'

'Were you armed?'

'No.'

Lapointe added, perhaps unthinkingly:

'There was no danger.'

The local police could not understand. Nor could the men from the flying squad. Even had they read the newspaper reports of the trial, they were not aware of the details of the case.

'Meurant made no attempt to run away. He remained in the same spot watching the corpse disappear, then reappear again two or three times, always a little further on, until it sank altogether.

'When I reached his side, he dropped his gun. I didn't touch it.'

The revolver was embedded in the mud of the lane, beside a dead branch.

'He said nothing?'

'Two words only:

' "It's over." '

The struggle was indeed over now for Gaston Meurant. His body seemed flabbier, his face puffy with tiredness.

He did not look triumphant, felt no need to explain himself, to justify himself. It was entirely his own affair.

In his view he had done what he had to do.

Would he have ever found peace otherwise? Would he find it from now on?

The public prosecutor's men from Melun would soon be arriving on the spot. The mad woman, on her threshold, was still nodding her head, never having seen so many people around her house before.

'It's quite likely,' Maigret said to his colleagues, 'that you may make some discoveries when you go through the cottage.'

He could have remained with them, helped in the search.

'Gentlemen, I shall send you all the information you will need.'

He would not be taking Meurant back to Paris, since Meurant no longer belonged to Quai des Orfèvres, nor to the public prosecutor's department for the Seine district.

It would be in another law-courts, in Melun, where he would appear for the second time before the Assizes.

Maigret asked Lapointe and Janvier in turn.

'Are you coming, lads?'

He shook hands all round. Then, as he was turning away, he took his last look at Ginette's husband.

Suddenly conscious of his weariness, probably, the man had leaned against the tree again and watched the chief-inspector leave, a look almost of melancholy in his eyes.

VIII

FEW words were exchanged during the drive back. Several times Lapointe opened his mouth, but Maigret's silence was so deep, so deliberate, that he did not dare say anything.

Janvier was driving and, little by little, he had the feeling that things were slipping into place.

But for the difference of a mile or two, they would have been taking Gaston Meurant back themselves.

'Perhaps it's just as well that way,' murmured Janvier as if he were speaking to himself.

Maigret did not approve nor disapprove. To what, besides, had Janvier been alluding exactly?

The three of them climbed the staircase together at Headquarters, separated in the corridor, Lapointe and Janvier going into the duty room, while Maigret entered his office, where he hung his coat and hat in the cupboard.

He did not touch the bottle of brandy which he kept handy for some of his visitors. He had hardly had time to fill a pipe when Lucas knocked on the door and put in front of him a thick file.

'I found that upstairs, Chief. You might say it all hangs together.'

And it did, in fact, all hang together. It was the file of a certain Pierre Millard, called Pierrot, thirty-two years old, born in Paris in the Goutte-d'Or district.

He had had his police record since he was eighteen years old, when he appeared for the first time at the Seine police-court for procuring. Later he had two other convictions on the same count, with a period in Fresnes gaol, then a conviction for assault and battery at Marseilles, and finally five years in the prison at Fontévrault, for breaking into a factory at Bordeaux and violent assault on a night-watchman who had been discovered half dead.

He was released from prison a year and a half ago. Since then, they had lost track of him.

Maigret lifted the receiver, called Toulon.

'Is that you, Blanc? Well, old man, it's all over up here. Two bullets in the hide of a certain Pierre Millard, called Pierrot.'

'A short dark fellow?'

'Yes. They are busy searching for his body in the Marne, where he fell in head first. Does the name mean anything to you?'

'I'd have to have a word with my men about it. I seem to remember that he was prowling around here a little more than a year ago.'

'That's more than likely. He came out of Fontévrault about then and was therefore prohibited from staying here. Since you've not got his name, could you perhaps put a few definite questions to Alfred Meurant? Is he still with you?'

'Yes. Do you want me to ring you back?'

'Yes, please.'

In Paris, at any rate, Millard had been prudent. Though he probably came frequently, almost every day, he was careful not to sleep the night there. He had found a safe refuge beside the Marne, in the cottage belonging to the old woman, who was probably his grandmother.

He had not budged since the double murder in the Rue Manuel. Ginette Meurant had made no attempt to visit him. She had not sent him any message. She was probably kept in the dark about his hiding-place.

If things had happened differently, if Nicolas Cajou, in particular, had not given his evidence, Gaston Meurant would have been condemned to death, or to forced labour for the rest of his life. At the best, considering the slight doubt in his favour and his unblemished past, he might have got off with twenty years.

Whereas Millard, once the verdict had been brought, could have left his hole, gone to the provinces or abroad, where Ginette Meurant could easily have joined him.

'Hello, yes . . .'

They were calling him from Seine-et-Marne. The flying squad at Gournay informed him that they had discovered the gold pieces, the bearer-bonds, and a certain number of bank-notes in an old wallet.

The whole lot had been buried, hidden in a tin, in the geese and ducks pen.

They had not yet fished out the body, which they hoped to find, like most bodies drowned in that reach, at the Chelles weir, where the lock-keeper was quite accustomed to it.

They had made some discoveries in the old woman's house, amongst them, in the loft, an ancient trunk containing a Second Empire wedding-dress, a suit, other dresses, some made of puce or pale blue silk, embroidered with yellowed lace. The most unexpected find was a Zouave's uniform of the beginning of the century.

Mother Goose could scarcely remember anything about her family, and the death of her grandson didn't seem to have affected her. When they had spoken of taking her to Gournay for questioning, she was only concerned about her birds, and they had had to promise to bring her back the same evening.

They would probably hardly bother about her past, or her children, of whom no trace could be found.

She would probably still live for years in her cottage by the waterside.

'Janvier!'

'Yes, Chief.'

'Will you take Lapointe with you and go along to the Rue Delambre?'

'Am I to fetch her here?'

'Yes.'

'You don't think I ought to take a warrant with me?'

Maigret, as an officer of Paris Police Headquarters, was empowered to sign an order to appear and he did it on the spot.

'What if she asks any questions?'

'Say nothing.'

'Shall I handcuff her?'

'Only if it's absolutely necessary.'

Blanc rang back from Toulon.

'I've just been asking some interesting questions.'

'Did you tell him of Millard's death?'

'Of course.'

'Did he seem surprised?'

'No. He didn't even bother to put on a pretence of it.'

'Did he come clean?'

'More or less. That's up to you to judge. He was careful not to say anything that might incriminate him. He admits that he knew Millard. He met him several times, more than seven years ago, in Paris and Marseilles. Then Millard copped five years and Alfred Meurant heard nothing from him.

'When he got out of Fontévrault, Millard came back to hang around Marseilles, then Toulon. He was pretty down on his luck and was trying to get back on the game. His plan, according to Meurant, was not to do the odd job any more, but to bring off something big which would set him up once and for all.

'As soon as he'd refurbished his wardrobe, he was intending to return to Paris.

'He only stayed a few weeks on the Coast. Meurant admits that he gave him small sums, that he introduced him to his pals, and that they helped him in their turn.

'As for the matter of Ginette Meurant, her brother-in-law talks of her jokingly. He apparently said to Millard, just as he was leaving:

' "If you're ever short of a woman, there's always my little sister-in-law; she's married to an imbecile and she's pretty bored."

'He swears that was all. He gave Ginette's address and also told him that she liked going to a dance-hall in the Rue des Gravilliers.

'If you can believe him, he heard no further news of Pierre Millard, nor of Ginette either.'

This was not necessarily true, but it was plausible.

'What shall I do with him?'

'Get a statement from him and release him. But don't let him out of your sight, because we'll need him for the trial.'

If there was a trial! New investigations would begin, as soon as Lapointe and Janvier brought Ginette Meurant into Maigret's office.

Would they be able to establish with sufficient certainty her complicity with her lover?

Nicolas Cajou would go to identify Millard's body, then the chambermaid, and others as well.

Afterwards, there would be the preliminary examination, then, eventually, the file would be referred to the Grand Jury.

During all that time it was more than probable that Ginette would remain in prison.

Then, one day, she would appear at the Assizes in her turn.

Maigret would be summoned as a witness once more. The jury would try to understand something of this story which was taking place in a world so different from their own familiar universe.

Before that, since the case was more straightforward and the list was not so full at the Seine-et-Marne Assizes, Maigret would be summoned to Melun.

With other witnesses he would be shut up in a gloomy, hushed room like a vestry where he would await his turn, watching the door and listening to the dull echoes from the courtroom.

He would see Gaston Meurant again between two policemen, would swear to tell the truth, the whole truth, nothing but the truth.

Would he really tell the whole truth? Hadn't there been one particular moment, while the telephone was ringing incessantly in his office, where he kept some control on all the characters, when he had accepted a responsibility which was hard to explain away?

Might he not have been able to . . .?

In two years he would no longer have to worry about other people's problems. He would be living with Madame Maigret far from the Quai des Orfèvres and the courts where men are judged, in an old house like a presbytery, and for hours on end he would sit in a punt moored to some stakes, watching the water flow past, fishing.

His office was full of his pipe-smoke. Next door he could hear typewriters tapping away, telephones ringing.

He gave a start when there came a light tap on the door and it opened to reveal Lapointe's young figure.

Had he really jerked back guiltily, as if somebody were coming to call him to account?

'She's here, Chief. Do you want to see her straight away?'

And Lapointe waited, seeing clearly that Maigret was slowly coming to from a dream – or a nightmare.

Noland
23 November, 1959

MAIGRET AFRAID

MAIGRET AFRAID

(*Maigret a Peur*)
*was first published in France in 1953
and in Great Britain in 1961
Translated from the French by Margaret Duff*

*Copyright © 1953 by Georges Simenon
Translation copyright © 1961 by Hamish Hamilton Ltd.*

MAIGRET AFRAID

I

Quite suddenly, between two small stations, whose names he could not make out, and of which he saw hardly anything in the darkness, except the driving rain against a large lamp and figures of men pushing trolleys, Maigret wondered what he was doing there.

Perhaps he had dozed off for a moment in the over-heated compartment? He could not have lost consciousness completely, because he knew he was in a train; he could hear its monotonous noise; he would have sworn that he had continually seen, every so often in the dark expanse of fields, the lighted windows of an isolated farm. All this, and the smell of soot mingling with that of his damp clothes, remained real, and also a steady murmur of voices in a near-by compartment, but it was in some way not entirely real, it was no longer very clearly situated in space, let alone in time.

He might have been somewhere else, in any little train travelling through the countryside, and he himself might have been a fifteen-year-old Maigret returning from college on a Saturday on a local train exactly like this one, with ancient carriages, their couplings creaking at each pull of the engine. With the same voices, in the night, at each stop, the same men bustling around the mail van, the same whistle-blast from the station-master.

He half-opened his eyes, pulled at his pipe which had gone out, and his glance rested on the man sitting in the opposite corner of the compartment. He might have seen this man too, in those days, in the train that took him home to his father's. He could have been the Count, or the owner of the château, the most important person of the village or of any little town.

He was wearing a golfing suit of light tweed, and a raincoat of the kind one sees only in certain very expensive shops. His hat was a green sportsman's hat, with a tiny pheasant's feather tucked inside the ribbon. In spite of the heat he had not taken off his fawn gloves, for such men never remove their gloves in a train or in a car. And despite the rain, there wasn't a spot of mud on his well-polished shoes.

He was probably sixty-five years old. He was already an elderly gentleman. Isn't it strange that men of that age take so much care over

405

the details of their appearance? And that they still try to set themselves apart from the ordinary run of mortals?

His complexion was of that pink peculiar to the species, with a small silvery-white moustache marked by the yellow circle left by cigar-smoking.

His expression, however, did not have quite the assurance it should have had. From his corner Maigret watched the man, and he, for his part, glanced back several times and on two or three occasions appeared to be on the point of speaking. The train was setting off again, dirty and wet, into a dark world sprinkled with widely scattered lights, and now and then, at a level-crossing, one could make out someone on a bicycle waiting for the last carriage to pass.

Was it that Maigret was depressed? It was vaguer than that. He wasn't feeling quite himself. And anyway, these last three days, he had drunk too much, not with any pleasure but out of necessity.

He had been attending the International Police Congress which, that year, was held at Bordeaux. It was in April. When he had left Paris, where the winter had been long and monotonous, spring seemed to be not far off. But at Bordeaux it had rained all three days, with a cold wind which made your clothes cling to your body.

By chance, the few friends he usually met at these congresses, like Mr. Pyke, had not been there. Each country, it seemed, had contrived to send only young representatives, men of thirty to forty whom he had never seen before. They had all shown great kindness to him, had been very deferential, as one is to an older man one respects and finds slightly old-fashioned.

Could that be it? Or had the unending rain put him in a bad humour? And all the wine that they had had to drink in the cellars which they had been invited to visit by the Chamber of Commerce?

'Are you enjoying yourself?' his wife had asked on the telephone.

He had replied with a grunt.

'Try to rest a little. You looked tired when you left. At any rate, it'll be a change for you. Don't catch cold.'

Perhaps he had suddenly felt old? Even their discussions, which were almost all to do with new scientific methods, hadn't interested him.

The banquet had taken place the previous evening. That morning there had been a final reception, at the Town Hall this time, and a lunch with lots to drink. He had promised Chabot that he would take advantage of not having to be in Paris until Monday morning and stop off to see him at Fontenay-le-Comte.

Chabot wasn't getting any younger either. They had been friends, in the old days, when he had done two years of medicine at the university of Nantes. Chabot, himself, had been a law student. They lived in the same lodgings. On two or three Sundays he had gone with his friend to his mother's house in Fontenay.

And since then, across the years, they had seen each other perhaps ten times all told.

'When are you coming to visit me in Vendée?'

Madame Maigret had had a hand in it too.

'Why don't you call and see your friend Chabot on your way back from Bordeaux?'

He should have been at Fontenay two hours ago. He had taken the wrong train. At Niort, where he had waited a long time, having a number of glasses of brandy in the waiting-room, he had hesitated to telephone for Chabot to come and fetch him by car.

He hadn't done so, in the end, because if Julien came to meet him, he would insist on Maigret's staying at his place, and the chief-inspector hated sleeping in other people's houses.

He would go to the hotel. Once there, and not before, would he telephone. He had been wrong to make this detour instead of having these two days' holiday at home, in the Boulevard Richard-Lenoir. Who knows? Perhaps in Paris, it was no longer raining and spring had arrived at last.

'So, they have sent for you . . .'

He jumped. Without realizing it, he must have gone on staring vaguely at his fellow-passenger, and the latter had just made up his mind to speak to him. He seemed to be embarrassed about it himself. He felt he had to put on a slightly ironical tone of voice.

'I beg your pardon?'

'I said that I suspected they would call for someone like you.'

Maigret still not seeming to understand, he continued:

'You are Chief-Inspector Maigret, aren't you?'

The traveller became once more the man of the world, rose from his seat to introduce himself:

'Vernoux de Courçon.'

'How do you do?'

'I recognized you immediately, from having often seen your photograph in the newspapers.'

He said that rather as if he were apologizing for being one of those who read newspapers.

'It must happen to you often.'

'What?'

'That people recognize you.'

Maigret did not know what to reply. He hadn't yet come firmly down to earth. As for the man, little drops of sweat had appeared on his forehead, as if he had got himself into a situation from which he didn't know how to recover advantageously.

'Was it my friend Julien who telephoned you?'

'Do you mean Julien Chabot?'

'The examining magistrate. I'm only surprised that he said nothing to me about it when I met him this morning.'

'I still don't understand.'

Vernoux de Courçon looked at him more attentively, frowning.

'You mean to say that it's just by chance that you're coming to Fontenay-le-Comte?'

'Yes.'

'Aren't you going to see Julien Chabot?'

'Yes, but . . .'

Maigret reddened suddenly, furious with himself, because he had just replied subserviently, as he used to do in the old days when he was addressed by people of this type, 'the people from the château'.

'Curious, isn't it?' said the other ironically.

'What is so curious?'

'That Chief-Inspector Maigret, who has probably never set foot in Fontenay . . .'

'Has someone told you that?'

'I only presume so. At any rate, you have not been seen there often, and I have never heard any mention of it. It's curious, I say, that you should be arriving just at a time when the authorities are baffled by the most puzzling mystery that . . .'

Maigret struck a match, took little puffs at his pipe.

'I did part of my studies with Julien Chabot,' he announced calmly. 'Many times in the past, I have been a guest at his house in the Rue Clemenceau.'

'Indeed?'

Coldly, he repeated:

'Indeed.'

'In that case, we shall surely see you tomorrow evening at my house in the Rue Rabelais, where Chabot comes every Saturday for a game of bridge.'

It was the last stop before Fontenay. Vernoux de Courçon had no luggage, only a chestnut-coloured leather brief-case placed by his side on the seat.

'I shall be curious to see if you'll unveil the mystery. Chance or no, it is lucky for Chabot that you're here.'

'Is his mother still alive?'

'As fit as ever.'

The man got up to button his raincoat, smooth on his gloves, adjust his hat. The train was slowing down, a string of lights went past and men began to run along the platform.

'I am very glad to have met you. Tell Chabot that I look forward to seeing you both tomorrow evening.'

Maigret merely replied with a nod and opened the door, took hold of his bag, which was heavy, and made his way to the exit without looking at the people he passed.

Chabot could not be expecting him off this train, which he had only caught by accident. From the front of the station, Maigret looked down the length of the Rue de la République, where it was pouring with rain.

'Taxi, sir?'

He nodded.

'Hôtel de France?'

He said yes again, settled himself irritably into the corner. It was only nine o'clock in the evening, but there was no longer any sign of life in the town, where only two or three cafés were still lit up. The door of the Hôtel de France was flanked by two palm-trees in barrels painted green.

'Have you got a room?'

'With a single bed?'

'Yes. If it's possible, I should like something to eat.'

The hotel was already in half darkness, like a church after vespers.

They had to go and ask in the kitchen, switch on two or three lights in the dining-room.

To save going up to his room he washed his hands in a porcelain wash-basin.

'Some white wine?'

He was sick of all the white wine he had had to drink in Bordeaux.

'Haven't you got some beer?'

'Only in bottles.'

'In that case, give me some ordinary red wine.'

They had re-heated some soup for him, and cut him some slices of ham. From his seat, he saw someone enter the hall of the hotel, dripping wet and, finding no one to ask, this man peered into the dining-room and seemed reassured to see the chief-inspector there. He was a red-haired fellow, of about forty, with large, ruddy cheeks and cameras slung over his shoulder outside his beige raincoat.

He shook his hat for the rain to drop off, came forward.

'First of all, do you mind if I take a photograph? I am the correspondent for *Ouest-Eclair* in this district. I just saw you at the station, but I wasn't able to catch up with you in time. So, they have sent for you to throw some light on the Courçon case.'

A flash of light. A click.

'Chief-Inspector Féron didn't tell us anything about you. Neither did the examining magistrate.'

'I am not here on the Courçon case.'

The young red-head smiled, the smile of someone in the game, who can't be fooled.

'But of course.'

'Why, of course?'

'You're not here *officially*. I understand. It doesn't mean that . . .'

'It means nothing at all!'

'The proof is that Féron's told me he is hurrying over.'

'Who's Féron?'

'The Fontenay police chief-inspector. When I spotted you, at the station, I dived in to a telephone kiosk and rang him up. He told me he woulb meet me here.'

'Here?'

'Certainly. Where else would you stay?'

Maigret emptied his glass, wiped his mouth, growled:

'Who is this Vernoux de Courçon with whom I travelled from Niort?'

'Yes, he was on the train. He's the brother-in-law.'

'Whose brother-in-law?'

'Courçon's, the murdered man's.'

A short brown-haired figure now entered the hotel and at once noticed the two men in the dining-room.

'Hullo, Féron,' called the journalist.

'Good evening to you. Forgive me, Chief-Inspector. Nobody told me of your arrival, which explains why I wasn't at the station. I was having a quick snack after a harassing day, when . . .'

He pointed to the red-head.

'I hurried and . . .'

'I was telling this young man,' said Maigret, pushing away his plate and grasping his pipe, 'that I have nothing to do with this Courçon affair of yours. I've come to Fontenay-le-Comte, by purest chance, to pay a visit to my old friend Chabot and . . .'

'Does he know that you're here?'

'He was supposed to be expecting me on the four o'clock train. As he didn't see me, he probably thought that I wouldn't come until tomorrow, or that I wouldn't come at all.'

Maigret rose.

'And now, with your leave, I shall go and call on him before retiring to bed.'

Both the police chief-inspector and the journalist looked equally disconcerted.

'You really know nothing?'

'Absolutely nothing.'

'You haven't read the newspapers?'

'The past three days, the organizers of the congress and the Bordeaux Chamber of Commerce haven't left us a moment to ourselves.'

They exchanged dubious glances.

'You know where the magistrate lives?'

'Yes, indeed. That is if the town hasn't changed since I paid my last visit.'

They couldn't bring themselves to let him go. On the pavement they stood on either side of him.

'Gentlemen, I must bid you farewell.'

The reporter persisted:

'Have you no statement to make for *Ouest-Eclair*?'

'None. Goodnight, gentlemen.'

He reached the Rue de la République, crossed the bridge and passed hardly anyone as he climbed the hill to Chabot's house. Chabot lived in an old house, which in his youth had excited Maigret's admiration. It was still the same, of grey stone with a flight of four steps and tall windows with lattice panes. A little light filtered between the curtains. He rang the bell, heard quick short steps on the blue paving-stones of the corridor. A spy-hole was opened in the door.

'Is Monsieur Chabot at home?' he asked.

'Who is it?'

'Chief-Inspector Maigret.'

'Is that you, Monsieur Maigret?'

He had recognized the voice of Rose, the Chabots' maid, who had been with them already thirty years ago.

'I'll let you in straight away. Just wait while I take off the chain.'

At the same time, she called inside the house.

'Monsieur Julien! It's your friend Monsieur Maigret . . . Come in, Monsieur Maigret . . . Monsieur Julien went to the station this afternoon . . . He was disappointed not to find you. How did you come?'

'By train.'

'You mean, you took the local train this evening?'

A door had opened. In the beam of orange-shaded light stood a tall, thin man, slightly stooping, wearing a maroon velvet smoking-jacket.

'Is that you?' he said.

'Indeed it is. I missed the good train. So I took the bad one.'

'Your luggage?'

'It's at the hotel.'

'How silly! I shall have to have it collected. We agreed that you would stay here.'

'No, wait, Julien . . .'

It was funny. It was an effort to call his old friend by his first name, and it sounded strange. Even the '*tutoiement*' didn't come easily.

'Come in. I hope you haven't dined?'

'Yes, I have. At the Hôtel de France.'

'Shall I inform Madame?' asked Rose.

Maigret intervened.

'I expect she's in bed?'

'She has just gone upstairs. But she won't be in bed before eleven o'clock or midnight. I . . .'

'Don't you dare. I refuse to let her be disturbed. I shall see your mother tomorrow morning.'

'She won't be pleased.'

Maigret calculated that Madame Chabot would be at least seventy-eight. Deep down, he was sorry he had come. Nevertheless, he hung up his overcoat, which was heavy with rain, on the old coat rack, followed Julien into his study, while Rose, who was herself in her sixties, waited for orders.

'What will you have? An old *fine*?'

'Yes, if you wish.'

Rose understood the magistrate's unspoken instructions and disappeared. The smell of the house had not changed, and this too was something Maigret had envied in the past, the smell of a well-kept house, where the floors were wax-polished and the cooking was good.

He would have sworn that not a single article of furniture had changed position.

'Sit down. I am very glad to see you . . .'

He would have been tempted to say that Chabot hadn't changed either. His features, his expression, were just the same. As both of them had aged it was difficult for Maigret to judge the effect of the passing years. He was, all the same, struck by some kind of lifelessness, uncertainty, a little feebleness that he had never observed before in his friend. Had he been like that in the old days? Had Maigret simply not noticed it?

'Cigar?'

There was a pile of boxes on the mantelpiece.

'Still the pipe.'

'Of course, I had forgotten. I myself haven't smoked for twelve years.'

'Doctor's orders?'

'No. One fine day I said to myself that it was stupid to cause a lot of smoke and . . .'

Rose entered with a tray on which there was a bottle, covered in fine cellar dust, and a single crystal glass.

'Don't you drink any more, either?'

'I gave it up at the same time. Just a little wine with a dash of water at meal-times. You haven't changed.'

'Don't you think so?'

'You seem to enjoy wonderful health. I'm really delighted that you have come.'

Why did he not seem altogether sincere?

'You have promised to call here so often, then put it off at the last moment, that I confess I gave up counting on you too much.'

'Everything comes right in the end, you see!'

'Your wife?'

'She's very well.'

'She didn't accompany you?'

'She doesn't like congresses.'

'Did it go off well?'

'We all drank a lot, talked a lot, ate a lot.'

'I do less and less travelling.'

He lowered his voice, for footsteps could be heard on the floor above. 'With my mother, it's difficult. Besides I cannot leave her alone now.'

'Is she still as fit as ever?'

'She doesn't change. Her sight is the only thing which has weakened a little. It distresses her not to be able to thread her needles nowadays, but she obstinately refuses to wear glasses.'

There was the feeling that he had his mind on other things, as he watched Maigret in rather the same way as Vernoux de Courçon had watched him in the train.

'Have you heard the news?'

'What about?'

'What's been happening here.'

'I haven't read a paper for almost a week. But I travelled up just now with a certain Vernoux de Courçon, who calls himself a friend of yours.'

'Hubert?'

'I don't know. A man of about sixty-five.'

'That's Hubert.'

Not a sound came from the town. One could hear only the rain beating against the window-panes and, from time to time, the crackling of the logs in the hearth. Julien Chabot's father, before him, had been examining magistrate at Fontenay-le-Comte and the study had not changed from father to son.

'In that case, you must have been told . . .'

'Almost nothing. A journalist descended upon me with his camera in the hotel dining-room.'

'A man with red hair?'

'Yes.'

'That's Lomel. What did he say to you?'

'He was convinced that I was here to take part in some case or other. I hadn't had time to disabuse him before the police chief-inspector arrived as well.'

'In fact, by now the whole town knows you're here?'

'Does that worry you?'

Chabot barely managed to hide his hesitation.

'No . . . it's only . . .'

'Only what?'

'Nothing. It's very complicated. You have never lived in a county town like Fontenay.'

'I lived at Luçon for more than a year, you know!'

'There was no case of the kind of thing I have on my hands now.'

'I remember a certain murder at L'Aiguillon . . .'

'That's true. I was forgetting.'

It was actually a case in the course of which Maigret had found himself obliged to arrest, on a charge of murder, an ex-magistrate whom everybody considered perfectly respectable.

'That wasn't so serious, however. You will realize that tomorrow morning. I shouldn't be surprised if the Paris newspapermen arrived on the first train.'

'A murder?'

'Two.'

'Vernoux de Courçon's brother-in-law.'

'You see, you do know!'

'That's all I've been told.'

'Yes, his brother-in-law, Robert de Courçon, was murdered four days ago. That alone would have been enough to make a fuss about. The day before yesterday, it happened to the widow Gibon.'

'Who's she?'

'Nobody of importance. Far from it. An old woman who lived alone right at the end of the Rue des Loges.'

'What's the connection between the two crimes?'

'Both were committed in the same way, probably with the same weapon.'

'A revolver?'

'No. A blunt instrument, as we say in reports. A bit of lead piping, or a tool like a spanner.'

'Is that all?'

'Isn't that enough? . . . Hush! '

The door opened silently, and a very small, very thin woman, dressed in black, came forward with her hand outstretched.

'There you are, Jules!'

How many years was it since anyone had called him by that name?

'My son went to the station. When he returned, he assured me that you wouldn't be coming and I retired upstairs. Haven't they given you any dinner?'

'He dined at the hotel, mama.'

'What do you mean, at the hotel?'

'He is staying at the Hôtel de France. He refuses to . . .'

'Oh, no never! I shall not allow you to . . .'

'Madame, please. There's all the more reason for me to stay at the hotel, now that the reporters are already after me. If I accepted your invitation, tomorrow morning, if not tonight, they would be hanging on your door-bell. Besides, it's better that nobody should suppose I'm here at your son's request . . .'

It was this, after all, which was bothering the magistrate, and Maigret saw it confirmed in his face.

'They will say that, anyway!'

'I shall deny it. This case, or rather, these cases are no concern of mine. I haven't the slightest intention of being involved in them.'

Had Chabot been afraid that he would interfere in things which didn't concern him? Or had he imagined that Maigret, with his occasionally somewhat personal methods, might put him in a delicate situation?

The chief-inspector had arrived at an awkward moment.

'I wonder, mama, if Maigret isn't right.'

And, turning to his old friend:

'You see, this isn't an ordinary case. Robert de Courçon, who's been murdered, was a well-known man, more or less closely related to all the big families in the district. His brother-in-law Vernoux is also an important figure. After the first crime, rumours began to get around. Then the widow Gibon was murdered, and that slightly altered the course of the gossip. But . . .'

'But . . .?'

'It's difficult to explain to you. The police chief-inspector is in charge of the investigations. He's a good chap, who knows the town, though he comes from the Midi, from Arles, I believe. The Poitiers flying squad is also on the spot. So, in my position . . .'

The old lady had sat down, as though she were paying a call, on the edge of a chair, and was listening to her son speaking as she might have listened to the sermon at High Mass.

'Two murders in three days is a lot in a town of eight thousand inhabitants. Some people are getting frightened. It's not simply because of the rain tonight that you don't meet anyone about the streets.'

'What does the public think?'

'Some maintain it's a lunatic.'

'There was no robbery?'

'In neither case. And in both cases the murderer was able to get himself let in the door without his victims being suspicious. It's a clue. And it's about the only one we've got.'

'No fingerprints?'

'None. If it's a lunatic, he'll probably commit other murders.'

'I see. And you, what do you think?'

'Nothing. I am trying to puzzle it out. I'm worried.'

'By what?'

'It's still too confused for me to explain. I have a terrible responsibility on my shoulders.'

He said this like an over-worked official. And it was indeed an official Maigret had before him now, a small-town official living in terror of making a false step.

Had the chief-inspector, too, grown like this, with age? He felt older himself, because of his friend.

'I wonder if I wouldn't do better to take the first train back to Paris. After all, I only came to Fontenay to say "How do you do". That's done. My presence here may cause complications for you.'

'What do you mean?'

Chabot's first reaction had *not* been one of protest.

'Already the red-head and the police chief-inspector are convinced that you have called me to the rescue. They will say that you're scared, that you don't know how to deal with it, that . . .'

'Oh no.'

The magistrate rejected this notion only rather weakly.

'I shall not allow you to leave. I may still receive my friends as I please.'

'My son is right, Jules. And for my part, I think you should stay with us.'

'Maigret prefers to have his freedom of movement, is that it?'

'I have my own habits.'

'I don't insist.'

'It will still be better if I leave tomorrow morning.'

Perhaps Chabot was going to agree. The telephone rang and its ring was not like any other, a quaint sound.

'Will you excuse me?'

Chabot lifted the receiver.

'Chabot, examining magistrate, speaking.'

The way in which he said that was yet another sign and Maigret forced himself not to smile.

'Who? . . . Ah, yes . . . It's you, Féron . . . What? . . . Gobillard? . . . Where? . . . At the corner of the Champ de Mars and . . . I'll come immediately . . . Yes . . . He's here . . . I don't know . . . Tell them not to touch a thing until I arrive . . .'

His mother looked at him, her hand held to her breast.

'Another one?' she stammered.

He nodded.

'Gobillard.'

He explained to Maigret:

'An old drunkard, whom everybody in Fontenay knows because he spends the best part of his days fishing beside the bridge. They have just found him on the pavement, dead.'

'Murdered?'

'His skull's been fractured, like the other two, most likely the same instrument.'

He had risen, opened the door, unhooked from the stand an old trench-coat and a battered hat which he probably only used on rainy days.

'Are you coming?'

'Do you think I ought to accompany you?'

'Now that it's known you're here, they would wonder why I didn't bring you. Two crimes was a lot. With a third, the town is going to be frightened out of its wits.'

As they were going out, a nervous little hand seized Maigret's sleeve and old mama whispered in his ear:

'Look after him, Jules! He is so conscientious that he doesn't realize the danger.'

II

WITH such a degree of obstinacy, of violence in it as this, the rain was no longer just rain, nor the wind a mere icy wind, it was becoming a vicious conspiracy of the elements, and already previously, on the poorly sheltered platform of the station at Niort, harassed by this winter whose final convulsions seemed determined not to end, Maigret had been put in mind of a beast which refuses to die and struggles to bite, to the very last.

It was no use now trying to protect oneself. Water was not only pouring from the sky, but falling from drain-pipes in large, cold splashes, and trickling onto the doors of houses, along the pavements where streams of it roared like a torrent, there was water all over one, on one's face, down one's neck, into shoes and even into the pockets of clothes, which were past drying out between excursions.

They were walking against the wind, without speaking, leaning forward, the judge in his old raincoat, with its skirts flapping like flags, Maigret in his overcoat which weighed two hundred pounds, and after a few paces, the tobacco sizzled out with a sputter in the chief-inspector's pipe.

Here and there, the odd lighted window could be seen, but not many of them. After the bridge, they passed the windows of the Café de Poste, and were aware that people were watching them over the tops of the curtains; the door opened after they had gone on a bit farther, and they heard footsteps, voices behind them.

The murder had taken place very near there. At Fontenay, nothing is ever very far away, and it is usually pointless to take your car out of the garage. A short street struck off to the right, joining the Rue de la République to the Champ de Mars. In front of the third or fourth house a group of people was standing on the pavement, near the headlights of an ambulance, some of them holding pocket-torches in their hands.

A little man detached himself from the group, Superintendent Féron, who almost put his foot in it by addressing Maigret rather than Chabot.

'I telephoned you immediately from the Café de la Poste. I also telephoned the public attorney.'

A human form was lying across the pavement, one hand hung in the gutter stream, and the gleam of his pale skin could be seen between his black shoes and the bottom of his trousers-legs. Gobillard, the dead man, was wearing no socks. His hat lay a yard away. The superintendent directed his torch on the face and, as Maigret and the judge were both bending over, there was a flash, a click, then the voice of the red-haired journalist asking:

'One more, please. A bit closer, Monsieur Maigret.'

The chief-inspector stepped back, groaning. Near the body, two or three people were observing him, then, quite separate, five or six yards away, there was a second group, bigger in number, where they were talking in whispers.

Chabot enquired, in a manner both official and exhausted:

'Who found him?'

And Féron answered, pointing to one of the nearest figures standing by, 'Doctor Vernoux'.

Did he, too, belong to the same family as the man in the train? As far as one could judge in the darkness, he was much younger. Perhaps thirty-five? He was tall, with a long nervous face, wore glasses across which drops of rain were sliding.

Chabot and he shook hands mechanically, in the manner of men who meet every day and even several times a day.

The doctor explained in a low voice:

'I was calling on a friend, on the other side of the square. I saw something on the pavement. I bent over. He was already dead. To save time, I dashed to the Café de la Poste, from where I telephoned the superintendent.'

Other faces were caught one after another in the beams of the torches, always with streaks of rain haloing them.

'Is that you, Jussieux?'

A handshake. These men knew each other like pupils in the same class at school.

'I was in the café just now. We were playing bridge and we've all come . . .'

The judge remembering Maigret, who was keeping in the background, introduced:

'Doctor Jussieux, a friend of mine. Chief-Inspector Maigret . . .'

Jussieux was explaining.

'Same methods as with the other two. A violent blow on the top of the skull. The weapon slipped slightly to the left, this time. Gobillard, too, has been attacked from in front, without attempting to protect himself at all.'

'Drunk?'

'You have only to lean over and sniff. At this time of night, besides, as you know him well . . .'

Maigret was listening with only half an ear. Lomel, the red-haired journalist, who had just taken a second picture, was trying to draw him to one side. What struck the chief-inspector was something rather difficult to define.

The smaller of the two groups, the one standing near the corpse, appeared to be composed only of men who knew each other, who belonged to a particular set: the judge, the two doctors, the men who, doubtless, had just been playing bridge with Doctor Jussieux, all of whom were probably local worthies.

The other group, less in the light, was not keeping so quiet. Without strictly speaking showing it, it emanated a kind of hostility. There were even two or three derisive snorts.

A dark car had just parked behind the ambulance and a man got out, who stopped short on recognizing Maigret.

'You here, Chief!'

He did not appear too pleased to meet the chief-inspector. It was Chabiron, a Flying Squad detective, for the past few years attached to the Poitiers force.

'Did they send for you?'

'I'm just here by chance.'

'That's what they call striking lucky, eh?'

He too laughed derisively.

'I was busy patrolling the town in my jalopy, which explains why it took so long to inform me. Who is it?'

Féron, the superintendent of police, explained to him:

'A certain Gobillard, a chap who goes around Fontenay once or twice a week collecting rabbit-skins. He also buys up hides of cattle and sheep-skins from the municipal slaughter-house. He has a cart and an old horse and he lives in a hut outside the town. He spends most of his time fishing near the bridge, using the most disgusting bait, marrow-fat, chicken guts, clotted blood . . .'

Chabiron must have been a fisherman.

'Does he catch any fish?'

'He's practically the only man who does. Every evening he goes from bar to bar drinking a jug of red wine in each, until he reaches his limit.'

'Ever any trouble?'

'Never.'

'Married?'

'He lived alone with his horse and a large number of cats.'

Chabiron turned to Maigret:

'What do you think, Chief?'

'I don't think anything.'

'Three in one week, it's not bad for a little spot like this.'

'What are we to do?' Féron asked the judge.

'I don't think it's necessary to wait for the attorney. Wasn't he at home?'

'No. His wife's trying to get him on the 'phone.'

'I think we might move the body to the morgue.'

He turned to Doctor Vernoux.

'You saw nothing else, heard nothing?'

'Not a thing. I was walking quickly, my hands in my pockets. I all but stumbled over him.'

'Is your father at home?'

'He returned this evening from Niort; he was dining when I came out.'

As far as Maigret could understand, this was the son of the Vernoux de Courçon with whom he had travelled in the local train.

'You can take him away, the rest of you.'

The journalist would not leave Maigret alone.

'Are you going to take charge of it, this time?'

'Certainly not.'

'Not even in a private capacity?'

'No.'

'Aren't you curious?'

'No.'

'Do you, too, believe in these being the crimes of a lunatic?'

Chabot and Doctor Vernoux, who had heard, looked at each other, still with that air of belonging to the same set, of knowing each other so well that words are no longer necessary.

It was natural. It exists everywhere. Rarely, nevertheless, had Maigret had such a strong sense of a clique. In a little town like this there are, of course, the local worthies, few in number, who, through force of circumstances, meet each other, if only in the street, several times a day.

Then there are the others, those, for example, who were gathered together to one side and seemed discontented.

Without the chief-inspector having asked at all, Chabiron was explaining to him:

'A couple of us have come over. Levras, who was accompanying me, had to leave this morning, because his wife's expecting a baby any time now. I'm doing what I can. I'm tackling the case from all angles at once. But as for getting those people over there to talk . . .'

It was the first group, the local worthies, whom he indicated with a jerk of his chin. His sympathies were obviously with the others.

'The superintendent of police, too, does his best. He has only four policemen at his disposal. They've been working on it all day. How many have you out on patrol at the moment, Féron?'

'Three.'

As if to confirm his statement, a cyclist in uniform stopped by the kerb and shook the rain from his shoulders.

'Anything?'

'I've checked the papers of the half-dozen people I've met. I'll give you the list. They all had good reasons for being out of doors.'

'Will you come back home for a moment?' Chabot asked Maigret.

He hesitated. He only chose to do so because he wanted something to drink in order to get warm again, and he didn't expect he would be able to get anything at the hotel any longer.

'I'll come along with you,' Doctor Vernoux announced. 'That is, if I'm not intruding?'

'Not at all.'

This time, they had the wind behind them and were able to talk. The ambulance had departed with Gobillard's body, and its red tail-lamp could be seen going towards the Place Viète.

'I haven't properly introduced you. Vernoux is the son of Hubert Vernoux whom you met in the train. He's a qualified doctor, but doesn't practise, and is chiefly concerned in research.'

'Research! . . . ' the doctor protested half-heartedly.

'He was a houseman for two years at Sainte-Anne, now he's keenly interest in psychiatry, and two or three times a week he goes to Niort lunatic asylum.'

'Do you believe these three crimes are the work of a madman?' asked Maigret, more out of politeness than anything else.

What he had just heard had not made him take kindly to Vernoux, since he didn't care for amateurs.

'It's more than likely, if not certain.'

'Do you know any mad people in Fontenay?'

'There are some everywhere, but usually one only discovers them at the critical moment.'

'I suppose it couldn't be a woman?'

'Why not?'

'Because of the force with which the blows have been struck on each occasion. It can't be easy to commit a murder like that, three times, without ever needing to strike twice.'

'In the first place, many women are as strong as men. Again, when you're dealing with lunatics . . .'

They had already arrived.

'Anything you want to talk about, Vernoux?'

'Not for the moment.'

'Shall I see you tomorrow?'

'Almost certainly.'

Chabot searched in his pocket for the key. In the passage, he and Maigret shook themselves so that the rain would fall off their clothes and immediately there were trails of water on the flagstones. The two women, the mother and the maid, were waiting in a badly-lit drawing-room, which looked onto the street.

'You can go to bed, Mother. There's nothing more to be done tonight, except to ask the police station to put all available men out on patrol.'

Only then did she decide to go upstairs.

'I feel really ashamed that you're not staying with us, Jules!'

'I promise you that if I stay more than twenty-four hours, which I doubt, I shall be making demands on your hospitality.'

They returned to the motionless atmosphere of the study, where the bottle of brandy was still in its place. Maigret helped himself and went to stand with his back to the fire, his glass in his hand.

He sensed that Chabot was ill at ease, that it was for this reason he had brought him back. Before anything else, the judge telephoned to the constabulary.

'Is that you, lieutenant? You were in bed? I'm sorry to disturb you at this hour . . .'

A clock with a bronzed dial, on which the hands could hardly be seen, showed half-past eleven.

'Yet another one, yes . . . Gobillard . . . In the street, this time . . . And from the front, yes . . . They've already taken him to the morgue . . . Jussieux is probably busy doing the post-mortem now, but there's no reason why we should learn anything from it . . . Have you some men at hand? . . . I think it would be a good thing if they patrolled the town, not so much tonight as in the early hours of the morning, so as to reassure the townspeople . . . You understand? . . . Yes . . . I felt that just now too . . . Thank you, lieutenant.'

Replacing the receiver, he murmured:

'A charming fellow, he passed out of Saumer . . .'

He must have realized what that signified—always a question of class!—and blushed slightly.

'You see! I'm doing what I can. It must seem childish to you. We probably give you the impression of being desperately old-fashioned. But we don't have the advantages of an organization such as you are used to in Paris. For finger-prints, for example, I'm obliged every time to send for an expert from Poitiers. So it is with everything. The local police are more used to petty offences than to crimes. The Poitiers detectives, for their part, don't know the people of Fontenay . . .'

He went on after a pause:

'I'd have given anything, with only three years left before my retirement, not to have been saddled with a case like this. In fact, we're about the same age. You, too, in three years' time . . .'

'Me, too.'

'Have you any plans?'

'I've even bought a little house in the country already, on the banks of the Loire.'

'You'll be bored.'

'Are you bored, here?'

'It's not the same. I was born here. My father was born here. I know everyone there is to know.'

'The townspeople don't seem very happy.'

'You've barely arrived and you've already realized that? It's true. I think it's inevitable. One crime, and it wasn't so bad. Especially the first one.'

'Why?'

'Because it happens to have been Robert de Courçon.'

'Wasn't he liked?'

The magistrate did not reply straight away. He appeared to be choosing his words first.

'Actually, the ordinary people hardly knew him, except by sight.'

'Married? Children?'

'An old bachelor. An eccentric, but a good fellow. If he had been the only one, the people would have remained fairly cool about it. Just the little excitement that always accompanies a crime. But, one after the other, there's been the widow Gibon, and now Gobillard. Tomorrow, I'm prepared to find . . .'

'It's already begun.'

'What?'

'The group which was keeping to one side, the ordinary people, I suppose, and those who'd come out of the Café de la Poste, seemed rather hostile to me.'

'It won't stop at that. However . . .'

'Is the town very left-wing?'

'Yes and no. It's not altogether that, either.'

'The Vernoux are unpopular?'

'Have you been told that?'

To gain time, Chabot asked:

'Won't you sit down? Have another glass? I'll try and explain to you. It's not easy. You know the Vendée, if only by repute. For a long time, the only people who counted were the owners of châteaux, counts, viscounts, anyone who had a "de" to his name, who lived amongst themselves and formed a closed society. They still exist, almost all impoverished, and they hardly matter any longer. A few of them still continue nevertheless to put up a certain show, and they are regarded with a kind of pity. Do you understand?'

'It's the same in all country districts.'

'Now, others have taken their place.'

'Vernoux?'

'Well, you have seen him; guess what his father did.'

'Haven't the least idea! How do you mean . . .?'

'Cattle dealer. The grandfather was a farm-hand. Father Vernoux bought up the livestock in the district, and drove them to Paris, in whole herds, along the roads. He made a lot of money. He was a brute, always half-drunk, and what's more, he died of *delirium tremens*. His son . . .'

'Hubert? The one in the train?'

'Yes. He was sent to college. I believe he did one year at university. In the last years of his life, the father started buying farms and land as well as cattle and it was that business which Hubert continued.'

'In fact, he's a property-dealer.'

'Yes. He has his offices near the station, the large freestone house, that was where he lived before he married.'

'He married a nobleman's daughter?'

'In one way, yes. But not exactly, either. She was a Courçon. Does this interest you?'

'Very much!'

'It will give you a better idea of the town. The Courçons were really called Courçon-Lagrange. Originally, they were just Lagranges, who added Courçon to their name when they bought the Château de Courçon. That happened three or four generations ago. I can't remember what the founder of the dynasty sold. Probably cattle, also, or scrap-iron. But that was all forgotten by the time Hubert Vernoux arrived on the scene. The children and grandchildren no longer did any work. Robert de Courçon, the one who's been murdered, was recognized by the aristocracy and he was the most expert man in the country around on matters of heraldry. He's written several works on the subject. He had two sisters, Isabelle and Lucile. Isabelle married Vernoux, who at once began to sign himself Vernoux de Courçon. Have you followed me?'

'It's not too difficult! I suppose that, at the time of this marriage, the Courçons had descended the scale again and found themselves without money?'

'Pretty well. They still had a mortgaged château in the forest of Mervent and the town-house in the Rue Rabelais, which is the handsomest residence in the town, and which they've several times tried to get scheduled as a historical monument. You'll be seeing it.'

'Is Hubert Vernoux still a dealer in property?'

'He has heavy liabilities. Emilie, his wife's elder sister, lives with them. His son, Alain, the doctor, whom you've just met, refuses to practise and devotes himself to research which brings in nothing.'

'Married?'

'He married a Mademoiselle de Cadeuils, from the real nobility this time, who's borne him three children already. The youngest is eight months old.'

'They live with the father?'

'The house is large enough, as you'll realize. That's not all. In addition to Alain, Hubert has a daughter, Adeline, who married a certain Paillet, whom she met while on holiday at Royan. What he does for a living, I don't know, but I have reason to believe that it's Hubert Vernoux who provides for their needs. Most of the time they live in Paris. Now and then, they turn up for a few days or a few weeks, and I suppose that means that they're hard-up. Do you understand now?'

'What have I got to understand?'

Chabot smiled mournfully, which for a moment reminded Maigret of his former comrade.

'It's true. I'm talking to you as though you came from here. You've seen Vernoux. He out-squires all the squires of the neighbourhood. As for his wife and her sister, they seem to contrive with all their skill to make themselves odious to the ordinary run of people. The whole thing constitutes a clique.'

'And this clique is on visiting terms with only a small proportion of the people.'

Chabot blushed for the second time that evening.

'Inevitably,' he murmured, rather as if he were guilty.

'So that the Vernoux, the Courçons and their friends have become a world apart in the town.'

'You've guessed right. Through the very nature of my position, I am obliged to see them. And, basically, they are not so odious as they appear to be. Hubert Vernoux, for example, is in fact, I would swear, a man overwhelmed with worries. He has been very rich. He is less so now, and I even wonder if he still is at all, because, since the majority of farmers have bought their own properties, the trade in land is no longer what it used to be. Hubert is weighed down with expenses, is obliged to provide for all his relatives As for Alain, whom I know better, he's a young man obsessed with one idea.'

'What's that?'

'You'd better hear about it. At the same time, you will learn why, just now, in the street, he and I exchanged anxious glances. I've told you that Hubert Vernoux's father died of *delirium tremens*. On the mother's side, that's to say the Courçons, the antecedents were no better. Old Courçon committed suicide in circumstances sufficiently mysterious for them to have been hushed up. Hubert had a brother, Basile, of whom they never speak, who killed himself at the age of seventeen. It seems that, however far you go back, there have been lunatics or eccentrics in the family.'

Maigret was listening, all the while lazily smoking his pipe, and taking a sip, every now and again, from his glass.

'That's the reason why Alain studied medicine, and went to Sainte-Anne as an interne. It's said, and it's plausible, that most medical men specialize in the illnesses with which they believe they themselves are threatened.

'Alain is obsessed by the idea that he belongs to a family of lunatics. According to him, Lucile, his aunt, is half-mad. He hasn't said so to me, but I'm convinced that he keeps looking for signs, not only in his father and mother, but in his own children.'

'Is it known in the locality?'

'Some people talk about it. In little towns, there's always a lot of gossip and a certain amount of mistrust of people who don't live exactly like everybody else.'

'They talked about it after the first crime particularly?'

Chabot hesitated only a second, nodded his head.

'Why?'

'Because they knew, or thought they did, that Hubert Vernoux and his brother-in-law Courçon didn't get on together. Perhaps also, because they lived immediately opposite one another.'

'Did they see each other?'

'I wonder what you're going to think of us. I fancy no similar situation could exist in Paris.'

In fact, the examining magistrate was ashamed of a milieu which was somewhat his own, as he lived in it year in, year out.

'I told you that the Courçons were ruined, when Isabelle married Hubert Vernoux. It's been Hubert who's given his brother-in-law, Robert, an allowance. And Robert's never forgiven him for it. When he mentioned him, he would say sarcastically:

' "*My brother-in-law, the millionaire.*"

'Or else:

' "*I'll go and ask the Rich Man.*"

'He wouldn't set foot in the big house on the Rue Rabelais, where he could follow all the comings and goings from his own windows. He lived opposite, in a smaller house, but a decent one, where he had a daily woman. He polished his boots and got his meals himself, ostentatiously setting off to do his shopping, dressed like a lord on the round of his estates, and he would bring home his bunches of leeks or asparagus as if they were trophies. He must have imagined it would make Hubert angry.'

'Did Hubert get angry?'

'I don't know. Possibly. He continued to support him nonetheless. Several times they've been seen, when they met in the street, exchanging politely cutting remarks. A small detail, which is no fabrication: Robert de Courçon never drew the curtains of his windows, with the result that the family opposite could see how he lived all the time. Some people make out that he occasionally put out his tongue at them.

'The next step is to make out that Vernoux had him got rid of, or killed him in a fit of temper . . .'

'That has been said?'

'Yes.'

'Have you thought so too?'

'Professionally, I can reject no hypothesis *a priori*.'

Maigret could not help smiling at this pompous phrase.

'Have you questioned Vernoux?'

'I haven't summoned him to my office, if that's what you mean. After all there haven't been sufficient grounds for suspecting a man like him.'

He had said:

'*A man like him.*'

And he realized that he gave himself away, that this was acknowledging that he was more or less part of the clique. The whole evening, this visit from Maigret, were probably torture for him. Nor was it a pleasant experience for the chief-inspector, although, by now, he no longer felt the same desire to leave.

'I met him in the street, as I do every morning, and asked him a few questions, without appearing to do so.'

'What did he say?'

'That he had not left his rooms that evening.'

'At what time was the crime committed?'

'The first one? About the same time as today, round about ten o'clock in the evening.'

'What are they usually doing at the Vernoux at that time?'

'Apart from bridge on Saturdays, which brings them all together in the drawing-room, each one leads his own life without bothering about the rest.'

'Vernoux doesn't sleep in the same room as his wife?'

'He would regard that as middle-class. Each one has his or her own suite of rooms, on different floors. Isabelle is on the first, Hubert in the wing of the ground floor, which looks onto the courtyard. Alain's household occupy the second floor, and the aunt, Lucile, two rooms on the third, which are attics. When the daughter and her husband are there . . .'

'Are they there at present?'

'No. They're expected in a few days.'

'How many servants?'

'A married couple, who've been with them for twenty or thirty years, and two fairly young maids as well.'

'Where do they sleep?'

'In the other wing on the ground floor. You'll see the house. It's almost a château.'

'With a way out at the back?'

'There's a door in the wall of the courtyard, which leads into an alleyway.'

'So that anyone can go in or out without being seen?'

'Probably.'

'You haven't checked?'

Chabot was on the rack and, because he felt himself at fault, he raised his voice, all but furious with his friend.

'You're talking the way some of the common people do here. If I had gone to question the servants, when I hadn't any evidence, not the slightest clue, the whole town would have been convinced that Hubert Vernoux or his son was guilty.'

'His son?'

'He too, definitely! Because, from the moment he stopped work and became interested in psychiatry, there have been people who regard him as mad. He doesn't go to either of the town's two cafés, doesn't play billiards nor belotte, doesn't run after girls and sometimes, in the street, will stop abruptly to stare at someone, his eyes enlarged through the lenses of his spectacles. They're so disliked that . . .'

'You're defending them?'

'No. I must keep my detachment, and, in a county town, it's not always easy. I'm trying to be fair. I, too, thought that the first crime was probably a family affair. I studied the matter under all aspects. The fact that there was no robbery, that Robert de Courçon did not attempt to defend himself, worried me. And doubtless I would have taken certain measures if . . .'

'Wait a moment. You haven't asked the police to follow Hubert Vernoux and his son?'

'In Paris, that's practicable. Not here. Everyone knows our four unfortunate policemen. As for the Poitiers detectives, they were spotted before they even got out of their car! It's seldom there are more than ten people at any one time in the street. You mean that, under such conditions, someone should be followed without his suspecting it?'

He calmed down suddenly.

'Forgive me. I'm talking so loud I shall wake my mother. It's just that I'd like you to understand my position. Until there is proof to the contrary, the Vernoux are innocent. I would swear to it that they are. The second crime, two days after the first, has almost proved it. Hubert Vernoux could be driven to kill his brother-in-law, to strike him in a moment of rage. He had no reason to take himself off to the end of the Rue des Loges in order to assassinate the widow Gibon, whom he probably didn't know.'

'Who is she?'

'A retired midwife, whose husband, long since dead, was a police constable. She lived alone, half-crippled, in a three-roomed house.

'Not only has there been the old Gibon woman, but Gobillard this evening. The Vernoux knew him all right, as the whole of Fontenay did. In every town in France, there's at least one drunkard of his kind, who becomes a sort of popular figure.

'If you can cite me a single reason for killing a fellow of that sort . . .'

'Suppose he had seen something?'

'And the widow Gibon, who never left her house any longer? Would she have gone to the Rue Rabelais, past ten o'clock at night, to witness the crime through the windows? No, come, come! I know the methods of criminal investigation. I didn't attend the Bordeaux Congress, and I may be a little behind-hand, perhaps, on the latest scientific discoveries, but I think I know my profession and carry it out conscientiously. The three victims belonged to completely different backgrounds, and there was not the slightest connection between them. All three were killed in the same manner and, by the look of the injuries, one might conclude with the same weapon, and all three were attacked from in front, which presupposes that they had no suspicions. If it is a lunatic, it's not a wild or raving one, of whom everyone would steer clear. It's therefore what I might call a clear-headed lunatic, who's following a definite line of activity and is sufficiently circumspect to take precautions.'

'Alain Vernoux hasn't fully explained his presence in the town, this evening, in such pouring rain.'

'He said he was going to see a friend on the other side of the Champ de Mars.'

'He didn't give any name.'

'Because it's not necessary. I know that he often goes to visit a certain Georges Vassal, a bachelor, whom he knew at college. Even without that knowledge, I wouldn't have been surprised.'

'Why not?'

'Because the case fascinates him even more than me, for more personal reasons. I'm not suggesting that he suspects his father, but I don't think he's far from it Some weeks ago, he talked to me about him and the family failings . . .'

'Just like that?'

'No. He was coming back from La Roche-sur-Yon and was quoting a case that he had been studying. It concerned a man in his sixties, who up to that time had behaved normally, but on the day when he should have presented the long-promised dowry to his daughter, went off his head. It was not immediately detected.'

'In other words, you're saying that Alain Vernoux might have been wandering around Fontenay at night on the look-out for the murderer?'

The examining magistrate was roused to fresh indignation.

'I presume he is more qualified to recognize a demented person in the street, than our worthy policemen grubbing around the town, or than you or me?'

Maigret didn't reply.

It was past midnight.

'Are you sure you wouldn't like to sleep here?'

'My bags are at the hotel.'

'Shall I see you tomorrow morning?'

'Of course.'

'I shall be at the Palais de Justice. You know where it is?'

'In the Rue Rabelais, isn't it?'

'A little farther up than the Vernoux' house. You'll notice the prison railings first, then a not very imposing building. My office is at the end of the corridor, near that of the public attorney.'

'Good night, old man.'

'I have welcomed you poorly.'

'Of course not!'

'You must understand my state of mind. It's the kind of case which could put the whole town against me.'

'Indeed!'

'You're laughing at me?'

'No, I promise you.'

This was true. Maigret was sad rather, as one is each time one sees a little of the past vanish. In the passage, as he struggled into his sodden overcoat, he sniffed again the smell of the house which had always appeared so pleasant to him, and now seemed musty.

Chabot had lost practically all his hair, which left uncovered a pointed cranium, like that of certain birds.

'I'll drive you back . . .'

He did not really want to. He said it out of politeness.

'Certainly not!'

Maigret added a not very subtle joke, for something to say, to finish on a cheerful note:

'I know how to swim!'

Whereupon turning up the collar of his coat, he plunged into the storm. Julien Chabot remained for a while in the rectangle of pale yellow light, then the door closed again, and Maigret had the impression that, in the streets of the town, there was no one else still about besides himself.

III

THE streets presented a more depressing sight in the light of morning than at night, because the rain had dirtied everything, leaving its dark traces on the façades of buildings, turning their colours ugly. Large drops still fell from cornices and electric wires, occasionally from the sky, which was draining itself, still in a dramatic style, as though gathering strength for fresh convulsions.

Maigret, having risen late, had not felt in the mood to go downstairs for his breakfast. Ill-tempered, with no appetite, he simply wanted two or three cups of black coffee. In spite of Chabot's brandy, he thought he could still discern in his mouth the after-taste of the over-sweet white wine he had consumed in Bordeaux.

He pressed a little pear-shaped bell, hanging by the head of his bed. The chamber-maid, in black with a white apron, who answered his call, looked at him so strangely that he felt obliged to check that he was decently covered.

'Are you sure you wouldn't like some hot croissants? A man like you needs to eat in the morning.'

'Only coffee, my dear. An enormous jug of coffee.'

She noticed the suit of clothes which the chief-inspector had put to dry over the radiator the night before, and seized them.

'What are you doing?'

'I'm just going to press them.'

'No thank you, it's not worth it.'

She took them, all the same!

Judging by her physical appearance, he would have said that she was usually rather a cross-patch.

Twice while he was dressing she came and disturbed him, once to make sure he had some soap, and again to bring a second jug of coffee which he hadn't ordered. Then she returned with his suit, dry and pressed. She was thin, flat-chested, with a look of having poor health, but was probably as tough as iron.

It crossed his mind that she had seen his name on the register, downstairs, and that she was an avid reader of news-items.

It was nine-thirty in the morning. He dawdled, in protest against something or other, something he vaguely considered to be a conspiracy of the fates.

As he descended the red-carpeted staircase, an odd-job man, coming up, greeted him with a respectful:

'Good morning, Monsieur Maigret.'

On arriving in the hall, he understood, for *Ouest-Eclair* was displayed on a small table, with his photograph on the front page.

It was the photo taken when he was bending over Gobillard's body. A double-size headline announced across three columns:

Chief-Inspector Maigret engaged on the Fontenay Crimes
A rabbit-skin dealer the third victim

Before he had time to glance through the article, the hotel manager came up to him, with as much eagerness as the chamber-maid.

'I hope you slept well and that Number 17 didn't disturb you too much?'

'Who's Number 17?'

'A commercial traveller who drank too much last night and was noisy. We eventually put him in another room, so that he shouldn't wake you.'

He had heard nothing.

'By the way, Lomel, the *Ouest-Eclair* correspondent, came in to see you this morning. When I told him you were still in bed, he said there was no hurry and that he would see you shortly at the Palais de Justice. There's a letter for you, as well.'

A cheap envelope, such as are sold in packets of six, in six different colours, in grocery stores. This one was greenish. Just as he was opening it, Maigret realized that there were half a dozen people outside, pressing their faces to the glass-door, between the palm-trees in tubs.

Don't let yourself be inflewenced by them that's High Sossiety.

The people waiting on the pavement, two of them being women dressed for market, drew aside to let him pass, and there was something trusting, friendly in the way they looked at him, not so much out of curiosity, not so much because he was a celebrity, but as if they counted on him. One of the women said, without daring to come nearer:

'You'll find him, Monsieur Maigret, you will!'

And a young lad, who looked like a delivery boy, kept pace with him on the opposite pavement, the better to look at him.

On the doorsteps, women were discussing the latest crime and broke off to watch him go by. A group came out of the Café de la Poste, and there, too, he read sympathy in their eyes. They seemed to want to encourage him.

He passed Judge Chabot's house, where Rose was shaking dusters out of the first-floor window, didn't stop, crossed the Place Viète and ascended the Rue Rabelais, where on the left stood a vast town house, a coat of arms emblazoned on the pediment, which must surely be the Vernoux mansion. There was no sign of life behind the closed windows. Opposite, a little house, also an old one, with closed shutters, was probably where Robert de Courçon had lived out his solitary days.

From time to time there blew a small gust of damp wind. Clouds were driving low, dark against a sky the colour of frosted glass, and drops of water were falling from their fringe. The railings of the prison seemed blacker for being wet. Some ten people were standing about in front of the Palais de Justice, which was not at all imposing, being less big, in fact, than the Vernoux house, but which was nevertheless graced with a row of columns and a low flight of steps.

Lomel, with his two cameras still slung round him, was the first to hurry forwards, and there wasn't a trace of remorse on his baby-face nor in his bright blue eyes.

'Will you let me have your impressions before you give them to my Paris colleagues?'

And as Maigret scowlingly pointed to the newspaper sticking out of his pocket, he smiled.

'Are you annoyed?'

'I thought I'd told you . . .'

'Listen, Inspector. I have to do my job as a journalist. I knew you would eventually become concerned in the case. I've simply anticipated by a few hours . . .'

'Another time, don't anticipate.'

'Are you going to see Judge Chabot?'

Amongst the group there were two or three reporters from Paris already and he had difficulty in getting rid of them. There were also a few inquisitive people who seemed determined to spend the day on guard outside the Palais de Justice.

The corridors were dark. Lomel, his self-appointed guide, went ahead. and showed him the way.

'Along here. It's much more important for us than for the rag-mongers in the capital! You must realize that! "He" has been in his office since eight o'clock this morning. The public attorney's here too. Last night, when they were looking for him everywhere, he was at La Rochelle, where he'd popped over by car. Do you know the attorney?'

Maigret, who had knocked and been called to enter, opened the door and closed it behind him, leaving the red-headed reporter in the passage.

Julien Chabot was not alone. Doctor Alain Vernoux was sitting opposite him in an armchair and got up to greet the chief-inspector.

'Did you sleep well?' the judge enquired.

'Not at all badly.'

'I've been reproaching myself for my poor hospitality last night. You know Alain Vernoux. He's dropped in to see me.'

That wasn't true. Maigret was sure that it was himself for whom the psychiatrist was waiting and even, perhaps, that this interview had been arranged between the two men.

Alain had taken off his overcoat. He was wearing a suit of rough wool, which with its indeterminate creases, could have done with being ironed. His tie was badly knotted. A yellow sweater protruded from under his waistcoat. His shoes had not been polished. Even like this, he still, nonetheless, belonged to the same class as his father, whose appearance was so meticulous.

Why did it make Maigret wince? One was too well-groomed, dressed up to the nines. The other, on the contrary, affected a negligence which a bank employee, a school-master, or a commercial traveller could not have allowed himself; yet, one surely did not find suits of such material except at an exclusive tailor's in Paris, or possibly Bordeaux.

There was a rather embarrassing silence. Maigret, who was doing nothing to help the two men, went and stood in front of the meagre log-fire beneath the chimney-piece, which was surmounted by the same black marble clock as the one in his own office at the Quai des Orfèvres. At some time the authorities must have ordered them in hundreds, if not thousands. Perhaps they all alike lost twelve minutes a day, like Maigret's?

'Alain was just telling me some interesting things,' murmured Chabot at last, his chin in his hand, in a pose very much that of an examining magistrate. 'We were speaking of criminal lunacy . . .'

Vernoux's son interrupted him.

'I haven't asserted that these three crimes are the work of a lunatic. I said that, *if they were the work of a lunatic . . .*'

'That comes to the same thing.'

'Not exactly.'

'Let's put it that it's I who said everything seems to indicate that we are confronted by a lunatic.'

And, turning to Maigret:

'We talked about this yesterday evening, you and I. The absence of motive, in the three cases . . . The similarity of method . . .'

Then, to Vernoux:

'So, will you repeat to the chief-inspector what you were explaining to me?'

'I'm not an expert. In these matters I am only an amateur. I was developing a general idea. Most people suppose that lunatics invariably act as lunatics, that is to say, without logic or continuity of ideas. Now, in reality, it is often the contrary. Lunatics have their own logic. The difficulty lies in detecting that logic.'

Maigret was looking at him, with his large eyes slightly sea-green in the morning light, without saying anything. He was sorry he hadn't stopped on the way to have a drink, which would have put new life in his belly.

This small office, where a layer of smoke from his pipe was beginning to float and the little flames from the logs were dancing, seemed scarcely real to him, and the two men discussing madness, watching him out of the corner of their eyes, appeared to him rather like wax figures. They too formed no part of real life. They were making gestures they had learnt, speaking as they had been taught to.

What could a man like Chabot know of what went on in the street? And, still more so, in the mind of a killer?

'It is that logic, since the first crime, I have been trying to penetrate.'

'Since the first crime?'

'Let's say, since the second. From the first, however, from the murder of my uncle, I thought it was the act of a madman.'

'Have you found anything out?'

'Not yet. I've only noted a few elements of the problem, which might provide a clue.'

'Such as?'

'Such as, that he strikes from in front. It's not easy to express my idea simply. A man who wanted to kill in order to kill, that's to say, to do away with other living beings, and who at the same time wouldn't like to be caught, would choose the least dangerous method. Now, this one certainly doesn't want to get caught, because he avoids leaving any traces. Do you follow me?'

'It's not too complicated, up to now.'

Vernoux frowned, sensing the irony in Maigret's voice. It was possible that, fundamentally, he lacked confidence. He did not look people in the eyes. From the shelter of the large lenses of his spectacles, he merely gave furtive little glances, then gazed at some point in space.

'You admit that he'll do anything rather than be caught?'

'It looks like it.'

'Nevertheless he attacks three people in the same week, and all three times he brings it off.'

'True.'

'In all three cases, he might have struck from behind, which would have reduced the chances of a victim starting to call out.'

Maigret stared hard at him.

'As even a madman does nothing without reason, I deduce from this that the murderer feels the need to fly in the face of fate, or in the face of those whom he assaults. Certain characters need to assert themselves, whether by one crime or by a series of crimes. Sometimes, it's in order to prove their power, or their importance, or their courage to themselves. Others are convinced they have to avenge themselves on their fellow men.'

'This one, up to now, has only attacked the weak. Robert de Courçon was an old man of seventy-three. The widow Gibon was a cripple and Gobillard, at the time he was assaulted, was dead drunk.'

It was the judge this time who had spoken, his chin still in his hands, evidently pleased with himself.

'I thought of that too. Perhaps it's a clue, perhaps it's a coincidence. What I'm trying to discover, is the sort of logic that directs the actions and conduct of this unknown person. When we have discovered that, it won't be long before we get our hands on him.'

He said 'we' as if he were participating in the investigation as a matter of course, and Chabot didn't object.

'Was it for that reason you were out last night?' enquired the chief-inspector.

Alain Vernoux started, blushed slightly.

'Partly. I was actually calling on a friend, but I do admit to you that, for the last three days, I have been going about the streets as often as possible, studying the behaviour of the passers-by. The town isn't large. It's more than likely the murderer isn't hiding out at home. He is about on the pavements, like everyone else, maybe having a drink in the cafés.'

'Do you think you would recognize him if you met him?'

'I think that Alain may be invaluable to us,' Chabot murmured with a touch of embarrassment. 'What he has said to us this morning seems to me full of good sense.'

The doctor rose, and at the same time a noise was heard in the passage, someone knocked at the door, Inspector Chabiron put his head round.

'You're not alone?' he said, looking not at Maigret, but at Alain Vernoux, whose presence appeared to displease him.

'What is it, Inspector?'

'I have someone with me I should like you to question.'

The doctor announced:

'I shall go.'

Nobody stopped him. As he was going out, Chabiron said to Maigret, not without some bitterness:

'So it seems you're taking a hand, Chief?'

'The newspapers says so.'

'Perhaps the case won't take long. It might be all over in a couple of minutes. Shall I bring my witness in, Judge?'

And, turning to the half-darkness of the corridor:

'Come on! Don't be afraid.'

A voice replied:

'I'm not afraid.'

They saw a small thin man enter, dressed in navy-blue, with a pale face, eager eyes.

Chabiron introduced him:

'Emile Chalus, schoolmaster at the boys' school. Sit down, Chalus.'

Chabiron was one of those policemen who invariably use '*tu*' to both offenders and witnesses in the belief that it would impress them.

'Last night,' he explained, 'I began interrogating people living in the street where Gobillard was killed. You may say, perhaps, it's just routine . . .'

He threw a glance at Maigret, as if the chief-inspector were a personal enemy of routine.

'. . . But sometimes routine produces results. The street is not a long one. Early this morning I went on combing the area minutely. Emile Chalus lives thirty yards from the spot where the crime was committed, on the second floor of a house, which has offices on the ground and first floors. Tell them your story, Chalus.'

The latter was longing to say his piece, in spite of the fact that he obviously had no sympathy for the judge. It was to Maigret that he turned.

'I heard a noise like the sound of feet on the pavement.'

'At what time?'

'A little after ten in the evening.'

'And then?'

'The footsteps went away.'

'In which direction?'

The examining magistrate was asking the questions, each time looking at Maigret as though to offer him the chance to speak.

'In the direction of the Rue de la République.'

'Hurried footsteps?'

'No. Normal steps.'

'A man's?'

'Definitely.'

Chabot looked as though he thought it was not a very startling revelation, but the inspector intervened.

'Wait for the rest. Tell them what happened afterwards, Chalus.'

'A few minutes went by and then a group of people came into the street, coming from the Rue de la République, too. They gathered together on the pavement, talking loudly. I heard the word doctor, then the words police inspector, and I got up to look out of the window.'

Chabiron was gloating.

'Do you understand, Judge? Chalus heard running footsteps. Just now he informed me that there had also been a muffled noise, like that of a body falling on the pavement. Repeat what you said, Chalus.'

'That is correct.'

'Immediately after, someone went off in the direction of the Rue de la République, where the Café de la Poste is. I have other witnesses waiting outside, customers who were in the café at that time. It was ten-past ten when Doctor Vernoux went in there, without saying anything, and went straight to the telephone box. After he had telephoned, he noticed Doctor Jussieux playing cards, and whispered something in his ear. Jussieux announced to the others that a crime had just been committed and they all rushed outside.'

Maigret gazed at his friend Chabot, whose expression had stiffened.

'You see what that means?' the inspector went on, with a kind of aggressive delight, as though he were taking a personal revenge. 'According to Doctor Vernoux, he found a body on the pavement, a body already almost cold, and he went off to the Café de la Poste in order to telephone the police. If this were so, there would have been two lots of footsteps in the street, and Chalus, who wasn't asleep, would have heard them.'

He didn't yet dare to exult, but they could sense his excitement growing.

'Chalus has no criminal record. He's a respectable schoolmaster. He has no motive for inventing a story.'

Maigret refused once again the invitation to speak which his friend offered him with a glance. There followed quite a long pause. To hide his feelings, probably, the judge scribbled a few words in a file which he had in front of him, and when he raised his head again, he was looking tense.

'Are you married, Monsieur Chalus?' he asked in a dull voice.

'Yes, sir.'

The hostility between the two men was palpable. Chalus was tense, too, and his manner of replying aggressive. He seemed to be challenging the magistrate to destroy his evidence.

'Any children?'

'No.'

'Was your wife with you last night?'

'In the same bed.'

'She was asleep?'

'Yes.'

'You went to bed at the same time?'

'As usual, when I haven't too much home-work to correct. Yesterday was Friday and I had none at all.'

'At what time did you and your wife go to bed?'

'Half-past nine, perhaps a few minutes later.'

'Do you always go to bed so early?'

'We get up at half-past five in the morning.'

'Why?'

'Because we make use of the freedom accorded to all French people to get up at whatever hour they please.'

Maigret, who was watching him with interest, felt pretty certain that he took part in politics, belonged to a left-wing party, and was probably what is called militantly so. He was the kind of man to march in processions, to speak at meetings, the kind of man, also, to slip pamphlets in letter-boxes and refuse to move on, in spite of injunctions from the police.

'So you were both in bed at half-past nine, and I presume you fell asleep?'

'We went on talking for about ten minutes.'

'That takes us to twenty to ten. You both fell asleep?'

'My wife went to sleep.'

'And you?'

'No. I find it difficult to get to sleep.'

'So that, when you heard the noise on the pavement, thirty yards from your house, you were not asleep.'

'That is correct.'

'You hadn't been to sleep at all?'

'No.'

'You were wide awake?'

'Enough to hear running footsteps and the noise of a body falling.'

'Was it raining?'

'Yes.'

'There isn't a floor above yours?'

'No. We are on the second.'

'You must have heard the rain on the roof?'

'You don't notice it after a bit.'

'Water running down the gutter?'

'Certainly.'

'So that the sounds you heard were just sounds amongst other sounds?'

'There is an appreciable difference between running water and the trample of men's feet or a body falling.'

The judge was not giving up yet.

'You hadn't the curiosity to get up?'

'No.'

'Why not?'

'Because we aren't far from the Café de la Poste.'

'I don't understand.'

'Frequently, at night, men who have drunk too much pass our house, and sometimes they collapse on the pavement.'

'And stay there too?'

Chalus could find nothing to answer to that straight away.

'As you have spoken of trampling feet, I presume you got the impression that there were several men in the street, at least two anyway?'

'That goes without saying.'

'Only one man disappeared in the direction of the Rue de la République. Is that right?'

'I suppose so.'

'Since there was a crime, two men at the very least were thirty yards from your house, at the time you heard running footsteps. Do you follow me?'

'It's not difficult.'

'You heard one going off again?'

'I've already said so.'

'When did you hear them arrive? Did they arrive together? Did they come from the Rue de la République or from the Champ de Mars?'

Chabiron shrugged his shoulders. Emile Chalus was pondering with a stern expression.

'I didn't hear them arrive.'

'You don't suppose, however, that they had been standing in the rain for a long time, one of them awaiting a propitious moment to kill the other?'

The schoolmaster clenched his fists.

'Is that all you've got out of it?' he muttered between his teeth.

'I don't understand.'

'It embarrasses you that someone from your own circle may be involved. But your question is ridiculous. I don't necessarily hear someone walking along the pavement, or rather I don't pay particular attention to it.'

'However . . .'

'Let me finish, will you, instead of trying to trap me. Up to the time of the running footsteps, I had no reason to pay any attention to what was happening in the street. Afterwards, on the other hand, my mind was alert.'

'And you maintain that from the time the body fell on the pavement until the time when several people arrived from the Café de la Poste, not a soul passed along the street?'

'There wasn't a single footstep.'

'Do you realize the importance of this statement?'

'I didn't ask to make it. It was the inspector who came to question me.'

'Before the inspector questioned you, you hadn't the slightest idea of the significance of what you had noticed?'

'I was unaware of Doctor Vernoux's testimony.'

'Who has told you about any testimony? Doctor Vernoux hasn't been called to testify.'

'Let's say that I was unaware of his story.'

'Was it the inspector who told you?'

'Yes.'

'Then you realized?'

'Yes.'

'And I suppose you were delighted with the effect you were going to produce? You hate the Vernoux?'

'Them, and all like them.'

'Have you specifically attacked them in your speeches?'

'It has happened.'

The judge, very frigid, turned to Inspector Chabiron.

'Has his wife confirmed what he says?'

'Partly. I didn't bring her, because she was busy in the house, but I can go and fetch her. They certainly went to bed at half-past nine. She is sure of this, because it is she who winds the alarm-clock each evening. They talked for a little while. She went to sleep and was woken up again by finding that her husband was no longer beside her. She saw him standing at the window. At that time, it was a quarter past ten, and a group of people were standing round the corpse.'

'Did neither of them go downstairs?'

'No.'

'They weren't curious to know what was happening?'

'They opened the window a little, and heard someone saying that Gobillard had just been murdered.'

Chabot, who still avoided Maigret's eyes, seemed discouraged. Without conviction, he asked yet a few more questions:

'Do any other people living in the street support his evidence?'

'Not so far.'

'Have you questioned them all?'

'Those who were at home this morning. Some had already gone off to their work. Two or three others, who were at the cinema last night, know nothing.'

Chabot turned to the schoolmaster.

'Do you know Doctor Vernoux personally?'

'I've never spoken to him, if that's what you mean. I've passed him in the street often enough, like everyone else. I know who he is.'

'You don't have any particular animosity against him?'

'I have already replied to that.'

'Have you ever appeared in court?'

'I've been arrested a good dozen times, over political demonstrations, but after a night in the cells and the usual rough handling, they have always let me out.'

'I am not concerned with that.'

'I realize that it doesn't interest you.'

'Do you stick to your statement?'

'Yes, even if it upsets you.'

'It doesn't affect me.'

'It affects your friends.'

'Are you so sure of what you heard yesterday evening that you wouldn't hesitate to send someone to prison or to the scaffold?'

'I haven't done any killing. The murderer himself didn't hesitate to do away with the widow Gibon and poor Gobillard.'

'You are forgetting Robert de Courçon.'

'About him, I couldn't care a f . . .!'

'Well, I shall call the clerk of the court so that he can take down your statement in writing.'

'I'm at your disposal.'

'Then we shall hear your wife's evidence.'

'She won't contradict me.'

Chabot was already reaching out his hand towards an electric bell on his desk, when the voice of Maigret, who had almost been forgotten, asked quietly:

'Do you suffer from insomnia, Monsieur Chalus?'

The latter quickly turned his head.

'What are you trying to insinuate?'

'Nothing. I believe I heard you say, just now, that you find it hard to get to sleep which explains why, though you were in bed by half-past nine, you were still awake at ten o'clock.'

'For some years now I've had insomnia.'

'Have you consulted a doctor?'

'I don't like doctors.'

'Haven't you tried any remedy?'

'I take some tablets.'

'Every day?'

'Is it a crime?'

'Did you take some yesterday before going to bed?'

'I took two of them, as I generally do.'

Maigret nearly smiled, seeing his friend Chabot revive, like a plant long deprived of moisture which has been watered at last. The judge couldn't resist resuming the direction of operations himself.

'Why didn't you tell us you had taken a sleeping-tablet?'

'Because you didn't ask me and because it's my affair. Should I also tell you when my wife takes a purgative?'

'You swallowed two tablets at half-past nine?'

'Yes.'

'And you weren't asleep by ten-past ten?'

'No. If you were in the habit of taking such drugs, you would know that in the end they have almost no effect. To start with, one tablet was enough for me. Now, with two, it takes me more than half an hour to feel drowsy.

'It's possible, then, that when you heard the noise in the street, you were already drowsy?'

'I wasn't asleep. If I had been asleep, I should have heard nothing.'

'But you could have been dozing. What were you thinking about?'

'I don't remember.'

'Can you swear you were not in a state between waking and sleeping? Consider my question seriously. Perjury is a grave offence.'

'I was not asleep.'

The man was basically honest. He had certainly been delighted to be able to bring down a member of the Vernoux clan and he had done it with glee. Now feeling the triumph slip through his fingers, he was trying to cling onto it, without quite daring to lie.

He cast Maigret an unhappy look tinged with reproach but not anger. He seemed to be saying:

'Why have you let me down, when you aren't on their side?'

The judge wasted no time.

'Suppose that the tablets had begun to take effect without, however, putting you to sleep completely, it may be that you did hear the noises in the street and your drowsiness would explain why you had not heard any footsteps before the murder. It needed a scuffle of feet, the fall of a body, to attract your attention. Isn't it plausible that immediately after the footsteps died away, you fell again into a drowsy state? You didn't get up. You didn't wake your wife. You weren't worried, you told us so yourself, as if the whole thing had happened in another world. It wasn't until several men, talking in loud voices, stopped on the pavement that you were completely roused.'

Chalus shrugged his shoulders and let them fall again wearily.

'I might have expected this,' he said.

Then he added something like:

'You and your type . . .'

Chabot wasn't listening any more, he was saying to Inspector Chabiron:

'You can still draw up a report of his statement. I shall hear his wife this afternoon.'

When he and Maigret were alone, the judge made a show of taking some notes. A good five minutes went by before he murmured, without looking at the chief-inspector:

'Thank you.'

And Maigret, sucking his pipe:

'There's nothing to thank me for.'

IV

THROUGHOUT the entire luncheon, the main course of which was a stuffed shoulder of mutton, the like of which Maigret could not remember ever having eaten, Julien Chabot had the air of a man suffering from a bad conscience.

As they entered the front door of his house, he had felt it necessary to mutter:

'We mustn't mention any of this in front of my mother.'

Maigret had had no intention of doing so. He noticed that his friend bent down to the letter-box, from which, discarding a few circulars, he took an envelope similar to the one he had been handed that morning in the hotel, with the difference that this one, instead of being pale green, was salmon-pink. Perhaps it had come from the same packet? He wasn't able to make sure then, since the judge slipped it negligently into his pocket.

They had hardly spoken a word while returning from the Palais de Justice. Before leaving there, they had had a short interview with the public prosecutor, and Maigret had been considerably surprised to find that he was a man barely thirty years old, hardly out of college, a handsome fellow who did not seem to take his duties too seriously.

'I'm sorry about last night, Chabot. There's a good reason why they didn't manage to get hold of me. I was at La Rochelle and my wife didn't know about it.'

He added with a wink:

'Fortunately!'

Then, suspecting nothing:

'Now that you have Chief-Inspector Maigret to help you, it won't be long before you catch the murderer. Do you also think he's a lunatic, Chief-Inspector?'

What use was there in discussing it? You could tell the relations between the judge and the public prosecutor were not overfriendly.

In the corridor there was the onslaught of journalists who already had wind of Chalus' evidence. The latter had probably talked to them. Maigret would have wagered that it was known about all over the town, too. It was difficult to explain the atmosphere there. From the Palais de Justice to the judge's house they saw only about fifty people, but it was enough to take the local pulse. The looks the two men received showed a lack of confidence. The working-class people, particularly women returning from shopping, had an almost hostile attitude.

At the top of the Place Viète there was a little café where quite a number of people were taking their *apéritifs* and, as they passed it, they heard a somewhat disturbing buzz of talk and derisive laughter.

Some people were probably starting to panic, and the presence of policemen patrolling the town on bicycles was not sufficient to reassure them; on the contrary they added a touch of drama to the appearance of the streets, by reminding people that somewhere about there was a murderer at large.

Madame Chabot had not attempted to ask questions. She was full of little attentions for her son, for Maigret too, whom she seemed to be asking, from her expression, to protect him and she was doing her best to introduce perfectly innocuous subjects into the conversation.

'Do you remember the young girl with a squint, with whom you had dinner here one Sunday?'

She had a terrifying memory, reminding Maigret of people he had met more than thirty years before, during his visits to Fontenay.

'She made a fine marriage, a young man from Marans who started a successful cheese-factory. They had three children, each more beautiful than the last, then all of a sudden, as if fate had decided they were too happy, she was struck down by tuberculosis.'

She mentioned others who had become invalids or had died, or had suffered similar misfortunes.

For dessert, Rose brought in an enormous dish of *profiterolles* and the old woman watched the chief-inspector mischievously. He wondered at first why, feeling that something was expected of him. He didn't care very much for *profiterolles* and he put one of them on his plate.

'Go on! Help yourself. Don't be ashamed! . . .'

Seeing she was disappointed, he took three.

'Don't tell me you've lost your liking for them! I remember the evening you ate twelve. Each time you came I made *profiterolles* for you and you used to maintain that you'd never eaten such good ones anywhere else.'

(Which was, incidentally, true: he never ate them at all anywhere else!)

It had all passed out of his memory. He was even surprised that he had ever shown a taste for pastries. He must have said so, once, for politeness' sake.

He did his duty, exclaimed his appreciation, ate all he had on his plate, took some more.

'And the partridge with cabbage! Do you remember that? I am sorry it's the wrong season now, for . . .'

When coffee was served, she withdrew discreetly, and Chabot, as was his custom, placed a box of cigars on the table, together with a bottle of brandy. The dining-room was as little altered as the study and it was almost painful to find things so much the same, including Chabot himself, who, in some ways, hadn't altered much either.

To please his friend, Maigret took a cigar, stretched his legs out towards the hearth. He knew that the other man wanted to broach a particular subject, that he had been thinking about it ever since they had left the Palais. It took time. The judge's voice, as he looked the other way, lacked confidence.

'You think I should have arrested him?'

'Who?'

'Alain.'

'I see no reason for arresting the doctor.'

'Yet Chalus seemed sincere.'

'He's that undeniably.'

'You too think he wasn't telling lies.'

Deep down, Chabot was wondering why Maigret had intervened, because but for him, but for the point about the sleeping-tablet, the schoolmaster's statement would have been much more damaging for the younger Vernoux. It perplexed the judge, made him ill at ease.

'First of all,' said Maigret, smoking his cigar awkwardly, 'it's possible that he really had dozed off. I always mistrust the evidence of people who have heard something from their beds, perhaps because of my wife.

'Time and again she insists that she hasn't got to sleep until two o'clock in the morning. She says it in all good faith, ready to swear to it. Now, quite often, I've woken up myself during her so-called insomnia and I've seen her asleep.'

Chabot wasn't convinced. Perhaps he imagined that his friend had simply wanted to save him from an awkward situation?

'Furthermore,' continued the chief-inspector, 'even if the doctor is the murderer, it's better he should not be put under arrest yet. He's not the sort of man from whom one can extort a confession through plain interrogation, still less through any rough-handling.'

The judge was already rejecting this idea with an indignant gesture.

'In the present state of the investigations there isn't even a particle of proof against him. By arresting him, you would give satisfaction to a section of the population who would come and demonstrate under the prison windows, shouting: "Kill him." Once such a disturbance had begun, it would be difficult to suppress it.'

'Do you really think so?'

'Yes.'

'You aren't saying so in order to reassure me?'

'I say so because it's the truth. As always happens in a case of this kind, public opinion points pretty frankly to one suspect or other, and I've often wondered how it chooses him. It's a mysterious phenomenon, rather a frightening one. From the first day, if I'm not mistaken, the people have turned against the Vernoux family, without caring too much whether it's the father or the son.'

'That's true.'

'Now it's on the son that they're venting their anger.'

'And supposing he is the murderer?'

'I heard you, before leaving, giving orders for him to be watched.'

'He may escape his watchers.'

'It wouldn't be wise of him to do so, because if he shows himself much in the town, he runs the risk of being torn to pieces. If it is he, he will do something sooner or later which will give us a clue.'

'Perhaps you are right. I really am glad that you're here. Yesterday, I admit, it bothered me a little. I told myself you would be watching me and that you'd find me clumsy, awkward, old-fashioned, and I don't know what else. In the provinces, we almost all suffer from an inferiority complex, especially in the face of people from Paris. Even more so when it's a man like you! Do you blame me?'

'For what?'

'For the stupid things I've been saying.'

'You've said some very sensible things. In Paris, we too have to take into account different situations and put ourselves in other people's shoes.'

Chabot already felt better.

'I shall spend my afternoon interrogating the witnesses Chabiron has hunted out for me. Most of them have neither seen nor heard anything, but I don't want to miss any chance.'

'Be nice to Chalus' wife.'

'Yes, certainly!'

'Will you come with me?'

'No. I'd rather scout around the town, drink a glass of beer here and there.'

'Well now, I haven't opened this letter. I didn't want to do so in front of my mother.'

He took the salmon-coloured envelope from his pocket and Maigret recognized the hand-writing. The paper definitely came from the same packet as the note he had received that morning.

Find out what the doctor was doing at the Sabati girl's.

'Do you know her?'

'Never heard that name.'

'I think I remember you told me that Doctor Vernoux doesn't run after girls.'

'He's reputed not to. Anonymous letters are going to pour in now. This one comes from a woman.'

'As most anonymous letters do! Would you mind 'phoning the police station?'

'About the Sabati girl?'

'Yes.'

'Straight away?'

Maigret nodded.

'Let's go into my study.'

He lifted the receiver, called the police station.

'Is that you, Féron? The examining magistrate speaking. Do you know a woman called Sabati?'

They had to wait. Féron had gone to ask his men, perhaps to examine the files. When he came on the phone again, Chabot took down a few words in pencil on his blotter, while he listened.

'No. Probably no connection. What? Certainly not. Don't do anything about her for the moment.'

In saying this, he looked for Maigret's approval and the latter nodded his head vigorously.

'I'll be in my office in half an hour. Yes. Thank you.'

He hung up.

'There is indeed a certain Louise Sabati in Fontenay-le-Comte. Daughter of an Italian builder who's supposed to be working in Nantes or thereabouts. For some time she was a waitress at the Hôtel de France, then a barmaid at the Café de la Poste. She hasn't worked for several months. Unless she's moved recently, she lives on the bend in the La Rochelle road near the barracks, in a large dilapidated house with six or seven families living in it.'

Maigret, who had had enough of his cigar, crushed out the glowing stub in the ash-tray, before filling a pipe.

'Are you thinking of going to see her?'

'Perhaps.'

'You still think that the doctor . . .?'

He stopped short, his eye-brows puckered.

'Well, what shall we do this evening? Normally I would be going to the Vernoux' for bridge. From what you've told me, Hubert Vernoux is expecting you to come with me.'

'Well?'

'I'm wondering if, in the present climate of opinion . . .'

'Are you in the habit of going there every Saturday?'

'Yes.'

'In that case, if you don't go, people will conclude that they're under suspicion.'

'And if I do go, they'll . . .'

'They'll say you're protecting them, that's all. They're saying so already. One way or another . . .'

'Do you intend to come with me?'

'Without the slightest hesitation.'

'All right then . . .'

Poor Chabot had given up resisting, left all the initiative to Maigret. 'It's time I went up to the Palais.'

They went out together, and the sky had still the same whiteness, at once bright and blue-green, the kind of sky one sees reflected in the water of a pool. The wind was still fierce and, at street corners, women's dresses clung to their bodies, sometimes a man would lose his hat and have to run after it waving his arms grotesquely.

They were going off in opposite directions.

'When shall I see you again?'

'I may call in your chambers. If not, I'll be at your house for dinner. What time is bridge at the Vernoux'?'

'Half-past eight.'

'I warn you I don't know how to play.'

'It doesn't matter.'

Curtains moved as Maigret passed along the pavement, his pipe between his teeth, his hands in his pockets, his head bent to stop his hat flying off. Now he was on his own, he felt a little less confident. All that he had just said to his friend Chabot was true. But when he had intervened, that morning, at the end of Chalus' interrogation, although he had acted on impulse, there was still, at the back of it, the desire to rescue the judge from an embarrassing situation.

The atmosphere of the town remained disquieting. Even though people had gone to work as usual, one sensed nonetheless a certain anxiety in the looks of the passers-by, who seemed to be walking more quickly, as if they expected to see the murderer suddenly spring out. On other days, Maigret felt sure, the housewives would not have gathered in groups on doorsteps as they did today, talking in low voices.

Their eyes followed him, and he thought he could read a silent question in their faces. Was he going to do something? Or would the unknown person be able to go on killing with impunity?

Some of them addressed him a timid greeting as if to say:

'We know who you are. You have a reputation for solving the most difficult cases. And *you* won't let yourself be impressed by certain individuals.'

He almost entered the Café de la Poste to drink a half-pint. Unfortunately, there were at least a dozen people inside whose heads all turned towards him when he approached the door, and suddenly he had no desire to have to reply to the questions they would put to him.

In the end, in order to reach the barracks district, he had to cross the Champ de Mars, a vast bare expanse, bordered by trees recently planted which were shaking in the icy wind.

He took the same little street the doctor had taken the evening before, the one in which Gobillard had been struck down. As he passed one house, he heard the sound of angry voices on the second floor. It was doubtless where Emile Chalus, the schoolmaster, lived. Several people were arguing passionately, some of his friends who had probably come for news.

He crossed the Champ de Mars, skirted the barracks, took the street to the right and looked for the large dilapidated building his friend had described to him. There was only one of this type, in a deserted street, between two pieces of waste ground. What it had formerly been was hard to tell, a warehouse or a mill, perhaps a small factory? Some children were playing outside. Others, younger ones, with bare bottoms, were crawling about in the corridor. A fat woman with hair falling down her back, put her head round the narrow opening of a door, and she had never before heard the name of Chief-Inspector Maigret.

'Who are you looking for?'

'Mademoiselle Sabati.'

'Louise?'

'I think that's her Christian name.'

'Go right round the house and in by the door at the back. Go up the stairs. There's only one door. That's it.'

He did what he was told, brushed past dustbins, stepped over rubbish, and all the time he could hear the bugles sounding in the barracks square. The outside door he had just been told about was open. A steep staircase, without a banister, led him to a floor which wasn't on the same level as the rest, and he knocked on the blue-painted door.

At first, no one answered. He knocked louder, heard the footsteps of a woman in old slippers, yet still had to knock a third time before he was asked:

'What is it?'

'Mademoiselle Sabati?'

'What do you want?'

'To talk to you.'

He added on the off-chance:

'The doctor sent me.'

'One moment.'

She went off again, probably to slip on some suitable garment. When she at last opened the door, she was wearing a flowered dressing-gown, of cheap cotton, under which she probably only had on a nightdress. Her feet were bare in her slippers, her black hair undone.

'Were you asleep?'

'No.'

She studied him from head to foot with mistrust. Behind her, beyond a diminutive landing, could be seen an untidy room which she didn't invite him to enter.

'What does *he* want me to say?'

As she turned her head slightly to one side, he noticed a bruise round her left eye. It wasn't altogether a fresh one. It was beginning to turn from blue to yellow.

'Don't be scared. I'm a friend. I'd just like to talk to you for a few minutes.'

What probably decided her to let him enter was the fact that two or three kids had come to look at them from the bottom of the stairs.

There were only two rooms, the bedroom, of which he only caught a glimpse and where the bed was unmade, and a kitchen. On the table, a novel was open beside a bowl still containing some coffee, a lump of butter was left on a plate.

Louise Sabati was not beautiful. In a black dress and white apron, she must have had that tired look which one notices in most chambermaids in provincial hotels. There was however something appealing, almost pathetic, in her pale face, where her dark eyes were intensely alive.

She cleared things off a chair.

'Did Alain really send you?'

'No.'

'He doesn't know you're here?'

As she said this she glanced with a terrified look at the door, remained standing, on the defensive.

'Don't be scared.'

'You're from the police.'

'Yes and no.'

'What's happened? Where is Alain?'

'At his home, probably.'

'You're sure?'

'Why should he be anywhere else?'

She bit her lip and the blood rose to it. She was very strung up, with an unhealthy nervousness. He wondered for a moment if she took drugs.

'Who told you about me?'

'Have you been the doctor's mistress for long?'

'Have they told you that?'

He put on his most affable air and anyhow he didn't have to make an effort to show sympathy to her.

'You've only just got up?' he asked, instead of replying.

'What business is that of yours?'

She had retained a trace of an Italian accent, no more. She can have been hardly more than twenty, and her body, under her badly cut dressing-gown, was well built; only her bosom, which must once have been provocative, sagged a little.

'Would you mind sitting down beside me?'

She wouldn't keep still. With feverish movements, she seized a cigarette, lit it.

'Are you sure Alain won't come?'

'Does it make you scared? Why?'

'He's jealous.'

'He hasn't any reason to be jealous of me.'

'He is of any man.'

She added in an odd voice:

'He's right.'

'What do you mean?'

'He's entitled to be.'

'He's in love with you?'

'I think so. I know I'm not worth it, but . . .'

'Won't you really sit down?'

'Who are you?'

'Chief-Inspector Maigret, from Police Headquarters, Paris.'

'I've heard of you. What are you doing here?'

Why not speak frankly to her?

'I happened to come here, to meet a friend I hadn't seen for years.'

'Was it he who told you about me?'

'No. I've also met your friend Alain. In fact, I've been invited to his house tonight.'

She sensed that he wasn't lying, but still wasn't reassured. She nonetheless drew a chair towards her but didn't sit down straight away.

'If he's not in trouble at the moment, he may well be any time now.'

'Why?'

From the tone in which she uttered the word, he concluded that she already knew.

'Some people think he may be the man they're looking for.'

'Because of the crimes? It's not true. It's not him. He hadn't any reason to . . .'

He interrupted her by handing her the anonymous letter the judge had left with him. She read it, her face tense, frowning.

'I wonder who wrote that.'

'A woman.'

'Yes. And it must be a woman who lives in this house.'

'Why?'

'Because nobody else knows. Even in this house, I could have sworn nobody knew who he is. It's spite, a dirty trick. Alain never . . .'

'Sit down.'

She decided at last to do so, taking care to cross the folds of her gown over her bare legs.

'Have you been his mistress long?'

She didn't hesitate.

'Eight months and one week.'

This exactness almost made him smile.

'How did it start?'

'I was working as a barmaid in the Café de la Poste. He used to come there from time to time, in the afternoons, always sat in the same place, near the window, where he could look at the people passing. Everyone knew him and greeted him, but he didn't easily open a conversation. After a while, I noticed he was watching me.'

She looked at him suddenly, defiantly.

'Do you really want to know how it began? All right, I'll tell you, and you'll see he's not the kind of man you think. In the end, he used to come for a drink in the evenings. Once he stayed right up to closing-time. I was rather inclined to make fun of him because of his big eyes following me everywhere. That night, I had a date, outside, with the wine-merchant, whom you'll certainly meet. We turned right, down the little street, and . . .'

'And what?'

'Oh well! We settled down on a bench in the Champ de Mars. You understand? That sort of thing never lasted very long. When it was all over, I set off alone to cross the square and return home and I heard steps behind me. It was the doctor. I was a bit scared. I turned round and asked him what he wanted me for. Looking quite shamefaced, he didn't know what to reply. Do you know what he managed to murmur in the end?

' "*Why did you do that?*"

'And I burst out laughing.

' "*Does it upset you?*"

' "*It distressed me a great deal.*"

' "*Why?*"

'That's how in the end he admitted he loved me, that he'd never dared to tell me, that he was very unhappy. You're smiling?'

'No.'

It was true. Maigret was not smiling. He could very well see Alain Vernoux in such a situation.

'We walked about until one or two in the morning, right along the towpath, and, in the end, I was the one who was crying.'

'Did he accompany you here?'

'Not that night. It took a whole week. During those days, he spent almost all his time in the café, watching me. He was even jealous seeing me thank a customer when I received a tip. He's like that all the time. He doesn't like me to go out.'

'Does he hit you?'

She put her hand instinctively to the bruise on her cheek and, as the sleeve of her dressing-gown slipped down, he saw there were other blue marks on her arms, as if they had been gripped hard between powerful fingers.

'He's entitled to do so,' she retorted, not without pride.

'Does it often happen?'

'Almost every time.'

'Why?'

'If you don't understand, I can't explain to you. He loves me. He's obliged to live over there with his wife and children. Not only does he not love his wife, but he doesn't like his children either.'

'Has he told you so?'

'I know.'

'Are you unfaithful to him?'

She shut up, stared at him, with a ferocious look. Then:

'Has someone told you so?'

And in a lower voice:

'It did happen, to start with, when I hadn't yet realized. I thought he would be like all the rest. When you've begun, like me, at fourteen, you don't attach any importance to it. When he found out, I thought he was going to kill me. I really mean it. I've never seen a man so terrifying. For a whole hour, he lay stretched out on the bed, his eyes fixed on the ceiling, his fists clenched, without uttering a word, and I could tell he was suffering terribly.'

'Did you do it again?'

'Two or three times. I've been pretty stupid.'

'And since?'

'No!'

'Does he come to see you every evening?'

'Almost every evening.'

'Were you expecting him yesterday?'

She hesitated, wondering what her replies might involve him in, wanting at all costs to protect Alain.

'What difference can it make?'

'You must have gone out to do your shopping.'

'I don't go right into town. There's a little grocer on the corner of the street.'

'For the rest of the time, you're locked up here?'

'I'm not locked up. You know as much, because I opened the door to you.'

'He's never talked of locking you up?'

'How did you guess?'

'He has done so?'

'For one week.'

'Did the neighbours realize?'

'Yes.'

'That's why he gave you back the key?'

'I don't know. I don't understand what you're getting at?'

'Do you love him?'

'Do you suppose I would live this sort of life, if I didn't love him?'

'He gives you money?'

'When he can.'

'I thought he was rich.'

'Everybody thinks that, whereas he's in exactly the same position as a young man who has to ask for a little money from his father every week. They all live in the same house.'

'Why?'

'How should I know?'

'He could work.'

'That's his business, isn't it? For weeks on end, his father leaves him without money.'

Maigret looked at the table where there was only some bread and some butter.

'Is that the position at the moment?'

She shrugged her shoulders.

'What difference does it make? I too, at one time, used to have notions about people who are supposed to be rich. It's all on the outside! A large house with nothing indoors. They're always squabbling to squeeze a bit of money out of the old man and the tradesmen sometimes wait months to get paid.'

'I though Alain's wife was rich.'

'If she had been rich, she wouldn't have married him. She imagined that he was. When she found out to the contrary, she began to hate him.'

There was a fairly long silence. Maigret filled his pipe, slowly, dreamily.

'What are you busy thinking now?' she enquired.

'I'm thinking that you really love him.'

'You've got there already!'

Her irony was bitter.

'What I'm wondering,' she continued, 'is why all at once people are taking against him. I've read the newspaper. It doesn't say anything definite, but I feel they're suspecting him. Just now, at the window, I heard some women talking in the yard, very loud, on purpose, so that I shouldn't lose a word of what they were saying.'

'What were they saying?'

'That the moment they started to look for a lunatic they wouldn't have to go far to find him.'

'I suppose they heard the scenes that took place up in your room.'

'So what?'

She suddenly became almost furious and got up from her chair:

'Are you too, because he's fallen in love with a girl like me and because he's jealous of me, are you going to presume that he's mad?'

Maigret got up in turn, tried, in order to calm her, to put his hand on her shoulder, but she pushed him away in anger.

'Say so, if that's how you see it.'

'It is *not* how I see it.'

'You think he's mad.'

'Certainly not because he loves you.'

'But he's mad all the same?'

'Until there's proof to the contrary, I've no reason for coming to that conclusion.'

'What does that mean exactly?'

'It means that you're a good girl, and that . . .'

'I'm not a good girl. I'm a whore, a piece of dirt, and I don't deserve . . .'

'You're a good girl, and I promise you I'll do my best to discover the true culprit.'

'Are you convinced it's not him?'

He sighed, embarrassed, and in order to hide his feelings, began to light his pipe.

'So you see, you don't dare say so!'

'You're a good girl, Louise. I shall probably come back again to see you . . .'

But she had lost confidence and, on shutting the door behind him, she growled:

'You and your promises! . . .'

On the stairs, at the bottom of which the kids were watching out for him, he thought he heard her add to herself:

'You're nothing but a dirty policeman after all!'

V

At a quarter-past eight, when they left the house in the Rue Clemenceau, they almost shrank back in surprise at the suddenness with which so much calm and silence enveloped them.

Towards five in the afternoon, the sky had turned as black as at the Crucifixion and lights had to be put on all over the town. Two brief, rending claps of thunder had rung out, and at last the clouds had emptied themselves, not in rain but in hail, people on the streets had disappeared, as though swept away by the squall, whilst white bullets rebounded on the paving-stones like ping-pong balls.

Maigret, who was in the Café de la Poste at that moment, had got to his feet with the rest and everyone had remained standing by the windows, looking at the street as though they were watching a fire-works' display.

Now, it was all over and it was a bit disconcerting to hear neither the rain nor the wind, to walk out in the still air, to see stars between the rooftops, when one lifted one's head.

Possibly because of the silence only broken by the sound of their footsteps, they walked without saying a word, going up the street towards the Place Viète. Just at the corner of it, they almost bumped into a man standing motionless in the darkness, a white arm-band on his overcoat, a cudgel in his hand, who watched them pass without breathing a word.

A few steps farther on, Maigret was on the point of asking a question, and his friend, guessing this, explained in a constrained voice:

'The police superintendent telephoned me just before I left my office. It's been boiling up to this since yesterday. This morning, boys distri-buted notices in people's letter-boxes. They held a meeting at six o'clock and have organized a watch committee.'

'*They*' obviously did not refer to the boys but to the hostile elements in the town.

Chabot added:

'We can't stop them doing so.'

Right outside the Vernoux' house, in the Rue Rabelais, three more men with arm-bands were standing on the pavement and watched them approach. They were not patrolling, simply standing there on guard, and one might almost have thought they were waiting for them, were perhaps going to stop them entering. Maigret thought he recog-nized, in the smallest of the three, the thin figure of Chalus the school-master.

It was quite impressive. Chabot hesitated to go up to the entrance, was probably tempted to continue along the road. There was no sign as yet of a riot, nor even a disturbance, but it was the first time they had come across such a tangible sign of public discontent.

Calm in appearance, very dignified, not without a kind of solemnity, the examining magistrate eventually mounted the steps and raised the door-knocker.

Behind him, there wasn't a murmur, not even a joke. Still not moving, the three men watched what he did.

The noise of the knocker reverberated inside as though in a church. Immediately, as if he were there to await them, a butler manipulated the chains, the bolts, and received them in reverent silence.

It could not usually have been like this, because Julien Chabot paused on the threshold of the drawing-room, sorry perhaps that he had come.

In a room the size of a ballroom, the great crystal chandelier was lit, other lights glittered on tables, enough armchairs were grouped in different corners, and around the fireplace, to seat forty people.

Yet only one man was there, at the farthest end of the room, Hubert Vernoux, with his white silky hair, who sprang from an immense Louis XIII armchair and came to meet them, hand outstretched.

'I told you yesterday, in the train, that you would be coming to see me, Monsieur Maigret. Besides, I telephoned today to our friend Chabot to make sure he would bring you.'

He was dressed in black and his coat was something like a dinner jacket, a monocle was dangling from a ribbon across his chest.

'My family will be here in a moment. I don't understand why they haven't all come down.'

In the poor light of the train compartment, Maigret had hardly seen him. Here, the man appeared older. When he had come across the drawing-room, his step had the mechanical stiffness of people with arthritis, whose movements seem controlled by springs. His face was puffy, almost artificially pink.

Why was the chief-inspector reminded of an aged actor, forcing himself to carry on playing his role and living in terror that the public will notice he's already half-dead?

'I must have them told you're here.'

He had rung, was addressing the butler.

'See if Madame is ready. Tell Mademoiselle Lucile too and the doctor and Madame . . .'

Something wasn't quite right. He was vexed with his family for not being there. To put him at ease, Chabot said, looking at the three bridge tables prepared:

'Is Henri de Vergennes going to come?'

'He excused himself by telephone. The storm has wrecked the drive of the château and he finds it impossible to take his car out.'

'Aumale?'

'Our friend the lawyer developed 'flu this morning. He went to bed at mid-day.'

Nobody would be coming, in fact. And it was as if the family itself was hesitating to come down. The butler hadn't reappeared. Hubert Vernoux pointed to the liqueurs on the table.

'Help yourselves, will you? I must ask you to excuse me for a moment.'

He went to fetch them himself, climbed the great stone staircase with its wrought-iron banisters.

'How many people usually come to these bridge parties?' Maigret enquired in a low voice.

'Not many. Five or six apart from the family.'

'Who are usually in the drawing-room when you arrive?'

Chabot nodded, reluctantly. Someone entered noiselessly, Doctor Alain Vernoux, who had not changed and was wearing the same creased suit as he had had on in the morning.

15*

'Are you alone?'

'Your father has just gone up.'

'I met him on the staircase. What about the women?'

'I believe he's gone to call them.'

'I don't think anyone else will come.'

Alain jerked his head towards the windows, concealed by heavy curtains.

'You saw?'

And, knowing that they had understood what he meant:

'They're keeping watch on the house. There's probably some of them on guard by the door in the lane, too. It's a very good thing.'

'Why?'

'Because, if another crime is committed, they won't be able to attribute it to someone in the house.'

'Do you foresee another crime?'

'If it's a lunatic, there's no reason why the number should stop where it is.'

Madame Vernoux, the doctor's mother, at last made her entrance, followed by her husband, who had a flushed face, as if he had had to argue to persuade her to come down. She was a woman of sixty, her hair still brown, with very dark-ringed eyes.

'Chief-Inspector Maigret, of Police Headquarters in Paris.'

She barely inclined her head, and went to sit down in an armchair, which must have been her own particular one. As she passed them, she merely greeted the judge with a furtive:

'Good evening, Julien.'

Hubert Vernoux announced:

'My sister-in-law will be down immediately. We had an electricity cut earlier on, which made dinner late. I suppose the current was off all over the town?'

He was talking for the sake of talking. It didn't matter what he said. He had to fill the void in the drawing-room.

'A cigar, Chief-Inspector?'

For the second time since he had been in Fontenay, Maigret accepted one, because he didn't dare bring his pipe out of his pocket.

'Isn't your wife coming down?'

'She's probably being held up by the children.'

It was already obvious that Isabelle Vernoux, the mother, had consented to put in an appearance, after God knows what haggling, but that she was determined not to participate actively in the gathering. She had taken up her tapestry and was not listening to what was being said.

'Do you play bridge, Chief-Inspector?'

'I'm sorry to disappoint you, but I never play. I hasten to add that I get a great deal of pleasure just watching a game.'

Hubert Vernoux looked at the judge.

'How shall we play? Lucile will certainly play. You and I. I suppose, Alain . . .'

'No. Don't count on me.'

'That leaves your wife. Would you go and see if she's nearly ready?'

It was becoming painful. Nobody, apart from the mistress of the house, had decided to sit down. Maigret's cigar enabled him to keep up appearances. Hubert Vernoux had also lit one and was busy filling the brandy glasses.

Could the three men standing guard outside guess that such things were happening indoors?

Lucile came down at last, and, though thinner and more angular, she was the image of her sister. She, too, accorded no more than a brief look at the chief-inspector, walked straight to one of the card tables.

'Shall we begin?' she enquired.

Then, pointing vaguely at Maigret:

'Is he playing?'

'No.'

'Who is playing, then? Why have you made me come down?'

'Alain has gone to fetch his wife.'

'She won't come.'

'Why not?'

'Because she's got one of her headaches. The children have been impossible the whole evening. The governess has given notice and left. Jeanne is looking after the baby . . .'

Hubert Vernoux mopped his brow.

'Alain will persuade her.'

And, turning to Maigret:

'I don't know if you have any children. No doubt it's the same in all big families. Everyone wants his own way. Everyone has his own pursuits, his particular likes . . .'

He was right: Alain brought in his wife, somewhat ordinary, rather dumpy, her eyes red from crying.

'Forgive me . . .' she said to her father-in-law. 'The children have given me a lot of trouble.'

'I gather that the governess . . .'

'We'll talk about it tomorrow.'

'Chief-Inspector Maigret . . .'

'I am delighted to meet you.'

She offered her hand, but it was a limp hand, without warmth.

'Are we playing?'

'We are.'

'Who?'

'You're sure, Chief-Inspector, you don't want to take a hand?'

'Positive.'

Julien Chabot, already seated as if at home in the house, was shuffling the cards, stacking them up in the centre of the green baize.

'It's your pick, Lucile.'

She turned up a king, her brother-in-law a knave. The judge and Alain's wife drew a three and a seven.

'We're partners.'

All this had taken almost half an hour, but at last they were settled. In her corner, Isabelle Vernoux, the mother, looked at no one. Maigret was sitting in the background, behind Hubert Vernoux, whose hand he could see as well as that of his daughter-in-law.

'Pass.'

'One club.'

'Pass.'

'One heart.'

The doctor had remained standing, with the air of not knowing what to do. Everybody was as at his post. Hubert Vernoux had gathered them together, almost forcibly, to preserve an appearance of normal life in the house, perhaps for the chief-inspector's benefit.

'Well now, Hubert?'

His sister-in-law, who was his partner, was calling him to order.

'Sorry! . . . Two clubs . . .'

'You're sure you shouldn't say three? I bid a heart against your club, which means I've at least two and a half honours . . .'

From that moment Maigret began to be fascinated in the game. Not in the play itself, but for what it revealed to him of the players characters.

His friend, Chabot, for instance, was as steady as a metronome, his calls exactly as they should have been, neither rash nor timid. He played his hand calmly, didn't pass a single remark to his partner. Barely a shade of annoyance came over his face when the young woman didn't respond correctly.

'I beg your pardon. I should have replied three spades.'

'It doesn't matter. You couldn't know what I've got in my hand.'

At the beginning of the third game, he announced and succeeded in winning a small slam, apologized for it:

'Too easy. I had it all in my hand.'

The young woman herself was absent-minded, tried to pull herself together and, when it was her turn to play, looked around her as though asking for help. Once she turned to Maigret, her fingers on a card, asking his advice.

She didn't like bridge, was only there because she had to be, to make up a fourth.

Lucile, on the other hand, dominated the table with her personality. It was she who, after each game, commented on the play and delivered sarcastic remarks.

'Since Jeanne bid two hearts, you should have known which way to finesse. She was bound to have the queen of hearts.'

She was right, moreover. She was always right. Her little black eyes seemed to see through the cards.

'What's wrong with you today, Hubert?'

'Why? . . .'

'You're playing like a novice. You're hardly listening to the bids. We'd have been able to win that game with three no-trumps and you ask for four clubs which you can't manage.'

'I expected you to say that . . .'

'I didn't have to tell you about my diamonds. You should have . . .'

Hubert Vernoux tried to make up for it. He was like one of those roulette players who, once having lost, cling to the hope that their luck is going to turn any moment and try every number, furious to see the number coming up that they have just abandoned.

Almost always, he bid beyond his own hand, relying on his partner's cards and when they weren't there, he would bite the end of his cigar nervously.

'I assure you, Lucile, that I was perfectly entitled to call two spades straight off.'

'Except that you had neither the ace of spades nor the ace of diamonds.'

'But I did have . . .'

He enumerated his cards, the blood rose to his head, while she regarded him with savage coldness.

To restore his losses, he bid still more recklessly, to the point where it was no longer bridge but poker.

Alain had gone to keep his mother company for a while. He came back to install himself behind the players, looking at the cards without interest, with his large eyes blurred through his spectacles.

'Do you understand it at all, Chief-Inspector?'

'I know the rules. I'm able to follow the game, but not play it.'

'Does it interest you?'

'Greatly.'

He scrutinized the chief-inspector with more attention, seemed to realize that Maigret's interest lay much more in the behaviour of the players than in the cards, and he watched his aunt and his father with a bored expression.

Chabot and Alain's wife won the first rubber.

'Shall we change?' Lucile suggested.

'Unless we take our revenge as we are.'

'I'd sooner change partners.'

This was a mistake on her part. She found herself playing with Chabot, who made no slips and with whom it was impossible for her to

find fault. Jeanne was playing badly. But, perhaps because she invariably bid too low, Hubert Vernoux won two games in succession.

'It's luck, nothing else.'

This was not quite true. He had had the cards, certainly. But if he
hadn't bid with so much boldness, he would not have won, for he had
no good reason to hope for the cards his partner held.

'Shall we continue?'

'Let's finish the round.'

This time Vernoux was with the judge, the two women together.
And it was the men who won, which meant that Hubert Vernoux had
won two rubbers out of three.

It seemed as if he was relieved, as though this bridge-party had had
considerable importance for him. He mopped his brow, went to pour
himself a drink, brought a glass for Maigret.

'You see, in spite of what my sister-in-law says, I'm not so imprudent.
What she doesn't understand is, that if one manages to grasp the way in
which your opponent's mind works, one is half-way to winning the
game, whatever the cards be. It's the same thing in selling a farm or a
piece of land. Know what the buyer has in mind and . . .'

'Please, Hubert.'

'What?'

'Couldn't you refrain from talking business here?'

'I'm sorry. I forgot that women like one to make money, but prefer
not to know how it's done.'

This too was imprudent. His wife, from her distant armchair, called
him to order.

'Have you been drinking?'

Maigret had seen him drink three or four cognacs. He had been
struck by the way Vernoux filled his glass, furtively, as if in a hurry, in
the hope that his wife and sister-in-law wouldn't see him. He would
swallow the alcohol in one gulp, then to reassure himself, would fill up
the chief-inspector's glass.

'I've only had two glasses.'

'They've gone to your head.'

'I think,' Chabot began, rising and taking his watch from his pocket,
'it is time we left.'

'It's hardly half-past ten.'

'You forget that I've a lot of work to do. My friend Maigret must be
beginning to get tired too.'

Alain seemed disappointed. Maigret felt sure that, all through the
evening, the doctor had hung around him, in the hope of drawing him
into a corner.

The others didn't attempt to keep them. Hubert Vernoux didn't dare
to insist. What would happen when the players had departed and he
would be left alone with the three women? Because Alain did not count.

That was obvious. Nobody bothered about him. Doubtless he would go up to his room or his laboratory. His wife was more a member of the family than he was.

It was a family of women, in fact, Maigret could see that straight away. They had allowed Hubert Vernoux to play bridge, on condition that he behaved himself well, and they had continually watched him like a child.

Was this the reason why, outside his own home, he clung so desperately to the personality he had created for himself, attentive to the smallest sartorial details?

Who knows? Perhaps, earlier on, when he had gone upstairs to fetch them, he had begged them to be nice to him, to allow him to play his role of master in the house without humiliating him with their remarks.

He was looking askance at the brandy decanter.

'One last glass, Chief-Inspector, what the English call a *night-cap*?'

Maigret, who did not really want one, said yes in order to give him the opportunity to drink one as well, but while Vernoux was raising the glass to his lips, he caught sight of his wife's fixed gaze, saw his hand hesitate, then, regretfully, put the glass down.

As the judge and the chief-inspector were reaching the door, where the butler was waiting for them with their coats, Alain murmured:

'Perhaps I'll accompany you part of the way.'

He himself did not seem to trouble over the women's reactions, though they seemed surprised. His own wife didn't object. It can't have made any difference to her whether he went out or not, seeing how little he counted in her life. She had gone over to her mother-in-law, whose work she was admiring, nodding her head up and down.

'You don't mind, Chief-Inspector?'

'Not at all.'

The night air was fresh, with a different freshness from that of the preceding nights, and one wanted to fill one's lungs, to greet the stars back in their places after so long.

The three men with arm-bands were still on the pavement and, this time, they stepped back a pace to let them pass. Alain had not put on his overcoat. As he passed the coat-stand, he had put on a soft felt hat, rendered shapeless by the recent storms of rain.

Seen like this his body leaning forward, his hands in his pockets, he was more like a student in his last year than a married man and father of a family.

In the Rue Rabelais, they weren't able to talk, because voices carried a long way and they were conscious of the presence of the three watchers behind them. Alain jumped when he brushed against the one on guard at the corner of the Place Viète, whom he hadn't seen.

'I suppose they've got them all over the town?' he muttered.

'Definitely. They're going to work in shifts.'

Few windows were still alight. People were going to bed early. One could see, far down the long vista of the Rue de la République, the lights in the Café de la Poste, still open, and two or three isolated people on the streets disappeared one after the other.

When they reached the judge's house, they had still not had time to exchange a dozen sentences. Chabot murmured reluctantly:

'Will you come in?'

Maigret said no:

'No point in waking your mother.'

'She won't be asleep. She never goes to bed before I'm back.'

'We'll see each other tomorrow morning.'

'Here?'

'I'll call at the Palais.'

'I've a certain number of telephone calls to make before I go to bed. Maybe there'll be something new?'

'Goodnight Chabot.'

'Goodnight, Maigret. Goodnight, Alain.'

They shook hands. The key turned in the lock; a moment later the door was shut again.

'May I come with you to the hotel?'

They were the only people in the street. For a split second, Maigret had a vision of the doctor taking his hand out of his pocket and knocking him on the skull with a hard object, a bit of lead piping or a spanner.

He replied:

'Gladly.'

They set off. Alain could not bring himself to speak straight away. When he did so, it was to ask:

'What do you think of it?'

'Of what?'

'Of father.'

What could Maigret have replied? What was interesting was the fact the question was being asked, that the young doctor had left his own home with no other reason than to ask it.

'I don't think he has had a happy life,' the chief-inspector murmured nonetheless, without much conviction.

'Are there people who do have a happy life?'

'For a while, at least. You are unhappy then, Monsieur Vernoux?'

'Oh, I don't count.'

'Yet you try to get your share of pleasure.'

The big eyes stared at him.

'What do you mean?'

'Nothing. Or, if you like, that totally unhappy people don't exist. Everyone clings to something, creates a kind of happiness for himself.'

'Do you realize what that means?'

And as Maigret did not reply:

'Do you know that it's this search for what I would call compensation, this search for some kind of happiness in spite of everything, that produces neurotics and, often, completely unbalanced people? The men who, at this moment, are drinking and playing cards at the Café de la Poste, are trying to convince themselves that they are enjoying themselves there.'

'And you?'

'I don't understand the question.'

'Don't you look for compensations?'

This time, Alain was worried, suspected Maigret of knowing more, reluctant to question him.

'Are you going to dare to go to the barracks district tonight?'

It was rather out of pity that the chief-inspector asked that, in order to relieve him of his doubts.

'You know?'

'Yes.'

'Have you talked to her?'

'For quite a time.'

'What did she tell you?'

'Everything.'

'Have I done wrong?'

'I'm not judging you. You're the one who brought up the subject of the instinctive quest for compensations. What are your father's compensations?'

They had lowered their voices, for they had reached the open door of the hotel, where a single light was lit in the hall.

'Why don't you answer?'

'Because I don't know the answer.'

'Does he have no affairs?'

'Certainly not in Fontenay. He's too well known and it would get about.'

'And you? Does it get about too?'

'No. My case isn't the same. When my father goes to Paris or Bordeaux, I suppose he treats himself to a little amusement.'

He murmured to himself:

'Poor papa!'

Maigret looked at him in surprise.

'Are you fond of your father?'

Modestly Alain replied:

'Anyhow, I'm sorry for him.'

'Has it always been like that?'

'It's been worse. My mother and aunt have calmed down a bit.'

'What have they got against him?'

'That he's a self-made man, the son of a cattle dealer who used to get drunk in village inns. The Courçons have never forgiven him for having needed him, do you understand? And in the days of old Courçon his position was more painful for Courçon was even more scathing than his daughters and his son Robert. Until the death of my father, every Courçon in the land will reproach him for the fact that they live off his money.'

'How do they treat you, yourself?'

'As a Vernoux. And my wife, whose father was Vicomte de Cadeuil, is hand in glove with my mother and aunt.'

'Did you intend to tell me all this, this evening?'

'I don't know.'

'You meant to talk to me about your father?'

'I wanted to know what you thought of him.'

'Weren't you chiefly anxious to know if I'd discovered the existence of Louise Sabati?'

'How did you find out?'

'Through an anonymous letter.'

'Does the judge know about it? The police?'

'They aren't doing anything about it.'

'But will they?'

'Not if the murderer is discovered fairly soon. I have the letter in my pocket. I haven't spoken to Chabot about my interview with Louise.'

'Why not?'

'Because I don't think, in the present state of the case, it has any bearing on it.'

'She has nothing to do with it.'

'Tell me, Monsieur Vernoux . . .'

'Yes.'

'How old are you?'

'Thirty-six.'

'How old were you when you finished your studies?'

'I left the Faculty of Medicine at twenty-five and then I was a houseman at Sainte-Anne for two years.'

'You've never been tempted to live on your own?'

He seemed suddenly disheartened.

'Don't you want to answer?'

'I've nothing to answer. You wouldn't understand.'

'Lack of courage?'

'I knew you would call it that.'

'Nevertheless you didn't return to Fontenay-le-Comte in order to look after your father?'

'Look, it's both simpler and more complicated than that. I came back one day to spend several weeks holiday here.'

'And you stayed on?'

'Yes.'

'Aimlessly?'

'If you like. Though it's not exactly that.'

'You felt you couldn't do anything else?'

Alain dropped the subject.

'How is Louise?'

'The same as ever, I imagine.'

'She isn't worried?'

'Is it long since you saw her?'

'Two days. I went to her house yesterday evening. After that, I didn't dare. Nor today. This evening, it's worse, with men patrolling the streets. Do you understand why it is, since the first murder, public opinion has turned against us?'

'It's a phenomenon I've often noted.'

'Why choose us?'

'Whom do you think they suspect? Your father or you?'

'It doesn't matter to them so long as it's one of the family. My mother or aunt would suit them just as well.'

They had to stop talking, for steps were approaching. It was two men with arm-bands, cudgels, who took stock of them as they passed. One of them shone the beam of an electric torch on them and, as they moved off, said in a loud voice to his companion:

'It's Maigret.'

'The other is Vernoux's son.'

'I recognized him.'

The chief-inspector advised his companion:

'You'd better go home.'

'Yes.'

'And don't get involved with them.'

'Thank you.'

'For what?'

'Oh, nothing.'

He didn't hold out his hand. His hat on one side, he went off, bent forward, in the direction of the bridge, and the patrol, which had stopped, watched him pass in silence.

Maigret shrugged his shoulders, went into the hotel and waited for someone to hand him his key. There were two letters for him, probably anonymous, but neither the paper nor the hand-writing was the same.

VI

WHEN he realized it was Sunday, he began to dawdle. Already before this, he had been playing a secret game from his early childhood. He occasionally played it still, in bed beside his wife, taking care that she should guess nothing. And she would be taken in, saying, when she brought him his cup of coffee:

'What were you dreaming of?'

'Why?'

'You were smiling in your sleep.'

This morning, at Fontenay, before opening his eyes, he felt a ray of sunshine passing through his eyelids. He didn't merely feel it. He had the impression of seeing it through the fine skin, which was tingling, and, probably because of the blood circulating there, it was a sun redder than the one in the sky, glorious as in a painting.

He could create a whole world with this sun, showers of sparks, volcanoes, cascades of melted gold. He simply had to keep his eyelids moving lightly like a kaleidoscope, using his lashes as a grid.

He heard pigeons cooing on a cornice above his window, then bells ringing from two directions at once, and he could imagine the steeples pointing up into the sky, which was surely an unclouded blue today.

He went on with his game, all the while listening to the noises in the street, and it was then, from the echo that lingered after footsteps, from a certain quality of the silence, that he recognized it was Sunday.

He hesitated some time before stretching out his arm to reach his watch on the bedside table. It showed half-past nine. In Paris, in the Boulevard Richard-Lenoir, if spring had at last reached there too, Madame Maigret would certainly have opened the windows and tidied the room, in dressing-gown and slippers, while a stew would be simmering on the stove.

He promised himself he would telephone her. As there were no telephones in the bedrooms, he would have to wait until he went down to call her from the telephone booth.

He pressed the electric bell. He thought the chamber-maid looked neater, more jolly than on the day before.

'What would you like to eat?'

'Nothing. I want a lot of coffee.'

She had the same curious way of looking at him.

'Shall I run your bath?'

'Not until I've finished my coffee.'

He lit a pipe, went to open the window. The air was still sharp, he had to put on his dressing-gown, but little waves of warmth could already be felt. The façades of houses and the roads had dried out. The street was deserted, but for now and again a family going by in their Sunday best, a country woman holding a bunch of mauve lilac in her hand.

The life of the hotel must have slowed down for he had to wait a long time for his coffee. He had left the two letters he had received the night before on the bedside table. One of them was signed. The hand-writing was as neat as on an engraving, in black ink like Indian ink.

Are you aware that the widow Gibon was the midwife who delivered Madame Vernoux of her son Alain?
It may be useful to know.
Best wishes.
Anselme Remouchamps.

The second letter, anonymous, had been written on a sheet of paper of excellent quality, the top of which had been cut off, doubtless to remove the heading. It was written in pencil.

Why don't you question the servants? They know more about it than anyone.

When he had read these two lines, the previous evening, before going to bed, Maigret had had an intuition that they had been written by the butler at the Rue Rabelais who had received him without a word and who at his departure had handed him his overcoat. The man, dark complexioned, strongly built, was between forty and fifty years of age. He gave the impression of being a farmer's son who has refused to cultivate the land, and harbours as much hate for rich people as he pours scorn on the peasants from whom he has sprung.

It would probably be easy to obtain a specimen of his hand-writing. Perhaps even the paper was the Vernoux' own?

All this had to be checked. In Paris, the task would have been simple. Here, actually, it was no business of his.

When the chamber-maid came in at last with the coffee, he asked her:

'Are you from Fontenay?'

'I was born in the Rue des Loges.'

'Do you know anyone called Remouchamps?'

'The shoemaker?'

'His Christian name's Anselme.'

'He's the shoe-maker who lives two doors away from my mother, he has a wart on his nose as big as a pigeon's egg.'

'What sort of man is he?'

'He's been a widower for I don't know how many years. I've always known him as a widower. He leers strangely when girls go by to frighten them.'

She looked at him in surprise.

'Do you smoke your pipe before drinking your coffee?'

'You may get my bath ready.'

He went to have it in the bath-room at the end of the corridor and spent a long time in the warm water, day-dreaming. Several times he opened his mouth as if to speak to his wife, who, when he was having a bath, he usually heard going to and fro in the next room.

It was a quarter-past ten when he came downstairs. The hotel proprietor was behind the desk, in consultation with the cook.

'The examining magistrate telephoned twice.'

'At what time?'

'The first time, a little after nine o'clock, the second a few minutes ago. The second time I replied that it wouldn't be long before you were down.'

'May I make a call to Paris?'

'Being Sunday, perhaps it won't take long.'

He gave his number, went to take the air outside the front door. There was no one there, today, to watch him. A cock crowed somewhere, not far off, and one could hear the waters of the Vendée flowing past. When an old woman in a mauve hat came by, he would have sworn he caught a whiff of incense from her clothes.

It was well and truly Sunday.

'Hullo! Is that you?'

'You're still at Fontenay? Are you telephoning from Chabot's? How is his mother?'

Instead of replying, he enquired in turn:

'What's the weather like in Paris?'

'Since midday yesterday it's been spring.'

'Midday yesterday?'

'Yes. It began immediately after lunch.'

He had lost half a day of sunshine!

'And what's it like there?'

'It's fine too.'

'You haven't caught a cold?'

'I'm very well.'

'Are you coming back tomorrow morning?'

'I think so.'

'Aren't you sure? I thought . . .'

'I may be detained a few hours.'

'What with?'

'Some work.'

'You told me . . .'

. . . That he would seize the chance of having a rest, of course! Wasn't he having a rest?

That was practically all. They exchanged the remarks they usually exchanged by telephone.

After which he rang Chabot at his home. Rose answered that the judge had left for the Palais at eight in the morning. He called the Palais de Justice.

'Anything fresh?'

'Yes. They have recovered the weapon. That's why I called you. They told me you were asleep. Can you come up here?'

'I'll be along in a few minutes.'

'The gates are closed. I'll watch out for you at the window and let you in.'

'Has something gone wrong?'

Chabot's voice on the phone seemed dejected.

'I'll talk to you about it.'

Maigret nonetheless took his time. He was determined to savour the Sunday and was soon walking slowly along the Rue de la République, where the Café de la Poste had already set out its chairs and little yellow tables on the terrace.

Two houses farther on, the baker's shop-door was open and Maigret slowed down still more to inhale the sugary smell.

The bells were ringing. There was starting to be more life about the street, roughly opposite Julien Chabot's house. It was the crowd beginning to come out of the half-past ten mass at the church of Notre Dame. It seemed to him that the people were not behaving quite as they would do on other Sundays. There weren't many of the faithful making straight for home.

Groups were forming on the square, who were not arguing noisily but talking in low voices, often quietening down completely as they watched the doors out of which the stream of parishioners was flowing. Even the women were in no hurry, holding their gilt-edged missals in their gloved hands, and almost all of them were wearing bright spring hats.

Outside the porch stood a long, gleaming motor-car, with, standing by its door, a chauffeur in black uniform, whom Maigret recognized as the Vernoux' butler.

Did these people, who lived no more than four hundred yards away, generally drive to High Mass by car? It was possible. It was, perhaps, part of their tradition. It was also possible that they had taken the car today in order to avoid contact with inquisitive people in the streets.

They were just coming out and the white head of Hubert Vernoux stood out above the others. He was walking with slow steps, his hat in his hand. When he reached the top of the steps, Maigret recognized, beside him, his wife, sister-in-law and daughter-in-law.

The crowd dispersed imperceptibly. Strictly speaking they didn't clear the way, but there was, nevertheless, a wide space around them, and all eyes converged on their group.

The chauffeur opened the door. The women entered first. Then Hubert took his place in the front seat and the limousine glided off in the direction of the Place Viète.

Perhaps at that moment, a word uttered by someone in the crowd, a shout, a gesture, would have sufficed to make popular fury assert itself. Anywhere else than at the exit from church it might well have happened. People's faces were hard, and though the clouds had been swept from the sky, there yet remained a sense of unrest in the air.

A few people greeted the chief-inspector timidly. Did they still trust him? They watched as he, in his turn, went up the street, his pipe in his mouth, his shoulders hunched.

He circled round the Place Viète, turned into the Rue Rabelais. Outside the Vernoux' on the opposite pavement, two young men, not yet twenty, were standing guard. They didn't wear arm-bands, carried no cudgels. These accessories seemed reserved for the night patrols. Still they were on duty and they showed themselves proud of it.

One of them raised his cap to Maigret as he went by, but not the other.

Six or seven journalists were grouped on the steps of the Palais de Justice, where the big gates were closed, and Lomel had sat down, his cameras placed beside him.

'Do you think they'll let you in?' he called to Maigret. 'Have you heard the news?'

'What news?'

'It seems they've found the weapon. They're in full session in there.'

The gate half-opened, Chabot signed to Maigret to come in quickly and, as soon as he had passed through, pushed back the gate, as if he feared a mass invasion of reporters.

The corridors were gloomy and all the dampness of the past few weeks clung to the stone walls.

'I should have liked to have spoken to you, privately, first, but it was impossible.'

It was brighter in the judge's office. The public prosecutor was there, sitting in a chair which he was tipping backwards, a cigarette in his mouth. Superintendent Féron was there too, as well as Inspector Chabiron, who could not help throwing Maigret a look at once triumphant and mocking.

On the desk, the chief-inspector saw immediately a piece of lead piping, about nine inches long and two inches in diameter.

'Is that it?'

Everybody nodded in assent.

'No fingerprints?'

'Only some traces of blood and two or three hairs stuck to it.'

The pipe, painted dark green, had once been part of the plumbing in a kitchen or a cellar or garage. It had been cleanly cut off, in all probability by a professional several months before, because the metal had had time to tarnish.

Had the length been cut when someone was removing a sink or some other such fitting? It was possible.

Maigret was on the point of asking where the object had been discovered when Chabot spoke:

'Tell your story, Inspector.'

Chabiron, who was only waiting for the signal, put on a modest look:

'We, in Poitiers, still stick to the good old methods. With the result that I, and my colleague, have questioned everyone living in the street, I've searched in every nook and cranny. A few yards from the place where Gobillard was attacked, there's a big door leading into a yard belonging to a horse-dealer and surrounded by stables. This morning, I was curious enough to go and look there. And, in the midst of the manure all over the ground, I soon found the object you see there. The chances are that the murderer, on hearing footsteps, threw it over the wall.'

'Who examined it for finger-prints?'

'I did. Superintendent Féron helped me. We may not be experts, but we know enough to take finger-prints. It's certain that Gobillard's murderer was wearing gloves. As regards the hairs, we went to the morgue in order to compare them with those of the dead man.'

He concluded with satisfaction:

'They tally.'

Maigret took care not to give any opinion. There was a pause, which the judge finally broke.

'We were in the middle of discussing what it would be best to do now. This discovery appears, at least at first sight, to confirm Emile Chalus' statement.'

Maigret still said nothing.

'If the weapon had not been discovered on those premises, one could have maintained that it was difficult for the doctor to have got rid of it before going to telephone at the Café de la Poste. As the inspector points out with good reason . . .'

Chabiron decided to say what he himself thought:

'Let us suppose that the murderer had, in fact, gone away, having committed his crime, before the arrival of Alain Vernoux, as the latter claims. It is his third crime. The other two times he took the weapon away with him. Not only have we found nothing in the Rue Rabelais, or in the Rue des Loges, but it seems evident that he dealt the blow on all three occasions with the same piece of lead piping.'

Maigret had realized this already, but he deemed it better to let him continue.

'The man had no reason, this last time, to throw the weapon over a wall. He wasn't being followed. Nobody had seen him. But if we admit that the doctor is the murderer, it was essential that he should get rid of such a compromising object before . . .'

'Why tell the authorities?'

'Because that would put him in the clear. He thought no one would suspect the man who gave the alarm.'

This seemed logical too.

'That's not all. As you know very well.'

He had pronounced these last words with a certain embarrassment, because Maigret, without being his immediate superior, was nevertheless a gentleman whom one does not attack directly.

'Go on, Féron.'

The superintendent of police, embarrassed, first of all stubbed out his cigarette in the ash-tray. Chabot, gloomily, avoided looking at his friend. Only the public prosecutor, who looked every now and again at his wrist-watch, seemed like a man with more agreeable things to do.

After a cough, the little police superintendent turned towards Maigret.

'When, yesterday, somebody telephoned me to enquire whether I knew a girl called Sabati . . .'

The chief-inspector realized and was suddenly afraid. He had an unpleasant sensation in his chest and his pipe began to taste nasty.

'. . . I wondered naturally if it had any connection with the case. It only struck me again towards the middle of the afternoon. I was busy. I was on the point of sending one of my men, then I thought I might call to see her on the off-chance, on my way to dinner.'

'Did you go there?'

'I heard you had seen her before me.'

Féron lowered his head, as though it upset him to bring an accusation.

'She told you so?'

'Not straight away. At first she refused to open the door for me and I had to resort to drastic measures.'

'Did you threaten her?'

'I told her she might have to pay dearly for playing such games. She let me in. I noticed her black eye. I asked her who had done it. For over half an hour she kept as tight as a clam, watching me suspiciously. It was then that I decided to take her to the police station, where it's easier to make *them* speak.'

Maigret felt weighed down, not just because of what had happened to Louise Sabati, but because of the police superintendent's attitude. In spite of his hesitations, his apparent humility, the man was fundamentally very proud of what he had done.

One could tell he had blithely set upon this uneducated girl who had no means of defence. Yet he must have come from common stock himself. He had taken it out of one of his own kind.

Almost every word he uttered now, in a voice increasing in assurance, was hateful to hear.

'The fact that she hasn't worked for more than eight months means she is legally without means of support; this was the first thing I pointed out to her. And as she receives a man regularly, that ranks her in the category of prostitutes. She understood. She was afraid. She fought back for a long time. I don't know how you fixed it, but she finally confessed that she had told you all.'

'All what?'

'Her relations with Alain Vernoux, his behaviour, how he fell into
blind rages of passion and beat her black and blue.'

'Did she spend the night in a cell?'

'I released her this morning. It's done her some good.'

'Did she sign her statement?'

'I wouldn't have let her go without that.'

Chabot addressed a look of reproach to his friend.

'I knew nothing of this,' he murmured.

He had probably said so to them already, Maigret had not told him
of his visit to the neighbourhood of the barracks and, now, the judge
probably considered this silence, which put him in an awkward
position, as a betrayal.

Maigret remained outwardly composed. His glance wandered musingly over the little weak-looking superintendent, who seemed to be
waiting for congratulations.

'I suppose you have drawn some conclusions from this story?'

'It puts Doctor Vernoux, at any rate, in a new light. This morning,
early, I interrogated the women neighbours, who confirmed that, at
almost every one of his visits, violent scenes broke out in her rooms, to
such an extent, that several times, they almost called the police.'

'Why didn't they do so?'

'Probably because they thought it was no concern of theirs.'

No! If the women neighbours did not raise the alarm, it was because
it gave them satisfaction that the Sabati girl, who had nothing to do all
day, should be beaten. And, probably, the more Alain hit her, the more
pleased they were.

They might have been sisters of little Superintendent Féron.

'What's become of her now?'

'I instructed her to return home and to consider herself under the
examining magistrate's orders.'

The latter coughed as well.

'Certainly this morning's two discoveries put Alain Vernoux in a
difficult spot.'

'What did he do last night when he left me?'

It was Féron who replied:

'He returned to his home. I'm in touch with the watch committee.
Since I couldn't prevent this committee from forming, I have thought
it best to assure myself of its collaboration. Vernoux returned home
straight away.'

'Does he usually attend mass at half-past ten?'

Chabot, this time, replied.

'He doesn't go to mass at all. He's the only one of the family not to
do so.'

'Did he go out this morning?'

Féron made a vague gesture.

'I don't think so. At half-past nine nothing had as yet been reported to me.'

The public prosecutor at last joined in the conversation, as though he was beginning to feel he had had enough of it.

'All this is getting us nowhere. What we need to know is whether we have enough charges against Alain Vernoux to put him under arrest.'

He stared hard at the magistrate.

'It concerns you, Chabot. It's your responsibility.'

Chabot, in turn, looked at Maigret, whose expression remained solemn and neutral.

Then, instead of replying, the examining magistrate delivered a speech.

'The situation is as follows. For one reason or another, public opinion has pointed to Alain Vernoux, ever since the first murder, that of his uncle Robert de Courçon. I am still wondering on what grounds people have adopted this attitude. Alain Vernoux isn't popular. His family is more or less disliked. Indeed, I've received twenty anonymous letters referring to the house in the Rue Rabelais and accusing me of being in league with the rich people with whom I have social contacts.

'The other two crimes have not lessened these suspicions, far from it. For a long time, Alain Vernoux has been considered by certain people as "a man apart".'

Féron interrupted him:

'The Sabati girl's statement . . .'

'. . . Is damning for him, as is Chalus' statement, now that the weapon has been retrieved. Three crimes in one week is a lot. It's natural that the townspeople are worried and seeking to protect themselves. Up to the present, I have hesitated to act, judging the evidence insufficient. Indeed, as the public prosecutor has just remarked, it's a heavy responsibility. As soon as he is put under arrest, a man of Vernoux's character, even if guilty, will tell nothing.'

He surprised a smile, which was not without irony or bitterness, on Maigret's lips, blushed, lost the thread of his ideas.

'The question is whether it's better to arrest him now or wait for . . .'

Maigret could not help muttering between his teeth:

'They've arrested the Sabati girl and shut her up the whole night, all right!'

Chabot heard him, was about to answer, probably to retort that it wasn't the same thing, but at the last moment changed his mind.

'This morning, because it's a fine Sunday, because of mass, we are experiencing a sort of respite. But already by this time, at their *apéritifs*, in the cafés, people will have started talking again. Some of them, going for a walk, will deliberately go past the Vernoux' house. It's known that I played bridge there yesterday evening and that the chief-inspector accompanied me. It's hard to make them understand . . .'

'Are you going to arrest him?' the public prosecutor enquired, rising to his feet, thinking the beating about the bush had lasted long enough.

'I'm afraid that, as tonight comes on, there may be an incident which could have grave consequences. It needs only the smallest thing, a youngster throwing a stone at the windows, a drunkard starting to shout insults outside the house. In the present state of public feeling . . .'

'Are you going to arrest him?'

The public prosecutor was looking for his hat, couldn't find it. The little superintendent, obsequiously, was saying to him:

'You left it in your study. I'll go and get it for you.'

And Chabot, turning to Maigret, was murmuring:

'What do you think?'

'Nothing.'

'In my shoes, what . . .?'

'I'm not in your shoes.'

'Do you believe the doctor is mad?'

'That depends on what you call mad.'

'That he's the murderer?'

Maigret did not reply, looked for his hat too.

'Wait a moment. I've something to talk to you about. First, I must finish this. It can't be helped if I'm wrong.'

He opened the drawer on the right, took from it a printed form, which he began to fill in, whilst Chabiron threw a look at Maigret more mocking than ever.

Chabiron and the little superintendent had won. The form was a warrant for arrest. Chabot hesitated yet another second on the point of signing it and adding the official stamp.

Then he wondered to which of the two men to hand it. Such an arrest as this had never occurred before in Fontenay.

'I suppose . . .'

At last:

'Anyway, you can both go. As discreetly as possible, so as to avoid demonstrations. You'd better take a car.'

'I've got my own,' Chabiron put in.

It was an unpleasant moment. It seemed, for a few seconds, that everyone felt a little ashamed. Perhaps not so much because they doubted the doctor's guilt, of which they felt pretty sure, but because they knew, deep down in themselves, that it was not on account of his guilt that they were acting, but from fear of public opinion.

'Keep me informed,' muttered the public prosecutor, who went out first and added:

'If I'm not at home, call me at my parents-in-law's house.'

He was going to spend the rest of Sunday with his family. In their turn Féron and Chabiron left, and it was the little superintendent who had the warrant carefully folded in his wallet.

Chabiron retraced his steps, after a glance out of the corridor window, to ask:

'What about the press?'

'Don't say anything to them now. Make for the centre of the town first. You can tell them that I'll have a statement to make them from here in half an hour and they'll stay here.'

'Are we to bring him here?'

'Straight to the prison. In case the crowd should be tempted to lynch him, it will be easier to protect him there.'

All this took some time. They were at last alone. Chabot was not proud of himself.

'What do you think of it?' he decided to enquire. 'D'you think I'm wrong?'

'I am afraid,' admitted Maigret, who was smoking his pipe, looking gloomy.

'Of what?'

He did not reply.

'In all conscience, I couldn't act otherwise.'

'I know. It's not that I am thinking about.'

'About what then?'

He did not want to admit that it was the attitude of the little superintendent towards Louise Sabati that lay heavy on his heart.

Chabot looked at his watch.

'In half an hour, it will be over. We'll be able to go and question him.'

Maigret continued to say nothing, as though he were following God knows what mysterious thoughts.

'Why didn't you tell me about it, yesterday evening?'

'About the Sabati girl?'

'Yes.'

'To try and avoid what's happened.'

'It's happened all the same.'

'Yes. I didn't foresee that Féron would do anything about it.'

'Have you got the letter?'

'Which letter?'

'The anonymous letter I received about her and which I handed to you. Now, I'm obliged to enter it in the file.'

Maigret searched his pockets, found it, crumpled, still damp from last night's rain, and dropped it on the desk.

'Would you mind seeing if the journalists have followed them?'

He went to glance out of the window. The reporters and photographers were still there, looking as if they expected something to happen.

'Have you the right time?'

'Five-past twelve.'

They had not heard the chimes sound. With all the doors shut, they were as though in a cellar there, where not a ray of sun could penetrate.

'I wonder how he will react. I wonder too what his father . . .'

The telephone rang suddenly. Chabot was so taken aback that for a moment he sat still, without answering it, at last muttered, staring at Maigret:

'Hullo . . .'

He frowned, his eyebrows puckered:

'Are you sure?'

Maigret could hear the noise of a loud voice coming from the receiver, without being able to make out the words. It was Chabiron speaking.

'Have you searched the house? Where are you at the moment? Good. Yes. Stay there. I . . .'

He passed his hand over his head in anguish.

'I'll call you back in a few minutes.'

When he hung up, Maigret contented himself with one word.

'Gone?'

'Were you expecting it?'

And, as he didn't reply:

'He returned home last night immediately after leaving you, that we know for certain. He spent the night in his room. This morning, early, he asked for a cup of coffee to be brought up to him.'

'And the newspapers.'

'We have no papers on Sunday.'

'To whom did he speak?'

'I don't know yet. Féron and the inspector are still in the house and questioning the servants. Shortly after ten o'clock the whole family, except Alain, set off for mass in the car, driven by the butler.'

'I saw them.'

'On their return, no one worried about the doctor. It's a house where, except on Saturday evening, everyone lives in his own quarters. When my two men arrived, a maid went up to inform Alain. He wasn't in his room. They called all over the house for him. Do you think he has run away?'

'What does the man on guard in the street say?'

'Féron questioned him. It seems that the doctor left shortly after the rest of the family and went down into the town on foot.'

'Wasn't he followed? I thought . . .'

'I had given instructions he should be followed. Perhaps the police thought that on Sunday morning it wasn't necessary. I don't know. If they don't catch him, they'll make out that I allowed him time to escape on purpose.'

'They'll certainly say so.'

'There's no train before five o'clock this afternoon. Alain hasn't a car.'

'So he can't be very far.'

'You think so?'

'It wouldn't surprise me if they found him at his mistress's. Normally, he slips out to see her only in the evenings, under cover of darkness. But it's three days since he saw her.'

Maigret did not add that Alain knew he had been to see her.

'What's wrong?' the examining magistrate enquired.

'Nothing. I am afraid, that's all. You'd better send them over there.'

Chabot telephoned. After which, both of them sat in silence, face to face, in the office where spring had not yet entered and where the green lamp-shade gave them a sickly look.

VII

WHILE they were waiting, Maigret suddenly had the embarrassing impression that he was watching his friend through a magnifying-glass. Chabot appeared to him even older, more worn-out than when he had arrived the night before last. There was just enough life, energy, personality in him, to lead the kind of existence he had been leading, and when, unexpectedly, as was the case now, he was called upon to make an extra effort, he collapsed, ashamed of his listlessness.

Yet, the chief-inspector was sure it was not just a question of age. He must always have been like that. It was Maigret who had been mistaken, long ago, during the time they had been students and he had been envious of his friend. Chabot had then been for him the symbol of happy adolescence. At Fontenay, a mother, full of little attentions for him, was there to welcome him in a comfortable house, where everything had a robust, permanent appearance. He knew he would inherit, apart from the house, two or three farms and he received enough money each month to be able to lend some to his friends.

Thirty years had passed and Chabot had become what he was bound to become. Today, it was he who was turning to Maigret for help.

The minutes passed. The judge made a pretence of glancing through a file but his eyes were not following the typewritten lines. The telephone still wouldn't ring.

He drew his watch from his pocket.

'It takes only five minutes to get there by car. The same again to return. They should have . . .'

It was a quarter-past twelve. One had to allow the two men a few minutes for going to look in the house.

'If he doesn't confess, and if, in two or three days, I haven't discovered undeniable proof against him, I'll be simply obliged to ask for my retirement to be brought forward.'

He had acted through fear of the bulk of the population. At the moment it was the reactions of the Vernoux and their social equals which frightened him.

'Twenty-past twelve. I wonder what they're doing.'

At twenty-five-past twelve he got up, too nervous to remain sitting down.

'Haven't you got a car?' the chief-inspector asked him.

He seemed embarrassed.

'I had one which I used on Sundays to take my mother for drives in the country.'

It was odd to hear someone speak of the country, living in a town where cows were grazing only five hundred yards from the main street.

'Now that my mother no longer goes out except for Mass on Sunday, what would I do with a car?'

Had he, perhaps, grown mean? It was quite likely. Not so much through his own fault. When one owns a tidy little property like his, one is inevitably scared of losing it.

Maigret felt that, since his arrival in Fontenay, he had come to understand things about which he had never thought, and he was building up a different picture of a small town from that which he had imagined until then.

'Something's certainly happened.'

The two policemen had left more than twenty minutes ago. It wouldn't take long to search Louise Sabati's two-roomed lodgings. Vernoux was not the kind of man to make his escape by a window and it was hard to imagine a manhunt taking place in the streets around the barracks.

There was a moment of hope when they heard the engine of a car climbing the sloping street and the judge stood still, expectant, but the motor passed without stopping.

'I give up.'

He pulled his long fingers, covered with pale hairs, threw brief glances at Maigret as though begging him to reassure him, while the chief-inspector persisted in resting inscrutable.

When, a little after half-past twelve, the telephone rang at last, Chabot literally threw himself at the instrument.

'Hullo!' he cried.

But, immediately, he was discomfited. A woman's voice could be heard, a woman who was probably unused to the telephone and spoke so loud that the chief-inspector could hear her from the other side of the room.

'Is that the judge?' she asked.

'Yes, the examining magistrate, Chabot. Speaking.'

She repeated in the same tone of voice:

'Is it the judge?'

'Yes, of course! What is it you want?'

'You are the judge?'

And he, furious:

'Yes. I am the judge. Can't you hear me?'

'No.'

'What do you want?'

If she had asked him once more if he was the judge, he would probably have thrown the instrument on the floor.

'The superintendent wants you to come.'

'What do you mean?'

But now, speaking to someone else, in the room from where she was telephoning, she said in a different voice:

'I've told him. What?'

Someone ordered:

'Hang up.'

'Hang up what?'

A noise was heard in the Palais de Justice. Chabot and Maigret pricked up their ears.

'Someone knocking loudly at the door.'

'Come on.'

They ran down the corridors. The knocks redoubled. Chabot hurriedly pulled the bolt and turned the key in the lock.

'Did they ring you?'

It was Lomel, in the midst of three or four of his colleagues. They could see others going up the street in the direction of the open country.

'Chabiron has just gone past, driving his car. There was an unconscious woman beside him. He must have been taking her to hospital.'

A car was parked at the foot of the steps.

'Whose is that?'

'Mine, or rather my newspaper's,' said a Bordeaux reporter.

'Will you drive us?'

'To the hospital?'

'No. First of all, go down to the Rue de la République. Turn right, towards the barracks.'

They all piled into the car. Outside the Vernoux' house, a score of people had gathered, who watched them pass in silence.

'What's happening, judge?' Lomel enquired.

'I don't know. An arrest should have been made.'

'The doctor?'

He hadn't the courage to say no, to carry on a battle of wits. A few people were sitting on the terrace of the Café de la Poste. A woman, in her Sunday clothes, was coming out of the pastry-shop with a white cardboard box suspended from her finger by a piece of red string.

'That way?'

'Yes. Now, to the left . . . Wait . . . Turn just past that building . . .'

There was no mistaking it. Outside the house, in which Louise had her rooms, it was swarming with people, mostly women and children, who rushed to the car-doors when it stopped. The fat woman who had answered Maigret the evening before, stood in the front row, her hands on her hips.

'It was me who went to 'phone you from the grocer's. The super-intendent's upstairs.'

It was developing into confusion. The little company of people went round to the back of the house; Maigret, who knew the way, took the lead.

The onlookers, more numerous on this side, were blocking the outside door. There were even some of them on the stairs, at the top of which the little police superintendent had been obliged to mount guard in front of the broken-down door.

'Make room . . . Stand aside . . .'

Féron's face had fallen, his hair over his forehead. He had lost his hat somewhere. He seemed relieved that he had been rescued.

'Have you told the police station to send me help?'

'I didn't know that . . .' the judge began to say.

'I instructed that woman to tell you . . .'

The newspapermen were trying to take photographs. A baby was crying. Chabot, whom Maigret had made go ahead, reached the last few steps as he asked:

'What's going on?'

'He's dead.'

He pushed the wooden door, which had been partly shattered.

'In the bedroom.'

The room was in disorder. Sunshine and flies were entering through the open window.

On the unmade bed, Doctor Alain Vernoux was lying, fully dressed, his spectacles on the pillow next to his face, which already looked bloodless.

'Tell us, Féron.'

'There's nothing to tell. We arrived, the inspector and I, and were shown to this staircase. We knocked. As no one answered, I issued the usual orders. Chabiron used his shoulder two or three times on the door. We found him just as he is, where he is. I tested his pulse. It was no longer beating. I place a mirror in front of his mouth.'

'And the girl?'

'She was on the floor, as though she had slipped off the bed, and she had been sick.'

They were all treading on what she had thrown up.

'She wasn't moving, but she wasn't dead. There's no telephone in the house. I couldn't run round the neighbourhood searching for one. Chabiron carried her over his shoulder and took her off to hospital. There was nothing else to do.'

'You are sure she was breathing?'

'Yes, with a strange rattle in her throat.'

The photographers were still busy. Lomel was taking notes in a little red book.

'The whole building descended on me. At one time, some kids managed to slink their way into the room. I couldn't leave here. I wanted to warn you. I sent the woman who appears to act as concierge, instructing her to tell you . . .'

Indicating the disorder around him, he added:

'I haven't even glanced over the rooms.'

It was one of the journalists who held up an empty tube of veronal. 'Anyway, there's this.'

It was the explanation. As far as Alain Vernoux was concerned, it was surely a case of suicide.

Had he persuaded Louise to kill herself with him? Had he administered the drug to her without saying anything?

In the kitchen, a bowl of coffee still contained some liquid at the bottom and they saw a bit of cheese beside a slice of bread, with a piece bitten out of the bread by the girl.

She used to get up late, Alain Vernoux must have found her in the middle of eating her breakfast.

'Was she dressed?'

'In her nightdress. Chabiron rolled her up in a blanket and carried her off like that.'

'The neighbours didn't hear a quarrel?'

'I haven't been able to question them. The kids are always hanging around in front and the mothers do nothing to shift them away. Listen to them.'

One of the journalists had his back against the door, which could no longer be shut, to stop it being pushed from outside.

Julien Chabot was going to and fro as if in a bad dream, like a man who has lost control of the situation.

Two or three times, he went over to the corpse before daring to put his hand on the dangling wrist.

He repeated several times, forgetting he had already said it, or determined to convince himself:

'It's obviously suicide.'

Then he asked:

'Shouldn't Chabiron be coming back?'

'I presume he'll stay there to question the girl if she recovers consciousness. He would have had to notify the police station. Chabiron promised to send me a doctor . . .'

Here he was, knocking on the door, a young interne who went straight over to the bed.

'Dead?'

He nodded his head.

'What about the girl who was brought to you?'

'They're seeing to her. She's got a chance of pulling through.'

He looked at the tube, shrugged his shoulders, muttered:

'Always the same stuff.'

'How is it he's dead, if she . . .'

He pointed to the vomit on the floor.

One of the reporters, who had disappeared without anyone noticing, came back into the room.

'There wasn't a quarrel,' he said. 'I've questioned the neighbours. They can be all the more sure about it because most rooms had their windows open this morning.'

Lomel himself was unabashedly rummaging through the drawers, which didn't contain much, underclothes and cheap dresses, knick-knacks of no value. Then he bent down to look under the bed, and Maigret saw him lie flat on the ground, stretch out his arm, bring out a cardboard shoe-box, with a blue ribbon round it. Lomel withdrew to one side with his find, and there was enough confusion for him to be left alone in peace.

It was only Maigret who went up to him.

'What is it?'

'Some letters.'

The box was practically full of them, not only letters but brief notes, written in haste on scraps of paper. Louise Sabati had kept everything, perhaps unbeknown to her lover, almost certainly so in fact, otherwise she wouldn't have hidden the box under the bed.

'Let me see.'

Lomel seemed affected as he read them. He said in a rather unsure voice:

'They're love letters.'

The judge noticed at last what was going on.

'Letters?'

'Love letters.'

'From whom?'

'From Alain. Signed with his Christian name, sometimes only with his initials.'

Maigret, who had read two or three of them, would have liked to stop them being passed around from hand to hand. They were probably the most moving love letters he had ever been privileged to read. The doctor had written them with the ardour and sometimes the naïveté of a young man of twenty.

He called Louise '*My little girl*'.

Sometimes: '*My own poor little girl*.'

And he would tell her, as all lovers do, about the long days and nights without her, the emptiness of his life, the house where, like a hornet, he would bang himself against the walls, he told her he wished he could have known her earlier, before any man had touched her, and of the rages that took hold of him, in the evenings, alone in his bed, when he thought of the caresses she had submitted to.

In certain places, he addressed her like an irresponsible child, and in others he gave way to cries of hate and despair.

'Gentlemen . . .' Maigret began, with a lump in his throat.

They paid no attention to him. It was none of his business. Chabot, blushing, his glasses misty, continued to look through the sheets of paper.

I left you half an hour ago and have regained my prison. I need your touch again . . .

He had known her a bare eight months. There were nearly two hundred letters there, and on certain days, he had written three, one after the other. Some of them had no stamp. He must have brought them with him.

If I were a real man . . .

It was a relief to Maigret when he heard the arrival of the police, moving aside the crowd and the kids.

'You'd better take them with you,' he whispered to his friend.

They had to be collected from everyone. The men seemed embarrassed as they handed them over. They hesitated now to turn towards the bed, and when they did glance at the outstretched body, it was only furtively, as though to apologize.

As he was now, without his glasses, his face relaxed and serene, Alain Vernoux looked ten years younger than when alive.

'My mother must be getting anxious . . .' Chabot remarked, looking at his watch.

He was forgetting about the house in the Rue Rabelais, where there was a whole family, a father, a mother, a wife, children, whom he would have to bring himself to inform.

Maigret reminded him. The judge murmured:

'I would much sooner not go there myself.'

The chief-inspector did not like to offer to do so himself. Perhaps his friend, on his side, did not like to ask him.

'I shall send Féron.'

'Where?' asked the latter.

'To the Rue Rabelais, to inform them. Speak to the father first.'

'What shall I tell him?'

'The truth.'

The little superintendent muttered under his breath:

'That's a nice job!'

They had nothing more to do here. No more to discover in the room of a poor girl, whose sole treasure consisted in a box of letters. Probably she hadn't understood them all. It didn't matter.

'Are you coming, Maigret?'

And, to the doctor:

'Will you take charge of moving the body?'

'To the morgue?'

'A post-mortem will be necessary. I don't see how . . .'

He turned to the two policemen.

'Don't let anyone enter.'

He went down the stairs, the cardboard box under his arm, and had to squeeze his way through the crowd gathered below. He hadn't considered the question of a car. They were on the far side of the town. Of his own accord, the Bordeaux journalist hurried forward.

'Where would you like me to drive you?'

'To my home.'

'In the Rue Clemenceau?'

For the most part, they made the journey in silence. Only when they were a hundred yards from his house, did Chabot murmur:

'I suppose that's the end of the case.'

He couldn't have been too sure, because he examined Maigret out of the corner of his eye. And the latter gave no sign of concurrence, said neither yes nor no.

'I can see no reason, if he wasn't guilty, for . . .'

He stopped short, because, on hearing the car, his mother, who must have been consumed with impatience, was already opening the door.

'I was wondering what had happened. I saw people running as though something was going on.'

He thanked the reporter, felt he had to offer him something:

'A brandy?'

'No, thanks. I must telephone my paper quickly.'

'The joint will be overcooked. I was expecting you at half-past twelve. You look tired, Julien. Don't you think, Jules, that he looks pale?'

'You must leave us for a moment, Mother.'

'Don't you want to eat?'

'Not straight away.'

She clutched hold of Maigret.

'Is there anything wrong?'

'Nothing to worry you.'

He preferred to tell her the truth, or at least part of the truth.

'Alain Vernoux has committed suicide.'

She simply said:

'Ah!'

Then, shaking her head, she went off to the kitchen.

'Let's go into my study. Unless you are hungry?'

'No.'

'Help yourself to a drink.'

He would have liked a glass of beer, but he knew there was none in the house. He looked in the liqueur cupboard, took out, at random, a bottle of pernod.

'Rose will bring you water and ice.'

Chabot had collapsed into his armchair where his father's head, before his own, had worn a darker patch in the leather. The shoe-box was on the desk, with the ribbon which had been re-tied.

The judge urgently needed to be reassured. His nerves were on edge.

'Why don't you take a little brandy?'

From the way Chabot glanced at the door, Maigret realized that it was at his mother's wish that he had given up drinking.

'I prefer not to.'

'As you please.'

In spite of the mild temperature that day, a fire continued to blaze in the hearth, and Maigret, who was too hot, had to move away from it.

'What do you think of it?'

'Of what?'

'Of what he's done. Why, if he were not guilty . . .'

'You read some of his letters, didn't you?'

Chabot lowered his head.

'Superintendent Féron invaded Louise's rooms yesterday, questioned her, took her to the police station, kept her all night in a cell.'

'He acted without my instructions.'

'I know. He did it, all the same. This morning, Alain hurried to see her and learnt everything.'

'I don't see what difference that made.'

He could tell very well, but was refusing to admit it.

'You think it's because of that . . .?'

'I think that was enough. Tomorrow, the whole town would have known. Féron would probably have gone on badgering the girl, they would have finally condemned her on grounds of prostitution.'

'He has been imprudent. But it's not a reason for taking one's own life.'

'It depends who you are.'

'You're convinced he is not guilty.'

'And you?'

'I think that everyone will believe him guilty and be satisfied.'

Maigret looked at him in surprise.

'You mean to say you're going to close the case?'

'I don't know. I just don't know any more.'

'Do you remember what Alain told us?'

'What about?'

'That a lunatic has his own logic. A lunatic, who's lived all his life without anyone perceiving his madness, does not set out all of a sudden to kill without reason. There must be a provocation at least. There must be a cause, which may appear insufficient to a person in his senses, but which appears sufficient to him.

'Robert de Courçon was the first victim, and, in my opinion, that's the one which counts, because it's the only one which might provide us with a clue.

'Public opinion doesn't just spring up out of nothing, either.'

'You trust the ideas of the masses?'

'It can be mistaken in its demonstrations. However, almost always, I've been able to recognize over the course of the years, that there's some serious foundation for it. I would say that the masses have an instinct . . .'

'So that it really is Alain . . .'

'I haven't come to that yet. When Robert de Courçon was killed, the townspeople associated the two houses in the Rue Rabelais, and, at that time, there was no question of madness. Courçon's murder was not necessarily the deed of a madman or a maniac. It was possible there were precise reasons for someone deciding to kill him, or to do it in a moment of anger.'

'Carry on.'

Chabot was giving up the struggle. Maigret could have told him anything, and he would have concurred. He felt that his career, his life, was in process of being destroyed.

'I know no more than you. There have been two more crimes, one after the other, both inexplicable, both carried out in the same manner, as if the murderer meant to emphasize there was only one and the selfsame guilty party.'

'I thought that criminals generally kept to one method, always the same.'

'I'm wondering, myself, why he was in such a hurry.'

'In such a hurry over what?'

'To kill once more. Then to kill yet again. As though to establish fully, in the public mind, that a criminal lunatic was going about the streets.'

At this, Chabot raised his head sharply.

'You mean it's not a lunatic?'

'Not exactly.'

'Well?'

'It's a question I'm sorry I didn't discuss more thoroughly with Alain Vernoux. The little that he told us about it sticks in my mind. Even a lunatic does not necessarily act like a lunatic.'

'That's obvious. Otherwise, there would be none left at large.'

'Nor is it, necessarily, because he's a lunatic that he kills.'

'I don't follow you any more. What's your conclusion?'

'I've come to no conclusion.'

16*

They jumped when they heard the telephone. Chabot lifted the receiver, changed his attitude, his voice.

'But of course, Madame. He is here. I'll pass him on to you.'

And, to Maigret:

'Your wife.'

She was saying at the other end of the line:

'Is that you? I'm not disturbing your lunch? Are you still at the table?'

'No.'

It served no purpose to tell her he had not yet eaten.

'Your chief 'phoned me half an hour ago and asked me if you were definitely returning tomorrow morning. I didn't know what to reply, because when you telephoned me you didn't seem certain. He told me, if I was 'phoning you again, to inform you that the daughter of some senator or other disappeared two days ago. It's not yet in the newspapers. It seems that it's very important, that there's some risk of a scandal. Do you know who it is?'

'No.'

'He gave a name, but I've forgotten it.'

'In fact, he wants me to return without fail?'

'He didn't put it quite like that. But I gathered he'd be glad if you'd take charge of the case yourself.'

'Is it raining?'

'It's wonderful weather. What are you going to decide?'

'I shall do my utmost to be in Paris by tomorrow morning. There must surely be a night train. I haven't yet looked in the time-table.'

Chabot signed to him that there was a night train.

'Is everything going well at Fontenay?'

'Everything's going well.'

'Give my regards to the judge.'

'I shan't forget.'

When he had hung up, he couldn't have told whether his friend was dejected or delighted to find that he was leaving.

'You have to return?'

'It would be best.'

'Perhaps it's time we went to luncheon?'

Maigret left the white box, which affected him somewhat as a coffin might, with regret.

'Don't let's mention any of this in front of my mother.'

They had not yet reached the dessert when there was a ring at the door. Rose went to open it, came back to announce:

'It's the superintendent of police asking for . . .'

'Show him into my study.'

'I have done that. He's waiting. He says it's not urgent.'

Madame Chabot was making an effort to talk of one thing or another as if nothing were going on. She dug up names from her memory, people who were dead, or who had left the town a long time ago, whose history she reeled off.

At last they got up from the table.

'Shall I have the coffee brought to your study?'

It was served to all three men, and Rose placed glasses and the bottle of brandy on the tray with an almost ritual gesture. They had to wait for the door to be shut again.

'Well?'

'I went there.'

'A cigar?'

'No, thanks. I haven't had lunch yet.'

'Would you like me to order something for you?'

'I rang my wife to say I wouldn't be long coming home.'

'How did it go?'

'The butler opened the door to me and I asked him if I could see Hubert Vernoux. He left me in the passage while he went to inform him. It took a long time. A boy of seven or eight came to look at me from the top of the stairs, and I heard his mother's voice calling him. Someone else observed me through the crack of a door, an old woman, but I don't know if it was Madame Vernoux or her sister.'

'What did Vernoux say?'

'He appeared from the end of the passage and, when he was three or four yards from me, he enquired, still coming forward:

' "Have you found him?"

'I told him I had bad news for him. He didn't invite me into the drawing-room, left me standing on the mat, looking at me from his full height, but I could see clearly that his lips and fingers were trembling.

' "Your son is dead," I eventually told him.

'And he replied:

' "You've killed him?"

' "He committed suicide, this morning, in his mistress's room." '

'Did he seem surprised?' asked the examining magistrate.

'It seemed to me that it gave him a shock. He looked as though he was about to ask a question, but merely murmured:

' "So he did have a mistress!"

'He didn't ask me who she was, nor what had become of her. He went towards the door to open it, and his last words, on ushering me out, were:

' "Now, perhaps, these people will leave us in peace."

'He jerked his chin towards the onlookers gathered on the pavement, the groups standing on the other side of the street, the journalists who were taking advantage of the moment he stood on the doorstep to photograph him.'

'He didn't try to avoid them?'

'On the contrary. When he saw them, he paused, facing them squarely, looking them in the eyes, then, slowly, he closed the door, and I
heard him fasten the bolts.'

'How's the girl?'

'I called in at the hospital. Chabiron is still at her bedside. They aren't
sure yet whether she will pull through, because of something wrong
with her heart.'

Without touching his coffee, he gulped down his glass of brandy, rose
to his feet.

'May I go and eat now?'

Chabot nodded and rose in his turn to see him out.

'What shall I do next?'

'I don't know yet. Call in at my office. The public prosecutor's
meeting me there at three o'clock.'

'Just in case, I've left two men outside the house in the Rue Rabelais.
The crowd's filing by, stopping, arguing in low voices.'

'Is it quiet?'

'Now that Alain Vernoux's committed suicide, I don't think there's
any more danger. You know how it is.'

Chabot looked at Maigret as though to say:

'You see!'

He would have given anything for his friend to have replied:

'Of course. It's all over.'

Only, Maigret made no reply.

VIII

A LITTLE before the bridge, as he was coming down from the Chabots'
house, Maigret had turned to the right and, for the past ten minutes,
he had been following a long road which was neither in the town nor in
the country.

To start with, the houses, white, red, grey, including the large residence and storehouses of a wine merchant, were still attached one to
another, but it didn't bear the stamp of the Rue de la République, for
instance, and some of them, whitewashed, without an upper floor, were
almost cottages.

Then there had been some gaps, alleyways which allowed glimpses of
kitchen gardens descending the slight slope towards the river, once or
twice a white goat attached to a stake.

He hardly encountered a soul on the pavements, but through
open doors he noticed, in the half-light, families seemingly motionless,

listening to the wireless or eating pastries, or else a man in his shirt-
sleeves reading the newspaper, somewhere else again a little old woman
dozing beside a grandfather clock with a copper pendulum.

Little by little, the gardens encroached more and more, the gaps
between the walls grew wider, the Vendée curved in close to the road,
bringing down with it the broken branches from the last squalls.

Maigret, who had refused to let himself be driven by car, was starting
to regret it, for he hadn't thought it was such a long way, and the sun
was already hot on the back of his neck. He took almost half an hour to
reach the Gros-Noyer crossroads, beyond which there seemed to be
only meadows.

Three young men dressed in navy-blue, their hair oiled, who were
leaning against the door of an inn and probably did not know who he
was, looked at him with the aggressive irony of peasants for the town-
dweller who has strayed amongst them.

'Madame Page's house?' he asked them.

'You mean Léontine's?'

'I don't know her Christian name.'

That was enough to set them laughing. They found it odd that anyone shouldn't know Léontine's Christian name.

'If you mean her, try that door over there.'

The house they pointed out to him consisted only of a ground floor, so
low that Maigret could touch the roof with his hand. The door, painted
green, was divided in two, like some stable doors, the upper part being
open, the lower closed.

At first, he saw no one in the kitchen, which was very clean, with a
white earthenware stove, a round table covered with a check oilcloth,
some lilac in a multi-coloured vase, doubtless won at a fair; the mantelpiece was crowded with knick-knacks and photographs.

He pulled a little bell hanging from a piece of string.

'What is it?'

Maigret saw her come out of the bedroom through a door on the
left: these were the only rooms in the house. The woman could have
been anything from fifty to sixty-five years old. As dry and hard as the
chamber-maid in the hotel had been, she looked him over with peasant-
like mistrust, without coming to the door.

'What do you want?'

Then straight away:

'Isn't there a photograph of you in the newspaper?'

Maigret heard someone move in the room. A man's voice enquired:

'Who is it, Léontine?'

'The chief-inspector from Paris.'

'Chief-Inspector Maigret?'

'I think that's his name.'

'Ask him to come in.'

Without moving, she repeated:

'Come in.'

He himself lifted the latch to open the lower part of the door. Léontine did not invite him to sit down, said nothing to him.

'You were Robert de Courçon's housekeeper, weren't you?'

'For fifteen years. The police and journalists have already asked me all sorts of questions. I know nothing.'

From where he was, the chief-inspector could now see a white bedroom with the walls adorned with coloured prints, the foot of a high walnut bed topped by a red eiderdown and the smoke of a pipe which reached his nostrils. The man was still moving about.

'I want to see what he looks like . . .' he was muttering.

And she, to Maigret, in an unfriendly voice:

'Did you hear what my husband said? Go in. He can't leave his bed.'

Sitting there, was a man whose face was covered in a beard; newspapers and popular novels were strewn around him. He was smoking a clay pipe with a long stem and, on the bedside table, within reach of his arm, was a litre of white wine and a glass.

'It's his legs,' explained Léontine. 'Ever since he was jammed between the buffers of two trucks. He used to work on the railway. It affected his bones.'

The lace curtains softened the light and two pots of geraniums brightened up the window-sill.

'I've read all the stories they tell about you, Monsieur Maigret. I read all day. I never used to read before. Bring a glass, Léontine.'

Maigret could not refuse. He clinked glasses. Then, taking advantage of the fact that the wife was still in the room, he brought out of his pocket the bit of lead piping which he had managed to be allowed to take with him.

'Do you recognize this?'

She did not turn a hair. She said:

'Of course.'

'Where did you last see it?'

'On the big drawing-room table.'

'At Robert de Courçon's?'

'At the master's place, yes. It was left over from the repairs, when part of the plumbing had to be changed, last winter, because the frost had burst the water-pipes.'

'He kept this bit of pipe on his table?'

'All sorts of things were there. It was called the drawing-room, but it was the room in which he spent all his time and where he worked.'

'You did his housework?'

'As much as he allowed me to do, sweep the floor, dust — but without moving a thing! — and wash the dishes.'

'He was a bit dotty.'

'I didn't say that.'

'You can tell the chief-inspector,' her husband whispered to her.

'I've no complaints to make about him.'

'Except there were months when you weren't paid.'

'It wasn't his fault. If the others, opposite, had given him the money they owed him . . .'

'You weren't tempted to throw away this pipe?'

'I tried to. He told me to leave it where it was. He used it as a paper-weight. I remember he added that it might be useful if burglars tried to break into his house. It was a funny idea, because there were lots of guns on the walls. He collected them.'

'Is it true, Chief-Inspector, that his nephew's killed himself?'

'It's true.'

'Do you think he's the murderer? Have another glass of wine? As far as I'm concerned, as I was telling my wife, I don't try to understand these rich folk. They don't think, they don't feel like us.'

'Did you know the Vernoux?'

'Like anyone else, from meeting them in the street. I've heard it said their money's run out, that they'd even borrowed from their servants, and that's probably true since Léontine's boss wasn't getting his allowance any longer and couldn't pay her.'

His wife was signing to him not to talk so much. He hadn't much to say, anyway, but he was glad to have company and to meet Chief-Inspector Maigret in the flesh.

The latter left them with a slightly sour taste in his mouth, from the white wine. On his walk back, he found few people about. Some young men and girls on bicycles were returning to the country. A few families were slowly making their way into town.

They were probably still in conference, at the Palais, in the judge's office. Maigret had refused to join them, because he did not want to influence the decision they were going to make.

Would they decide to close the inquiry and take the doctor's suicide as an admission of guilt?

It was most likely and, in that case, Chabot would feel a sense of remorse to the end of his life.

When he reached the Rue Clemenceau and could see right down the length of the Rue de la République, there was quite a crowd, people were walking on both pavements, others were coming out of the cinema, and, on the terrace of the Café de la Poste, all the chairs were occupied. The sun was already taking on the pinkish hues of sunset.

He made for the Place Viète, passed his friend's house, where he caught sight of Madame Chabot behind the first-floor windows. In the Rue Rabelais, some inquisitive onlookers were still posted in front of the Vernoux' house, but, perhaps because there had been a death in the household, people kept at a respectful distance, most of them on the opposite pavement.

Maigret repeated to himself once more that this case was no concern of his, that he had a train to catch that same evening, that he was running the risk of upsetting everyone and falling out with his friend.

After which, incapable of resisting, he reached up his hand to the door-knocker. He had to wait a long time, in full view of the passers-by, before he at last heard footsteps and the butler half-opened one side of the door.

'I'd like to see Monsieur Hubert Vernoux.'

'Monsieur can't see anyone.'

Maigret had entered without being asked. The hall was still in half-darkness. No noise could be heard.

'Is he in his rooms?'

'I think he's lying down.'

'One question: do the windows of your room look onto the street?'

The butler seemed uneasy, spoke in a low voice.

'Yes. From the third floor. My wife and I sleep in the attics.'

'And you can see the house opposite?'

Though they had heard nothing, the drawing-room door opened and Maigret recognized the figure of the sister-in-law in the gap.

'What is it, Arsène?'

She had seen the chief-inspector but did not address him.

'I was telling Monsieur Maigret that Monsieur can't see anyone.'

She finally turned to him.

'You would like to speak to my brother-in-law?'

She resigned herself to opening the door wider.

'Come in.'

She was alone in the vast drawing-room, with the curtains drawn; one lamp only was alight on a small table. There was no book open, no newspaper, no piece of needlework nor anything else. She must have been sitting there, doing nothing, when he had raised the knocker.

'I can receive you instead of him.'

'It's him I wish to see.'

'Even if you go to his room he probably won't be in a state to answer your questions.'

She walked over to the table where there were a number of bottles, picked up one of them which had contained Marc de Bourgogne and was now empty.

'It was half-full at midday. He wasn't more than a quarter of an hour in this room, while we were still at table.'

'Does this often happen?'

'Practically every day. Now he will sleep until five or six and then he will be glassy-eyed. My sister and I have tried to lock up the bottles, but he finds ways to get round it. It's better it should happen here than in some bar or other.'

'Does he go to bars now and again?'

'How could we tell? He goes out by the little door, without our knowing, and then later, when we see his big eyes, when he begins to stammer, it's obvious what it means. He'll end up like his father.'

'Has this been going on for a long time?'

'For years. Perhaps he drank before too, and it had less effect on him. He doesn't look his age, but he's sixty-seven after all.'

'I'm going to ask the butler to take me to him.'

'Won't you come back later on?'

'I am going back to Paris this evening.'

She realised it was useless to argue and pressed a bell. Arsène appeared:

'Take the chief-inspector to Monsieur.'

Arsène looked at her, surprised, as though asking her if she had thought it over.

'We can't help what happens!'

Without the butler, Maigret would have lost himself in the large, echoing passages inter-crossing like those of a convent. He glimpsed a kitchen where copper pots were gleaming and where, as at Le Gros-Noyer, a bottle of white wine was standing on the table, doubtless Arsène's bottle.

The latter seemed not to be able to understand Maigret's attitude any more. Since the question on the subject of his room, he had been expecting a veritable interrogation. Yet he was being asked nothing.

In the right wing of the ground floor he knocked at a carved-oak door.

'It's me, Monsieur!' he said, raising his voice so as to be ard inside.

And, as they heard a groan:

'The chief-inspector is with me and insists on seeing you, Monsieur.'

They stood there without moving, while someone moved about the room, and eventually opened the door a crack.

The sister-in-law had not been mistaken when she spoke of his big eyes, which fixed on the chief-inspector in a sort of stupor.

'It's you!' Hubert Vernoux stammered out, in a thick voice.

He must have been lying down completely dressed. His clothes were crumpled, his white hair fell down over his forehead and he passed his hand over it in a mechanical gesture.

'What do you want?'

'I would be glad of an interview with you.'

It was difficult to turn him away. As though he had not yet recovered his senses, Vernoux drew aside. The room was very large, with a canopied bed of carved wood, very dark, with faded silk draperies.

All the furniture was antique, nearly all of the same style, and made one think of a chapel or a sacristy.

'Will you excuse me a moment?'

Vernoux went through into a bathroom, ran himself a glass of water and gargled. On returning, he already seemed a little better.

'Sit down. In this armchair if you wish. Have you seen someone?'

'Your sister-in-law.'

'She told you I had been drinking?'

'She showed me the bottle of marc.'

He shrugged his shoulders.

'Still the same old story. Women can't understand. A man who's just been brutally informed that his son . . .'

His eyes moistened with tears. The tone of his voice had lowered, almost to a whimper.

'It's a hard blow, Chief-Inspector. Especially since he was the only son. What's his mother doing?'

'I've no idea . . .'

'She will fall ill. It's her little trick. She falls ill and one daren't say anything to her after that. Do you understand? Then, her sister takes her place: she calls it taking charge of the house . . .'

He reminded one of an old actor trying, at all costs, to stir one's emotions. On his slightly puffed face, the features changed expression at an astonishing rate. In the course of a few minutes, he had successively expressed boredom, a kind of fear, then paternal grief and bitterness with regard to the two women. Now it was fear returning to the surface.

'Why have you insisted on seeing me?'

Maigret, who had not sat down in the armchair indicated to him, took the piece of piping out of his pocket and placed it on the table.

'. . . you often visit your brother-in-law?'

'About once a month, to take him his money. I suppose they've heard that I made him a living allowance?'

'Then you've seen this piece of piping on his desk?'

He hesitated, realizing that the reply to this question was of vital importance, and also that he had to make a rapid decision.

'I think I have.'

'It's the only material clue they've got in this case. Up to now, they don't seem to have grasped its full significance.'

He sat down, took his pipe out of his pocket and filled it. Vernoux remained standing, his features drawn as though he had a violent headache.

'Will you listen to me for a while?'

Without waiting for a reply, he carried on:

'It has been asserted that there were three, pretty well identical crimes, without it being noticed that the first one is, in fact, completely different from the others. The widow Gibon, like Gobillard too, was

killed in cold blood, with premeditation. The man who rang at the
former midwife's door went there in order to kill her and did it without
waiting in the passage. On the doorstep, he already had his weapon
in his hand. When, two days later, he attacked Gobillard, he may not
have had him in mind particularly, but he was out of doors in order to
kill. Do you understand what I mean?'

Vernoux, at any rate, was making an almost painful effort, to guess
what Maigret was trying to get at.

'The Courçon case is a different one. On entering his house, the
murderer had no weapons. We may deduce from that that he did not
come with homicidal intentions. Something occurred, which drove him
to the deed. Perhaps Courçon's attitude, often provocative, maybe even
a threatening move on his part?'

Maigret interrupted himself to strike a match and draw on his pipe.

'What do you think of it?'

'Of what?'

'Of my reasoning.'

'I thought this case was ended.'

'Even supposing it were, I'm trying to understand it.'

'A madman would not worry himself over these considerations.'

'And if it were not a mandman, at any rate not a madman in the
usual sense of the word? Listen to me a moment more. Someone calls to
see Robert de Courçon, in the evening, without concealing his identity,
since he hasn't yet any evil intent, and, for reasons we don't know, is
driven to kill him. He leaves no trace behind him, takes the weapon
away, which indicates that he doesn't want to be caught.

'It must, therefore, be a man who knows the victim, who's in the
habit of going to see him at that time of night.

'The police are bound to search along these lines.

'And there's every chance they'll find the culprit.'

Vernoux looked at him with an air of reflection, as though weighing
the pros and cons.

'Let us now suppose that another crime is committed, at the other
end of the town, on someone who has nothing to do with the murderer
nor with Courçon. What's going to happen?'

The man did not entirely repress a smile. Maigret continued:

'They will not *necessarily* search amongst the acquaintances of the
first victim. The idea which will occur to everybody is that it's a case of
madness.'

He was silent for a while.

'That is what happened. And the murderer, as an extra safeguard, in
order to strengthen the theory of madness, committed a third crime, in
the street this time, on the first drunkard he happened to meet. The
judge, the public prosecutor, the police all fell for it.'

'Not you?'

'I wasn't the only one to disbelieve it. Sometimes public opinion is mistaken. Often, too, it has the same kind of intuition as women and children.'

'You mean it pointed to my son?'

'It pointed to this house.'

He rose, without pursuing the matter, went towards a Louis XIII table, which served as a desk and on which some writing-paper was lying on a blotting-pad. He took one of the sheets, drew a piece of paper from his pocket.

'Arsène wrote,' he remarked negligently.

'My butler?'

Vernoux approached quickly, and Maigret noticed that, in spite of his corpulence, he had the lightness of movement that fat men frequently display.

'He wants to be questioned. But he doesn't dare come of his own accord to the police or to the Palais de Justice.'

'Arsène knows nothing.'

'Maybe, though his room looks onto the street.'

'Have you spoken to him?'

'Not yet. I wonder if he bears you a grudge for not paying his wages and having borrowed money from him.'

'You know that too?'

'Have you nothing to tell me yourself, Monsieur Vernoux?'

'What could I tell you? My son . . .'

'Let's not talk about your son. I suppose you've never been happy?'

He did not reply, gazed at the dark, floral carpet.

'So long as you had money, the satisfaction of your vanity was enough for you. After all, you were the rich man of the place.'

'These are personal questions I don't like discussed.'

'Have you lost a lot of money, in the last few years?'

Maigret adopted a lighter tone, as though what he was saying was of no importance.

'Contrary to what you are thinking, the case is not finished and the inquiry remains open. Up to now, for reasons which are no business of mine, the investigations haven't been conducted according to the rules. The interrogation of your servants can't be put off much longer. They will also want to pry into your affairs, examine your bank accounts. They will learn, what everybody suspects, that for years now you have been struggling in vain to save the remains of your fortune. Behind the façade there is nothing left, merely a man treated without consideration by his own family, since he's no longer capable of making money.'

Hubert Vernoux was about to speak. Maigret did not allow him to begin.

'They will also call in psychiatrists.'

He saw his companion raise his head with a sudden jerk.

'I don't know what their opinion will be. I'm not here in any official capacity. I'm returning to Paris this evening and my friend Chabot still has responsibility for the investigation.

'I told you just now that the first crime was not necessarily the work of a lunatic. I added that the other two were committed for a precise purpose, following a pretty devilish line of reasoning.

'Now, it would not surprise me if the psychiatrists regarded that line of reasoning as an indication of madness, a particular kind of madness more common than one might think, which they call paranoia.

'Have you read the books your son must have in his study?'

'I've sometimes looked through them.'

'You should re-read them.'

'You're not suggesting that I . . .'

'I am suggesting nothing. I saw you yesterday playing cards. I saw you win. You're probably convinced you will win this game in the same way.'

'I am not playing any game.'

He protested weakly, flattered, really, that Maigret paid so much attention to him, rendering an indirect homage to his astuteness.

'I just want to put you on your guard against committing one error. It wouldn't help matters, quite the reverse, if there were to be more killings, or even a single crime. Do you understand what I mean? As your son emphasized, madness has its own rules, its own logic.'

Once more Vernoux was about to speak and still the chief-inspector would not let him do so.

'I have finished. I'm catching the half-past nine train and I must go and pack my suitcase before dinner.'

His companion, dismayed, disappointed, was looking at him as if completely lost, made a movement as though to retain him, but the chief-inspector was moving to the door.

'I shall find my own way.'

It took him some time, but then he found the kitchen, out of which Arsène sprang, with a questioning look.

Maigret said nothing to him, followed the central passage, himself opened the front door which the butler closed behind him.

There were no more than three or four persistently curious people left on the pavement opposite. Would the watch committee, this evening, continue its patrols?

He very nearly went to the Palais de Justice, where the meeting was doubtless still continuing but decided he would do what he had said he would and went to pack his suitcase. After which, in the street, he felt he wanted a glass of beer and sat down on the terrace of the Café de la Poste.

Everyone was looking at him. They talked in lower tones. Some of them started to whisper.

He drank two big glasses, slowly, savouring them, as if he had been on a terrace on the Grands Boulevards, and parents were stopping to point him out to their children.

He saw Chalus, the school-teacher, go past, in company with a pot-bellied gentleman, to whom he was relating a story, gesticulating all the while. Chalus didn't notice the chief-inspector and the two men disappeared round the corner of the street.

It was almost dark and the terrace had become empty when he got painfully to his feet to make his way to Chabot's house. The latter came to open the door for him and cast him a troubled glance.

'I was wondering where you were.'

'On a café terrace.'

He hung his hat on the hall-stand, saw the table laid in the dining-room, but dinner wasn't ready and his friend ushered him first into his study.

After quite a long silence, Chabot muttered without looking at Maigret:

'The inquiry continues.'

He seemed to be saying:

'You've won. You see! We aren't so feeble after all.'

Maigret did not smile, made a little sign of approval.

'From now on, the house in the Rue Rabelais is being guarded. Tomorrow, I shall get on with interrogating the servants.'

'By the way, I was almost forgetting to return this to you.'

'Are you really going this evening?'

'I must.'

'I wonder if we shall arrive at a result.'

The chief-inspector had laid the lead pipe on the table, was searching his pockets for Arsène's letter.

'How's Louise Sabati?' he enquired.

'She seems to be out of danger. Her vomiting save her life. She had just eaten and hadn't begun to digest.'

'What has she said?'

'She only answers in monosyllables.'

'She knew they were both going to die?'

'Yes.'

'Was she resigned to it?'

'He told her that they would never leave them happily alone.'

'He didn't talk to her about the three crimes?'

'No.'

'Nor about his father?'

Chabot looked him in the eyes.

'Do you think he's the man?'

Maigret merely blinked his eyes.

'Is he mad?'

'The psychiatrists will decide.'

'In your opinion?'

'I'm glad to say again that people in their senses do not commit murder. But it's only an opinion.'

'Perhaps not very orthodox?'

'No.'

'You seem uneasy.'

'I'm waiting.'

'For what?'

'For something to happen.'

'You think something will happen today?'

'I hope so.'

'Why?'

'Because I paid a visit to Hubert Vernoux.'

'You told him . . .'

'I told him how and why the three crimes were committed. I let him know how the murderer would normally react.'

Chabot, so proud a moment ago of the decision he had taken, appeared frightened again.

'But . . . in that case . . . aren't you afraid that . . .'

'Dinner is served,' Rose came in to announce, while Madame Chabot, on her way to the dining-room, smiled at them.

IX

ONCE again, because of the old lady, they had to be quiet, or rather to speak only of this and that, without any bearing on what was on their minds, and, that evening, the topic was cooking, in particular the method of dressing hare *à la royale*.

Madame Chabot had made *profiterolles* again and Maigret ate five of them, feeling slightly sick, his eyes ceaselessly fixed on the hands of the old clock.

At half past eight, still nothing had happened.

'You needn't hurry. I've ordered a taxi to go to your hotel first and pick up your luggage.'

'Still, I must go there to pay my bill.'

'I telephoned to say they were to charge it to me. That'll teach you not to stay with us when, once in a whole twenty years, you deign to come to Fontenay . . .'

Coffee was served, and brandy. He accepted a cigar, because it was the tradition, and his friend's mother would have been upset if he had refused.

It was five minutes to nine and the car was purring at the door, the driver was waiting, when the telephone bell rang at last.

Chabot hurried over, lifted the receiver.

'Speaking, yes . . . How? . . . Is he dead? . . . I can't hear you, Féron . . . Don't speak so loud . . . Yes . . . I'll come immediately . . . See that he's taken to hospital, I don't need to tell you . . .'

He turned to Maigret.

'I must go up there straight away. Is it vital for you to return tonight?'

'Without fail.'

'I shan't be able to accompany you to the station.'

Because of his mother, he said no more, seized his hat, his light coat. Only when they were on the pavement did he murmur:

'There's been a dreadful scene at the Vernoux', Hubert Vernoux, dead-drunk, started smashing up everything in his room, and in the end, in a frenzy, gashed his wrist with his razor.'

The chief-inspector's composure astonished him.

'He isn't dead,' Chabot continued.

'I know.'

'How do you know?'

'Because men like him don't commit suicide.'

'Yet his son . . .'

'You go. They're waiting for you.'

The station was only five minutes away. Maigret went over to the taxi.

'We've just enough time,' said the driver.

The chief-inspector turned one last time to his friend, who seemed lost in the middle of the pavement.

'Write to me.'

It was a monotonous journey. At two or three stations, Maigret got off to have a glass of brandy, and finally dozed off, vaguely conscious, at each stop, of the station-master's shouts and the creaking of the trolleys.

He arrived in Paris in the early morning and a taxi drove him home, where from below he smiled up at the open window. His wife was waiting for him on the landing.

'Not too tired? Did you sleep a little?'

He drank three large cups of coffee before relaxing.

'Are you going to have a bath?'

Certainly he was going to have one! It was good to find Madame Maigret's voice again, the smell of the flat, the furniture and objects in their place.

'I didn't quite understand what you said to me on the telephone. Were you involved in a case?'

'It's over.'

'What was it?'

'A fellow who couldn't face losing.'

'I don't understand.'

'It doesn't matter. There are people who are capable of anything rather than tumble down the slope.'

'You must know what you're talking about,' she murmured philosophically, without bothering more about it.

At half-past nine, in the Commissioner's study, they gave him the known facts about the disappearance of the senator's daugther. It was a sordid story, with almost orgiastic meetings in a cellar and drug-taking as the main item.

'It's pretty certain that she didn't leave of her own free will and it's unlikely she was kidnapped. Most probably she's died from too strong a dose of drugs and her friends, in panic, have got rid of her body.'

Maigret copied a list of names, addresses.

'Lucas has already heard some of them. Up to now no-one's prepared to talk.'

Wasn't it his job to make people talk?

'Did you enjoy yourself?'

'Where?'

'In Bordeaux.'

'It rained the whole time.'

He did not mention Fontenay. He hardly had time to think about it for three days, which he spent hearing the confessions of young idiots who thought themselves smart.

Then, in his mail, he found a letter with the postmark of Fontenay-le-Comte. From the newspapers, he already knew, roughly, the epilogue to the case.

Chabot, in his neat, regular writing, rather sharply pointed, which might have been taken for a woman's hand, furnished him with the details.

At some point, shortly after your departure from the Rue Rabelais, he stole down to the cellar and Arsène saw him come back up with a bottle of Napoleon brandy, which had been kept in the Courçon family for two generations.

Maigret could not help smiling. Hubert Vernoux, for his last drunken bout, had not been content with any old spirit. He had chosen the rarest in the house, a venerable bottle they had preserved partly as a proof of nobility.

When the butler came to tell him that dinner was served, his eyes were already haggard, red-rimmed. With a great theatrical gesture, he ordered him to leave him alone, shouted at him:

'Let the bitches dine without me!'

The women sat down to table. About ten minutes later, heavy thumps were heard coming from his rooms. Arsène was sent to see what was happening, but the door was locked, and Vernoux was meantime smashing up all he could lay hands on and shrieking obscenities.

When they told her what was happening, it was his sister-in-law who suggested:

'*The window . . .*'

They did not disturb themselves, remained sitting in the dining-room while Arsène went out into the yard. One window was half open. He drew the curtains apart. Vernoux saw him. He already had a razor in his hand.

He yelled again to leave him alone, that he had had enough, and, according to Arsène, continued to utter filthy words nobody had ever heard him use before.

While the butler was calling for help, because he did not dare enter the room, the man began to slash his wrist. The blood spurted out. Vernoux looked at it in terror, and thereupon stopped what he was doing. A few seconds later, he fell quite limp on the carpet, unconscious.

Ever since, he refuses to answer any questions. At the hospital, the next day, they found him ripping up his mattress and they had to lock him in a padded cell.

Desprez, the psychiatrist, came from Niort to give him a first examination: tomorrow he will have a consultation with a specialist from Poitiers.

According to Desprez, there is scarcely any doubt of Vernoux's madness, but, because of the publicity the case is receiving in the district, he prefers to take every precaution.

I have given permission for Alain's burial. The funeral takes place tomorrow. The Sabati girl is still in hospital and is doing very well. I don't know what to do about her. Her father must be working somewhere in France, but we can't get hold of him. I can't send her back to her lodgings, since she still has ideas of suicide.

My mother talks of taking her as a maid in the house so that she can give a little help to Rose, who is getting old. I'm afraid that people . . .

Maigret did not have time to finish reading the letter that morning, because they were bringing him an important witness. He stuffed it in his pocket. What became of it, he never knew.

'By the way,' he announced that evening to his wife, 'I had a letter from Julien Chabot.'

'What does he say?'

He searched for the letter, could not find it. It must have fallen out of his pocket when he was pulling out his handkerchief or his tobacco-pouch.

'They are going to take on a new maid.'

'Is that all?'

'Practically.'

It was a long time after, while looking at himself anxiously in the mirror, that he muttered:

'I found that he had aged.'

'Who are you talking about?'

'Chabot.'

'How old is he?'

'Within two months of me.'

Madame Maigret was tidying the room, as she always did before going to bed.

'He should have got married,' she concluded.

Shadow Rock Farm,
Lakeville, Connecticut
27 March, 1953